DON'T MISS ANDREA KANE'S BLOCKBUSTER CONTEMPORARY NOVEL OF ROMANTIC SUSPENSE

RUN FOR YOUR LIFE

"A knockout! Andrea Kane expertly juggles suspense and romance in this fast-paced story of good vs. evil."

—*New York Times* bestselling author Iris Johansen

"A real page-turner! Andrea Kane's *Run for Your Life* is a keep-you-up-all-night romantic suspense."

—Karen Robards, bestselling author of *Paradise County*

PRAISE FOR

THE SILVER COIN

"*The Silver Coin* leaves readers wondering what Andrea Kane can do next. . . . The action-packed story line never eases up."

—*Affaire de Coeur*

"The tension and suspense remain at a high level throughout the book, punctuated by the escalating romance and passionate love scenes."

—Bookbug on the Web

THE GOLD COIN

"Kane's engrossing plot and her quick-witted, passionate characters should make readers eagerly await this novel's companion. . . ."

—*Publishers Weekly*

"A superb novel. . . . The story line is nonstop and loaded with romantic tension and intrigue."

—*Affaire de Coeur*

ALSO BY ANDREA KANE

ANDREA KANE

THE
GOLD COIN

THE
SILVER COIN

POCKET BOOKS

New York   London   Toronto   Sydney

This book is a work of fiction. Names, characters, places and incidents are products of the author's imagination or are used fictitiously. Any resemblance to actual events or locales or persons, living or dead, is entirely coincidental.

 POCKET BOOKS, a division of Simon & Schuster, Inc.
1230 Avenue of the Americas, New York, NY 10020

The Gold Coin and *The Silver Coin* copyright © 1999 by Andrea Kane
These titles were originally published individually by Pocket Books.

All rights reserved, including the right to reproduce
this book or portions thereof in any form whatsoever.
For information address Pocket Books, 1230 Avenue
of the Americas, New York, NY 10020

ISBN: 1-4165-1316-7

This Pocket Books trade paperback edition January 2005

10 9 8 7 6 5 4 3 2 1

POCKET and colophon are registered trademarks of
Simon & Schuster, Inc.

Manufactured in the United States of America

For information regarding special discounts for bulk purchases,
please contact Simon & Schuster Special Sales at 1-800-456-6798
or business@simonandschuster.com.

Contents

꧁

THE GOLD COIN

To family—those special people
whose hearts and lives
are tied to yours.

Acknowledgments

To Gryphon Books, for their commitment, patience, and professionalism in digging up reference books for me on the 19th-century English banking system. Many thanks—you've spared me more sleepless nights than I can count.

To my family, the true-to-life embodiment of what Anastasia and Breanna's grandfather believed family ought to be. I love you.

Prologue

❧

*T*hey made the pact when they were six.

They hadn't planned on making it. But drastic circumstances required drastic actions. And drastic circumstances were precisely what they found themselves in on that fateful night.

Fearfully, the two little girls hesitated at the doorway.

Crackling tension permeated the dining room. They peeked inside, freezing in their tracks as angry voices assailed them. They scooted backward, pressing themselves flat against the wall so as not to be spied.

"What the hell is wrong with discussing profits?" Lord George Colby barked, his sharp words hurled at his brother. "The fact that our business is making a fortune should please you as much as it does me."

"Tonight is not about profits, George," Lord Henry reminded him in a voice that was taut with repressed ire. "It's about family."

"Family? As in brotherly devotion?" A mocking laugh. "Don't insult me, Henry. The business is the only meaningful thing you and I share."

"You're right. More and more right every day. And I'm getting damned tired of trying to change that."

"Well, so much for sentiment," George noted scornfully. "And so much for this whole sham of a reunion."

"It wasn't meant to be a reunion." Clearly, Henry was striving for control. "It's Father's sixtieth birthday celebration. Or had you forgotten?"

"I've forgotten nothing. *Nothing.* Have you?"

The pointed barb sank in, blanketing the room in silence.

"They're fighting loud," Anastasia hissed, inching farther away from the doorway, and shoving one unruly auburn tress off her face. "Especially Uncle George. We're in trouble. *Big* trouble."

"I know." Her cousin Breanna gazed down at herself, her delicate features screwed up in distress as she surveyed her soiled party frock—which was identical to Anastasia's, only much filthier. "Father sounds really mad. And if he sees I got all dirty . . . and ruined the dress Grandfather gave me . . ." She began rubbing furiously at the mud and grass stains, pausing only to wipe streaks of dirt from her forearms.

Anastasia watched, chewing her lip, knowing this whole disaster was her fault. She'd been the one who insisted they sneak out of Medford Manor to play while the grown-ups talked. Now she wished she'd never suggested it. In fact, she wished it had been she, rather than Breanna, who had fallen into the puddle outside. Her father would have forgiven her. He was gentle and kind—well, at least when it came to her. When it came to almost everyone, in fact. Except for one person: his brother. He and Uncle George, though twins, were practically enemies.

Maybe that was because they were so different—except for their looks, which were identical, right down to their vivid coloring: jade green eyes and thick cinnamon hair, both of which she and Breanna had inherited. But in every other way their fathers were like day and night. Her own father had a quick mind and an easy nature. He embraced life, creative business ventures, and his family, while Uncle George was stiff in manner, rigid in expectations, and downright intimidating when crossed.

Especially when the one who crossed him was his daughter.

"Stacie!" Breanna's frantic hiss yanked Anastasia out of her reverie. "What should I do?"

Anastasia was used to being the one whose ideas got them both in and out of trouble. But this time the trouble they'd be facing was bad. And the person who'd be paying the price would be Breanna. Well, that was something Anastasia couldn't—*wouldn't*—allow.

Her mind began racing, seeking ways to keep Uncle George from seeing Breanna—or at least from seeing her frock.

Absently, Anastasia studied her own party dress, noting that other than a fine layer of dirt along the hem, it was respectably clean.

Now *that* spawned an idea.

"I know! We can change dresses." Even as she spoke, she spied Wells, the Medford butler, striding down the endless corridor, heading in their direction. Any second he would spot them—if he hadn't done so already. It was too late for scrambling in and out of their dresses.

"No," she amended dejectedly. "We don't have time. It would've worked, too, 'cause our dresses look exactly the same—" Abruptly she broke off, her eyes lighting up as she contemplated another, far better and more intriguing possibility. "So do we."

Breanna's brows drew together. "So do we . . . what?"

"Look exactly the same. Everyone says so. Our fathers are twins. Our mothers are sisters—or at least they were until yours went to heaven. No one can ever tell us apart. Even Mama and Papa get confused sometimes. So why don't you be me and I'll be you?"

"You mean switch places?" Breanna's fear was supplanted by interest. "Can we do that?"

"Why not?" Swiftly, Anastasia combed her fingers through her tangled masses of coppery hair, trying—with customary six-year-old awkwardness—to arrange them in some semblance of order. "We'll fool everyone and save you from Uncle George."

"But then *you'll* get in trouble."

"Not like you would. Papa might be annoyed, but Uncle George would be . . ."

"I know." Breanna's gaze darted toward Wells, who was now almost upon them. "Are you sure?"

"I'm sure." Anastasia grinned, becoming more and more intrigued by the notion. "It'll be fun. Let's try it, just this once."

An impish smile curved Breanna's lips. "A whole hour or two to speak out like you do. I can hardly wait."

"Don't wait," Anastasia hissed. "Start now." So saying, she lowered her chin a notch, clasping the folds of her gown between nervous fingers in a gesture that was typically Breanna. "Hello, Wells," she greeted the butler.

"Where have you two been? I've looked everywhere for you." Wells's eyes, behind heavy spectacles, flickered from Anastasia to Breanna— who had thrown back her shoulders and assumed Anastasia's more brazen stance. "All of us, most particularly your grandfather, have been worried sick. . . . Oh, no." Seeing the condition of Breanna's gown, Wells's long, angular features tensed.

"It's not as bad as it looks, Wells," Breanna assured him with one of Anastasia's confident smiles. "It was only a little trip and a littler fall."

A rueful nod. "You're right, Miss Stacie," he agreed. "It could have been worse. It could be Miss Breanna who'd taken the spill. I shudder to think what the outcome of *that* would have been. Now then . . ." He waved them toward the dining room, frowning as he became aware of the heavy silence emanating from within. "Hurry. Tell them you're all right. It will certainly brighten your grandfather's birthday."

With an uneasy glance in that direction, he scooted off, retracing his steps to the entranceway.

The girls' eyes met, and they grinned.

"We fooled him," Breanna murmured in wonder. "*No one* fools Wells."

"No one but us," Anastasia said with great satisfaction. She nudged her cousin forward. "Let's go." An impish twinkle. "After you, Stacie."

Breanna giggled. Then, head held high, she preceded Anastasia into the dining room—despite the soiled gown—just as her cousin would have.

Once inside, they waited, assessing the scene before them.

The elegant mahogany table was formally set, its crystal and silver gleaming beneath the glow of the room's ornate chandelier. At the head of the table sat their beloved grandfather, his elderly face strained as he looked from one son to the other. At the sideboard, George bristled, splashing some brandy into a glass and glaring across the room at his brother, who was shaking his head resignedly. Henry nodded as he listened to the soothing words his wife, Anne, was murmuring in his ear.

Grandfather was the first to become aware of his granddaughters' presence, and he beckoned them forward, his pursed lips curving into a smile of welcome. "At last. My two beautiful . . ." His words drifted off as he noted Breanna's stained and wrinkled gown. "What on earth happened?"

"We took a walk, Grandfather," Breanna replied, playing the part of Anastasia to perfection. "We were bored. So we went exploring. We climbed trees. We tried to catch fireflies. It was my idea—and my own fault that I fell. I forgot all about the time, and I was rushing too fast on my way back. I didn't see the mud puddle."

The Viscount Medford's lips twitched. "I see," he replied evenly.

Anastasia walked sedately to her grandfather's side. "We apologize, Grandfather," she said, intentionally using Breanna's sweet tone and respectful gaze. "Stacie and I were having fun. But it is your birthday. And we should never have left the manor."

"Nonsense, my dear." He leaned over and caressed his granddaughter's cheek. His insightful green gaze swept over her, his eyes surrounded by the tiny lines that heralded sixty years of life. Then he shifted to assess her cousin's more rumpled state. "You're welcome to explore to your hearts' content. The only reason for our concern was that it's becoming quite dark and neither of you knows your way around Medford's vast grounds. But now that you're here, no apology is necessary." He cleared his throat. "Anastasia, are you hurt?" he asked Breanna.

"No, Grandfather." Breanna shot him one of Anastasia's bold, infectious grins. "*I'm* not hurt. But my gown is."

"So I noticed." The viscount looked more and more as if he were biting back laughter. "How did you fall?"

"I slipped and landed in a puddle. As I said, I was in too much of a hurry."

"Aren't you always?" George muttered, abandoning the sideboard and marching over to the table. Purposefully, he ignored the girl he assumed to be his niece, instead gesturing for his daughter—or at the least the girl he thought to be his daughter—to take the chair beside him. "Sit, Breanna. You've already delayed our meal long enough." A biting pause. "Perhaps your cousin should change her clothes before she dines?" he inquired, inclining his head to give his brother a pointed look.

"Papa? Mama?" Breanna glanced at her uncle Henry and aunt Anne. "Would you prefer I change?"

Anastasia's father shook his head. "I don't think that will be necessary."

"Darling," Anne inserted, her brows drawn in concern, "are you sure you aren't hurt?"

"Positive," Breanna assured her with that offhanded shrug Anastasia always gave. "Just clumsy. I really am sorry."

"Never mind," the viscount interrupted, gesturing for the girls to be seated. "Dirty or not, you're a welcome addition to the table." He tossed a disapproving scowl in George's direction. "A breath of fresh air, given the disagreeable nature of the conversation."

"It wasn't a conversation," George replied tersely. "It was an argument."

"When isn't it?" his father countered, shoving a shock of hair—once auburn, now white—off his forehead. "Let's change the subject while we enjoy the fine meal Mrs. Rhodes has prepared."

Despite his urging, the meal, however delicious, passed in stony silence, the only sound that of the clinking glassware and china.

After an hour, which seemed more like an eternity, the viscount placed his napkin on the table and folded his hands before him. "I invited you all here tonight to celebrate. Not only my birthday, but what it represents: our family and its legacy."

"Colby and Sons," George clarified, his green eyes lighting up.

"I wasn't referring to the business," his father replied, sadness making his shoulders droop, his already lined face growing even older, more weary. "At least not in the economic sense. I was referring to us and the unity of our family—not only now, but in years to come."

"All of which is integrally tied to our company and its profits." George sat up straight, his jaw clenched in annoyance. "The problem is, I'm the only one honest enough to admit that's what business—*and* this family—are all about: money and status."

Viscount Medford sighed. "I'm not denying the pride I feel for Colby and Sons. We've all worked hard to make it thrive. But that doesn't mean I've forgotten what's important. I only wish you hadn't either. I'd hoped . . ." His glance flickered across the table, first to Anastasia, then to Breanna. "Never mind." Abruptly, he pushed back his chair. "Let's take our brandy in the library."

Anne rose gracefully. "I'll get the girls ready for bed."

"We won't be staying," George said, cutting her off, his jaw clenching even tighter as he faced his brother's wife. "So you needn't bother."

She winced at the harshness of his tone and the bitterness that glittered in his eyes. But she answered him quietly, and without averting her gaze. "It's late, George. Surely your trip can wait until morning."

"It could. I choose for it not to."

Anastasia and Breanna exchanged glances. They both hated this part most of all—the icy antagonism Breanna's father displayed when forced to address his brother's wife.

The antagonism *and* its guaranteed outcome.

They'd be split up again soon. And Lord knew when they'd see each other next.

Quickly, Breanna rose. "Breanna and I will wait in the blue salon, Uncle George," she said, still playing the part of her cousin. "We'll stay there until you're ready to leave."

George was too caught up in his thoughts to spare her more than a cursory nod.

It was all the girls needed.

Without giving him an instant to change his mind, they scampered out of the room. Pausing only to heave sighs of relief, they bolted down the hall and dashed into the blue salon.

"We were wonderful!" Anastasia squealed, plopping onto the sofa. "Even *I* wasn't sure who was who after a while."

Breanna laughed softly. "Nor I," she agreed, squirming onto the cushion alongside her cousin.

"Let's make a pact," Anastasia piped up suddenly. "Whenever we're together and one of us gets in trouble—the kind of trouble that would go away if people believed I was you or you were me—let's switch places like we did tonight. Okay?"

After a brief instant of consideration, Breanna arched a brow. "Good for me, but what about you? When could you ever be in enough trouble to need to be me?"

"You never know."

"I suppose not." Breanna sounded decidedly unconvinced.

"So? Is it a pact?" Anastasia pressed, bouncing up and down on the sofa.

Apparently her enthusiasm was contagious, because abruptly Breanna grinned. "It's a pact."

With proper formality they shook hands.

A knock interrupted their private moment together.

"Girls?" Their grandfather entered the salon, closing the door behind him. "May I speak with you both for a moment?"

"Of course, Grandfather." Anastasia eased over and patted the space between her and Breanna, a curious glint in her eye. "Come sit with Brea—with Stacie and me," she hastily rectified.

"Thank you—Anastasia." With a whisper of a smile, the viscount lowered himself between the girls, chuckling as he saw surprise, then disappointment, flash across Anastasia's face.

"You knew?" she demanded.

"Of course, my headstrong Stacie. *I* knew," he clarified, leaning over and patting each of their hands. "But no one else did. Especially not your father," he assured Breanna. "A brilliant tactic on both your parts. I do, however, suggest you swap frocks right after our chat, in case your visit is cut short. I'll do my best to keep peace in the library, but I'm not sure how long your fathers will stay in the same room together."

"Good idea," Anastasia agreed at once.

"Not good," Breanna amended with utter resignation. "Just wise."

Both girls fell silent.

A shadow crossed the viscount's face, and he gazed sadly from Anastasia to Breanna and back. "You're both extraordinarily special. I only wish your fathers could share the bond you do. But I'm afraid that's impossible."

"Why do they fight, Grandfather?" Breanna asked. "And why does Papa dislike Aunt Anne so much?"

The viscount sighed, feeling far older than his sixty years. What could he say? How could he tell them the truth when they were far too young to understand?

He couldn't.

But what he could do was to ensure their futures. Their futures and that of the Colby family.

"Tell me, girls," he asked, "which would you value more, gold or silver?"

Anastasia shrugged. "That depends on which of us you ask. I love gold—it's the color of the sun when it rises and the stars when they glow in the sky. Breanna loves silver—it's the color of the trim on her favorite porcelain horse, and the color of the necklace and earrings her mama left her."

"It's also the color of the pond here at nighttime," Breanna pointed out. "When the moon hits it, it looks all silvery and magical."

Their grandfather's smile was gentle. "I'm glad you feel so much at home at Medford Manor," he said, moved by the irony that neither of his granddaughters had equated value with actual monetary worth. "You do know that gold is worth more than silver, like a sovereign is worth more than a crown?"

Breanna frowned. "Of course. Father says things like that all the time. But that's not what you asked."

"No," the viscount agreed in an odd tone. "It's not, is it?" With that, he dug into his pocket, extracted two shiny objects, one silver, one gold. "Do you see what I have here?"

Both girls leaned closer, studying the objects. "They're coins," Anastasia announced.

"Indeed they are. Identical coins, other than the fact that one is silver, the other gold." He held them closer. "They're also very special. Can you see what's engraved on them?"

"That's Medford Manor!" Anastasia exclaimed, pointing. "On both coins."

"Um-hum. And on the back of each coin is the Colby family crest." The viscount caressed each veneer lovingly, then slipped the gold coin into Anastasia's hand, the silver one into Breanna's. "They remind me of you two: very much alike and yet so very different, each unique and rare, both worth far more than any bank's holdings." He squeezed their little fingers, closing them around their respective coins. "I want you both to promise me something."

"Of course." Breanna's eyes were wide.

"Each of you hold on to your coin. They're special gifts, from me to you. Keep them safe, somewhere you'll always be able to find them. Don't tell anyone else about the coins, or about your hiding places. We'll make the whole thing our secret. All right?"

Solemnly, the girls nodded.

The viscount gazed intently from one girl to the other. "The day may come when you're asked to give up your coins, for what might seem to be a very good reason, even one that's offered by someone you trust. Don't do it. Don't *ever,* under any circumstances, give the coins to anyone else, not even to your fathers." His mouth thinned into a grim line. "They wouldn't understand the coins' significance, anyway. But you will—perhaps not now, not entirely, for you're too young. Someday, however, you will. These coins represent each of you, and your commitment to our family. Wherever your lives take you, let them remind you of this moment and bring you back together again, to renew our family name and sustain it, knowing that you yourselves are the riches that bequeath it its value. Do that for me—and for each other."

Somehow both girls understood the importance, if not the full meaning, of what they were being asked. Together, they murmured, "We will, Grandfather."

"Good." With that, he rose, kissing the tops of each of their heads. "I'll leave you now, so you can exchange clothes. Remember what I said: you're extraordinarily special. I don't doubt you'll accomplish all your fathers didn't and more." He straightened, regarding them for a long, thoughtful moment. "I only wish I could make your paths home easier," he murmured half to himself.

Crossing the room, he stepped into the hall, shutting the door behind him to ensure the girls' privacy and protect them from discovery. Then he veered toward the entranceway, determined to complete one crucial task before returning to the library to assume his role as peacemaker.

"Wells," he summoned, beckoning to his butler.

"Yes, sir?"

The viscount withdrew a sealed envelope from his coat pocket. "Have this delivered to my solicitor at once. It's imperative that he receive it— and that I receive written confirmation of that fact."

"I'll see to it immediately, my lord," Wells replied.

Nodding, the viscount handed over the envelope, fully aware of how drastic an action he was taking, how explosive the results might be.

He only prayed the rewards would outweigh the consequences.

1

Kent, England
July 1817

She was home.

Glancing out the carriage window, Anastasia drank in the sprawling countryside and the lovingly familiar roads of Kent, the winding path of oak trees and lush, colorful gardens that led to Medford Manor.

More than ten years had passed since she'd last been here. And yet she remembered that final day as if it were yesterday—a foggy, drizzly March morning when she and her parents had left England.

It had been the worst day of her life.

No, actually it had been a culmination of worst days, beginning a fortnight earlier when her beloved grandfather had died. Then had come the funeral—where she'd wept and wept—and the reading of the will, a formality that did nothing to ease her hollow sense of loss. She and Breanna had huddled together in the back of Mr. Fenshaw's office, alternately crying and comforting each other as the solicitor summarized the provisions their grandfather had made—something about dividing his assets in half and passing ownership of Colby and Sons to their fathers, to be shared equally.

Those are only things, Anastasia had wanted to scream. *None of them can bring Grandfather back.*

But she'd bitten her lip, swallowed her grief, and said nothing.

The next day, the unthinkable had happened.

Her father had taken her aside, explained that he, Mama, and she were about to embark on the adventure of a lifetime. They were sailing for the States, opening an American branch of Colby and Sons in the thriving city of Philadelphia, starting a whole new life in a whole new country.

Anastasia had understood—far more than he'd realized.

With Grandfather's passing, the Colby family had ceased to exist. The final vestiges of it had died along with him, been dispensed along with his possessions. Uncle George and her father no longer had a reason to strive for the mutual tolerance they'd exerted during their father's lifetime. In fact, they wanted nothing more than to put an ocean between them.

Well, to her father that might have meant new beginnings and the thrill of expansion.

To Anastasia, it had meant something entirely different: that she'd never see Breanna again.

Which was why, on that foggy spring morning, she'd felt as if she were living a nightmare. She was bidding a final farewell to everything she held dear: Grandfather, England, Medford Manor—and Breanna.

She and her cousin had exchanged a tearful good-bye on the steps of Medford Manor—a brief one, given that Uncle George refused to take Breanna to see them off. Not only didn't he share her anguish, he was also far too busy moving into his new home. He was, after all, the new Viscount Medford, a title he'd craved for years and which passed to him by right since he was older than his twin by twelve minutes.

Thus, Breanna and Anastasia had parted, hugging each other fiercely, exchanging their good-byes amid promises to write every week.

They'd kept their word.

Throughout the years, weekly letters had sailed back and forth from England to the States, as the girls kept each other apprised of their lives. How different those lives had become—Breanna being groomed for the role of a proper English lady and Anastasia enjoying the slightly less sophisticated but more independent role afforded by life in Philadelphia. She'd never quite felt she belonged; she wasn't an American, for England was still, would always be, her home. Yet she wasn't a traditional English noblewoman either. And while she never stopped yearning for her country, she had to admit she felt a tremendous admiration for the American ideals and those who held them.

She'd also seen a thousand opportunities for expansion in the States; a great untapped world of natural resources to cultivate and trade. She'd asked her father dozens of questions, learned as much as she could about Colby and Sons: what an import and export company did, the kinds of goods her father traded, the contacts he made, even the lengths he went to to ensure neutral trade continued during the years America and Britain were at war.

Abruptly, eighteen months after the war ended, Anastasia's foundation was snatched away. Her mother died of a fever, leaving her father grief-stricken and in shock. He never recovered. Eight months later, he passed away in his sleep, leaving Anastasia utterly, excruciatingly, alone.

Henry Colby's American solicitor, Mr. Carter, had sent for Anastasia, explaining that her father's will was held in England, given that Henry had assumed his daughter would choose to return there upon his death.

However, if such was not the case, Mr. Fenshaw could forward the will to Philadelphia, where Mr. Carter would read it.

Anastasia had smiled softly, realizing how well her father had understood where her heart was. She'd thanked Mr. Carter, arranged to have him continue to oversee her father's local assets and to act as the American agent to Colby and Sons—a role he'd been groomed for—then packed her bags and booked passage on the next packet ship to Liverpool.

Breanna's letter had arrived in Philadelphia that very day, begging Anastasia to come home, to come straight to Medford Manor and move in with them. *Even Father agrees this is the best thing for you,* she'd added with a touch of ironic amusement.

Gratefully, Anastasia had decided to do just that. The last thing she wanted was to be totally alone. And being with Breanna again would bring great joy at a dismal time.

The ship had docked three days ago, at which time Uncle George's carriage had been ready and waiting. She'd spied the family crest instantly, and had nearly wept with happiness at the familiar sight.

She hadn't minded the length of the drive from Liverpool to Kent. She'd used the time to savor the winding country roads, the quaint villages and towns the carriage rolled through. She'd reacquainted herself with her country, reveled in the sheer joy of being back after more than a decade away.

And now, at long last, Medford Manor loomed ahead, a beacon of light at the end of a very dark tunnel.

Anastasia leaned out the carriage window, watching the manor draw closer, the gardens flowing around her like a cluster of dear friends, welcoming her home.

The front door burst open as the carriage rounded the drive, and a young woman rushed down the steps.

Anastasia didn't need to ask who it was.

It was like peering into a looking-glass, seeing a mirror image of herself gazing back at her. Even now, at almost twenty-one years old, they still looked like twins.

"Stacie!" Breanna waved frantically, and Anastasia nearly knocked over the footman in her haste to alight.

"Breanna!" She flung her arms around her cousin, alternately laughing and crying, more overwhelmed by this moment than even she'd realized.

The two girls, now women, drew back, stared at each other in joy and wonder.

"After all this time, I can't believe I'm seeing you." Anastasia grinned. "Seeing *me,*" she corrected, taking in Breanna's delicate features and vibrant coloring.

"It is amazing," Breanna agreed, returning her cousin's scrutiny with rapt fascination. "I always wondered if we'd still look alike after all this time. Well, now I know." Her eyes sparkled. "I have a twin." She gripped Anastasia's hands. "I can't believe you're finally here."

"Nor can I. I feel as if an eternity's passed since I left. And yet, in some ways, it's like I never left at all. Never and forever all rolled into one." As she spoke, Anastasia gazed up at the manor, a knot of emotion tightening her throat. Here, after all these years, was the estate on which she and Breanna had frolicked as children. Only now their childhood was over, and she was entering Medford Manor with the maturity and self-sufficiency of an adult.

It was a sobering thought.

"Forever and never . . . yes, I feel the same way," Breanna agreed. "But more the former than the latter. Without your letters, I don't know what I would have done. I can't tell you how I missed you." She paused, watched the play of emotions on her cousin's face. "Stacie," she added softly. "I'm so sorry about your parents."

"I know you are." Anastasia blinked away her tears. "Now let's go inside. We have a decade to catch up on."

As if on cue, Wells stepped outside—an older, grayer Wells, perhaps, but Wells nonetheless, his sharp features softening as he gazed at Anastasia.

"Miss Stacie . . . forgive me, Lady Anastasia—welcome."

Anastasia abandoned the formalities and hurried up the steps to hug the elderly butler. "Thank you, Wells," she whispered, a tremor catching in her voice. "And I'm still Stacie. Everything else might have changed, but that's the same."

He chuckled, looking a bit misty-eyed. "I'm glad to hear that." He shook his head in wonder. "There's one other thing that hasn't changed. You and Miss Breanna still look too much alike to distinguish one of you from the other. It's startling. I remember your father saying he couldn't tell . . ." Wells's mouth snapped shut.

"It's all right," Anastasia told him gently. "Mentioning Papa doesn't make it hurt any more than it already does. Besides—" Her chin came up a notch as she sought the internal strength she'd come to count upon. "He's with Mama now. Which is precisely what he wanted."

"And you're with us." Breanna ascended the stairs, squeezed Anastasia's shoulders, and led her inside the house. "Let's get you settled. You must be exhausted. Mrs. Charles has made sure your room is all ready. We gave you the one right next to mine—so we can talk all night, just like we used to."

Anastasia stepped into the house, feeling a surge of warmth encompass her. It was like greeting a long-lost friend, or being enfolded in safe, loving arms. Medford Manor was precisely as she remembered it, its tasteful Oriental carpet running the full length of what had seemed to a child's eyes to be an endless hallway filled with paintings and flanked on either side by two elegant, winding staircases.

All that was missing was Grandfather.

Again, grief coiled in her stomach.

"It's just the same as it was then," Breanna told Anastasia, touching her arm gently. "Just as Grandfather would have wanted it."

"Yes. It is." Anastasia drank in every tiny beloved detail, a twinge of surprise accompanying the realization of just how true Breanna's statement was. "Actually, I thought Uncle George would have made a few changes, given that this is his home now and that he and Grandfather didn't exactly have similar taste. Or similar views, for that matter."

"The same honest Stacie," Breanna noted with fond amusement and perhaps a touch of awe. "You're right. They didn't. I suspect Father scarcely notices what the house looks like. Decorating doesn't interest him—business does."

"Breanna, you didn't tell me your cousin had arrived." George Colby interrupted their conversation, emerging from the sitting room and making his way slowly toward them. "Anastasia—welcome to Medford Manor."

Anastasia tensed a bit at the well-remembered patronizing tone, and her gaze darted over to study the man who was her father's twin.

She'd been almost afraid to see him again; afraid he'd remind her so much of her father that her loss would become impossible to bear. But that wasn't the case. Uncle George hadn't aged well. He was far grayer than her father had been, his face more lined, his shoulders stooped. And his eyes, though the same striking jade green hue as that of all the Colbys, were lackluster, devoid of the intelligent spark that had lit her father's eyes or the laughter and insight that had glistened in her grandfather's.

The years had not been kind to her uncle. Then again, kindness was not a trait he valued—nor one he deserved.

"Thank you, Uncle George," she greeted him cautiously. "It's good to see you. And I'm very grateful to you for inviting me to stay here."

He nodded, surveying her with a cool, assessing look. "I wouldn't have it any other way. After all, you shouldn't be alone—not at a time like this, and certainly not in a strange country. Not when you have family right here in England to help ease your loss." He cleared his throat. "I trust your journey was uneventful?"

"It was tiring, but fine." She realized he was making an attempt at polite conversation. Still, she couldn't help feeling as if he were delivering a rehearsed speech, and she were responding in kind.

"Stacie's exhausted, Father." Breanna spoke in that same measured, respectful tone she'd used as a child. "I'd like to show her to her room, perhaps let her rest awhile."

"Yes, of course." The viscount gestured toward the second level. "Go ahead. Wells will see that your bags are brought up. Luncheon will be served promptly at two."

"Thank you," Anastasia murmured, already heading toward the stairs. She was tired, yes, but she was also eager to see her new room, to spend time with Breanna.

To find a place for herself again.

Waiting for Breanna to catch up, Anastasia ascended the steps, rounding the second-floor landing and following her cousin down the corridor to the fourth room on the right.

"I hope you like it," Breanna said, waving her into her new chambers. "Gold and green used to be your favorite colors. I hope they still are."

"They are," Anastasia assured her, smiling at the sight of the drapes and bedcovers, both a deep green brocade, and the floral needlepoint hanging over the canopied bed—a path of goldenrods amid a tree-lined grove. "Oh, Breanna, it's lovely."

"I wanted to do more. I also wanted to meet you at the ship. But there's only so much Father will allow . . ." Breanna's voice trailed off, and she shut the door behind them. "Anyway, feel free to decorate any way you choose," she continued. "From this moment on, it's your room."

Anastasia dropped onto the edge of the bed, tucking a strand of hair behind her ear as she assessed the chambers. "My room. At Medford Manor. It's hard to believe." She studied her cousin with compassionate awareness. "Don't give another thought to not having met me at the ship. I know Uncle George too well to have contemplated the notion. Oh, he's being very solicitous. Still—" Her voice dropped to a mock baritone. "—'Breanna, you didn't tell me your cousin had arrived' and 'luncheon will be served promptly at two.'" She rolled her eyes. "Something tells me he hasn't changed a bit."

"No, he hasn't." Breanna's lips curved slightly. "Then again, neither have you. You're still as forthright as ever. Only your accent has changed."

"My accent?"

"Um-hum. You no longer speak proper English. Now you sound like . . . like . . ."

"Like I've lived ten years in America?" Anastasia teased.

"Well . . . yes." Breanna's eyes sparkled with curiosity. "Tell me about Philadelphia. Your letters made it sound so different from here."

"Not entirely different. But less restrictive." Anastasia leaned back on her elbows. "Protocol isn't valued as highly as it is in England.

Chaperons aren't mandatory, there isn't as wide a chasm between servants and those who employ them. America is less set in its ways than
England is. Which makes sense, given that it's a new country."

Breanna lowered herself to a chair. "It sounds a lot like you—
unorthodox, set on forging its own path. Will you miss living there?"

"Some aspects of it, yes. Others, no. It's true I fit in, but I never
really belonged. We were always glaringly English. It was especially
obvious during the war. If Papa hadn't had such a good rapport with
the American farmers and manufacturers, we probably would have had
to leave, to go to Canada or come home. But they trusted him. He had
integrity—and connections in nearly every neutral country. I guess
that when it comes right down to it, profits are profits. And Colby and
Sons ensured a healthy revenue for all, war or no war. Father was his
usual inventive self, devising creative routes to deliver goods without
violating either England or America's war policies." She broke off,
shot her cousin a questioning look. "Why are you staring at me like
that?"

"How do you know so much about your father's business?" Breanna
demanded.

"It's not just Father's business. It's our entire family's business, yours
and mine included." Seeing Breanna's incredulous expression, Anastasia
felt her lips twitch. "Now that I consider it, I suppose my interest in
Colby and Sons must seem rather extreme to you. A proper
Englishwoman involved in matters of business and money-making?
Shocking."

"Not shocking, just . . . unusual." Breanna sighed. "We *do* have a lot
of catching up to do."

"Let's start with you." Anastasia leaned forward, propping her chin on
her hand. "Your letters left far more to the imagination than mine did.
For example, I know Uncle George brought you out two Seasons ago.
Yet you never went into any detail about the balls you attended, the gentlemen you met. And when I pressed you for details, you avoided the
subject altogether. Why is that?"

Breanna lowered her lashes, contemplated the folds of her gown.
"The truth? Or what everyone believes to be the truth?"

"I think you know the answer to that."

A nod. "I've never told this to a soul. Then again, I'm not in the habit
of discussing my private life with anyone—other than you." Breanna
inhaled sharply. "Father is very specific about his plans for my future.
Yes, he brought me out, but it was all a formality. My first Season was
scarcely under way when a business emergency—an alleged business
emergency," she amended, "necessitated our returning here, where we
stayed for the duration of the Season. Last year we didn't go to London

at all—supposedly because I was recovering from a severe bout of influenza. A bout of influenza, which, to be blunt, I never had."

Anastasia sat straight up, her gaze fixed on her cousin's veiled expression. "I don't understand. You're saying Uncle George is intentionally keeping you from meeting eligible noblemen? That makes no sense. Knowing him, I should think he'd be eager to marry you to the Prince Regent himself."

Breanna's lashes lifted, but she didn't smile. "If that were feasible, I'm sure Father would try to arrange it."

"Breanna, what aren't you telling me?" Anastasia felt the old surge of protectiveness swell inside her. "You know you can trust me," she added, when her cousin remained silent.

"Of course I do. It isn't that. Frankly, it's just that this whole situation is horribly embarrassing." Breanna laced her fingers together, stared down at them. "I feel like a prize horse."

"A prize horse." Anastasia's mind was racing, fitting pieces together. "Then you're being groomed for something." A pause. "Or some*one*."

"A very specific some*one*," Breanna acknowledged. "Father's plans are to wed me to the wealthiest and most successful nobleman he's acquainted with, and then share in his wealth and position."

"And who would that be?"

"The Marquess of Sheldrake."

"Oh." Anastasia's mouth snapped shut.

She needn't ask who the Marquess of Sheldrake was. He was the one and only Damen Lockewood.

She'd heard his name all her life; first, from her grandfather, who had begun his company at the same time that Damen's father had opened his first bank, and later from her father, who had developed his most powerful contacts in America thanks to Damen and the long-standing relationship between the Colbys and the Lockewoods.

According to Anastasia's father, it was Damen who'd always been the true genius of the family, even though in official terms he'd become head of the House of Lockewood only nine years ago, upon his father's death. Since that time, however, he'd made the House of Lockewood the most influential merchant bankers in England, if not perhaps the world. His advice and counsel were sought by nearly all the nations of Europe, and his business acumen and powerful connections with statesmen and financiers alike garnered his family its reputation.

So, yes, Anastasia knew who the Marquess of Sheldrake was.

She also knew her Uncle George. And, given that Lord Sheldrake was rich, titled, and acclaimed throughout Europe—not to mention serving on the Board of Directors at Colby and Sons—it stood to reason he'd be Uncle George's choice for a husband for Breanna.

Money. Wealth. Status. *And* enhancing his business. Those were the only things that mattered to Uncle George.

Obviously, he truly was the same man her father had disliked, had turned away from all those years ago.

"Stacie? Aren't you going to say anything?"

"I presume you've met the marquess," Anastasia replied. "Because I haven't. He was still at Oxford when we sailed for Philadelphia."

"Yes, I've met him. Many times, right here at Medford Manor. He advises Father on all his important business matters."

"And?"

"And . . . what?"

"What do you think of him?"

Breanna sighed. "He's very handsome, very charming, and—as you would expect—very intelligent."

"But . . . ?"

"But nothing. He kisses my hand when he arrives and again when he leaves. The rest of the time he spends talking with Father, except on those embarrassing occasions when Father coerces him into having dinner with us. On those nights, he sits across the table from me—doubtless feeling as uncomfortable as I—makes polite conversation, and says good night." A tiny shrug. "He's very gracious, considering how obvious Father's intentions are. Still, gracious and enamored are a far cry from each other. And the ability to exchange pleasantries is hardly a basis for a marriage. Although Father insists otherwise."

"Uncle George would insist the sky was green if that would convince you and Lord Sheldrake to marry," Anastasia stated bluntly. "What I want to know is what *you* think. You've spoken of the marquess's reaction to you. What about your reaction to him? Could you have feelings for this man?"

"Feelings." Breanna repeated the word as if it tasted foreign on her tongue. "I'm not sure how to answer that. Lord Sheldrake is a fine man. I like and admire him. Are those feelings?"

"No."

Breanna started at her cousin's adamant reply, the resolute lift of her chin, and burst out laughing. "Oh, Stacie, I've missed your audacity more than you can know. I'm so glad you're home." She dismissed the subject of Damen Lockewood with a wave of her hand. "Enough about me. Let's discuss you. You must have met dozens of gentlemen in Philadelphia."

Anastasia frowned, but took her cousin's cue, letting the subject drop—for now. "I did. And they were all pleasant enough. But I suppose I never thought of them as anything other than acquaintances passing through my life. Part of me always knew I'd be returning to England.

Papa knew that, too, which is why he never pressed me toward a commitment. Except once in a while when he'd remember that I was no longer eighteen. Then he'd push me, ever so gently, toward a particular gentleman." A pointed look. "Only I'd push back. I won't even consider marriage unless I fall in love. Neither should you."

A tentative knock on the bedchamber door interrupted their conversation.

"Yes?" Breanna called.

A young, uniformed girl poked her head in and glanced uneasily about as if she were afraid of intruding. "Pardon me . . ." Spying Breanna—and then Anastasia—her eyes widened in amazement. "My goodness."

Swiftly, Breanna rose and beckoned her in. "You're not losing your mind, Lizzy. Come in and meet my cousin. Anastasia—this is Lizzy. She assists Mrs. Charles at just about everything."

"Hello, Lizzy," Anastasia greeted her.

The young girl continued to stare. "I can't believe it. You're the same. I mean, you look the same. I mean . . ." Blushing, she dropped a curtsy. "I'm sorry. Pleasure to meet you, my lady."

"As it is to meet you."

"Did you need something, Lizzy?" Breanna pressed gently, as the maid continued to shake her head in wonder.

"Oh, yes." Lizzy stuck her hand in her apron pocket, fumbling until she'd extracted an envelope. "This just arrived for Lady Anastasia. Mrs. Charles asked me to bring it right up."

"Thank you." Anastasia stepped forward and took the letter with a smile. "And thank Mrs. Charles. I can't wait to see her again."

Nodding, Lizzy backed away until she butted up against the door. Reluctantly, she turned and slipped out.

"I think we're going to be getting a lot of that sort of reaction," Anastasia commented in amusement. She tore open the envelope.

"I suspect you're right." Breanna watched Anastasia read her message. "What is it?"

"A letter from Mr. Fenshaw. He's arranged the reading of Father's will for tomorrow. Uncle George and I are expected at his office at one o'clock." Anastasia paused, her brows knitting together in puzzlement. "He asks that you be there as well. Not for the will reading, but for another matter. A matter of great importance to both you and me. He's instructing us to bring the confidential gifts Grandfather gave us when we were six."

Her chin shot up, and her gaze met Breanna's. "The coins."

2

❧

$\mathcal{M}$r. Fenshaw's office was in an unassuming brick building on Chancery Lane in London. George Colby's carriage arrived there just before one—not a surprise, given that the viscount was never late—at which time he hurried Anastasia and Breanna out of the carriage and up the steps.

The slight bang that accompanied the closing of the door alerted the solicitor to their arrival, for he walked out of his inner office, slipping his spectacles onto his nose as he came forward to greet them.

"Good day, George, Breanna." He blinked as his pale gaze shifted to Anastasia. "Or is this Breanna?"

Anastasia shook her head. "No, Mr. Fenshaw. You were right the first time."

He blinked again. "Anastasia, goodness. The resemblance is astonishing." He bowed ever so slightly, giving her a gentle smile. "I don't suppose you remember me. But I remember you—an active little girl with a mind of her own. I'm terribly sorry about your parents. They were fine people, both of them."

"Yes, they were." A flash of memory flitted through Anastasia's mind; a gray-haired gentleman with red cheeks, thick spectacles, and a kind smile offering her a peppermint stick. "Actually, I do remember you. You had the most delicious peppermint sticks in London."

Fenshaw chuckled. "You did so enjoy that candy." He inclined his head, his expression compassionate. "How are you, my dear? Under the circumstances, that is."

"Not as devastated as I was a few months ago. I'm very fortunate to have Uncle George and Breanna. Returning to them and to Medford Manor has made my loss a little more bearable."

"I'm glad."

"I realize we're early, Fenshaw," George interrupted. "But if it's all right with you, we'll proceed. I have another business matter to see to this afternoon and I want to leave for Kent before dusk."

"As you wish." Fenshaw gestured them into his inner office. "Please, come in. Now that everyone is here, we can begin at once."

"Everyone?" George shot him a perplexed look as he crossed the threshold behind his daughter and niece. "Who else . . . ?" He broke off, staring in surprise at the tall, broad-shouldered man who rose to his feet as they entered. "Sheldrake. I don't understand."

Sheldrake? Now *that* brought Anastasia's head around quickly.

"Nor do I," the marquess was replying, shrugging his dark head. He extended his hand to shake George's. "All I know is that Fenshaw asked me to attend. So here I am." He glanced past George, then bowed politely at Breanna—whom he clearly had no difficulty recognizing, despite the presence of Anastasia by her side. "Breanna, how are you?"

"I'm well, my lord."

"I'm glad to hear that." Damen Lockewood's gaze flickered to Anastasia, and a slight smile curved his lips. "Ah, it seems I don't need an introduction."

"Nor do I," she returned. "Although in your case, it's your name I recognize, rather than your appearance." Eager to remedy that fact, Anastasia stepped forward, curtsying quickly so she could rise and inspect this man she'd heard so much about.

He was tall—over six feet—and powerfully built, with steel-gray eyes, a square jaw, and hard, patrician features. His raven-black hair was cut short at the nape, yet a few strands of it swept over his broad forehead—perhaps the only aspect of him that was even remotely disheveled. His blue tailcoat, silk waistcoat, and white shirt and trousers were of the latest style, worn with the casual elegance of a man who was accustomed to such attire. He carried himself with an air of self-assurance—not arrogance, exactly, but more an awareness that he knew his own capabilities and was not afraid to acknowledge them.

There was something infinitely intriguing about the Marquess of Sheldrake.

"I'm pleased to meet you, my lord," Anastasia continued, watching a corner of Damen Lockewood's mouth lift at her flagrant scrutiny. "My father spoke very highly of you. So did my grandfather. Which leads me to believe that your reputation as a shrewd banker and clever investment adviser is more than just a rumor."

A chuckle escaped his lips. "I'm relieved to hear that. My clients will be as well." He brought Anastasia's fingers to his lips. "Welcome home, my lady." His amusement vanished. "With regard to your father and grandfather, I had the utmost respect for them both. They were fine men and, as I remember, your mother was a lovely, gracious lady. Please accept my condolences on your loss."

"Thank you," she replied softly.

"It's always a pleasure to see you, Sheldrake," George spoke up. "But I still don't understand why you're here." He arched a questioning brow at Fenshaw.

"All of you, have a seat," Fenshaw responded, retreating behind his desk and extracting a folded document from his drawer. "I believe the next few minutes should answer all your questions."

Everyone complied, and Anastasia's interest in Damen Lockewood was forgotten as the finality of what was about to occur sank in. She steeled herself for yet another facet of this painful good-bye with her father, seating herself between Breanna and Lord Sheldrake, and clutching Breanna's hand as Mr. Fenshaw commenced the will reading.

" 'I, Henry Colby, being of sound mind, do hereby give, devise, and bequeath . . .' "

The words droned on, stating her father's last wishes, the provisions he'd made for his sizable assets. Initially, there were no surprises. Henry had left everything he possessed—including his funds in both England and America, together with his share in Colby and Sons—to his beloved Anne. And, in the event that his wife predeceased him, to his daughter Anastasia, and to her children thereafter.

With regard to Anastasia's proper guardianship: Should she choose to remain in Philadelphia upon his and Anne's death, and should she, at that time, be unmarried and under the age of twenty-one, appropriate instructions had been left with Frederick Carter, his American solicitor, and would be read and carried out by the same. Should she, however, choose to return to England as he believed she would, his brother George would assume the role of her guardian, to properly reintroduce her to English society and to do his best to ensure her future happiness and well-being. To that end, and for that sole purpose alone, the sum of ten thousand pounds had been deposited at the House of Lockewood, from which George could withdraw whatever amounts were necessary to provide for Anastasia's coming-out.

At that point, Mr. Fenshaw paused and looked up, something about the intensity of his expression, the gravity of his stare as he glanced from one of them to the other, making them all aware that something unexpected was about to occur.

"Continue, Fenshaw," George instructed, waving his hand impatiently so as to hear the remainder of his brother's provisions.

Fenshaw cleared his throat. " 'With regard to the above guardianship, I have several stipulations to make. First, Anastasia shall not be forced to abide any circumstances she finds intolerable; specifically, unduly harsh or unfeeling treatment, or excessive discipline that might result in squelching her spirit. Second, she shall never be forced to marry against her will, for while she needs a guardian's hand to guide her through the portals of society, she must be allowed to wed as her heart dictates.

" 'If either of these stipulations is violated, if Anastasia should find herself unhappy or ill-treated in any manner, she will advise Mr. Fenshaw of such, at which point alternate provisions will be made for her guardianship. Should that occur, the funds set aside for Anastasia's coming-out will be transferred to her newly appointed guardian and will no longer be available to my brother, George.

" 'Second, and more painful, is the matter of managing my daughter's newly acquired inheritance. It is no secret that my brother, George, and I do not agree about the importance of money, nor about the fervor through which it is earned or hoarded. Therefore, and excepting the sum set aside for Anastasia's coming-out, I specify that George's guidance and control over my daughter's life be limited only to nonfinancial matters. Specifically, in the event Anne and I should both die either before Anastasia is well and truly wed, or before her twenty-first birthday, I hereby appoint an administrator to oversee my daughter's inheritance, including her interest in Colby and Sons, and to advise her in her capacity as beneficiary. The man I have chosen to serve as that administrator is Damen Lockewood.

" 'His lordship is a man of great honor and integrity, as well as one whose knowledge of my assets is surpassed only by his wisdom at investing them. He shall, therefore, be the sole overseer of Anastasia's financial resources, until or unless she weds, at which point the responsibility shall be transferred to her husband, or in the event of her death without husband or issue prior to the age of twenty-one, at which point my funds shall be equally divided between my brother, George, and his daughter, Breanna.' "

Halting, Mr. Fenshaw took an uncomfortable sip of water from the glass perched on his desk. "That, in essence, is that."

Scarcely had the words been uttered when George rose to his feet. His movements were controlled, deliberate, but Anastasia could feel the anger emanating from him.

"Those stipulations are absurd, Fenshaw," he stated, pressing his palms flat on the desk and leaning toward the solicitor. "Henry must not have been himself when he devised them."

"I assure you, he was quite himself, my lord," Fenshaw replied with the kind of quiet certainty that indicated he'd readied himself for just such a reaction. "The will was drawn eleven years ago, just before Henry took his family to America. We've been in constant touch ever since, and he remained adamant that the will stay as is. Mr. Carter, Henry's

American solicitor, was advised to adhere to the terms and conditions as well, the only difference being he was given different guardianship provisions to comply with in the event Anastasia chose to remain in Philadelphia. However, in either case, the marquess was designated to administer Henry's estate for the next three months."

"Three months?" Damen spoke up for the first time, his tone probing rather than stunned. His expression was intent as he studied Mr. Fenshaw, his entire demeanor suggesting that he liked to be in possession of all the facts before he reacted.

"Yes," Anastasia heard herself reply, her voice sounding thin to her own ears. She was grappling with an onslaught of emotions besieging her all at once—emotions that required all her energy to sort out and master. There was bittersweet comfort that her father had taken the time to so carefully consider her future, weak-kneed relief that her uncle George would have minimal control over her life.

And bone-deep resentment that this total stranger sitting beside her would have ultimate say over her financial decisions. Especially given the plans she'd made in her father's memory.

Just pondering this unexpected constraint made her chin come up a mutinous notch. "Yes," she repeated, staring directly at Damen Lockewood. "Three months. I'll be twenty-one in October."

One dark brow lifted ever so slightly. "I see." His sharp gaze flickered past Anastasia and Breanna, focusing on George and assessing his obvious displeasure. "Does this provision of Henry's will present a problem for you, George?"

The marquess was certainly direct, Anastasia thought, automatically tensing as she awaited her uncle's response. No one spoke so boldly to George Colby—not without expecting to be cut off at the knees. Then again, few if any had Damen Lockewood's power.

She sneaked a peek to her left. Sure enough, her uncle was shaking his head, even as a muscle worked furiously in his jaw.

"No, Sheldrake," he managed to say. "A shock, perhaps, but not a problem."

"Are you certain?" Damen pressed. "Because if so, we'd best discuss it—now."

Curiously, Anastasia angled her gaze at the marquess, noting his unwavering stare and unruffled composure.

Doubtless her uncle George noted them, too.

"Consider it from my standpoint," he offered. "By appointing you to administer his funds, my brother has all but labeled me a financial buffoon. It's bad enough he intimated—in a less-than-subtle manner— that I might somehow mistreat Anastasia. But this . . ." He shook his head. "I always knew how deeply he disliked me, and how deeply he disapproved of my preoccupation with our business. But I never thought he'd doubt my judgment to the point where he'd refuse to grant me control, not only of his funds but of his interest in Colby and Sons. It's disgraceful."

Damen frowned. "I don't think Henry is doing any such thing. I think he wants an unbiased eye kept on the family business—which I do anyway, given my involvement in your company—and a knowledgeable banker who will advise Lady Anastasia in a manner that reflects the way her father would advise her were he alive. Dislike is not the issue here, George. Objectivity is."

Even as he spoke, Damen nodded his conviction. "Actually, I think Henry's decision is a prudent one, one that will ensure his daughter's happiness and continued prosperity, as well as that of his company. Remember, I have far more contacts in America than you. I can easily oversee the Philadelphian branch of Colby and Sons." A pointed cough, and Anastasia could swear the marquess was speaking more to her than to her uncle. "Besides, it's only for three months. After that, your niece will be mistress of her own fate." His lips twitched the tiniest bit. "Unless, of course, some gentleman sweeps her off her feet before that time and she decides to wed."

"I seriously doubt that will happen, my lord," Anastasia informed him, torn between annoyance at his absurd comment and admiration at the shrewd, concise way he had of explaining things so as best to soothe her volatile uncle's pride. "My feet are planted firmly on the ground and not likely to be swept anywhere."

This time Damen made no attempt to hide his grin. "Very well, then, three months it is." He made to rise. "Shall we set up an appointment to review your newly acquired assets?"

"Wait." Fenshaw forestalled Anastasia's reply, holding up a deterring palm. "There's another matter to be addressed before you leave."

Anastasia frowned. "I thought you said you'd concluded Papa's will reading."

"I have." The solicitor folded up the will and tucked it away, extracting a second document from inside his desk. "But now that you've returned to England, I have another legal matter to conclude." He paused, amending his own choice of words. "Actually, your return to England made this far easier for me. Had you opted to remain in Philadelphia, I would have had to summon you anyway. The terms must be carried out by you and Breanna prior to your respective twenty-first birthdays—which will occur in October and December of this year."

"Is this matter you're referring to the reason I was summoned to this meeting as well, Mr. Fenshaw?" Breanna asked.

"Yes, Breanna. It is."

"Henry left a document other than his will?" George demanded.

"No, my lord. Your father did."

George blinked, although neither Breanna nor Anastasia were stunned by Mr. Fenshaw's announcement. Given the wording of his written message, they'd expected something of this sort.

Fenshaw smoothed out the page, looking from one cousin to the other. "The late viscount's provisions are simple. Prior to his death, he set aside a sizable trust fund for each of you, to be inherited upon your respective twenty-first birthdays."

"How large a trust fund?" George asked.

"Fifty thousand pounds apiece."

"Good Lord." George sucked in his breath. "I was never told about this fund."

"Nor was your brother," Mr. Fenshaw advised him. "No one knew of the trust funds' existence but your father and myself. And, of course, Lord Sheldrake, whose bank holds the funds." His gaze flickered in Damen's direction, then leveled on Anastasia and Breanna. "There is a condition to your receiving this money. Many years ago, your grandfather gifted each of you with a coin. Do you recall that fact?"

"Yes, Mr. Fenshaw," Anastasia replied, answering for them both. "We do."

"And did you bring those coins with you today, as instructed?"

"No, Mr. Fenshaw, we did not."

The solicitor looked intrigued. "And why not?"

"Because when Grandfather gave us the coins, he told us to put them in a safe place—permanently. Which is what we've done."

"I see." Mr. Fenshaw turned a quill over in his hands. "That presents a problem."

"What coins?" George bit out. "What problem? What is this all about?"

"In a minute, my lord," Mr. Fenshaw assured him. He continued addressing the girls. "You say you don't have the coins with you. Let me explain why you need to produce them. At the time your grandfather gifted them to you, did he not tell you the coins had great significance, if not great value?"

"He did."

"You're about to discover what he meant. In order to collect your inheritances, you must both turn your coins over to me. At that time, I will sign the money over to you, due and payable on your twenty-first birthdays."

Neither girl moved.

"Breanna, what coin is Mr. Fenshaw referring to?" George demanded, turning to face his daughter. "You've never spoken a word to me of a coin."

Breanna paled but didn't falter. "Grandfather asked that we keep it between us. No one was to know about the coins but him, Stacie, and me."

Her father drew a harsh breath, looking as if he wanted to lash out at her for deceiving him, yet unwilling to do so given the advantageous outcome of her silence. "An odd arrangement," he said at last, his syllables clipped. "However, there's no point in berating you for something you did as a child. We'll simply go home, get the coin, and you can give it to Mr. Fenshaw, thus satisfying your grandfather's peculiar terms."

"I can't do that, Father."

George started. "What did you say?"

"We can't turn over the coins, uncle George," Anastasia confirmed. "Not even for an inheritance, no matter how vast. Grandfather's instructions were for us to keep the coins safe, and to never, under any circumstances, give them to anyone else." An uncomfortable pause. "Not even to our fathers."

Her uncle George swore softly under his breath.

Trying to ignore his anger, Anastasia focused her gaze on Mr. Fenshaw. "When I was six, I didn't fully understand Grandfather's reasons. But I think I do now. He wanted Breanna and me to hold fast to something he feared was doomed to die along with him: our family. The coins display our family crest on one side, and Medford Manor on the other. They're a symbol—one that Grandfather felt was up to us to sustain. He said nothing about trading them in; in fact, he emphasized the contrary, insisting we keep them with us always. Well, if those were his wishes, then keep them we will. Unless you can read something from that document that gives us reason to believe Grandfather changed his mind. But in all due respect, an inheritance isn't that reason."

"Your logic is ridiculous . . ." George began anew.

Again, Mr. Fenshaw held up his palm, never looking away from Anastasia. "You refuse to give me your coin?"

"Yes, Mr. Fenshaw, I do. Please understand. I mean you no disrespect. You're a dear family friend. But even if my own father were to have asked, I wouldn't have given him that coin. Not when Grandfather specifically told me not to."

"I see." Fenshaw averted his head, studied Breanna. "And you?"

Breanna straightened her shoulders and folded her hands rigidly in her lap—as defiant a gesture as Anastasia had ever seen her make. "I feel the same way Stacie does," she declared without hesitation. "My coin remains where it is."

"You're both mad," George exclaimed, coming to his feet. Briskly, he rubbed the back of his neck. "Fenshaw, let me talk to them. We still have several months before their birthdays. I'm certain they'll change their minds by then."

"There's no need," Fenshaw responded.

"Pardon me?"

"I said, there's no need. I've heard all I must." He set down his quill, interlacing his fingers on the desk. "Clearly, your grandfather was right about you. You have all the qualities he most prayed you would have, loyalty not being the least of them. You've more than passed his test."

"Test?" both girls asked simultaneously.

"Yes. The viscount did indeed want you to keep those coins, not only then but forever—for all the reasons Anastasia just enumerated. He wanted to be certain you couldn't be tempted to part with them, not even for a large inheritance." Fenshaw's round cheeks glowed. "A fabricated inheritance, I might add."

George seemed to wilt on his feet. "You mean, there is no inheritance?"

"Oh, there's an inheritance, just not the one I spoke of."

"You said fifty thousand pounds apiece."

"Yes. The actual inheritance is one the late viscount began amassing the day Anastasia was born, compiled from profits he made over the ensuing years. It totals over four hundred thousand pounds—two hundred thousand pounds apiece."

"Four hundred thousand . . ." George murmured faintly.

"Actually, it's closer to six hundred thousand pounds," Damen supplied. "Including all the interest that's accrued over the years."

George swallowed, his eyes a bit glazed as they shifted from Damen to Fenshaw. "You're saying my father kept that amount of money separate and apart from what he left Henry and me?"

"That's exactly what I'm saying," Fenshaw confirmed. "For reasons of his own, your father wanted that sum to go directly to his granddaughters, rather than by way of his sons. So he made provisions to do just that—and modified those provisions the day he gave your daughter and niece their coins. Had Breanna and Anastasia willingly turned over their coins for fifty thousand pounds apiece, the entire four—pardon me—six hundred thousand pounds would have been donated to charity. Further, if both the girls were to die childless, the remainder of the fortune would go to charity after their deaths."

Mr. Fenshaw pointed to the bottom of the document. "It's clearly stipulated here that the money is to pass only to Breanna and Anastasia, then on to their children; or, should either of them die childless, the full amount is to pass to the other cousin. Under no circumstances were either you or Lord Henry to have access to this fortune."

"He would donate it to charity," George repeated woodenly. "My own father would have given away his money rather than leave it to me."

"To you *or* Lord Henry," Fenshaw reminded him. "Sir, I don't think the late viscount's decision was meant as an indignity, either to you or your brother. It was simply his way of ensuring the continuity of the Colby family."

Anastasia was scarcely listening at this point, so dazed was she by the steps her grandfather had taken. The six hundred thousand pounds was staggering enough. But what it represented—his faith in her and Breanna, in their ability to preserve what their fathers could not—*that* was even more overwhelming.

"Stacie?" Breanna touched her sleeve, speaking in an undertone so as to keep their conversation separate and apart from her father's discussion with Mr. Fenshaw. "Are you as astounded as I am?"

"I'm reeling," Anastasia replied. She inclined her head toward her cousin. "Breanna, do you realize how sure Grandfather was that you and I could do what our fathers could not?"

Solemnly, Breanna nodded.

"We won't let him down," Anastasia said fiercely. "Not under any circumstances." She tensed as her uncle snapped out a few final words to Mr. Fenshaw, reminding herself that—on the subject of not-under-any-circumstances—her uncle's resentment was at the top of the list. Combating it was going to be a formidable challenge, indeed.

"Pardon me, my lady." Damen Lockewood's voice broke into her thoughts.

Anastasia pivoted in her chair, watching as the marquess rose, regarding her from beneath hooded lids.

"I have two meetings I'm already late for," he informed her in a crisp, businesslike tone. "Before I leave, I'd like to set up that appointment regarding your inheritance. Would tomorrow at eleven be convenient?"

Feeling dwarfed by his height and less than pleased by that decided disadvantage, Anastasia stood as well, tilting back her head to meet his gaze. "Tomorrow?" A rush of irrational resentment surged anew. What was the man's hurry? Did he hope to quickly rid her of all financial responsibilities, take over full authority of her financial investments?

If so, he was going to be in for the surprise of a lifetime.

"I admire your initiative, my lord," she replied coolly. "You're certainly eager to assume your role as my business adviser. By the way, how is it possible to be late for two meetings at the same time?"

He looked more amused than put off. "The House of Lockewood has its main offices right here in London. The building runs almost the full length of Bishopsgate Street. Inside are many offices in which I confer with clients. Sometimes I meet with one while another reviews documents I've prepared." His lips curved. "I assure you, I give my full attention to each and every person I advise. You won't be neglected."

Anastasia had a strong urge to strike him. "Trust me, my lord, being neglected was the least of my worries. As for our meeting, it will have to wait. I can't possibly impose upon Uncle George to return to London again tomorrow."

"Understandable." The marquess acknowledged the obstacle she'd erected, never breaking stride as he scaled it. "Fine. I'll ride to Kent, then. Expect me tomorrow morning at eleven."

The more insistent he became, the deeper Anastasia dug in her heels. "That's very considerate of you. But I have no need of your assistance. Rest assured, I won't squander my funds away by morning. And I don't want to inconvenience my uncle."

"Ah, of course not. Let's address that issue, shall we?" Without awaiting her reply, the marquess glanced over her head, assessing George's fervent conversation with Mr. Fenshaw and interrupting it with the slightest lift of his brows. "Pardon me, George. I need to meet with your niece about her inheritance. Would it be possible for me to drop by Medford Manor at eleven o'clock tomorrow?"

"H-m-m? Why, yes, I suppose so." George's forehead was still deeply furrowed, his lips thinned in a tight line of annoyance as he contemplated the morning's revelations.

Abruptly, Damen's request sank in, and George whipped out his timepiece, blinking in surprise when he saw it was nearing three o'clock.

"Actually your visiting tomorrow morning would work out nicely," he announced with a frown. "As I mentioned earlier, I have another meeting this afternoon—one I'm already an hour late for, and which I suspect will go on for some time. Your riding out in the morning would ease my time constraints. If it's agreeable with you, I'll have my driver take Breanna and Anastasia back to Kent directly from here, while I stay on to conduct my business. After that, I can spend the night in Town and ride home with you tomorrow."

Lord Sheldrake nodded. "That's perfectly acceptable."

"Good." For the first time since entering Mr. Fenshaw's office, Uncle George looked pleased by an outcome. "We'll arrive at Medford Manor by eleven o'clock. You'll stay for lunch, of course."

"How can I resist one of Mrs. Rhodes's fine meals?" the marquess responded, gathering up his portfolio and putting a purposeful end to the discussion. "So, on that pleasant note, I'll be on my way. Fenshaw, I'll be in touch. George, Breanna—I'll see you both tomorrow. And Lady

Anastasia—" He bowed, a corner of his mouth lifting as his gaze found hers. "It was a pleasure meeting you. Oh, and by the way," he added in an offhanded tone—although Anastasia could swear she saw a baiting look flash in those steel-gray eyes—"I wasn't concerned about your squandering your funds, at least not for the next three months. You can't. You'd need my signature to do so."

3

❧

*T*he Thames was bustling as the business day came to a close.

Iron cranes loaded and unloaded cargo from the various ships tied up in the harbor, and a stream of workers shuttled freight into the slew of waiting warehouses.

This surge of activity was clearly visible from the offices of Lyman Shipping Company. Overlooking the river, the company's spacious front room window provided a lovely view of Westminster Bridge and of the dignified cluster of buildings surrounding Westminster Hall.

The charm of the view was lost on George Colby.

Scowling, he peered into the gathering dusk, feeling choked by fate and its unexpected limitations.

"I expected to be paid today, Medford," Edgar Lyman reminded him for the second time, his voice fraught with tension. Abandoning his chair, the stocky man with the square jaw and watery blue eyes paced about his office, palms sweating as he rubbed them together. "I need that money."

"I know. I thought I'd have it." George ran a hand through his hair, then rubbed the nape of his neck in frustration. "Unfortunately, the cash I expected to come into will be delayed—temporarily."

"Then the shipment will have to be delayed—temporarily."

"The hell it will." George's head whipped around, his eyes darkening with anger. "Don't threaten me, Lyman. You won't like the results."

"I wasn't threatening you." Lyman recoiled from George's menacing tone, taking a precautionary step backward. "I'm just stating a fact. Expenses are mounting. So are risks. Meade's pressuring me. He wants higher wages. Says there's more at stake now."

"Then deal with him," George snapped. "Meade's your problem, not mine. But that merchandise is expected. Arrangements have been made to receive it. It will go out—*on* schedule. I don't care if you have to use your personal funds to get it there. I've certainly spent enough of mine. You'll make your profit. You always do. So does Meade—more than that browbeating son of a bitch is worth. Now get that shipment out by week's end."

A resigned nod. "Fine. I'll take care of it. But with regard to payment . . ."

"I said, I'm working on it. An unexpected obstacle's been thrown in my path."

"An insurmountable obstacle?"

George's lips thinned into a grim line. "No obstacle is insurmountable. I'll either bypass it or remove it. Just as Meade is your problem, this is mine. And I'll resolve it. Soon." He walked to the door. "Contact me when the shipment reaches port."

Alone in his London Town home, George abandoned the facade of self-assurance. Cursing under his breath, he poured himself a brandy, tossing it off in three swallows.

Damn life and its ugly, unforeseen twists. Damn Anne for giving birth to that little chit. Damn Henry for his exasperating stipulations. And now, the most stunning twist of all—damn their father for leaving a bloody fortune to two stupid girls who hadn't a notion what to do with it.

Six hundred thousand pounds. *Six hundred thousand pounds.* Every pence of which should have been his. Instead, he hadn't even known of its existence. And, now that he did know, he'd been advised—in the very same breath—that he couldn't touch a single pound of it. Not now. Not ever.

Furiously, he refilled his goblet, his thoughts jumping from his father to his brother.

Henry's estate wasn't worth a third of their father's unexpected trust fund, but it was a sizable estate nonetheless. More important, it was money George had counted on having access to. Why else would he have invited his niece to come live at Medford Manor? Oh, he'd expected Henry to have found a way to limit his power, probably by directing Fenshaw to keep an eye on things, possibly even assigning the solicitor some say in the management of Anastasia's inheritance. Neither of those restrictions would have amounted to a major stumbling block. The situation would simply have required a touch of creativity—something George was more than capable of providing. But for Henry to snatch his inheritance away entirely? To leave full control of it to a nonfamily member, no matter how trusted? That was a blatant slap in the face—and a major impediment to his plan.

Which brought him to the man Henry had entrusted his funds to:
Damen Lockewood.

Having the marquess in charge was indeed a double-edged sword. On
the one hand, George felt confident that his own relationship with
Sheldrake was good—good enough that he might be able to use it to
make inroads to Henry's money. On the other hand, Sheldrake was smart
as a whip *and* ethical—especially when it came to financial matters. So
how the hell could George avail himself of Henry's estate without alerting the marquess to his intentions?

Then there was the additional matter of Colby and Sons, which
George had fully anticipated having to himself after today's will reading.
Not directly, of course. He'd second-guessed Henry's decision to
bequeath his shares of the company to Anastasia. Nevertheless, that
wouldn't have posed a major problem. After all, George's grieving niece
was living under his roof now. And things being what they were, he was
confident he could have convinced her, with relative ease, to let him represent her interests in the family business. But now, with Sheldrake managing her shares? George would have to tread very carefully. As it was,
the marquess was integrally involved in their company. This new duty
would make his role that much more pivotal—and the profits that much
more difficult for George to skim.

He *had* to get his hands on those profits—fast.

That realization brought him full circle, back to the ultimate shock:
his father's six hundred thousand pounds. The old man had always been
too bloody sentimental. But to leave a fortune of that size to a pair of
women? Mere girls at that, he reminded himself. The pathetic old fool
must have snapped altogether.

George's fist struck the sideboard. None of this was doing him any
good. The bottom line was that his hands were tied. He had no access to
his father's trust fund and—thanks to Henry—he'd also be hard-pressed
to get at the remaining Colby resources. Dammit, he needed that cash.
And he needed it now.

But how to get it, without answering any questions or arousing any
suspicions . . . now *that* was his dilemma. He'd have to go about things
slowly. And the logical approach was to begin with what was legally
available to him.

Anastasia's coming-out funds.

True, it was only ten thousand pounds. But it *was* a start. And a start
was all he needed—for now.

Late morning sunlight trickled into Anastasia's bedchamber, a sticky
summer breeze heralding yet another July day.

Breanna sat, perched at the edge of the carved armchair, watching as

Anastasia brushed her hair at the dressing table. "Stacie, what is it?" she asked. "You've been frowning since we left Mr. Fenshaw's office yesterday. What's troubling you so much?"

"H-m-m?" Anastasia looked up, realizing Breanna had spoken to her. "I'm sorry. What did you say?"

"The same thing I said to you last night before we went to bed. You're obviously upset. Is it grief? Are you missing your parents? Did yesterday's will reading worsen the pain? If so, tell me. I'd like to help."

Anastasia lowered her eyes, staring at the handle of her brush with a wistful expression. "If anyone could help, it would be you. And, yes, I miss Mama and Papa. I always will. That's what's weighing on my heart. But my mind—now that's another story."

"And what story is that? Is it the money Grandfather left us? Are you worried over how he'd want us to spend it?"

"Oddly enough, no. I have a feeling we'll know just what to do with that money when the time comes. I think Grandfather believed that, too."

"I agree." Breanna fell silent, waiting expectantly.

Anastasia chewed her lip, met her cousin's gaze in the looking glass, and sighed. "Actually, it's the money Father left me that's on my mind. Or, more specifically, the man who'll be overseeing how I spend it." She lay down her brush, turning to face Breanna. "It's nearly eleven o'clock," she blurted. "Before I force myself to go downstairs and attend this meeting, tell me more about Damen Lockewood."

"Ah." Breanna propped her chin on her hand, regarding her cousin with amused interest. "Damen Lockewood. That was my third guess. He really rankled you, didn't he?"

"Why do you say that?"

"Oh, I don't know—probably because you sprang up and confronted him like a hissing cat about to strike."

A rueful grin. "Was I *that* obvious?"

"Let's say you weren't subtle."

"Wonderful." Anastasia rolled her eyes. "Now I'll not only have an arrogant, opinionated overseer, I'll have an arrogant, opinionated overseer who dislikes me."

"I didn't say he dislikes you," Breanna refuted, tucking a stray ringlet back into her smooth knot of upswept hair. "In fact, if I had to wager a guess, I'd say he was more fascinated by you than annoyed. You are unique, Stacie. What's more, I doubt many women challenge Lord Sheldrake's authority, much less his skill."

"I didn't challenge his skill." In one impatient motion, Anastasia gave up trying to arrange her own auburn waves, letting them tumble unimpeded down her back. "I'm sure he's every bit the financial genius Papa claimed him to be. But that doesn't mean I want him as a guardian—monetary or otherwise."

"So I gathered." Breanna gave a quizzical shrug. "Why not? Surely you can benefit from his knowledge."

"I'm sure I can. But I'm *not* sure I want to." Rising, Anastasia shook out the folds of her lime green day dress. "What do you know of him—besides the fact that he's brilliant, wealthy, and, if Uncle George has his way, your future husband?"

A flush stained Breanna's cheeks. "I wouldn't place much faith in the last. As for the rest, yes, he's both brilliant and wealthy. He's also charming, handsome, and polite. I'm not sure how much more I can tell you. From what little I saw during my sole London Season, I suspect he's never at a loss for female companionship. On the other hand, I truly believe business is his primary passion—and his primary pastime. While he did attend a few balls that Season, he didn't seem particularly enthused and he didn't stay long. I only danced with him twice. As for other women . . ."

"What type of investor is he?"

Breanna blinked. "Pardon me?"

"When he invests your father's money, is he narrow-minded in his choices, rigid in his approach? Or is he willing to try new things, hear new ideas?"

"How on earth would I know?"

Anastasia's hand balled into a frustrated fist, her arm helplessly slicing the air before falling to her side. "I suppose you wouldn't. But I need to. I have specific ideas for how that money should be invested—how Papa would *want* it to be invested. And I must know if . . ."

A knock on the door interrupted them.

"Come in," Anastasia called.

"Pardon me." Kate, the rotund, smiling, middle-aged woman who'd been assigned—in whatever limited capacity her new mistress would allow—the role of Anastasia's lady's maid, entered the room. "The viscount and Lord Sheldrake have arrived," she informed Anastasia. "They're awaiting you in the yellow salon." A concerned, motherly look. "Shall I fix your hair, m'lady? I can put it up like Lady Breanna's, or weave some pearls through the crown and—"

"Thank you, no, Kate." Anastasia waved away the suggestion. "I'll just tie it back. That should suffice. After all, I'm going to a meeting, not a ball." So saying, she snatched up a satin ribbon, tugging it into place as she walked. "Very well. Let's get this over with." She glanced at Breanna. "Are you coming?"

Her cousin stood, a spark lighting her eyes. "I wouldn't miss it for the world."

* * *

Both George and Lord Sheldrake rose to their feet when Anastasia and Breanna entered the salon. Anastasia's gaze bypassed her uncle altogether, going straight to the man who, for the next three months, held her financial future in his hands.

The marquess was as impeccably groomed and mannered today as he had been yesterday, his commanding presence—those bold good looks and that profound self-assurance—seeming to fill the room. Alongside his chair was propped the same portfolio he'd carried to Mr. Fenshaw's office yesterday, only this morning it was twice as thick as it had been then.

"Excellent," George pronounced, nodding his approval at the girls' promptness. "You're both here." His glance flickered from Anastasia to Breanna and back again—and Anastasia had the distinct impression he hadn't a notion which of them was his daughter.

"Ah, Breanna." Clearly, Lord Sheldrake didn't suffer from the same affliction. He stepped forward and walked straight to Breanna, bowing and kissing her hand. "Good morning. You look lovely, as always." He turned to Anastasia, his expression altering from cordial to assessing. "Good morning, my lady. I trust you slept well and are ready for our meeting?"

Staring into those probing silver-gray eyes, Anastasia wondered if he was taunting her or merely making light conversation. "I slept soundly, my lord," she assured him. "I'm quite rested and ready to discuss my inheritance."

"Good. Then let's get started." The marquess turned to George. "Where can your niece and I meet in private?"

The viscount's jaw dropped. "In private? I don't think—"

"You know very well how I do business, George," Lord Sheldrake broke in quietly. "My discussions with my clients are confidential. As of yesterday, Lady Anastasia is my client. Now, where can she and I meet?"

George inhaled sharply, then gave a terse nod. "Why don't you stay right here? Breanna and I will busy ourselves elsewhere and meet you in the dining room in, say, an hour."

"Fine." The marquess moved back to his chair, gathered up his portfolio and removed some papers, placing them on the end table alongside the sofa. That done, he drew himself up, hands clasped behind him, and shot George an expectant look.

Reluctantly, the viscount signaled Breanna, then strode out of the salon. Breanna followed suit, but hovered in the doorway for an instant, tossing Anastasia an I-can't-wait-to-hear-the-details look. Then she followed her father into the hallway, shutting the door in her wake.

Lord Sheldrake waited until the quiet click heralded the privacy he'd sought.

"Have a seat," he instructed Anastasia, gesturing offhandedly at the mahogany settee opposite the sofa. Brow furrowed, he resumed perusing his stack of papers. "This shouldn't take long. I'll explain all your father's assets to you as simply as I can, then give you my recommendations with regard to investments. Or, if you'd prefer, I can just take care of things myself, and not trouble you at all. Whatever your preference, I will, of course, keep records of all the transactions I conduct on your behalf in the event you want to see where your inheritance has been invested and how its value grows."

"Stop." Anastasia held up her palm, certain she'd scream if he continued for one more moment. "First, you needn't exert yourself searching for simple words of explanation. I am very familiar with financial terms. I'm also well acquainted with the options available to me—especially those I'd be interested in pursuing. In addition, given that the money in question is mine and not yours, I insist not only on being apprised but on approving each and every investment decision involving my inheritance. And last, *I* have some recommendations to offer *you.*"

Damen Lockewood's head came up, and he stared at her, utter astonishment written all over his face. "Do you now?" he murmured at length. Abruptly, his lips twitched. "I suppose that shouldn't surprise me."

"But it does."

"Yes, it does—this time. Which is quite a coup for you, given that I'm rarely caught off-guard. However, what I *never* am is stupid—stupid enough to make the same mistake twice. So, from here on in, I won't be surprised."

He tossed down his papers and folded his arms across his chest—scrutinizing her in a way that indicated he was abandoning his customary tactics. Then he advanced toward her, a challenging gleam in his eye. "Very well, my lady. I suggest we try a different approach. You tell me what you already know of your assets, what additional information you need, and how and where you suggest investing them. First, I'll listen. Then I'll give you my input, after which decisions will be made. How would that be?"

Anastasia's brows rose. "You'd really agree to that kind of exchange? You'd actually hear me out?"

"I would." A slow smile spread across the marquess's face. "It appears that now *I've* surprised *you.*"

"I have to admit you have. Somehow, I didn't expect you to be so . . . so . . ."

"Open-minded?" he supplied.

Anastasia nodded. "Yes. Open-minded."

"Well, I am—sometimes. Other times, I'm every bit as rigid as you anticipated I'd be. Which quality I demonstrate depends upon the wisdom of what I hear. Fair enough?"

"I suppose it will have to be."

One dark brow shot up. "Meaning?"

"Meaning you were careful to say that decisions would be made. I notice you didn't qualify who would make those decisions."

A corner of Lord Sheldrake's mouth lifted. "No, I didn't, did I?" He chuckled, gesturing toward the sofa. "Nonetheless, I did agree to listen to your ideas, if not to defer to them. So, can we sit down, or must we continue to do battle standing up?"

Reluctantly, Anastasia gathered up her skirts and crossed over, perching at the edge of the settee and waiting, stiff-backed, until the marquess had followed suit. Only after he'd lowered himself to the adjoining sofa did she relax. Bad enough that the man towered over her when they were both on their feet. But with him standing and her seated, she felt dwarfed by his size and power—a perception that made her feel at a distinct disadvantage, something she was unwilling to allow.

"I'm neither armed nor dangerous," he interrupted, as if reading her mind.

"I realize that." Anastasia started, taken aback by the magnitude of his insight. She eyed him intently. Armed? Dangerous? That was a matter of opinion. This man needed no weapon to be a formidable adversary. He was intelligent, powerful, and self-assured. He also had an impressive array of contacts and an unrivaled level of success—both of which she intended to profit from, and which had factored heavily into the amended strategy she'd devised last night.

"Is it true you privately convene with kings all over the Continent to offer them financial counsel?" she blurted out, inspired by the possibilities her own thoughts had conjured up. "Is your courier system really faster than that of any sovereign? Is that one of the reasons for your success? Do you get advance information that gives you an edge in determining your own investments, as well as those of your clients'?"

At first, amusement flickered in his eyes, but as the questions continued to be fired, it faded, eclipsed by a hint of wariness. "What inspired this deluge of questions?" he asked when she'd paused for air. "Is it idle curiosity? Or is it more? Because if you're prying, I don't discuss my clients or the nature of their business ventures with anyone. And if you're verifying my credentials, I assure you, I'm as qualified as your father deemed me to be."

Anastasia couldn't help but feel a grudging admiration for the marquess's integrity. "Part harmless curiosity, my lord," she assured him candidly. "And part personal interest. I wasn't doubting you, nor was I prying. I'm simply fascinated by how extensive your dealings are, and how notable your contacts. As I told you yesterday, your reputation precedes you."

The wariness vanished as quickly as it had come. "In that case, I'll merely say thank you." A twinkle. "I'm glad I've piqued your interest— and equally glad I've impressed you."

"I didn't say I was impressed," Anastasia amended, her own eyes dancing. "Not yet, anyway. You'll have to work harder to accomplish that feat."

To her surprise, Lord Sheldrake laughed aloud. "You, Lady Anastasia, are quite a handful. Physical resemblance aside, it's hard to believe you and Breanna are related."

"Breanna has had more restrictions than I," Anastasia said, defending her cousin swiftly. "I was fortunate. I lived in America, and my parents encouraged my curiosity and, to a great extent, my independence. Breanna's situation is quite different."

"Yes, I know. Quite different." The marquess pursed his lips, diverting the subject before Anastasia had a chance to figure out his underlying meaning. "Tell me, what makes you think I meant that as a compliment?"

"Pardon me?"

"You rushed to Breanna's defense, and I commend you on your loyalty. Still, what makes you think I find being a handful an admirable trait?"

"*You* might not, my lord, but *I* do."

Again, laughter rumbled from Lord Sheldrake's chest. "I rather expected as much."

"Good. I'm glad I didn't surprise you," she returned with a perky grin. "That would have violated your one-surprise-per-person rule."

"True." Schooling his features, Lord Sheldrake leaned back and crossed one long leg over the other in a deceptively casual stance. "Tell me what you had in mind for your father's inheritance."

Anastasia realized instantly that the abrupt change in subject was meant to catch her off-guard. Well, it wouldn't. She was too well-prepared with this particular response. She'd rehearsed it half the night, modifications and all.

Gripping the folds of her gown, she raised her chin, met the marquess's gaze head-on. "What I have in mind is twofold: to invest directly in America's expanding industry, and to open a bank that will meet a growing nation's demands—one that will make an enormous profit in the process."

Lord Sheldrake's expression never changed. "Were these your father's ideas?"

"I believe they were his wishes. But the ideas are mine."

"I see." He cleared his throat. "There are already banks in America."

"Not like the one I have in mind. Mine would be as vital to America as the House of Lockewood is to Europe. Which is why I want your cooperation—not only as my adviser, but as my partner."

Dead silence.

Then: "You want me to co-invest in this endeavor?"

"Yes. Although, to be blunt, I never considered the idea until yesterday. I intended to do this on my own. Then, when I found out that Papa had appointed you to oversee my funds, my mind began to race. Your insights, your contacts, my firsthand knowledge of the States; abruptly, it struck me that my bank—*our* bank—would be twice as successful, twice as quickly, if we combined our resources. Surely you can see what a splendid opportunity it is?"

Lord Sheldrake rubbed his palms together, contemplating his answer. "Lady Anastasia," he said at last, "part of being a sound investor is avoiding putting all your eggs in one basket. Another is determining which ventures have a higher percentage of success, and which have greater risks and somewhat uncertain rewards. England and the Continent offer both stability and proven opportunities. The colonies are still a vast unknown."

Anastasia's jaw set. "They're not colonies anymore, my lord. They're states. And just because you've always done things one way doesn't mean there isn't a better way to do them. It only means you have yet to find that other way. Reluctance breeds complacency, which often leads to failure."

An astute glance. "You've rehearsed this argument well."

"I had all night to do so. I anticipated your reluctance since yesterday afternoon when Mr. Fenshaw proclaimed you my financial adviser. I just didn't know whether that reluctance would extend only to investing your own money or whether you'd be dubious of the entire notion. I suppose now I have my answer."

Lord Sheldrake raised his head, met her stare. "I suppose you do. But I want you to understand why I'm reluctant. It's not because I refuse to explore new avenues, nor because I resent your suggestions. It's because I'm not convinced this is the right time to do what you're suggesting. In a few years, maybe. But not now. Not with a country that's still as wobbly on its legs as a new colt—a country, I might add, with whom we've just been at war."

"A few years? That makes the issue rather moot, since I won't need to consult with you then. Nor will I need to do so in a few months, for that matter." Anastasia's hand balled into a fist, pressed into the brocaded cushion of the settee. "But I don't want to wait a few months. I intend to get started right away—for my father. He was a man of great foresight; he welcomed new, creative business challenges. Several times we talked about expanding the role of Colby and Sons in the States, finding a way to lend capital to the growing number of merchants we did business with. He would have been the first to applaud my endeavors."

"I agree that Henry was very enterprising. But he was also smart. He wouldn't have suggested throwing away money. Nor would he have poured all his assets into one risky investment."

Anastasia bit back her disappointment, reminding herself that this was only a setback, not a defeat. "We could argue this point all day. You see things one way; I, another." She rose. "You've given me your answer. You won't be taking part in my venture. Very well. I'll manage it alone. Father's estate is worth over a hundred fifty thousand pounds, and that's not including his home in England and his home in Philadelphia, nor his shares in Colby and Sons. Tell me exactly how much of the estate is in cash assets which are, therefore, immediately available to me."

"None of it."

Anastasia's head jerked around, and she stared at the marquess. "Pardon me?"

"Your father's cash assets total close to two hundred thousand pounds—*none* of which is available to you." Calmly, Lord Sheldrake unfolded himself from the sofa and came to his feet. "My job is to advise you—and to manage your funds. I can't, in good conscience, allow you to squander away your inheritance."

Twin spots of color stained Anastasia's cheeks. "Are you saying you're refusing me access to my own money?"

"No, I'm merely saying I'm refusing to let you invest that money in an American bank." He regarded her intently, clearly aware that she was angry and, therefore, trying to soften the blow. "I'm not doing this to be cruel or tyrannical. I hope you believe that. But if you don't . . ." A shrug. ". . . that's something we'll both have to live with. I won't compromise my integrity just to convince you that my intentions are honorable. Think of it this way: I can't stop you forever. Starting in October, you'll be overseeing your own funds, and you can invest as you choose. I only hope that three months gives me enough time to influence your thinking; that, with a little financial guidance from me, you'll have regained your senses by then."

"Or perhaps I'll have used those three months to influence other businessmen, those who aren't afraid to try something new by financing my venture," Anastasia shot back, feeling angry and frustrated and resentful—more so because she wasn't wholly sure where those emotions stemmed from. Oh, she was furious at being thwarted, at having someone else in control of her life. But she was also bothered by Lord

Sheldrake's rejection, more bothered than she'd anticipated. And she couldn't help but feel a grudging surge of admiration at his utterly principled way of doing business—even if she did loathe the outcome.

So who was she angry at, him or herself?

An intrigued spark had lit the marquess's eyes. "You intend to seek out other investors?"

"Given your negative response, yes."

His lips twitched. "I wish you luck."

Damn, the man was arrogant.

"This meeting is over, my lord." Anastasia gathered up her skirts and started to walk by him. "I appreciate your time, and your integrity. I *don't* share your opinions."

Unexpectedly, he caught her arm as she passed. "And I respect your passion for this venture. Can we agree to disagree, or is that too unconventional a notion, even for you?"

Anastasia froze, uncomfortably aware of the strong hand gripping her forearm, more aware of her own powerful, if confusing, reaction to it. Half of her wanted to yank herself away, the other half to stay precisely as she was, to explore the odd sensations elicited by Lord Sheldrake's touch. Both reactions were too extreme, too irrational, given the inconsequence of the contact, the casual nature of their acquaintance. Perhaps it was just the fervor of their discussion, the intensity of their differing opinions. And yet . . .

Slowly, her gaze lifted to meet his. "No, my lord," she replied, trying to read his thoughts, and to understand her own. "It's not too unconventional for me. As of now, we agree to disagree."

"Excellent."

Was it her imagination, or did his grip tighten? She wasn't certain. What she was certain of was that his gaze narrowed, probed hers, and that despite the finality of his tone, he made no move to release her.

A heartbeat later, he spoke. "I, in return, promise that I won't interfere with your efforts to win over England's businessmen. If you find someone eager to invest—wonderful. I not only won't stand in his way, I'll applaud your abilities of persuasion."

Anastasia felt an unwilling smile tug at her lips. "Is that a challenge, my lord?"

His teeth gleamed. "And if it is?"

"Then I accept." Her gaze shifted back to her arm, where she could actually feel the warmth of his fingers seeping through her gown, singeing her skin with an unknown and strangely disconcerting heat. "We'd best go to lunch," she suggested, her tone oddly strained.

Slowly, he nodded. "Yes. We'd best."

4

$\mathcal{L}$unch was an hour and a half of delicious food, fine wine, and tension so thick you could cut it with a knife.

It wasn't for lack of conversation. George saw to that. Seated at the head of the table, he scarcely let a moment pass before directing yet another financial question at Damen Lockewood. The marquess, seated on George's left, answered every question, his gaze politely encompassing not only George but Breanna—who sat directly across the table from him—and occasionally Anastasia, seated to her cousin's right. For his part, George never spared a glance at either girl, keeping his body angled toward the marquess, and his eyes, which seemed overly bright, glued to him as well. George's voice and expression were strained, and Anastasia suspected he was still peeved that he hadn't been privy to her financial advisory session.

She stifled a smile. How relieved her uncle would be if he knew he'd missed nothing of consequence. No grand business ventures had been planned, no innovative ways to invest her inheritance had been explored. To the contrary, other than learning the value of her father's estate and having Lord Sheldrake shoot down her investment plans, the entire meeting had been immaterial.

She looked up at that moment, met the marquess's scrutinizing gaze, and instantly averted her eyes.

Perhaps not *entirely* immaterial.

"Before we finish dessert, I have a bit of news I'd like to share." George leaned forward, for the first time addressing everyone at the table. "I've given Anastasia's situation a great deal of thought. It was Henry's wish that I bring her out, introduce her to all the right people. I've decided to do just that."

With a tight smile of self-approval, he continued. "I'm going to host a house party—a *substantial* house party—in Anastasia's honor. Several hundred people will be invited. It will include two or three days of diversions, including a grand ball to introduce Anastasia to high society. My niece will be brought out in true Colby style, with all the grace and distinction Henry would have wanted."

Anastasia started. This was the *last* thing she'd expected, especially knowing her uncle as she did. His mind was preoccupied with business, not parties, and his motives were never selfless—even if he was using her father's money to pay for all this. The bottom line was, what possible benefit could holding an event of this magnitude have for him?

"Uncle George," she responded carefully. "That's really not necessary. I appreciate your sentiments, but I don't think Papa expected . . ."

"Nonsense." George waved away her protest. "You're the only daughter of my only brother. I insist." He turned to Damen Lockewood, who was watching him with an unreadable expression on his face. "What do you think of the idea, Sheldrake?"

The marquess cleared his throat. "I think it has merit. After all, Henry set aside ten thousand pounds for this occasion. So there are more than enough funds available, as I'm sure you know." A pointed pause ensued—enough to make Anastasia wonder if Lord Sheldrake was thinking along exactly the same lines as she was. "When did you want to hold this party?"

George shifted in his chair, noticeably flustered by the marquess's reference to his source of capital. "As soon as possible. In a week, perhaps. I'll send out the invitations this very day."

"A week?" Anastasia echoed. "Isn't that a little ambitious? From what I recall, Mama and Papa used to receive invitations to parties of this size at least a fortnight in advance. That was the only way to ensure none of the balls would conflict."

"During the Season, that's true," her uncle returned. "But the Season is long past. So we don't run the risk of such conflicts."

"Yes," Damen agreed. "Which brings up a different problem. Much of the *ton* is either in Brighton, Bath, or traveling abroad. Why not wait for the fall when everyone is back?"

"Because by then, Anastasia will have endured two months of loneliness and grief," George replied with a generosity of spirit that nearly made Anastasia gag. "This way, she'll remember her first summer here as a joyous one, filled with laughter and festivities." He gave a careless shrug. "The majority of those I know have remained in England for the summer. As for Brighton and Bath—neither are too far from here to travel."

"I suppose not." Lord Sheldrake brought his wineglass to his lips, savoring the final drops. "Fine. A house party it is."

"Excellent." George sank back in his chair. "I'd appreciate your advice with regard to the guest list. I want the most influential members of society here."

"Influential—does that include businessmen?" Anastasia came abruptly to life.

"Yes." Her uncle shot her an odd look. "Of course. Businessmen, nobles, landed gentry. Everyone worth meeting."

"It sounds wonderful," she declared, interlacing her fingers in her lap to curb her excitement. "Thank you, Uncle George."

Lord Sheldrake coughed—a cough that sounded suspiciously like smothered laughter. "Of course, Medford. I'd be glad to advise you on your guest list. We'll include prominent noblemen, respected gentry . . . oh, and affluent businessmen, of course." He tossed Anastasia a quick, wry grin—one she pretended not to notice.

"Good." Uncle George was oblivious to the exchange. Instead, he was scrutinizing his knife and fork, visibly preoccupied by another detail yet to be addressed.

Anastasia soon found out what that other detail was.

"Ah, Sheldrake." George abandoned his silverware, casually refolding his napkin. "You will do me the honor of escorting Breanna to the ball."

"Father." Hot color rushed to Breanna's cheeks, and she lowered her eyes, torn between embarrassment and fear of defying her father. "I don't think . . ."

"It would be my pleasure to escort Breanna to this grand ball of yours," Lord Sheldrake interrupted, giving Breanna a warm smile. "Together, she and I will see to it that Lady Anastasia enjoys her first taste of English society." He slanted a look at Anastasia, a decided twinkle in his eye. "In fact, I personally vow that between her own efforts and ours, your niece won't be bored for a moment."

"What did Lord Sheldrake mean by that last comment of his?" Breanna demanded as she and Anastasia enjoyed a late afternoon stroll through the gardens.

"H-m-m-m?" Anastasia shaded her eyes from the sun, drinking in the vibrant colors and intoxicating scents of Medford's flowers. The goldenrod, the honeysuckle, the wild roses—she'd missed this most of all. England's glorious countryside, unhurried and unrivaled. The beauty of nature, the freedom to walk for hours and never reach a destination, the sense of peace and adventure all rolled into one.

Lord, it was good to be home.

"Stacie?" Breanna prompted.

Smiling, Anastasia paused at a massive oak, whose profusion of branches overhung the lawns and headed up a grove of now-blossoming trees that lined the estate's south gardens.

"Remember this tree?" she asked Breanna, caressing the trunk. "It's the one I climbed when we were four. I wanted to be taller than anything else, so that nothing could impede my view of the grounds."

"I remember," Breanna returned dryly, folding her arms across her chest. "You fell out, caught your gown on one of the branches, and slashed the top of your thigh. You bled for half an hour—it took three of Grandfather's handkerchiefs to stop the bleeding."

Anastasia chuckled. "I still have the scar." Her smile faded. "I remember how frightened you were, and how much the gash hurt. I even cried—no, I sobbed—and you know how seldom I do that. But I also remember how incredible it felt, for one fleeting instant, to stand on top of the world. And do you know what? It was worth it. Tears, pain, scar and all. It was worth it."

"Stacie, are you going to tell me what Lord Sheldrake was alluding to or aren't you?" Breanna interrupted her cousin's reminiscing. "For that matter, are you going to fill me in on what happened at your meeting this morning? Whatever it was, it couldn't have been *too* dire. You and the marquess seemed to be getting along reasonably well at lunch; certainly better than you were yesterday."

Anastasia wasn't sure why, but she had the sudden urge to sidestep her cousin's question—at least that part which dealt with her attitude toward Lord Sheldrake.

"That's probably because I was too taken aback by Uncle George's surprising announcement about his ball in my honor," she replied instead. "A costly frivolity like a party? Hardly typical of your father."

"I agree," Breanna said. "It stunned me, as well. And then to insist that Lord Sheldrake escort me . . ." She flushed. "I'm sure that was part of Father's plan. I assume he wants to make a grand display of some kind, to show the *ton* that the Colbys are still every bit as influential as they ever were—despite Grandfather's death, and now Uncle Henry's."

"You have a point." Anastasia tucked her gown around her and lowered herself to the grass. "Either that, or perhaps he's in the midst of a business deal he feels will progress faster in a social setting." She patted the large, flat stone embedded in the earth beside her. "Let's sit for a while, savor the sunshine. You can use this as your chair. That way, you won't get grass stains." A mischievous twinkle. "I assume soiled garments still enrage Uncle George."

Breanna's lips curved at the memories Anastasia's comment elicited, but there was a kind of sad resignation in her eyes. "Everything enrages Father," she replied. "Some things more than others—such as soiled gowns." Gingerly, she gathered up her skirts and perched at the edge of the stone's clean surface.

That all-too-familiar fist of worry knotted Anastasia's gut, worry she'd known since childhood but had been too afraid to address.

Now she did.

"Breanna—he doesn't hurt you, does he? Physically, I mean."

Her cousin stared out across the grounds. Then, she slowly shook her head—a half-hearted gesture that looked suspiciously like she was shading the truth, trying to keep Anastasia from worrying. "No. Not really. Not yet." A pause. "He's always been volatile. You know that. But most of the time he expends his anger by lashing out verbally. Once or twice it's gone beyond that—usually when I question his decisions at the wrong times. I usually know when those times are, and I make myself scarce. But sometimes I approach him before I have time to recognize the signs."

"What signs?"

"Long, bitter silences. Excessive drinking and brooding—usually following tense business meetings behind closed doors. You know how preoccupied Father is with making money. When things don't go right, he explodes."

"And he strikes you?"

"Sometimes. Nothing I can't bear."

"You said yet. What does that mean?"

Breanna plucked a blade of grass and rubbed it between her fingers. "I don't know. Lately, his moods seem more intense than they've ever been. It's like he's seething beneath the surface, fighting the need to erupt. The way he used to act when your mother was in the room."

"I remember." Anastasia fell silent, reminding herself that there were pieces to this puzzle Breanna still didn't know—pieces she herself would supply when the time was right.

"I didn't mean to worry you, Stacie. I'm probably overreacting. It's just that this situation with Lord Sheldrake is causing an inordinate amount of friction. My misgivings are infuriating Father. When the marquess is here, I'm embarrassed, ill at ease—and, yes, dubious. I know what Father expects of me. But I can't promise him I can supply it."

"Of course not," Anastasia proclaimed, feeling faintly guilty, and unwilling to ponder why. "You can't force affection the way you can obedience. Surely Uncle George realizes . . ."

"He doesn't. Nor am I apt to convince him." Breanna propped her chin on her hand, angling her face toward her cousin's. "I'm not a coward, Stacie," she said quietly. "It's important to me that you know that. I'm also not the same frightened little girl I was ten years ago. When I feel strongly enough about a situation, I do challenge Father, regardless of how angry he gets. If Lord Sheldrake turns out to be one of those situations, so be it. The point is, I just don't defy my father often or without good cause. Frankly, given the outcome, it isn't worth it."

"I never thought of you as a coward." Anastasia took her cousin's hand and squeezed it. "You're a survivor. We both are. Sometimes survival means holding one's tongue—a feat you're far better at than I. That doesn't make you fainthearted. It makes you wise. I'd be wise to learn some of your self-restraint. And to use it—such as earlier today." A sigh. "Ah well. This time survival will have to mean deviating from my original plan."

Breanna's expression turned quizzical. "What on earth are you talking about?"

Another sigh, and Anastasia leaned back on her hands, letting her palms sink into the plush green bed of grass. "We're talking about me and my grand scheme to leave the Colby mark—*my* mark—on the world. A scheme that now needs to be modified, thanks to Lord Sheldrake."

"You've lost me."

"I wanted to use my inheritance to open a bank in Philadelphia—one that would grow and expand and eventually offer all the resources and stability to Americans that the House of Lockewood offers to the Continent and to England. I announced my intentions to Lord Sheldrake, asked him to share in this venture as my partner. He refused. He also refused to let me use Papa's funds to pursue this investment on my own, either now or for the duration of time in which he's in control of my inheritance. So I told him I'd seek backing elsewhere, from other prominent businessmen willing to take a chance on something new. He was amused, but dubious. He also realized—right after Uncle George's announcement—exactly where I meant to begin my campaign for capital: at this gala house party. Thus, his taunt about my never being bored at the ball."

Breanna's jaw had dropped a bit farther with each word. "Stacie, you spent your meeting with Lord Sheldrake informing *him* how *you* intend to invest your money?"

"Yes. For all the good it did me. Not that I plan to be dissuaded. I don't. I'll simply find another way."

"A bank. You mean to open a bank—in Philadelphia." A disturbing possibility, secondary or not, struck Breanna—hard. "Does this mean you'll be going back to the States?"

"Only to visit," Anastasia assured her. "England is my home. Breanna, I don't mean to build the bank's walls with my bare hands or count out each shilling that's dispersed. Between the relationships Papa formed and Lord Sheldrake's contacts and experience, that won't be necessary. I'm supplying the idea. Now all I need is the capital to get things started. It would succeed. I *know* it would. But the marquess is so damned stubborn . . ."

"Stacie, he's a financial genius. Surely he knows better than you what would make a profitable investment."

"I'm sure he does—or would, if he were willing to listen. But he's not. He's convinced that Europe is a sure thing and America an uncertainty. Well, vast empires were founded on risk. Ventures require nothing less. And if Damen Lockewood is too pigheaded to see that, I'll simply go elsewhere."

"Seeking funds from whomever you meet at the ball."

An anticipatory grin lit Anastasia's face. "Exactly. Which is where you come in. I'll ask Uncle George for an advance copy of the guest list. Don't worry," she added, seeing the anxious pucker form between Breanna's brows. "I'll use the excuse that I want to review the names in advance so I don't embarrass him by mispronouncing anyone's title. That's just the type of dutiful gesture Uncle George would applaud."

"That's true," Breanna concurred. "But where do I come in?"

"You'll study the list with me, and tell me who's who. I need you to distinguish which guests could be potential backers." Anastasia waved away Breanna's anticipated protest. "I realize you don't involve yourself in Uncle George's business, but surely you know who his colleagues are, and who are the most successful of the bunch. Then, on the night of the ball, you'll point those particular gentlemen out to me, and make the proper introductions. I'll do the rest. By the time my coming-out is complete, my venture will be fully funded."

Breanna couldn't help but chuckle at her cousin's enthusiasm. "Tell me, are you going to enjoy a single hour of this party? In the traditional sense, that is. You know—chatting, meeting interesting people, even dancing. Or are you going to spend the entire time doing business?"

Anastasia's grin widened. "That depends on how quickly I accomplish my goal."

Accomplishing his goal, George reflected bitterly one short week later, was a damned, bloody nuisance—one he resented with every fiber of his being.

Fixing a polished smile on his face, he assessed the grand ballroom, which, a mere hour ago, had been empty. Now, it was bursting at the seams, a profusion of color and movement as streams of arriving guests made their entrance, while those already in attendance whirled about the dance floor, chatted in ever-growing groups, or made their way over to the refreshments.

The typical onset to an extravagant house party.

Clasping his hands behind his back, George resumed his role as host.

He milled about, dropping a smile to his left and a greeting to his right, all the while mentally tabulating how much this wretched affair had wound up costing. Oh, he'd padded the receipts as best he could, adding fifty pounds here and a hundred pounds there. But he hadn't dared get too carried away. Not with Sheldrake's watchful eye overseeing every pence of Henry's money. As a result, George had scarcely been able to squeeze out enough profit to make this whole bloody affair worth his while. In fact, he'd be willing to bet that, once the final numbers were tallied up, he'd be lucky to come out a thousand pounds ahead.

And what would a thousand pounds buy him? A two- or three-week reprieve, perhaps. No more. It certainly wouldn't restore his business to its necessary peak.

Dammit.

George paused as he heard Wells announce Lord and Lady Dutton, and cursed under his breath as he watched them make their entrance. So, the pompous windbag had convinced his tyrant of a wife to leave Bath for the occasion after all. That was hardly an inspiring discovery. It wasn't as if he and Dutton were doing business at the moment. The problem was, that could change at any time. The man was too damned influential to snub, and he had enough money to keep himself that way. Fine, George decided. He'd go over there and do his duty. Then, he'd take a moment or two to find the man he needed to see and set his own dealings back on track.

Resignedly, George headed for the doorway, raising his chin in greeting, and steeling himself for a quarter hour of annoying chatter.

"Good evening, Lady Dutton." George bowed, kissing her gloved hand and wondering idly how her husband's protruding belly was going to allow room for the other two hundred guests. "Dutton," he added, stepping back to welcome the man without slamming into his stomach.

"Medford. Good evening. This is a splendid party," Dutton proclaimed, nodding his approval as he assessed the other attendees. "I give you credit. You've managed a fine gathering on very short notice. And at a very inconvenient time of year. As you know, Penelope here had to be coaxed away from Bath. I'm relieved to see it was worth my efforts in doing so . . ." A swift man-to-man look together with a subtle roll of the eyes. ". . . or she'd never let me forget it."

Ignoring the poisonous glare Lady Dutton threw at her husband, George nodded his understanding. "I'm delighted you could both come." He gestured for them to enter, half-hoping he could cut the conversation short. "Please, enjoy yourselves."

"Which young lady is your niece?" Dutton pressed, dashing George's hopes of an abbreviated chat by remaining where he was, peering over as many heads as his stubby height would allow. "Ah," he interrupted himself. "I see a familiar face: your Breanna. She's over there by the French doors—alone, surprisingly. It's been quite some time, but I'd know her anywhere. Although I do believe she's grown even lovelier; she's a veritable vision in yellow."

Tensing, George pivoted, followed Dutton's line of vision, and visibly relaxed. "You're mistaken, Dutton. My daughter is among the crowd enjoying the strings." He waved his arm in the direction of the musicians. "Her gown is blue, not yellow. And she's dancing with Sheldrake. The young lady you spied is my niece, Anastasia."

Dutton's jaw dropped, and he stared from one girl to the other. "My goodness, they could be sisters. Twins, actually."

"They've been mistaken as such." George was in no mood to pursue this particular line of conversation. In fact, he'd had about all he could stand of Dutton. Having made the requisite amount of small talk, and having assured himself that Breanna was, indeed, where she was supposed to be—at Sheldrake's side—he had more important business to attend to than answering this buffoon's nosy questions. "I'll be officially presenting Anastasia to everyone once the majority of guests have arrived. In the interim, if you'll both excuse me, I have a few matters to attend to. Please—partake. My home is yours."

"Yes. Most gracious of you, Medford." Dutton licked his chops, easing his wife—and his belly—farther into the room, doubtless toward the refreshments, George thought in disgust.

"Hello, Medford."

George had scarcely taken a step when Lyman appeared at his elbow, nursing a cup of Regent's punch and speaking in an undertone. "This ball is elegant—*and* expensive. I'm relieved to see that your financial reverses have righted themselves."

George stiffened. "Not now," he muttered under his breath. Without sparing Lyman another look, he moved deeper into the crowd.

He was more determined than ever to conduct his business.

Just inside the double doors leading onto the balcony, Anastasia watched the short, chunky man leave Uncle George's side and steer his wife into the room. Impatiently, she shifted from one foot to the other, willing the minuet to end so Breanna could perform the introductions. From the description her cousin had provided, Anastasia was almost certain that the new arrival was Lord Dutton. Based on what Breanna had said, Lord Dutton was an affluent nobleman who owned several enormous estates, a shipbuilding company, and a string of smaller businesses. And *that* made him an ideal candidate to finance her bank.

She frowned, her gaze—with a will all its own—shifting back to the same place it had traveled a dozen times: to the dance floor where Lord

Sheldrake was gliding Breanna about. Not for any personal reason, she assured herself hastily. Only to see if they were concluding their dance so she could proceed with her plan.

Even as she assured herself of that fact, she knew it was a lie.

The truth was, she couldn't stop staring at Damen Lockewood. He was easily the most compelling man in the room, his dynamic presence seeming to overshadow everyone around him. He looked devastating in his formal evening clothes, a fact that was evidenced by all the admiring glances cast his way by women of all ages.

Breanna looked breathtaking at his side. She was poised, graceful, incredibly beautiful; her upswept hair—a shimmering crown of auburn laced with pearls—as perfectly in place as if she were reposing rather than dancing. She was refined, captivating, the consummate lady, and Anastasia felt incredibly proud of her.

Ruefully, she tucked a stray tendril of her own hair behind her ear, almost laughing aloud at the realization that, in this one way, little had changed since their childhood. She was still the hoyden, Breanna the lady. And while Breanna might admire her for her forthrightness, Anastasia was in perpetual awe of Breanna's natural grace and composure.

Still, Anastasia knew her cousin better than anyone. And, composed or not, Breanna looked very strained at the moment, almost as if she were silently willing the minuet to end.

Or was that only wishful thinking on her own part?

Stop it, Anastasia admonished herself. *Whatever you think happened last week in the yellow salon was all in your mind. Lord Sheldrake is the overseer of your inheritance—and the main obstacle in your path. He's fervent in his beliefs, which explains the intensity you felt during those unexpected final moments of your meeting. Stop reading anything more into it.*

As if on cue, Damen Lockewood raised his head, his gaze spanning the ballroom and finding hers.

Their eyes met—and held.

Feeling that same warmth shimmer through her, Anastasia jerked her gaze away. This reaction was unacceptable, for many reasons. Least of all was the role the marquess had been assigned to play in her life. Most of all was the role he'd been assigned by Uncle George to play in Breanna's.

Anastasia sucked in her breath. She had to stop staring. The last thing she needed was for Lord Sheldrake to think she was assessing his and Breanna's suitability. She had enough to handle, just trying to line up her backers—and holding Lord Sheldrake to his vow not to undermine her attempts to do so. Provoking him would hardly serve her best interests.

Besides, his relationship—or lack thereof—with Breanna was their concern, not hers.

With staunch determination, Anastasia shifted her attention to locating Lord Dutton, who'd disappeared somewhere in the crowd. Not that his girth would allow him to remain unnoticeable for long, she reminded herself with a grin. On impulse, she turned toward the refreshment table, her lips curving as she saw that her instincts had been correct. The rotund fellow was in the process of gobbling down a large pastry, simultaneously inching away from his wife and her gossiping circle of friends.

Perhaps it was time to take matters into her own hands . . .

"It would be far easier if I supplied the introduction."

The sound of Lord Sheldrake's amused baritone from directly behind her made Anastasia start.

"Pardon me?" She whipped about to face him, spotting Breanna by his side and wondering when the two of them had finished their dance and made their way over.

"Lord Dutton," Sheldrake supplied, tipping his head in that direction. "I assume you're about to ask him for money. If you stroll up to him alone, I doubt he'll make the connection between a beautiful woman and a business deal. Shall I pave the way, or would you prefer to ask your uncle to do the honors?"

Anastasia sucked in her breath. "Tell me, my lord, how do you read minds and execute a minuet at the same time, without missing a step? Or is that similar to conducting two business meetings simultaneously?"

The marquess's teeth gleamed. "I'm flattered you were watching. As for my mind-reading abilities, they're uncanny—whether or not I'm otherwise occupied. However, in your case, they're hardly necessary. You're eyeing Dutton like a wolf circling a sheep. And given that the gentleman in question is married, over fifty, and wider than he is tall, I ruled out any romantic interest on your part."

An impish grin curved Anastasia's lips. "Perhaps I prefer fat, married men. Have you considered that?"

All humor vanished from Lord Sheldrake's eyes. "No," he replied quietly. "I haven't. That would be too great a waste to consider."

Anastasia's breath lodged in her throat, the marquess's words burning through her like a kindled flame. She searched his face, his expression no longer teasing but probing, intense.

Tearing her gaze away was even more difficult this time.

"I—I'd appreciate the introduction," she managed, struggling to regain her composure. "Plus any others you'd care to provide. I had asked Breanna to present me, but I'd be a fool not to realize that they'd take me far more seriously if the introductions came from you."

"Consider it done." Lord Sheldrake took her arm, arching a questioning brow at Breanna. "You're sure you don't mind?"

Breanna shook her head. "As I told you on the dance floor, I'd be thrilled to be relieved of the awkward duty. Approaching a dozen overbearing men is hardly my idea of an enjoyable evening." She gestured gratefully at a cluster of young women who were chattering in the far corner of the room. "Besides, Margaret Warner has been trying to catch my eye for the past hour. She and her friends want to hear all about my long-lost cousin who's finally returned from America."

Anastasia wrinkled up her nose. "Why would they want to know about me?"

Breanna's sigh was the essence of exasperation. "Because while you're preoccupied with business, most women are not. My guess is that Lady Margaret and her chums want to assess their competition. You're far too pretty to suit the unmarried ones." A flash of recall flickered in her eyes and, without thinking, she muttered, "Don't forget, I did experience one London Season. And I learned that although the men might be lechers, the women are lethal."

Laughter rumbled in Lord Sheldrake's chest. "I'll refrain from comment."

"Oh—" Breanna flushed, looking startled by her own uncharacteristic frankness. "I suppose that was incredibly rude."

"No, it was merely accurate." Anastasia grinned. "I encountered similar types of women in Philadelphia. In my case, I avoided them. Otherwise, I shudder to think what trouble my quick tongue would have gotten me into. But with your inherent gift of tact, you won't run that risk. Lethal or not, those girls will be charmed by you. Everyone is."

That comment made Breanna smile—a fleeting smile that tugged at her lips, then vanished—almost as if she'd enjoyed a private joke she alone was privy to. "If you say so." She gathered up her skirts. "Anyway, if you'll both excuse me, I'll head over to the ladies' corner. It will be entertaining to hear the latest gossip." She paused, squeezing Anastasia's arm. "Good luck finding investors, Stacie. My fingers are crossed."

Anastasia watched her cousin weave her way across the room. "Sometimes I forget how much Breanna is deprived of," she murmured to herself. "So much so that a chat with a group of women is like an extraordinary gift. How in God's name can Uncle George . . ." She broke off, realizing she'd spoken her thoughts aloud.

"I don't know," Lord Sheldrake surprised her by answering. "But it can't stay that way. Nor will it, now that you're home. You're very good for Breanna. I've never heard her speak her mind before. It's a healthy sign."

Before Anastasia could respond or even contemplate the marquess's words, he dropped the subject. Turning on his heel, he tightened his grasp on her arm and began drawing her toward the refreshment table. "Come. It's time to accost Lord Dutton."

Anastasia complied, although Lord Sheldrake's subtle taunt was not lost on her. In response, she tossed him a saucy look. "I'm not going to accost him," she retorted. "I'm going to offer him the chance of a lifetime."

5

Unfortunately, Lord Dutton didn't seem to share Anastasia's-opinion. Oh, he gleefully acknowledged Lord Sheldrake's introduction, swaggered his fat little body when he heard she wanted to speak with him alone, then gobbled her up with his eyes when the marquess walked away. But when he heard the nature of her business—or rather, that all she wanted to discuss was business—his entire demeanor changed. He looked shocked, then offended, and finally scornful, not even waiting to hear the details before he brought the conversation to a rapid close and made his way back to the desserts.

She received similar responses from the other eleven businessmen she approached—from Edgar Lyman, the shipbuilder, to Arthur Landow, the wealthy manufacturer, to Viscount Crompton, a retired military general who invested his inherited fortune just for diversion, even to William Bates, a London magistrate who received huge stipends for keeping dangerous criminals off the streets and who reputedly had a knack for making large amounts of money through various business ventures—to every other prospective investor on her list.

No one was interested in conducting business with a woman, much less investing their funds in an American bank.

An hour later, Anastasia was more discouraged than she could bear.

Easing her way through the throng of intoxicated guests, she slipped out onto the balcony, hoping to have a few minutes to herself. She needed to collect her thoughts before her uncle summoned her for the inevitable formal introduction to the room at large—an introduction that would be happening at any moment, given that almost all the guests had now arrived.

The night sky was clear, and filled with stars. Anastasia leaned against the railing, gazing up at the bright specks of light and remembering when she and Breanna used to count them, trying to get closer to the heavens by climbing that favorite oak of theirs.

Somehow Anastasia never felt she'd climbed high enough.

But Grandfather always believed she would someday, that both she and Breanna would reach their own symbolic peak.

With a wistful smile, Anastasia gazed off to the right, fond memories of her grandfather and her childhood surging to the forefront of her mind.

It was too dark to make out the outlines of specific buildings, but she knew the stables were in the direction she was facing. She remembered the dawn when she and Grandfather had walked there to see a new foal being born. Life, Grandfather had explained to her, was the most precious gift God offered. And the ties born of that life were equally precious. Even animals knew that, he'd explained. Even they possessed that unique, priceless instinct to love those who belonged to them.

He'd shown her the natural affinity between mare and foal, a bond that was only a fraction of what human beings felt toward their young.

Family. That was even more important than personal accomplishments—not only to Grandfather, but to her. But what if one was integrally tied to the other? What if accomplishing a feat was the first step in carrying on a lineage, perhaps even in restoring ties that should never have been broken?

Anastasia massaged her temples, contemplating not only her immediate goals—to pay tribute to her father and unite and expand Colby and Sons—but the enormous sum of money Grandfather had left her and Breanna. How would they put that money to work in order to do their grandfather justice, to reap the rewards he was determined that they reap, not only for themselves, but for their children, their future?

If tonight was any indication, then Anastasia feared Grandfather's hopes and dreams would fall by the wayside.

Dear God, what if she let him down?

"Here you are."

Damen Lockewood strolled out onto the balcony, coming up to stand beside her. He leaned his elbow on the railing and angled himself to face her. "You're discouraged. After twelve fruitless efforts, I can't blame you."

Anastasia continued to stare off into space, hovering somewhere between dejection and nostalgia. "Have you come out here to gloat?"

"Hardly." He fell silent for a moment, studying her profile intently as he chose his next words. "Tell me something, my lady. Is your original offer still open—the one regarding a potential partnership between us?"

Whatever Anastasia had been expecting, it hadn't been this.

She whirled about, her eyes wide. "What did you say?"

"I asked if your original offer still stands. Because if it does, if you're still interested in having me co-finance this venture of yours, I'd like to accept."

Pensively, she studied the marquess's face, puzzled and curious all at once. What had prompted this total turnaround? she wondered. Certainly not some absurd sense of gallantry. Not with a man like Damen Lockewood, who regarded business above all else.

Except perhaps loyalty. Was that it? Did the marquess feel a sense of commitment to her father, a responsibility not to let Henry's daughter falter?

If that was the case, she wanted no part of his charity.

"Why?" she demanded, giving voice to her thoughts. "Why would you change your mind so suddenly and completely? Out of duty? Pity?"

One dark brow shot up. "Neither. To begin with, I don't pity you. Doing business means experiencing disappointment, sometimes even coping with failure. What's more, even if I did feel sorry for what you're going through, I don't allow emotions to dictate my business decisions. And that includes loyalty to fine men like your father. Henry would laugh in my face if he heard me suggest investing in something I didn't believe in just out of respect for him. So, no, put those foolish notions out of your mind. I'm reversing my decision because it's prudent to do so."

Sheldrake lifted one shoulder in a careless shrug. "As it turns out, I spent the better part of last week researching your ideas. I made some inquiries, pored over long columns of numbers. And I discovered that you were right. I didn't give your proposal a fair chance. Well, now I'm ready to. If you're still interested."

Anastasia eyed him skeptically. "Why didn't you mention this change of heart before an hour ago when I went on my futile crusade to solicit backers?"

"Because I wanted you to explore all your options before I made my offer. After all, there was every chance you'd reject it at this point, given my initial response. Especially if you'd found someone else to finance your venture."

"Which I didn't." Anastasia frowned, contemplating another, equally important, question. "Let me ask you this: what if I say no? Will that preclude me from using my own funds to finance the bank? Will I have to wait until October, when you're no longer managing my inheritance, to get started?"

Lord Sheldrake's jaw tightened fractionally. "What you're effectively asking is whether or not I'd resort to blackmail. The answer is no. I don't do business that way. You'll have access to your funds immediately, whether or not we form a partnership. I'll sign the necessary documents at my bank on the morning after this party ends. No strings attached."

"I see." Anastasia wet her lips with the tip of her tongue. "Forgive me if I insulted you. But I had to be sure."

"No insult taken—this time. However, I don't expect my integrity to be questioned again."

"Fair enough." The first ray of hope she'd experienced all evening dawned inside her. "You really believe in my bank?"

"*Our* bank," Sheldrake corrected with a cocky grin. "At least if you accept my offer. And, yes, I do."

With visible relief and excitement, Anastasia extended her hand. "Then consider us partners."

"Splendid." Solemnly, he shook her hand, his fingers lingering far longer than necessary. "Tell me, now that we're partners, do you think we might dispense with the formalities?"

Anastasia swallowed, her pulse picking up speed. "Which formalities in particular, my lord?"

"The ones you just employed." His gaze held hers. "I believe it's fitting for partners to call each other by their given names."

"I suppose that makes sense."

"Good." Abruptly, his grip tightened, refusing to let go, and his stare delved deep inside of her. "When I first walked out here, you weren't only thinking about the bank, were you? There was far more on your mind."

Anastasia blinked—startled by the abrupt change of subject, taken aback by the marquess's boldness and his insight. She had no idea what prompted her to answer. Perhaps it was the camaraderie of the past few minutes; perhaps it was the vulnerable state in which he'd found her or the compassion she heard in his voice.

Or perhaps it was the heat that emanated from their joined hands.

In any case, she stared at his strong fingers wrapped around her slender ones and replied, "Yes, I was pondering far more than the bank. I was thinking about many things—my grandfather, my father, how much I missed Medford Manor while I was away, how much I still . . ." She bit her lip, then blurted out, "Is it possible to miss home even when you're right there in it?"

"Yes," the marquess responded without pause. "When that home is no longer the same as the one you remember. And the one you remember is the one you miss."

Slowly, Anastasia tilted her face up to his. "You're a very perceptive man, Lord Sheldrake."

"Damen," he corrected. "And you're a very intriguing woman, Anastasia."

Without any warning, he stepped closer, caught her chin between his fingers, and lowered his mouth to hers.

Anastasia had no time to think, no time to prepare.

She only had time to feel.

Damen's lips brushed hers in a whisper of sensation, a warm, fleeting caress that sent tiny shivers up her spine. He repeated the motion, and Anastasia caught her breath, her eyes sliding shut as she reeled with newfound awareness.

She'd been kissed before—on the hand, an occasional peck on the cheek, even one tentative sampling of her mouth, given by a brazen though unimpressive suitor. But never before had she felt this tingling sensation, this quivering that rippled from her head to her toes.

The odd thing was that Damen's kiss was no less chaste than those that had preceded it. It was a mere grazing of the lips—the only difference being that it lingered, its motion retraced in slow reversal—first right to left, then left to right.

And then it ended.

Damen raised his head, his eyes smoky as he gazed down at her. His knuckles brushed her cheeks—first one, then the other—before gliding down to skim the side of her neck. Then, he framed her face between his palms and bent to take her mouth again.

This time his lips settled more fully on hers, moving back and forth in a purposeful dance of discovery, and Anastasia leaned closer, instinctively seeking a closer contact.

His mouth was warm, firm, as intense and insistent as he, and equally as restrained. There was fire burning beneath the surface, fire she could sense, but he kept it carefully in check, smoldering beneath the surface.

When finally they eased apart, it was gradual, their lips brushing softly—once, twice—before relinquishing contact altogether. Anastasia's lashes lifted as the night air fluttered across her damp mouth, gently prodding her back to reality.

Damen was watching her, his stare intense, his steel-gray eyes alive with sparks. Still cupping her face, he murmured, "If I apologize for doing that, will you stay out here a while longer?"

"No. But I'll stay out here a while longer if you don't apologize."

He chuckled, lifted a few loose strands of burnished hair off her face. "Fair enough. Also far more honest. The truth is, I'm not sorry. I've been wanting to do that all night." He took a reluctant step backward, dropped his arms to his sides. "But I won't press my luck. If we stay out here, it's to talk."

"About our bank?"

"About whatever it is you'd like to talk about."

Anastasia nodded, still somewhat off-balance, besieged by too many emotions to ponder. "Tonight is certainly a night of surprises," she managed.

Damen's stare was deep, contemplative. "Is it?" he asked huskily. "Odd, it doesn't feel that way to me."

Inside the ballroom, George greeted the last of his arriving guests, then moved briefly into the hallway, standing alone to ponder the evening's accomplishments.

All in all, things were moving along nicely. Breanna was dutifully stationed at Sheldrake's side, Lyman and his curiosity had been deferred to a more appropriate place and time, and his own business discussion— handled earlier as planned—had yielded the necessary results.

Silently, George congratulated himself on the excellent argument he'd presented. The necessary party now understood what needed to be done in order to ensure the highest profits were reaped and maintained. Not only understood the situation, but intended to act upon it.

Yes, the response had been gratifying, and as a result, more attention would now be paid to the details. With that extra supervision, the quality of their next shipment would be better, the quantity greater. And the profits, higher. Hopefully, much higher.

Now, if Sheldrake would only propose to Breanna, and he himself could somehow gain access to Anastasia's inheritance . . .

"Medford." Lyman joined him outside the doorway, glancing about to ensure that no one could hear them. "I've been looking for you. You were swallowed up by the crowd before we could finish talking."

"We *were* finished talking," George replied tersely. "As for where I was, I was greeting my guests—and solidifying our future success. That was part of my reason for holding this ball. From now on, we can expect our shipments to be more substantial, and our merchandise of finer quality."

"Ah. Excellent. And imperative." Lyman took a step closer, and George could see the beads of perspiration on his brow. Clearly, the man was even more rattled than he'd realized. But why?

"Imperative?" he repeated carefully. "That sounds rather ominous."

Lyman's tongue wet his lips. "It is. That's what I was trying to tell you earlier. I'm glad you've corrected your business reverses, and equally glad our shipments will be improved. Because our costs have just gone up. Significantly. Fifty percent, to be exact. Effective imme- diately."

George's brows drew together in a scowl. "Where did this information come from?"

"From Meade. He's flatly refused to work another day without getting paid—in full. He won't accept your credit any longer, not for past shipments and definitely not for future ones. There have been too many late payments. He insists on your debt to him being satisfied immediately—in pound notes. As for upcoming deals, he wants his money up front and with a fifty percent increase. He says the risks are just too great, and your ability to pay too uncertain. I tried everything to convince him to reconsider, to bend a bit, but to no avail." Lyman whipped out a handkerchief, dabbed at his face. "So I'm glad we can meet his demands. Otherwise . . ."

Anger surged through George's veins. "Are you telling me Meade is blackmailing us?"

"I'm telling you he wants his money. He's not going to be deterred, not this time."

"Oh, yes he is." George drew himself up, his mind already racing over possible solutions, and settling on a logical one. "I'm tired of Meade and his threats. It's time I eliminated them."

"You're going to confront him?"

"In effect. Nothing *too* uncivilized." George's jaw set. "Let's just say I'm going to see that the wind is knocked out of his sails." His hand sketched a dismissive wave, as Lyman began asking another question. "It's no longer your problem. I'll attend to it."

"Very well." Lyman appeared to be relieved. Still, he hesitated, lingering in the hallway as if he had something more to say.

"Is there something else?" George snapped, eager to bring this conversation to a close.

"Frankly, yes." A frown creased Lyman's forehead, and he blurted out, "Do you actually approve of your niece's behavior—involving herself in business, investing in, of all things, an American bank, seeking backers right here at her own coming-out party?"

The questions struck George like a series of blows.

"What in the name of heaven are you babbling about?" he demanded.

"Your niece. Anastasia. You mean you don't know? She's intent on starting a bank in the colonies. And she's asking Lord knows how many of your guests to finance this venture."

Silence.

"I didn't think you'd approve of it," Lyman concluded, seeing George's livid expression. "Not only Anastasia's choice of ventures, but the very idea of her being actively involved in business. And using this ball to acquire her . . ."

"Are you certain about this?" George interrupted.

"Of course I am. She approached me directly, requested my backing. She also approached Landow, Crompton, Bates . . ."

"Where is she?" George broke into Lyman's explanation, whipping about to scrutinize the ballroom from the entranceway door, only to find his niece was nowhere in sight. "Where's Anastasia now?"

"With Sheldrake. I assume she's soliciting his help as well."

"That's impossible. Sheldrake is with . . ." George's mouth snapped shut as he spied Breanna, chatting with a group of girls near the punch. "Dammit," he muttered. He turned to glare at Lyman. "You say Anastasia is with Sheldrake?"

"Yes. On the balcony. They've been out there for quite some time. Then again, as I understand it, the man is her financial overseer. Perhaps he's trying to talk some sense into her. I hope he succeeds."

George's hands balled into fists at his sides. Bad enough that Sheldrake wasn't with Breanna, as planned. But this? This was disastrous. It had never occurred to him that Anastasia might have made plans with regard to her father's money. But he'd obviously underestimated her. And if she squandered that inheritance before he got his hands on it . . .

Slowly, he sucked in his breath. Ludicrous. In order to spend her money, Anastasia needed Sheldrake's permission, something the marquess would never provide, not for a stupid venture such as this. And as far as getting other backers to finance her endeavor, that was equally preposterous. Not one man in this room, even the most outlandish of gamblers, would agree to do business with a woman. On the contrary, the stupid chit had probably succeeded in alienating every member of the peerage, a likelihood that posed an entirely different set of problems.

It was time to contain the damage.

"Excuse me, Lyman," George told his colleague. "All the guests have now arrived. I'm going to summon Anastasia and make her formal introduction."

"A wise idea."

George wasn't interested in Lyman's blessing. He weaved his way through the ballroom, forcibly restraining himself from plowing his way to the balcony. He had to look unconcerned, to avoid arousing suspicions. No one must think anything was amiss, that he was at all distressed by his niece's outrageous behavior. Oh, he didn't doubt the room was abuzz with gossip. But he'd deal with that later, address the comments, one by one. As for now, as host of an elaborate party, all that mattered was saving face.

Schooling his features, he edged closer to the open French doors, mentally rehearsing how he'd introduce Anastasia, diffuse the gossip, and find a way to stifle his niece's campaign for funds long enough to get through this house party, after which he'd deal with her privately.

He paused and, in a tone that echoed loud and clear, ordered the footmen to refill everyone's glasses. He was well aware that by doing so he was alerting the whole ballroom to the fact that an announcement was about to be made.

Satisfied, he strolled out onto the balcony.

Anastasia and Sheldrake stood near the railing, engaged in heated debate. George couldn't hear their actual words, but it was obvious his niece was uttering something decisive, her gloved hand slicing the air in emphasis. Sheldrake responded with an adamant shake of his head, refuting her position in no uncertain terms, his arms folded tightly across his chest, his baritone firm, uncompromising.

Thank goodness.

George could actually feel a bit of the tension drain from his body. But only a bit. Because he had an excellent memory. And if his now-grown niece bore any similarity to the willful child she'd once been, it would take sheer wizardry to alter her intentions.

Wizardry or a heavy hand.

He'd decide later which of the two to employ.

"Anastasia." George bore down on her, determined to aid Sheldrake's efforts and divert Anastasia's attentions—at least temporarily—before she decided to seek support elsewhere in the room. "I've been looking for you. It's time for your formal presentation."

Anastasia inclined her head and blinked, looking as if she had forgotten the whole purpose of this bloody ball. "Oh—yes. Of course. I'm coming, Uncle George." She gathered up her skirts, giving the marquess a measured look. "You'll have to excuse me."

Sheldrake gestured for her to join her uncle, then followed politely behind. "By all means. We'll continue this discussion later."

"My announcement will only take a minute, Sheldrake," George informed him. "After which I'm going to ask the musicians to strike up a waltz to commemorate the occasion. I'm sure Breanna would enjoy dancing with you. So feel free to interrupt and ask her."

With that, he guided Anastasia into the room, well aware that hundreds of eyes were upon them.

"Ladies and gentlemen," he began, a polished smile on his face. "It's no secret why I've invited you all here. My niece, Anastasia, who's been living abroad for the past ten years, has returned to England. It was my late brother Henry's fondest wish that his only daughter be properly brought out and introduced to English society—a society that Henry so deeply missed and that Anastasia has yet to experience. Tonight is her first foray into that society, and she's eager to embrace it, to leave the colonies and all they represent behind." A pointed pause. "I'd appreciate your joining me in helping her do that, and in welcoming her back home to England. Everyone—my lovely niece, Anastasia."

There was a round of applause, accompanied by some heated whispers among the ladies and a healthy number of fervent nods among the gentlemen—gentlemen who were openly proclaiming their approval of George's tacit message; that is, relegating Anastasia to her proper place.

In response, Anastasia smiled and thanked her uncle, although she nearly had to bite off her tongue to manage it, so great was her outrage. She recognized only too well the less-than-subtle admonishment she'd just received, and she harbored no illusions as to why it had been given. Obviously, one or more of the gentlemen she'd approached with her business offer had gone to her uncle to complain. And Uncle George was furious at what he'd perceive as nothing short of flagrant disrespect and indignity.

Inwardly, Anastasia frowned, realizing that, in her haste to acquire financial backing, she hadn't fully considered this. Oh, she'd expected her uncle to be annoyed when he learned of her behavior. But after a ten-year separation, she'd forgotten just how severe his reaction could be.

In any case, she'd have to deal with this later.

The musicians struck up the promised waltz, and Anastasia found herself automatically glancing about for Damen. She spotted him without too much trouble, across the ballroom, watching her with an enigmatic expression.

"Well, Anastasia." Her uncle's voice cut into her thoughts. "I see you already have a captive audience." He drew her attention back to him—and away from Damen—gesturing toward the opposite wall. "There are three gentlemen on their way toward us, all arguing over who will have the honor of dancing with you first. I'll let you decide. It will keep that active mind of yours occupied with something useful."

Anastasia didn't pretend to misunderstand. Nor did she flinch. She simply nodded, seeing beyond her uncle's practiced smile, noting that his eyes were icy chips of jade. "I'm sure it will," she replied.

Fortunately, the three eager suitors reached her side at that moment—bickering among themselves about the order in which they'd dance with her ladyship—so Anastasia wasn't forced to contend with her uncle's antagonism any longer, at least for the time being.

She turned away from him, as one simpering fellow, Edward something-or-other, claimed her, bowing and grasping her gloved hand simultaneously, leading her onto the dance floor and into the waltz.

The second young man, fair-haired and thickset, whose name she didn't catch nor cared to, hovered nearby like a hungry lion, whisking her away the instant the waltz ended and a minuet began. And the third chap, Lord Percy Gilbert, a handsome, ebony-haired fellow whose opinion of himself had to exceed any plausible reality, swept her into a reel, his dark eyes glued to her, rife with promise.

Somehow, Anastasia managed to enjoy herself, more as a consequence of the dancing than the company. She did, however, find herself glancing about the room, involuntarily seeking out Damen, only to spy him dancing with Breanna.

She forced herself to look away, and to stifle the unwelcome surge of envy that welled up inside her.

"You dance magnificently, my lady," Lord Percy informed her as the music stopped.

"Thank you." Anastasia smiled. "I've always loved to dance. Then again, I love any kind of activity that involves physical exertion: climbing trees, racing horses. But dancing is a pleasure unto itself."

He gave a warm chuckle. "You must have learned to dance at the same time as you learned to climb trees—as a child."

A puzzled tilt of her head. "No. I learned at the customary age of thirteen or fourteen. Why would you think otherwise?"

Lord Percy looked utterly taken aback. "But you were in the colonies at that time. Do they actually teach English dances there?"

Anastasia wasn't sure whether to laugh aloud or shout in frustration. "The dances we're enjoying tonight weren't English inventions, my lord," she reminded him, rectifying his ignorance in as gentle a tone as she could muster. "That particular reel was Scottish, the minuet came to us from France, and the waltz originated in Vienna. We simply borrowed them. As did the States. Might I also remind you that America, too, is not an extension of the Crown. It's a country all its own now."

Gilbert stared at her, astonishment reflected on his chiseled features. "I stand corrected." He cleared his throat, a gleam of anticipation lighting his eyes. "You're a very frank and knowledgeable young woman, my lady. Also refreshingly unconventional. I hope to sample more of your free-spiritedness—and of you."

Before Anastasia could open her mouth to reply, a hard hand closed about her forearm. "Here you are, Lady Anastasia." Damen's deep baritone sliced the air. "That waltz you promised me is about to begin." He guided her firmly away from her companion. "Excuse us, Gilbert."

Whether or not Gilbert excused them was irrelevant, since they were already halfway across the floor. Damen signaled the musicians with a purposeful lift of his brows. In response, they commenced playing.

Anastasia began waltzing before her mind fully grasped what had just occurred.

When her thoughts finally caught up with her feet, she began to smile. "Why don't I recall discussing this particular dance?" she inquired. "In fact, why don't I think this waltz was planned at all, but, rather, was requested at the last minute—by you?"

"Because it was." Damen's expression was hard, and a muscle flexed at his jaw. "Your earlier scrutiny of the guest list might have told you who the investors were, but they didn't shed much light on the lechers. Gilbert is one of the latter."

Anastasia felt an irrational rush of pleasure. Was Damen being protective? Or was it just possible he was jealous? "Thank you for disclosing that bit of information. However, I'd already guessed as much."

"Really? Did you also guess that what he just suggested sampling wasn't another reel?"

"Indeed I did." Anastasia bit back her laughter. "I'm not stupid, my lord. I know when I'm being approached for an immoral liaison. Just as I know when I'm being rescued. Speaking of which, now that you've accomplished your valiant rescue, could you stop looking so fierce? People will think I'm an excruciating dancer, too trying to endure."

Damen's lips twitched. "We can't have that now, can we?" He whirled her about. "Very well. I'll try to look as if I'm having a wonderful time."

"And is that so difficult to manage?"

His smile faded. "The only difficulty tonight will be my keeping the proper distance from you. That, and restraining myself from breaking Gilbert's nose."

Anastasia's heart gave a tiny leap, and she studied Damen's face, wondering at the precise meaning of his comment. Was he referring to retaining the immediate physical distance between them, or to a far more significant, long-term distance?

Their gazes locked.

"Are you all right?" Damen asked quietly. "Your uncle's announcement obviously upset you."

She gave a small shrug. "Not upset me, angered me. The reasons why have nothing to do with the announcement itself, but with its underlying meaning. I'm not sure I can explain."

"You don't have to."

Taking in Damen's hard tone, the grim lines about his mouth, Anastasia tried to figure out whether he was alluding to the fact that he didn't want to pry or to the fact that he already knew what she was feeling.

Either way, his compassion warranted some sort of response.

"Perhaps not," she conceded. "But I'll try just the same. You see, Uncle George made that pointed reference to my severing all ties with the States for a reason. He was blatantly condemning the idea of my starting a bank there. Knowing my uncle, I suppose I should have been prepared for his reaction to my plan. But after ten years, it seems I'm out of practice."

Memories flickered to the surface and brought a wave of sadness to Anastasia's eyes. "Once upon a time I was accustomed to Uncle George's rules, especially with regard to anything that might undermine him or cause him embarrassment. Both of which would definitely result from a Colby pursuing a business venture that not only excludes him but that puts a woman—his niece, no less—at the helm." She stared at the wool of Damen's coat, reflecting on how foolish she'd been to forget her uncle's rigid beliefs. "It was naive of me not to realize he'd feel that way. And it was equally naive not to realize that one of his colleagues would tell him what I'd been up to. In any case, that announcement was Uncle George's way of putting me in my place."

"I wonder if he has any idea what your place is."

Anastasia blinked, her gaze darting back to Damen's. She was taken aback by the fervor of his statement, and its remarkable accuracy. "I doubt it, Lord Sheldrake," she replied softly.

"Damen."

"Damen," she corrected herself, with a small smile. Abruptly, that smile vanished. "Something else just occurred to me, something I should have thought of before now. Will the outcome of my actions tonight— namely, our partnership—jeopardize your business relationship with Uncle George?"

The severe lines on Damen's face softened, and a hint of satisfaction glinted in his eyes. "I like the sound of my name on your lips," he murmured. "And, no, your uncle won't let his disapproval of our partnership interfere with his dealings with my bank or me."

Anastasia pursed her lips, still unconvinced. Given Damen's role in Uncle George's life and the powerful position he held on the board of Colby and Sons, it was doubtful he'd even seen the dark side of Uncle George, much less dealt with it. But Anastasia had. And she didn't want to be responsible for Damen's encountering it now. "Perhaps I shouldn't mention the partnership to him."

"If you don't, I will. And not only because the man is your guardian." Damen's fingers tightened around hers. "Anastasia, I'm not in the habit of explaining or defending my investment decisions, not unless those decisions involve my clients' funds. But when the funds in question are my own, I answer to no one but myself. If your uncle is uncomfortable about the partnership you and I struck, that's his problem, not mine. And definitely not yours. All right?"

A hesitant nod. "All right."

"There's still something troubling you," he pressed.

Anastasia quirked a brow. "You really do read minds."

"Um-hum." Damen shot her a broad grin. "Even while I'm dancing. As you yourself said, without missing a step."

His teasing relaxed her into her customary candor. "Very well, then. It's Breanna. I feel guilty. You should be dancing with her, not me."

Damen frowned, although he didn't look startled by her admission. "You worry about your cousin a great deal, don't you?"

"Yes. I did, even as a child. Probably because I had reason to."

"Well, you don't now; not at this particular minute. Breanna is surrounded by a large crowd of admirers. You can see for yourself after we round the next corner of the dance floor. Just look over my shoulder, to the left of the musicians." So saying, Damen whisked Anastasia about, angling her so she could see her cousin, who was, indeed, chatting with three or four gentlemen, obviously having a wonderful time.

"If you ask me, she's catching up on the Seasons she never had," Damen continued quietly. "She's enjoying all the newfound attention. Which is why it's too soon for her to be dancing with the same partner all night, and far too soon for her to be tied down to just one suitor. She knows I'm dancing with you. In fact, she urged me to go. Especially when she saw the predicament you were in. She was nearly as eager as I to rescue you from Percy Gilbert's lascivious hands."

Anastasia's eyes twinkled. "You just got to me first."

"Exactly."

"Tell me, Damen, how is it you know so much about Breanna and me? According to her, you've spent little time in her company. And I met you less than a fortnight ago. So where do these accurate perceptions come from?"

He drew her a tad closer. "Come riding with me and I'll tell you."

"What?" Anastasia was so surprised that she missed a step.

"Tomorrow. Before breakfast." Damen's grip about her waist tightened, steadying her on her feet. "I heard you tell Gilbert that you love to race. As it happens, so do I. We can take Medford's course at a rushing gallop. The winner gets to decide the order of surnames in our new partnership: Lockewood and Colby, or Colby and Lockewood. He or she also gets to choose the name of our new bank. Remember? That was what we were arguing about on the balcony when your uncle interrupted us."

"I remember." Anastasia wondered if she'd ever breathe again. This man affected her more powerfully than she ever would have believed possible. She was actually trembling, and she wasn't even sure why. "You have yourself a deal, my lord. We'll race at dawn. And *when* you lose," her eyes sparkled, "I want to hear how you come upon your insights into my cousin and me. *Then* I'll name our bank."

"Agreed." Damen's eyes were smoldering clouds of smoke. "I look forward to it—to the ride, to the conversation, and to whatever follows."

Across the room, Lord Dutton finished his fourth pastry and tapped George on the shoulder.

"Your niece and Sheldrake appear to be getting on famously," he noted, dabbing at his mouth with a napkin and pointing. "It seems that he's spent half the evening with her and the other half with Breanna." A chuckle. "Then again, perhaps he's lost track of which one is which."

"Yes. Perhaps," George muttered, watching intently as Sheldrake swept Anastasia about the room. They were too far away to make out their expressions, and he found himself fervently hoping that Sheldrake's sole purpose in sharing this prolonged waltz with Anastasia was to shake some sense into the outspoken chit.

Because if not . . .

"Pardon me, sir."

Wells came up behind him, and cleared his throat before continuing. "I apologize for interrupting, but this message just arrived from the Continent. It's marked urgent."

George pivoted, glancing down at the envelope and recognizing the familiar hand. "Thank you, Wells," he said, taking the message and giving Dutton a terse nod. "Pardon me, Dutton. There's some business I must attend to."

"Of course, of course." Dutton waved him away, hungrily eyeing the new platter of food that had just been carried in. "Business first."

"Right." George weaved his way through the room, again reminding himself to behave calmly, not to alert anyone to the urgency that was swelling inside him with each passing step.

He made his way to the hall, veering left, then striding purposefully down the corridor.

At last, he crossed the threshold to his study, shutting the door behind him.

Swiftly, he tore open the envelope, palms sweating with anticipation as he extracted the single sheet of paper and unfolded it.

It was inside the note.

George scanned the draft, then swore under his breath. The payment might have been anticipated, but the amount was not.

Determined to find answers, he turned his attention to the note.

Your last shipment was of poor quality and insufficient quantity, it read. *As a result, the agreed upon price of three thousand pounds is reduced to fifteen hundred pounds. Draft enclosed. Next shipment best arrive in a fortnight, prompt and up to previous standards, or no payment will be made and our association will be terminated.—M. Rouge*

"Goddammit." George crumpled the note into a ball and flung it into the fireplace. Broodingly, he watched it fray, then burn, turning to ashes before his eyes.

Raking a hand through his hair, he began pacing the room, sweat beading on his brow.

This was the last complication he'd expected. First Lyman, then

Meade, now Rouge. The obstacles were closing in on him like steel walls.

He'd be damned if he'd get crushed.

He *had* to regain control. And to do so, he had to get his hands on some money. Now.

Time was running out.

6

❦

$\mathcal{D}$awn was slicing the sky in wide streaks of orange and yellow when Anastasia made her way down to the stables the next morning.

She wasn't sure what to expect. Damen hadn't specified a time, and she hadn't had the opportunity to ask. In fact, they hadn't had a minute alone after their waltz together had ended. Immediately after the strings fell silent, a group of businessmen had cornered Damen, and Lord Percy Gilbert had whisked Anastasia into the next dance. After that, Gilbert had monopolized her attention, relinquishing her only when one of his persistent friends wedged his way between them, demanding a dance.

Breanna had eventually saved her, tactfully summoning her over to where the young women were clustered. According to her, the ladies were eager to make Lady Anastasia's acquaintance.

Anastasia didn't care whether that were true or not. She was thrilled to escape Gilbert's bold innuendos and wanton stares.

But as it turned out, it was true, and Anastasia had found herself the center of a hundred questions about life in the States, the gentlemen she'd met there, and the parties she'd attended.

Sometime after midnight, Damen had wandered over, politely interrupting only to bid both Colby girls good night.

Now it was morning—barely—and Anastasia wondered if Damen was even awake to keep their scheduled appointment. And if so, was he alert enough to race?

She rounded the path leading to the stables and got her answer.

There, leaning against the stable door, clad in a brown riding coat, beige breeches and black Hessian boots, arms folded across his chest as he awaited her arrival, was Damen.

He straightened when he saw her, his lips curving with pleasure, and a touch of surprise.

"I wasn't sure whether or not to expect you," he stated bluntly, walking toward her. "When I said good night, you were still very involved with your guests. I had visions of you dancing till dawn."

"No, only till one," Anastasia assured him, smoothing the folds of her bottle-green riding dress. "And I must admit, I, too, wasn't sure I'd find you here this morning. I thought you might be exhausted from hours of dancing and dispensing business advice."

Damen chuckled. "I don't tire that easily." He stopped, mere inches away from where she stood, his gaze sweeping over her appreciatively. "You look beautiful this morning. As you did last night, by the way. I never had the chance to tell you so. Not one man in your uncle's ballroom could tear his eyes away from you."

"Including you?" Anastasia asked boldly.

"Yes," Damen replied without the slightest hesitation. "Including me." With that, he gestured toward the stable door. "I took the liberty of having two horses saddled, in the event that you did arrive as planned."

"Really?" Anastasia baited. "And are they equally matched? Or can I expect you to be riding Uncle George's swiftest stallion while I'm on a sweet old nag?"

"Now how did I know you'd ask that?" he questioned with a wry grin. "Don't worry. I specifically asked the head groom to choose two well-matched, exceedingly swift mounts for our race." A grand sweep of his arm. "You're welcome to verify it for yourself."

"That won't be necessary." Anastasia tucked a strand of hair behind her ear, studying Damen as she spoke. "Any man who's as honorable in business as you wouldn't resort to cheating in a race. Besides, if you recall, I did promise never to question your integrity again."

"So you did." Damen glanced up as a leathery-faced groom led two horses out—both alert, both sleekly beautiful, their tails flicking in anticipation.

"This here is Sable, on account of her being all black." The groom indicated the first horse. "She's yours, m'lord. And this is Whisper, 'cause she's real quiet, likes to keep her ears up and listen to the other horses. She's for Miss Stacie here. Both these mares can run like the wind."

Anastasia looked at Whisper and frowned.

"What is it?" Damen asked.

"I intend to win this race. And I won't do that if I ride sidesaddle." She inclined her head at the groom. "Hughes, would you mind very much switching saddles for me? I'm going to race astride."

Hughes's gaze widened, but he nodded, dragging a forearm across his brow. "Whatever you say, Miss Stacie." He led Whisper back into the stable.

A corner of Damen's mouth lifted. "A wise decision."

"One that might cost you the race."

"I'll take my chances, and I'll take them with fair odds." His gaze narrowed quizzically. "I notice people call you Stacie."

"Only those who have known me since I was a child." A fond smile touched her lips. "When we were little, Breanna couldn't pronounce my name. Not that I blame her. It was hard enough for *me* to pronounce. Anyway, she shortened it to Stacie when we were three. The staff seemed to like it, so the name stuck. Those household members who are still here now—Wells, Hughes, Mrs. Rhodes, and a handful of others—seem to have reverted back to it since I returned. It makes me feel a little more at home." Anastasia's smile faded, and a wistful look crossed her face. "Grandfather called me Stacie. He said it suited me because I never stood still long enough for anyone to say Anastasia."

"An astute observation," Damen replied, his tone curiously gentle. "Then again, your grandfather was an astute man."

"Yes. He was."

"Here you are, Miss Stacie." Hughes led Whisper out, a standard saddle strapped on her back. "Just make sure to tuck those fancy skirts of yours out of the way," he advised, averting his face, which had gone beet red.

Anastasia's smile returned. "Don't worry. I will." She tossed Damen a challenging look. "Ready?"

"Ready."

They led the horses down the path to the open, grassy fields where the Medford horses were exercised. There, they stopped.

"You choose our course," Damen offered, gripping Sable's reins and squinting to assess the area. "Since you obviously know Medford Manor better than I do."

"Do I? You've probably spent more hours here than I have."

"That might be true, but my hours here have been spent in your uncle's library and study, while yours were spent racing horses and climbing trees. So you're far more familiar with the grounds than I."

"Agreed." Anastasia blew yet another loose strand of hair off her cheek, considering Damen's words. "In which case, I'll not only lay out our course, I'll deliberately alter it from the one I used to take as a child. That way, you won't be at a disadvantage." A sparkle danced in her eyes. "You see, my lord, you're not the only fair and ethical adventurer."

"So I see."

Giving up on her stubborn wisps of hair, Anastasia pointed across the field. "Do you see that fence? The one way down near the stream? We'll ride from here to there. Then, we'll veer left and make our way across to that line of hedges over there." She pivoted, drawing an imaginary line with her forefinger. "From that point, we'll race back to our starting point. How would that be?"

"Excellent. We'll use my coat as our makeshift finish line." Damen shrugged out of his coat and lay it on the ground, stretching the sleeves out to reach their maximum span. He gazed across the field intently, visually reviewing their path. Then, he turned and eyed Anastasia with a hint of a grin. "Can I offer you my assistance in mounting? You're going to have your hands full tucking those skirts out of the way."

She conceded, reluctantly, turning toward Whisper and frowning at the notable distance between the ground and the saddle. "This is not going to be one of my more graceful maneuvers."

"It won't be so bad. Watch." Damen came up behind her, his hands anchoring her waist. "Go ahead and put your left foot in the stirrup." The instant she complied, he lifted her off the grass, gently rotating her frontward as he did. "Now swing your right leg over. Gather up your skirts first. You'll worry about rearranging them once you're settled." A teasing note crept into his voice. "I won't peek. I promise."

Anastasia was laughing as she followed his instructions—a fact that slowed down the process considerably.

At last, she sank into the saddle, taking the handfuls of muslin she'd gathered up and shoving them beneath her.

"You don't look particularly comfortable," Damen noted, his gaze traveling up her bare legs and settling on the bulky cushion that separated her and the saddle.

"I thought you weren't going to peek."

His teeth gleamed. "That was when you were mounting. I couldn't resist watching this preparation ritual of yours."

Anastasia tossed him a saucy look. "Fine. Then, to answer your question—I don't feel particularly comfortable. However, I do intend to win."

"That remains to be seen." Damen walked around to Sable's left and mounted her in one smooth motion. "Shall I act as starter or would you like to?"

"By all means, my lord, you do the honors." Anastasia gathered up her reins. "I trust in your integrity." She leaned forward, her eyes straight ahead, her heels pressed close to Whisper's sides.

"Very well." Damen followed suit, a fine tension permeating his body as he leveled his stare at the fence. "On your mark . . . get set . . . go!"

The two horses took off like bullets, tearing down the path, Sable just a neck ahead of Whisper.

Sable reached the fence with two seconds to spare, then veered to the left, heading toward the line of hedges. Anastasia picked up speed, and she and Whisper caught up just as Damen rounded the hedges, prepared to make a break for their goal.

They galloped the last lap neck-and-neck.

Itching to glance over and see Damen's expression, Anastasia fought the impulse to do so. Even a small gesture like that would break her concentration and cost her precious seconds. And *that* could cost her the race.

Blood thrummed through her veins as she urged Whisper on, feeling the mare's instantaneous response. Her gallop increased, her legs literally flying off the ground, propelling her forward.

The problem was, Damen had the same idea.

Crouching low and forward, he and Sable moved as one, tearing toward the finish line, undaunted by Anastasia and Whisper's remarkable show of horsemanship.

Two pairs of front hooves struck the jacket simultaneously, one pair on the left sleeve, one pair on the right.

"Well, what do you know—a tie," Damen observed, his breath coming rapidly as he brought Sable around.

"Yes. It was." Anastasia sounded not only winded, but positively stunned. Patting Whisper's neck, she gave Damen a look of grudging respect. "You're a splendid rider, my lord. I didn't expect such fine competition."

Damen chuckled, gripping the front of the saddle as he dismounted. "What you really mean is, you expected to win." He walked over, inclined his head. "Right?"

Anastasia didn't hesitate. "You're right."

Laughter rumbled from Damen's chest. "Candid, if not modest. Then again, given your skill in the saddle, modesty would be misplaced." Idly, he stroked Whisper's muzzle, his brow creased in thought. "You do realize that our dilemma remains: the christening of our partnership and our bank."

"No," Anastasia corrected at once. "Only half our dilemma remains. With regard to our partnership, it will be Lockewood and Colby, just as I would have declared it had I won."

Damen looked startled. "But I thought . . ."

"You thought wrong. You assumed that, like most women, I'd be swayed by emotion. I'm not. The truth is, your family name carries a great deal more weight in the financial community than mine does. Colby and Sons is a trading company. The House of Lockewood is the most influential merchant bank in England, if not the world. The power of its name is invaluable. I'd be stupid not to use it to promote our bank. And, just as you claimed about yourself, I'll echo about me: I'm *never* stupid." An impish smile curved her lips. "However, I'm not entirely magnanimous either. I do demand equal say in naming our bank—just as a tie commands."

Rather than bantering back, Damen sobered, an odd expression flitting across his face—one that made Anastasia's own banter fade and caused her throat to tighten. "You're astonishing," he murmured.

"Is that a compliment?" she managed to ask.

"Yes." His gaze intensified, and he reached up, indicating his desire to help her dismount. "May I?"

Nodding, Anastasia leaned toward him, her breath catching as he lifted her up and out of the saddle.

She swung her right leg over to join her left, letting the damp folds of her gown flow free as Damen lowered her to the ground.

Their gazes caught—and held.

His hands lingered, and she could feel the pressure of his gloves, generating a heat that seeped through her clothes and into her skin, which was moist from the exertion of the race.

"Your riding is extraordinary," he told her. "As is your candor, your determination—and you."

"I'm also a mess." Anastasia couldn't believe those words had just popped out of her mouth. When had she ever been preoccupied with her appearance? When had it ever mattered to her how she'd looked after a wild dash on horseback?

Only now.

Tearing her gaze from Damen's, Anastasia regarded herself; the ruined gown flowing around dirt-stained stockings, not to mention her hair, which now tumbled free, cascading over her shoulders and back and sticking to her perspired neck and cheeks. She considered trying to rearrange it, then gave up the idea as hopeless. "It seems to me I'm in a perpetually rumpled state."

Damen shook his head slowly from side to side. "Not rumpled. Genuine. Uninhibited. Free-spirited. There's a big difference." He tugged off one of his gloves, capturing a strand of her hair and rubbing it between his fingers. "You embrace life, live it to its fullest. Never make light of that. It's a great blessing."

Anastasia's heart began hammering against her ribs. "You're speaking from experience."

"Um-hum." His knuckles caressed her cheek, his forefinger slipping beneath her chin to tilt it upward. "I'm much the same way. I seize life with both hands, savor every opportunity it hands me." His gaze fell to her lips. "Every one."

He lowered his head, capturing her mouth beneath his.

This kiss was nothing like the one he'd given her last night; nothing like anything she'd ever experienced. It was intense, commanding, his lips molding and shaping hers, urging them apart, his hands gripping her shoulders, gliding down the sleeves of her gown, then settling on her waist, tugging her closer as he deepened the kiss.

Anastasia shivered as his tongue touched hers, then claimed it in a slow, purposeful melding she felt down to the soles of her feet.

She moaned, torn between dizziness and drowning, and clutched at Damen's waistcoat, much more for balance than resistance. The truth was, resistance was the farthest thing from her mind. Not when what was happening was so unbearably exquisite.

"Put your arms around me," Damen instructed hoarsely, seizing her arms and bringing them up and around his neck. "Yes. Like that." His own grasp tightened, one arm anchoring her at the waist, the other tangling in her already disheveled hair. "Now give me your mouth."

"Damen, I . . ."

"Kiss me." He gave her no time to reply before swallowing her words, tasting and awakening her in a way that made her entire body start to tremble.

She sank into the kiss, her fingertips feathering over the nape of his neck, discovering the damp strands of hair that lay against his cravat, and exploring their silky texture. In contrast, his body was hard and powerful, his muscles flexing beneath her touch, his entire frame taut even through the confines of his shirt and waistcoat.

As if sensing her thoughts, Damen sharpened her awareness of him, drawing her closer, then crushing her fully against the unyielding wall of his chest. Anastasia's breath expelled in a rush, her breasts tingling beneath the onslaught, her entire body shimmering to life.

The kiss burned on and on.

When they finally broke apart, it was long minutes later, and they stared at each other in mutual astonishment, their breath coming in harsh rasps.

"God," Damen muttered, half to himself. His fingers, of their own volition, continued sifting through her hair, letting damp strands trail across his palm, between his fingers, then watching as they feathered slowly to her shoulders. "I expected fireworks. But *that*—that was . . ." He shook his head, as if words escaped him.

Anastasia licked her lips, trying desperately to gain control of herself. She felt wobbly, as if she'd run a great distance, and her heart was racing its accord. Her skin felt hot and shivery all at once, and there was a dull ache inside her—one that made her feel strangely empty and yet simultaneously full. Worst of all was her reeling mind, which seemed unable to grasp even a thought, or much of anything else for that matter.

Damen framed her face between his palms, his expression still reflecting amazement, his tone husky. "Are you all right?"

Reflexively, she nodded, although she doubted it was true. "I . . . yes."

A corner of his mouth lifted. "I'm not either."

"I'm not sure what just happened," Anastasia blurted out. A bright flush stained her cheeks. "I mean, I realize what happened, I just don't . . ."

"I understood what you meant." Damen's thumbs stroked her cheeks. "And I felt it, too."

Swallowing, Anastasia tried once again to collect herself, to right her upended emotions. "Our bank," she said, grabbing hold of the first coherent thought that flitted through her brain. "We should name it."

"Coward," Damen teased gently. But he followed her lead, letting his arms drop to his sides and taking a deliberate step away. "Very well, do you have a suggestion?"

"Yes." Anastasia was glad she'd mulled this over last night. There was no earthly way she could conjure up something profound in her current dazed state. "I think we should call it by the terms through which it was formed: Fidelity Union and Trust."

Damen's nod was almost instantaneous. "I agree. Lockewood and Colby. Fidelity Union and Trust. Fitting. Consider it done. I'll issue instructions to my assistant, have him draw up the papers with Fenshaw this very day. I'll look them over when I return to London tomorrow night. And you and I can sign them the next morning in my office."

"Wonderful." Anastasia averted her gaze, gripped Whisper's reins securely in her hand. "I think we should bring back the horses. It's nearly time for breakfast."

Silently, Damen studied her, and she could feel his steel-gray stare bore through her, even without turning her head for firsthand confirmation. "Fine," he said at length. "But we *will* talk about what happened here, Anastasia. Count on it."

George rose from behind his study desk, scanning the note he'd just penned.

Rouge, it read. *Received your meager draft. Consider it an installment on our agreed-upon sum. Be advised that, as my costs have risen, so have yours. Therefore, the shipment you received was fair and adequate. Nonetheless, you'll be pleased to learn that I've found a new source of supply, which will improve both the quality and the quantity. To demonstrate my good faith, a more extensive lot will be leaving in two to three weeks. The cost of that shipment is seven thousand five hundred pounds, including the fifteen hundred pounds due on the previous shipment. I'll advise you when the cargo is ready to sail. Rest assured, if you don't want the merchandise, another buyer will.—Medford*

That said it all. Clear, direct, and without revealing any of the worry that gripped his gut.

With a terse nod, George folded the note in two, slipping it into the envelope he'd addressed beforehand and sealing it.

Two could play this game of threats.

Unfortunately, only one could win.

Pressing his lips tightly together, George yanked open his drawer and returned his writing paper to its proper home. He hated leaving things out of place. In fact, he hated disorder of any kind.

In the process of shutting the drawer, he paused, extracting the miniature portrait he kept hidden in back. Staring at the delicate features and flawless skin, captured so perfectly on the tiny canvas, he scowled, the familiar rage starting to churn in his blood. Damn her. Damn them both. Things could have been so different. If only this part of his life had fallen neatly into line, everything else would have followed suit. His life, his family, his business—everything would have been in perfect order.

Well, it hadn't. And now chaos was everywhere.

With that, he shoved away the picture, shut and locked the drawer, and snatched up his letter. There was no time for brooding. He had work to do.

Purposefully, he strode down to the entranceway door, signaling for Wells as he did.

"I need this delivered immediately for dispatch to the Continent," he instructed the butler.

"Of course, sir." Wells glanced at the envelope as he took it. "Is it going to the customary address in London?"

"Yes."

"I'll see to it at once, my lord."

"Good." George glanced at the grandfather clock in the hallway. "It's after ten. Have the first guests awakened yet?"

"A few have made their way in for breakfast. A dozen or so of the gentlemen went out early, some to fish, others to hunt. All the ladies are still abed." A tender smile. "With the exception of Miss Stacie, of course."

"Anastasia? Is she in the dining room?"

"No, my lord. Although I should think she'd be ravenous. She was up and out before the sun, and returned to the manor, along with Lord Sheldrake, before eight."

"Returned?" That brought George up short. "Returned from where?"

"Why, from their ride, sir."

George stiffened. "You're sure it was Anastasia and not Breanna who went with Sheldrake?"

"Quite sure, sir. According to Miss Stacie, she and the marquess had some business to discuss."

"They left together?"

"No. Lord Sheldrake left the manor first, Miss Stacie about a quarter hour later." Wells frowned. "They were only gone a few hours, my lord."

"And then what?"

Wells's frown deepened. "Then they returned, each requesting that hot water be sent up to their respective bedchambers. After that, they went their separate ways. Lord Sheldrake came downstairs for breakfast and left the manor again about a half hour ago. And Miss Stacie is upstairs, waiting for Miss Breanna to awaken. She wants to have breakfast with her cousin."

"Did the marquess mention where he was going?"

"No, he didn't, my lord. He sent a message off to Mr. Cunnings at the bank, then headed out. I didn't get the impression he'd be gone long. Perhaps he joined the other gentlemen at the stream."

"Perhaps," George muttered, his lips thinning into a tight line of disapproval. "Then again, perhaps not."

Upstairs in her bedchamber, Anastasia paced restlessly about. She'd been unable to sit still—with the exception of her long soak in the tub—since she'd returned from the stables. And she knew exactly why.

It was that kiss she'd shared with Damen. Not only the kiss, but its significance—*and* its complications.

A deluge of guilt crashed down upon her shoulders, shattering the last vestiges of her earlier daze and bringing to light an issue she'd been evading since last night's ball.

Breanna. Or rather, Damen and Breanna.

Last night the prospect had hovered on the periphery of her consciousness, but had been eclipsed by her quest for financial backing, and later by her fascination for Damen. But there was no longer any excuse for dodging the all-too-crucial questions that today's kiss had accentuated.

Could a relationship between her cousin and Damen ever exist—not now, but in the future? True, they were merely acquaintances now, but might that change? Might they develop feelings for each other—feelings stemming from mutual respect and compatibility? After all, Breanna was changing, coming into her own. Damen himself had noticed that. Was it possible her feelings for him might change, too—or, if not change, grow? She *had* said she found the marquess charming, handsome, and intelligent. And as for Damen . . .

Almost against her will, Anastasia remembered Damen's observation of Breanna last night, what he'd said as they'd waltzed by.

She's enjoying all the newfound attention. Which is why it's too soon for her to be dancing with the same partner all night, and far too soon for her to be tied down to just one suitor.

By one suitor, had he meant himself? And if so, had he meant it as a response to Uncle George's obvious attempts to push him in Breanna's direction, or as a response to his own inclinations? Could Damen's comments be an indication, inadvertent or otherwise, that he intended to wait for Breanna, to indulge her until she came into her own? Was he destined to be the partner who ultimately stood at Breanna's side?

If so, Anastasia thought wildly, *then what happened this morning could completely undermine Breanna's future.*

She chewed her lip, her mind racing. Whatever had occurred between her and Damen, it had been based on passion, attraction, fascination; call it what you will. But it wasn't the kind of emotion that futures are based on. And if he and Breanna were meant to share a future—not one inspired by Uncle George's selfish whims, but one rooted in devotion—then what had she been doing, kissing Damen, losing herself in his arms and wanting never to stop?

Dejectedly, Anastasia dropped onto the edge of her bed, wondering how in the name of heaven she was going to deal with this. She couldn't speak to Breanna about it. She knew her cousin only too well. Breanna would always place her cousin's happiness above her own. If Anastasia so much as hinted at her attraction to Damen, Breanna would immediately squelch any feelings she might be developing just so as not to stand in Anastasia's way.

My way to what? Anastasia questioned herself. *There's no reason to assume Damen thinks of me as anything more than an exciting diversion.*

But if he did . . .

If he did, then there was something else to consider, something just as critical as Breanna's feelings, and perhaps a great deal more dangerous.

Uncle George. Uncle George and *his* reaction if a relationship were to develop between his niece and the man he intended to be his daughter's husband. Lord only knew how angry he'd get—and how he would vent that anger.

Or on whom.

Anastasia's jaw tightened. That settled it. She couldn't let this flirtation between Damen and her continue. She'd have to put an end to it—now—before it really began.

George was in a foul mood.

He continued to trudge across the eastern portion of the grounds, having already covered the western and northern sections, searching for any sign of Damen Lockewood. The marquess hadn't been in the expected locations: the stream, the hunting or riding areas, as the other guests had been. In fact, wherever he was, it was becoming increasingly apparent that he was alone. Because the only guest who, according to the others, was out and about and whom George had yet to come upon during this unwelcome excursion about Medford's grounds, was Viscount Crompton.

Predictably, the viscount had left the group he'd been hunting with to engage in target shooting on his own. As a retired military general, he prided himself on his superior skill with both rifles and pistols—a passion the other guests soon grew tired of hearing about and being forced to watch. And, as far as George knew, Damen had no particular affinity for the viscount and no interest in marksmanship. So, unless the two men were chatting about business, Sheldrake was alone.

The question was, why? Had Anastasia said or done something to give the marquess food for thought? Because Lord help her if she had. She'd already caused more trouble than she was worth, standing between him and Henry's assets, then embarrassing the hell out of him by approaching his guests for money to pour into some idiotic venture in the States. And now, this unexpected affinity between her and Sheldrake. It was trouble, any way you viewed it. Either the marquess was intrigued by her business ideas—or worse, by her.

Neither was acceptable.

But he'd find out exactly what was going on.

Then, he'd stop it.

7

ᗢ

The crack of a pistol brought George's head up.

Crompton, he thought, turning in the direction of the sound. He must be nearby.

Striding forward, he found himself hoping that the viscount might at least have spied Sheldrake. Hell, who was he kidding? That self-absorbed loon probably hadn't noticed a bloody thing. No doubt he was too caught up praising himself over his incomparable aim.

At that moment, he spied Crompton, standing in a clearing and reloading his pistol, his stance every bit as arrogant as he.

George approached quietly, coming up behind the viscount as he raised his head and surveyed a line of trees.

"Do you see that cluster of oaks over there?" Crompton inquired conversationally, never turning around. He smoothed his gloves more snugly into place, then gripped the handle of the pistol and raised it. "I'd judge them to be about a hundred feet away. See that center oak—the short one that's dwarfed by the others? There's a good-sized knot about halfway down. You can see it if you look closely. I'm going to hit that knot directly in the center." So saying, he aimed and fired, striking the knot dead-center.

"Excellent," George commended, wondering if Crompton was talking to himself or if he actually knew someone was behind him, given that he'd yet to look. And, once he realized he had company, did he plan on launching into an endless lecture on the fine art of marksmanship; or worse, recounting long-winded stories of his years in the infantry, fighting the French, the Americans, and whoever the hell else he'd fought?

"Thank you." The viscount turned, his lean, tanned face relaxing into a smile. "Ah, Medford. I thought you might show up, acting as a good host and checking to see if I'm enjoying myself. Well, I am. And I must say, it's nice to have an appreciative audience." He sighed, waving his arm, presumably in the direction of the gentlemen who were out hunting.

"I grew tired of shooting pheasants with amateurs. Anyone can strike a fat, slow-moving bird. It's mastering difficult targets that makes one feel truly accomplished."

George was in no mood for small talk, and less in the mood for Crompton's eccentric babbling. "I'm sure that's true. Actually, I can't stay and join you, much as I'd like to. I need to find Sheldrake. You haven't seen him, have you?"

"As a matter of fact, I have." Crompton flexed his shoulder, relaxing his lanky but well-muscled build for a moment. Despite the fact that youth had long since passed him by, extensive military training had left him as fit as a man twenty years his junior. "Sheldrake stopped by here a short while ago, said he was taking a walk." A knowing gleam. "And this time he was actually alone—not with that beautiful niece of yours."

A knot formed in George's stomach. "Why would you comment on that?"

"Oh, come now. Surely you saw the amount of time Sheldrake spent dancing with Anastasia last night. And they went riding early this morning. I saw them on their way back. They were laughing and joking like old friends. At first I thought it might be Breanna—I've heard rumors that you were encouraging a match between those two. But then I over-heard snippets of their chatter: financing, business endeavors, and the like. Not to mention the woman's less clipped articulation. And I real-ized it was Anastasia."

In one smooth motion, Crompton reloaded his weapon. "Maybe she managed to convince Sheldrake to invest in that bank of hers. She cer-tainly tried to convince me." A definite shake of his head. "But I have other ideas for how to increase my assets—ideas that can be furthered right here in England. And once those assets are mine, I'll deposit them in the bank of the very man you're looking for. He went in that direction, by the way." Crompton pointed toward the gardens on the south side of the estate. "He's a shrewd man, that Sheldrake. Smart as a whip."

"I agree." George was already walking. "That's why I need to find him. I'll catch up with you later, Crompton."

"Fine." The viscount adjusted his gloves, raised his pistol, and resumed his target practice.

Unaware he was being discussed, Damen continued along the path that led through the southern gardens. Hands clasped behind his back, he was lost in thought, scarcely noticing the colorful array of flowers at his feet.

His rule about never allowing anyone to surprise him more than once had long since fallen by the wayside. And the person responsible was the same person he couldn't seem to get out of his mind—not for a minute, not since she'd first confronted him in Fenshaw's office, fire burning in those beautiful jade-green eyes as she'd battled her resentment over finding out that he'd been appointed her financial administrator.

Anastasia.

Damen paused, staring out across the manicured lawns beyond the garden, marveling at the unprecedented effect this one woman had on him. While he was definitely a man of passionate views and commitments—and an equally passionate sense of adventure—he was not a man given to sentiment, nor was he particularly romantic in nature. He enjoyed women, their company and their charms, as they enjoyed his. But as for anything deeper, more significant—no woman had ever inspired that sort of response from him.

Then again, Anastasia was nothing like any other woman he'd ever known.

She was beautiful, yes, but her beauty was just the outermost layer of something far more compelling. It was like the sugar drizzled over a tantalizing confection: initially, it lured you over, made you want a taste. And yet, having sampled one, you suddenly realized that the icing was but the finishing touch on a cake that was distinctively luscious unto itself.

God, he was thinking like either a starving man or a romantic. And since he'd already eaten, that left the latter alternative.

So much for his lack of sentiment.

Damen stopped, leaning against a tree and contemplating the facts, if not the emotions, of the situation, with the careful deliberation he applied to investment matters.

Anastasia was drawn to him. She was too open to hide that. She was also enthralled by his knowledge, his contacts, and his influence in the financial community. She enjoyed his company, whether on the dance floor or on horseback, and she especially enjoyed matching wits with him, a fact that kept both their conversations and their arguments vibrant and interesting.

He, for his part, was fascinated by her quick mind, her untainted spirit, and her determination to overcome impossible odds—namely, becoming a successful businesswoman in a world dominated by men. He was impressed as hell by her intelligence and insight; it had been her absolute belief in their banking venture that had provoked him into doing additional research and, ultimately, into reversing his decision.

On a more intimate level, he was aroused by her boldness and her fire—aroused, he reminded himself ruefully, to the point of behaving like a rash schoolboy. Bad enough that he'd overstepped his bounds with last night's kiss. This morning, he'd all but devoured her—and that was nothing compared to what he'd wanted to do.

She hadn't pulled away, he reminded himself. Quite the opposite, in fact. She'd come alive in his arms, responded to his kiss—no, *shared* his kiss—with an intensity that had nearly brought him to his knees. And the bewilderment he'd seen in her eyes afterward: awe and pleasure combined with reluctance at having to stop, that only served to heighten the already unbearable ache in his loins.

He'd known her less than a fortnight, yet he wanted her to the point of distraction. He wanted her ardor, her innocence, the wealth of untapped passion he yearned to ignite, then go up in smoke with.

On a completely different note, he was also touched by the tender-hearted side of her; the side that wanted to shield Breanna, to recapture the past, to change and shape the future. He was moved by her unwavering loyalty and commitment to her cousin; to the entire Colby family, actually. He'd seen the sadness in her eyes that first day in Fenshaw's office, watched her reaction during her father's will reading. She'd been heartbroken by the loss of her parents—something that no inheritance could abate.

And she'd adored her grandfather.

Figuring out what made people tick was one of Damen's finest abilities—an ability that made him damned good at his profession. He'd watched Anastasia carefully as Fenshaw told her about the six hundred thousand pounds; first noting her zealous refusal to produce her coin, then perceiving her inner turmoil as she struggled to understand just what her grandfather had wanted of her and Breanna, what he'd hoped to accomplish with his elaborate provisions.

And last night, when he'd come upon her on the balcony, when she'd spoken of a Medford Manor that no longer was—the late viscount was the person she'd been speaking of, the person she'd been missing.

Obviously, Anastasia's grandfather had been very close to his grand-daughters—far closer than he'd been to his sons.

But George and Henry Colby were very different people, not only from their father, but from each other. And given George's unfeeling nature—well, there was no doubt in Damen's mind that Anastasia saw herself as Breanna's protector.

The question was, did Breanna need a protector?

"Sheldrake. At last."

The very man Damen was about to ponder headed toward him.

"Hello, George." Damen turned, arched a quizzical brow. "I assume you were looking for me."

"Indeed I was." George stopped alongside the tree where Damen was lounging, mopping his brow after the exertion of his walk. "I was beginning to fear you'd left Medford Manor entirely."

"Why would I do that?"

A stiff shrug. "It's just that no one knew your whereabouts. Wells said only that you'd taken a stroll, and it became clear to me that you did so alone. Is everything all right?"

Damen's eyes narrowed. "Of course. Why wouldn't it be?"

George hesitated, as if he were trying to decide how to phrase his answer. "I was concerned that someone might have offended you."

"Anyone in particular?"

"To be blunt, yes. My niece."

"Anastasia?" Damen feigned surprise, although he'd been expecting something like this. "Why would you think that?" A flicker of supposed realization—and a chuckle. "Do you mean because of her preoccupation with business? You know me better than that, George. I'm not bound to convention. Your niece is a very bright young woman."

"But she *is* a woman," George returned, his tone crisp. "And many of my guests were put off by her inane chatter about investing in an American bank."

Damen smiled, idly adjusting his cuffs. "Then your guests are fools. Because the notion is an excellent one. I've looked into it and I fully support Anastasia's efforts."

George's jaw looked as if it might drop into the peonies at his feet. "Are you saying you're allowing my niece to squander away a portion of Henry's money on a bank? In the States?"

"It's Anastasia's money now, George," Damen reminded him. "*All* of it. And, yes, I'll be authorizing the release of the necessary funds. In fact, I'll be doing more than that."

His complexion turning a sickly shade, George wet his lips with the tip of his tongue. His heart raced frantically as he tried to fathom just how much of Anastasia's inheritance was about to be lost to him forever. "You aren't suggesting . . ." He broke off, falling deadly silent as the final part of Damen's statement sank in.

Abruptly, the knot in his gut tightened to the point where he could barely speak. "More than that?" he repeated woodenly. "Are you suggesting that, on top of wasting Henry's funds, you're considering aiding Anastasia, acting as her backer in this absurd venture?"

"Her backer? No, I'm not considering that."

A tinge of relief crept into George's veins. "Thank goodness. You had me worried for a minute. I actually thought you were going to allow her to commit a large chunk of her inheritance to this, then make up the difference by loaning her your own funds . . ."

"I'm her partner," Damen interrupted. "We'll be investing equally in our new bank."

Another lethal silence.

Then: "You aren't serious."

"Oh, I'm very serious. The papers are being drawn up as we speak."

Unable to hide his outrage, George straightened, his eyes green chips of ice. "Why wasn't I consulted on this matter?"

Damen tensed ever so fractionally. "Because it wasn't necessary. If you recall, your guardianship doesn't extend to Anastasia's finances."

A flinch, the anger wavering a bit. "How much will each of you be investing?"

"That's not your concern either. Not unless Anastasia wants to share that information with you. The choice is hers." Damen's eyes narrowed on George's face. "Why does this bother you so much, George? It's not as if it's *your* money Anastasia is committing."

Sucking in his breath, George brought himself under rigid control. "You're right. It's not. But she is my niece; Henry's only child. And I worry that she'll squander the funds he provided for her future. Surely you can understand that?"

"Oh, I understand perfectly." A meaningful pause. "But don't lose a moment's sleep over Anastasia's financial security. I take my role as her administrator very seriously, just as Henry intended. I'd never allow her to compromise her inheritance."

"Of course you wouldn't." Damen's pointed tone had found its mark, and George flushed, cleared his throat. "Why don't we just drop the entire matter? I spoke without thinking. Of course my concerns are unfounded. With you managing Anastasia's assets, she'll never want for anything. I'm just glad you weren't offended by her rather forthright nature."

"I wasn't."

"Then why are you out here alone?" George forced a smile to his lips. "Or is that because you're passing time waiting for my lovely daughter to awaken from her long night of dancing?"

"Actually, there are several matters at the bank weighing heavily on my mind," Damen replied, choosing his words with purposeful care. "I only wish it *had* been Breanna I was contemplating. Your daughter has been one of the bright spots in my week. It occurred to me last night just how drab the past Seasons' balls have been without her there to light up the room."

This time there was a genuine, if still weak, quality to George's smile. "I'm pleased to hear that." He clapped Damen on the shoulder in an awkward gesture of friendship. "Then why don't we stop talking about finances and return to the manor? I'm sure Breanna is awake by now."

"A fine idea."

Breanna and Anastasia had just finished breakfast and were descending the stairs when the two men entered the manor.

"Ah, Breanna." George took a step forward, then paused, glancing uncertainly from one girl to the other.

"Yes, Father?" Breanna gathered up her skirts and moved forward, automatically touching her smooth knot of upswept hair to ensure it was in place.

"Lord Sheldrake was wondering where you were," George responded, totally ignoring his niece. "I assured him you'd be awake by now."

"We were experimenting with Stacie's hair," Breanna responded, glancing proudly at Anastasia, whose hair had been arranged in much the same fashion as hers. "Doesn't it look lovely?"

"H-m-m-m?" George gave his niece a perfunctory look. "Oh. Yes, yes, of course."

A grin curved Anastasia's lips. "It's stayed put for nearly ten minutes now. That's a record, at least for me." Her laughing eyes met Damen's, and instantly she averted her gaze. "If you'll excuse me, I promised Mrs. Rhodes I'd give her Mama's recipe for glazed cross-buns. They were the talk of Philadelphia."

"I'm sure they were." George gave a dismissive wave. "By all means, go." He waited until she'd complied, then turned to Damen. "I'd best check on the rest of my guests. I'll leave Breanna in your capable hands."

"My pleasure." Damen gave a half-bow, smiling at Breanna as George turned and walked off.

But once George was gone, and for the briefest of instances, Damen's gaze flickered toward the kitchen, watching as Anastasia disappeared from view.

Dammit, George thought, hovering on the threshold of the billiards room, observing his guests as they played. What else could go wrong at this bloody party? First the news about Meade and his threats, then Rouge trying to renegotiate their deal, and now Sheldrake and his unexpected affinity for Anastasia.

Bad enough that Sheldrake was actually condoning the chit's squandering away funds that by all rights should have been his—and believing in her enough to invest his own money, to actually form a partnership. But the amount of time the marquess was spending with her—the waltzes, the early morning rides—how much of that was business and how much personal interest?

George had taken steps to find out how much money was being invested in that partnership—the right steps. It had been a stupid blunder on his part to ask Sheldrake outright how much of Anastasia's inheritance she was committing. With any luck, he'd withdrawn the question in time to avoid permanent damage. He'd find out in his usual fashion, from his usual source, who'd be receiving his instructions within the hour. As for the personal aspect of Sheldrake and Anastasia's relationship, he'd take care of that himself.

He needed Sheldrake. He needed more and better quality merchandise. He needed the money both would yield. And he needed time to get them—time he didn't have.

Only ten weeks until Anastasia's twenty-first birthday. If he didn't get his hands on Henry's money by then, it would slip through his fingers. Anastasia would be an independent woman, no longer under his guardianship; free to go where she pleased, live where she pleased, marry whomever she pleased.

And take her bloody inheritance with her.

Damn. He *had* to get Henry's money while Anastasia was still living at Medford Manor, under his roof and his guidance. He had to eliminate all the obstacles. They were cluttering his path. Especially Anastasia.

First things first. One obstacle at a time.

Shifting his weight, George peered into the billiards room, waiting for just the right moment to catch Bates's eye.

The magistrate must have sensed something because he missed his shot, then glanced up to find George studying him from the doorway. Ever so slightly, George angled his head in the direction of the French doors, indicating to Bates that he wanted to see him alone.

Bates gave an almost imperceptible nod.

"That's enough for me," he announced, tugging his waistcoat down over his portly belly and backing away from the table. "My luck is definitely not here today. Perhaps I'll do better at the gaming table."

A few grumbling retorts followed, but on the whole the men accepted Bates's quitting without question and resumed their play.

Bates checked the doorway again, noticed that it was now empty. Confirming that everyone's attention was no longer on him, he ambled toward the rear of the billiards room and strolled through the French doors. There, he paused, whistling as he idly surveyed the grounds.

As if by chance, George joined him, coming around the side of the manor and greeting his guest.

The two men walked off, chatting amiably.

"What's wrong?" Bates murmured when they were beyond hearing range. "I thought we'd taken care of your problem when we spoke last night. I told you I'd find you a new source. And I will."

"There's another problem I need to discuss with you—one I couldn't get into at the ball," George replied.

"Which is?"

"Meade."

A sigh. "Is he giving you trouble again? What is it this time—stealing the goods or tampering with them?"

"Worse. He's refusing to deliver my merchandise without a hefty pay increase. He's also making some threatening noises that sound disturbingly like blackmail. And *that* is something I will not tolerate."

No, but you'll inflict it, Bates thought bitterly. Aloud, all he said was, "What do you need?"

"An arrest warrant." George pursed his lips. "I need something to hold over Meade's head. A warrant would do the trick nicely. The charges are certainly real enough. The bastard is guilty of smuggling, privateering, maybe worse. You've conveniently overlooked all that to suit our purposes. Well, now our purposes have changed. And, as we both know, Meade is terrified of being sent to the gallows."

"So if you remind him that we can send him there, you ensure his cooperation." Bates nodded his balding head. "A sound idea. Consider it done."

George came to a halt. "When can you get it to me?"

"Is tomorrow soon enough? I can have my messenger deliver it by nightfall."

"Tomorrow is fine. I'll pay Meade a visit the next morning, wave the warrant in his face." A bitter smile. "That will do a great deal toward ensuring his cooperation, and his flexibility about payment."

"Then it's settled." Bates relaxed, as he always did when he'd satisfied Medford's demands. In truth, he hated dealing with the man. It made him jittery every time the viscount sent for him. But he owed Medford, and would continue to owe him as long as he wanted to keep his position of power.

How many times had he berated himself for accepting Medford's first offer, thus allowing the snake to have this much control over his life? But it was too late now. Medford's support, his connections, were what had ensured that Bates received—and kept—his appointment as magistrate of, not one, but three thriving districts, including this one in Kent. Undermining Medford would cost him everything: his reputation, his appointment, and, knowing Medford, perhaps even more.

The prospects were chilling.

"Your party is a rousing success," Bates commented, switching to the safer ground of casual conversation. "Your niece was welcomed with open arms by nearly every unattached man, as well as many of the attached ones. And the added attraction of having Breanna among us again—" A chuckle. "If I weren't so old, I'd give Sheldrake some competition myself. I'd happily choose either of the women he's pursuing."

George's head snapped up. "Either of the women he's pursuing?"

Instantly, Bates realized his error. "Not to worry. He spent most of the evening with Breanna."

"And the rest of it with Anastasia," George amended bitterly.

"I'm sure he was just being cordial. I wouldn't give it a thought."

"I have to give it a thought. More than a thought, in fact." George's hands balled into fists at his sides, his mutterings only half audible. "If she does anything else to ruin my life . . ." He stopped, sucked in his breath. "Just take care of the warrant," he snapped at Bates. "I'll deal with Anastasia."

8

❧

$\mathcal{T}$he House of Lockewood was even more impressive than Anastasia had imagined. Running almost the full length of Bishopsgate Street, it was a veritable world unto itself—a dignified world, with high, molded ceilings, polished marble floors and, at the head of the room, a bronze plaque of a coin bearing the Lockewood family crest, set on a pedestal and flanked by twin columns. One side of the bank boasted a triple set of doors that admitted patrons, and between the doors were rows of floor-to-ceiling windows, adorned by deep-green velvet drapes.

The uniformed staff, properly spaced along the entire periphery of the room, stood behind walnut gates, ready to assist the bank's clientele. In the rear of the room were small, private cubicles, where bank officers could meet with customers on matters that required additional attention. Behind the cubicles stood a towering walnut door bearing a bronze plaque etched with the word PRIVATE—a clear divider between the main room and whatever lay beyond.

Anastasia wandered farther into the bank, her gaze shifting to the bustle of activity taking place around her. How many dozens of people must come and go from here over the course of a day, contributing to the aura of importance that permeated the House of Lockewood? How many of those people had Damen Lockewood advised, turned profits for, vitally impacted with respect to their financial success?

"My lady." A reedy gentleman, whose sleek top hat and dark green uniform heralded him as an employee of the House of Lockewood, hurried forward, bowing the instant Anastasia entered the bank. "We've been expecting you."

As he spoke, the bank's clock chimed eleven, precisely the hour Anastasia had told Damen she'd be arriving.

Curiously, she inclined her head. "Forgive me, sir, but how do you know who I am?"

A polite smile curved his lips. "I'm the head gatekeeper here. It's my job to recognize all our clients. Lord Medford visits our bank often, sometimes with Lady Breanna. And Lord Sheldrake told me how much alike you and your cousin look."

Anastasia smiled back. "I'm impressed, Mr. . . . ?"

"Graff," he supplied. Another bow. "And it's my pleasure to assist you, my lady." He stepped back, making a grand sweep with his arm. "If you're ready, I'll show you to Lord Sheldrake's office. Mr. Fenshaw is expected shortly."

"Thank you, Mr. Graff." Anastasia cast another awed look around, then gathered up her skirts and followed him across the marble floors, past the individual cubicles, and through the massive walnut door.

A semicircular expanse of imposing offices loomed before her.

"This way, my lady." Graff gestured toward the farthest—and, clearly, the grandest—office; the one nestled in the corner by itself. He paused, knocking briskly on the gleaming door.

"Yes?" Damen's deep baritone rumbled from within.

"Lady Anastasia is here, my lord."

"Show her in, Graff."

"Yes, sir." Graff turned the handle and eased open the door. "Go right in, my lady," he instructed, carefully remaining outside.

"Thank you." Wondering what on earth to expect, Anastasia gripped the folds of her lilac gown, and crossed the threshold.

Instantly, the door shut behind her—so firmly that she jumped.

Chuckling, Damen rose from behind his desk, smoothing his striped silk waistcoat as he walked around to greet her. "Alone in the lion's den," he teased, taking her gloved hand and kissing it.

"That's a bit what I feel like." Anastasia studied her surroundings, taking in the walnut furnishings and green velvet drapes, similar to the ones that accented the rest of the bank, along with a few personal touches: stacks of leather-bound books on the desk and shelves, an Oriental carpet atop the polished floor, and two magnificent landscape paintings adorning the walls.

"Are you pleased with what you see; actually, with everything you've seen throughout the bank thus far?"

Anastasia nodded in amazement, her gaze returning to his. "I'm astounded. In fact, it's good I met you elsewhere first, or I'd probably be very intimidated."

Laughter rumbled from Damen's chest. "I can't imagine anyone or anything intimidating you."

* * *

"You're right." An impish grin. "Then let's just say I wouldn't have been nearly as relaxed around you as I have been." A bright flush stained her cheeks. "By relaxed, I didn't mean . . ."

"I know what you meant." He was still holding her hand, brushing her gloved fingers against his lips. "I also know that something's going on in that beautiful head of yours, something that's making you keep your distance from me. You barely spoke a word to me at the party—*after* our ride, that is. Those few minutes following the race, when we were together—did I offend you?"

She didn't pretend to misunderstand. "You know you didn't."

"Good. I didn't think so." Without warning, Damen tugged her closer, brought her arms around his neck. "In that case we'll discuss your misconceptions later, whatever they might be. Because Fenshaw's due here soon with our papers, after which we won't be alone. And since I've been unable to stop thinking about you—the feel of you in my arms, the taste of your mouth under mine—and since I can't seem to act rationally around you, I need to do this." His palms slid down the length of her arms, capturing her face and angling it toward his.

Anastasia's breath caught, but she had no time to react before Damen's mouth swooped down, seized hers in a hot, bone-melting kiss. Demonstrating none of the other morning's gradual onset, he let the powerful pull between them take over, his lips moving purposefully over hers, his arms rigid as they shifted to her waist, bringing her against him.

"Anastasia." He said her name, and the sound made shivers go through her. She opened her mouth to respond, and his tongue slid inside, teasing and caressing hers until a low moan escaped her.

Damen tightened his grip, drawing her closer still, kissing her more deeply, his hands moving restlessly up and down her spine.

For a moment, Anastasia gave in, her eyes sliding shut as she sank into the kiss, pleasure drenching her senses as she felt Damen's warmth, his incredible power, engulf her. She pressed against the solid wall of his chest, felt the silk of his waistcoat against her cheek, the crisp muslin of his shirt collar beneath her fingertips. It was exquisite, this intoxicating feeling that flowed through her, making her limbs go weak and her heart pound like a drum. The sensations were just as they had been two days ago, only stronger, more potent. She could drown in this feeling, her body too alive to protest, her mind too dizzy, too clouded . . .

Much too clouded.

That triggered a warning bell—one that screamed its reminder about her decision—and its basis.

Abruptly, Anastasia tensed, planting her hands firmly on Damen's shoulders and wrenching herself away. "Don't," she managed, her breathing shallow. "Please."

Damen caught at her elbows, his tone and expression raw. "What is it? Why are you pulling away?" He frowned. "Dammit, Anastasia, answer me. Are you upset with me?"

Resolutely, she stepped backward, folding her arms across her breasts—whether for emphasis or emotional support, she wasn't certain. "I'm not upset with you. I'm upset with me. With us. With the situation." She inhaled slowly, determined to stand her ground. "Why don't we pretend this never happened, and just get to the purpose of my visit: signing our partnership papers?"

His eyes narrowed on her face. "I can't do that. Neither, for that matter, can you. As for the papers, we can't sign them until Fenshaw gets here. And he's not due for twenty minutes."

Anastasia blinked. "Your note said the appointment was at eleven."

"It said *your* appointment was at eleven. Fenshaw's is at half after. I wanted some time alone with you."

Why did that notion elicit a rush of pleasure she couldn't squelch? "Damen, this is a bad idea," she informed him, knowing how unconvincing she sounded.

"On the contrary, it's the best idea I've had in ages." He moved closer again, threaded his fingers through her hair. "What happened to the new style you were trying?" he murmured, sifting strands of burnished copper off her shoulders.

"It failed miserably. By last night I gave it up. I simply can't keep my hair from toppling to my shoulders, no matter how hard I try."

"Stop trying." Damen brought one tress to his lips, savoring its texture. "You weren't meant to look prim. You were meant to look unaffected, sometimes disheveled, always beautiful—and always unique, the way you looked on horseback." His forefinger slid beneath her chin, raised it until their gazes locked. "The way you look now, with your lips still moist from mine and your eyes asking me to kiss you again."

"Damen . . ." Anastasia had no idea what she was going to say. Her palms were on his lapels, smoothing up the cloth of his blue tailcoat.

"H-m-m?" His lips brushed hers, once, twice, then hovered as he awaited her consent. "One more kiss," he said, his breath teasing her mouth. "Just one. Then we'll talk."

She took an unconscious step closer. "And this kiss will be the last?"

"If you want it to be."

Her eyes searched his face. "You know I don't want it to be."

"Um-hum. And I also know why you believe it should be." His knuckles caressed her cheek, the side of her neck, the curve of her shoulder, absorbing the tiny shivers his touch elicited. "What you're thinking—it's not true, Anastasia," he said huskily. "I promise you, it's not. Now stop fighting the inevitable and kiss me."

"You don't understand . . ."

"Yes I do. Now kiss me."

She gave up. She didn't have the strength not to. Not when she wanted more than anything to feel the incredible pleasure of his mouth on hers again.

With a breathy sigh, she leaned up, closing the distance between their lips and giving him exactly what they both wanted.

Damen took over, penetrating and devouring her mouth in hungry, relentless possession. His arms locked around her like steel bands, and he drew her up on tiptoe, crushing her body to his in a way that made her blatantly aware of his hardening contours.

"Don't pull away," he muttered against her lips. "Just lose yourself. For a minute. That's all I ask."

Ask? He didn't need to ask. Anastasia was already complying, molding her body instinctively to his, twining her arms about his neck as their tongues melded, parted, melded again.

With a rough, appreciative sound, Damen relinquished another modicum of control, his hand gliding around to find and cup her breast. His thumb found her already hardened nipple, rubbing it sensuously through her gown, sending skyrockets of sensation shooting through her.

"Damen . . ." She gasped his name, every nerve ending in her body centered beneath this new, incredibly spectacular sensation. His only answer was a harsh groan, a tremor racking his body as he pressed more urgently against her, his thumb continuing its motion—faster, more voracious.

Long minutes passed, time and the world held at bay, the kiss, the embrace, blazing hotter, growing more abandoned.

Abruptly, with what was clearly a herculean effort, Damen yanked up his head, dragged his hand away from Anastasia's breast. He planted both hands on the safety of her waist, gripping her tightly as if to anchor not only her but himself. Neither of them spoke, just stared at each other, their breathing labored, uneven.

"Anastasia," Damen managed at last, her name a hoarse, awed caress. "Ending that was the hardest thing I've ever had to do." His gaze sharpened, delved inside her. "But the kiss is all I ended. Make sure you understand that. Everything else between us is just beginning."

Pangs of guilt and worry intruded on the moment. "It can't."

An astute look. "Because of Breanna. Or rather, Breanna and me. And whatever it is you perceive about us."

She started. "You *do* know."

"I told you I knew. I also told you you're wrong."

"If you'd already guessed the reason for my aloofness, why did you question me?"

"Because I wanted to make sure there wasn't something else bothering you—something more than the foolish conclusions you'd jumped to. I saw my answer in your eyes."

Anastasia sighed, still reeling from the impact of their embrace. "What you saw there was real; I'm not denying that. I wanted you to kiss me. But that does nothing to change what can and cannot be."

Damen's jaw set. "Don't you think *I* should have some input into that decision? Or have you already sent me marching down the aisle with your cousin?"

Confusion knotted Anastasia's stomach, and she broke Damen's grasp, turned away. "I'm not planning your life, Damen. That was done before I arrived."

"By your uncle," he supplied.

"Or by fate."

"Fate?" Damen made a frustrated sound, gripping Anastasia's shoulders and whirling her around to face him. "I'd say fate is playing a much bigger hand in fanning the flames that burn between you and me, than in pushing me toward Breanna."

That Anastasia couldn't deny. "I'm not saying you're in love with Breanna. Nor, for that matter, is she in love with you. But you do enjoy being in each other's company. That was obvious at the ball. And given time . . ."

"Given time, she and I would be nothing more than good acquaintances who like and respect each other," Damen finished. "Just as we are now. And, before you ask, that would have been the case whether or not you returned to England."

"How can you be so sure?"

A wry grin tugged at Damen's lips. "If you'd given me the chance to tell you about my insights into you and your cousin, you'd know why. That was one of the unfulfilled terms of our racing bet, remember?"

Anastasia felt her lips curve in return. "I remember." She inclined her head, studying Damen's expression. "Very well. Share your insights with me."

"All right. I'll begin with my assessment of you." Damen's fingers caressed her shoulders, his touch warming her skin through the fine muslin of her gown. "You, Lady Anastasia Colby, are a strong-willed, intelligent, spirited nonconformist. You're always the leader, never the follower. You believe in yourself, in your ideas and your principles, and you believe life was meant to be savored, not nibbled at. You have keen instincts, a quick mind, and an independent nature. You also—as you're first discovering—have a rush of untapped passion just waiting to burst free." Damen's gaze fell to her mouth. "And I unlock that rush of passion in you. Just as you do in me."

Anastasia swallowed. "I think I've just been called a bluestocking," she managed weakly. "A bluestocking and a wanton."

"I think you've just been called breathtaking," Damen replied. "Breathtaking, enticing, and so beautiful you bring a man to his knees." He lowered his head, brushed her lips with his. "All of which you are." Another whisper of a kiss. "Shall I continue?"

A heartbeat of a pause.

"With my insights," Damen clarified.

"Oh." Why did she have to sound so disappointed? Probably because she was. "Yes—go on."

The glitter in Damen's eyes said he knew precisely what she was thinking, and that he shared her hunger. "Now for Breanna," he said, his lips hovering just above hers. "Breanna is like a beautiful flower: sweet, vivid, always pleasing to the eye, every petal perfectly in place. She's delicate, yes, but she's stronger than she appears to be—*if* she's cared for. *When* she's cared for," Damen amended. "Which she will be—by the right man." He framed Anastasia's face between his palms. "I'm not that man, Anastasia. I never will be. Breanna and I just aren't right for each other—not now, not ever."

Anastasia wet her lips with the tip of her tongue. "Does Uncle George know that?"

"No. He doesn't *want* to know that. And I've been reluctant to tell him—probably for the same reason you are."

She hesitated, then blurted out, "How well do you know my uncle—on a personal basis?"

Damen considered the question. "Not well. But the way a man conducts himself in business tells you a lot about the way he conducts his life."

"Business *is* Uncle George's life," Anastasia replied bitterly. "Business and the money it generates."

"I'd be a nice source of income, wouldn't I?" Seeing the startled look on Anastasia's face, Damen quirked a brow. "Did you think I was so arrogant—and naive—as to believe your uncle wanted me for his son-in-law because of my outstanding character and kind heart?"

Anastasia's lips twitched. "I suppose not."

"My suspicions are that he's not faring as well financially as he would have liked. Frankly, he just doesn't have either your grandfather's business acumen or your father's innovativeness and flair with people."

"Are you saying he's having monetary problems?"

Damen shrugged. "I only know as much as George lets me know. Colby and Sons is doing fine. But as for your uncle's private investments—those he doesn't conduct through me—I have no idea. Still, it would certainly explain his eagerness for Breanna and I to wed."

Anastasia's laugh was humorless. "You don't know my uncle. He doesn't need a reason to crave money and power. He could be the second richest man on earth, and he'd still battle for first place. And you: the head of the House of Lockewood, rich, titled, renowned everywhere and by everyone; you're an asset that's far too desirable to let slip through his fingers—whether or not he's short of funds." She averted her gaze, her expression drawn with worry. "Uncle George is such a cold, hard man. My only fear is that . . ."

"You think he'll take out his anger on Breanna? That he'll blame her for not winning me over, so to speak?"

A chill permeated Anastasia's heart. "I don't know. Nor do I know just how severe a form that anger might take. But I don't want to find out."

"At some point, we'll have to."

"Perhaps by then, Breanna will have met someone else—someone even wealthier and more influential than you." Anastasia sighed. "I don't suppose your scores of contacts could arrange that, could they?"

Damen gave a rueful chuckle. "They could summon extraordinary gentlemen from all four corners of the globe. But they couldn't ensure that one of those men would be right for Breanna."

"No, I suppose not."

Gently, Damen tilted up her chin. "Would you feel better if I spoke to your uncle? I could take full responsibility for not pursuing Breanna."

Anastasia's inner chill intensified. "And then do what, pursue me instead?" A hard shake of her head. "That would be the worst possible course to take. Rejecting Uncle George's daughter, then showing an interest in his brother's? You have no idea of the reaction you'd trigger. I shudder to think." She chewed her lip, chose her next words carefully. "The resentment Uncle George feels for Papa—for all three of us: Papa, Mama, and me—runs deep."

Again, Damen's eyes narrowed. "And you don't want to discuss why."

"No. I don't. But please, Damen, I need your word that you won't say anything to my uncle—not about what you don't feel for Breanna or what you might be feeling for me."

"I can't do that. Not when I fully intend to see you again. Not just once, but over and over." Damen's voice grew husky, and he threaded his fingers through her hair, that hot light flaring in his eyes. "We can't ignore what's happening between us. I *won't* ignore it."

A shiver ran through her. "Nor can I. But we'll have to be discreet about seeing each other. We'll have to say we're meeting just to discuss my inheritance."

"And our partnership," Damen reminded her.

She frowned. "I have to ask again, are you sure you want Uncle George to know about that?"

"He already does. I told him the morning of our race."

"You did?" Anastasia's eyes widened. "He hasn't said a word." She contemplated that fact. "Then again, I haven't seen him alone for a minute. He was with his guests until the final ones took their leave late last night. And this morning, he left right after breakfast." An uncertain look. "How did he react?"

Damen shrugged. "Much as you'd expect. He wasn't happy—not with the partnership, nor with the fact that a portion of your inheritance will be leaving the country. But he'll get over it. He'll have to. He has no choice." A quick glance at the clock. "Speaking of our partnership, Fenshaw is due here any minute. I'm afraid our private moments together are running out, for now."

That brought a sparkle to Anastasia's eyes. "Tell me, Lord Sheldrake, now that we've enjoyed this half hour alone, what would you have done if I'd brought my lady's maid with me? May I remind you that most women don't travel to London alone?"

"True. Most women don't, but you do." Damen's teeth gleamed. "You would never allow a chaperon to attend this meeting, or any other business meeting that involved you, for that matter. Even if your uncle insisted, you'd have asked your maid to wait in the carriage." A cocky look. "Another splendid insight?"

"Definitely."

Damen snapped open his gold pocket watch and realized Fenshaw's arrival was imminent. "We'll decide later how to handle your uncle—and what the best strategy is for seeing each other. In the meantime . . ." He buried his lips in hers for a brief, heated kiss that singed her down to her toes. "As I said before—only the beginning," he muttered as Graff's knock sounded. "Remember that, Anastasia. We're going to find out where this fire blazing between us is going to lead. Soon."

Forty-five minutes later, Damen sat back in his chair, nodding as he scanned the final page of the document he held. "Excellent," he praised Fenshaw. "You've put in all the terms we discussed."

"I'm glad you're pleased." Mr. Fenshaw, seated on the other side of the massive desk, pushed his spectacles higher onto the bridge of his nose, and gestured at Damen's quill. "Shall we summon Cunnings and you can begin signing . . . ?"

"Not yet." Damen held up his palm, glancing at Anastasia, who sat beside Fenshaw. "There are two of us involved in this partnership. I have yet to hear Lady Anastasia's final word on these papers."

Fenshaw's red cheeks grew redder. "Forgive me. I'm just not used to . . . I'm not in the habit of . . ."

"I understand, Mr. Fenshaw," Anastasia soothed him. With a twinkle, she turned back to Damen, sliding her copy of the document onto his desk. "The terms are not only fair, they're even readable to those of us who are new to the world of finance. I thank both you and Mr. Fenshaw for being so considerate." She inclined her head. "One question: once we sign, what's the procedure?"

"Before we sign, John Cunnings will be joining us. He's my senior officer, and my right-hand man. He's also in charge of the House of Lockewood's overseas investments. He'll be joined by another officer of the bank. Together with Mr. Fenshaw, those gentlemen will witness our signatures. Graff will then see to it that one copy of the sealed document is sent by courier to Mr. Carter in Philadelphia. Authorized funds from both my account and yours will be transferred to the States, after which, the building of our new bank will commence." A corner of Damen's mouth lifted. "Any other questions?"

"Not for now." Anastasia folded her hands primly in her lap. "I'll let you know if that situation should change."

"I'm sure you will." Damen rang for Graff, who hurried in, the essence of professionalism.

"Yes, my lord?"

"Tell Cunnings we're ready for him. Ask Booth to join him."

"Right away." Graff rushed off, leaving the door ajar.

Not a minute later, two men entered: one an older fellow with a round face and a full head of white hair, the other—who led the way—younger, in his mid thirties perhaps, tall and broad, with dark, close-cropped hair, a square jaw, and intelligent blue eyes.

"You're ready for us?" the younger man asked Damen, waiting respectfully just inside the office.

"Yes. Come in." Damen rose to his feet. "You both know Mr. Fenshaw, of course. And this is Lady Anastasia Colby, my partner in the business venture we're consummating today. Anastasia, may I present John Cunnings and William Booth."

"A pleasure, my lady." Mr. Cunnings bowed, kissing Anastasia's hand and clearly trying not to stare.

"Yes, she is beautiful and yes, she does bear a remarkable resemblance to Lady Breanna," Damen supplied, as if Cunnings had spoken.

"She certainly does." If Cunnings was embarrassed by Damen's remark, he gave no indication of such.

"It's uncanny." Mr. Booth—who upon closer inspection was not old as Anastasia had first thought, but rather prematurely white-haired—shook his head in amazement, assessing her thoroughly as he bowed, brought her hand to his lips. "Are people actually able to tell you apart?"

"Not most people, no." Anastasia fought the urge to look at Damen who, thus far, was one of the few people who seemed never to confuse her and Breanna. "Often not even our parents."

"I'm not surprised." Booth made another sound of disbelief, then recovered himself. "Forgive me for staring. I've seen your cousin only twice, but she has such vivid coloring, such striking beauty—suffice it to say she's not easy to forget. And the resemblance between you two is staggering." Roughly, he cleared his throat. "I apologize for rambling on like that. I hope I haven't embarrassed you."

"Not at all," Anastasia assured him. "Actually, your compliment was lovely; sincere enough to be appreciated, yet indirect enough to avoid making me feel self-conscious." A smile. "After all, it was Breanna you were describing, not me."

Damen interrupted the exchange with a purposeful rustle of the papers that were the subject of today's meeting. "Now that we've completed the introductions, let's get our signatures on these, shall we?" He produced a second quill from his desk drawer, handed it to Anastasia. "Ready?"

A definite nod. "Ready."

Ten minutes later, the papers were ready to dispatch.

"Do you miss America?" Cunnings asked conversationally as they awaited Graff's return.

"Some aspects of living there, yes," Anastasia replied with total candor. "I miss the people; they were lovely. I miss some of the freedom I had in Philadelphia that isn't possible now that I'm home. But most of all, I miss the essence of my life in the States: my parents." A reflective pause. "Actually, that's not a fair statement. I'd miss Mama and Papa no matter where I lived, possibly more so if I'd stayed on in America without them."

She dispelled the sober mood with a dismissive wave. "On the other hand, it's wonderful to be back in England. I longed for so many aspects of home: the bustle of London, the beauty of the countryside and, of course, Medford Manor and Breanna. It means the world to me that I'm with my cousin again. Breanna and I have always been more sisters than cousins."

"That's true." A half-smile touched Fenshaw's lips. "I remember the stories your grandfather used to regale me with—tales of your antics, of your deep attachment to each other. Even as tots, you girls were inseparable, whenever you had the opportunity, that is . . ." Fenshaw broke off, gave an uneasy cough, as if he realized he'd said too much. Frowning, he removed his spectacles, began polishing them furiously. "It would do the late viscount's heart good to see you and Breanna reunited after all these years. As for the ties you and your parents forged with the States, those will be sustained through the opening of this bank."

"I agree." Cunnings rubbed his palms together. "What's more, I think that launching an American bank will prove beneficial, not only on a personal level, but on a financial one, as well. Like Lord Sheldrake, I believe this investment is going to be a lucrative one."

"As do I," Booth concurred. His gaze flickered from Anastasia to Damen and back again. "It's also gratifying to see how amenable a partnership you're forming. Too many business associations are clouded by emotion. Clearly, you and Lord Sheldrake don't suffer from that problem—which is good, since it only gets in the way. Personal feelings of any kind have no place in business."

Anastasia squirmed in her seat, made distinctly uneasy by Booth's assessment. Why would he make such an odd, extraneous comment about her partnership with Damen?

Maybe it hadn't been extraneous. Maybe it had been deliberate. Maybe Booth sensed the attraction between her and Damen and was tactfully chiding her for it.

Or was she being overly sensitive, projecting her own feelings onto others since she herself was so vitally aware of the pull that existed between her and Damen?

She studied Booth carefully—a tactic that yielded no results. He was simply gazing at her politely, his hands clasped behind his back. Damen, for his part, seemed oblivious to the remarks, his attention focused on Graff, who now hovered in the doorway.

He signaled for the gatekeeper to enter. "You know what to do with these."

"Yes, sir." Graff collected both sets of documents. "One envelope will be secured right here in the bank. The other will be on its way to the States before nightfall."

"Excellent." Damen rose to his feet, nodding to each man in turn. "Thank you all. That completes everything we came here to do." He extended his hand to Fenshaw. "Thank you for your time and attention in preparing the documents."

"Not at all." Fenshaw clasped Damen's hand. "I'm glad things went so smoothly. If there's anything else I can do, just let me know."

"I will." Damen frowned as he saw Anastasia rise, shake out her skirts. "We have more business to discuss," he reminded her.

"I know, my lord."

Anastasia felt Damen's brooding stare, knew he wanted to continue their private talk, to work out how they should handle her uncle. But now was not the time, for a variety of reasons. First, she'd told Breanna she'd be away only a few hours; and second, she didn't want to arouse suspicions about the nature of her relationship with Damen—suspicions that, judging from Mr. Booth's reaction, might already have been kindled.

"I realize we still have some unfinished business," she said, meeting and holding Damen's gaze. "But it will have to wait. I must get home. As it is, I've been away far longer than I expected. I don't want Breanna to worry." *Or to get in trouble with my uncle,* she added silently.

As if reading her mind, Damen relented. "Very well. I'll drop by tomorrow then. Right after breakfast."

"That would be fine."

"I'll escort Lady Anastasia to her carriage," Booth offered, taking a step toward her.

"There's no need for you to inconvenience yourself," Fenshaw said, waving away Booth's offer before Anastasia could respond. "I'll be leaving now anyway, to return to my office. I'll personally escort Lady Anastasia to her carriage." He offered Anastasia his arm. "My lady."

"Thank you, Mr. Fenshaw." Anastasia complied, wondering why Booth was so eager to get rid of her. Was he anxious to get back to his work, or was he just trying to prevent her from being alone with Damen?

"It was a pleasure meeting you, my lady." John Cunnings interrupted her thoughts, bowed as he moved toward the doorway.

"I return the compliment, sir," she replied. "And I appreciate your belief in our venture." She turned to Damen, gave him a cordial, businesslike smile. "Lord Sheldrake—I look forward to a profitable association."

"As do I." Damen came around the front of his desk and kissed her gloved hand, his silver-gray gaze boring inside her, telling her he was far from happy with this abrupt departure. "I'll see you first thing tomorrow morning."

The noon hour came and went.

The skies remained gloomy, a fine drizzle dampening the London docks, turning the bank of the Thames to mud.

Still, activity was at a peak. Crewmen yelled back and forth to each other as they readied ships about to set sail. Cranes hoisted cargo from arriving vessels. Porters stood at wharfside, ready to unload incoming coal, and watermen adeptly rowed passengers out to catch departing ships they'd missed. Dock workers, their skin glistening with raindrops, strained as they jumped on and off ships, some loading, others unloading cargo. This all-important hustle and bustle dominated the wharf, and warehouse doors were flung wide as able-bodied men carried thick bags of cargo in for storage.

Meade made his way up the path leading to the warehouses, two heavy sacks pitched on his back, their cumbersome weight doubling him over until his chin could practically touch his protruding belly. He entered the warehouse, falling to his knees and letting the bags drop to the rotted wooden floor beside him.

The relief was blessed.

He rose up, shaking strands of unkempt hair out of his face and dragging a sleeve across his sweaty forehead.

Sugar. Pounds and pounds of wretched sugar.

What a waste. Granules—useful only to make cake. Pretty poor chance of making any real money out of that.

Then again, there hadn't been much money made out of anything else lately either. At least not for him. And his belly was the only one he cared about feeding.

Well, all that was about to change. After his talk with Lyman, everything would change.

The warehouse door flung wide, striking the wall with a thud.

Meade whipped around to see who had joined him, automatically stooping to snatch his knife from his boot.

He straightened, the blade glinting in the dimly lit warehouse.

Faint or not, the lighting was good enough. He recognized Medford right away by his haughty air and deceptively hunched shoulders.

"Put the knife away, Meade." The viscount advanced toward him in slow, predatory steps. "I think it's time we had a talk."

Meade wasn't alarmed. He'd expected a visit like this the minute he made his demands. Of course Lyman would go straight to Medford. He was the one who paid their wages. As for Medford's anger, well, he'd expected that, too. The son of a bitch didn't take threats lightly. He liked being in control. That suited Meade just fine. He didn't want control. He wanted money. Which, after this little talk, was just what he'd get. Because Medford needed him. They both knew that.

Steeling himself, Meade ignored Medford's command. How the hell did he know the bastard wasn't armed? He couldn't take that chance. No, he'd keep his blade right where it was—clutched and ready.

"I don't wanna talk." The privateer's eyes glinted, his whiskered jaw tightly set. "I want me money. *All* me money. And more of it from now on."

"So I heard. Fifty percent more." Undeterred by Meade's weapon, Medford never paused, walking forward until he could almost touch the gleaming blade—then halting. "The fact is, you won't be getting your money. Not yet. I don't have it. And your generous wage increase? *That* you won't be getting at all."

"Then I won't be deliverin' yer merchandise."

"Ah, but you're wrong. You *will* be delivering my merchandise—willingly and without further threats." Medford slipped his hand into his pocket, and Meade tensed, his fingers tightening about the handle of his blade.

"I told you to put that away, Meade," the viscount commanded.

"And let ye shoot me? Not a chance."

"I don't plan to shoot you." George withdrew his hand and flourished a sheet of paper. "I won't have to. That task will be taken care of for me."

Meade's eyes narrowed. "What are ye talkin' about?"

A tight smile. "If you'll hold this up to the light, you'll see it's an arrest warrant. It was issued by the magistrate himself. You're a wanted man, Meade—a renowned privateer and smuggler. Why, if I turn you in, you'll be in the gallows before you know it, hanging by the neck at the end of a very short, tight rope. How does that sound?"

Lowering his blade, Meade snatched the page, brought it over to the window. He swore at the official-looking seal at the bottom of the document, knowing right away what it meant.

"Now, can we renegotiate our terms?" George inquired. "Instead of your demands for an increase and your threats to expose me, why don't we settle for keeping things just as they are? In return, I'll pretend I never heard of you, should I be asked. I'll simply ignore the dictates of my conscience, refrain from turning you in. I think that's a fair arrangement, don't you?"

Silence.

"Good. Then we understand each other. Right, Meade?"

Another long silence, during which Meade felt his heart drumming wildly in his chest. Hanging. Dying. Feeling his neck crack in two.

Nothing was worth that.

Resignation sank deep in his gut, and he saw his fortune go up in smoke. "Yeah, Medford," he muttered bitterly. "Right."

Triumph glittered in the viscount's eyes. "Excellent. The next shipment will be ready in ten days. Be prepared to deliver it on time. And Meade? Don't *ever* blackmail me again."

9

*T*he victory was little cause for celebration.

George leaned back in his carriage, his teeth gritting as he assessed the situation.

All well and good that Meade would deliver the shipment as planned. First, the damned merchandise had to be secured, a reality that Bates was supposedly seeing to. And even if both tasks went smoothly, George had to pray that his note to Rouge had been convincing enough to inspire a modicum of patience; that, as a result of George's threat to take his business elsewhere, Rouge would adhere to the specified terms and pay the full amount due.

And if that happened?

Even the full amount was a mere drop in the bucket compared to George's ocean of debt:

His colleagues, his creditors, his informants.

The very thought of how many thousands and thousands of pounds he owed made him ill.

And then there was Anastasia.

Just pondering his niece, the fact that she held his fate in the palm of her hand, made his skull pound with rage. Oh, Henry's precious brat had no idea of the power she wielded. But George did. And he loathed her for it.

What had his contact found out? he wondered bitterly. How much of Henry's money had been committed to this wretched bank Anastasia hoped to open? And what were the details of her partnership with Sheldrake—and any other unwelcome bond that might be developing between them?

George wasn't stupid. He knew only too well that business associations often led to personal ones. And given that it was a man and a woman who were involved in this particular partnership—well, suddenly the word *personal* took on a whole new meaning. If Anastasia and Sheldrake were to spend any substantial amount of time together . . . George's hands balled into fists at his sides. Damn her. She would not rob him of that, too.

He'd have another talk with Breanna—immediately—and make his intentions for her future unmistakably clear. Then he'd find ways to throw her and Sheldrake together, and ways to keep the marquess and Anastasia apart. He needed Sheldrake in the family, not only to provide money and status, but to shed a favorable light on George's reputation, and to ensure his silence if he were to learn anything damning about his new father-in-law.

Perhaps there was something to say for family after all.

A humorless smile twisted George's lips. Family hadn't been enough motivation for Henry, not when it came to including his brother as a beneficiary to his estate. Well, with the right manipulation, Henry's funds would find their way into the right hands after all.

Whatever was left of those funds, that is.

George stared out the window, watched as the gates of Medford Manor came into view.

He had to find out how much of Henry's inheritance had been allocated to that bloody bank. And he had to find out *now.*

He was in trouble. Big trouble. His options were vanishing before his very eyes. With Anastasia controlling half of Colby and Sons, and Sheldrake acting as her trusty administrator, there was little hope of doctoring receipts to Lyman or any other supplier without getting caught. As for a more readily available source, there were only a few thousand pounds left to drain of the funds Henry had set aside for Anastasia's coming-out.

He needed that inheritance.

Ten weeks. After which, it would be too late. Everything would blow up in his face. Rouge would find another supplier, the creditors would close in, and Anastasia would walk away with her inheritance, her half of Colby and Sons, and—Lord help her—Damen Lockewood.

No. George sat upright, his fingers reflexively gripping the door handle, ready to twist it the instant the carriage came to a halt. He wouldn't allow it. He'd talk to Breanna right now. Then, he'd summon his contact, learn the details of that bloody partnership.

And then, he'd do whatever he must to save his neck.

Wells stood in the open doorway, his expression nondescript as he watched the viscount stalk up the stairs and into the manor.

"Where's Breanna?" George bit out, glaring at his butler.

"In the library, my lord. Shall I summon her?"

"No. I'll do my own summoning. Besides, the library is as good a place as any."

Wells stiffened a bit. "For what, sir?"

"Nothing that concerns you." George strode down the hall, jerking open the library door and stepping inside.

"Father." Breanna started, as she looked up from the settee upon which she was curled, thumbing through a novel. She studied her father's expression, a certain wariness coming over her. Slowly, she shut the book. "Did you wish to see me?"

"Indeed I did." George shut the door firmly behind him. He crossed over to the sideboard, poured himself a drink. Tossing it down in three gulps, he slammed the goblet onto an end table and walked across the room until he loomed directly over his daughter. "You and I are going to talk. Or rather, *I'm* going to talk. *You're* going to listen. And then, you're going to do as I say."

Instinctively, Breanna scooted to the far corner of the settee. "What is it we're talking about?"

"You and Lord Sheldrake." George pressed his palms together, studying his hands as if that act could help him maintain his self-restraint. "It's time we took definite steps to ensure your future as Mrs. Damen Lockewood."

Color suffused Breanna's cheeks, and she lowered her lashes, contemplating the cover of her book. "I think any steps we take would be futile," she said at last. "In fact, I think we should both accept the fact that I don't have a future with Lord Sheldrake."

Her breath lodged in her throat, as George swooped down, gripping her shoulders and nearly lifting her off the settee. "I don't think you understand. So let me make it clear. Giving up is not an option. Not in this case." His eyes blazed with jade fire, his fingers bit into her flesh. "You *will* marry Lord Sheldrake. Soon. What I'm here to discuss is how best to speed up this courtship."

Breanna's eyes widened in fear, but she didn't retreat. "What courtship, Father? There is none."

"Then there will be one as of now." George lowered Breanna back to the settee, his forefinger jerking up her chin to meet his gaze. "Besides, you underestimate yourself. The marquess was very attentive at the ball. He danced with you for most of the evening. Afterward, he spoke highly of you. I think all he needs is a little encouragement—not from me, from you. And you're going to give him that encouragement."

"Why? Why is it so important to you that I marry Lord Sheldrake? Are you hoping he'll offer you money for my hand?"

A flicker of astonishment, after which George's lips thinned into an angry line. "Where is this newfound impertinence coming from—having Anastasia living with us?"

Breanna swallowed. "I apologize if I sounded rude. But it's only natural for me to have questions. After all, it is *my* life we're discussing. And I'd like to understand what you hope to gain by wedding me to Lord Sheldrake. I know how much wealth and position mean to you. We wouldn't be having this conversation if the marquess were poor and unrenowned. Is it that you hope to gain access to his fortune? If so, I don't think that's an unspoken certainty—not unless Lord Sheldrake chooses it to be. And, to be honest, I don't think he's so enchanted with me that he'd pay handsomely just to give me his name."

George twisted Breanna's chin until she whimpered, then shoved her away. "My motives, daughter, are my own. Your job is to make them a reality. Now, I'm going to invite the marquess to breakfast tomorrow. Once the meal is over, I'll suggest that you two take a private stroll. During that time, I expect you to make it blatantly clear that you enjoy his attentions, and that you'd welcome his affections. Is that understood?"

Silence.

Renewed anger flared in George's eyes, and he leaned menacingly over her. *"Is that understood?"*

Breanna nodded, but didn't flinch. "Yes, Father. You've made your expectations perfectly clear."

"Good." George backed away, walked over to freshen his drink. "Where is Anastasia—in her room?"

Steeling herself for the inevitable explosion, Breanna shook her head. "No, she went out several hours ago. She should be back any minute."

Something about Breanna's tone must have aroused George's suspicions, or perhaps it was the fact that Anastasia rarely went out alone that made him leery.

He turned, goblet in hand. "Where did she go?"

"To the House of Lockewood." Breanna tried not to react to the fury that twisted her father's features. "She said something about a meeting."

"Dammit." George raised his arm over his head, and Breanna braced herself for the crash of the goblet striking the floor.

The crash never came.

Slowly, George lowered his arm, visibly trying to control his wrath.

"Send her to my study," he ground out between clenched teeth, "the minute she returns. It's time your cousin and I had a little talk, as well."

"She's only gone to finish settling Uncle Henry's affairs," Breanna defended at once, trying to ward off whatever confrontation her father had in mind. "I'm sure she would have told you about this meeting herself, but you'd already left the estate."

"I'm sure she is and I'm sure she would have." George's words were as caustic as his smile. "But the fact remains that I'm her guardian. And, as such, I can't have her gallivanting about without permission or, knowing Anastasia, without a proper chaperon. I'm concerned for her safety, and for her reputation. After all, this is England, not America."

"Still, I don't think . . ."

"Stop shielding her, Breanna. Just send her to my study. Immediately." George's eyes narrowed into glittering jade chips. "And remember what I said. I expect to be announcing your betrothal to Lord Sheldrake in a matter of weeks."

Anastasia sensed something was wrong the minute she saw Wells's drawn expression.

Glancing about, she noted the empty hall, felt the tension permeating it.

"Wells?" she murmured, inclining her head. "What is it?"

The butler didn't mince words. "Your uncle arrived home an hour ago. He was unusually distressed."

"Distressed," Anastasia repeated. "You mean angry. Especially when he learned I wasn't here—and probably where I was." Another swift glance down the hall. "Is he with Breanna now?"

"Not anymore. He was with your cousin in the library for about twenty minutes. Then, he emerged rather briskly, and disappeared into his study."

Anastasia's uneasiness intensified. "What about Breanna? Is she still in the library?"

"Yes, Miss Stacie. She's come out twice asking if you were home yet. I promised to send you down the moment you arrived."

"I'm on my way." Anastasia hurried down the hall, tiptoeing past her uncle's study, and made her way to the library.

She pushed open the door and stepped inside.

Breanna was pacing in front of the windows.

"Stacie. Thank goodness." She motioned for her to enter and shut the door behind her.

Anastasia complied, frowning as she studied her cousin. Breanna was noticeably upset, just as she always was after dealing with her father. But this time she was more; this time she was totally distraught.

"What happened?" Anastasia didn't mince words. She crossed over, seized Breanna's hands.

And went utterly cold inside when she saw the bruise on her cousin's chin—a bruise that could have been caused by nothing but the punishing grip of a thumb and forefinger.

"Oh, no." She reached out, touched the mark ever so gently.

"It doesn't hurt." Breanna waved away her cousin's concern.

"Honestly, Stacie. I don't even think Father knew he was doing it. He was desperate to make his point, to push me into doing his bidding. And when I balked . . . well, I truly think he lost his reason."

"You're defending him?" Anastasia asked incredulously.

"No, of course not. All I'm saying is, he didn't beat me. He didn't even shout. It's as if he's desperate—desperate enough to be even more callous than usual."

"But it's *me* he's angry at, not you."

"Actually, it's both of us." Breanna smoothed a shaky hand over her upswept hair. "You, for going to Lord Sheldrake's bank; me, for not yet wearing his wedding ring." She dismissed Anastasia's onslaught of questions with a firm shake of her head. "Listen to me, Stacie. You and I can discuss this in detail tonight after Father's gone to bed and we're alone. Right now, he's awaiting your arrival like a hungry lion awaits its dinner. He's angry, he's unnerved, and he's determined to have his say. All that's important is for you to know what you're in for. Father feels threatened by your relationship with Lord Sheldrake—both personally and financially. He has his own plans for the marquess's fortune—and his future. Father wants me to marry Lord Sheldrake. You and I both know that. We also know it's never going to happen, and why. How we get Father to accept it is another matter entirely. I tried, and failed. It's your turn. But tread carefully. This is not going to be a pleasant meeting."

Anastasia listened closely, appreciating Breanna's worry, at the same time captured by her cousin's adamant statement: *We also know it's never going to happen, and why.*

The way Breanna said that—with the certainty of one who knew rather than surmised—clearly, she was referring to something more concrete than the fact that she and Damen were mere acquaintances. And, given how finely attuned she and Anastasia were, given that they'd always been able to read each other's thoughts, it didn't take a genius to figure out that Breanna had sensed the attraction between her cousin and Damen.

A dozen questions hovered on Anastasia's tongue, and were silenced as she stared at the bruise on Breanna's chin.

At the moment, none of her questions mattered; not those concerning Breanna's underlying meaning, nor those pertaining to how much of the truth she'd guessed. What mattered was Uncle George—Uncle George and his violent determination to shape the future his way.

Anastasia clenched the folds of her gown, her resolve strengthening twofold. She knew how she must handle this impending confrontation, and it included keeping her bloody tongue in check. Otherwise, it wouldn't be she who would suffer. It would be Breanna.

"Don't worry," she said lightly, squeezing her cousin's arm. "You've prepared me. I can handle Uncle George. Who knows? Maybe I can even mollify him a bit."

Breanna gave her a small smile. "I wouldn't count on it. He's incensed. And he'll be more incensed once you've spoken your piece."

The girls' eyes met.

"Tell him, Stacie," Breanna said quietly. "He'll find out anyway."

Anastasia was still puzzling over her cousin's words as she approached Uncle George's study. What exactly had Breanna been urging her to disclose? That she'd opted to invest in an American bank? That she'd formed a partnership with Damen Lockewood?

Or was it more?

Sucking in her breath, Anastasia paused at the study door. She'd get her answer later. Whatever it was, it wouldn't affect her decision.

She raised her hand, rapped on the door.

"Who is it?" her uncle barked.

"Anastasia."

A dozen purposeful strides sounded from within, after which the door was yanked open, and her uncle stood before her, his expression taut, his eyes burning with suppressed ire.

"You wanted to see me?" Anastasia asked, as nonprovokingly as she could.

"Indeed I did. Come in." He snapped out the words, gesturing for her to enter, then shutting the door firmly in her wake. He stared at the carpet for a moment—doubtless trying to curb his anger—then jerked up his head to meet her gaze. "You went to the House of Lockewood this morning while I was out. You traveled alone, unchaperoned, and you never mentioned to me that you had an appointment. Why is that?"

Anastasia forced what she hoped was an apologetic look on her face. "I'm not accustomed to taking a chaperon with me when I go out for a simple ride. I realize that's inappropriate now that I'm home, and I'll try to be mindful of that in the future. As for my appointment, I intended to tell you about it. But you'd already left. So I asked Breanna to do it for me."

"And what was your business at the bank?"

He's testing me, Anastasia thought. *He's trying to catch me in the act of lying; or rather, of hiding the truth. Well, I'm about to surprise him.*

"I had business with the marquess," she answered, looking her uncle squarely in the eye. "Regarding an investment I'm about to make. I want to use a portion of Papa's inheritance to invest in an American bank."

A flicker of surprise—one that was quickly replaced by a dark scowl. "An American bank," he repeated icily. "I heard that you approached a number of my guests about financing that ludicrous venture. But I assumed that, once you saw their aversion to the notion—and to the notion of even discussing business with a woman—you'd been wise enough to abandon the idea. Really, Anastasia, isn't it enough that you offended a roomful of prominent noblemen with your unprecedented audacity? Did you then have to force your ideas on Lord Sheldrake?"

"I didn't force my ideas on Lord Sheldrake," Anastasia replied, fighting to keep her temper in check. "I merely presented them."

"Call it what you will." Her uncle's steely tone told her he was unwilling to be deterred. "It still adds up to one thing: you've forgotten who and where you are. You're my niece. You're also no longer in America. Perhaps there it's common for women to take an active role in financial matters, but . . ."

"It's not," Anastasia interrupted. "I was bolder than American women, too."

George's mouth thinned into a grim line. "I don't find your cheekiness amusing. Need I remind you that this is my home? Therefore, you will abide by my rules. And one thing I will not permit is impertinence."

Silently, Anastasia counted to ten. "I didn't intend to be impertinent," she said at last. "Just honest."

"I don't require honesty, not unless I specifically demand it by way of a direct question. What I do require is obedience. Further, I won't tolerate having my guests insulted."

This was becoming more difficult by the minute.

"Insulting your guests was never my intention, Uncle George. My intention was to gain support for my bank." Anastasia made a wide sweep with her hands. "In any event, I was unsuccessful. Obviously, your guests feel as you do about women in business. So I won't try that tactic again." She literally forced out her next words. "I apologize for any embarrassment I caused you."

"Fine." A terse nod. "Then, let's return to today's meeting at the bank. What is it you hoped to accomplish?"

You already know, Uncle George, she reflected. *What you* don't *know is that I'm aware of that. Very well. There's no harm in reiterating what Damen already told you.*

"As that was a direct question, I have to assume you're expecting honesty," she responded, rubbing her skirts between her fingers in a seemingly nervous gesture. "Therefore, I'll provide it. The purpose for my meeting this morning was to sign a partnership agreement with Lord Sheldrake. He's joining me in this banking venture—not as a backer, but as an equal partner."

George started—his surprise prompted not by her news, she fully recognized, but by her unanticipated frankness. It was plain that this was one time he *had* expected her to lie, after which he'd planned to throw that lie in her face.

"I see." He scowled, clasping his hands behind his back and regrouping his thoughts. "I'm astounded that Lord Sheldrake would agree to involve himself in this pointless endeavor."

"He doesn't expect it to be pointless. He expects it to be profitable. As do I." Anastasia raised her chin a notch. "I realize you and I have differing opinions on this subject, Uncle George. However, with all due respect, you're not my financial guardian. Lord Sheldrake is. So while I'll abide by your rules of behavior, I won't seek your approval on how I invest my money. Fortunately, Lord Sheldrake and I are of the same mind with regard to that."

"You and Sheldrake seem to be of the same mind with regard to many things," George bit out, a vein throbbing at his temple.

Anastasia's brows lifted. "I don't understand."

"Oh, I think you do. Especially given the amount of time you and he spent together at your coming-out party."

"He's the administrator of my inheritance, and now my business partner. Of course we spent time together."

"And that's all there is to it?"

"What else could there be?"

Thunderclouds erupted on George's face, and he sliced the air with his palm. "Don't be coy with me, Anastasia. I'm not stupid. Nor are you. So I'll spell out the situation for you. I intend for Lord Sheldrake to marry Breanna. In fact, I expect to be announcing their betrothal any day now. Your cousin will have a wonderful life with the marquess. He'll give her everything she could ever want or need. And I don't plan to let anything, or any *one,* stand between them. Am I making myself clear?"

Anastasia swallowed—hard—keeping her expression as nondescript as possible. "Perfectly clear."

"Good. I'll hold you to that. One, because I know how much Breanna's happiness means to you, and two, because I know you'd never purposely undermine me. Not when you know how dire the consequences could be. And I *do* mean dire."

A chill ran up Anastasia's spine at the biting intensity of her uncle's words. She stared at him, trying to decipher his precise state of mind. She saw bitterness and anger in his eyes, as well as a dislike and resentment that was far older than she. But she also saw desperation—a desperation she couldn't quite fathom.

What was prompting it? Was it simply a grasping desire for Damen's money and power—greed combined with a need for retribution? Or was it more? Just how depleted were Uncle George's personal funds? Colby and Sons might be flourishing, but that told her nothing about what her uncle did with his portion of the profits, nor about how he handled any of his personal investments. Damen himself had bluntly told her he didn't have much faith in her uncle's business acumen, adding that he suspected her uncle might be struggling financially. Just how badly *was* he struggling? Enough to breed this level of desperation?

A sixth sense told Anastasia there was more here than met the eye.

"I take your silence to signify agreement." Her uncle interrupted her thoughts, his gaze narrowed on her face. "Am I correct?"

Careful, Anastasia. Don't provoke him. Not until you have all the facts. He'll only take it out on Breanna.

"You know how deeply I care for Breanna." She lowered her chin in a gesture of compliance. "I'd never do anything to stand in the way of her happiness. Never."

"Fine. Then we understand each other."

Anastasia nodded, still staring at the carpet. "Yes, Uncle George. We understand each other very well."

"Was it as bad as I expected?" Breanna asked the minute Stacie slipped into her room that night. Anxiously, she scrutinized her cousin, returning the porcelain figurine she'd been holding to the top of her nightstand.

Anastasia shrugged, tying her wrapper more firmly about her waist and pacing restlessly about. "Let's say there were no surprises."

She headed toward a chair, pausing to glance at her cousin's nightstand. A reminiscent smile touched her lips, and she walked over, gingerly touching the porcelain horse that had always been Breanna's favorite. "Every one of them, just as I remembered," she murmured, her gaze shifting to the bureau where rows of delicate figurines stood—tiny statues depicting everything from children to animals to vases with flowers. "The entire collection, as if time stood still. Then again, I suppose for these beautiful statues, it does."

"There are a few you haven't seen. I added them over the years." Breanna pointed out the new additions, including one of two little girls, laughing and picking flowers. "This one reminded me of us," she said, lifting it up and cradling it tenderly in her hands. "I first saw it about a year after you left England. I admired it in the shop window for months. I fully intended to save my pence, one at a time, until I could buy it. But Wells—dear man that he is—surprised me instead. He bought it for me that Christmas. It's the most precious figure in my collection. If you look closely, you'll see why."

Quizzically, Anastasia inclined her head, taking the porcelain object and inspecting it up close. Two little girls, their bright heads bent over the row of flowers they were picking.

A glistening object caught Anastasia's eye, and she peered closer,

spotting the sliver of metal wedged between the flowers and the children.
    The silver coin.
    She reached out, touched it ever so gently. "So this is where you keep
it. I thought it was under the base of your porcelain horse."
    "It was. Until Wells bought me this. It reminded me so much of us, I
couldn't help but feel the coin belonged here."
    A tender nod. "The gold coin is still in my jewel box—the one Mama
got me when I was four. It was supposed to hold my hairpins and ribbons, so I'd find them in time to make my hair look presentable when
need be. Of course, I lost every ribbon and hairpin I ever owned, so the
box was never used for that. Instead, I kept my treasures in it: that wonderful multicolored stone you and I found near Medford Manor's pond,
that odd-shaped leaf I plucked off our oak—things like that. Years later, I
added new, equally precious treasures: every letter I received from you
when I was in America, special mementos of Mama and Papa. The gold
coin has never left that box. Except when I needed to see it, touch it,
hold it to feel closer to Grandfather—and to believe that you and I really
would be reunited one day."
    "Well, now we are." Breanna's voice was choked, and Anastasia felt
her own heart constrict with emotion.
    Her gaze returned to the exquisite figure in her hands, and she studied
the tiny glazed sculpture. Two girls, sharing laughter and confidences,
and an absolute trust that not even distance could sever.
    A trust as precious as the gold and silver coins themselves—and all
they represented.
    "Breanna, we need to talk." On that thought, Anastasia acted, setting
down the delicate statue and marching over to the bed. She perched at
the edge, her expression determined.
    Nodding, Breanna gathered up the folds of her night robe, tucking
them around her as she lowered herself to the armchair alongside the
bed. "Tell me what Father said," she urged, her green eyes searching
Anastasia's face.
    "He lectured me about approaching his guests on such a scandalous
matter as business. He interrogated me about my partnership with Lord
Sheldrake. And he warned me not to come between you and the marquess." Anastasia dispensed with the facts as quickly as possible, sensitive to Breanna's concern, yet focused on getting at the more significant
matter of Damen, and how Breanna perceived—or *didn't* perceive—her
future with him.
    "I see," Breanna reflected aloud. "And did you set Father straight
about Lord Sheldrake?"
    There it was again. That feeling that Breanna was referring to some-
thing far deeper than that which they'd already discussed.

"That depends on what you mean by setting Uncle George straight," Anastasia replied, carefully gauging her cousin's reaction. "I apologized for upsetting his guests. With regard to Damen, I told him the truth about our partnership . . ."

"And about your feelings for each other? Did you tell him about those, as well?"

Anastasia caught her lower lip between her teeth, taken aback—not by Breanna's insight, but about the forthright way she gave voice to it. It was unlike her cousin to be so direct. Then again, it was better that she'd chosen this opportunity to be as such. This issue needed to be resolved—now.

"No," Anastasia responded, equally blunt. "I said nothing about my feelings. For many reasons." She scrutinized Breanna's expression, looking for some sign—any sign—that her cousin was upset. But all she saw there was curiosity; curiosity and a touch of confusion. "Breanna," she blurted, leaning forward and clutching the folds of her robe. "I'd rather die than hurt you. I wish you hadn't guessed my feelings, because I'm determined to know yours before I even allow myself to contemplate mine. If you love this man, if you *could* love this man, if you can even imagine—by some remote chance—that you might be happy with him . . ."

"Stop right there," Breanna interrupted, holding up a deterring palm. "Is that what's holding you back? *My* feelings?" Shaking her head, she reached over, took Anastasia's hand in hers. "I already told you there's nothing between the marquess and me. He's a charming, charismatic man. He's been very kind about diffusing Father's anger—pretending to be captivated by me, spending hours at my side. But, Stacie, I have no romantic interest in Lord Sheldrake." An impish grin. *"You,* on the other hand, do. And as for the marquess, he's so smitten, he can scarcely tear himself from your side."

"Did he actually tell you that?" Anastasia heard herself ask.

Breanna's eyes twinkled. "No. But he stepped on my feet four times when you were dancing with Lord Percy. Also, twice he mistakenly called me by your name—and not because he didn't know who he was dancing with."

Despite her best intentions, Anastasia couldn't deny the rush of pleasure that revelation brought. Still . . .

"I wouldn't lie to you, Stacie," Breanna assured her softly. "Not about something as important as this. I'd sooner challenge you for the marquess's affections—*if* I had feelings for him. Not because I'd place my needs above yours, but because I know you'd forever blame yourself if I forfeited a man I cared for just to ensure your happiness. But that's not the case. So put the notion out of your head." Her grip tightened, her cheeks glowing with excitement. "Instead, tell me what it feels like. Has he kissed you yet?"

Anastasia's lips curved as relief swept through her—relief more powerful than even she'd anticipated. "Yes. I thought my knees were going to buckle." She eased back, tugged her hand free to run it through her tumbled waves of hair. "It's all happening so fast—and I'm not even sure what *it* is."

A dubious glance. "Aren't you?"

"No. All I know is that I want to find out." Abruptly, Anastasia's smile faded. "But I can't. Not with Uncle George as vehement as he is."

"Don't be a fool, Stacie. You never let Father stop you before. You certainly can't start now, not when your whole future could be at stake."

"It's *your* future I'm worrying about—and what will happen to it if your father discovers the truth."

Breanna's jaw set in that rare but unyielding way of hers. "He'll get over it. He'll have to."

"I doubt it will be as simple as that. Not given all the instigating factors involved." Anastasia paused, knowing it was time to fill Breanna in on the pieces of the past she'd never been told, praying it wouldn't cause her cousin too much distress. "This adamancy of Uncle George's is prompted by more than just his plans for you, even more than his plans for himself. It's prompted by feelings of bitterness and resentment that began over two decades ago and have sprouted like ugly weeds ever since."

"You're talking about our fathers' hostility for each other," Breanna murmured. Her forehead creased with puzzlement. "You think Father wants to wed me to Lord Sheldrake just to outdo Uncle Henry?"

"Not to outdo him—to punish him. More specifically, to punish him through me."

"Now you've lost me. How would my marrying Lord Sheldrake punish Uncle Henry? It might satisfy some warped need on Father's part to attain a higher level of power and position than Uncle Henry ever did. But that's all."

"No, that's not all." Slowly, Anastasia rose to her feet, gripping the bedpost and turning to face her cousin. "Uncle George hated Papa for more than just their differing principles. He hated him for marrying Mama."

A baffled pucker formed between Breanna's brows. "It's no secret that Father disliked Aunt Anne. You and I both sensed that, even as children. But how does his dislike for her . . ." Abruptly, her eyes widened. "You know the reason for that animosity, don't you?"

"Yes," Anastasia confirmed. She paused, wet her lips with the tip of her tongue, and provided the truth. "It was because Uncle George wanted—no, expected—that it would be *he* who wed Mama."

Breanna started. "What?"

"Mama told me the whole story several years ago." Anastasia leaned her head against the bedpost. "Evidently, she was introduced to Uncle George during her very first London Season. He began courting her, intent on winning her hand. A month later she and Papa met. It was by sheer chance. She was coming out of a shop on Bond Street when she saw a man—whom she presumed to be Uncle George—leap from the path of a speeding carriage. He fell against a lamppost, twisting his ankle in the process, after which he crept to a nearby bench to nurse the swelling. Naturally, Mama hurried over to help—only to discover that the victim was not Uncle George, but his twin brother. They fell in love during that first chance encounter. Papa tried everything to make Uncle George understand, but to no avail. He never forgave either of my parents."

"Nevertheless, they married," Breanna murmured, the pieces falling rapidly into place. "And Father's hatred festered. That explains so much: why he always acted so strained around Aunt Anne; why he never stayed in the room with her unless he had to." A quizzical tilt of her head. "Did he love my mother? Or did he marry her as a substitute for Aunt Anne?"

Anastasia chewed her lip. "I honestly don't know. Your parents got married a few months after Mama wed Papa."

"Our mothers were sisters. They looked so much alike. They were only a year apart. And Father married my mother right after he lost Aunt Anne to Uncle Henry. Surely that can't all have been a coincidence."

"Knowing Uncle George, I'd have to agree." Anastasia frowned, intent on clarifying what she *did* know. "I've hesitated telling you this because I didn't want to upset you. But, Breanna, please believe this: you *were* wanted. Quite fiercely, from what Mama told me. Aunt Dorothy was a gentle, caring person. She yearned with all her heart for a child—possibly so she could share her love with someone who craved it, given that her husband undoubtedly didn't. If she were still alive, I'm sure . . ."

"Stacie, don't." Breanna waved away her cousin's assurances. "I don't doubt that my mother wanted me. Aunt Anne told me stories about her, too—as did Wells. Enough so that I know what kind of a person she was, and how eagerly she awaited my birth. As for my father, I also recognize what kind of a person he is. Still, it's crucial that I know all the details of the past so I can comprehend why Father hated—*hates* . . ." She corrected herself. ". . . Uncle Henry so vehemently. What you just divulged saddens me, but it doesn't shock or wound me."

"I'm glad." Anastasia felt as if a great weight had been lifted from her shoulders, until she remembered why she'd told Breanna the truth in the first place. "Surely now you realize why Uncle George is so hell-bent on winning this battle to see you become Mrs. Damen Lockewood. It's not just about ensuring that you end up with Damen, but about ensuring that *I* don't. I shudder to think how he'd react if the reverse were to occur. Couple that with the fact that he seems to need Damen's wealth and influence so badly . . ." Anastasia gave a hard shake of her head. ". . . and the thought of telling him the truth becomes untenable. I refuse to put you in that position."

"*You're* not putting me in that position. *I* am. And since it's my fate in question, I'm the one to decide whether or not I'll walk into the lion's den . . ." Abruptly, Breanna broke off, a sudden, reminiscent spark lighting her eyes. "Let me amend that," she murmured, the spark igniting to a full-fledged glow as her idea took hold. "There is a way for you to explore this fascination between you and Lord Sheldrake without arousing my father's wrath."

"And just how am I going to accomplish that? It's you Uncle George wants to see with Damen."

"Then that's precisely what he'll see. Beginning tomorrow morning, when Lord Sheldrake comes for breakfast, as per Father's invitation." Breanna stood, reaching up to pull the pins from her hair, shaking the tresses free. "You said once that a day might come when you'd need to be me. Well, that day has arrived." She smiled triumphantly. "Come, *Breanna.* It's time to tousle my hair and restore your accent to its former clipped tones. Tomorrow morning we reinstate our pact."

The pub was small, dark, almost unnoticeable from the main road. Its walls were chipped and peeling, but the ale was cheap—a factor that was most crucial to those who frequented the establishment. And nobody asked questions, not if your money was good.

Which made it the perfect place for these meetings.

George rubbed his palms distastefully down the front of his coat, as if by doing so he could dispel the odious feel of the room. He hovered in the entranceway, wincing at the filth and clutter, and trying to ignore the raucous laughter that exploded as drunken sailors sank deeper into their cups. It took every ounce of his self-control not to gag at the offensive smells accosting his nose.

But right now he had more important things on his mind.

Swiftly, he perused the room, eager to conduct his business and be gone.

At last, he spied the telltale flare of light from the pub's far corner.

He crossed over, slipped into his seat.

"What did you find out?" he demanded.

His companion lit a cheroot, gazed calmly back at him. "The partnership's real. The terms are standard. They each invested twenty-five thousand pounds."

"Twenty-five thousand . . . dammit!" George nearly forgot himself and slammed his fist to the table.

"Easy, Medford. That's going to get you noticed. Which is the one thing you don't want."

A terse nod. "What about my niece and Sheldrake? What can you tell me?"

"Your niece is beautiful. Every bit as beautiful as your daughter."

"I didn't ask for your opinion. I asked you what was going on between her and Sheldrake."

"Nothing I could see. Then again, they were alone in his office for about a half hour. I have no idea what went on during that time. But otherwise, it was only business."

"Make sure it stays that way," George hissed. "And if it changes, let me know. Immediately." He scowled. "Any word on that damned trust fund my father set up?"

"I had the terms checked into. They're solid as steel. Forget that money, Medford. You won't be touching it—ever."

A bitter laugh. "All the more reason why I've got to get my hands on the rest of that inheritance. Before my bloody niece squanders away every last pence." He leaned forward, glared at his companion. "Did you get that message off to the Continent?"

"The very night I got it."

"Good. Now keep your eyes on Sheldrake. And make sure he keeps his eyes off Anastasia."

10

$\sim$

$\mathcal{B}$y half after nine that morning, the girls were—even to the most discerning observer—each other.

The transformation took a surprisingly short time to complete: a swap of gowns, a few quick pointers on how to keep Anastasia's hair from tumbling free, some powder on Breanna's bruise, and a few practice sessions—Anastasia on the proper articulation of words, and Breanna on the fundamental points underlying Anastasia and Damen's partnership.

"I'd forgotten how much I enjoy being assertive," Breanna teased, parading around the bedchamber in Anastasia's bolder, more confident stride. "I'll be sure to voice all my opinions between mouthfuls."

"I wouldn't," Anastasia cautioned dryly, holding her perfectly coiffed head at just the right angle. "Uncle George made it clear to me he doesn't welcome honesty. He's also not too thrilled with me right now. So I would curb my forthrightness, if I were you."

"But you *are* me." Breanna grinned. "Remember?"

Anastasia couldn't stifle a smile. "You're really enjoying this, aren't you?"

"Absolutely. I'll enjoy it even more when I see you and Lord Sheldrake go off for a private stroll. I wonder what he'll say when you tell him who he's really strolling with."

That brought an impish spark to Anastasia's eyes. "*When* I tell him who he's really strolling with. I plan to savor my secret, wait until the right moment to disclose it. I'm looking forward to outwitting Damen Lockewood. So far, I've managed only to equal him—in intelligence, in inventiveness, even on horseback. It's time I won at something."

Breanna rolled her eyes. "You're impossible. I hope the marquess is up for the challenge he's about to face. He might be a financial genius, but no transaction he's concluded has prepared him for you. Of that, I'm certain."

A knock at the door interrupted their chatter.

"Yes?" Anastasia called out, given that it was Breanna's room—supposedly *her* room—in which they were dressing.

Lizzy poked her head in. "Pardon me, m'lady," she said, her gaze fixed on Anastasia. "But your father asked me to tell you that the marquess has arrived. They're awaiting you and Lady Anastasia in the dining room."

"Thank you, Lizzy," Anastasia replied serenely. "We'll be down in a moment."

"Very good, m'lady." The door shut behind her.

"Now *that* was a good start," Anastasia commented. She gathered up her skirts in Breanna's customary graceful manner.

"Indeed," Breanna agreed. She tied her hair back with a ribbon, making sure to let one or two burnished strands tumble onto her cheeks. "Come, Breanna," she urged with a twinkle. "Your suitor awaits."

Damen rose the minute the girls entered the room, his keen silver gaze shifting from Breanna to Anastasia and back again. "Good morning, ladies. It's a pleasure to see you both."

"And you, my lord," Breanna returned immediately. She smiled, then walked over to Anastasia's seat, giving her father a measured look. "Good morning, Uncle George."

George's nod was customarily aloof. "Anastasia." He turned to the girl he presumed to be his daughter. "Breanna." With that, he reseated himself, signaling for the footmen to serve their meal.

"Anastasia, I was just telling your uncle about our meeting yesterday," Damen said, sipping at his tea. "But it seems you'd already spoken to him about it."

"Yes, I did," Breanna replied, choosing the strawberry jelly rather than her customary apple, just as Anastasia would have. "Right after I returned. Actually, I should have told him about my plans before I left Medford Manor. As it was, he was terribly worried about me. I'm going to have to learn to curb my independent streak. As Uncle George rightfully pointed out, this is England, not the States."

"True." Damen bit into a biscuit, chewing it thoroughly, then swallowing before he spoke. "But you were hardly in danger. The viscount's carriage took you directly to my bank, where my entire staff had been alerted to your arrival." A pointed look at George. "Your niece was in good hands."

"I'm sure she was." George's jaw tightened as he spoke. "Nevertheless, we have her reputation to consider—even though her business with you was just that—*business*. She still should have secured my permission and taken her lady's maid with her." He dismissed the matter with an adamant flourish, his shoulders stiff as he commenced eating his meal.

Anastasia and Breanna exchanged glances.

Silence descended, punctuated only by the clinking of china and crystal—and a few undisguised, meaningful glares by George, aimed at the girl he thought to be Breanna.

Anastasia shifted uncomfortably in her chair, fully aware what she was being ordered to do—what *Breanna* was being ordered to do. But how did one initiate a courtship? More important, how would her cousin do so?

The truth was, she wouldn't.

Weighing that knowledge against the unspoken command in her uncle's eyes, Anastasia wracked her brain for a solution. Deliberately, she avoided her uncle's blistering stare, choosing instead to toy with her breakfast as she pondered how on earth to approach Damen in a manner that even remotely fit her cousin's more reserved demeanor.

"Breanna, what did you do yesterday while your cousin and I were hard at work?" Damen inquired, breaking the silence and providing just the opening Anastasia needed.

Nearly sagging with relief, she folded her napkin neatly in her lap. "I have to admit, I was lonely." *Good start, Anastasia,* she commended herself. *It makes you sound wistful. Keep it up and Damen will have no choice but to gallantly offer you some time in his company.* "The truth is, I've grown accustomed to having Stacie home," she confessed in Breanna's quiet, vulnerable tone. "I never realized until now how seldom I'm among people, and how much I enjoy sharing my thoughts with a sympathetic listener."

Self-consciously, she broke off, pausing to sip at her tea. "In any case, that's not what you asked. Let's see. I took an early morning walk, before it became too hot. Then I went to the library and read. That helped the morning pass. And Stacie returned before lunch."

Damen nodded, giving her a warm smile. "After which, I'm sure you spent the afternoon together."

"We usually do." Anastasia smiled back, responsively but demurely. "Stacie and I have a lot of years to catch up on, my lord."

"And you've come alive since she returned," he noted, polishing off the last bite of his breakfast. "You're like another woman these days. It's wonderful to see—a beautiful butterfly emerging from its cocoon."

"Goodness, I hope that doesn't mean I was a caterpillar before."

"Not at all." Damen chuckled. "Just a shyer butterfly."

George shoved away his plate—his food only half-eaten. "I have a splendid idea," he declared, looking decidedly more cheerful than he had a few minutes earlier. "Breanna, I recall your mentioning something about wanting to seek Lord Sheldrake's advice on that trust fund your grandfather left you. Why not do so now, right after you finish breakfast? I have some papers to go through before I'm ready to meet with the marquess. And it's a shame for him to sit here idle, especially given that it's such a beautiful day. Why don't you walk down to the stream, stroll through the gardens?"

Anastasia gave her uncle an obedient smile. "Of course, Father. That's a good idea." She inclined her head uncertainly at Damen. "If Lord Sheldrake wouldn't mind, that is."

"Mind? I'd enjoy the company." Abandoning his own meal, Damen pushed back his chair and stood. "I'm ready whenever you are."

Gracefully, Anastasia rose, resisting the urge to do her usual bolting to her feet. "Would you excuse us, Father?"

"Of course. Anastasia and I still have to finish our meal. So take your time."

The real Anastasia shot her cousin a questioning look. "You don't mind, do you, Stacie?"

"Of course not," Breanna retorted in her cousin's bold tone. "You two go and enjoy yourselves."

It took all Anastasia's restraint not to succumb to laughter. Instead, she took Damen's arm and let him lead her from the dining room through the hallway, toward the entranceway door.

From his post, Wells watched their approach, straightening in surprise. "Miss Breanna. Are you leaving?"

"No, Wells. Lord Sheldrake and I are just going for a walk. We'll be back soon."

"I see." The butler frowned. "Your father knows this?"

"Of course."

"Very well then." He opened the door. "Don't wander far."

Anastasia stifled another grin. "We won't."

"Your butler is very protective," Damen commented, tucking Anastasia's arm through his as they headed away from the manor.

"Yes, he is." She kept her stare fixed on the path. "I don't often leave the manor—certainly not unchaperoned and escorted by a gentleman."

"I suppose not." A corner of his mouth lifted. "So, where is it George ordered us to go—to the stream?"

"Yes." She sighed. "It's on one of the more remote sections of the estate."

"Giving us the maximum amount of time alone." Damen chuckled. "Why am I not surprised? And why don't I believe you had any plans of asking my advice about your inheritance?"

"Because I didn't." Anastasia peeked up at him through the fringe of her lashes. "Although perhaps I should. You know how little I understand about money or how to invest it."

"Would you like to learn?"

She pretended to consider the notion. "I don't think I'd enjoy it very much. Nor would my father approve. Business is a man's forte."

"Anastasia would disagree."

"You're right. Then again, Stacie's not a typical woman."

"I can't argue with you there." Damen fell silent, and Anastasia would have given anything to be able to read his thoughts.

They continued walking, and when Anastasia couldn't bear the silence for another instant, she blurted out, "Have I offended you?"

"No, of course not. Why would you think so?"

"I don't know. Maybe because I'm not enthused by business. Or maybe it's because I said what I did about Stacie," she added, unable to resist the urge to probe.

"Ah. That." He gave an offhanded shrug. "Well, neither comment offended me. I don't expect everyone to share my fascination for investments. As for Anastasia, she *is* different. *Very* different."

"Is that approval or disapproval I hear?"

"Neither. It's captivation. Anastasia intrigues me in a way no other woman ever has." He shot her a questioning look. "Now I hope *I* haven't offended *you.*"

"H-m-m? No, not at all." Anastasia had to firmly remind herself that it was Breanna he was addressing, not she. Therefore, emitting a gleeful shout would be totally out of place.

"Are we headed in the right direction?" Damen asked, slowing his steps as their path wound its way into a thick grove of trees.

"Yes."

"Good." He guided her through the profusion of oaks, walking steadily until the sun and the grounds were eclipsed by greenery.

Abruptly, he stopped, lush branches enveloping them as he tugged her around to face him.

Anastasia blinked in the filtered daylight. "Is something wrong?"

"Wrong? No."

She looked puzzled, studying his nondescript expression, cast in the shadows of the encompassing trees. "Then why are we stopping?"

"To talk." He brushed a leaf off the top of her smoothly coiffed hair. "You did say you were lonely, didn't you?"

Anastasia didn't have to feign the astonishment that flashed across her face. "Well, yes. But . . ."

"I'd like to eliminate that loneliness."

"By talking?" she asked cautiously.

"Among other things." He traced the delicate curve of her jaw with his fingertips. "You're incredibly beautiful."

"*That's* what you want to talk about?" Anastasia's surprise rapidly transformed to anger. "My beauty?"

"Um-hum." He caressed her cheek, her chin. "That, and everything else about you."

"Such as?"

"Such as—you said Anastasia's forte was business. What are *your* interests?"

Retreating from his touch, Anastasia rubbed the folds of her gown between her fingers, frantically trying to sort out what was happening here.

The problem was, she knew *exactly* what was happening. There was no mistaking this flagrant a seduction.

But Damen Lockewood—the *principled* Damen Lockewood—was not only trying to seduce an innocent woman, but trying to seduce Breanna. *Breanna.* After promising Anastasia he felt nothing for her cousin but friendship; after, just moments ago, proclaiming how captivated with Anastasia he was.

She didn't know whether to strike him or scream.

"Tell me," he coaxed, clasping his hands behind his back—as if he were exercising great restraint—"what is it *you* like to do?"

Slap you, she thought furiously. "My interests?" she repeated instead. "Reading. Drawing. Ah, and collecting porcelain figures. Nothing you'd find exciting."

"Never make assumptions." His tone was as intimate as a caress. "What type of porcelain figures?"

"All types—people, animals, flowers, objects. I began my collection when I was a child. It's grown to be quite extensive at this point."

"Really? You'll have to show it to me sometime."

When? she wanted to blurt out. *When you carry me—rather,* Breanna—*off to your bed?* "Don't tell me you're actually interested in examining little statues."

A quizzical lift of his brows. "You sound surprised."

"I am. I never imagined a man like you would enjoy such a thing. Then again, I never imagined a man like you would stoop to . . ." She snapped her mouth shut before she said something that would give her away.

"Would stoop to what?" Damen inquired. Undeterred by her obvious distress, he stepped closer—much closer—reaching out to capture her hands in his. "And a man like me—tell me, what type of man is that?"

"An honorable one. One who's absorbed in investments rather

than . . ." Her breath caught as he brought her hands to his lips, and simultaneously eased her deeper into the shelter of the trees.

"Rather than . . . ?" he prompted, tugging off one of her gloves and pressing his open mouth into her palm.

"What are you doing?"

"What does it look like I'm doing?" Damen tugged off the other glove, tossed them both aside. Then, he drew her closer, and planted his hands firmly on her waist.

"Lord Sheldrake, really." Anastasia twisted free, her fury as genuine as if she were truly being violated. How *dare* he? Given what was supposedly happening between him and Anastasia, how dare he make blatant advances toward Breanna? "I think you'd better take me back to the manor," she instructed sharply.

"I'd rather not."

"Fine. Then I'll take myself." She attempted to walk around him.

"No—you won't." His arm snaked out, caught her around the waist, and dragged her back to him. "Not when I've sat through an entire breakfast in order to get you alone."

That did it.

"Release me this instant." She slapped at his arms, stiffening as he lowered his head, brushed the curve of her shoulder with his lips. "Stop," she commanded, an inadvertent quiver rippling through her, "Let me go. Before I . . ."

"If I'm to be honest, I prefer your hair down," he murmured, kissing the pulse at her neck, working his way down the column of her throat. "But it does look more convincing this way. And I wouldn't want to upset your brilliant plan. So I'll restrain myself from pulling out all the pins." His thumb tilted up her chin, and he lowered his mouth to hers. "Instead, I'll concentrate on doing this." His lips brushed hers. "Kiss me."

Something in his husky mutterings struck her as significant, but she was too besieged by conflicting feelings to determine what that something was.

Her hands balled into fists, shoved against his chest, even as the warmth of his kiss surged through her. "I don't want . . ."

"Kiss me, Anastasia."

Realization struck her like a tidal wave.

Her eyes snapped open, peered directly into his, and she saw the utter awareness in his gaze. "You . . . knew?" she managed.

"From the instant I saw you." He silenced her protest with a heated nudge of his mouth against hers. "Berate me later. For now, just kiss me."

Whatever indignation Anastasia felt was dwarfed by the hypnotic effect of being in Damen's arms. Without another word, she relented, stepping closer and angling her mouth to his.

Damen made a rough sound of approval, capturing her arms and bringing them high around his neck, then pulling her against him, covering her lips with his.

Fire ignited Anastasia's mouth, spread through her like a rampaging blaze. She flung herself into the kiss, parting her lips to Damen's seeking tongue, meeting his sensual strokes with her own.

Growling her name, Damen lifted her from the ground, carrying her backward three steps until she felt the cool bark of a tree behind her. Using that as an anchor, he crushed her body to his, devouring her mouth and letting his hands roam over her soft curves, awakening her through the confines of her gown.

He cupped her breast, molded it to his palm, and Anastasia moaned aloud, shifted restlessly to afford him greater access.

He took it.

Slipping his hand inside her bodice, he worked his way beneath her chemise to the warm, responsive flesh that craved his touch. His thumb found her nipple, already hardened with desire, and circled it, teasing the aching peak with unrelenting strokes.

The fire inside Anastasia grew.

Shuddering from the intensity of sensation, she heard herself whimper, arch instinctively closer. Damen's breath rasped at her lips, and he tore his mouth away only long enough to drag in air. Then, he buried his lips in hers again, consuming her mouth with an intensity that jolted through her like bolts of lightning.

"Damen . . ." Her arms twined more tightly around his neck, and she clung to him, succumbing more deeply to the flames scorching her from the inside out.

With a muffled oath, Damen dragged down her bodice, and tugged open her chemise.

There was a brief rush of cool air as her breasts sprang free, and then it was gone, as Damen lowered his head, captured her nipple between his lips.

This time she sobbed aloud, unable to stifle the unbearable pleasure screaming through her veins. She clutched at his head, cradled it closer, silently urging him to take more and more of her.

Damen indulged her—and himself.

He shifted, his lips closing around her other nipple, his tongue lashing across it as his thumb stroked its already dampened mate in slow, arousing circles.

A twig snapped just beyond where they stood.

Damen's head shot up, and he surveyed the area, instinctively shielding Anastasia's body with his.

The culprit scooted into view: a red squirrel who, startled by Damen's sudden motion, dropped his acorn and darted off.

Slowly, Damen lowered his head, staring down at Anastasia, his normally silvery gaze almost black with passion. Sanity warred with desire as his hot stare moved restlessly from her face down to her naked breasts, then back up again.

"You're so bloody beautiful," he muttered, his breath coming in hard, uneven rasps. "And all I want to do is . . ."He bit off his remaining words, his jaw working as he brought himself under control. In a few taut motions, he lowered her feet to the ground and tugged up her bodice. "Anastasia . . ." He cupped her hot face between his palms, uttered her name in a husky whisper. "I never meant to let it go this far. I'm sorry."

"No, you're not," she managed in a shattered voice that bore no resemblance to her own. "And neither am I." She leaned her head weakly against his chest, willing her trembling limbs and wildly pounding heart to calm.

Damen seemed to understand, because he gathered her closer, enfolding her against him and resting his chin atop her head. He was as affected as she, his arms shaking with reaction, his heart thundering against her ear. "You're right," he said hoarsely. "I'm not sorry. What's more, if that damned squirrel hadn't interrupted . . ."

Anastasia nodded, still trying to regain her wits and her thoughts.

"Are you all right?" Damen's breath ruffled her hair.

That question jogged the memory of what had preceded these erotic moments.

"You knew." Anastasia's pronouncement was weak, more a statement than an accusation, her words muffled by Damen's waistcoat. "All the time—you knew."

She felt him smile against her hair. "From the instant you walked into that dining room—yes, I knew."

Her hand balled into a fist, struck ineffectually at his shoulder. "Damn you, Damen Lockewood. Can't you *ever* be outdone?"

His smile vanished. "I just was," he confessed raggedly. "Not just outdone, but brought to my knees."

Anastasia leaned back, watching him solemnly as she shook her head. "That's not what I meant."

"I know. But it's true nonetheless."

"For me, as well." She swallowed. "How long were you going to play your little game of cat and mouse with me?"

Again, his lips twitched. "I could ask you the same question. How long did you want me to think you were Breanna?"

An impish grin. "Until I told you otherwise."

Damen chuckled. "Honest to a fault." His thumbs caressed her cheeks. "Let's get this straight here and now. I'm never going to confuse you and Breanna. So you might as well give it up. Although I am curious as to why you're carrying out this little masquerade. I suspect it has more to do with your uncle than with your desire to outwit me."

Anastasia sighed. "You're right. Uncle George has all but forbidden me to see you. He's planning on announcing your betrothal to Breanna in a matter of weeks. And he's warned me not to do anything to jeopardize that announcement, or Breanna's future."

Glints of anger flared in Damen's eyes. "This delusion of his is going too far."

"I agree. But the situation is more complicated than that." Anastasia disengaged herself from Damen's arms, stooping to pick up her gloves. She tugged them on, then tucked her stray tendrils of hair back in the smooth knot atop her head. "We'd best keep walking," she advised, indicating the path. "I don't want to have to lie to Uncle George about where you and I went for our stroll. As you yourself pointed out, I'm not a terribly convincing liar."

"True." Damen caught her arm, tucked it through his. "But let's take advantage of the fact that you're supposed to be Breanna. After all, nothing would please George more than if he peered out the window and saw his daughter and I walking arm in arm."

"Nothing except if he saw his daughter and you walking arm and arm down the aisle as man and wife," Anastasia amended dryly.

Damen's lips thinned into a grim line. "Tell me what happened," he commanded as they resumed their walk. "What took place after you returned from the bank yesterday?"

Omitting nothing, Anastasia relayed the details of her conversation with her uncle, and those of the lecture Breanna had endured from him earlier. Having done that, she told Damen her theories on the reasons for her uncle's extreme behavior.

"I understand your concern," Damen said thoughtfully when she'd finished. "And I agree that George must be deeper in debt than we know. But how will this pretense of yours make things better? Sooner or later, he'll have to be told there's no future for Breanna and me."

"We'll deal with that if it becomes necessary."

"*If?*" Damen stopped, caught her shoulders in his hands. "It's already necessary," he stated flatly, his gaze boring into hers. "As I told you, what's happening between you and me is not going to go away. It's only going to grow stronger, more consuming. So if you're waiting for it to end . . ."

"I'm not," Anastasia interrupted. She pressed her lips together, trying to decide how much to say. "Damen, I'm afraid he'll hurt her."

His eyes narrowed. "Does he strike her?"

"Sometimes. I don't know how hard or how often. But I suspect it's a lot more frequent and more severe than Breanna will admit—even to me. She's very close-mouthed about that part of her life. But she did say her father has been unusually short-tempered these days, even for him. He's been tense, brooding, ready to explode at the slightest provocation. When I came home yesterday, she had a bruise on her chin—a bruise bad enough to need a half hour of powdering in order to conceal, especially given she was supposed to be me. And that was only as a result of his wanting to stress a point. What would he do if she failed to give him the prize he wants—you?"

Damen's breath expelled in a hiss. "And how do we protect her from that?"

"By continuing this charade. By my pretending to be Breanna whenever you visit—unless that visit pertains to our partnership. Then, I'll be me."

"Until when?"

"Until I figure out just how heavily in debt Uncle George is, and how violent he'd become if he were crossed. And until I think of a way to protect Breanna from that violence. Damen, I'm all Breanna has, at least until she meets the right man. I can't turn my back on her."

"I wouldn't expect you to." Damen guided her into the clearing, then toward the glistening stream across the way. "That's one of the traits you and Breanna do have in common," he remarked. "You're both soft-hearted." He paused as they reached the stream, tipped up her chin. "Although you're the true romantic. I didn't miss your pointed 'until she meets the right man.' " A smile. "Forward-thinking or not, you believe in the age-old sentiment of one man for one woman."

"So do you," Anastasia reminded him. "I distinctly recall your assuring me that Breanna would flourish once she met the right man."

"So I did." A corner of Damen's mouth lifted. "I never thought of myself as a romantic. But damned if I'm not finding out that I am one."

"Romantic about love, but pragmatic about business." A reminiscent light dawned in Anastasia's eyes. "That's the way my father was. Practical in his work, emotional about Mama and me." She sighed. "If I'm a romantic, it's not a surprise, nor an accident. My parents were deeply in love. I grew up seeing that, knowing that love was a rare, priceless treasure—one to be fervently sought and captured as a prerequisite to marriage. Breanna never had the chance to learn that firsthand. Her mother died when she was born."

"I remember how much Henry adored your mother," Damen reflected. "He couldn't take his eyes off her when they were together, and he spoke of her often when they were apart. As for Breanna's parents, I was a boy when her mother died. Tell me, did your uncle feel the same way about his wife as your father did about his?"

Anastasia lowered her lashes. "I was only a few months old when Aunt Dorothy died in childbirth. I never knew her."

"Surely your mother spoke of her. She was her sister, after all."

"Her younger sister, yes." Anastasia had no desire to pursue this subject—not again. Telling Breanna was one thing; she had a right to the truth. But opening up to Damen was another matter entirely. His role in her life was too new, too fragile, to share the sordid details behind her uncle's hatred for her father. Perhaps someday . . . but not yet.

"Mama and Aunt Dorothy looked very much alike," she offered instead. "Between that and the fact that our fathers are twins, it's no wonder Breanna and I are identical."

"You're not identical. And you're changing the subject, just as you did in my office when we touched on your uncle's resentment toward you and your parents. It's obvious these two subjects are related. It's also obvious you're not ready to discuss either one with me."

"For now—no, I'm not. Please understand, this is all very personal."

"All right." Damen nodded slowly, his eyes hooded. "I won't push you."

"I appreciate that." Anastasia cleared her throat. "You said that softheartedness was one of the traits Breanna and I have in common. What other ones do you perceive?"

"Loyalty." Damen followed her lead, abandoning the prior topic and picking up the current one. "Loyalty and love—especially for each other. And, I suspect, for your grandfather."

Anastasia blinked, taken aback, yet again, by the depth of Damen's insight. "I'll repeat what I said to you that night on the balcony: you're a very perceptive man, Lord Sheldrake."

"And I'll repeat what I answered you then: you're a very intriguing woman, Anastasia." He caressed her cheek, let his fingers trail down the side of her neck. "Intriguing and intoxicating. So intoxicating that I can't keep my mind—or my hands—off of you." He wrapped an insistent arm around her waist, pulled her against him. Then, he lowered his head, buried his lips in hers for a long, dizzying minute. "Tell me you feel the same way," he murmured, ending the kiss with the greatest reluctance. "Tell me."

"I do," she replied breathlessly.

Abruptly, his mood altered, and he gripped her arms, searching her face with those smoky, compelling eyes. "Then let me help you. Let me help unravel this puzzle."

"How?"

"I have many contacts. I'll make some inquiries, find out just what George's financial situation is. The sooner we know what we're up against, the sooner we can set things right."

A surge of relief flooded through her, and for the first time she realized how alone she'd felt in this dilemma. Her parents were gone, her uncle was suspect, and Breanna was too much at risk to call upon for help. She'd had no one to turn to, no one to ask for help.

Until now.

"Stacie," Damen said softly, mistaking her silence for refusal. "You sought me out as a partner for your bank. This is no different. I know you value your independence. But sometimes success requires drawing upon additional resources in order to achieve the most profitable outcome. This is one of those times."

Anastasia arched a teasing brow. "Spoken like a true investment adviser. Tell me, Lord Sheldrake, are you proposing yet another partnership between us?"

He grinned. "Um-hum. And I'd jump at this one if I were you. I'm a damned good risk."

"Yes," she agreed. "You are." This time it was she who initiated things, reaching up to tug Damen's mouth down to hers. "Consider this my signature."

He made a rough sound against her lips, his arms tightening, drawing her closer. "Much better than a quill," he muttered.

"And far more binding."

Slowly, Damen raised his head, stared deeply into her eyes. "Binding. I like the sound of that." He smoothed his fingers over the shining crown of her hair. "And speaking of binding, I hope that soon you'll decide to tell me the details of whatever caused George's hostility toward you and your parents. And after that . . ." His thumb caressed her soft lower lip. ". . . I want to hear all about the special tie you shared with your grandfather."

An ardent sparkle lit her eyes, and she kissed his fingertips. "That will take long hours in private, my lord. Do you think you can arrange that?"

"Oh, yes. I can definitely arrange that." On the heels of his vow, all teasing vanished, and Damen's expression grew intense. "But, Stacie, if I do—I'm not sure I can promise to display that honorable quality you obviously believe I possess."

Anastasia's heated gaze met his. "Good. Because I'm not sure I want you to."

11

✧

$\mathcal{T}$he next few weeks were fraught with tension.

Some of it was internal, coiled deep within Anastasia's gut—tension incited by the deception she and Breanna were fostering each time Damen visited Medford Manor. Despite the sheer joy that pretending to be Breanna afforded her—namely, spending long hours alone with Damen—Anastasia couldn't escape the worry that her uncle would discover the truth: that his plan to snare Damen Lockewood as a son-in-law was doomed to failure *and* that he was being tricked and defied by his daughter and his niece. And if he were to uncover that truth, Anastasia knew very well who would bear the brunt of his rage: Breanna.

Still, regardless of all that, she sensed that the tension was being triggered by something far more vast than her own personal apprehension. She just didn't know what that something was.

But she knew very well who was at its center: her uncle.

George was drawn taut as a bowstring these days, barking at everyone, snapping at the servants, and generally slamming about the manor as if nursing a barely controllable rage. Every day, he'd closet himself in his study for hours, muttering loudly to himself—loud enough for his voice, if not his words, to be heard in the hallway. That only served to arouse Anastasia's curiosity, compelling her to try to decipher the muffled sounds. Several times a day, when no one else was about, she'd hover outside the locked study door and eavesdrop intently, pressing her ear to the doorway and straining to listen. But the wood was thick, and all she could make out was her uncle's tone, which was undeniably agitated, vacillating from bitter to apprehensive to sullen.

To make matters worse, he'd been drinking heavily, commencing each day with a full goblet of brandy, then steadily increasing his intake until, by midafternoon, he was actually slurring his words, so deep in his cups was he.

Clearly, it wasn't Breanna's relationship with Damen that was insti-gating these drinking bouts. In fact, quite the opposite was true. Given Damen's seemingly avid courtship of Breanna, George had ceased pres-suring Breanna, and appeared to be satisfied with the way things were going—at least on that score.

No, it was something else that was tormenting her uncle, something that eclipsed even acquiring Damen as a son-in-law.

One thing was certain. Whatever was plaguing him, he was like a can-non waiting to explode.

Tucking her legs beneath her, Anastasia settled herself more comfort-ably on the sitting room window ledge and gazed across the grounds. The head gardener was manicuring the shrubs that lined the length of the drive, but she scarcely noticed him, so preoccupied was she with ponder-ing her uncle's state of mind.

Especially after hearing all that Damen had relayed to her yesterday during their meeting at the House of Lockewood.

She'd gone there—presumably—just for business purposes: to receive an update on the status of their joint venture. But only a portion of their conversation had been allocated to Damen's recounting of how things in America were progressing, including an estimated forecast on when the doors of Fidelity Union and Trust would open for the first time. By mid fall, he speculated. Excellent timing indeed.

The rest of their meeting had been about George, as Damen told Anastasia about what his contacts had unearthed and just how deep a financial hole her uncle had dug himself.

That hole was pretty damned deep.

George owed thousands of pounds to his creditors. On top of that, he'd invested thousands more in foolish, unsuccessful ventures and, in the process, had lost every last shilling. In short, he was a man facing monetary ruin. The only thing in his favor was the continued success of Colby and Sons. But even that success he seemed to be destroying, in Damen's judgment.

"I don't understand. Aren't the profits of the business enough to sus-tain him?" Anastasia had asked.

"They might be, *if* he managed them wisely," was Damen's reply. "The problem is that all signs indicate he hasn't. He certainly never deposited any recent profits at the House of Lockewood, which is where he keeps the bulk of his savings, or whatever's left. Nor have those prof-its turned up at any other reputable institution, according to my contacts. In my mind, that means George probably squandered them away. What's more, he probably did so carelessly, based on his original expectation that your father would bequeath his half of the business to him, rather than to you."

"Yes," Anastasia had agreed dryly. "Uncle George didn't exactly hide his indignation at Papa's will reading, did he?"

"He wanted Henry's half of the business—badly," Damen responded. "In that way, he would have had a greater amount of profits to gamble with, and would hopefully have recouped some of his losses."

"Only to lose them again," Anastasia had pointed out.

Damen had given her a terse nod.

Well, that explained why George was so desperate for Breanna and Damen to wed. He was frantic to get his hands on Damen's wealth. But it didn't explain the magnitude of his growing anxiety—given the fact that, in his mind, Breanna's relationship with Damen was secure. Based on the frequency of Damen's visits and the obvious attraction that existed between him and the woman George thought to be Breanna, their union was on the verge of becoming a reality. But instead of the relief Anastasia expected her uncle to display, it was almost as if he were waiting for something pivotal to occur—something that could either restore or destroy him.

What was it?

Or was she just dramatizing things in her mind? Was her uncle's strain simply the cumulative effects of a downward monetary spiral?

Somehow she didn't think so.

A flash of motion from outside caught her eye, and Anastasia sat up straighter, peering more closely at the drive just in time to see a carriage come to a screeching halt.

A familiar-looking man—middle-aged, stocky, with a square jaw— emerged, speaking sharply to his driver and eyeing the house nervously before sucking in his breath and hastening up the steps.

Anastasia watched him, racking her brain as she tried to put a name to the familiar face. She'd met hundreds of people at her coming-out party, but this one she recalled. He was one of the gentlemen she'd approached with her business proposition, one of the men who'd turned her down. He was an affluent businessman, not titled, but prominent nonetheless. He owned a shipping company, she remembered in a rush. Lyman. That was it. Mr. Edgar Lyman.

Obviously, he was here to see Uncle George.

And judging from his agitated stance, whatever news he brought, he wasn't looking forward to sharing it.

Squirming to the edge of the window seat, Anastasia waited, poised like a cat ready to spring. Not yet, she cautioned herself. Wait. Five, maybe ten minutes. After that, she'd casually meander down the hall and hover near Uncle George's study. Perhaps she'd overhear something that would shed a ray of light on whatever was at the root of his agitation.

*   *   *

Down the hall in his study, George tossed off his goblet of brandy and ordered Wells to show Lyman in.

"What are you doing here?" he demanded the instant they were alone. "I told you I'd contact you as soon as I got word from our envoy that the shipment had reached port."

"You won't be hearing from him." Lyman's forehead was dotted with sweat, his palms trembling as he rubbed them together. "The ship isn't going to reach port."

George started. "What are you talking about?"

"I'm talking about that horrible storm we had two nights ago." Lyman wasn't mincing words. "My ship was caught right in the middle of it. Lightning struck the main mast. The ship went down."

All the color drained from George's face. "It went down? What about the cargo?" he demanded. "Surely the crew was able to save . . ." His voice drifted off as he watched Lyman's adamant shake of the head.

"No, Medford. No one was saved. It happened in the dead of night. Everyone was probably asleep. I assume that by the time they realized what was happening, it was too late." He clutched his head in a helpless gesture. "What point is there in speculating? The fact is that no one survived. No one and nothing. Oh, except Meade. He took the one bloody longboat that wasn't destroyed or lost and rowed to shore. Isn't that ironic? He's the one who came and told me about all this. And don't bother asking me if he's lying. He's not. I had it checked out. Our entire shipment is lost." A tremor quivered through his voice. "And I needn't tell you there was no insurance. How could . there be, in this case? So it's gone. All the merchandise, all the profit. Gone."

George swore viciously, sweeping his arm across his desk in one violent motion and sending everything on it crashing to the floor. "No. Goddammit, *no*." He snatched the bottle of brandy off the side table and refilled his goblet with shaking hands. "We'll sail out there ourselves, comb the waters. Surely some part of the cargo can be rescued . . ."

"No. It can't. Four of my best men have already done what you just described. Other than the wreckage, there's no sign of anything, except a few dead bodies floating in the water."

"Dead bodies?" George bellowed. "Dead bodies don't do me a damned bit of good." He tossed back three healthy gulps of brandy. "What the hell am I going to do? That merchandise was worth a fortune—you saw the quality Bates came up with. We would have gotten thousands for it. *Thousands*. And Lyman, it was our last chance. *Our last bloody chance!*" George flung his glass against the wall, where it shattered into a dozen fragments. "Damn Meade to hell! The son of a bitch should have saved the most valuable cargo and pulled it into the longboat. Instead, he sacrificed the whole shipment just to save his own miserable neck—a neck we could well do without."

In the hallway just outside the study, Anastasia pressed herself against the wall, her eyes wide with shock as she struggled to assimilate all the information that had just been hurled in her face—and the resulting unanswered questions.

Who was this stranger she called her uncle—a man who would place cargo above human life? And what kind of cargo could be so important as to cause such a frenzy at its loss?

Illegal cargo. *That* much was a certainty. It was the only explanation for Uncle George and Mr. Lyman's drastic reaction, and the only explanation as to why no insurance had been obtained before the merchandise was shipped.

But what kind of illegal cargo?

What in God's name was her uncle involved in?

She had little time to contemplate the possibilities. A thud of approaching footsteps from inside the study crossed toward her, separated only by the still-locked door.

Panic gripped her. She couldn't let her uncle find her standing here. Lord only knew what his reaction would be—and how severe a form it would take.

She had to get away.

Squelching her panic, Anastasia took off at a run, rounding the corner of the hallway and darting up the stairs. She didn't pause until she'd crossed the threshold of her bedchamber and shut the door. Her heart slamming against her ribs, she pressed her ear to the door, listening intently to see if she'd been followed.

Silence.

Her shoulders sagged with relief. No one was coming after her. Whatever she'd learned was her secret.

For now.

Damen. She had to get to Damen.

But how? What excuse could she use to go to the House of Lockewood when she'd just been there yesterday and, upon returning, had made no mention of a subsequent meeting scheduled for today?

She'd have to elicit help—not from Breanna, because involving her cousin would be too dangerous.

Then from whom?

From Wells. Yes, Wells held a special, affectionate place in his heart for her and Breanna. He might be willing to help—if she managed to convince him how vital his part in her plan might be. Of course, she'd have to accomplish that without revealing too much or betraying her uncle—both of which would compromise Wells's integrity and perhaps even threaten his position in the household.

She'd simply ask him straight out—without providing any details.

That decided, Anastasia walked over to the window, shifting the curtain just enough so she could peek out without being seen. Her guess—if the purposeful footsteps she'd heard within her uncle's study had been any indication—was that Mr. Lyman would be making his exit any moment now.

Sure enough, the door opened and their agitated visitor hurried down the steps and into his waiting carriage.

The carriage rounded the drive and sped off.

For a long minute Anastasia waited, peering outside to see if any further activity would ensue.

She was greeted with nothing but stillness.

Stepping away from the window, she rubbed her temples, trying to imagine what her uncle was doing right now—or more importantly, where he was. Clearly, he wasn't rushing off to meet anyone. What that suggested, given his recent behavior, was that he'd bid Mr. Lyman good-bye, then retreated back into the refuge of his study, where he'd promptly drowned himself in more brandy.

On the other hand, he could be making provisions to go out, perhaps getting some papers in order or composing himself enough to ride off and deal with this Meade person he blamed for the loss of his cargo.

If that was the case, Anastasia could very well come face-to-face with her uncle in the entranceway door. Fine. That was a chance she'd have to take. And if it happened, she'd have to pray that Wells would sense her dilemma and choose to follow her lead.

Sucking in her breath, Anastasia smoothed her gown, tucked a few loose tendrils of hair behind her ear, and left her bedchamber. She paused outside Breanna's door, wondering if her cousin was inside. Her fingers automatically reached for the door handle, then, just as quickly, fell away. It didn't matter whether or not Breanna was in her room. She couldn't be involved in this. In fact, the less she knew of Anastasia's intentions, the less vulnerable she'd be to Uncle George's outrage. That way, when interrogated by her father, Breanna could honestly declare she'd been totally unaware of her cousin's last-minute decision to travel to Town.

Staunchly, Anastasia continued on her way, descending the stairs while forcing herself to appear as casual as possible.

The ground floor was deserted.

Slowly, nonchalantly, Anastasia headed toward the entranceway door, half expecting her uncle to spring out at her and demand to know where she was going and why.

No such confrontation occurred.

Wells looked up as she approached, inclining his head in question. "Miss Stacie." He determined her identity upon seeing the loose waves of hair that tumbled about her shoulders. "Are you going out?"

"Yes, Wells, I am." Stacie glanced about quickly, ensuring that they were alone. "I need your help," she confessed in a whisper. "And, unfortunately, in this case that means lying to Uncle George. I wouldn't ask it of you unless the matter was critical."

The butler cleared his throat, appearing less surprised by her request than she'd expected. "What sort of lie is it you require?"

"A minor one," Anastasia assured him. "It's crucial that I speak with Lord Sheldrake—at once. And since the marquess isn't due here today, I need a reason to go to the House of Lockewood. I'd like you to advise Uncle George that the marquess contacted me with regard to our investment; that his message said something had come up—something that required my immediate attention—and my immediate presence at his bank. Can you do that without feeling disloyal?"

"Crucial, you said." Wells's gaze remained steady. "May I assume you're choosing me to provide this lie in order to protect Miss Breanna?"

"You may."

A flicker of resolve. "In that case, I can manage to live with my guilt. Consider your favor granted." He pivoted, tugging open the door. "Go. If your uncle asks, Lord Sheldrake summoned you to his bank. You left immediately thereafter. We won't expect you back until late this afternoon." The barest hint of a smile. "In fact, you were in so much of a hurry that you dashed off without your lady's maid."

Anastasia's head snapped up, and she studied Wells's face, wondering if the astute butler understood even more than she'd suspected. "Thank you," she murmured, recognizing that now was not the time for questions. "That explanation would be ideal."

"You're quite welcome, Miss Stacie." Wells's expression turned sober, and a note of concern crept into his voice. "Good luck. And be careful."

Solemnly, Anastasia nodded. "I will."

The House of Lockewood was buzzing with activity when she burst in several hours later.

Graff spotted her immediately, and strode rapidly to her side. "Lady Breanna," he greeted her. A quick scan of the doorway told him that she was unaccompanied by the Viscount Medford. "Or is it Lady Anastasia?" he amended, with a questioning lift of his brows. "Forgive me, but I still can't seem to tell you two apart."

Anastasia grinned. "And since you saw I was unchaperoned, you made an educated guess as to which cousin I was—a correct guess, I might add. Very good, Graff. Lord Sheldrake is lucky to have you in his employ."

A bow. "Thank you, my lady." He pursed his lips. "Is the marquess expecting you?"

"No, but it's imperative that I see him." For the first time, the untenable possibility that Damen might not be at the bank occurred to her. "Is he available?"

"He's in his office, meeting with a client. But let me tell him you're here. I'm sure he'll make time to see you."

With a crisp bow, he headed off toward the private section of offices.

Anastasia paced about the lobby of the bank, plucking at her gloves as she awaited Graff's return. She hoped he'd be persistent enough to yank Damen off to a side, at least long enough to tell him not only who was here, but how anxious she was to see him.

"Why, hello."

A masculine voice, faintly familiar, brought her head around, and Anastasia found herself looking up into Mr. Booth's round face and thoroughly pleased expression.

"My lady." He bowed, lifting her hand to his lips. "I had no idea you and your father were expected today. It's a pleasure to see you."

"Good afternoon, Mr. Booth." Anastasia shifted a bit, thinking there was something about this man that made her feel vaguely uneasy. Perhaps it was his obvious captivation with Breanna, and now with her. "It's no surprise you weren't expecting me," she added. "My visit to your bank wasn't planned. It just came up. By the way, I think you've confused me with my cousin."

Booth had clearly come to that conclusion on his own, given Anastasia's easily detected, diminished accent. "Lady Anastasia," he corrected himself. "Forgive my error." He offered her a small, apologetic smile. "It's hard to believe that two such lovely young women exist, much less how identical in appearance they are."

"I . . . thank you for the compliment," she replied, more self-conscious than flattered. "But I assure you, Breanna and I are anything but identical, other than in our appearance."

"Anastasia."

Before she could elaborate—in whatever as-of-yet undetermined manner she intended to do that—Damen came up behind her, his tone clearly commanding her full attention. "Is everything all right?"

She whipped about, met his penetrating gaze, and nodded. "Yes. I apologize for interrupting your meeting. But I needed to see you right away."

He scrutinized her for another long, probing minute, then nodded, lifting his head and fixing his hard stare on Booth. "Crompton's in my office. You'll have to take over for me—at least until John gets back from his meeting at Lloyds."

"I'm here, Damen." As luck would have it, John Cunnings happened back at that moment, reaching his employer's side in ample time to deduce what was going on. "I'll handle Crompton. The investment he's contemplating extends to several European countries as well as to Singapore. I'm familiar with the risks and rewards of the transaction."

"Excellent. I'll send him to your office." Having resolved the matter to his satisfaction, Damen gestured to Anastasia, careful to maintain the aloof, professional air they'd established between them in public. "Come, my lady."

Anastasia preceded Damen to his office, pausing only to greet Mr. Crompton as he gathered up his portfolio, nodding his agreement to join John Cunnings.

"I see you found a backer," Crompton noted in that crisp, military way he had. "Good for you, dear girl."

"Thank you." Anastasia didn't bother correcting him about Damen's role in her venture. She was far too preoccupied to concern herself with how Lord Crompton perceived her business acumen. "I'm grateful to be working with the marquess."

"As well you should be. He and his officers are among England's finest." Crompton smoothed his waistcoat, then tugged each finger of his gloves snugly into place. "Sheldrake," he continued, snapping his lean body into formal erectness. "I appreciate your preliminary advice. Cunnings can handle things from here. I'll stop by your office after he and I have conducted our business. I assume by then you and Lady Anastasia will have completed yours."

"That will be fine." Damen held the door ajar, waiting politely until the older man had left. Then, he shut the door and turned the key in the lock.

An instant later, he was across the room, gripping Anastasia's shoulders, his eyes boring into hers. "What's wrong? You're white as a sheet."

She swallowed, realizing for the first time how unnerving this day had been. "I overheard something. A conversation. Frankly, I don't know what to make of it."

"What kind of conversation? Between whom?"

Carefully, Anastasia recounted whatever snatches she could recall of her uncle's discussion with Edgar Lyman.

"Dammit," Damen hissed when she'd finished. "I was afraid something like this might be going on." His grip on her shoulders tightened. "You're sure neither of them saw you? That they had no idea you were there?"

"I'm sure. I was gone before they opened the study door." She made a helpless gesture. "Damen, obviously whatever my uncle is involved in is illegal. The question is, what? And who else—besides Mr. Lyman—is involved in this sordid scheme?"

"This Meade person, for one." Damen frowned. "But my guess is he's just some unsavory seaman who works for Lyman. He might not even know what the hell it is he's carrying aboard his ship. If we go to the trouble of finding and confronting him, it's very likely we'll learn nothing, and risk exposing ourselves in the process."

Anastasia nodded. "Meade would doubtless tell Mr. Lyman about our visit. And he, in turn, would tell Uncle George. After all, that's where Meade's loyalties—and his wages—lie."

"Exactly." Damen pressed his lips together. "Did your uncle or Lyman mention any other names?"

"I'm not sure. It's possible." Anastasia squeezed her eyes shut, trying to recall every word of the conversation. A nagging feeling plagued her, the vague awareness that she was forgetting something—something important. Whatever it was, it hovered just beyond the periphery of her memory—tangible, but out of reach. "I was so overwhelmed by what my uncle is doing—not to mention his cold-blooded attitude about the loss of all those lives—that I had trouble focusing on the rest of what he and Mr. Lyman were saying. Also, their voices were muffled. The study door is thick."

Damen nodded his understanding. "If there's something more, you'll remember it. In the meantime, whatever goods George is transporting, they're obviously damned valuable. Otherwise, he'd never take this kind of risk. Then again, I don't know how desperate he is. Maybe his finances have deteriorated to the point where he'll do anything just to recoup a portion of his losses."

Anastasia inhaled sharply, then blew out her breath. "We need answers. And to get them, we need proof. Without it, there's nothing we can do, except put ourselves—and most of all, Breanna—at risk."

"I have scores of contacts, Stacie. But even my resources can reach just so far, especially when it comes to unethical dealings. I'm not exactly an expert on those."

"I know."

With an exasperated sound, Damen scowled, racking his brain as he sought the right avenue to pursue. "Meade is inconsequential. For that matter, so is Lyman. He'd never tell us a thing, not when talking would incriminate him as much as it would your uncle. No, what we need is someone who can get us concrete evidence. Someone who can gain access to actual records—written documentation of these dealings your uncle is involved in. Those records have got to exist, even if they're disguised as innocent exchanges of money for merchandise. If I could get my hands on them, I could figure out what George's arrangement is, and with whom—possibly even what they're transporting. But who's close enough to your uncle to gain that sort of access? Wells?"

Anastasia gave a definitive shake of her head. "No. Asking Wells to betray Uncle George would be dangerous and unfair. Besides, Wells knows the household like the back of his hand, but he hasn't an inkling how Uncle George conducts his business. Nor would my uncle agree to share that sort of information with a servant. No, whoever does this bit of detective work has to delve beyond whatever sketchy records Uncle George most likely keeps in his study. They have to have access to ... ."

Breaking off, Anastasia met Damen's gaze, the obvious choice exploding in her mind like fireworks. "Me." She gripped the lapels of Damen's coat. "Why didn't I think of it before? I've been so fixed on the fact that our answers lie at Medford Manor, that I overlooked the obvious—the place where records could more easily be hidden: Colby and Sons."

A dark scowl blackened Damen's face. "I don't like the sound of this."

"I'm sure you don't." She chewed her lip, her mind racing as she followed her idea through to completion. "But it's the logical choice—the only choice. Damen, you yourself said that Uncle George's sole source of income seems to be coming from the profits of Colby and Sons. Couple that with what we've just learned, and the fact that no one else has the key to his private office." A smug smile. *"Yet,"* she amended. "All that's about to change. I now own all Papa's shares of Colby and Sons. It's only natural that I show an interest in the running of our family business. I'll tell Uncle George I want to visit the offices, to see the ledgers, the receipts, all the records of our recent profits. I'll ask to meet our suppliers—*all* of them—one of which you and I know to be Mr. Lyman. Uncle George will have no choice but to comply. Not unless he wants me to discuss his lack of cooperation with Mr. Fenshaw."

Damen's jaw had dropped, a look of disbelief slashing his features. "You must be joking. Do you honestly believe your uncle would willingly, and without suspicion, share the details of his business operations with you?"

"It's not *his* business. It's our family's. He won't have a choice. And, knowing me as he does, he won't suspect anything but that I'm being my usual audacious, bluestocking self. It would never occur to him that I'm actually searching for something incriminating, nor that I'm clever enough to find it. I am a woman, after all." She shot Damen an impish grin. "I assume you noticed."

"Oh, I noticed, all right." Damen's scowl deepened. "I also noticed you're reckless and overconfident. What you're planning—it could be incredibly dangerous."

"Or incredibly informative." Anastasia's resolve was strengthening more with each passing instant. "Damen, my uncle is bitter and greedy. As we've just learned, he's also unlawful. My worry is that he's dangerous, as well. Any man who would do what he's doing, speak as he spoke . . ." A distasteful shudder. "My concern is Breanna."

"It should also be you." Damen dragged her against him, tucking her head beneath his chin and stroking the tumbled waves of her hair. "Stacie, if your uncle is the criminal we suspect, you represent a major obstacle in his path. If he should suspect . . ."

"He won't." Anastasia drew back, offered Damen an appealing look. "Give me a few days. That's all I ask. Let me poke around the offices at Colby and Sons. If I don't stumble on anything, or if I sense I'm walking into any sort of danger, I'll stop. You have my word. I'll come straight to you, and we'll think up another tactic. Agreed?"

"Two days," Damen clarified. "Beginning tomorrow. And at the end of each of those two days, I'll be riding to Medford Manor for dinner. To call on Breanna," he added with a meaningful look. "She and I will take two very long walks on those nights. After which, we'll determine our next step. *Now* are we agreed?"

Something warm and wonderful unfurled in Anastasia's chest. "Yes," she murmured, reaching up to kiss his chin. "Agreed."

Damen tugged back her head, lifted her face to his for a profound, lingering kiss. "You and I have things to discuss," he muttered against her lips. "You know that, don't you?"

She nodded, not daring to allow herself the sheer joy of contemplating what those things might be.

"We've put off this conversation far longer than I care to contemplate—*weeks* longer." He drew back, threaded his fingers through her hair. "But no more. These feelings between us—feelings that started that first day in Fenshaw's office and have intensified every moment since—they're very real. Very real and *very* permanent. And the instant this dilemma with your uncle is resolved . . ."

"Yes. That instant." Anastasia pressed her fingertips to his lips, silencing his declaration. "But until then . . ." She shivered, her eyes sliding shut as Damen drew her fingers into his mouth, caressed them with his tongue.

"Until then?" he prompted.

"Oh, Damen, I'm falling in love with you," she confessed breathlessly. "Surely you know that."

He pulled her against him, covered her mouth with his. "Yes, I know that," he murmured huskily. "But I had to hear it. Because I'm so in love with you I can hardly think."

He sealed his vow with a kiss that both cherished and consumed her, wrapped itself around her heart with a force that nearly made her legs give out.

A knock sounded at the door, interrupting their precious moments of discovery, and Damen gave a disgusted grunt deep in his throat. "We could ignore it," he said, his voice rumbling against her lips as he continued to kiss her.

"We could." Anastasia sighed. "But we'd only arouse suspicions. And that's the last thing we want."

"Is it?"

Their gazes met—and held.

"A few days, Damen," she said in a pleading whisper. "Just to ensure Breanna's safety. Remember, I can challenge Uncle George's guardianship any time I please, request that Mr. Fenshaw find a more appropriate person to oversee my well-being. But Breanna doesn't have that option. She's completely at his mercy. Please—a few days is all I ask."

"A few days," Damen agreed. "No more. After that, I'll break into Colby and Sons myself if I have to, find the bloody evidence we need to put your uncle in prison. And once Breanna is safe, nothing is going to stop me from making you mine. Nothing, Anastasia."

Another knock.

Muttering a curse, Damen walked over and turned the key, flinging the door open to admit a startled Cunnings. "What can I do for you?"

One of Cunnings's dark brows arched. "Have I interrupted something?"

Damen pivoted, stalking over to his desk. "I'm trying to review some details with Lady Anastasia. Which I can't do if I'm interrupted." His head came up, and he met Cunnings's curious gaze. "I repeat, what can I do for you?"

Cunnings took a few tentative steps into the office. "I just wanted to see if Lord Crompton's portfolio was in here. He seems to have misplaced it."

"Here it is, Cunnings." Booth stood in the doorway, waving the portfolio in the air. "Evidently, Crompton left it in the waiting area. Graff retrieved it and brought it directly to your office."

"Ah. Good." Cunnings smiled, heading for the door and pausing only to shoot Damen an odd look. "I apologize for interrupting your meeting. Lady Anastasia . . ." He bowed. "Good day." His heels echoed down the corridor.

Booth hovered in the doorway for a minute, staring at Anastasia as if she were a priceless painting.

"Yes, Booth?" Damen prompted.

"H-m-m? Oh, nothing, sir. If you'll excuse me . . ." One last reverent glance, and he left, shutting the door behind him.

"That man makes me very uncomfortable," Anastasia declared. "He gapes at me as if I were a valuable jewel of some kind."

"You are." Damen's tone was fervent.

"Thank you." Anastasia smiled. "Coming from you, that's a lovely compliment. Mr. Booth, however, is another story entirely. He's not my suitor, Damen, he's your employee. And he ogles me every time I walk through those doors."

"It's not ogling, it's admiration. He does the same to Breanna." Damen shrugged carelessly. "Booth is a shy man who doesn't spend much time with women. My guess is he's lonely. But he's harmless, believe me."

"If you say so." She sounded dubious.

"I do." Damen walked over, brushed his knuckles across her cheek. "I'll see you tomorrow night."

A faint smile. "No, you'll see Breanna."

"Everyone else might see Breanna. I see you."

Anastasia leaned reflexively closer, half-wishing she could just fling herself into Damen's arms and let the rest of the world take care of itself.

"Two days," he reiterated quietly, as if reading her mind. "Two risky days in which I'll probably worry myself sick. After that, we're taking whatever steps are necessary to bring down your uncle and end this ridiculous charade."

Today had been a nightmare, George reflected bleakly. Hovering inside the dingy pub, he peered about through bloodshot eyes, trying to clear his muddled brain. The room swam around him, and he wobbled a bit, then glared at the buxom barmaid who shot him a curious look. *Cast your wretched gaze in a different direction,* his icy stare seemed to command.

That did the trick.

She hurried off, and George leaned against a pillar so as not to make the same mistake again. The last thing he needed was to call attention to himself. Or maybe it didn't matter. Maybe nothing mattered anymore.

Brushing droplets of rain off his coat, he blinked, trying to focus on the rear of the tavern where his contact doubtless awaited him. He was rankled that he'd been summoned in the first place—today of all days. After Lyman's devastating news and all the havoc it prophesied, he had enough to contend with without traveling to this filthy hovel for yet another meeting.

He'd spent the entire afternoon and evening closeted in his study, buried in his brandy as he desperately tried to conjure up a solution to his crumpling life. Rouge wouldn't be assuaged or bullied, not this time. No, this time all George could expect was fury, condemnation, and a complete severing of business ties between himself and his Paris buyer. And then what would he do? How would he find another interested party? He couldn't exactly advertise for one in the newspaper. Further, how would he recoup his staggering losses? He'd invested nearly every last pence in this final shipment—a shipment whose exceptional quality Rouge would never see, nor believe existed.

Perhaps that's what this late-night meeting was about, he thought with a surge of panic. Perhaps Rouge had already sent him a message terminating their association, and he was about to receive it. But no, he decided, commanding his frayed nerves to quiet. His contact never accepted or delivered messages in person. He hired a courier to do that, for the obvious purpose of protecting his own identity.

Then what the hell was tonight about?

The note had said it was important.

What could possibly be important when his entire life was falling apart?

Damn Meade. Damn the storm. And damn the fates for once again shattering his life.

The fates—and Anne. Nothing had been right since she betrayed him.

Squelching that unwelcome thought, he straightened, sharpening his search of the darkened pub.

From the far corner, a telltale flicker of light caught his eye, and he strode toward it.

"I'm not in good humor," he bit out, dragging out his chair and dropping heavily into it. "So make this brief."

"Fine." His contact lit his customary cheroot, assessing George curiously as he blew out a ring of smoke. "Are you all right?"

"I didn't hire you to inquire about my health," George snapped back. "Just tell me why the hell you needed to see me so I can go home."

An offhanded shrug. "Very well. I thought you should know that your niece was at the House of Lockewood today. It was a most unexpected visit."

"*That's* what you dragged me out here for—to talk about my wretched niece?" George shoved back his chair, ready to stagger to his feet and leave. "The only good news you could give me about Anastasia is that she'd been struck by a carriage and killed."

"I was under the impression you wanted me to keep an eye on her, at least with regard to Sheldrake."

"I did." George gave a dismissive wave. "But a visit to the bank hardly constitutes a tryst. Besides, I already knew about her little excursion. My butler gave me the message right after she left Medford Manor. He said Sheldrake sent for her about some nonsensical matter. I think he needed to review some details of that contemptible venture of theirs."

"Did he?" Another slow draw of the cheroot. "That's not the way it seemed to me. To me, it seemed like Sheldrake was as surprised by Lady Anastasia's visit as I was—and even more pleased than he was surprised."

George went still. "You're saying this visit wasn't at Sheldrake's initiation?"

"It certainly didn't look that way. What's more, they were in his office for nearly an hour, with the door locked. After which, their physical appearance was . . . shall we say, distinctly mussed."

"Mussed." George scowled. "You're crazy. Sheldrake's been at the manor three or four times a week, hovering at Breanna's side like a hawk circling its prey. There's nothing between him and my niece. He scarcely acknowledges her, except for some polite conversation over dinner."

"Whatever you say. But when that office door opened it didn't look to me as if he and Lady Anastasia had been discussing business of any kind. Sheldrake was brusque and out of sorts, while your niece's hair was tousled, her cheeks flushed . . ."

George gave a derisive laugh. "Anastasia is perpetually disheveled. She has been since childhood. If looking rumpled was deemed grounds for punishment, she would have been thrown in prison long ago." A pause. "Did you actually *see* the two of them in a compromising state?"

"No. As I said, the door was locked. And in public, well, in public they behave like business associates."

"Then there you have it." A worried frown creased George's brow as a sudden, untenable thought struck. "This business meeting—Anastasia isn't planning on squandering any more of Henry's inheritance, is she?"

"I've seen no papers to indicate that. So far, it's been only the American bank."

"Good." George felt only a minor surge of relief, the most current dilemma still weighing heavily on his mind. "And your courier's brought you no messages for me from the Continent?"

"If so, you'd already have received them."

"I suppose I would have." A wave of futility swept over George. "It doesn't matter. It's inevitable anyway. Damned, bloody inevitable. All of it. Except Sheldrake. He's my last hope. He—and whatever I can recover of my brother's funds before that miserable bitch invests it all away." George teetered to his feet. "In any case, this whole meeting's been a waste of time. I'm going home for a brandy."

The other man studied George thoughtfully, simultaneously grinding out his cheroot. "You can get a drink here."

George eyed him as if he were insane. "I don't drink the swill they serve in this place." He buttoned his coat, missing the second buttonhole twice. "Good night." He paused, blinking to make the room right itself, reflecting on what he'd just said. An inner voice penetrated his foggy state, warning him that he couldn't afford to be too lax, too sure of himself, when it came to Sheldrake. Marrying the marquess off to Breanna might very well turn out to be his last hope, his last chance of survival.

"Whether or not you're imagining things, I want you to continue as you were," he instructed his contact. "Keep your eye on these meetings between my niece and Sheldrake. Make sure all they share is that bank. Because if it's more . . ." Rage momentarily twisted his features. "Just make sure it's not."

12

❧

George's late-night brandy was just burning its way down to his stomach when a knock sounded on the study door.

He scowled, staring down at the miniature portrait of Anne and willing whoever was summoning him to go away.

His wishes went unheeded.

A second knock sounded, this time more firmly.

"What is it?" he barked, carefully replacing the portrait and rearranging the drawer before sliding it shut.

The study door opened and a young woman who was either Breanna or Anastasia stepped inside. The girl's hair tumbled about her shoulders, and her bold gaze flickered from the near-empty goblet to the neatly stacked desk to George's bloodshot eyes, blatant disapproval registering in her own.

Anastasia.

"What do you want?" George snarled.

"I need to speak with you, Uncle George."

"Not tonight." He waved her away, fuming at the intrusion. The last thing he wanted to deal with tonight was this outspoken bitch—a bitch who was the living embodiment of Anne's betrayal. "I'm too tired. Whatever it is can wait."

"No, it can't." Anastasia walked toward him, her unwavering stare meeting his head-on. "Uncle George, it occurs to me that I'm neglecting my role as Papa's heir. I've been so caught up with my own coming-out party and my reunion with Breanna, that I've completely overlooked my responsibility to Colby and Sons."

George went rigid. "What are you talking about?"

"Our company. I own half of it now. In America, Papa spent long years teaching me about the family business. He'd want me to continue with my education, to share with you the full responsibility of running Colby and Sons. I intend to do that. Starting tomorrow."

Bile rose in George's throat, and he quickly washed it down with another gulp of brandy. "I must be misunderstanding you."

"I don't think so," she countered brightly. "What I've planned is to visit our London offices tomorrow. I'll go through our current list of business associates, our suppliers, our contacts throughout the Continent. I'm sure most of those names will be familiar to me—after all, we dealt with them from our American offices, too." She inclined her head quizzically. "Would you like to join me? Or shall I just take the plunge on my own?"

George felt as if his head was about to split in two. How dare this impertinent little bitch walk in here and announce that she was assuming a role in his company? How dare she presume she had the right?

His knuckles whitened around the periphery of his glass.

The trouble was, she *did* have the right.

"Uncle George?" she pressed. "Shall I tell Wells that I'll be traveling to London alone, or . . ."

"No," he ground out, fighting the vise of panic that gripped him at the thought of Anastasia having access to his doctored receipts, his veiled correspondence. *Stop it,* he commanded himself. *She'll never see through it—not if you don't condemn yourself by acting guilty.* "I'll go with you," he continued, in as calm a voice as he could muster. "I'll show you around the office. I'll ask my carriage driver to wait, so you can run along home immediately thereafter."

"Oh, I don't want to run along," Anastasia declined with a reassuring smile. "I want to stay—to read through the ledgers, the ongoing contracts, everything." Her smile faded, and she gave him an apologetic look. "I know you find the prospect of a woman in business outrageous. But I think you'll be surprised to see how quick my mind actually is. I suppose I take after Papa. I find the import–export business fascinating." With that, she glanced at her uncle's half-empty brandy bottle, and backed away. "Anyway, I won't keep you. You mentioned you were tired. And I, too, had best get a good night's rest. I want to be especially alert tomorrow."

George stared after her as she left, watching blindly as the door shut in her wake. A fury like he'd never known surged inside him, pulsed through his veins. Violently, he seized his bottle of brandy, hurling it at the now-closed door, staring at the dark splotches of color that splattered the walls, stained the carpet.

If only it was Anastasia he'd shattered, her blood he'd spilled.

Then maybe retribution could blot out adversity.

*   *   *

It was just past dawn when Breanna knocked on her cousin's bed-chamber door.

"Stacie, are you awake?"

Anastasia opened the door, a surprised expression crossing her face. "Awake and dressed," she assured her cousin. "Is everything all right?"

"You tell me." Breanna walked into the room, shutting the door and leaning back against it. "I tossed and turned all night. I couldn't shake the feeling that you're in some kind of trouble. Are you?"

Rubbing her palms together, Anastasia contemplated how to answer that. It didn't surprise her that Breanna sensed her turmoil, not given the uncanny connection that existed between them. But what could she possibly say to ease her cousin's mind?

"Don't skirt the issue or try lying to me," Breanna second-guessed her to warn. "You're terrible at hedging and even worse at lying."

A grin. "That certainly limits my options, now doesn't it?" Her smile faded. "Breanna, I'm not trying to hide things from you. I'm only trying to protect you."

"From my father," Breanna concluded.

"Yes. From your father."

A contemplative pause, during which time Breanna studied her cousin, tapping her chin thoughtfully. "But you *have* shared this dilemma of yours with someone. And I'd be willing to bet that someone is Damen Lockewood."

"You'd be right." This, at least, was something Anastasia could share with Breanna—something she was aching to share with her. "I'm in love with him," she admitted, gauging her cousin's reaction. "And what's even more wonderful, he's in love with me."

Genuine joy erupted on Breanna's face, and she rushed over, hugged Anastasia tightly. "I'm so happy for you—for you both." She drew back, teasing laughter dancing in her eyes. "Of course, *I've* known this for weeks. I was wondering how long it would take the two of you to figure it out. You're both so miserably stubborn."

"You're right." Anastasia smiled. "But we finally declared our feelings aloud."

"When?"

"Yesterday. At the House of Lockewood."

That elicited an entirely different reaction, worry clouding Breanna's face. "You didn't mention to me that you were going to the bank."

"The visit wasn't planned." Anastasia fell silent, torn between the attempt to protect her cousin and the realization that Breanna had a right to the truth—especially if that truth turned out to be a dangerous one. "Breanna, I overheard something yesterday, something terribly unnerving. I went to Damen for advice, and perhaps for help."

"And that something involves Father."

"Yes."

"Tell me what it is. I deserve to know." Breanna's jaw set as if to steel her for what was to come. "Even if I won't like what I hear."

"All right." Anastasia sank down on the bed, relaying the entire conversation she'd overheard, ending with her talk with Damen and her subsequent decision to visit the offices of Colby and Sons. "If there's anything incriminating to be found, I'm sure that's where it will be. It's the only place Uncle George would feel secure about leaving such records."

"God." Breanna sank down beside her cousin. "This is even worse than I suspected." She massaged her temples, then abruptly stopped. Twisting about, she faced Anastasia. "But if my father is involved in something ugly, you could be endangering yourself by going there and trying to uncover evidence."

"That was Damen's argument. It didn't deter me. Nor will it now."

"Fine. Then I'm going with you."

"No." Anastasia leapt to her feet. "You're not."

"Stacie, he's *my* father. You're not putting yourself at risk alone."

Anastasia gave a hard shake of her head. "Breanna, listen to me. I'm not trying to be heroic. I'm trying to find answers. Thus far, I've succeeded in arranging all this without arousing Uncle George's suspicions. But if you suddenly appear by my side, insisting on learning a business you've never before expressed any interest in, all that will change. Your father's not a stupid man." Anastasia took Breanna's hand in hers. "I have to do this alone—for all our sakes, to get at the truth as soon as possible. And if our worst suspicions are confirmed, if Uncle George is indeed dangerous . . ." A swallow. "Then he must be dealt with before he can harm anyone."

"Anyone—meaning me."

"Yes, meaning you." Anastasia never diverted her gaze. "I asked you this once before, in a less than straightforward fashion. Now I'm asking you directly: does Uncle George strike you?"

"Strike me, yes. Beat me senseless, no. Do I sense an element of cruelty in him? Of course. But can I say I've ever feared for my safety? I . . . I don't think so."

"You've never given him reason to threaten your safety, or to become truly enraged, for that matter. But if you did, especially now, when he's constantly drinking, when his humor is as black as night and his temper so short that everyone cringes the minute he enters the room . . ." Anastasia's voice trailed off. "I can't vouch for what he might do. Nor can I vouch for his stability. The bottom line is, he's your father. That's not something you can undo. You're his responsibility until your twenty-first birthday. I can sever ties with him if need be. You can't. And I won't leave you here at his mercy." A pause. "Can you shoot a pistol?"

Breanna sucked in her breath. "What?"

"Humor me. Can you shoot?"

A nod. "At targets and pigeons, yes. But not at people." Breanna gave her cousin an incredulous look. "Do you honestly believe I'll need to defend myself to that degree?"

"I don't know what to believe. And I'm not thinking only of the possible danger Uncle George represents. If he's involved in something illegal, who knows what type of people he consorts with? Or how many of those unsavory contacts won't get paid—and, as a result, will become very agitated—because that shipment of Uncle George's went down?" Anastasia counted off on her fingers. "There are those who supplied the illegal cargo, those who awaited its arrival, investors—the possibilities are too vast too contemplate. Will any of those lowlifes show up here to retaliate? I'm not going to speculate. But I have a very uneasy feeling about all this. And I'd feel better if you kept a pistol nearby, just in case."

Breanna frowned, unable to dispute her cousin's reasoning. "Very well. As I recall, Father keeps an extra pistol in the library, to have on hand in case of a burglary. Since he never uses it, he wouldn't notice if it were to disappear, at least not for a few days. I'll go downstairs and get it after you and he leave for the office. I'll hide it in my bureau drawer." Her frown deepened. "What about you? How will you protect yourself?"

"If I sense anything out of the ordinary today, I'll slip off and go straight to the House of Lockewood. If need be, I'll borrow a pistol from Damen. But Uncle George wouldn't dare harm me in public—especially not once I casually mention that I informed Damen during yesterday's meeting that I'd be going to Colby and Sons today."

"I see your point. My father would never want to tarnish his image—not in the eyes of Lord Sheldrake." Breanna captured both Anastasia's hands, squeezed them tightly. "Please. Be careful. And try not to act too cheeky. Things will go much better with Father if you don't challenge his opinions or his authority."

A rueful smile tugged at Anastasia's lips. "I hear the message you're giving me loud and clear. I promise to do my best to keep my place and not antagonize Uncle George."

That promise wasn't going to be easy to keep, she fumed silently, after traipsing along behind her uncle for an hour, exploring the wonders of the outer office at Colby and Sons. The sum total of the room was a desk, occupied by their mild-mannered clerk, Mr. Roberts; a row of chairs and a file cabinet against one wall; and, against the wall adjacent to George's private offices, a settee and two end tables, before which rested a long, rectangular table. Not a sheet of paper lay exposed upon the desk or any of the tables, nor was there visible evidence of any other business-oriented material.

Did her uncle actually think she'd be content with this inane tour and then run along home like a good little girl?

If so, he had quite a surprise in store.

She'd begin with the obvious file cabinet.

"Uncle George, if it's all right with you, I'd like to start familiarizing myself with the company." She gestured toward the cabinet. "What if I begin by glancing through the files so I can acquaint myself with our current transactions, as well as the names of those suppliers we deal with most frequently."

Her uncle bristled and Mr. Roberts's head shot up as he awaited his employer's reply.

"Fine," George bit out, practically choking on his words. "I have some papers to sort through in my office." He turned to his clerk. "Roberts, give Lady Anastasia whatever she needs."

"Certainly, my lord." The poor little man whipped off his spectacles, wiping at an imaginary speck of dust before shoving the spectacles back on his nose and rising to his feet. "Why don't you have a seat, my lady? I'll bring the files to you."

"Thank you, Mr. Roberts. That would be very kind." Anastasia settled herself on the settee. Surreptitiously, she peeked at her uncle from the corner of her eye, watching him approach his private office, then extract a key from his pocket, which he used to unlock the door. That done, he pushed open the door and stepped inside.

It took all her self-restraint not to dash in after him.

Leaning forward, she peered around the open doorway and caught a glimpse of a tidy room with a walnut desk and sideboard. Ledgers were neatly stacked on the far left-hand corner of the desk alongside a tray of papers—correspondence, perhaps—and what looked to be an appointment book. The sideboard was uncluttered, although she'd bet her last pound that it was stocked with liquor.

She was dying to go through those ledgers and that appointment book. But she'd have to wait, bide her time, until she could find the means to get in.

The door slammed shut.

Sighing, Anastasia resettled herself on the settee, awaiting Mr. Roberts, who was gathering files for her from the cabinet. Instinct told her she'd find nothing incriminating in what she was about to be given. Whatever her uncle was involved in, he certainly wouldn't want Roberts having access to those records. Still, she had to be sure. She also had to start somewhere.

Two hours later, she had three stacks of files piled up on the long table before her, and she'd learned nothing other than the fact that Colby and Sons had a healthy clientele and a substantial number of ongoing transactions. The only curious detail that struck her was the high prices charged by several of their shippers. If all the shipping companies' fees had been uniformly higher, she would have assumed that shipping costs in England simply exceeded those in America. But that didn't seem to be the case, not when most of the companies appeared to be charging fees that were comparable to what she was accustomed to seeing in her father's records. Further, of those few shippers who commanded a higher price, one was Mr. Lyman, whose very name sent off warning bells in Anastasia's head. This she'd have to investigate further.

She was just about to plow through yet another pile of receipts when the entrance to Colby and Sons was flung open.

"Roberts, I need to see Lord Medford right away." A stout man who looked distinctly familiar burst into the room, his pudgy cheeks bright red, whether from the exertion of hurrying or something more, Anastasia couldn't determine. But he certainly seemed agitated, and urgent about his demand to see her uncle.

Before Roberts could respond, the inner office door nearly flew off its hinges, and Uncle George stalked out, brushing by the settee where Anastasia sat, and crossing over to join his caller. "I didn't expect you today," he greeted, his entire demeanor strained as he backed the other man toward the entranceway. "Roberts, you may go to the bank for me now," he instructed brusquely over his shoulder.

The nervous clerk jumped to his feet, and George waited, keeping his back to Anastasia and remaining silent until Roberts had excused himself and left. Then, he continued speaking to his guest, his voice, and that of his companion, scarcely audible.

Casually, Anastasia rose, twisting about to eye her uncle's now-vacant office longingly. She turned back, studying the two men and grappling over which to do: Should she sidle closer to them, try to eavesdrop on the conversation, and learn what this visit was all about? Or should she use this time to try to slip into her uncle's private domain and glance at his personal records?

Since the men's voices were so quiet that eavesdropping was a virtual impossibility, and coupled with the fact that she might never have another chance, she opted for the latter.

Slowly, she edged toward the inner office, never looking away from her uncle and his visitor. They were engrossed in heated discussion, their agitated tones escalating into hisses, both men totally unaware of her presence.

At the precise moment, Anastasia eased inside, then halted, deciding quickly where to spend the few seconds she had. Scrutinizing the room, she made an impulsive decision, and acted upon it. She rushed to the desk, snatched up the appointment book, and tucked it in the pocket beneath her skirts. Holding her breath, she inched back to the threshold, peeking outside and feeling a surge of relief when she saw the two men still talking. She slipped out, sidled over to the settee, and resumed her position.

"Uncle George, may I help myself to the next drawer of files?" she inquired brightly.

"What?" Just the sound of her voice made George's shoulders go positively rigid. "Oh, yes, yes. Mister . . . my guest and I will be going out for a few minutes." He turned, hurried over to lock his office door. Pausing beside Anastasia, he glanced down at what she was perusing, and looked subtly but discernibly relieved at whatever he saw. "Browse through the files as you please," he forced himself to offer. "Save any questions you have for Roberts. He'll be back within the half hour."

"Thank you. I will." She smiled, holding her breath until her uncle and his portly guest—who had retreated into the hallway to wait—had left.

She heard their footsteps fade away, and waited an extra moment to be safe.

Then, she whisked the appointment book out from under her skirts, and began scanning the entries.

Rather than starting at the beginning, she focused on the 7th of August, about one week ago, hoping to see a name that would leap out at her and correspond with the timing of the shipment of that questionable cargo.

Lyman's name appeared several times, but that was no surprise. So did a few other names. Curiously, they were all the shippers whose rates were higher than their competitors.

A rather clipped entry dated two days ago caught her eye: *Rouge— receive Paris shipment.*

No further details were provided, an oddity, given that the other entries in the book were thorough, described in full.

And neat.

That was another thing. Unlike George's other entries, which were precisely penned, as fastidious as he, this one was uneven, its awkwardly scrawled letters crammed in the corner, almost as if he wanted them hidden.

Which he probably did.

The date on the entry was August 12th—just one day after the shipment had gone down.

Paris. Was that where that illegal cargo had been headed? And, if so, who was Rouge?

Quickly, Anastasia flipped through the appointment book, noticing two additional, equally obscured entries that indicated other occasions when this Rouge was expecting something from Uncle George—something to be delivered to Paris.

But what?

A noise in the hallway caught Anastasia's ear, and swiftly she slipped the appointment book back into its hiding place beneath her skirts. When Mr. Roberts entered an instant later, she was calmly leafing through a stack of receipts.

"Have you everything you need, my lady?" he asked timidly.

"Yes." Anastasia gave him a grateful smile. "Thank you, Mr. Roberts. Oh, Uncle George said he'd be back shortly. He went for a stroll with Mr. . . . Mr. . . . ." She screwed up her face, seemingly searching for the name of their visitor. "I'm sorry. I've received so many introductions since I returned to England. I completely forgot the surname of that pleasant gentleman who was just here."

"Bates," Roberts supplied, nodding his understanding as he resumed his place at his desk. "Mr. Bates. The magistrate."

"Yes, that's right. Mr. Bates." Anastasia nearly leaped out of her seat as the name fell into place. Of course. Bates—the magistrate. No wonder Uncle George hadn't wanted her to get too good a look at him. He knew that if she saw him up close she'd recognize him, and wonder why a magistrate was visiting the offices of an import–export company.

Mr. Bates. *Now* she remembered. He'd been one of the potential backers she'd approached at her coming-out party. He was financially secure and well-connected.

And his was the name she'd overheard her uncle speak to Mr. Lyman in their meeting yesterday.

Anastasia had to keep herself from shouting aloud as that snippet of memory fell into place, and she recalled her uncle's words.

That merchandise was worth a fortune—you saw the quality Bates came up with. We would have gotten thousands for it. Thousands. And Lyman—it was our last chance. Our last bloody chance!

Bates. *That* had been the name that had hovered out of reach when she'd recounted the conversation to Damen.

And now that she did recall it, a whole new set of questions emerged. Why in the name of heaven was a magistrate involved in supplying goods? What stolen or illegal merchandise had he gotten his hands on that Uncle George had shipped to someone named Rouge in Paris? Valuable jewels? Opium?

She'd be willing to bet that the sunken cargo was the reason for

Bates's visit today—*and* the reason for his unsettled state of mind. He'd probably just found out that whatever he'd provided to Uncle George was never going to reach its destination.

Anastasia massaged her temples. She had to assimilate all this information, to review it with someone she trusted—the same someone who could help her make sense of all she'd gleaned today.

Damen.

Half tempted to make some excuse and head out, she suddenly remembered the appointment book. If she left the office without returning it, her uncle would undoubtedly come back and discover it missing. Then he'd know she was up to something, which would arouse his suspicions and, consequently, undo everything she'd accomplished thus far.

She eased back on the settee. She had to have patience, to find a way to replace the appointment book before leaving the office.

How was another matter entirely—one she wished she'd given some thought to before she'd snatched the bloody thing. Then again, there hadn't been time. If she'd taken one extra minute to think things through, her opportunity to seize the book would have vanished and she never would have had the chance to read those potentially incriminating entries.

Somehow, some way, she had to await her uncle's return and accompany him into his office, then find a way to slip the appointment book back onto his desk—before he noticed it was missing.

Lord only knew what she was letting herself in for, especially given the wretched mood her uncle would doubtless be in after his heated discussion with Bates.

Well, she'd just have to contend with that, as well.

She lowered her head, resuming her perusal of the files. Being she was stuck here, she might as well make the most of it. She'd pore over as many receipts as time permitted.

Twenty minutes later, George stalked into the office, a black scowl darkening his face. His breath was coming quickly—as if he'd been running or, perhaps, arguing strenuously. He barely glanced at Roberts or Anastasia, but headed straight for his office door. His hand shook as he fitted the key into the lock, and it took him three attempts to get the door open.

Either he's been drinking or, more likely, he craves a drink, Anastasia mused silently.

Just the thing she needed to save her.

Moving to the edge of the settee, she waited until her uncle had taken a few steps inside his office. Then, she shot to her feet, following him in as quietly as she could.

Sure enough, he had crossed the room and was pouring himself a generous helping of brandy.

Without pause, Anastasia yanked the appointment book from beneath her skirts and placed it silently on the desk where she'd found it.

"Uncle George?" she said, pretending she'd just entered the room. "I want to thank you for giving me free rein to explore. It's been exciting to learn just how vast our company has become."

George's head jerked around, and he stared at Anastasia as if she were a loathsome insect. "I'm glad your morning was exciting. Mine wasn't." He drowned his bitterness in two deep swallows of brandy, clearly trying to squelch his obvious hostility toward his niece—hostility rooted in something far harsher, more deep-seated than mere disapproval over her business acumen. "Have you seen enough for one day, or are you intent on further upsetting my filing system and my schedule?"

Anastasia chewed her lip in apparent distress. "I didn't mean to be disruptive. But perhaps you're right. Perhaps I did overstay my welcome a bit, especially in the case of poor Mr. Roberts. He's been waiting on me all morning, probably to the exclusion of his other work." She glanced over her shoulder at the outer office, a rueful expression on her face. "The more I think about it, the more I think I'll be going."

A spark of relief flickered in George's eyes. "I'm sure Roberts would appreciate that. We still have quite a bit of paperwork to review today."

"Then I'll be on my way."

"Fine. Take the carriage."

"But how will you get home?"

"I'll find a way," George snapped. "Just go."

"All right." Anastasia wasn't waiting for her uncle to change his mind. "I'll thank Mr. Roberts and be off."

A half hour later she walked into the House of Lockewood.

Impatiently, she looked around for Graff, eager to have him announce her to Damen.

She needn't have bothered.

Damen himself was pacing about the bank, his gaze flickering from his customers to the entranceway and back.

The instant he saw Anastasia, he broke away from the crowd, making his way to her side.

"Are you all right?"

"Fine. May we talk?"

"Right now." He gripped her arm, led her across the floor, through the rear door, and directly into his office.

He shut and locked the door.

"What happened?" he demanded, turning to face her. "I've been watching the clock and worrying since I got up this morning. Actually, I worried all night, too. I didn't shut an eye. I never should have agreed to this. The risk is too great."

"But well worth it." Anastasia rushed forward, clutched his forearms. "Damen, I got results. At least I think I did." She blurted out everything she'd discovered, from the odd discrepancy in the receipts to the entries in her uncle's appointment book, to the most damning information of all: Bates's visit and the fact that it had been his name she'd overheard in her uncle's conversation with Lyman yesterday—all of which added up to the fact that the magistrate was somehow involved in these shady dealings.

Damen's scowl deepened with each passing word. "That's it," he declared the minute she was finished. "Your part in this is officially over. Whatever your uncle is involved in is more serious than I thought, and even more dangerous. Magistrates and affluent businessmen who risk their positions in society are desperate men. When they're backed into corners, they react like trapped animals. They attack when threatened. As do unscrupulous viscounts who already despise their nieces and find out those nieces have played a major role in bringing them down. I'll take it from here, Stacie. I mean it."

Anastasia sucked in her breath. "What will you do?"

"I'll have Bates investigated. It should be easy enough to find out if George is compensating him in some way. My guess is it's with power, not money—being that your uncle has none of the latter to offer. But he does have influence, or at least his title does. I wouldn't be surprised if he's had a hand in broadening Bates's area of jurisdiction."

"That makes sense," Anastasia concurred. "What about Rouge? How do we get information on him?"

"I'll notify one of my contacts in Paris, see what they can dig up. Whoever this Rouge is, he can't be too hard to find, especially if he doesn't know we're looking for him." Damen considered the rest of what she'd told him, and his lips thinned into a grim line. "As for the companies you mentioned—the ones whose prices were higher than the others—my guess is that either your uncle's cohorts padded those receipts and split the difference with him, or that the companies in question have investments in his seedy operation, in which case, he's giving them a percentage of what he's making by paying their inflated bills."

"In other words, he's embezzling from Colby and Sons—my grandfather's company." Anger flared deep within Anastasia's gut.

"Yes. He's nothing but a common criminal—he and his despicable partners. A common criminal, *and* a dangerous one."

The anxiety in Damen's voice dispelled Anastasia's ire, supplanted it with concern. "You're worrying about me," she stated quietly.

"I bloody well am. As your grandfather would be if he were alive.

Funds can be recouped. People can't. Besides, I know firsthand that Colby and Sons is in no financial danger. You, on the other hand, are another matter entirely. As of this moment, you're to stay as far away from your uncle as the walls of Medford Manor permit. I'd recommend the same for Breanna—although I doubt George would be suspicious of her. Just steer clear of him. Live there, eat there, but keep your distance. No more visits to Colby and Sons, no more inflammatory confrontations. And no more deceptions."

That brought Anastasia's head up. "If you're referring to Breanna and me switching places, the only way we can end that deception is if you stop visiting me. Is that what you want?"

A muscle worked in his jaw. "You know it isn't." He dragged her against him, buried his lips in her hair. "I can't—*won't*—stay away from you."

"Nor I from you." She rested her forehead against his chest. "We'll just have to make sure Uncle George doesn't figure us out. Because until you gather enough evidence to have him thrown into jail, he's a threat to Breanna. Especially now, when your supposed preoccupation with her is my uncle's main source of hope. If he were to discover there's to be no future between Breanna and you . . ." Anastasia sighed. "I shudder to think what he'd do."

"And if he discovered the lengths you and she are going to to deceive him into believing that lie? What would he do to her then?"

Silence.

Damen's embrace tightened. "I've got to get that evidence—fast. It's the only way to ensure your and Breanna's safety, and allow us the future I intend us to have."

Anastasia inhaled sharply and broke away, crossed over toward the desk.

Her abrupt movement startled the shadowy figure that hovered outside the office door.

Tension rippling through him, he pressed close to the wall, waiting to see if bolting would become a necessity. It didn't. The office door remained shut. Better still, the voices from inside, until now too muffled to discern, loomed within clear, distinguishable range.

"Stacie? What is it?" Unaware he was being eavesdropped upon, Damen walked over, turned Anastasia about to face him.

She squeezed her eyes shut, wishing she could explain how badly she needed the balm Damen's words provided, how impossibly thrilling a future with him sounded. "Tell me about our future together."

He seemed to understand, because his hand stroked her hair, moved it out of the way so he could caress the nape of her neck. "Later. For now, I'd rather show you."

"That would be heaven," she breathed, feeling shivers go up her spine. "Far more wonderful than telling me. Certainly better than talking about my uncle and whatever criminal activities he's involved in. And much, much better than your lecturing me about the dangers Breanna and I are flirting with by switching places."

Damen tilted back her head, his hot gaze probing hers with burning intensity. "I wish I didn't want you so damned much," he muttered. "Because, despite your insistence to the contrary, my every instinct is screaming that I should continue lecturing you. It's time for you and Breanna to stop this insanity, to stop pretending to be each other during my visits. Sweetheart, you're playing with fire."

"M-m-m," Anastasia murmured, only half-listening to Damen's words. She was still contemplating his vow to show her what was in store for them. She turned her head, brushed her lips against his throat. "Playing with fire—well, maybe I am. Fortunately, I only burn when I'm with you."

Damen's muscles went rigid. "You're trying to distract me."

"And if I am?" She slipped her fingers into the knot of his cravat, untied it. "It's working, isn't it?"

"Yes, it's working. Too damned well."

"Good," she breathed, kissing the strong column of his throat. "Because I don't want to talk about my uncle anymore, at least not now. In fact, I don't want to talk at all."

With a rough groan, Damen tugged back her head, lowering his mouth to hers. "You make me crazy," he muttered against her lips. "I want to protect you and throttle you all at once. And I want to strip away every last barrier between us and make love to you until neither of us can breathe."

"Um-m-m, the last sounds spectacular," Anastasia murmured, sliding her hands beneath his waistcoat, gliding them up the fine linen of his shirt. "Terribly improper, but spectacular."

"This discussion is not over," he warned, his fingers automatically reaching around, dispensing with the buttons of her gown. Hungrily, he tugged the bodice down to expose the upper slope of her breasts. "Understood?" His lips blazed a path to her chemise, dipping lower as he untied the ribbons, one by one. "We have to come up with a different plan for us to be together—one I can live with."

Anastasia urged him closer, welcoming his caresses, the all-encompassing surge of heat that claimed her, obliterated all else from her mind. "Understood," she managed. "We'll fight this battle out—later." She shifted restlessly, eager to free herself from the confinement of her chemise. "Much later."

Outside the door, the eavesdropper straightened, stepped away. He'd learned all he had to. He didn't need to tarry any longer—not when every moment meant risking discovery. Besides, it didn't take a scholar to guess what was about to take place behind that door.

Glancing around to confirm he'd remained undetected, he made his way toward the privacy he sought. His mind was racing, reminding him that time was of the essence. He'd send a message off right away, arrange for a meeting tonight.

What he'd just heard explained everything. He was pleased to discover his instincts hadn't failed him, contrary to what Medford claimed. He'd been right about Lady Anastasia and Lord Sheldrake.

As for Medford—well, the viscount certainly wasn't going to be happy with the news he was about to receive. Especially since the courier was already en route to his lordship's residence with that letter from the Continent he'd been dreading.

Two pieces of bad news in one night.

The man scowled. Ah, well. Making the viscount smile wasn't his job. Giving him information was.

With that, he stepped into the empty room and quietly shut the door.

Inside Damen's office, Anastasia, oblivious to anything but what was happening between them, lost patience. She reached around, untying the final ribbon of her chemise and shrugging the garment off her shoulders.

Damen drank in her beauty, his eyes darkening to that smoky gray that made her heart pound. "You're pushing me to a dangerous brink," he whispered roughly, bending his head to draw one aching nipple into his mouth. "Perhaps *too* dangerous."

"I don't care." She arched, offering him more of herself, quivering as he took it. "For once, I don't want to think. I want to go wherever this takes us. And when we get there—I don't want you to stop."

With a harsh shudder, Damen caught her about the waist, backing her up until she collided with the edge of his desk, then lifting her onto it. Urgently, he pushed up her skirts and wedged himself in the cradle of her thighs. "I won't stop," he vowed huskily. "I can't." His forefinger lifted her chin, and he lowered his head again, sealing their lips in a kiss that was slow and hot and deep. His tongue slid across hers, taking it in blatant possession, and his fingers tangled in her hair, cradling her head so she couldn't move away.

Moving away was the farthest thing from Anastasia's mind.

She moaned softly, wriggling closer to the warmth of Damen's body, knowing she was testing his control and half-hoping it would shatter.

It nearly did.

He gripped the bunched muslin layers of her gown, pushing them higher, gliding his palm up her stocking-clad inner thighs. He kept kissing her, his mouth eating at hers, devouring her with an intensity he'd never before allowed. He muttered her name, his fingers shifting higher, finding the spot where her stockings left off and her bare skin began.

"Damen." Anastasia clutched at him, sensing what he was about to do, frantic for him to do it.

"Do you want this?" he rasped against her mouth.

"Yes. Please. Yes." She nodded wildly, her hips lifting instinctively toward him, silently begging for his touch.

His palm climbed that last tantalizing inch, grazed the burnished nest between her thighs. Then, his fingers parted her, stroked the delicate flesh that screamed for his touch.

Anastasia's breath lodged in her throat. Time seemed to stand still, all sensation concentrated beneath Damen's heated caress. She heard him groan, felt the tremor that racked his body. But all she knew was the unbearable stirring inside her, the rush of wet warmth that surged through her core, the tight knot of need that coiled inside her, an awakening and an emptiness all at once.

"Silk," Damen breathed into her lips. "Hot, flawless silk. God, I want to be inside you." His fingers responded to his command, gliding into her warm wetness, caressing and exploring her, only to emerge, circle the tight bud that throbbed with yearning.

Anastasia whimpered into Damen's open mouth, parting her thighs shamelessly and moving against his hand, unable to get close enough, to deepen his presence in her body fully enough.

Somehow he understood.

His fingers withdrew, then entered her again, only this time they began an unbearable rhythm of plunge and retreat, moving faster and deeper, reaching high inside her, pushing toward that unendurable tightness curled in her very center. At the same time, his thumb found that tight little bud, circled it enticingly, first once, then again and again and again.

Abruptly, bright colors exploded inside Anastasia's head, and her entire body clenched and convulsed, shimmering and shattering into a million fragments of sensation. She tore her mouth from Damen's, burying her face against his shoulder as spasms racked her body. She cried out, the sound muffled by Damen's woolen coat, and he held her as she came apart in his arms, his fingers heightening her pleasure until the final spasm had subsided and she sagged against him, everything inside her melting and sliding away into nothingness.

From a distance, the faint sounds of the bank trickled back into consciousness, and gradually, Anastasia became aware of her surroundings again. Damen was holding her, stroking her back in slow, soothing motions, gently kissing the crown of her hair, his own breath emerging in harsh, shallow rasps.

With a herculean effort, Anastasia raised her head, gazed into the blazing inferno of Damen's eyes. "God," she whispered, her voice as unsteady as her heartbeat. "That was . . ."

"Inconceivable," Damen supplied, smoothing damp tendrils of hair off her cheeks. "It defied words, surpassed even my wildest fantasies. And it was only the beginning, Stacie. There's more—so much more."

Anastasia heard the strain in his voice and her gaze fell reflexively to his trousers, noting the obviously rigid contours of his body and, despite her innocence, realizing precisely what they meant. "But you . . ."

". . . will survive—at least for the time being." Damen smiled at the stricken expression on her face. "I'm not being selfless, sweetheart. Trust me. I intend to succumb to this relentless craving inside me, to pour myself into you until every last drop of me is spent. But I want more than a few stolen minutes in my office. Once I make you mine . . ." A profound light flickered in his eyes. "I don't intend to let you go. Not ever. You asked me to tell you about our future. Well, now I will. I'm going to marry you, Anastasia. I'm going to place my ring on your finger and declare my love for you before God and all mankind. And I'm going to do it the instant this insanity is behind us—after which, nothing and no one is going to stop me."

Tears glistened on Anastasia's lashes. "Have I any say in this new partnership you're describing?" she asked in a small, quavery voice.

"One word. That's all the say you have."

A tremulous smile. "Very well. Then here's that word: yes. Yes to everything you just described. Yes to everything you want but have yet to describe. Yes."

13

❦

*I*t was the first time George had ever arrived at this filthy establishment before his contact. Then again, he was early. Ordinarily, he kept a close eye on his pocket watch, never riding off to their meeting place one moment sooner than was necessary. But tonight, he hadn't so much as glanced at his timepiece. He'd been too preoccupied with Rouge's message.

It couldn't have come at a better time.

The day had been nerve-racking. After a sleepless night—filled with dark dreams of Anastasia discovering his doctored receipts, then flourishing them before the authorities—he'd been forced to escort her into London, through the doors of Colby and Sons, all the while treating her as if she belonged there. And then, as if that hadn't been enough, he'd been forced to watch the bitch tear his office apart file by file as she immersed herself in *his* company.

On the heels of that, Bates had arrived.

Of all the days for the fool to find out about the lost cargo, it had to be today. Calming him down, assuring him his identity had been kept secret, never mentioned in the records of the lost shipment, had taken the better part of an hour.

But dealing with Bates had been more aggravating and time-consuming than it had been alarming. George knew the magistrate would never betray him. He enjoyed his position too much. As long as his name stayed unsullied, he'd be cooperative and keep his mouth shut.

What had been alarming was the prospect of Anastasia recognizing Bates, wondering what a magistrate was doing bursting into the office of an import–export company, sputtering on as if he'd lost his last dollar here.

The very thought of the interrogation that would have followed made George's insides clench.

Thankfully, he'd kept Bates well-concealed, and too far away from Anastasia for her to recognize him, especially given the fact that they'd only been introduced once, at Anastasia's coming-out ball, where they'd chatted only long enough for Anastasia to seek the magistrate's financial support in her banking venture.

Still, it was hardly time for self-congratulations. Who knew how many more trips that miserable wretch intended to make to Colby and Sons, how many more visitors she'd glimpse that would give her pause, would make questions crowd her head?

How long would it be before she discovered just a little too much?

Damn, how he wished he could snuff her out like an unwanted candle.

He'd arrived home, waved away dinner, and gone straight to his study and his brandy. He'd yanked out Anne's miniature portrait, gripped it so tightly his knuckles had turned white, and sworn at her as he drank himself into oblivion.

That's when the courier had arrived.

He'd nearly thrown the man out, weaving back to his desk and ripping open the envelope with enough venom to tear it in two.

Fortunately, the message had remained intact. Because it had been anything but the terse rending of ties he'd expected.

He'd read it through five times, and was almost totally sober by the time the second message came.

Its urgency had been palpable, unable to be ignored. It demanded that he be at the customary location at 1 A.M. sharp, to discuss information that would alter his plans, his perspective, his life.

And so he'd come, arriving at half after twelve so he could read and ponder Rouge's message once again before the arrival of his contact.

Resettling himself on the hard, rotting chair at the pub's far corner table, George unfolded the letter again, reread the unexpected contents.

Ordinarily, I'd be severing our association at this time, as this extraordinary shipment you promised never arrived. However, circumstances allow me to give you one last chance. As luck would have it, I've been approached by a wealthy client with very specific tastes and an unreasonable sense of urgency. Nothing in your previous supply would have suited him, extraordinary or not. To be brief, he requires a specimen of rare beauty and breeding—a specimen as untouched as she is well-bred. A lady in speech, manner, and upbringing. And he requires her within one week's time, after which he'll be taking her and sailing for India. To this end, he is willing to pay an enormous sum. Your compensation would be fifty thousand pounds and a resumption of our business alliance—ONLY if your shipment meets my client's needs. Don't even consider sending that gutter trash you've shipped in the past. If you do, it will be discarded, no payment made, and our business together permanently terminated.

George stared broodingly off into space, contemplating this unforeseen opportunity he was being handed. Fifty thousand pounds—an astounding amount of money. Certainly enough to pay off some of his debts, to keep his life from crumbling into bits.

And all in exchange for one girl.

But where could he get such a girl—a lady rather than a common wench? Oh, Bates's latest crop had been exceptional—clean, attractive, a bit more refined and less dissipated than the previous ones. But they were still a workhouse crop—poor, uneducated, of questionable origins.

A well-bred young lady . . . that was another matter entirely. Where would he find someone of that caliber, someone who was not only polished, beautiful, and untouched, but who also came without the ties that would cause her to be missed if she were to disappear—permanently?

His mouth twisted into a bitter smile as, for the dozenth time, the ideal candidate sprang to mind—or if not ideal, at least the one young woman he *really* wanted to send.

Anastasia.

Every time he remembered the way he'd had to bow and scrape before her this morning, offer her unrestricted access to those files when all he'd really wanted to do was to choke her with his bare hands . . . the very memory sickened him. She was everything ugly and painful in his life—the embodiment of Anne's union to Henry, the usurper of Henry's inheritance, the intruder in his business.

The only thing she hadn't been able to take away from him was Sheldrake. The marquess was clearly enamored with Breanna. Lucky for Anastasia, or with God as his witness, she'd be on that ship to Paris right now.

How delightful it would be to send her off to become some rich man's whore—to reap that ultimate revenge and, in the process, earn a hefty sum *and* regain Henry's estate.

Reason intruded. Tempting as that prospect was, there would be too many unanswered questions, too many tracks to cover. And too little time to get it all done.

Still, the notion was enticing . . .

"Medford. You're unusually prompt tonight."

George's thoughts were interrupted by the arrival of his contact, who slid into the chair opposite his.

"Yes, well, I was preoccupied by the correspondence your courier delivered earlier. In fact, I brought it with me. I had to reread it."

"That bad?"

"Let's say it wasn't what I expected." George folded the letter and slipped it back into its envelope. "In any case, *your* message was extremely urgent, more so than ever before. What's happened?"

"Quite a bit." The other man leaned forward, not even taking the time to light his customary cheroot. "Your niece was at the bank again today."

George stiffened. "That's impossible. She spent the whole morning at . . ." His voice trailed off. "What time did she arrive?"

"Around noon. And to answer your unfinished bit of reasoning, she came directly from Colby and Sons. She made that clear during her meeting with Sheldrake."

"They met?"

"Oh, very much so." An uneasy cough. "Sheldrake was waiting for her. More than waiting. He was pacing. He'd canceled all his afternoon meetings so he'd be free whenever she arrived. The moment she did, he whisked her away to his office."

"And?" George could feel his stomach knot.

"And I went after them as soon as the area was deserted. I missed the first part of their conversation between the noise of the bank and the thickness of the door. But I sure as hell heard the last part."

"Stop playing cat and mouse games with me," George snapped. "Tell me what you heard."

"Two people making plans to spend the rest of their lives together, for starters."

Dead silence. Then: "You'd better explain."

"Your niece and Sheldrake are all but at the altar taking their vows. Your whole plan to see him married to your daughter is never going to happen."

"But his visits to my home . . . their walks . . . the way he looks at her . . ."

"That's Anastasia he's looking at, not Breanna." Suddenly realizing the magnitude of the fury he was about to incite, George's contact opted to have a cheroot after all. He shoved it between his lips, lit it with unsteady hands. "Your daughter and niece have been playing games with you," he continued, keeping his tone as light as he could. "Whenever Sheldrake visits, they change places, each one pretending to be the other. That way, Anastasia can spend time with the marquess without any interference from you—given that you believe it's Breanna he's out strolling with."

"*What?*" Rage contorted George's features. "You're saying —"

"There's more." The other man stabbed out his cheroot, lit another. "Evidently, Anastasia has some suspicions about you. She said something about your being involved in something illegal. I'm not sure what, only that it's criminal. Whatever it is has her all agitated."

George could feel the room spinning. "And she told this to Sheldrake?"

"I don't know what she told him. As I said, I couldn't hear the beginning of their conversation. And at the end . . . well, at the end they weren't doing very much talking. They were . . . absorbed in doing other things, shall we say."

"I don't believe this." George dragged a hand over his face, his heart pounding like a drum. "They were carrying on in Sheldrake's office?" His mind wouldn't stay still long enough to wait for a reply. "And Sheldrake—what did he say about Anastasia's suspicions? Did he believe her?"

A shrug. "He seemed more worried about what would happen to her if you found out what she and Breanna were up to. He knew you'd be furious."

George wet his lips, panic washing over him like an icy wave. It dragged him under, and mentally he thrashed about, desperately seeking a buoy to cling to. His wild gaze darted about the room, seeing nothing but the undoing of his life.

Questions erupted, screaming over the roaring in his head in their efforts to be heard. What part of this madness should he focus on first? What should he *do* first? How much did Anastasia know? What had she discovered in his office? It had to have been in his office—didn't it? Had she recognized Bates? Found something in the files? And how much had she told Sheldrake? Enough to convince him? Had her visit to his bank been to report on the embezzling going on at Colby and Sons, or had it been a prearranged tryst between her and Sheldrake?

The last made uncontrollable rage explode inside George's head, supplanting panic with fury.

The little trollop. All this time. Luring Sheldrake into private alcoves on the grounds of Medford Manor. Convincing Breanna to help her. Wresting away the final chance George had to restore himself and his fortune.

Henry's fortune . . . their father's fortune . . . the company . . . now Sheldrake . . .

Hatred, absolute and consuming, boiled up inside him, spilling over rather than abating. It extinguished all traces of panic and fear, permeated his very being with its intensity.

And in that frozen moment, George made his decision.

He'd see the bitch in hell.

"Medford, I'm getting you a drink." Observing the play of emotions on George's face, his mottled color, the other man signaled to a barmaid, gestured for her to bring two ales to the table.

Dutifully, she complied.

"Down that," the other man instructed, shoving the mug toward George. "I don't care what it tastes like. You need a drink."

"You're right," George replied in an odd, tight voice, staring at the mug for a long unseeing moment before grasping its handle, tossing down the entire contents in a few gulps. "I need a drink—and a great deal more. She thinks she's won, the wanton bitch, that she's taken it all. Well, she's about to learn otherwise. I'll see her dead before I let her destroy my life. *Dead.*" He slammed the mug to the table, undeterred by the few nearby sailors who turned to gape. At this point he didn't give a damn if he were noticed or not.

"Is there something I can do to help?" his contact asked carefully.

The question echoed eerily in George's head. Help? No, he didn't need help. He needed Anastasia to die—to die and take the threats and memories with her. Then, it would finally be over.

"Medford?" the other man pressed.

"No," George bit out. "You can't help. Not unless killing people is also your forte. Because my survival is contingent upon Anastasia's untimely death. Interested?" he added scornfully.

A heavy silence descended, during which his companion traced the rim of his mug thoughtfully.

"Actually, I might be able to help you," he offered in a low, intense tone. "I know someone who does just what you require. He's very proficient at it, and very much in demand."

George felt the ale burn its way to his stomach. It was potent, yes, but it hadn't dulled his senses *that* much. "You know an assassin?"

"As luck would have it—yes."

"How?"

"That doesn't matter. The point is, I can contact him, if you're serious about wanting your niece dead, that is."

"Serious?" Pure venom glittered in George's eyes. "I've never been more serious in my life. She should never have been born in the first place. I want nothing more than to erase her very existence, to make her vanish . . ." He broke off, his own words triggering the ultimate solution to his problem. Swiftly, he yanked out Rouge's letter, scanning the already memorized words. "I can," he muttered aloud. "I can make her vanish, rid myself of her forever—*and* get rich in the process. It'll be tricky, given the limited amount of time I have, and the number of people I'll have to convince—most especially Sheldrake—but I'll find a way. I have to." A triumphant laugh. "It's the ultimate vengeance."

His contact frowned. "What are you talking about? What do you intend to do?"

A brittle smile lingered on George's lips. "I intend to take care of everything in one fell swoop—to recoup my losses, to regain my company, my brother's inheritance, and Breanna's position in Sheldrake's life . . . and to condemn my niece to the very hell she deserves."

"It sounds complicated. A lot more complicated than my suggestion."

"But a lot more rewarding." George shoved back his chair and rose, stuffing Rouge's letter back into its envelope. "Thank you for the information. I'll be in touch."

Slowly, his contact came to his feet, eyeing George as if he were unsure whether or not he was in his right mind. "I assume you know what you're doing," he said at last. "But if you should change your mind . . ."

"I'll advise you immediately." Folding the envelope in half, George tucked it into his coat pocket. "Good night."

It was the ideal plan.

Unfortunately, there were obstacles mocking him at every turn.

Closeted in his study, George paced away the long hours of night, alternately drinking and swearing at the portrait of Anne.

It had seemed so simple when he thought it up in the pub—ship Anastasia off, claim what was his, and savor the revenge of a lifetime.

Since then, however, he'd examined the plan from every angle, pondered it when he was sober, then again and again as he sank deeper into his cups. It didn't matter whether he was drunk or clearheaded. There was no resolution that covered everything, made all the pieces fit.

Originally, George had intended to announce that Anastasia had grown restless here in England, sailed off to see more of the world. The problem was, he'd never convince Breanna and Sheldrake that she'd leave so abruptly, and without a word of good-bye. To further complicate the matter, even if Fenshaw were more easily convinced than they, even if he believed that Anastasia had just up and gone, the solicitor's hands would still be tied about transferring Henry's inheritance to George. That would only be possible if Anastasia was dead.

Had it not been for Rouge's offer, George would have been thrilled to make that happen.

But not now.

If he hired that assassin, arranged to have him kill Anastasia, that would eliminate any chance of fulfilling Rouge's request—an idea that was equally as untenable as forfeiting Henry's money. And not only because of the fifty thousand pounds he'd earn or his renewed association with Rouge.

But because of what it would do to Anastasia.

For the umpteenth time, George grasped Anne's portrait, stared bitterly at the beautiful features that gazed back at him. How fitting that Anne's daughter should become a whore. Just like her mother—the woman who'd claimed to care for him, then left him for his brother. Well, history was about to repeat itself. In more ways than one. Because just as he'd had to settle for Dorothy—the lesser sister, the one he didn't want—so Sheldrake would do the same with Breanna. Once Anastasia was gone, he'd turn to her cousin for comfort and, ultimately, for marriage.

Sheldrake.

George slammed down the portrait, dragged a hand through his hair. How much did the marquess know? More important, how much did he believe of what Anastasia had said?

Nothing, he assured himself for the dozenth time. If Sheldrake knew the truth, or even a portion of the truth, he'd be breaking down the doors with the authorities in tow. Whatever Anastasia suspected, it had to be a vague hunch only, something she couldn't substantiate with proof.

Still, the sooner he shipped her off, the better. Because knowing Anastasia, she wouldn't rest until she found that proof.

There *had* to be a way to reap the benefits of her death without killing her.

There was, George determined abruptly. He had to stage her death, convince everyone she was dead when she'd really be very much alive, warming the bed of Rouge's client, while he'd be reaping the rewards.

Poor Anastasia. She wouldn't *really* be dead—but she'd sure as hell wish she were.

An ugly laugh escaped George's lips, all the effects of the brandy vanishing as the pieces of his plan fell into place.

Bates. He'd begin with Bates. From there, the rest would be easy . . .

Just before dawn, George emerged from his study, feeling more in control than he had in months. He went directly to the entranceway, summoning Wells with a wave of his hand.

"Yes, my lord?" the butler said politely, trying not to stare at Lord Medford's disheveled state.

"Wells, I need you to do something for me." He stuffed a note in the butler's hand. "Have this delivered to Bates immediately. I want him here in one hour. When he arrives, show him directly to my study." A meaningful pause. "No one else is to know about the magistrate's visit. In fact . . ." He stroked his chin thoughtfully. "Arrange for Breanna and Anastasia to be at the stables, or in the far gardens, or somewhere equally remote when Bates arrives. Have their breakfast served there, if need be. I don't want them in this manor during Bates's visit. Is that clear?"

For a moment, Wells said nothing. Then, he nodded. "Quite clear, sir."

* * *

Anastasia hadn't slept a wink all night.

She and Breanna had talked until half after three, analyzing what Anastasia had found in that appointment book, trying to fit it together with Bates's visit and this mysterious Rouge. They were both frustrated by their lack of ability to do anything, although they saw the wisdom of leaving things in Damen's hands—for now. Still, they couldn't stop their minds from racing as they discussed the possibilities, the options, the dangers. Nor could they shake the feeling that they were hovering on the brink of something explosive, and that it was up to them to keep their eyes and ears open in order to prevent it. After all, Damen might be the wiser and safer choice to actively investigate matters, but *they* were the ones who were living here.

They'd retired to their separate chambers a few hours before dawn, agreeing to try to get some rest, then resume their discussion at dawn while taking a long walk through the gardens.

For Anastasia, sleep hadn't come.

She'd finally given up, climbing out of bed and taking her small, ornate strongbox out of the nightstand drawer. Opening it, she'd smiled fondly as she sifted through the mementos of her parents and the ten years of correspondence with Breanna, reaching beneath them to extract the precious gold coin her grandfather had bequeathed her a veritable lifetime ago.

What should I do, Grandfather? she pondered silently, leaving her bed and crossing over to the window, staring out across the grounds and clutching the coin in her hand. *I know you perceived Papa and Uncle George's animosity, but did you ever have any idea it would come to this?*

She glanced down at the coin, tracing the beloved imprint of Medford Manor, then flipping the coin over to caress the elegant seal that signified the Colby family name.

A name her uncle was bent on destroying.

"I see you couldn't sleep either." Breanna came up behind her cousin, sighing as she saw what Anastasia clutched in her hand. "I was cradling my coin for the longest time, too, hoping it would help supply the answers."

"And did it?" Stacie asked softly.

"I think we're going to have to do that on our own."

"I agree." Anastasia continued staring off into the distance, studying all the beloved places where she and Breanna had played as girls, then raising her eyes up to the heavens. "He's counting on us, Breanna," she murmured. "Somewhere up there, Grandfather is watching and counting on us to set things right."

"And we will." Breanna followed Anastasia's gaze. "He has faith in us, Stacie. Giving us the coins, leaving us that trust fund—those were his ways of making sure we'd always recall how deeply he believes in us. Just as he believes we'd never let him down."

"I know that," Anastasia replied. "I just wish . . ." She broke off, a fragment of memory from so long ago flashing through her mind.

You're extraordinarily special. I don't doubt you'll accomplish all your fathers didn't and more. Anastasia could hear her grandfather's voice as if he were standing there beside her, having just presented her and Breanna with their coins. *I only wish I could make your paths home easier . . .*

" 'I only wish I could make your paths home easier,' " she repeated aloud. "That's what Grandfather said when he gave us our coins. It's as if he had a sixth sense of how complex the situation would become— even if he was spared having to live through it firsthand."

"It wouldn't surprise me if he realized how deep my father's hatred ran—*and* what he was capable of," Breanna murmured in agreement, as Anastasia's memory triggered her own. "Grandfather was an extraordinary man. He seemed to know us better than we knew ourselves."

"Indeed he did. Our faults, our virtues, even our dreams."

Hearing the tremor in Anastasia's voice, Breanna intentionally lightened the mood. "Speaking of our dreams, one thing I'm sure Grandfather is extremely pleased about is you and Damen. I don't think he could have picked a more perfect man for you—someone who might actually manage to keep you in line. Occasionally."

That elicited a grin. "When *I'm* not keeping *him* in line. But you're right. Grandfather would be pleased. He and Papa both had great respect for Damen. I'm sure they'd applaud the idea of us sharing our lives." Anastasia hesitated a moment, then turned to meet her cousin's gaze. "Breanna, I didn't mention this last night because of the gravity of our discussion. Still, I want you to be the first to know—Damen's asked me to marry him. Not now, of course," she added quickly. "Not until this nightmare is behind us."

Breanna was already hugging her. "That's just the news I wanted to hear. And it's all the more reason for us to resolve things quickly. What a beautiful bride you're going to make," she added, drawing back to dab at her eyes. "Although I do wonder if you'll be able to make it through an entire ceremony *and* a wedding breakfast without tearing your dress or tousling your hair."

"I doubt it," Anastasia returned, squeezing Breanna's hands fiercely. "My saving grace will be having you as my bridal attendant—which you will be, right?"

"Just try and stop me." Breanna drew a calming breath. "We have lots of planning to do. First, we've got to think up a way to help Damen find out what Father is up to. After that, we have a wedding to arrange." Her fingertips grazed Anastasia's coin. "Put that treasure away. It's time to get dressed and go for our stroll. I have a feeling we're about to come up with something."

Savoring the coin's comforting shape, Anastasia could actually sense her grandfather's presence, as if he were gifting them with his love and his strength. "You know what, Breanna? I have the same feeling."

Wells was fidgeting.

Anastasia noticed it as soon as she and Breanna caught sight of him from the other end of the hallway.

Breanna noticed it, too, for she cast a swift, curious glance at her cousin, who shrugged in reply.

Something was definitely amiss.

Wells never fidgeted.

"Wells? Are you feeling all right?" Anastasia asked as they approached the entranceway door.

The butler started, his brows drawing together as he turned to study them. "I? Yes, Miss Stacie, I'm fine. I was actually just contemplating the two of you, wondering if I'd be overstepping my bounds if I were to awaken you."

"You could never overstep your bounds with us. But was there some reason you needed to awaken us; something in particular you wanted?"

"No, no. It's just that it's such a lovely day, I thought you might prefer having a private breakfast served to you in the east gardens. Right now—while the sun is still making its glorious assent."

"I see." Breanna was openly regarding him as if trying to decipher the cause of his odd behavior. "Ironically, Stacie and I were just headed to that very place for a stroll. Breakfast there would be lovely. Wells, are you *sure* you're feeling all right?"

Pressing his lips together, the butler nodded. "Quite all right, Miss Breanna, thank you." A distinct pause. "However, I *am* concerned about the two of you. You look peaked."

"I suppose we are. We've been up most of the night." Breanna hesitated, shot her cousin a sidelong look.

"We have a great deal on our minds," Anastasia added. She had the oddest feeling Wells was steering the conversation in a specific direction.

"Then a walk will do you good," the butler declared, adjusting his spectacles and peering intently at a stray thread on his sleeve. "And it all works out quite well—the timing, that is. You'll be gone for several hours, which should give the gentlemen ample time to conclude their meeting."

"What gentlemen?" Anastasia jumped on the butler's words at once. "What meeting?"

Slowly, Wells raised his head, met Anastasia's gaze head-on. "I really can't say, Miss Stacie. No one is to know who our guest is or when he arrives. My job is to maintain my silence, and to assure your uncle the privacy he's requested. You're both to remain absent from the manor, starting from about a half hour from now." With that, Wells clasped his hands behind his back, all traces of fidgeting gone. "I've done as I was asked. How you two respond is entirely up to you."

Anastasia's eyes had grown round as saucers. "You're advising us to stay here," she breathed. "You think we should know who Uncle George is meeting with—and what they're meeting about."

"Your grandfather did so enjoy the earliest hours of morning," Wells declared. "He always claimed he made his best discoveries then, before the world was awake to clutter his thinking."

"That *is* what you're saying," Breanna concurred.

Wells's glance flickered over them, and his voice quavered ever so slightly. "You two were the light of your grandfather's life. Nothing would mean more to him than ensuring your safety. Not duty, not faithfulness, not even loyalty. Nothing."

On impulse, Anastasia stepped forward, reaching up and kissing the butler's cheek. "Thank you, Wells. Grandfather was lucky to have you. And so are we."

A hard swallow. "Be careful," he cautioned. "Both of you."

"Don't worry. We will."

Tender amusement softened Wells's features. "You two were always the very finest of eavesdroppers. I suspect you still are."

The quality of Anastasia and Breanna's eavesdropping was never in question, at least not in their minds.

Still, certain precautions had to be taken before they could begin doing what they did so well.

To protect Wells and ensure things proceeded as planned, the girls left the manor that very instant, walking off in the direction of the east gardens as if they intended to spend the morning there, milling about and having breakfast.

But the minute they were far enough away from George's study window to avoid detection, they darted back toward the manor. Except that instead of retracing their steps to the front door, they headed for the rear, slipping in through the servants' entrance.

From there, they crept down the hall and into the alcove nestled just off the main hallway. Waiting, they listened intently until they heard two sets of footsteps—one belonging to Wells, the other to their surprise guest—along with Wells's clear, polite voice instructing their visitor to follow him. Clearly, the butler was ushering someone in the direction of George's study, and alerting them to that very fact.

The footsteps faded. Minutes later, Wells's resumed, this time alone. He paused mere feet from where they stood, and pulled out his handkerchief. Folding it in two, he blew his nose loudly—once, twice—then continued on his way.

Despite the tension permeating her body, Anastasia had to bite her lip to keep from laughing. "I believe that was our signal," she hissed.

Breanna nodded, her own lips twitching. "Let's wait another minute, make sure we've given Wells enough time to get back to his post. If anything should go wrong, I don't want him in trouble."

"Agreed."

They held their breath, counted slowly to sixty. Then, they tiptoed down the hall, rounding the corridor that led to George's study.

Outside, they halted, ears pressed close to the tightly shut door.

"No, I don't want a drink," a muffled voice was refusing. "I want an answer to my question. What in God's name possessed you to drag me here at six A.M.?"

"I know that voice," Anastasia muttered. "I've heard it recently."

"I dragged you here because I've thought up the solution to all our problems," George was replying. "With a little work on both our parts, our circumstances will be better than ever in one week's time."

"How can that be? Just yesterday you told me that the entire shipment I supplied you with is lost, with no chance for recovery."

"Bates," Anastasia determined in a low voice. "The magistrate. That's who Uncle George is talking to."

"I know what I told you, Bates," George confirmed with his next words. "But things have changed since then. Everything's changed."

"I don't care. I'm finished worrying myself to sleep every night, finished praying I'll have a job rather than a cell to go to in the morning. Whatever it is, Medford, count me out."

Footsteps, as Bates veered away, marched toward the door.

The girls tensed, preparing to bolt.

"I can't do that." George's icy statement halted the magistrate in his tracks. "And I wouldn't suggest you walk out of this study. Because if you do, I'll be forced to uncover records tying you to that final shipment, and all the others that preceded it." A pause. "Ah, I see I have your attention. Does that mean you'll be staying?"

"What choice do I have?" was the bitter response. "Tell me what you want of me. And it better not be another lot; I've exhausted my contacts."

"No, no, this time I've got my own merchandise to provide. As luck would have it, only one girl is required, not an entire crop. And I've got the perfect one picked out."

"Then why do you need me?" Bates sounded as puzzled as he did unnerved.

"Because this is going to take some creativity to pull off. And I need your cooperation to do that." The clinking of a glass . . . no, a cup and saucer. George wasn't drinking spirits, not this time. "As you know, I've recently ensured our friend Meade's continuing services. We'll need him for this particular assignment. He'll be our captain. Lyman will supply the ship, and the falsified records as to its destination. And I'll supply the passenger."

"What the hell are you talking about? What false destination? And where do I come in?"

"I'm just getting to that part. Unfortunately, soon after leaving England for America—which, in answer to your question, is our false destination—our ship will encounter some turbulent seas. Sadly, our homesick passenger, who will be strolling on deck when the harsh seas strike, will topple overboard and drown, despite Meade's frantic attempts to save her. Terribly upset, Meade will steer the ship back to London, bringing with him our passenger's personal effects—personal effects I can easily supply. At which point you will declare her legally dead. And the sun will, once again, shine."

"America." A nervous cough. "Where will this ship really have gone?"

"To Paris, as usual. To deliver the merchandise to Rouge."

"The merchandise. In other words, this girl isn't really going to drown. She's going to . . ." A long, uneasy pause—as if Bates had already guessed the answer to his question. "Who is it you're sending to Paris?"

"Why, Bates. I'm surprised you have to ask."

"My God, Medford. You wouldn't."

"Wouldn't I?" A biting laugh. "I'll get Henry's inheritance, Rouge's generous payment, and the perfect son-in-law from one swift, ingenious transaction. Who am I sending? Why, my niece, Anastasia, of course."

14

All the color drained from Anastasia's face, as she clapped a hand over her mouth to keep from crying out.

Uncle George was selling women. And *she* was next.

"Oh my God," she heard Breanna gasp. An instant later, distraught hands grasped her arms, and Breanna gave her a hard, insistent shake. "Stacie, come on. We've got to get out of here. We've got to go—*now.*"

Anastasia turned her head, stared blankly at Breanna as shock continued to ripple through her.

Abruptly, her cousin's words sank in and she sprang to life.

Gathering up her skirts so as not to make a sound, she slipped past Breanna to lead the way. They tiptoed halfway down the hall, then abandoned precautions and dashed the remaining distance to the stairway, tearing up the steps and down the corridor to Anastasia's room.

Breanna shut the door firmly behind them, turning to gape at her cousin.

"Do you realize what's been happening? Worse, what's going to happen?" She pressed her fingertips to her temples. "I can't believe what I just heard, what my father is capable of."

Now that the shock of discovery was fading, Anastasia felt reason seep back into her brain. "Even I never suspected . . ." She sucked in her breath. "Women. The man is actually peddling women, selling them as possessions." She shot her cousin a look of utter revulsion. "I shudder to think how many unsuspecting girls he's done this to."

"Obviously many. At least according to what Bates said."

"Bates," Anastasia echoed in disgust. "Well, he should certainly know. He's been supplying them. It's barbaric." With an appalled shiver, she wrapped her arms about herself, as if to ward off her uncle's vile intentions. "And lucrative," she continued bitterly. "And, in my case, the perfect way to even a long-unsettled score."

"Oh, Stacie." Breanna looked as if she were going to be sick. "I'm so sorry. I don't know what to say."

"Don't you dare apologize. You and I have always known that all you and Uncle George share is blood. You're *nothing* like him. And the onus of who he is, what he does—that's his alone to bear." Anastasia laced her fingers together, contemplating the current dilemma. "We could analyze this for hours, and we'd probably come up with all the missing details. Unfortunately, I seem to have run out of time. I suspect that Meade and his ship will be leaving soon—with me on it, if Uncle George has his way."

"Well, he won't." Breanna dashed across the room, pulling out Anastasia's bags and tugging her gowns from her wardrobe, one by one. "You're leaving Medford Manor. Today. Right away."

Anastasia frowned, stayed Breanna with her hand. "And do what—run away? I won't do that. Nor will I leave you here alone with that monster."

Breanna straightened, facing Anastasia, hands on hips, in that rare but unyielding stance she used when her mind was utterly made up. "I won't be alone. I'll have Wells—who is clearly more than a little suspicious of Father—and a houseful of servants, any of whom would come to my aid if need be. As for you, I think the more distance you put between yourself and Father, the safer you'll be. Go to Mr. Fenshaw, ask him to put you up at a local inn . . ." She broke off, seeing the insightful spark that lit Anastasia's eyes. "You have a plan," she realized aloud. "What is it?"

"I need a quill and some paper." Anastasia marched over to the desk, extracting both. "I'm going to write your father a note. Then, I'm going to help you pack my things. I'll be gone within the hour."

"A note? Saying what?"

"That I'm off to supervise the opening of my new bank."

Breanna started. "In Philadelphia?"

"Exactly." A hint of a smile. "Every new business needs overseeing in order to ensure a smooth onset. And if *I* know that, your father will, too. Actually," she added thoughtfully, beginning to write, "I have him to thank for my plan. After all, it was he who first came up with the idea that I should return to America—*allegedly*."

"Allegedly." Brows drawn, Breanna studied her cousin's face. "So you won't really be leaving England."

"No. Definitely not." Anastasia tossed her cousin a sideways look. "Did you actually think I'd leave you, leave all Grandfather wanted for us—especially now, when everything is about to explode in our faces?"

"Truthfully? No." A quizzical glance. "Where do you intend to go—or need I ask?"

"I doubt you need to ask. But I'll answer anyway. I'm going to Damen."

"So I assumed." Breanna peered over her cousin's shoulder, read her words. "Ah, you're telling Father that you're traveling to Philadelphia at Damen's request. That sounds believable. After all, half that investment money is his."

"Exactly." Anastasia paused, frowning. "I'll have to reach Damen right away, not only so he can make provisions to hide me, but so he'll know what I've told Uncle George and can play along."

"So you're going straight to the bank."

A hard shake of the head. "That would be too easy for Uncle George to trace, in the event he decides to verify my story. He could simply ask his driver, who'd say he drove me to the House of Lockewood. And why would I be going there if I'm leaving the country? No, I'll send Damen a note, asking him to meet me at the docks. I'll have Uncle George's driver deliver me there. That way, everything will appear legitimate."

"Fine. *I'll* find a way to get the message to Damen."

"Oh, no you won't. Getting you involved is the last thing we need. Wells will take care of it for me, quickly and discreetly. I'll pen the note to Damen as soon as I'm finished writing the one to your father. I'll give both notes to Wells as I leave the manor, ask him to dispatch Damen's right away, then wait a bit before handing Uncle George his. Damen will be at the docks before I know it."

"Not soon enough." Breanna frowned. "Those docks aren't safe."

"It's broad daylight. The warehouses will be swarming with activity."

"They'll also be swarming with lowlifes like that Meade person," Breanna countered. "Face it, Stacie—you're female, you're pretty, and you're alone." She leaned forward, snatching up another sheet of paper and motioning for Anastasia to make room for her at the desk. "You finish the note to my father. I'll write the message to Damen. Then, I'll give it to Wells while you pack the rest of your things. Wells will make sure the letter is on its way to London before you climb into that carriage. With any luck, Damen will be waiting for you when you get to the docks."

Reluctantly, Anastasia nodded. "You're right." She hesitated a minute, chewing her lip as she studied her cousin, contemplated Breanna's status in all this. "You *did* fetch that pistol from the library, didn't you?"

Breanna nodded, pivoting slowly to meet her cousin's gaze. "It's in my nightstand."

"Good. Keep it close by at all times."

"Stacie . . ."

Anastasia waved away whatever protest Breanna was about to make. "Your father is unstable. He must be, to actually sell women for profit.

We don't know how he'll react to my bolting like this. He might panic at the thought of losing out on his profit, or explode at the realization that I've eluded his sick attempt at revenge. In either case, he'll probably vent his emotion at you or, if he decides to try to stop me from leaving, he might try forcing you to tell him details of my departure—details you're going to claim not to know. I'm not sure what tactic he'll take. But, servants or not, you must keep up your guard. Promise me."

"All right. I promise." Breanna swallowed. "How will I contact you? How will I know you're all right? When will I see you?"

Anastasia squeezed her hand. "Damen is courting you, remember? He'll be sure to take you for many carriage rides. Well, I'll be the destination of those rides." Her jaw set. "It will be a matter of days, Breanna, not weeks. With what we overheard in that study, I have more than enough incriminating information to pass along to Damen. He'll use it to dig up whatever evidence we need." A frustrated sigh. "If we only had that evidence now, I'd go straight to the authorities, rather than dropping out of sight. But all we have is a conversation we'd attest to having heard. Your father would, of course, deny everything."

Pondering her own words, Anastasia gave an ironic laugh. "Not only would he deny everything, he'd probably arrange for his friend Bates to hear our charges. And we both know how that would turn out. Uncle George would walk out of that courtroom a free man, and you and I would bear the brunt of his rage. No, when we confront your father, I want to be sure we have all the evidence we need to send him to Newgate for a long, long time."

"I agree." Breanna dipped her quill into the inkwell, gesturing for Anastasia to do the same. "And speaking of time, let's not waste it. You have to leave Medford Manor—before it's too late."

Damen's carriage sped to a stop.

Leaping out, he stalked down to the wharf, peering between the masts of ships and rows of warehouses, pushing his way through the crowds of workers and searching for Anastasia.

Where the hell was she?

What was going on?

Why did she have to meet him here, now, without a single word of explanation?

And why had the note he received been written by Breanna rather than by Anastasia herself? What in the name of heaven had happened?

"Damen."

As if in answer to his fears, Anastasia called out to him, her voice shaky, barely audible above the surrounding din.

But Damen heard it.

He swerved, watching as she stepped out of a warehouse doorway and beckoned to him, her cheeks flushed, her entire body sagging with relief as he strode to her side. "I'm so glad you're here."

"Stacie." His own relief was absolute, and he gathered her against him, savoring the sheer joy of holding her, knowing she was safe. "Are you all right?"

"I am now."

"How long have you been waiting here alone?"

"Only a quarter hour or so. Breanna rushed the note off to you to avoid my having to linger here for an extended length of time."

Damen's sigh ruffled her hair. "Thank God for your cousin's cautious nature. I left my office the minute Graff brought me her message." His gaze fell to Anastasia's bags, which were hidden behind the open warehouse door. "Why are you packed? Where are you going?"

"With you." Reluctantly, she eased out of his embrace, gave an uneasy glance around. "Is your carriage nearby? I'd prefer if we talked there."

His jaw set, but he didn't press her. "It's just beyond these buildings, off to a side. I came alone, just as Breanna asked. Let's go." Without another word, he picked up her bags and led the way, weaving through the crowd until he reached his waiting phaeton. He tossed the bags inside, helped Anastasia into her seat, and climbed into his own. Then, he turned, gripped Anastasia's shoulders. "Now—tell me what's happened."

Anastasia drew a slow, shuddering breath. "I don't know where to begin. Yes I do. Damen, I'm in danger. I need somewhere to hide, somewhere Uncle George can't find me."

Thunderclouds erupted on Damen's face. "What has that bastard done to you?"

"Nothing—yet. Please, I'll explain everything. But first I need to know if you'll . . ."

"There's nothing to discuss on that score. You'll stay with me."

Another surge of relief shot through her. "Thank you."

Damen tipped up her chin, his silver-gray gaze scrutinizing her. "Why did we meet here? Are you being followed?"

Reflexively, Anastasia looked around. "No. Uncle George is probably first finding out I've gone. I asked Wells to wait as long as he could before giving him my note. We're meeting here to substantiate the story I made up."

"Which is?"

"In my note, I told Uncle George I was leaving England immediately. I said I was on my way to Philadelphia, that you'd foreseen some problems with the completion of our bank and that you'd advised me to sail home and oversee things." She clutched Damen's arms. "If he should come to see you at the House of Lockewood, if he should ask you any questions . . ."

"I'll confirm your story. You're on your way to the States." Damen's knuckles caressed her cheek, his insides growing colder by the minute. Medford must have done something brutal to incite this type of fear in a woman like Anastasia—a woman who'd never cowered in her life. "What did your uncle do? How did he frighten you like this?"

Anastasia wet her lips with the tip of her tongue, clearly still battling major shock.

"Stacie—did he hurt you?" Damen demanded, fear knotting his gut.

"No. Not yet. But he will. Rouge will. Rouge and whoever the man is who's paying him."

"Paying him? Paying him for what?"

"For me." Anastasia's shaken gaze met Damen's. "Uncle George intends to sell me. To an affluent bidder. In Paris. Through this Rouge. Just like the other women he's sold . . . that Bates has gotten him . . . like that illegal cargo that went down . . . we thought it was opium, or jewels—but it was women. And now I'm scheduled to be next . . ." Her voice broke, and her entire body began to shake. "My God, Damen. My own uncle . . ."

Damen swore under his breath, his fingers unconsciously biting into Anastasia's shoulders.

Women. The merchandise Medford had been selling, shipping to Paris, was women.

Bile rose in his throat.

Abruptly, urgency supplanted worry, and a self-imposed calm settled over Damen—a calm born of necessity.

"Stacie, listen to me." His palms framed her face. "Nothing is going to happen to you. I won't let it. Your uncle won't get close enough to touch you, much less ship you to Paris. I want to hear every bloody detail of what you and Breanna heard, to understand *exactly* what your uncle's been doing and with whom. But later. Right now, all I want is to get you to my Town house where you'll be safe. I don't want to give George one extra second to realize you're gone. All right?"

She gave a definitive nod.

"Good. Let's go."

With that, Damen released her, slapped the reins, and urged the horses forward.

The phaeton sped toward London's west end.

Damen's home was masculine and spacious, its heavy walnut furnishings richly appointed and refined, the rooms commanding yet unpretentious—much like Damen himself. His staff was small but incredibly effective, every one of them the essence of discretion. Not a question was asked when he ushered her inside, announced that Lady Anastasia would be staying here for a few days, and instructed them that no one outside the house was to learn a word about this arrangement.

Within minutes, Damen's housekeeper had arranged a bedchamber for Anastasia's use, his cook had begun preparations for dinner, and his butler had sent a footman up with Anastasia's bags and a serving girl to bring tea to the sitting room. Once that had been done, all the servants tactfully disappeared—including the marquess's valet—having assessed the situation with the realization that Lord Sheldrake's guest was far more than just a casual acquaintance.

"Your servants must think I'm a harlot," Anastasia noted, settling herself on the settee and sipping at the welcome cup of tea. "A harlot," she repeated in a hollow voice, staring into the delicate china. "How ironic. I almost was one."

Damen muttered an oath under his breath, began pacing about the room. "Don't talk that way. Don't even think that way." He stopped, slamming his fist against the sideboard. "Tell me everything you and Breanna overheard—slowly, word for word. We're going to assemble all the pieces. And then we're going to see your uncle rot in prison."

Anastasia placed her cup and saucer on the table, then folded her hands rigidly in her lap. "Bates was at the manor this morning. He and Uncle George had a conversation—one Breanna and I weren't supposed to overhear."

"But you did."

"Yes. We made sure of it, thanks to a few subtle hints from Wells. And it's a good thing we did, or I shudder to think what my fate would be."

A muscle in Damen's jaw began to work. "How did George intend to manage this . . . this . . . atrocity of his?"

Thoroughly, in as much detail as possible, Anastasia recounted the plan her uncle had shared with Bates. "He was going to stage my death—doubtless, so he could get his hands on Papa's inheritance—while actually selling me as a whore, earning a hefty profit from Rouge. Oh, and getting you in the bargain."

"Pardon me?" Damen's voice became deadly quiet.

Anastasia never averted her gaze. "Uncle George was quite clear on that point. He obviously assumed that whatever threat I represent to Breanna's and your future would be eliminated at the same time as I. His exact words were: 'I'll get Henry's inheritance, Rouge's generous payment, and the perfect son-in-law from one swift, ingenious transaction.' "

Fury slashed Damen's features. "The deluded son of a bitch actually thought I'd just accept your disappearance without question?"

"I assume so. Remember, he has no idea how much we mean to each other."

"I don't give a damn. Even if our relationship was strictly business, I'd never believe you'd run away like that. Certainly not after just having been reunited with Breanna after ten long years. And not with your grandfather having placed so much faith in yours and Breanna's ability to rebuild your family ties . . ." Damen made a harsh sound, dragged a hand through his hair. "What am I rambling on about? George is clearly unbalanced—unbalanced, immoral, and corrupt. Why would I expect him to think rationally?" A probing look. "How deep is Bates's involvement? From what I managed to dig up yesterday, his jurisdiction was definitely expanded as a result of your uncle's influence. And, just as I thought, his financial situation is moderate at best. So increased power was the bait George used to lure him in."

"And blackmail is what he's using to keep him there," Anastasia added. "Uncle George was quite clear in his threats this morning. Which is what kept Bates from walking out the door. As for the depth of his involvement, I'm not sure. Truthfully, I didn't stay to hear the rest of their conversation. I bolted as soon as I realized what Uncle George intended to do to me. But obviously Bates supplies the women—from where, I don't know. And Rouge, well, he's at the other end to receive them."

"And I'd be willing to bet that Lyman supplies the ships, and maybe even lowlifes like Meade to captain them. That would explain the inflated receipts you found."

Anastasia considered that, and nodded. "That makes sense. But it's all supposition. I don't know who else is involved, or how the payments are divided up. We'll need proof to determine that, and to guarantee they're all locked up, especially my uncle. What I do know is that in Uncle George's mind this is about more than money. He wants to punish me, to punish my parents."

"For what?" Damen approached the settee, dropped down on the cushion beside Anastasia, and angled her face toward his. "Isn't it time you told me what caused this deep-seated grudge your uncle bears?"

"It's not that big a mystery," Anastasia replied softly. "In fact, I'm sure you've guessed what it concerns."

"I suspect it has something to do with your parents, with how deeply they loved each other," Damen replied, not even feigning ignorance. "I sensed that the day I asked you about them, and about George's feelings for your aunt."

"He wanted my mother. She fell in love with my father instead. Uncle

George never forgave either of them. His hatred festered over the years, turned into an obsession. After Grandfather died, Papa decided that putting distance between himself and his brother would be for the best. Perhaps he even hoped Uncle George would soften with time. He never did."

"I see." Damen pursed his lips, contemplating Anastasia's revelation. He wasn't shocked. He'd guessed that something like this was at the root of George's bitterness. But to carry it to this extreme?

"I'm sure this factored into your grandfather's decision," he murmured. "Since I imagine he was privy to all the reasons behind George's animosity—not only his greed and thirst for power, but his antagonism over losing Anne to Henry. That's why your grandfather was so adamant about leaving the coins—and the inheritance that was tied to them—only to you and Breanna."

"Yes." A fond smile touched Anastasia's lips—the same fond smile that always accompanied mention of her grandfather. "Grandfather knew the facts. He also knew his sons. Thus, he concluded that any chance of seeing them bury the past and act like brothers was hopeless." Her smile faded, and that stunned disbelief returned to her eyes. "But I doubt he ever imagined Uncle George would stoop to the abduction and selling of women—including his niece."

With a rough sound, Damen drew her against him, buried his lips in her hair. "That's not going to happen. You're with me, and you're safe. I'll kill him before I let him near you." As he spoke, a fierce rush of protectiveness surged through his blood, heightened the all-encompassing emotion he already felt for this woman. "Marry me, Anastasia. Now. Today."

Anastasia started, leaning back to gaze up at him. "I can't," she whispered. "My birthday's still nearly two months away. I'd need Uncle George's permission—or Mr. Fenshaw's agreement to assign me another guardian, after which I'd need *that* guardian's permission."

"We'll ride to Gretna Green. We can be married in a matter of days." Damen's fingers tangled in her hair. "Dammit, Stacie, don't you see it's the only way I can protect you?"

"What I see is that you love me." She reached up, caressing his jaw with her palm. "Oh, Damen, I wish it were that simple. I want to be your wife. I want that more than you can imagine. But not under these circumstances." Her eyes begged for his understanding. "You said I was a romantic. Well, when it comes to marriage, I am. When you and I take our vows, I want it to be the most wonderful moment of our lives, not a rushed ceremony cluttered by worry and fear. Think about it. If we gallop off to Gretna Green, we'll be gone for nearly a week, leaving Breanna alone with that monster. I was reluctant to abandon her even for today, and I did so only after she promised to keep her pistol nearby. Lord only knows what Uncle George will do when he realizes I've gone. But whatever he does, he'll do it to Breanna. We've got to stay in London, find the proof we need, and bring this madness to an end. We've got to."

Jaw clenched, Damen struggled for reason. "Yes, and I'm going to get that proof. Hopefully, it's already on its way. I sent an urgent letter to the head of my Paris branch yesterday, seeking information on this mysterious Rouge. With any luck, what I find out will tie Rouge to George, and to the women they're transporting. Hell, I'd break into Colby and Sons and steal George's damned appointment book and private ledgers if I thought they'd give us what we need. But your uncle isn't stupid enough to actually pen the word 'women' under the heading 'merchandise being shipped.' He probably uses some code word. It doesn't matter. I'll get him. That bastard will soon be in Newgate, along with all his colleagues. I promise you that."

Anastasia sank gratefully into Damen's strength, rested her cheek against his waistcoat. "I believe you."

He heard the exhaustion in her voice, and frowned. "How much sleep have you gotten this week? Next to none," he answered for her. "Come." He drew her to her feet. "There's nothing more we can do right now. You're going upstairs and getting some rest."

"Rest? It's still afternoon."

"Then you'll be awake in plenty of time for dinner." Gently, Damen guided her across the sitting room and into the hallway, which was still deserted. "I'll take you up," he announced, looking unsurprised by the utter lack of activity.

"Where is everyone?" Anastasia asked. Her attention diverted, she glanced about as they ascended the stairway, curious over the odd, absolute silence.

"Occupied elsewhere, if they're smart."

Anastasia blinked, shot him a quizzical look. "Did you tell your staff we wanted privacy?"

"I didn't have to. They're very astute."

"I see." Anastasia was starting to become irritated by Damen's glib responses, and their implications. She frowned as they rounded the second-floor landing and headed down the hall. "Are you in the habit of entertaining women here?"

A corner of Damen's mouth lifted, and he came to a halt outside the bedchamber his housekeeper had prepared for Anastasia. "No," he replied, a self-satisfied gleam lighting his eyes. "Although I'm delighted by the fact that you're jealous."

"I'm not jealous. I'm . . ."

"Jealous," he supplied. His knuckles caressed her cheek, and he moved closer, stopping only when mere inches separated them. "You have no cause to be." He traced the bridge of her nose, his voice husky. "I've never brought a woman here before. As for my staff's perceptiveness, it isn't coincidental. It's based on the fact that I called them together last night to say there would be some changes occurring here soon."

"Changes?" Anastasia sounded breathless.

"Um-hum." Damen's thumb grazed her lips. "I told them that this manor would, within the month, be acquiring a mistress. And that that mistress would be Lady Anastasia Colby, who would, by then, be the Marchioness of Sheldrake . . ." He lowered his head, his lips brushing hers. "Mrs. Damen Lockewood," he clarified, kissing her again. "My wife."

"Oh," Anastasia managed.

Damen smiled at the wonder in her voice, her eyes. "Any further questions?"

Mutely, she shook her head.

"Good." He turned the handle and pushed open the door, gesturing for her to enter. "I hope you'll be comfortable here." He watched her cross the threshold; then, after a heartbeat of a pause, he followed her in. "At least for now. These quarters are only temporary. After we're married, your chambers will be adjoining mine."

"I can't wait." Anastasia turned to face him, never even glancing about to view her surroundings. Her gaze—a luminous jade green—was fixed on him. "Although I can't imagine I'll be using my bedchamber much, not with yours right next door."

The tension that had permeated the day intensified, shifting its focus to something equally powerful, but far more inspiring.

"Shall I send up a maid?" Damen inquired, hearing the jagged edge to his tone.

"Definitely not." Anastasia reached up, tugged out the few hairpins she wore. "I'm very efficient at dressing and undressing myself. I lived in America, remember?"

"I remember."

"Still," she added with a siren's smile, "I suppose some assistance would be nice." She shook out her auburn tresses, making no attempt to disguise her growing anticipation. "Better than nice—wonderful. But not from a maid. A maid is the last person I need—or want—right now."

Blood pulsed through Damen's veins, pounded at his loins. "And the first person you need—and want—right now?"

"You."

He shut the door, threw the bolt before he could stop himself. "I should leave—now, while I'm still able." Even as he spoke, he was disregarding his own words, walking toward her. He reached her side, taking over her task and freeing her hair until burnished waves tumbled over his hands. "Beautiful," he murmured, caressing the silken strands. "So impossibly beautiful." He brought a handful to his lips, savored it, as his other arm clamped about her waist. "Send me away."

"No." Anastasia stepped closer, gliding her hands beneath his coat, unbuttoning his waistcoat with trembling fingers. "I can't do that."

"Stacie . . ." Damen's fingers were already dispensing with the buttons of her gown. "I didn't intend . . ."

"I know." She stood on tiptoe, kissed the strong column of his throat as she untied his cravat. "Neither of us did. But it's so right." She sighed, opening his shirt and pressing her lips to his chest. "Don't leave me—not now."

"Leave you?" He gave a hoarse laugh, dragging her gown off her shoulders, letting it drop to her feet. "There's not a prayer of that. I'll never leave you. Not now. Not ever."

His mouth found hers, covering it, his lips parting hers with a hunger that was too powerful to stave off with light, teasing kisses. He grasped handfuls of her hair, angling her face closer to his, possessing her with his tongue, his breath, devouring her mouth totally, voraciously—again and again. Anastasia moaned, leaning into him to give him better access, clutching at his shirt and returning his hot, open-mouthed kisses with her own. Their tongues intertwined, melded, and caressed with dizzying sensuality.

They broke apart only to gasp in air, and Damen's gaze burned into hers, his fingers shifting to the ribbons of her chemise, yanking them free until the scanty garment joined her gown on the carpet.

He paused then, his ravenous stare raking her from head to toe, lingering on the burnished nest between her thighs, his fists clenching and unclenching at his sides as he struggled for control.

Anastasia wrested it away.

Boldly, she shoved off Damen's open coat, waistcoat and shirt, letting them drop to the floor. Her palms smoothed up the hard planes of his bare chest, exploring the hair-roughened texture, the solid muscle beneath. Then, she reversed her motion, her palms traveling down to his waist, lingering at the buttons of his trousers.

With a wonder and curiosity too arousing to bear, she descended lower, her fingers brushing the rigid length of him, reveling in discovery, then shifting impatiently to the buttons that separated her from her goal.

It was too much.

With a strangled groan, Damen shoved away her hands and dragged her against him. He lifted her in his arms, nuzzling the warm valley between her breasts as he carried her to the bed.

In one unsteady motion, he yanked back the bedcovers, lay her on the sheet, and stepped away only long enough to finish the task she'd begun, kicking free of his remaining clothes. He was literally shaking with need, his hands trembling so badly he could hardly believe this was he.

Naked, he loomed over her, slipping her stockings down her legs and off, already making love to her in a way that made her breath come in shallow pants.

"You're exquisite," he muttered in a raw voice. "My fantasies pale in comparison."

"And you're magnificent." She scrutinized his body with open fascination, shivering as he reached down, cupped her breast, his thumb rasping over the taut nipple.

"Damen." His name was a wisp of sound, a glimmer of heated longing. "Please." She opened her arms to him.

Another filament of control snapped.

"God, I want you," Damen ground out, coming down beside her, watching her breasts swell to his touch, unable to tear his eyes away. "There aren't words . . ."

"Then don't search for any." Anastasia stroked his shoulders, the muscled planes of his back. "Just make love to me."

A hoarse sound vibrated through him, and Damen covered her body with his, tangling his hands in her hair and lifting her mouth to receive his kiss. His mouth ate at hers, and his chest rubbed across her breasts, teasing her already hardened nipples with slow, tantalizing strokes.

Anastasia whimpered, shifted restlessly beneath him, her thighs instinctively parting to make room for him.

He nudged his hips into place, nestling within the cradle of her thighs and continuing to kiss her, fighting the urge to relinquish the next glorious minutes and just plunge into her, join himself to her in the most fundamental way possible.

This was one fight he intended to win.

Not only to avoid causing her pain—although he was determined to eclipse whatever pain was unavoidable with a deluge of pleasure so acute she'd remember nothing else—but to prolong what he inherently knew would be the most breathtaking of preludes.

One that would lead to the most breathtaking of joinings.

"Not yet," he murmured, shifting his weight to his elbows, staring into her beautiful flushed face.

Anastasia's eyes flew open, her expression rife with confused disbelief.

"Soon," Damen promised, answering her unspoken question, kissing her hot cheeks as he continued to fight the instinctive motion of his hips.

"Very soon." He kissed a slow path to her breasts, drawing first one nipple into his mouth, then turning his attentions to the other, teasing each with whisper-light strokes of his tongue.

He was rewarded with a shuddering moan.

Easing himself upward, he covered her mouth with his and kissed her—slow and deep—his tongue gliding forward to entwine with hers. Simultaneously, his palm drifted over her breast, his thumb circling the nipple, still damp from his mouth, then dropping lower, defining the curve of her waist, her hip, finally slipping between her thighs to claim the moist haven he craved above all else.

Anastasia's grip on his shoulders tightened and, reflexively, her back arched, her hips lifting to receive his caress.

Damen's thighs pushed hers farther apart, opening her completely to the heated stroke of his fingertips.

Too far gone to withstand tentative explorations, he slid two fingers inside her, nearly wild with his need to feel her softness close around him. "Yes," he muttered thickly, savoring her warmth, her wetness, her quivering welcome to his penetration. He stroked softly, his thumb teasing the tiny bud that cried out for his touch.

Abruptly he needed more.

He tore himself away, shoving himself downward on the bed. He felt her start of surprise, but he didn't—couldn't—pause to explain. In a few jerky motions, he raised her legs, draped them over his shoulders.

And buried his mouth in her sweetness.

Anastasia stifled a scream, nearly coming up off the bed as sensation slammed through her. Her fingers laced through Damen's hair, and her head tossed from side to side on the pillow, her hips arching wildly, lifting her closer to Damen's mouth, his seeking tongue.

Damen's own need surged inside him like a drowning wave. He gripped Anastasia's bottom, hauling her upward, anchoring her so she couldn't escape a fraction of the havoc he was lavishing on her senses. Her scent, her taste, were driving him insane, taking him so close to the edge, he wondered if he'd survive. He deepened his caresses, felt her body grow taut, tauter still, clenching and tightening as he drove her to the brink of climax.

"Damen . . . no . . ."

It took him a full minute to realize she was struggling, her hands shoving at his shoulders as if to push him away.

He raised his head, passion pounding through his brain, and stared at her in stunned noncomprehension.

"Not alone," she whispered, her entire body trembling with a need she refused to give in to. "Please . . . not this time, this first time. I want us together."

Damen sucked in his breath, blind desire transforming to comprehension.

"Stacie . . ." Rasping her name, he capitulated, crawling over her and hooking his elbows beneath her legs. With unerring precision, his throbbing shaft found the welcoming entrance to her body.

Slowly, erotically, he pushed into her.

"Oh . . . yes." Half-whimpering, half-sighing, Anastasia wound her arms and legs around him, undeterred by the pain she knew must follow, focused on nothing but the need to be one. "This way. It's perfect."

"Sweetheart, I . . ." Damen had no idea what he intended to say. His body was inadvertently thrusting, urging him into her, crowding him into her snug, clinging passage. His eyes slid shut, all his energies concentrated on the incomparable feeling of making this woman his. "Anastasia." Her name was a love word, uttered over the roaring in his head, the pounding in his loins. She was so incredibly tight, quivering, poised on the brink of climax. And he wanted to share that climax, to meld his fire with hers, to feel her pulse and shatter all around him while he poured his entire soul into hers.

He reached the barrier of her innocence, and reality intruded in a jarring blow.

Damen froze, his fists clenching on either side of Anastasia's head, leaving deep impressions in the soft pillow below. Every muscle in his body went rigid, tremors of restraint quivering through him as his body screamed its protest.

God, he wasn't sure he could stop.

"Damen."

Anastasia whispered his name—a frantic whisper—and his eyes snapped open. Their gazes met and locked—hers wild, pleading; his hot, frantic.

"Don't stop." Her fingers, which had been clenched in the damp strands of hair at the nape of his neck, moved down his spine, clutched at his buttocks with an urgency as palpable as his own. "Please." She swallowed, clearly at the edge of her control, scarcely able to speak, much less express her desperation. "I need you." Her hips undulated, wordlessly beckoning him deeper. "I ache. I can't . . . bear it . . ."

Damen groaned, gave in to the inevitable. Framing her face between his palms, he stared deeply into her eyes, his own glittering with emotion. "I love you," he said fiercely. His hands shifted to her hips, gripped them tightly. "I love you, and you're mine."

He thrust forward; she arched to meet him.

The delicate barrier gave, and Damen couldn't stifle his exultant shout as he buried himself to the hilt, stretching and filling her entirely. At the same time, he was acutely aware of the pain he must be causing her, and he forced himself to still, not daring to move until he was sure she was all right.

Her body gave him his answer.

For the briefest second, she tensed, her body recoiling from the sharp, first-time intrusion. Then, the pleasure took over. She emitted a wondrous sigh, softening and melting, wrapping herself around him and sheathing him in liquid fire.

"Damen." She undulated her hips to feel him deeper inside her, then moaned as the frantic need for completion screamed to life, this time unwilling to tolerate delay. "I'm . . . dying . . ." she gasped, her nails digging into his back. "Damen . . . please."

It was all the encouragement he needed.

Withdrawing slowly, he watched her face, memorizing her expression as he surged forward, pushed even higher inside her, then repeated the motion, penetrating her in one deep, inexorable stroke. He heard her sob, felt her clench all around him, and he thrust forward again, angling his body so he could caress her inside and out, take her over the edge.

She screamed, her entire body dissolving into wrenching spasms of completion, and Damen pushed deeper into her, matching the rhythm of her climax even as his own built to excruciating heights, clawed at his loins until holding back became an impossibility.

He erupted, hot bursts of seed exploding from inside him, gushing into her in torrents. He threw back his head, shouted her name again and again, every fiber of his being focused beneath the onslaught of sensation. Her climax retriggered his, and spasm after hot spasm wrenched at his loins, shuddered through his body.

Finally, they both collapsed, sinking deep into the bed, too weak to move or speak, too sated to try.

Inhaling the scent of their lovemaking, Damen drifted, savoring the tiny aftershocks of pleasure that rippled through him. He cradled Anastasia in his arms, marveling at the extraordinary sense of peace and contentment that pervaded him.

It was ironic. He'd spent his life making investments—for himself, for others—embarking on ventures that altered circumstances, lives. And yet, despite the magnitude of these investments, he'd just discovered one that was far more vast, one that required all one's resources but yielded immeasurable riches in return.

Love, he mused in wonder. The greatest venture of a lifetime. And it's made without forethought, without reason, and without a whit of control—all of which he prided himself on displaying.

Clearly, he wasn't quite the genius everyone believed him to be.

But, damn, he was lucky.

15

❧

Somewhere in the house, a grandfather clock chimed four, and Anastasia stirred, murmuring a protest at even that minimal an intrusion.

Interpreting her action as a sign of discomfort, Damen gathered his strength and rolled to one side, taking her with him. "I'm hurting you," he murmured.

She smiled, shaking her head against his chest. "You never hurt me. Not before. Not now." She stretched, then leaned back, gazed up at him. "I never imagined feelings like that were possible."

"Nor did I." His knuckles caressed her cheek. "Then again, I never imagined *you* were possible. Thank God I was wrong."

Tenderness softened Anastasia's eyes. "You're turning out to be quite the romantic, you know."

"I know." Regret slashed his handsome features. "And the romantic in me wishes I'd walked you down the aisle, made you my wife, and gave you the wedding night you deserve."

"You will." She lay her palm against his jaw. "Damen, dashing off to Gretna Green is not my idea of a wedding. As for what just happened between us, how could anything have been more romantic, or more perfect?"

He turned his lips into her palm. "It couldn't. Nor could you." He bent down, kissed her tenderly. "At least I compelled you to get some sleep."

An impish grin. "If that's your technique, you're welcome to encourage me to sleep any time you want—now, and for the rest of our lives."

"I'll remember that, with pleasure." He tucked a strand of hair behind her ear, noting the reminiscent light that glimmered in her eyes. "What were you just thinking?"

"About something Breanna said earlier. She said Grandfather would be delighted that you and I found each other. And I agree. He would."

Damen reflected on his memories of the late viscount, then nodded slowly. "I think you're right. Your grandfather was an exceptional man—intelligent, shrewd, and compassionate. To find all those qualities in one person is a rarity, believe me." A corner of Damen's mouth lifted. "He must have adored you—your spirit, your fire. And that incredibly sharp mind that puts the rest of the world to shame."

Anastasia smiled at Damen's assessment. "I don't recall putting *you* to shame. Try though I will, I've yet to best you."

"Ah, but I fully expect you to keep on trying," Damen teased. "Think how exciting our marriage will be—in bed and out."

"True." Her smile softened. "As for Grandfather, he adored Breanna *and* me—each for different reasons. He was the only person, until you, who never confused us. I suppose he saw differences that escape most people."

"He also saw the equally important similarities. Your loyalty and love for each other, your determination to preserve the Colby family. That's why he entrusted you both with that huge inheritance."

"Yes, I know." Anastasia sighed. "I think about that money often, about what Breanna and I can do with it that would ensure Grandfather's wishes are carried out. I feel as if the answer is right here in our own backyard, only we have yet to see it. But whatever it is, it has to be something that would bind our family together, not only now but for generations—actually, forever, if I had my way."

"I notice you don't speak of investing the money."

Anastasia's chin shot up and she gave an adamant shake of her head. "No. That's not what Grandfather wanted. He didn't regard the inheritance as an impersonal avenue through which to increase our funds. He regarded it as a uniting force, a means to entwine Breanna's and my futures, and the futures of our children. Allocating it to a business venture, or worse, to several different business ventures, is out of the question. If we divide it, it loses its impact. And if we invest it, however wisely . . ."

". . . all you could reap is more money," Damen finished for her. "When what you're really determined to secure is something far more valuable." He kissed the pucker between her brows. "I think you've just begun to answer your own question. The rest will come with time. You and Breanna will see to it."

Absorbing Damen's words, Anastasia recognized not only the truth they held, but Damen's part in helping her arrive at that truth. Emotion formed a tight knot in her chest, emotion inspired by his innate understanding of her, heightened by their earlier intimacy. Fervently, she leaned up to kiss him. "I love you, Damen Lockewood. More than you could possibly know."

He rolled her to her back, his own expression mirroring the profound intensity of hers. "Show me."

The knock startled them both.

Anastasia jolted out of a light doze, automatically reaching for the bedcovers as Damen sat up, swung his legs over the side of the bed, a black scowl darkening his face.

"Who could it be?" Anastasia whispered.

"I don't know. But I intend to find out."

He yanked on his trousers, striding to the door and opening it just enough to address whoever was on the other side of the threshold. "What is it, Proust? I thought I made it clear that I wasn't to be disturbed."

Proust. That was Damen's valet. Anastasia popped her head out from beneath the bedcovers, straining her ears to learn what the servant wanted.

"Forgive me, sir. I wouldn't have intruded, but you said to advise you the instant your response from the Paris office arrived. The courier just delivered it." He slipped a letter through the partially open doorway. "I took the liberty of bringing it up. I hope that was the right decision." A tactful silence.

Damen snatched the sealed correspondence, his entire demeanor having altered from infuriated to relieved. "It was absolutely the right decision. As usual, you know me well."

"I try, sir." Proust cleared his throat. "If that's all, I'll leave you to your privacy."

"Yes, that's all. I appreciate your diligence, Proust."

Anastasia heard the servant's footsteps fade away. Simultaneously, Damen shut and bolted the door, tearing open the envelope as he walked across the room.

"It's from Dornier," he informed her, perching on the edge of the bed and angling the correspondence toward the window to catch the late-afternoon sunlight. "He runs my Paris office."

By now, Anastasia had guessed that this letter concerned Damen's inquiries about Rouge, and she leaned forward eagerly, watching his face as he smoothed out the single sheet of paper. "What does it say?"

Damen scanned the letter, then reread it carefully, his brows knitting more severely with each passing word. "This makes no bloody sense," he muttered. "Dornier says he's totally baffled by my questions about Rouge and his background, given that I'm the one conducting extensive business with Rouge—business that's highly confidential in nature."

"What?" Anastasia sat bolt upright.

"According to Dornier . . . here, I'll read it to you: 'Some months ago,' Dornier writes, 'I received specific instructions from you advising that the Paris office would be receiving numerous sealed communications to one M. Rouge. Those confidential communications, you directed, were to be set aside and held while a note was immediately dispatched to a specific address . . .' "

Damen paused, reading the address aloud as if hoping that by doing so he would trigger some memory of its significance. " '4 Rue La Fayette.' " A blank shrug. " 'In that note'—" He resumed reading Dornier's words. "—'I was to state that a message addressed to M. Rouge had arrived and was waiting at the bank's main office. Soon after that, I was to expect a courier to appear, presenting my note for identification purposes. At that time I was to give the courier Rouge's envelope, no questions asked.

" 'Conversely, should a courier arrive at the Paris office bringing correspondence addressed to the House of Lockewood in London, with the designation, *To Lord Sheldrake, confidential—M. Rouge,* I was to dispatch that letter immediately, again no questions asked.' "

Damen looked up, an odd expression on his face. "Dornier closes by assuring me that he's followed my instructions to the letter, and asks whether my latest inquiry means I've decided to alter these arrangements. If so, I should advise him immediately. He's awaiting my reply. Dammit!" Bolting to his feet, Damen raked a hand through his hair and began pacing about the room. "Do you have any idea what this means?"

Anastasia's mind hadn't stopped racing since Damen had begun relaying the contents of the letter. Now, she nodded, feeling utterly sick—not only for the situation, but for Damen. "It means that someone is using the House of Lockewood as a conduit for sending information to and from Rouge." She pursed her lips. "Could it be my uncle?"

"No." Damen shook his head emphatically. "Although I'm sure whoever it is is working with your uncle. But there's no way George would have access to the bank's correspondence, most particularly to any letters addressed privately to me. Whoever sent Dornier those instructions has to work at the House of Lockewood." Damen stared at Anastasia, his expression pained. "Someone at my bank is using his position to undermine me and to help your uncle in his sick endeavors with Rouge. Well, I intend to find out who that is. And when I do, I pity him."

He stalked over to the writing desk, yanking out a quill and paper.

"You're writing back to Dornier," Anastasia deduced.

"Indeed I am."

"What are you planning?"

"I'm planning to beat this M. Rouge at his own game."

Anastasia inclined her head, considered Damen's statement. "How?

By having the French police storm 4 Rue La Fayette? I doubt Rouge lives there. My guess is that it's just a meeting place."

"I'm sure you're right." Damen dipped his quill and started writing.

"Then what are you advising Dornier to do—snatch the courier when he arrives at the bank? Damen, there's no guarantee the lad turns the letters directly over to Rouge. In fact, there's no guarantee he's even met Rouge. Nor, for that matter, is there reason to believe that Rouge sends the same messenger each time. Anyone who's clever enough to buy and sell women without getting caught is certainly clever enough to cover his tracks with the couriers he uses."

"Again, your logic is excellent. Grabbing the messenger would be futile." Damen paused, his features taut with concentration. "The only way to beat a man like Rouge is to catch him by surprise. I'm going to tell Dornier to continue business as usual. The next letter that arrives from *me* addressed to Rouge is to be handled precisely the way it's been handled up until now. With two exceptions . . ."

His jaw set. "One, that I'm to be notified immediately of the letter's arrival by a courier waiting to leave for London at a moment's notice. And two, that a private investigator—one hired by Dornier the instant he receives this reply—is to follow Rouge's messenger from the bank to wherever he takes the correspondence I supposedly sent. Even if Rouge himself doesn't meet up with his messenger, another of his paid lowlifes will. I don't care if this investigator has to follow a chain of gutter rats through Paris and all the way up to Calais—which is where I'm sure the shipments of women first dock. He's going to unearth Rouge. And when he does, we'll grab him *and* implicate your uncle. Correction—*further* implicate your uncle. By then, I'll have had George arrested on charges of theft, kidnapping, and Lord knows what else. I'm just getting started."

Anastasia pursed her lips thoughtfully. "How are you going to manage that? With what proof? Never mind," she added quickly, supplying her own answer. "I can guess. You intend to find out who the traitor is at the House of Lockewood and link his activities to Uncle George. I should have known you'd never wait long enough for Rouge to be captured and supply you with his informant's name. You want him now."

"You're bloody right I do. I'm going to expose that bastard myself." Damen stared at the tip of his quill. "My father started the House of Lockewood, Stacie. He opened our very first bank. He also invested a good portion of his money and all his heart and energy into making us the thriving merchant bankers we are today."

A small smile touched Anastasia's lips. "I think you're being a bit modest. From what Papa told me, you're the family genius—the one who made the House of Lockewood the most influential merchant bankers in England, maybe even in the world. Your business acumen, your powerful connections—why, every European nation seeks your advice and counsel. You might not have opened the bank's first doors, but I'd say you had a hand in establishing the House of Lockewood's reputation."

Damen waved away the compliment. "My financial insights enhanced our bank's reputation. But they didn't establish it. What established it was what brought people in initially, what convinced them to entrust us with their money, their investments. And that something was integrity. My father's integrity. He fostered loyalty and trust in our clients, and he did it by being a fine, decent, and honorable man. Shrewd investing might have increased our number of clients, expanded our number of contacts, but it was the knowledge those clients and contacts had—the knowledge that they could count on us, count on our honesty and dedication—that built our reputation. Well, no one's going to take that reputation away, certainly not some miserable scoundrel who's using his position in my bank to achieve his own crooked ends."

Anastasia watched Damen's face as he spoke, seeing, feeling his fervor, and realizing for the first time just how it was he understood so much about family loyalty and commitment.

His allegiance to his family ran as deep as her own.

"You've never spoken of your father," she said softly. "Were you close?"

Damen gave a vague lift of his shoulders. "Not in the way you mean. Not like you and your parents. In all fairness, we didn't spend very much time together. I was away at school most of the time, and he was either building up the bank or traveling abroad with my mother. When she died, he threw himself into the House of Lockewood. When I came home on holiday, I worked alongside him. He wasn't a demonstrative man, nor was he given to conversation. But he was a good man, a decent man. So were we close? Not tangibly. But we shared the same principles, maybe even part of the same dream."

"Expanding your bank."

A nod. "The House of Lockewood was a symbol of who my father was, what he believed in. I shared that commitment. The difference is that my father was driven solely by his dedication and integrity. Whereas I . . ." Damen shrugged, considering how best to explain. "Dedication and integrity are at the core of every good man, every worthwhile endeavor. But they're not the only factors that drive me. I revel in what I do. Running the House of Lockewood is a perpetual challenge, one that stimulates my mind and fires my excitement. It's so bloody fascinating—taking a sum of money, analyzing the possibilities of where it can be invested, choosing the right place to invest it. Then, watching that investment as it increases and thrives. That's where my father and I were different. He savored the end result, because it benefited people. I savor that, too. But I also savor the process of getting there." Damen quirked a brow in Anastasia's direction. "Do I make any sense?"

"Oh, a great deal of sense." She grinned. "You're talking to the one woman in England who finds business, investments, and earning profits riveting—even if that does get me labeled a bluestocking."

Damen's chuckle was husky. "A very beautiful, very passionate, very brilliant bluestocking." His smile faded, as his attention returned to the matter at hand. "In any case, perhaps now you can understand why I can't let that traitor at my bank go undetected—or worse, unpunished."

"I understand completely," Anastasia responded, pride welling up inside her. "You needn't explain. And, Damen, we'll figure out who that snake is. I promise you that. He and Uncle George will both be locked up at Newgate—soon."

For the tenth time, George reread the note Wells had given him earlier that day, muttering each word aloud as if to confirm it. Then, he crumpled the page and shoved it into his pocket, crossing the study to pour himself a much needed brandy.

Anastasia was gone. Anastasia had left England and gone home to America to supervise the opening of her new bank. And she'd gone at the request of Lord Sheldrake.

With a bitter oath, George tossed back the contents of his goblet and refilled it.

Who was the little bitch trying to fool?

She'd no more left England at Sheldrake's urging than he had. Damen Lockewood handled his own business matters; he didn't send a woman to manage them for him—even a woman as astute in business as Anastasia. No, if she'd left England, it was for another reason.

But what?

And given her sordid affair with Sheldrake, their supposed attachment for each other, why would she leave England at all?

On the other hand, why would she lie? Was she planning something, plotting something at his expense?

Another vicious oath escaped George's lips, and he dismissed his own stream of useless questions.

What the hell difference did it make *why* Anastasia had gone? The fact was, he had to get her back. *Now.* Because without her staged death, without her transport to Paris, there would be no payment from Rouge, no inheriting Henry's money, no Sheldrake as his son-in-law.

No future.

Dammit, he had to find her.

Furiously, George polished off his next brandy, then slammed down his empty goblet and abandoned it, for the time being.

There was only one place to turn to for answers. Because if anyone knew Anastasia's plans, her whereabouts, it was her loving cousin.

Fine. He'd get his information from Breanna.

He made his way down the hall and toward the stairway, pausing to grip the banister and right the dizziness in his head. He probably shouldn't have had that last brandy. He needed his wits about him so he'd recall every word Breanna said, as well as what she didn't say. And if she dared lie to him . . . His hand balled into a trembling fist. If she did, he'd thrash her.

"Can I help you with something, sir?" Wells approached the stairway, hands clasped behind his back.

"H-m-m?" George scowled at the butler. "Help me? No . . . yes. You can tell me where Breanna is."

Wells pursed his lips, his astute gaze flickering over his employer, taking in his besotted state, as well as the fact that he was angry. *Very* angry. "I believe Lady Breanna went upstairs to rest, my lord. She'd gone for an afternoon ride. And the sun is unusually strong today. She looked quite peaked when she returned. My guess is she's already asleep."

"Then I'll just have to awaken her." Ignoring Wells's protest, George climbed the stairs, rounded the second-floor landing, and marched down to Breanna's chambers.

He rapped purposefully at the door, simultaneously twisting the handle, only to find the door was bolted.

"Yes?" Breanna's voice was muffled, as if she had indeed been asleep.

"It's your father. Let me in at once."

Some muffled sounds, then footsteps as Breanna crossed the room. She turned the bolt and opened the door, peeking into the hall, her wrapper clutched tightly about her. "Can it wait, Father? I was resting."

"No. It can't." He shoved past her, striding into the room and veering about to face her. "I want to hear everything you know about Anastasia."

Breanna blinked, smoothing back her hair. "I don't understand what you mean. She explained everything in the note."

"Don't toy with me, daughter." George massaged his temples, feeling rage pound through his skull like gunfire. "I don't believe a word of that note. I want the truth. And I want it now."

With a wary expression, Breanna walked back toward her bed, doubtless considering her answer. She perched on a side chair, reaching for the cup of chocolate that was sitting atop her nightstand. "I don't know what truth you mean, Father. As I told you, Stacie didn't confide in me. She probably knew I'd try to talk her out of leaving—which I would have, given how long we've been apart. But you know how headstrong she is. She must have decided this was the best way to follow Lord Sheldrake's instructions without upsetting . . ."

"Sheldrake would *never* have sent her to oversee that bank," George bit out.

"He trusts Stacie," Breanna reasoned quietly. "She understands business better than most men do. And it is half her investment she's protecting."

"And what of the investment she's leaving behind?" he sneered. "Her *personal* financial adviser, the marquess. Her partner in business and in bed."

Breanna's eyes widened. "I don't know what you mean."

"Damn you, Breanna." George lunged forward, grabbing her shoulders and hauling her to her feet. He shook her—hard—sending her cup and saucer clattering to the floor. "I won't be lied to, do you understand? I want to know where Anastasia is. Did she really leave England? Where did she go—to the Continent? Is she doing something with that inheritance of hers?" His hand drew back, and he slapped Breanna across the face, not once but twice, sending her head jerking sideways from the impact. *"Where is she?"*

"You've had too much to drink, Father." Breanna twisted herself free, a defiant light flickering in her eyes as she rubbed her smarting cheeks. "I think we should discuss this later."

"We'll discuss this now." George reached into his pocket and flourished a strap. He gripped Breanna's arm, twisting her around so her back was to him. "I'll ask you again, where is Anastasia, and what were her real reasons for leaving?"

Breanna went rigid. "And I'll answer you again, I don't know anything more than you do."

The strap lashed out, striking Breanna's back and biting through the delicate material of her gown and wrapper, which did little to buffer the pain. She flinched, cried out.

"Answer me!" George bellowed.

It was as if something inside her snapped.

In one swift motion, Breanna wrenched herself away and yanked open the nightstand drawer. Whirling about, she faced her father, a pistol gripped tightly in her hands. "Don't strike me again," she commanded.

George's jaw dropped, and he stared at her, as taken aback by the vehemence of her tone as he was by the weapon in her hand.

"I mean it, Father. I won't be used as a whipping post."

"Why, you presumptuous little . . ." He took a step toward her, then hesitated as her fingers tightened, her jaw set in harsh, unyielding lines.

"Don't doubt that I'll use this," Breanna assured him. "I will—if I have to."

"You're not a killer, daughter." George's statement was absolute, but his voice held the tiniest shred of uncertainty. "You don't have it in you."

A shrug. "Perhaps not. At least not under these particular circumstances. Then again, I wouldn't have to kill you. I'd simply have to wound you. Just enough to incite an investigation—*and* the ensuing scandal that would occur. A daughter, so brutalized by her father that she'd be forced to shoot him to protect herself. That would do irrevocable damage to the reputation you're so eager to preserve. Or to restore."

Twin spots of red stained Breanna's cheeks as she watched the stunned amazement on her father's face. "I may be reserved, Father, but I'm not stupid. I've always understood your motivations. More often than not, I've bowed to them. But not this time. I won't be beaten to satisfy your belief that Stacie is anywhere except where she claims to be, or that I know more than I'm telling you. So it's up to you. Are you going to promise not to strike me again, or shall I shoot?"

Again, George hesitated. He massaged his temples, grappling with this insane twist of events, wondering if he was imagining this whole encounter, if it was really just some absurd nightmare—a product of his liquor-clouded mind.

He refocused, saw Breanna aiming the pistol at him, and realized this was no nightmare. It was real. Very real.

Disbelief surged to the forefront, penetrated his besotted state. "You'd threaten your own father?" he sputtered. "With bodily harm?"

"Only if *he* threatened *me* with the same. If you don't strike me again, you have nothing to fear—not a bullet or a scandal."

George dragged a shaky hand through his hair, wishing like hell he was sober. "I just want to know . . ."

"I have no information for you," Breanna interrupted. "Stacie's gone to Philadelphia. She'll be away several months." A tiny smile. "Perhaps she'll be back in time to help me celebrate my twenty-first birthday; it's less than four months away. And then Stacie and I will both be independent women."

Splotches of color suffused George's face as the reminder found its mark.

"What's more, I don't know why you're so upset about Stacie's leaving," Breanna added dryly. "We both know you're hardly fond of her."

Another swift glance at the pistol. "Regardless of my personal feelings, Anastasia is my responsibility."

"Not any longer, she's not. When she returns, she'll be of age. You'll no longer have to look out for her. Why, I should think you'd be celebrating."

George's jaw set, his gaze flickering to the nightstand as he considered his options, and how to effect them.

"You're right," Breanna acknowledged, reading his mind aloud. "I won't always have my pistol handy. But if you should try to strike me when I'm unarmed, I'll simply scream loud enough to alert the servants, then make it look as if you were beating me senseless. The staff is very fond of me, so they'll be more than willing to support my story. And if you're wondering how that could possibly harm your reputation, I'll explain. Hard as it is for you to believe, there are some noblemen out there—Lord Sheldrake, for one—who'd be appalled to learn how violent a man you are, how unduly cruel you and your strap are to me. Appalled enough to reconsider their alliances—both business and personal. Are you willing to take that risk, just to gain information I don't have?"

A choked sound of frustration and anger emerged from George's throat.

Simultaneously, a knock sounded on the bedchamber door. "Miss Breanna?" Wells's voice called out. "Are you all right? Are you hurt?"

Breanna inclined her head, staring down her father. "It's your choice," she prodded.

Drunk or not, George couldn't deny the truth of Breanna's logic. He'd obviously underestimated her; she'd anticipated his course of action, and developed tactics to combat it. And though he loathed her for putting him in this position, he was lucid enough to realize that to push her any further could yield disastrous results. It was also possible that Anastasia had acted without telling anyone her real plans, that Breanna was indeed speaking the truth, as far as she knew it.

And a scandal, at this particular time—he shuddered to think what damage that would do. No, livid or not, his best recourse was to back away, to let Breanna be. Then, he'd keep an eye on her, go through her mail each day to make sure she had no contact with Anastasia. And, in the meantime, he'd find that bitch himself.

"Miss Breanna?" Wells knocked louder. "Are you all right?"

"Answer him," George snapped.

"I'm not sure what to say," Breanna replied. "You tell me—am I all right?"

George shot her a dark look. "Physically, yes. But your behavior—I don't know what's happened to you. You're no longer my obedient, dutiful daughter." His eyes glittered with resentment. "But I do know who prompted the change: Anastasia."

"No, Father, Stacie didn't prompt my behavior. *You* did." Breanna never averted her gaze. "Just a minute, Wells," she called out. Another pointed look as she awaited her father's decision.

"Fine," George conceded, taking a symbolic step backward. "I'll do as you ask—even if it is my right as your father to discipline you as I see fit."

"Not any longer, it isn't," Breanna retorted. "I'm a grown woman, not a child. I've endured all the *discipline* I intend to from you."

He forced himself to nod.

Satisfied, Breanna lowered the pistol, pivoting about to replace it in her nightstand drawer. "Coming, Wells," she called. Walking boldly past her father, she crossed over and opened the door. "I'm fine, thank you," she assured the anxious butler. "Just clumsy. Father and I were chatting and I dropped my cup. I didn't mean to worry you." She made a wide sweep with her arm, throwing open the door so Wells could see everything—and every*one*—in the bedchamber.

Wells's gaze shifted from Breanna to George to the broken fragments of china on the floor, then returned to Breanna's face—and the clear imprint of her father's fingers on her cheeks. "As long as *you* aren't hurt. I'll summon a maid to clean up the mess."

"I'd appreciate that." Breanna smiled. "And then I'd like to resume my nap." She inclined her head quizzically in George's direction. "Unless, of course, there's something else you need to speak with me about, Father."

George cleared his throat. "No. As a matter of fact, I have some business to arrange." He left the room, pausing when he'd reached Wells's side. "I'll be gone a good portion of the day tomorrow," he said quietly, for the butler's ears alone. "Keep an eye out for the mail carriage. When it arrives, collect all correspondence, but distribute nothing. From this moment on, I want everything addressed to this manor to be held for my inspection. Is that clear?"

"Perfectly clear, my lord."

With a brooding glance at Breanna, George stalked off, his footsteps echoing down the hall.

Wells watched him go, then turned to meet Breanna's gaze.

A current of communication ran between them.

"I'll send up a pitcher of cold water and a cloth," the butler said in a tight voice. "It will take away the sting."

Breanna walked over, squeezed his arm. "Thank you. And don't look so worried. This won't happen again."

Over his spectacles, Wells's brows rose fractionally. "With all due respect, Miss Breanna, how do you know that?"

A twinkle. "Because I just threatened Father at gunpoint. I told him that if he ever struck me again, I'd shoot him and make sure it resulted in the scandal of the decade."

Wells started, studying Breanna as if to ensure she was telling the truth. At her emphatic nod, his lips began to twitch. "I'm sorry I missed it."

"So am I. It was a long time in coming." She leaned up, kissed the butler's weathered cheek. "I can't tell you how much I appreciate your rushing to my rescue."

"My pleasure." He cleared his throat, waited until his emotions were in check. "Now, if you'll excuse me, I'll arrange for the water and the cleanup. I'd do both myself, but I have a letter to dash off."

"A letter?"

"Indeed." The tiniest spark glinted in his eyes. "I want to advise Lord Sheldrake that tomorrow afternoon would be a splendid time for a visit—from him, and any other surprise guests he'd care to bring along."

16

❧

$\mathcal{A}$wakening in a man's arms was a novel experience.

But given those arms belonged to Damen—the experience was sheer heaven.

Anastasia smiled, snuggling farther beneath the bedcovers, reliving the exquisite hours that had flanked the arrival of that disturbing missive from Paris. First, there had been the dreamlike hour before Proust interrupted, the once-in-a-lifetime moment when Damen had made her his. And then, much later, after the return message to Dornier had been sent, after their immediate plans had been discussed and a late dinner consumed, they'd gone back to bed, spending hour after glorious hour discovering the magic their bodies made together.

Three A.M. had come and gone by the time they fell asleep, wrapped in each other's arms, their future a beckoning wonder they had only to reach.

After the obstacles blocking their way were eliminated.

That reality jogged Anastasia awake, and she shifted, wincing a bit in response. Her body ached in places she'd never known existed before last night, and it was strangely comforting to have those lingering twinges to remind her of the beauty she and Damen had shared, especially in light of the trying events that lay ahead.

Stretching, she opened her eyes, noting the weak sunlight that filtered through the windows. It couldn't be much past dawn, she mused in relief. And that suited her just fine. She and Damen had a lot to accomplish today which, much as she wished otherwise, meant they couldn't loll away the day in bed.

"Good morning." Damen's husky voice came from just above her ear, and she twisted around to see him propped on one elbow, gazing down at her. He looked uncharacteristically disheveled, his hair mussed, a shadow of a beard covering his face.

It was nice to know that the unrufflable Lord Sheldrake could sometimes be ruffled after all.

Nicer still to know it was only she who could manage that feat.

"Good morning," she replied with a radiant smile.

A corner of Damen's mouth lifted. "Don't we look self-satisfied this
morning." He lowered his head, brushed her lips with his. "Any reason in
particular?"

"M-m-m." Anastasia sighed, twined her arms around his neck.
"Several. Most of which are self-explanatory." She caressed his hair-
roughened jaw. "But at the moment I was thinking how smug it makes
me feel to know that I, and I alone, can demolish the composure of the
ever-commanding Damen Lockewood."

"Indeed you can." He rolled onto his back, pulled her over him, and
dragged her mouth down to his. "Again and again, if I remember correctly," he breathed into her lips.

Anastasia shivered, giving in to the demands of her watery muscles,
which clamored to relax, melt into Damen's solid strength.

Damen made a husky sound of approval, tangling his hands in her
hair and slanting her mouth to accept the full penetration of his.

Their tongues met, stroked, melded, and Anastasia's breath came
faster as their kisses deepened, turned more urgent. Her nipples hardened
against his chest, tingling as the hair-roughened surface rasped against
them. Damen's thighs slid between hers, nudged hers wide apart, and she
whimpered aloud as his rigid shaft probed the entrance to her body.

"Is it too soon?" he managed, his voice rough with passion. "Can you
take me again?"

Anastasia tried to answer, but the words lodged in her throat. Instead,
she let her body speak for her, her knees straddling his hips, her thighs
lowering her slowly, maddeningly onto him. He glided into her, a rumbling groan vibrating in his chest, and his mouth devoured hers as he
eased into her tight, clinging passage. She sank down farther, begging
him wordlessly for more, and Damen's hands slid down her back to her
bottom. He gripped her buttocks, hard, and pushed up and into her trembling wetness, burying himself to the hilt inside her.

Talons of pleasure shot through her, and Anastasia tore her mouth
from Damen's, arching her back and taking him deeper still. She began
the instinctive motion—up, down, up, down—the resulting sensations
too acute to withstand. She felt wild, frantic, her entire body burning
with a fever she'd only just discovered and couldn't imagine living without.

Clutching her waist, quickening the motion of his hips, Damen raised
up, capturing her nipple between his lips. He drew the entire peak into
his mouth, lashing at it with his tongue until a harsh sob escaped

Anastasia's lips. Still, he didn't relent, shifting to the other breast, lavishing that nipple with the same attention as the first.

"Damen." She cried out his name, so desperate for release that she hardly knew what she was saying. Her thighs gave out, the muscles too weak to keep setting the pace. She was close, so close, hovering right at the brink of where she needed to be, and yet unable to get there. Each tug of Damen's lips sent fire shooting from her breasts to her loins, each lunge of his hips brought her one degree closer to fulfillment. And yet . . . God, she couldn't reach it.

Her entire body tightened, reaching, shuddering with unappeased hunger. "Damen," she gasped again, his name an unspoken plea.

Damen understood it.

Abandoning her breasts, he dropped back down to the bed, his own body screaming its need for release. Staring into Anastasia's passion-flushed face, he raised his knees, pushed her backward until she was anchored by them. "Let me," he commanded. He grasped her waist with one hand, continuing the frenzied rise and fall of his hips as he thrust even higher, farther, into her, nudging the very mouth of her womb. "Stacie, look at me," he rasped. "I want to watch you. I want you to watch me."

She complied instantly, meeting his blazing silver gaze, his handsome features taut with unsated passion. Just seeing how close he was made her own need even sharper, and she whimpered again, quivering as she kept her eyes on his.

His other hand moved to the spot where they were joined, his fingers unerringly parting her, finding the straining bud. His thumb caressed it, scraped over it, then circled it with erotic precision. Her insides clenched violently and, the instant he felt her response, Damen lunged upward, lifting her off the bed with his total possession, his fingers burning into her as he filled her, stretched her, penetrated her, beyond bearing.

Her climax slammed through her like cannon fire, and she screamed, grabbing Damen's shoulders and watching his face as his own release took over, stormed through him. He threw back his head, the tendons in his neck straining, and he shouted her name, thrusting into her once, twice, then holding her there as he pumped his hot seed into her, meeting each of her wrenching contractions with a scalding burst of heat. She watched him until the pleasure became too acute, until she had to arch, fling back her head, then toss it from side to side as the spasms intensified, clasped rhythmically around Damen's turgid length as he poured himself into her.

She fell forward, collapsed against the wall of his chest, felt it heaving with the exertion of their lovemaking. She was shaking uncontrollably, her heart racing, her emotions as raw as her body.

Damen's arms closed around her, enfolded her tightly against him, and he pressed his lips into her hair, willing his senses to right themselves. "God," he panted, barely able to speak. "My God."

Anastasia closed her eyes, lay her cheek against his hot skin. "I love you," she whispered. "More than I ever thought possible."

"And I love you; although those words—any words—seem inadequate after what we just shared."

A lingering shiver rippled through her, along with all the romantic yearnings of a woman in love. "I wish . . ." Her voice trailed off.

Damen hooked a forefinger beneath her chin, angling it until her gaze met his. "So do I. And we will." He brushed damp strands of hair off her face. "We'll have it all, Stacie—a lifetime like this. Beginning with a church wedding, and all the guests you want to fill it. Once we've taken our vows and the entire world has witnessed you becoming my wife, we'll have a wedding breakfast fit for a king and his queen—most of which we'll miss because I'll be sneaking you off to a local inn, making love to you until you can't breathe and don't even want to. We'll leave for our wedding trip the next day, very little of which you'll remember because I'll be keeping you abed throughout it. And when we come home . . ." His fingertips caressed her lips. "When we come home, you'll be pregnant with my child, and I'll spend the next nine months doting on you and watching you grow more beautiful and radiant with each passing day. How does that sound so far?"

Tears glistened on Anastasia's lashes. "So far? Have you planned more than that?"

"Of course." A profound smile touched his lips. "I'd like four, maybe five, children."

"Five—is that all?" She smiled through her tears. "Girls? Or boys?"

"Both. The girls will look just like you; beautiful miniatures of their mother, with burnished hair that won't stay up and jade green eyes that flash when they're angry and glow when they've conjured up a brilliant idea."

Anastasia kissed his fingertips. "And the boys will be impossibly handsome and independent, and so astute in business that it will be obvious from the day they're born that they're destined to be brilliant." A peppery spark. "Then again, the brilliant part applies to the girls, too. After all, they'll be *our* children. Besides, we have more than enough companies for them to manage: the House of Lockewood, Fidelity Union and Trust—soon to be open and thriving—and, of course, Colby and Sons . . ." Anastasia halted, the very mention of her grandfather's company acting as a blatant reminder of the ugly dilemma they now faced.

She stared at Damen, apprehension eclipsing all traces of humor.

"We'll make things right, Stacie," he said softly. "I promised you that, and I meant it."

"We have to. Because none of the beautiful dreams you just described can happen until we put Uncle George and all his colleagues in prison." Fear knotted her gut. "By now, I'm sure he's interrogated Breanna to see if she knows anything more about my disappearance. I hope to God she's all right, that he didn't try to beat information out of her."

Damen gave an astute shake of his head. "Have faith in your cousin, sweetheart. I think she'll surprise you. She's stronger than you realize."

"I know." Despite the certainty of her words, Anastasia frowned, her brows knit in worry. "Breanna is very strong. But Uncle George is irrational. Lord knows how desperate he'll become when he discovers I'm gone, and to what lengths he'll go to find me."

Equally troubled as she by the prospects that conjured up, Damen rolled to one side, taking Anastasia with him. "Let's get our strategy under way. You'll feel better and, frankly, so will I." He kissed her ever so softly, held her for one more tantalizing minute before reluctantly withdrawing from her clinging warmth. "Remember where we left off," he murmured.

A watery smile. "Just try to make me forget."

He framed her face between his palms, brought her mouth back to his. "I'd rather make you remember. And I will, just as soon as we've destroyed your uncle and brought him and his crooked associates to justice."

It seemed days rather than hours before the grandfather clock in the hallway chimed twelve, heralding the noon hour and the time Damen had said he'd be returning to his Town house.

Anastasia spent the morning the only way her frayed nerves would allow her: she paced through every room in the house, covering both levels and never sitting down.

The servants were kind and understanding, offering her meals, tea, a library of books to read. But all she could think about was Damen and what he might be finding out at the bank. That, and Breanna, and whatever had taken place between her and her father yesterday.

Although she was significantly less worried about the latter since Wells's note had arrived this morning.

Actually, it had arrived last night, but Proust had waited until morning to present it to Damen, handing it to him the minute he and Anastasia strolled into the dining room. The two of them had read it together, and Anastasia had nearly wept with joy at how cheery the message sounded. According to Wells, he was writing at Miss Breanna's request. She was feeling lonely since her cousin's departure and would like some company. Therefore, she was cordially inviting Lord Sheldrake to either tea or a late lunch the following day.

Which meant today.

"That's Wells's way of assuring us Breanna is all right," Anastasia declared, rereading the message. "He's also suggesting that afternoon would be the best time for your visit. Uncle George probably has business away from Medford Manor." Anastasia sighed with relief. "I only wish Proust had delivered this note the instant it arrived. I would have slept much better."

Damen had cocked a brow, glancing about to make sure the dining room was deserted. "May I remind you that I practically accosted Proust the first time he interrupted us? I hardly think he'd choose to take me on again, especially when I hadn't mentioned expecting another piece of urgent correspondence last night." A provocative twinkle. "With regard to your sleeping better, that's a moot point since you didn't really sleep at all. I can attest to that fact."

Anastasia had been cheerfully unable to dispute that logic.

Right after breakfast, Damen had put their plan into motion. He'd gone to the bank as usual, ready to act as if nothing were amiss while keeping a keen eye on the mail, and on whoever touched it. Later in the morning, he intended to announce that he had an afternoon appointment, after which he'd ride out to Medford Manor.

Making an unscheduled stop at his Town house to pick up a passenger.

It was ten past twelve when Anastasia heard the key turn in the front door.

She flew to the entranceway, nearly knocking down Damen's butler in the process. "You're home," she gasped, seizing Damen's forearms and tugging him inside. "Tell me what happened."

He glanced back over his shoulder, then gestured for his butler to shut the door. "You're supposed to be staying out of sight," he reminded Anastasia with a dark scowl. "What if it hadn't been me at the door?"

She shot him a defiant look. "Just who else has a key to your home?"

He couldn't help but grin. "Good point. No one." He guided her into the sitting room, then drew her close, covering her mouth in a slow, lingering kiss. "Just so you know, that's how I'd like to be welcomed home each day."

"With pleasure, my lord." Anastasia leaned back in his arms, searched his face. She could see beyond the bantering, sense the strain beneath it. "You didn't figure out who he is."

Damen shook his head. "I know as little as I did yesterday. I saw the mail arrive. No one went near it during the quarter hour it sat up front. Then, Graff distributed it, leaving my personal letters on my desk. I glanced through my correspondence the moment he walked out. There was nothing from M. Rouge. I then intentionally left my door open and my room unattended to see if any of the bank officers went in, inspected my mail. They're the only people with access to that private section of the bank. Although it's hard for me to believe any of them could be guilty. They've been with me for years. Still, I can't be influenced by sentiment. I intend to catch this bastard, whoever he is. In any case, the point was a moot one."

"No one took the bait?"

"Not a soul so much as stepped into my office, much less examined my mail." Damen sighed, dragging a hand through his hair. "It was a wasted effort. In fact, the only productive thing I did all morning was to put on a convincing show. Anyone scrutinizing me would think it was a day like any other. That way, should my scrutinizer meet with your uncle, he can truthfully say I behaved in my typical fashion. George will have to conclude that your absence came as no unwelcome surprise to me, which would support your claim that it was I who advised you to go to Philadelphia."

"Or indicate that you haven't an inkling that I've gone at all," Anastasia pointed out. "Uncle George will probably try to find out, either directly or through his informant, which of the two it is. Not that it would alter his plans. Either way, I'm sure he'll be sending Meade after me." An ironic smile touched her lips. "But while it won't alter his plans, it will certainly improve his humor if he decides the latter is true. Just think, if I acted on my own, with no urging from you, Uncle George would have the pleasure of telling you what I'd done. You'd doubtless be furious at the recklessness of my actions, and more than ready to wash your hands of me."

"Turning my full attentions to Breanna."

"Exactly."

Damen sucked in his breath. "Every time I think about what that bastard has planned, what he means to do to you, I want to choke him with my bare hands."

"I know," Anastasia responded quietly. "But then you'd be the one in prison and I'd have to live without you. I don't intend to do that. Nor do I intend to let whoever's deceiving you continue on at the House of Lockewood, unknown and unpunished. The same applies to Bates, Lyman, Meade, and whoever else is involved in this."

"Like M. Rouge and his contemptible clients," Damen muttered. He straightened, shot Anastasia a probing look. "Are you ready to go on our little jaunt?"

A terse nod. *"Very* ready."

* * *

Damen's closed carriage rounded the drive at Medford Manor, coming to a halt before the front steps.

"Don't forget," he cautioned under his breath. "Stay under that blanket. Don't move or poke that curious head of yours out to see what's going on. We don't know for sure that your uncle is away. Nor do we want any of the servants to see you. Remember: you're on a ship on your way to Philadelphia."

"And you're alone in a carriage having a conversation with a horse blanket," came the muffled retort from beneath the opposite seat.

Damen rolled his eyes, torn between amusement and worry. He knew Anastasia. And she wasn't going to stay still for long—especially after a lengthy, cramped carriage ride from London, during which she'd been allowed to emerge and stretch her legs only when the roads they'd been traveling were deserted enough to ensure she wasn't detected—and, even then, only after the carriage curtains had been tightly drawn.

Oh, Damen knew how much Anastasia loathed confinement of any kind. But he wasn't taking any chances with her safety.

"I'll linger inside only as long as I have to," he advised the horse blanket. He bent down, as if to retrieve his glove. "Promise me you'll stay put."

"Promise me you'll bring Breanna."

He grinned. "I promise."

"Then so do I."

"Good." Damen straightened just in time for his driver to come around, open the door. "Wait here," he instructed the driver in a normal tone, as he alighted from the carriage. "I'll be out shortly. You'll be taking Lady Breanna and me for a ride in the country."

"Very good, my lord." The driver nodded, shutting the door and resuming his seat at the reins.

Damen climbed the steps and knocked.

Wells opened the door at once. "Ah, Lord Sheldrake," he greeted. "Lady Breanna will be delighted to see you."

"I'm looking forward to seeing her as well." Damen glanced down the hallway, trying to determine if George was at home.

"I hope you don't have pressing business to discuss with the viscount," Wells continued. "He had an appointment in Town and won't be back for several hours. He'll be sorry he missed you."

"Ah." Damen shot Wells a grateful look. "That's quite all right. My business with the viscount can wait. I really came to see Lady Breanna."

"Then I won't keep you waiting." Breanna reached the bottom of the staircase, smiling as she approached Damen. "I'm so glad you're here."

"As am I." Damen cleared his throat. "I realize you invited me for tea, but it's such a beautiful summer day that I thought perhaps you'd enjoy a ride in the country instead. Unless, of course, you haven't eaten."

"I've solved that problem," Wells interrupted. "Wait here." He hurried off, reappearing scant minutes later carrying a basket. "Mrs. Rhodes was kind enough to pack up these sandwiches. She'd prepared them for you to eat in the garden, but they'll taste just as good elsewhere. So long as you're enjoying the summer day, it doesn't matter where you are."

"Thank you, Wells." Breanna squeezed his arm.

"Go," he urged, gesturing toward the still-open door. "Have a good time." He leaned forward to hand Damen the basket, briefly whispering something to Breanna as he bent past her.

Her lips twitched, but she didn't reply.

Three minutes later, Breanna and Damen were both settled in the carriage, basket and all, and the driver was urging the horses around the bend.

"Not yet," Damen warned in a hard voice. "Don't move or speak. Not until we're beyond the gates and I've drawn the curtains."

Breanna blinked in surprise, thinking at first that Damen was addressing her. Then, she followed his line of vision and smiled as she spotted the lumpy blanket beneath her seat. "Why, Lord Sheldrake, is that for me—a token of your esteem, perhaps?"

"Don't sound so enthused," he retorted dryly. "You might return it once you see how much trouble it is."

A grunt of protest emerged from beneath the blanket.

Laughter bubbled up in Breanna's throat. "Does that mean *you* wish to return it?"

With a profound shake of his head, Damen leaned forward and stared at the blanket, all teasing having vanished. "No. You see, as fate would have it, this is one gift I can't seem to live without."

"Then, indeed, it should be yours." Visibly moved, Breanna followed Damen's gaze, her own filled with the joyful knowledge that Anastasia had found her future. "As you should be hers." She reached down, touched the blanket ever so lightly. "The gates are just ahead," she said soothingly. "We're almost there."

"Breanna, what did Wells say to you as we were leaving?" Damen asked curiously. "Or am I prying?"

"Not at all." Breanna's sparkle returned. "He said there's more than enough food in the basket to serve three."

Damen's lips curved. "So he *does* know."

"Wells knows everything." A smug lift of her chin. "Except when Stacie and I are switching places."

An impatient thump resounded from beneath the blanket.

"We're driving through the gates now," Damen answered. "I know you're eager. But I've got to make sure you're not seen. Concealing your presence by switching places with Breanna is one thing. But it would be a little hard to explain you away by claiming you're Breanna if you're both sitting beside me at the same time. Give me a minute or two to create the illusion that Breanna and I are seeking some privacy. Then you can come out."

The ensuing silence signified Anastasia's agreement.

They rounded the corner onto the road, and Damen rose out of his seat, jerked the curtains closed on both sets of windows. He squatted down and yanked the blanket off Anastasia's head. "You're free, little hellion." He offered her his hand. "Come on out."

Anastasia squirmed out of her hiding place, blowing strands of hair off her face. She accepted Damen's assistance, clutching his fingers and scrambling out and onto the seat beside Breanna.

The girls hugged, and Anastasia heaved an enormous sigh of relief. "Thank God you're all right."

"*I? You're* the one who dashed down to the London docks alone."

"I wasn't alone for long. Damen rode in and rescued me like a knight-in-shining-armor."

Her analogy made Breanna smile. "Still the same romantic Stacie. Clearly, you're none the worse for your adventure."

"And you?" Anastasia asked quietly. "Are you any the worse for yours?"

Breanna didn't pretend to misunderstand. "I'm fine. I thought you'd figure that out from Wells's note."

"I did." Anastasia drew back, gripped her cousin's hands. "But I needed to see for myself." She studied her cousin's face closely, seeing remnants of evidence that Damen had missed. "Uncle George hit you."

Breanna's shrug was nonchalant. "At first, along with a fair amount of shouting and threats. But that's over now."

"What do you mean?"

With more than a touch of pride, Breanna recounted her showdown with her father.

"You threatened to shoot him?" Damen repeated in amazement.

"I certainly did. Very convincingly, if I must say so myself. Believe me, Father won't touch me again. He's too terrified of a scandal, and of the possibility that he might lose you as an ally and future son-in-law."

"An ally," Damen muttered. "I'm hardly that."

"But Father doesn't know that, at least not yet."

"Where is Uncle George now?" Anastasia asked.

"With Mr. Lyman," Breanna supplied. "Wells said that's who Father dashed off a note to last night."

Anastasia and Damen exchanged glances.

"He's arranging for Meade to find me," Anastasia murmured, catching her lower lip between her teeth. "That doesn't give us much time. The ship I allegedly took is only one day ahead of him. And how many ships could have left for the States in that amount of time? Not many."

"You didn't necessarily have to have boarded a packet ship. You could just as easily have paid your way on a smaller craft," Damen pointed out. "Lyman will have to check every ship's manifest. He and Meade still have their work cut out for them."

"I'm not sure they'll be looking at all," Breanna inserted.

Anastasia's head whipped around. "What do you mean?"

Her cousin frowned, rubbing her gloved palms together. "Something Father said last night really puzzled me. I haven't been able to get it out of my mind."

"What did he say?"

"While he was accusing me of knowing your whereabouts, he demanded to know if you'd truly left England. He seemed to think you might not have. I tried to convince him that it was perfectly natural for you to be going to Philadelphia since it was half your investment you'd be protecting. He sneered at me and asked, 'What of the investment she's leaving behind? Her *personal* financial adviser, the marquess. Her partner in business and in bed.' I realize Father was drunk, but his words were quite lucid." Breanna gazed anxiously at her cousin. "He wasn't guessing, Stacie. It's as if he *knew* you and Damen are involved. But how could he?"

A ponderous silence, punctuated only by the *clack-clack* of the carriage wheels.

Abruptly, Damen muttered an oath, his fist striking his knee with furious awareness. "He *did* know about Stacie and me," he bit out. "How? From his informant."

"What informant?" Breanna demanded.

"The one in my bank."

Breanna sucked in her breath. "You'd better explain."

Tersely, Damen told her about the letter he'd received from his Paris office, and the information it conveyed, as well as what that information signified. He leaned forward, growing more definitive as he spoke. "Think about it. For the past few weeks, you and Anastasia have switched places every time I visited Medford Manor. Your father believed it was *you* I was courting, and he was thrilled with our presumably whirlwind courtship. If he'd realized the truth . . . well, suffice it to say, he would have made us aware of that realization. So, up to and including my latest visit, he had no idea it was really Stacie I was with. Right?"

"Right," Breanna concurred.

"Now let's get to Stacie and me. It was only during the last few days that we've let down our guard, spent any intimate time together. And where were we? At my bank, in my office." A muscle worked in Damen's jaw. "Which means that our secret is out. And that it was discovered at the House of Lockewood."

"Of course," Anastasia breathed, her eyes wide with realization. "That explains what pushed Uncle George over the edge. Not only was he worried about losing Papa's inheritance, he was now frantic about losing you, too. That's what he meant when he told Bates about his plan, and added the part about how he'd be getting the perfect son-in-law from this transaction. He must have just found out we'd been deceiving him."

"Yes. And he found out from one of my bank officers." Damen's voice was rough with anger and betrayal. "There's no other explanation, Stacie. No one but my officers have keys to that door marked 'Private.' Only they have access to my office area, which was the only place we talked and acted in any intimate manner. Whoever this son of a bitch is, he's someone I trust. He's also a duplicitous cad who's using my bank to communicate with Rouge and spy on me."

Anastasia inclined her head, her brows drawn in mystification. "There's a hole in that logic. If what you're saying is true, if this informant eavesdropped on our private conversations, then he'd certainly rush off and tell Uncle George everything he'd overheard, including our suspicions of my uncle's guilt. Well, if that's the case, why is Uncle George still counting on your welcoming him with open arms as your father-in-law? That makes no sense."

Damen stared broodingly at the carriage floor, analyzing Anastasia's well-taken point, and trying to remember the last few meetings the two of them had shared. "My office door was shut," he recalled aloud. "Maybe only snatches of what we said were audible. Or maybe George's snitch didn't wait around long for fear of getting caught. I don't know. But think about it. It wouldn't take more than thirty seconds of eavesdropping to figure out the way we feel about each other. That's the only explanation I can come up with. He knows some part of the truth, but not all of it." A scowl. "The question is, how much is some?"

Her mind darting from the issues to the suspects, Anastasia zeroed in on a possibility. "Damen, do you think it could be Booth? I've mentioned to you before how uneasy he makes me. He seems to hover around whenever you and I are together. On my last visit, he greeted me in the lobby and stayed right by my side, flattering my appearance, until you rescued me. A short while later, when Cunnings interrupted us to look for Mr. Crompton's portfolio, Booth magically appeared in your office doorway and flourished it. I told you—there's something about that man, the way he ogles me, rambles on and on about my beauty, and

about Breanna's." Anastasia paused, chewed her lip. "Maybe he hasn't
been ogling me at all. Maybe he's been spying for my uncle."

"Mr. Booth?" Breanna interrupted in surprise. "I never thought of him
as anything but harmless. You're right about the flattery; he's been very
solicitous of me on those few occasions when I visited the bank with
Father. Still, a spy for Father? That's hard to imagine."

"I agree," Damen said. "And not out of a stubborn sense of loyalty, by
the way. Hell, at this point, I don't know who to trust." He considered the
notion, shaking his head ever so slightly. "Booth has a keen mind when
it comes to managing money. But he's very awkward around people—
too awkward, I think, to serve George's purpose." A slight shrug. "Then
again, my instincts are apparently more flawed than I realized. Maybe
Booth is guilty. Maybe he's a superb actor. I don't know."

"We'll figure it out." Gently, Anastasia wrapped her fingers around
Damen's. "I'm sorry," she said softly. "I know how hard this is for you.
But at least what Breanna's told us narrows down our search." She
paused, watching his expression. "Damen, this doesn't demean your instincts. None of us is clearheaded when it comes to those we trust. And
in your case, the handful of men who are now potential suspects have
been valued colleagues—and friends—for years."

"You're right." Damen kissed her gloved fingertips, his brooding supplanted by determination. "And not just about my instincts. About the
fact that we've narrowed down the choices. There are only four men—
five, if you count Graff—who have access to my office. I'll do thorough
checks on all of them, find out if they've come into any recent funds
from unknown sources, if they've been seen coming and going from
their homes at unusual hours. By tomorrow, we'll have our informant."

"In the meantime, I'll keep my eye on Father," Breanna said thoughtfully. "Something you just said piqued my interest—the idea of comings
and goings at unusual times. Now that I consider it, Father's been guilty
of that, and more so recently. I never gave it much thought, until now."

"What unusual comings and goings?" Anastasia demanded, swooping
down on her cousin's words. "Why didn't I notice?"

"Because you've only lived with us since July. You wouldn't know
Father's habits as well as I do." Breanna fingered the folds of her gown
as she reflected. "Over the past months, he's been making late-night
jaunts, usually after drinking to excess. I assumed he was going out to
clear his head. Now I wonder. Could he be meeting this informant of
his?"

"How frequently does he do this, Breanna?" Damen asked. "How late
at night? And how long is he gone?"

"It used to be about once a fortnight. Lately, it's been more like twice
a week." She frowned. "I'm afraid I never paid much attention to the

hour or to the amount of time he was gone. I was usually in bed, reading, when I'd hear him drive off. So it had to be after midnight. As to when he'd return . . ." A shrug. "I was asleep. Lord only knows how late it was." Breanna broke off, a triumphant smile curving her lips. "Let me rephrase that: the Lord isn't the only one who knows how late it was. Wells knows, too."

"Of course." Anastasia's eyes lit up. "Wells knows everything. He'll give you any details he can."

"I'm sure he will." Unconsciously, Breanna smoothed a wisp of hair into place. "I'll talk to Wells—right away, if I can. I'll also keep an eye on Father. Maybe I can figure out how much he knows, and how much of the truth Lyman and Meade have pieced together by now. Damen, you do your checking into the suspects at the bank. Schedule another visit to Medford Manor for the day after tomorrow. That will unnerve Father, since he's now aware of the fact that you're not calling on me, at least not in the romantic sense." A triumphant gleam lit her eyes. "That doesn't mean we don't have things to discuss—things like Stacie's whereabouts. Which I'm sure is what Father will assume we're discussing. The very notion will throw him into a tizzy. The more off-balance we render him, the better. Because with any luck, after we combine whatever information we've uncovered, we'll have enough proof to confront him. And, if he's drunk enough, intimidated enough, we might just get a confession. Which would be the perfect finishing touch to the evidence we've amassed—and the perfect end to this nightmare."

"An excellent plan." Damen looked sufficiently impressed. "You and Stacie are more alike than I realized."

"At times, yes." Breanna grinned. "Although you've rarely seen that side of me. I must admit I find it much easier to be myself around you now that I know you're to be my cousin and not my husband." She shot him an apologetic look. "At the risk of sounding too brazen—even more so than Stacie—you and I are terribly suited."

Laughter rumbled in Damen's chest. "True. But there's a lucky man out there somewhere who's going to feel very differently about the two of you. And once you meet him, you'll agree. Unfortunately, he'll have to win both Stacie's and my approval before he can win your hand. Ah, the poor fellow." Still chuckling, Damen leaned over the basket. "On that intriguing note, let's enjoy some of Mrs. Rhodes's delicious sandwiches."

"Wait." Anastasia held up her palm, halting Damen in the process of unpacking the basket.

"Why?" Damen's head came up, and he frowned as he saw the rankled expression on Anastasia's face, the indignant set of her jaw. "What's the matter?"

"I'm delighted that the two of you have successfully worked out your strategies for capturing Uncle George and his colleagues," she retorted, folding her arms across her chest. "Just how am *I* supposed to contribute to all this?"

The lighthearted banter of the past moments vanished in a heartbeat.

"You're supposed to remain in hiding, unseen and undetected by the men who are trying to find you—*and* sell you," Damen replied, his expression grim. "Or have you forgotten that unpleasant tidbit?" Warning glints flashed in his steel-gray eyes. "I'm not taunting you, Stacie. I'm dead serious. Your life is in danger. You're going to stay put until that's no longer the case. Is that clear?"

Silence.

"Anastasia . . ."

"It's clear," she replied, her gaze as direct as his. "For now."

17

That's the last update, Medford. And still no luck. Lyman slapped the scribbled note on his desk, dismissing the lad who'd delivered it by tossing him a shilling, then gesturing for him to go.

He waited until the office door had shut before turning back to George, who was pacing furiously near the windows overlooking the docks. "My contacts have been at it all night, ever since I got your message. They've checked every bloody manifest. The fact is, no Lady Anastasia Colby booked passage to the States yesterday. Not in London, anyway. I won't know about Liverpool for a few days. But you and I both know how unlikely that is. Your driver said he brought her to the London docks. I doubt she found her way to Liverpool from there."

"I wouldn't put anything past Anastasia. Maybe she did that just to steer me in the wrong direction. Or maybe she boarded in London, but used another name." George halted, slicing the air with his palm. "Damn that miserable chit! Where the hell is she?"

"I don't know." Lyman looked grim. "But I don't think a false name is our answer. I had Meade and a few other men ask around at the docks. And no one matching Anastasia's description was seen boarding a ship, or even walking along the wharf or around the warehouses. So, unless she paid a coach to take her to Liverpool, my guess is your niece didn't leave England."

"Dammit. *Dammit!*" For the third time in the past hour, George crossed over to the sideboard and refilled his glass, taking two healthy gulps as he resumed pacing. "I've got to know for sure. There are so many ways she could have managed this—stowing away, disguising herself. You don't know Anastasia. She's the most resourceful female I've ever met."

Lyman drew a slow breath, then released it, crossing over to refill his own glass at the sideboard, then hurrying back to stand behind his desk.

When Medford was in this kind of mood—drunk, irrational, angry—he was more comfortable putting some distance between them, even if it was only half a room and the comforting presence of his desk that separated them.

Because when Medford was like this, there was a dangerous quality about him, one Lyman wasn't interested in provoking.

"I don't doubt your niece's resourcefulness," he replied in what he hoped was a soothing tone. "I've seen her attempt to charm a roomful of men to finance that bank of hers. The question is, why would she go to so much trouble to keep you from finding her? She left you a note, told you where she was going and why. Why would she suddenly decide to become secretive?"

"Maybe because she knows something—something that could lead to something more, and then more, and then more . . . all of which could eventually spell my end." George gulped down the remainder of his drink, slammed the glass down on the window ledge. "Maybe that's why she's sailing off—to protect herself while she assembles the pieces she's uncovered. Or maybe that's why she's not leaving England at all—to assemble the pieces here and now."

The shipping owner had gone very still. "Knows something?" he asked carefully. "As in, about us? What we've been doing?"

George stared broodingly across the room at the pile of papers on Lyman's desk—all letters stating that Anastasia Colby's name had not been listed on any ship's manifest. "Yes, about us," he bit out. "And what we've been doing. At first, I thought she was running off to squander more of Henry's money before I could stop her. Then, I thought about it more carefully, in light of some information that's recently been brought to my attention."

"What kind of information?" Lyman asked in a shaky voice.

"I have reason to believe Anastasia suspects I'm involved in something criminal. How many of the details she's privy to, who else she's told . . . all that is pure speculation, as is whether or not it ties into her reasons for disappearing."

"Christ." Lyman had gone white. "You never mentioned any of this."

"I just told you, I only recently found out. It's one of the reasons I'm so eager to find her, and to get rid of her."

"Under those circumstances, you should be glad she's gone. Instead of brooding over where she's gone, be grateful it's not to the authorities. Instead, concentrate on figuring out who she might have shared her suspicions with. They could be far more dangerous to us than Anastasia. She's your *niece*, for heaven's sake. Your brother's daughter. She might condemn you, but she'd never turn you in. Hasn't she proven that by running off? She wants no part of your illegal activities—or of you. Whereas someone else, someone outside your family, wouldn't hesitate to send you to the gallows." A cold shiver ran up Lyman's spine. "Getting rid of Anastasia should be secondary to . . ."

His mouth snapped shut as the meaning of George's words sank in, and he stared at him as if seeing a ghost. "By 'get rid of,' do you mean—kill her?"

An ugly laugh. "Yes and no. Figuratively, yes. Actually—well, actually, I mean for her to begin a brand-new life. Only *not* in America. And *not* at my expense. At my profit, as a matter of fact. My fifty-thousand-pound profit."

Realization struck, and Lyman sagged into his chair. "The ship . . . the falsified destination . . . the whole damned arrangement you're working on with Bates to supply Rouge with the girl he needs. My God, Medford, you're planning to send Anastasia?"

George shot him a disgusted look. "Stop looking so horrified. We've been sending women to Rouge for months."

"But your *niece* . . ."

". . . could be our downfall," George finished for him. He strode over to the desk, gripping the edge until his knuckles turned white. "Did you hear what I said?" he ground out, leaning forward to glare at Lyman. "She might know enough to send us both to prison. And you're a fool if you think she won't. My *niece* . . ." he spat, ". . . has no loyalty to me—hell, *Henry* had no loyalty to me. As for selling Anastasia to Rouge, stop sounding so bloody self-righteous. You've been more than content selling women all this time."

"But they're . . . she's . . ." Sweat was beading up on Lyman's forehead.

"Ah. In other words, it's acceptable to sell strangers, workhouse girls we don't know, but you're offended by my selling the one girl who could see us both in Newgate."

"Does she know what you intend . . ." An inadvertent shudder. ". . . what you intend to do to her?"

"No. That much, she's blissfully unaware of."

"Thank God for that."

"Stop thanking God. We've got to find the little bitch before she causes any more trouble."

"She could be anywhere," Lyman put in weakly.

"Not according to your sources." Rage against Anastasia was rebuilding inside George until he could taste it. "According to your sources, she's still right here in England." His eyes narrowed. "And if she is, I intend to find her."

"How?"

"To begin with, by keeping a close eye on my daughter—something my butler is taking care of in my absence. Breanna knows more than she's telling me. Although, in her case, she'd never be stupid enough to actually help Anastasia destroy me, not unless she was privy to my plans for her wretched cousin. In *that* instance, she would protect Anastasia with her life." George scowled, remembering the shocking confrontation he'd had with Breanna last night. Clearly, his daughter had more pluck than he'd given her credit for. "Fortunately, Breanna hasn't any idea what I intend for Henry's brat."

"And speaking of Anastasia," he continued, "assuming she's still in England, she doesn't have that many friends, certainly not friends who'd keep her from her legal guardian. I'll start with Fenshaw, see if he's heard from her. Then, I'll stop in at the House of Lockewood, find out what Sheldrake knows." He paused, rubbed his palm across his chin. "On second thought, that's too obvious. If Sheldrake knew anything about what we're doing, he'd have sent Bow Street over here to collect us by now. That's the only reason I'm sure Anastasia isn't with him. He's too damned ethical to ignore our crimes, even for a short while. No, she hasn't told him yet—either because she's only just figured it out or because, as I said, she's still missing pieces and dropped out of sight to do a little investigating on her own."

"Or maybe you're overreacting and she doesn't know a thing," Lyman burst out, his composure drawn taut to breaking.

"Then why did she run off?" George shot back.

"I don't know!" Lyman's control snapped. "To spend Henry's money! To see the world! Why does any young woman run off? Maybe she's with child!"

George recoiled as if he'd been struck. "With child?" Everything inside him went numb. "I never thought . . . but given their trysts . . . and if she is . . ." He could see it all dissipating before his very eyes—not just Rouge's payment now, but everything: Henry's inheritance, the balance of power from his own descendants to Henry's, not to mention Sheldrake . . .

Sheldrake.

White shock vibrated through George's being.

If Anastasia was pregnant, Sheldrake was the father.

"Dammit." His hands balled into fists, pounded the desk with all the rage of a wounded animal. "It can't be. *It can't be!*"

Lyman backed away, breathing heavily. "Take it easy, Medford. I only meant . . ."

"Give me a quill." George's tone was lethal, a drowning man clawing his way to the surface. "I've got to get a letter off. *Now.*"

"Fine. Here. Whatever you say." Lyman shoved a quill and some paper across the desk. "Who are you writing to?" he ventured.

"To the one person who can tell me just how Sheldrake fits into all this. Because if Anastasia knows something, if she puts the rest of the pieces together, she'll run straight to him. And if she's with child . . ." A bitter laugh. "She'll definitely run straight to him. Either way, I've got to get to her first. Even if it means taking a chance and passing off some substitute to Rouge. My wretched niece has got to be stopped."

In Medford Manor's sitting room, Breanna moved the heavy drapes aside, peeked out the window, and watched Damen's carriage disappear around the drive. She felt a sense of emptiness, of loss, knowing Anastasia was in there, leaving her home yet again. It shouldn't be this way. Stacie belonged here. Not just here, but safe, happy.

Breanna drew herself up, her chin set in staunch determination. It was *her* father who was responsible for this nightmare. And it was up to *her* to stop him.

"Miss Breanna?" Wells addressed her from the sitting room doorway. "Lord Sheldrake has taken his leave. You wanted to see me?"

Slowly, Breanna turned and nodded. "Come in, Wells. And please shut the door. I want this conversation to remain private."

The butler complied, looking not the least bit surprised at Breanna's request.

"I suspect you know what this is about," she began.

Wells's expression softened. "I suspect I do."

Breanna cast a nervous glance over her shoulder, scanning the deserted drive.

"We have another hour or so before your father returns," Wells supplied. "So you needn't worry."

"Good." Her mind at ease, Breanna turned her attention back to Wells, who was regarding her with an expectant look on his face. "I hate involving you in this," she said honestly, her brow furrowed. "But I'm afraid we no longer have a choice."

"I'm already involved, Miss Breanna." Wells adjusted his spectacles, then stood up straight, hands clasped firmly behind him, as if stating his position on the subject. "I've been involved since the day your grandfather died. I know what he wanted. And I mean to see that he gets it."

Tears glistened on Breanna's lashes. "Thank you," she managed. "From Stacie and me. And Grandfather, as well." She composed herself, clearing her throat to steady her voice. "I don't know how much you're aware of . . ."

"There's something *you're* not aware of," Wells interrupted. "Until your father returns from London—which, as I said, should be in another hour or so—I've been assigned to keep a close eye on you, to report back if you should meet with anyone unusual . . ."

Breanna gripped the back of the settee. "Anyone meaning Stacie."

"Or someone who knows her whereabouts."

Her eyes widened. "Does Father suspect Damen?"

"I don't know, Miss Breanna." The butler shrugged. "I'm sure it's occurred to him that Lord Sheldrake is somehow involved. From what I've gleaned from the viscount's mutterings, he realizes Miss Stacie and Lord Sheldrake are . . . close friends."

"Yes, he does." Breanna sighed, smoothing her palm over the settee's textured cloth and polished wood trim. "Wells, I want to use this time wisely, since Father will be home soon. I need to ask you some questions about his actions. Or, more specifically, his destinations—if you know them."

"I'll tell you anything I can. But *you* tell *me* one thing first: is she all right?"

A soft smile touched Breanna's lips. "She's fine. Eager to have this ordeal over with, but fine. And Wells—" For an instant, Breanna put the unpleasantness aside to tell their lifelong friend something she knew would delight him. "When all this is behind us, there's going to be a wedding. An incredibly joyful wedding."

Wells's smile was broad, but a fine mist veiled his eyes. "Our Miss Stacie—a bride. It's hard to imagine her as a wife—the little girl who climbed trees and spoke her mind no matter what the cost."

"She still speaks her mind, only now she speaks it to Damen." Breanna's eyes twinkled. "They're perfect for each other, Wells. Grandfather would be so happy."

"Indeed he would." Wells's gaze grew sober. "What questions can I answer to make this wedding happen more quickly, and more safely?"

"Father's late-night outings." With equal gravity, Breanna resumed their original subject. "The ones he's been taking more and more often these days. Do you have any idea where he goes? Who he meets?"

The butler pressed his lips together, contemplating his employer's activities. "I don't know the viscount's precise destination, nor the name of whomever he meets. What I can tell you is that he's only gone a few hours each time, which means he can't be going far. And, if I had to wager a guess, I'd say his meetings take place at a pub."

That brought Breanna up short. "A pub? Why would you think that?"

"Because whenever your father returns, he reeks of smoke, and there's a certain stench clinging to his clothing." A distasteful shudder. "The last time he got home, the smell of cheap ale was on his breath. It doesn't take a scholar to add up all those clues."

"That fits," Breanna murmured. "If Father were meeting a contact for some secret, unscrupulous purpose, he wouldn't want to be recognized. And what better place to remain anonymous than in a seedy pub filled with riffraff who don't know you and, quite frankly, don't care?"

Wells nodded. "There are only three or four such places I'm aware of within a half hour's carriage ride from Medford Manor. But then again, I'm not exactly an expert on taverns."

Breanna couldn't help but smile at Wells's offended tone. "Of course you're not." She reflected on what she'd just learned. So her father met his snitch at a pub. *Which* pub she'd have to determine later, perhaps by intercepting the next message between the two men.

And that led to her next question.

"How does my father make arrangements for these late-night excursions? I assume he communicates with his colleague by messenger."

"A courier brings the messages straight to Lord Medford."

"What about those messages initiated by Father, or his responses to those he receives?"

"One of our footmen delivers the viscount's correspondence directly to the courier's address. Where it goes from there, I have no idea."

"I see." Breanna's thoughts were racing. "They go to a great deal of trouble to keep the recipient's identity unknown." She pursed her lips. "This courier—I assume it's the same one each time?" She waited for Wells's nod. "Tell me, does he come here often?"

"Not too often. Other than to dispatch word on the late-night excursions we've just discussed, he generally comes only when the viscount receives business correspondence from the Continent." A frown, as Wells reconsidered his words. "Actually, that's not true. He handles only the viscount's most pressing business correspondence to and from the Continent."

Breanna jumped on that distinction. "How do you know the business involved is pressing?"

"Several reasons, the most obvious being that the letters are marked 'urgent.' Also, the viscount's instructions are that I bring these letters to him immediately, no matter what the hour or circumstances." Wells's frown deepened. "And they do arrive at the oddest hours. For instance, one such letter was delivered during Miss Stacie's coming-out party. Your father rushed off, closeted himself in his study, and read it. The next morning he arose at dawn, and dashed off an equally urgent reply."

"And this courier delivered it for him?"

"Again, our footman brought the letter to the courier's address. I assume from there it was dispatched to the Continent. I don't know who these messages are from or to, but they cause your father great agitation. Could that tie into anything you and Lord Sheldrake are considering?"

"Rouge," Breanna muttered. "That must be who Father is corresponding with. The courier you're describing is obviously hired by the informant at the House of Lockewood. It stands to reason he'd use the same person to handle everything else pertaining to these vile transactions." She met Wells's gaze. "I need that courier's address."

"Of course. It's number 17 Fleet Street." Wells's eyes narrowed a bit. "You're not thinking of doing something foolish, are you? Because confronting the courier . . ."

"No, no." Breanna waved away Wells's concern. "Confronting the courier would be stupid. He wouldn't tell me anything, since I don't pay his bills. And I'd only succeed in making him suspicious enough to go to Father. No, what I intend to do is give the address to Damen. I'm willing to bet that courier is someone who does frequent business with the House of Lockewood. That way, no one would notice a few extra charges on his bill—charges incurred by the snitch Father's working with. Damen can use the address as evidence when he confronts whoever that turns out to be."

"You've lost me, Miss Breanna."

"That's all right." Breanna released her grip on the settee, and began walking restlessly about the sitting room. "The sordid details can wait. Planning our tactics can't." She paused, pivoting slowly to face Wells. "My father's with Mr. Lyman. He's probably trying to locate Stacie, which we both know is not going to happen. So, Father's going to be unnerved. My guess is he'll want to find out exactly how much Damen knows, and how he factors into Stacie's plans. He won't ask Damen flat out; that would be too risky. Instead, he'll probably get his informant to do a bit of spying. After which . . ."

". . . after which, the viscount will need to meet with this snitch of his, to get the information he's seeking," Wells finished for her.

"Exactly." Breanna pressed her palms together, tightly interlaced her fingers. "Wells, I need you to tell me the minute Father gives you a message to send off to that courier. I'm going to steam open the seal and read it."

"There won't be time. Your father expects those particular messages to be dispatched posthaste. He'd notice even the slightest delay."

"Fine. Then I'll read his informant's reply."

"He'll be waiting for it." Wells gave an emphatic shake of his head. "It's not only implausible that you could manage to intercept the note without being spied, it's hardly worth your effort to try. Think about it. The viscount and his snitch have been holding their late-night meetings for months now. My guess is that their meeting place has remained the same. Why, then, would they bother spelling out the address in a note? Their communications are probably cryptic—stating the time they should arrive and the urgency of the topic."

"You're right." Breanna gave an exasperated sigh. "But I've got to . . ." Abruptly, she broke off, her jade green eyes darkening with resolve.

"Fine. I'll accomplish this in a bolder manner. The instant Father exchanges a message with this courier or informs you that he'll be going out late at night, tell me. I suspect we haven't long to wait until that happens. Things being as they are, I'm sure Father will want his answers right away, either tonight or tomorrow night."

"Why are you so eager to know when this meeting is going to take place?" Wells asked cautiously.

"Because whenever Father goes, I'm going, too."

Wells sucked in his breath. "You're going to follow the viscount to . . ."

"Yes. It's the only way I can learn who Father's meeting, how much he assumes we know, and what he's planning."

"Miss Breanna." Wells looked ill. "Do you understand how dangerous that is?"

"I understand it's the only way we're going to get the information we need quickly enough. Even if Damen figures out the name of my father's contact by tomorrow, all we'll have is an uncooperative snitch whose confession we can't count on. And even if his confession is genuine, there's no guarantee he can piece together the whole plot. Damen, Stacie, and I know aspects of my father's plan that this informant might not. I need to hear Father's conversation with him firsthand, hear what his instructions to him are. Then, I can combine what I learn with what I already know, and figure out the full scope of what Father's done—*and* what he plans to do next. Especially the latter, if we're going to ensure Stacie's safety and bring this nightmare to an end."

She hesitated, searching for the right words to explain to Wells how deeply, how personally, she felt about all this. "I'm his daughter, Wells," she said in a small, dignified tone. "It's up to me to stop him." Her chin set, and she met Wells's gaze with unyielding conviction. "Please don't try to deter me. It won't work. I can be as stubborn as Stacie when I want to be, if I believe what I'm defending is important enough. And this *is* important enough. It's more precious to me than anything else in my life. It's my family."

Wells cleared his throat, his lips pursed as he contemplated his reply. "I'll make sure the second phaeton is ready, both tonight and tomorrow night," he declared, the essence of efficiency. "We can follow behind, at a discreet distance, so we won't be spied."

"*We?*" Breanna's jaw dropped.

One of Wells's brows raised ever so slightly. "You didn't think I'd let you do this alone, did you? Now . . ." He continued as if that subject were closed. "Neither of us can go in our customary attire. Certainly not you, who'd be devoured by the pub's lowlifes, before your father could even recognize you to thrash you. And I . . ." He glanced down, scowling at his dignified uniform. ". . . I look far too stately to fit into the crowd we'll be mingling with, certainly if I hope to do so without being spotted by your father." A decisive sniff. "I'll borrow the necessary clothing, have it ready. We can leave at a moment's notice."

Emotion clogged Breanna's throat, made speaking difficult. "It's obvious that Grandfather realized something I've only just begun to comprehend," she managed. "Something that explains why Stacie and I are still blessed enough to have you looking out for us: that family isn't necessarily defined by ties of the blood. Family is defined by ties of the heart." She crossed over, abandoning protocol entirely to give Wells a huge hug. "Thank you, my dear friend. Thank you for being part of our family."

George stormed up the front steps of Medford Manor, pounding on the door with his fist.

Wells opened it, stepping aside to allow his employer to enter. "Good evening, sir. I didn't know you'd arrived."

"Obviously, I have." George marched inside, trying for the fifth time to smooth the wrinkles out of his coat. He hated wrinkles. They looked damned untidy, even if one had been drinking.

Besides, whatever liquor he'd consumed had long since worn off. As had its dulling effect.

"Is my daughter home?" George demanded, peering about as if expecting to see Breanna awaiting his return.

Wells stifled a cough. "She's in her room, sir."

"And the mail—did you put it aside for me?"

"Just as you asked, yes."

"Good. Were there any private messages delivered to Breanna?"

"No, my lord." This time, Wells relented, giving one or two raspy coughs. "But Miss Breanna did have a visitor."

George's head shot up. "Who?"

"Lord Sheldrake."

"Sheldrake." Suspicion and fear clouded George's eyes. "He came to see Breanna?"

"Actually, he was looking for you, as well. Something about business you two had to conduct. But I told him you'd be gone all day, so he said he'd return in a day or two to meet with you."

"That's all he said?"

"Sir?" Wells cleared his throat, looking puzzled.

"Did the marquess say anything else?" George snapped. "Was he in a good humor?"

"We exchanged pleasantries. And, yes, he seemed cheerful enough."

"I see." George digested that fact, although sweat still broke out on his forehead. Why the hell had Sheldrake come to Medford Manor—to get answers or to provide them? What had he and Breanna discussed?

Who, he could guess.

"You say Sheldrake visited with Breanna?"

"Indeed he did, sir. They took a picnic lunch and went off for a ride in the country. Lord Sheldrake thought Miss Breanna might need some cheering up, given that Miss Stacie had to leave so suddenly."

George's eyes narrowed into slits. "So Sheldrake knew Anastasia was gone?"

"Why, yes, sir." Wells plucked out a handkerchief, coughed discreetly into it. "As I understood it, she left at his suggestion. Nonetheless, it was clear he sympathized with Miss Breanna's loneliness. I'm sure he appreciated how much she missed her cousin—how much we all miss her. But then, I needn't explain that to you, my lord."

"No, you needn't," George muttered, wishing he had more concrete information, determined to get it. "I want to see my daughter," he barked.

Almost instantly, he realized his error, as he saw Wells start, tense ever so fractionally. *Dammit,* he berated himself. *I have to watch my tone.*

The very notion made him furious. *He* was the master of this household, the bloody head of the family. Why the hell shouldn't he rule it with an iron hand, or any other way he chose to? Worse, why should he allow his actions to be dictated by his acquiescent slip of a daughter?

Not so acquiescent, he reminded himself, recalling yesterday's incident, as well as the reproving look on Wells's face when he'd glanced into Breanna's bedchamber, assessed whether or not she'd been hurt—by her father.

Silently, George swore. The little chit was not only bolder than he'd realized, she was also smarter. Because she was right. He couldn't afford to alienate his servants, not given the precarious state of his life right now. The staff adored Breanna; they had since she was a child. If they believed he was physically harming her . . .

No. He couldn't risk the kind of scandal that would ensue. It could push things over the edge, eliminate any remaining chance he had with Sheldrake. There was no choice to be had. He must curb the severity with which he approached Breanna, lest she follow through with her threats. Besides, she wouldn't tell him a damned thing if he thrashed her. But if he was civil, perhaps that would yield different results.

So be it. However, when all this was over, when Anastasia had been found and his own world had been righted, then things would return to normal. Then, he'd once again be master of Medford Manor, and of his fate. And when he was—well, God help Breanna if she upset his plans for her future.

Inspired by that thought, George drew a slow breath, sought a more acceptable approach.

"Wells," he began, this time keeping his tone composed and even. "Give me a few minutes to peruse the mail. Then, ask Breanna to come to my study. I have a few questions I'd like to ask her."

He could actually see Wells's rigid stance relax a bit. "As you wish."

"Thank you. Oh, and once Breanna and I have finished talking, I'll take my dinner in my study. Alone. I'm not to be disturbed all evening. And Wells . . ." George leaned forward, lowered his voice to a secretive pitch. "I'm expecting the courier. When he arrives, bring his message to me at once. That also means I'll be going out tonight. At half after midnight. Have the phaeton ready."

"Of course, my lord." Wells winced a bit, his fingers shifting reflexively to his throat. "Pardon me, sir, but may I ask permission to retire early tonight? After I've taken care of your arrangements, that is. I'm feeling a bit under the weather. Of course, I'll direct one of the footmen to attend the entranceway door, if needed."

As grateful as George was that Wells's misgivings had been appeased, he wasn't interested in hearing about the butler's health. He had more important things on his mind. "H-m-m?" he asked, distracted by the reminder of all that had yet to be resolved. "Oh, that's fine. And don't bother with the footman. Other than my dinner, I won't be needing anything more tonight. Once the courier's gone and the phaeton's been readied, you can take the night off."

"Thank you, sir. I'll go see Mrs. Rhodes now, make sure she sends your dinner directly to your study. Then, I'll return to my post and await the courier."

Wells headed off to the kitchen, acutely aware of the viscount's footsteps as they moved down the hall in the direction of his study.

By the time the study door had clicked shut, and the bolt had been thrown, Wells had finished speaking with Mrs. Rhodes and was halfway to his own quarters.

Once there, he paused long enough to yank open his bureau drawer and scoop up the smaller of the two stable hands' outfits he'd found earlier in the laundry yard and had hidden in his room. He spread the clothes out on a serving tray, then draped a fine linen napkin over them, making the overall presentation look like an elegant dinner.

With a gleam of approval, he left his room, made his way calmly to the front hallway, then up the stairs. He rounded the second-floor landing, nodding his acknowledgment to the passing servants, who bowed respectfully and hurried on their way.

Without incident, Wells knocked on Breanna's door.

"Yes?"

"I have your refreshment, Miss Breanna."

A quick rustling sound, and Breanna tugged open the door. "Thank you, Wells," she said, her gaze searching his face. "Would you kindly put it on my nightstand?"

"Certainly." Wells walked over, placed the tray beside her bed. "I think you'll find everything to your liking," he assured her. He straightened, met her stare head-on. "Tonight. Half after midnight," he breathed, his voice nearly inaudible. "I'll bring the phaeton around and meet you on the east side of the drive, the side concealed by that awning of trees."

Slowly, she nodded, a glint of anticipation lighting her eyes. "I'll be there," she whispered. Then: "Thank you, Wells," she said in a more normal tone.

"My pleasure, Miss Breanna." The butler clasped his hands behind his back, a flicker of distaste crossing his face. "Your father wishes to speak with you. Please give him a quarter hour, then go to his study." A scratchy cough, followed by a meaningful look. "I'm feeling a bit under the weather, and the viscount has given me permission to retire early. But should you need anything, I'll be in my quarters."

"I appreciate that," Breanna replied, nodding her understanding. Wells had freed himself of having to man the entranceway door by claiming to be ill. But that didn't mean he wouldn't be available to her, if her father lost control. "I'll be fine," she said, giving his forearm a reassuring squeeze, then shooing him toward the door. "Go. Get some rest. That way, you'll be yourself again in no time."

Waiting only till Wells had gone, Breanna retreated into her chambers, tugging the napkin off the tray and nearly laughing aloud as she viewed her "refreshment." A shoddy pair of breeches, a threadbare shirt, some scuffed but serviceable boots and—ah, bless Wells's keen mind—a cap.

Breanna gathered up the clothes, tucked them away in her wardrobe. Then, with a thoughtful glance at her nightstand, she reminded herself of the one other article she'd need to bring with her.

Her pistol.

Given the risk involved in tonight's excursion, the full extent of which she didn't dare ponder, a little protection was in order. Because if her identity were discovered, she'd need that protection—not only from her father, whose wrath would be too fierce to imagine, but from his informant, with whom she was doubtless acquainted and could therefore identify, and from any riffraff who became unruly once they realized she was a woman.

In short, discovery was unthinkable. But, should it occur, the pistol was necessary.

As for now, her father had asked to see her. Well, that came as no great surprise. By now, Wells had doubtless told him that Damen had been at Medford Manor during his absence, which would make him frantic to find out what Damen knew of Stacie's whereabouts.

And what he knew of her father's guilt.

Bitterness surged through Breanna's veins. *Very well, Father. I'll come to your study. I'll play this cat and mouse game with you. But if you think you'll learn one wretched thing from me, you're wrong. Even I can't be browbeaten into helping you, not when it's lives you plan to sacrifice. Innocent lives—including Stacie's. No, not this time. This time you're going to get what you deserve.*

18

❦

George swore under his breath, examining each worthless letter that had been delivered today, then slapping them onto his desk. All trivial invitations and foolish announcements. Not one of them pertinent to the dilemma he now faced.

He *had* to find Anastasia.

Dragging a hand through his hair, he dropped into his chair, contemplating today's latest development.

Sheldrake had been here. He'd spent hours alone with Breanna. Why? Certainly not to woo her. That he knew, thanks to the information he'd received from his reliable contact. Then why? Did Sheldrake know where Anastasia was? Had he come to tell Breanna? Or was he corroborating Anastasia's story that it was he who'd sent her to America?

Tonight's meeting should yield some answers with regard to Sheldrake's involvement, not only in Anastasia's disappearance, but in whatever incriminating search she'd undertaken.

Perhaps, in the meantime, he could acquire a few of those answers from his daughter.

As if on cue, a knock sounded at the study door.

"Yes?" he responded impatiently.

"You wanted to see me, Father?" Breanna called back.

George rose, crossing over and unlocking the door. He gestured at his daughter, who was hovering on the threshold, eyeing him warily. "Come in." He stood aside, waiting for her to comply.

She took a few tentative steps into the room, then halted.

"Stop staring at me as if you expect me to whip you," George ordered. "Do you?"

George drew a slow, calming breath. "No." He shut the door, but refrained from locking it. "There. This is a private conversation, or I'd leave the door ajar. But the bolt isn't thrown. You can escape any time you fear for your safety." He paused, giving her a pointed glare. "Or did you bring your pistol as protection?"

"My pistol is in my drawer." Breanna interlaced her fingers in front of her. "I told you, I don't intend to walk around the manor armed."

"Ah. You'll just shout for the servants if need be, accuse me of thrashing you within an inch of your life." George walked across the room, stood before his desk, and leaned back against it. "Well, don't worry. I want only to talk."

Breanna's delicate brows rose. "About what—Stacie?"

"No, about Lord Sheldrake. He did visit you today, didn't he?"

"You must know he did. Just as you must know we went for a carriage ride."

"Indeed I do." George folded his arms across his chest, watching Breanna's face. "And tell me, how is your courtship progressing? I did advise you to encourage the marquess as much as possible, if you remember."

"I remember." Breanna never averted her gaze. "But, as I tried to tell you last time, no one can force feelings. Lord Sheldrake isn't in love with me. Nor, to be honest, am I in love with him. He's a fine man. But he's not destined to become my husband." A small smile played about her lips. "However, I do suspect he'll be a member of our family, nonetheless."

George's brows shot up. He'd expected to catch Breanna in a lie. Dammit, was she actually going to tell him the truth? "What does that mean?" he asked carefully.

"It means that Lord Sheldrake and Stacie are in love. I expect they'll be getting married. Whenever Stacie gets home, that is."

"I see." George's fingers dug into his sleeves, anger surging through him in wide, hammering waves. What kind of game was Breanna playing, admitting something she knew would enrage him? Was she testing him to see if he'd strike her?

He wouldn't. Furious or not, he'd keep this to a battle of words.

"Your cousin and Sheldrake," he said icily. "Interesting. Tell me, when did they become so enamored with each other?"

"Over the course of their business meetings, I suppose. I really don't know the details. Stacie hadn't time to divulge them to me before she left."

"If she and Sheldrake are so smitten with each other, why did she leave him and make this trip to the States?"

Breanna sighed. "We already discussed this, Father. I told you: Lord Sheldrake felt Stacie would be the right one to protect their interests in that new banking venture. Frankly, I think Stacie agreed. She's as leery as the marquess is about trusting others with their investments."

George leaned forward, scowling at Breanna. "Why didn't Sheldrake go himself?"

"I couldn't say. Probably because he's a busy man. He has dozens of clients who count on him."

"Yet he found time to see you."

"He came to see you, Father. But you weren't home."

"So he took you on a lengthy carriage ride?"

A grateful nod. "He's a very compassionate man. He guessed how much I miss Stacie, and tried to take my mind off it. Now that I've stopped trying to win his affections, I feel far more relaxed around him."

Good, George thought silently. *Then you'll slip easily into the role of the Marchioness of Sheldrake once I've rid myself of your cousin.* Aloud, he asked, "What did you and Sheldrake discuss during your ride?"

Breanna shrugged offhandedly. "Nothing special: Stacie. You."

George's insides clenched. "Me? How did I factor into this conversation?"

The slightest hesitation. "To be frank, Lord Sheldrake is relieved that Stacie will be of age when she returns to England. He didn't want to offend you by whisking her off to Gretna Green, but he is determined to wed her. Now you'll have several months to accustom yourself to the idea of their marriage and, upon Stacie's return, it will no longer be an issue. She'll be twenty-one and she and Lord Sheldrake can have the formal church wedding she wants so much, along with the presence and the blessings of those they love."

Over my dead body, George thought bitterly. *It's you who will be Sheldrake's bride. He'll get over Anastasia, learn to live with the closest substitute. Just as I did. And I'll get my respectability back, along with Henry's inheritance, and all the benefits of Sheldrake's wealth and acclaim.*

"Father?"

George blinked, refocused on Breanna. "What?"

"Was there anything else you wanted?"

Swiftly, he gathered his thoughts. "Sheldrake—did he say when Anastasia would be returning?" A pointed pause. "From the States, that is."

If Breanna felt flustered by the question, she didn't show it. "She'll leave the minute the bank is open and running smoothly. She'll be back before the holidays. After all, she won't want to be away for *too* many months. She has so many exciting announcements to make, so many life-altering events to look forward to—not only her wedding, but beyond."

A hard knot of dread gripped George's gut. "Beyond?" he echoed, unable to keep the strain out of his tone. "What kind of events are you referring to?"

Breanna met his gaze, her expression unreadable. "Fate is a miraculous thing, Father, whether or not you believe it. It takes a hand in putting the right people together, and seeing that the right people get what they deserve."

George could hear the thundering of his own heart. "What the hell does that mean?"

"Mean?" Breanna's brows drew together, but there was an odd glint in her eyes. "It was a philosophical statement. I don't think it requires further explanation."

The rage was beginning to take over. George could feel it. "I'll ask you again," he said, unconsciously pushing away from his desk, taking a step toward Breanna. "What life-altering events are you referring to? And who is it you expect to get what he deserves?"

Like prey being cornered by a hunter, Breanna tensed, swiftly assessing her father's approach, the controlled violence of his motions. She reacted instantly, reaching behind her to twist open the door handle. "I'm going to my room," she pronounced. "Before you do something you'll regret."

"Not before you answer my question." In three strides, George was beside her, slamming his palm against the door and holding it shut, his eyes blazing as he glared down at his daughter. "What events? And what *deserving* people?"

Although Breanna was clearly unnerved by the vehemence of his response, she didn't cower, nor did she evade the question. "Stacie's beginning a new life with a new husband here in England, the country she loves but spent ten years away from. If those aren't life-altering events, I don't know what is. I realize you don't feel about her as I do, but I happen to think Stacie is wonderful. She and Lord Sheldrake deserve a long and happy future together." Breanna drew a slow, shaky breath. "Now please take your arm away and let me pass. I'd like to go upstairs and rest."

"In a minute," George ground out from between clenched teeth. He grabbed her arm, his stare probing hers with seething intensity. "And don't bother shouting for the servants. I don't intend to thrash you—not this time. But I *do* intend to get an answer. You say you were referring to your cousin's future, her right to be happy. Let's say I accept that. But I *don't* accept that ludicrous explanation about your comment regarding fate." His grip tightened. "What do you know that I don't?"

"Nothing." Breanna shook herself free, wearing that same determined look she'd worn when she aimed her pistol at him. "You know everything I do, and you have for far longer than I. But knowing and accepting are two different things."

"Knowing and accepting what?" George shouted, abandoning his last filaments of control.

"Just what I said." Breanna raised her chin, twin spots of color staining her cheeks. "That the right people belong together. Like Stacie and Lord Sheldrake." A pointed pause. "And Uncle Henry and Aunt Anne."

George went rigid, his air expelling in a hiss. Anne? What did his daughter know about Anne?

"I might have been a child, but even I could see how much in love she and Uncle Henry were," Breanna supplied. "Your bitterness was wasted. Aunt Anne cared only for her husband, just as Lord Sheldrake cares only for Stacie." An astute look. "Or is that repetition of history exactly what's bothering you so much?"

Fury exploded in George's skull.

"And *I'm* getting what I deserve?" he bellowed, grabbing Breanna's shoulders, shaking her violently, his fingers biting into her flesh until she whimpered. *"I'm getting what I deserve?"* He flung her away from him, knowing that in another minute, he'd beat her so viciously, he'd ensure his own undoing. "Get out of here!" he thundered, wrenching open the door and shoving Breanna halfway across the hall. "Get out of my sight!"

He slammed the door in her wake, his entire body shaking with the force of his rage. That little bitch Anastasia had actually told the entire story to Breanna. It's the only way his daughter could have found out. Which meant that Anne, the faithless trollop, had confided the whole history of their lives to the child she should have had with him, but had given Henry instead.

Muttering an oath, George crossed over and sloshed a drink into his goblet. On the verge of tossing it down in a few hard gulps, he slammed it onto the sideboard and thrust it away. *No,* he ordered himself, eyeing his trembling hands. *I'm already out of control. I can't compound it by getting drunk.*

He gripped the edge of the sideboard, determined to stay, if not rational, then sober—sober enough to ponder all Breanna had just said.

And all she hadn't said.

Had she really told him all she knew? Or had that allusion to his getting what he deserved encompassed more than just her assessment of his bitterness, his solitary life? Had Anastasia confided in her cousin, told her she was close to exposing him as a culprit, a thief—or worse? Had she told her about Bates's visit to his office, wondered what urgent business a magistrate might have with Colby and Sons? Had she found something suspicious in his files—something she couldn't yet prove? Had she noticed anything out of the ordinary about his bills from Lyman and the few other shippers he had special financial arrangements with?

Was it even worse than that? Had she actually managed to fit together enough pieces to deduce what was *really* being transported to the Continent?

And what the hell had Breanna meant about the life-altering events Anastasia had to look forward to after her wedding? Oh, she'd explained it away nicely with that drivel about her cousin becoming a bride, starting a whole new life. But George sensed there was more—a lot more.

Icy fear prickled up his spine.

Could Lyman be right? Could Anastasia be with child? Could *that* have been what Breanna was alluding to? Had Anastasia divulged that to her, then sworn her to secrecy? Was his wretched niece giving Sheldrake a child? Is that why she'd run off, yet remained in England?

No. Dammit, no. If she was pregnant, she'd have gone straight to Sheldrake.

Maybe she had.

Not according to Breanna.

But Breanna wouldn't admit such a truth—not if it meant betraying her cousin.

Still, Sheldrake was so bloody noble. If Anastasia had gone to him, told him she was carrying his child, it would have been Gretna Green he'd be driving to today, not Medford Manor.

So where did Damen Lockewood fit into all this? What did he know, about Anastasia, about the illegal activities going on at Colby and Sons? How involved in Anastasia's investigation was he? And what life-altering results might have resulted from this liaison of theirs?

All the unanswered questions led back to Sheldrake. As did George's future. Because the minute Anastasia showed up on the marquess's doorstep, either with the news that she was carrying his child or with proof of her uncle's guilt, George's hopes, and his life, would be over.

Which meant one thing: he had to get to Anastasia before she got to Sheldrake.

And when he did . . .

When he did—what?

A better question would be how, he berated himself. *How do I find her? How do I get rid of her when I do—especially if the time frame on Rouge's requirement has elapsed?*

George scowled at the sideboard, ran his forefinger around the rim of his goblet. He'd questioned dozens of people today: from Lyman, Bates, and Fenshaw, to a slew of innkeepers in both London and Kent, not a single one of whom had an Anastasia Colby—or any young woman matching her description—staying in their establishment. George had even gone into shops, into coffeehouses, and made inquiries. Nothing. And, as of his last check with Lyman, made late in the day, not one of the shipping company owner's contacts had turned up anything, nor had Anastasia's name appeared on a single ship's manifest.

The bloody chit had vanished into thin air.

Unless she was with Sheldrake.

According to the marquess's conversation with Breanna, she wasn't. Unless, of course, Breanna was lying. But she wouldn't be that stupid. Not when she knew bloody well he'd confirm the story with Sheldrake the very next chance he got.

So, if Anastasia wasn't with Sheldrake, where was she? Where had she disappeared to? And who was equipped to find her?

That question incited a flash of recall, and George's mind darted to the conversation he'd had—the one about the professional assassin. Abruptly, he found himself considering the prospect.

A hired killer; one who'd hunt Anastasia down and end her miserable life.

It sounded more enticing by the minute—and more necessary.

Of course, it would mean forfeiting Rouge's money, but that was a moot point anyway, since if Anastasia didn't surface, there would be no fifty-thousand-pound compensation. Besides, perhaps a suitable substitute really could be found. He still had some time.

But not if Anastasia incriminated him.

Which she couldn't if she were dead.

With her demise, the threat to his freedom would be gone, Henry's inheritance would be his.

And hell, the bitch would be gone forever.

Wouldn't that be divine justice, Anne, George mused sardonically. *Destroying the one person you loved even more than you did Henry. Killing off Henry's legacy, his sole heir. Marrying Breanna off to Sheldrake, and having the Colby name to myself. Savoring the sheer joy of knowing I do.*

On that thought, George stalked over to his desk, dragging open the drawer and shoving everything aside until he found the miniature portrait. He glared down at Anne's likeness, loathing her with every fiber of his being, wishing he had her in front of him, alive and well, just so he could choke her to death with his bare hands.

Savagely, he flung the portrait across the room, watched it strike the wall and topple to the carpet, not giving a damn that its clutter upset the room's perfect sense of order. Fine. Anne was dead. Perhaps it was time he accepted it.

Perhaps it was also time for Anastasia to join her.

19

❧

*I*t was ten minutes past midnight.

Breanna shoved in her last hairpin, then tugged on the cap Wells had given her, relieved to see it was deep enough to cover all her hair, its brim reaching halfway down her forehead.

Excellent. She pivoted in front of the looking glass, grinning at the image she made. If someone didn't plant himself directly before her, they'd think she was a scrawny but wholly realistic sailor or workman.

Mentally, she reviewed what was left to do.

Her bed.

She crossed over, rearranging the bedcovers and stuffing the pillows beneath it until it looked as if someone was not only there, but deeply asleep. That way, if her maid should check on her, all would seem normal.

With a satisfied nod, Breanna completed the final detail of her attire. She slid open the nightstand drawer and extracted the pistol, shoving it into the pocket of her coat. Now she was ready.

Twelve fifteen. Almost time.

She wandered about the room, running her fingertips over her porcelain figures and reflecting back over the cryptic war of words she'd had with her father—a war that had ended with him exploding in a manner so irrational that it made her wonder if he'd truly gone over the edge. The enmity in his eyes, the trembling fury in his voice, the frenzied way he'd thrown her out . . . Even now Breanna shuddered.

Maybe she'd pushed him too far. She'd sensed his surprise and his anger when she freely offered him information on Stacie and Damen's feelings for each other. Clearly, he'd expected her to lie. Which also meant he had no recollection of what he'd blurted out yesterday while in a drunken rage—the reference to Stacie as Damen's partner in bed. If he'd recalled saying it, he would have known why she'd called his bluff, given him the truth she already knew he possessed.

But the rest of what she'd said to him . . .

Breanna frowned, unconsciously picking up the figure of the two little girls, holding it tightly in her hands. She'd known she would provoke him with that reference to people getting what they deserve. But she hadn't been able to restrain herself. It had been a stupid thing to say—she was fully aware that she'd made him suspicious of how much she knew. Nevertheless, she couldn't regret it. She hated him for what he was doing, and in some small way, she needed him to know that.

However, his control had snapped when she mentioned fate putting the right people together. She hadn't planned on telling him she knew about Aunt Anne; that had just slipped out in the heat of anger. Still, even she had never anticipated the intensity of his rage.

Well, it was too late now for regrets. She couldn't retract her words even if she wanted to. Whatever her father believed, however furious he was, the damage was done, the die cast.

As for his reaction to her statement about life-altering events, obviously he was worried about how Stacie's future would affect his. She'd be marrying Damen, joining her life with his . . .

Having his children.

Breanna's head shot up, the realization accosting her. Of course. *That's* what her father's fears stemmed from. He knew Stacie and Damen were intimately involved. He was probably terrified that she was pregnant. In his mind, that would explain why she'd run off.

It would also explain his absolute determination to find her. To find her and rid himself of her—especially if she was also carrying a child he wanted gone, its conception undiscovered. She could almost imagine her father's thoughts: if he shipped Anastasia off to Rouge quickly enough, he could pass this child off on another man and no one would ever be the wiser. But if he waited too long . . .

A surge of fear shot through Breanna. Her father's panic was escalating. He stood to lose more and more with each passing day. Lord only knew what lengths he would go to to find Stacie and transport her to Rouge.

She had to stop him.

Biting her lip, Breanna replaced the porcelain figure on her bureau, pausing only long enough to caress the edge of the silver coin, which was gently nudged in its slot between the little girls and the flowers. "Help me, Grandfather," she whispered aloud. "Help me find the strength to do what I must. And please—help Stacie."

She turned away from her bureau, dashed away the moisture from her lashes.

Her glance fell on the clock.

Twelve twenty-five. Time to act.

Savoring the reassuring weight of the pistol in her coat and her grandfather's presence in her heart, Breanna went to the door, eased it open.

The hallway was deserted.

She made her way to the landing, hiding in the alcove and listening for noises below—noises that would indicate her father's departure.

Three minutes later, she heard them.

Quick, purposeful strides—her father's—walked the length of the front hall to the entranceway. The door opened, then shut, its firm click echoing through the empty hallway.

Breanna counted to ten. Then, she scooted down the staircase and darted in the opposite direction, down the corridor that led to the manor's side door, and the eastern portion of the drive.

She glanced into her father's study as she ran by, shivering as she remembered the rage on his face when he'd shoved her out.

A shiny object near the threshold caught her eye.

Without the slightest notion why, Breanna stopped long enough to bend down and pick up the object. It turned out to be a small, ornate picture frame, one that housed a tiny portrait. The portrait was of a woman, one with delicate features, fair skin, and a cloud of honey brown hair.

At first glance, she thought it was her mother.

Instinct made her look more closely, and she realized her mistake in a flash.

It wasn't her mother. It was Aunt Anne.

Trepidation gripped Breanna's gut.

Her father had kept Aunt Anne's portrait all these years. Clearly, he'd been consumed for decades by a woman he adamantly believed should have been his.

But what really frightened her was that he'd chosen tonight to destroy it, as if he'd finally banished Aunt Anne from his life.

Just as he intended to banish Stacie.

Time was running out.

Stuffing the miniature into her pocket, Breanna took off at a tear, bolting down the hall and bursting out the side door.

Wells and the phaeton were waiting. Panting, Breanna climbed into the passenger seat, adjusting her cap and peering around the drive.

Silently, Wells pointed, indicating that her father's carriage was nearing the gates.

Breanna nodded.

They waited only until George's phaeton had turned the corner, disappeared from view.

Then Wells slapped the reins.

* * *

Damen's contacts were as good as their word.

By 1 A.M., they'd compiled and delivered personal details on every one of the five men—his four bank officers and Graff—who had access to the private offices at the House of Lockewood.

Proust brought the final papers to the sitting room, where Damen and Anastasia were already poring over what they'd received.

"That's the last of what you requested, sir," Proust announced.

"Thank you, Proust." Damen glanced at the grandfather clock, which heralded the hour as ten past one. "Go to bed. Anastasia and I can manage from here."

"Very good, sir." The valet bowed and took his leave.

"I see absolutely nothing incriminating about Booth," Stacie murmured. She was curled up on the settee, papers strewn all around her, and she frowned as she read and reread the pages on Booth. "He lives a simple life, doesn't gamble or attend parties, and resides in a modest flat several blocks from the bank. Even his savings account is adequate but not huge, although I doubt this snake would be stupid enough to deposit his illegal earnings in your bank."

"Probably not." Damen crossed over, sank into the armchair beside Anastasia. "However, you'd be surprised how arrogant some people become when they feel they've outsmarted the world. They become lax, make careless mistakes. I see it every day in business." He peered over Stacie's shoulder. "In Booth's case, though, I think we're barking up the wrong tree. I've reviewed everything three times, and I see nothing to label him as anything but a quiet, honest man."

With a frustrated sigh, Anastasia tossed the pages aside. "We've also reviewed the pages on Valldale and Lockhorn. They, too, appear to be as innocent as babes. Which means that all we have left are Graff and Cunnings. Both of whom have been with you longer than any of the others. Both of whom have handled your confidential papers for nearly a decade."

"All the more reason we have to investigate them." A muscle worked in Damen's jaw as he tore the seal of the newly delivered envelope. "I can't let sentiment interfere with learning the truth."

"Damen, I can't imagine . . ." Stacie broke off, waving away his oncoming rebuttal. "I know. We have to be sure. Fine. Let's be sure. But I'm beginning to wonder if this is all a waste of time."

"Someone told George about us. Someone is corresponding with Rouge. If these papers don't tell us who that someone is, we'll find another way. But I want that son of a bitch stopped."

Anastasia heard the pain in his voice, and she put aside her doubts, aching for what this part of the investigation was doing to him. "I love you," she said quietly, reaching out to caress his forearm.

Damen looked up, the tension on his face softening, although the fiercely protective light in his eyes seemed to intensify rather than diminish. "And I love you. I don't think you realize how much." He caught her palm, brought it to his lips. "I want my ring on your finger," he said fervently. "I want to flourish you before the world as my wife. I want my child growing inside you. And I mean to make all those wants realities the minute you're safe and those bastards are in Newgate. I intend to move heaven and earth to see that that happens."

Anastasia's fingertips caressed his jaw. "I hope you realize something, Lord Sheldrake," she murmured in a watery tone. "Brilliant as you are, some things are not even in your control."

"Such as?"

"Such as the last want you described." Her misty gaze met his. "It's very possible our child will decide not to wait for your permission to go ahead and be conceived. Especially if he's half as impatient as his mother." Anastasia's voice quavered. "Or *her* mother, as the case may be."

Damen put the envelope aside long enough to pull Stacie off the settee and drag her onto his lap. "That thought . . . the very possibility of you carrying my child . . ." His eyes darkened to a smoky gray, his hand tightened around the nape of her neck as he lowered his mouth to hers. "God, you don't know what it does to me."

"I think I do." She twined her arms around his neck.

"I love you," he breathed, burying his lips in hers. "And if I had my way I'd forget these bloody papers and carry you off to bed, create our first child. Tonight. This minute." A shuddering sigh, as he brought himself under control. "But I won't. Because I intend to have *all* those 'wants,' Stacie, not just one. And there's only one way that can happen."

"I know." Anastasia kissed him tenderly. Then, she leaned over, scooped up the envelope, and extracted the remaining papers. "Let's find him."

The pub was a forty-minute drive from Medford Manor, tucked off a dilapidated road in a village near Canterbury.

"As I suspected," Wells muttered, pulling the phaeton into a nearby alley, nestling it in the shadows between a carpenter shop and a blacksmith shop. "A shabby alehouse; one that's close enough to get to, but far enough—and crude enough—not to be recognized in."

"I see your point." Breanna peered about, tried to see around the corner. "Is Father already inside?"

A terse nod. "His phaeton is on the far side of the pub. I saw him leave it there and make his way inside."

"Good. Then we can follow." She began to descend.

"Wait." Wells stayed her with his hand. "Give the viscount an extra minute or two to get settled. I realize you're anxious. But he's not going to elude us, not at this point. And we certainly don't want to come face to face with him."

"You're right." Breanna hovered at the edge of her seat, poised and ready.

"Miss Breanna, maybe you should stay here while I . . ."

"Wells, I'm going in there with you," Breanna interrupted. "I came to find out who my father is meeting and what they have planned. And I'm not leaving until I do." She leaped lightly from the phaeton. "We've given him enough time. Let's go."

Wells alit as quickly as his less youthful bones would allow. Then, he walked around the phaeton, studying Breanna intently and ensuring, for the tenth time, that her identity and her gender were totally concealed. "I'll do the talking," he instructed. "I have only to remember to speak in a less refined manner. Whereas you'd have to do that *and* lower your voice to a much deeper pitch."

"I can manage."

A troubled frown creased Wells's forehead. "Miss Breanna," he said unsteadily. "If anything should happen to you, your grandfather would never forgive me." A deep swallow. "I would never forgive myself."

"Nothing will happen to me, Wells." Breanna squeezed his arm. "I promise. As for Grandfather, he's with us. I can feel his presence. Besides," she added, trying to soothe Wells's misgivings. "We'll fit right in. We both look like common workingmen." She patted the worn sleeve of his coat. "And our shillings will qualify us as patrons."

Accepting, however uneasily, her unwavering decision, Wells nodded. Together, they strolled out of the alley and toward the pub.

"We've got to act natural, as if we're used to frequenting alehouses," Breanna instructed. "The less attention we draw to ourselves, the better. We'll find Father, sit as near to him and his colleague as we dare. And remember . . ." She tapped her pocket. "If necessary, I have my pistol."

The butler's lips thinned into a grim line. "I haven't forgotten. I only pray you won't have to use it."

The pub was smoky and dim, the latter of which Breanna was thankful for. She scanned the room, scrutinizing the darkest corners first—the tables where it made the most sense for anyone trying to avoid detection to sit.

Sure enough. There he was. He and another man, whose back was turned toward them.

Silently, Breanna nudged Wells, jerking her chin in that direction so he could follow her gaze.

Wells's eyes narrowed as he saw the viscount and his associate, and he pointed to a table just beside theirs—one that was equally concealed by darkness, but that was close enough to attempt eavesdropping.

Pausing only to order two ales—which they paid for at the counter to avoid any immediate interruptions—Wells and Breanna carried their tankards to the table, lowering themselves to the rickety stools.

"You're sure Sheldrake acted normal? He didn't slip off during the day or receive any suspicious missives?"

It was her father's voice, audible even over the thrum of voices, clanking of glasses, and occasional bursts of raucous laughter.

Breanna leaned closer, listening for the reply.

"Perfectly normal. And the only time he slipped off was to go to your house. I'm telling you, he thinks she's on her way to the States. Whatever your niece is doing, she's doing it alone. Or with your daughter."

Clenching her teeth, Breanna stifled the anger that rose inside her.

She knew that other voice. And so did Damen. He knew it well.

"Dammit."

Damen uttered the word in a hiss of disbelief, his finger tracing the number of purchases listed on the page he was reading: jewelry, clothing—all bought over the past several months. In addition, there was a large quantity of food purchased and people hired—extra footmen, a cook, maids, a trio of musicians—for an extravagant party that had been held a fortnight ago at a private house. The house, whose address Damen had never before seen or heard mention of, was the property of the same man who'd paid for the party, a fact that was verified by the attached documents.

In short, John Cunnings was spending more than ten times what he was earning.

He was also conducting extra business with one of the House of Lockewood's couriers—business the courier believed to be sanctioned by the bank but which, upon closer investigation by Damen's contacts, showed no bank authorization whatsoever. And that business involved the delivery of messages to and from Medford Manor.

"Oh, Damen." Anastasia lifted her head, her stunned eyes meeting Damen's. "I can't believe this."

"Cunnings." Damen dragged both hands through his hair. "Of all people." A bitter laugh. "My senior officer, the man in charge of all my overseas investments. He's been with the House of Lockewood since before my father died, and he was by my side from the day I took over. I considered him to be my right-hand man, my friend. Yet it appears I don't even know him."

Anastasia interlaced her fingers with Damen's. "To some people, money means more than anything, including friendship and integrity," she reminded him softly. "I know that's foreign to you, as it is to me. But just look at Uncle George. Look at the extremes he's willing to go to for wealth and position."

"Yes. George." Damen's jaw set. "I wonder how deeply involved Cunnings is in his sick scheme. Is he just George's spy, his connection to the fastest courier? Or is he fully aware of the cargo George deals with? Worse, is he getting paid to help find you, ship you off on the next vessel to Rouge?"

"I don't know. But we'll have to . . ." Anastasia broke off, an odd expression crossing her face.

"What is it?" Damen asked.

"I'm not sure." She pressed her lips together, shifting restlessly on Damen's lap. "But I have the strangest feeling something's happening. Something that involves Breanna."

"You think she's in danger?"

Contemplating that possibility, Anastasia frowned, slowly shook her head. "No. At least I don't think so. I don't feel panicked. I feel . . . fidgety." Her gaze met Damen's. "Whatever it is, it won't be long now. My instincts tell me that this whole nightmare is beginning to unravel."

In the alehouse, Cunnings straddled his stool, lighting a cheroot and eyeing George warily. "Medford, isn't it time you told me what's going on? I know you want Sheldrake to marry your daughter. You've been doing everything you can to keep him and your niece apart. Well, now she's gone. So why aren't you celebrating?"

"Because I don't think she's gone." George's laugh was bitter. "And because 'gone' is no longer good enough."

"You're talking about your brother's inheritance."

"I'm talking about all of it: the inheritance, the company, Sheldrake. Everything. But I can't get my hands on those things as long as Anastasia's missing."

Cunnings brought the cheroot to his lips, inhaled. "I thought you had a plan."

"I did."

"But you need your niece for that plan."

"Exactly."

Cunnings took a swallow of ale. "She'd have to be dead for you to get any of what you want—including Sheldrake, at this point. I told you, he's head over heels in love with her."

George stared at his clenched hands. "If my plan had worked, the world would have believed she was dead."

"Where *would* she have been?"

"On a ship. En route to the Continent."

One of Cunnings's brows rose. "To Rouge?"

"Yes."

A low whistle. "That sounds like a damned good plan. How much were you getting paid?"

"It doesn't matter." George shoved aside his untouched tankard of ale, glaring at Cunnings. "What matters is, Anastasia's gone. I *know* she's still in England—although where, I haven't an inkling."

"And if she reappears—without your being able to grab her before she gets to Sheldrake, ship her off to Rouge—then your plan is a thing of the past. As, given your current financial situation, are you." Cunnings inclined his head. "Have you considered sending a substitute? Or is Rouge demanding only Anastasia?"

"What Rouge is demanding is a well-bred young woman who's chaste, beautiful, and highborn. And I've got five days to deliver her."

"Really." Cunnings stabbed out his cheroot. "Let me look over the bank's client list. Maybe we'll get lucky and find a lady we can send in Anastasia's place—someone who fits Rouge's specifications, *and* who won't be missed. How would that be? Would it be worth ten percent of whatever Rouge is paying you?"

"Fine. Fine." Whereas yesterday George would have jumped at that opportunity, today he was more preoccupied with finding Anastasia and eliminating her—permanently. "But first we deal with the problem of Anastasia. Which brings me to the other business we have to discuss tonight." He gripped the edge of the table, leaning forward to regard Cunnings intently. "That associate of yours—the one you mentioned last time—how good is he at tracking people down?"

Cunnings raised his chin, met George's stare head-on. "There's no one better."

"So he'll find her."

"No matter where she's hiding, yes. He'll find her."

"And then?"

"He'll kill her."

At the next table, Breanna bit off a cry. She grabbed her tankard of ale and pressed it to her lips, taking an enormous gulp to quell her shock.

Kill her? He was going to kill *Stacie?*

The bitter taste of ale burned its way to her stomach, but she scarcely noticed it.

Her horrified stare met Wells's.

"I've known him for quite some time," Cunnings was continuing. "And I'm well aware of his accomplishments. He's an expert tracker and an even better shot." A meaningful pause. "He's also expensive. *Very* expensive."

George waved away the warning. "That doesn't concern me."

"It should. You owe me almost a thousand pounds, plus that ten per-cent if I find you another girl for Rouge. You owe a fortune to your col-leagues and your creditors. How the hell are you going to pay the kind of professional we're discussing? His fees are a lot higher than mine."

"You forget about Henry's inheritance." Triumph curved George's lips. "You yourself told me Anastasia only invested twenty-five thousand pounds of that money. That leaves over one hundred seventy-five thou-sand pounds for me. I can pay you double what I owe you, and I can pay your friend. I'll be a rich man, Cunnings. I'll also be sole owner of Colby and Sons. In fact, handle both these assignments successfully—ending Anastasia's life and securing another candidate for Rouge—and I'll give you the notoriety you've always craved. No more second place. You'll have a seat on my Board of Directors. Why, you'll be right up there with Sheldrake."

Cunnings tossed off the rest of his ale with a flourish. "I've served like a faithful dog at my rich master's feet all these years. And what has it gotten me? Nothing but an occasional pat on the head. I deserve better. And I'm going to *get* better. You've got yourself a deal, Medford. Give me a day. I'll dig through the bank's files and contact my associate. Your niece is as good as dead."

George's eyes gleamed. "When can I meet this gifted assassin?"

"You can't. He never meets with anyone—other than me." Cunnings shoved back his stool, aiming a pointed look at George. "Surely, given his line of work, you can understand his desire to stay anonymous."

"I suppose so." George nodded reluctantly. "How long will this take? It must happen quickly."

"If she's nearby, as you claim? A day. Two at the most. Relax. The next time you see Anastasia, it will be at her funeral."

Breanna's breath was coming in sharp rasps as she dashed down the alley and jumped into the phaeton.

She'd had to dig her nails into her thighs to keep from leaping up and lunging after Cunnings. But she had to stay level-headed—for Stacie's sake. So, she and Wells had nursed their drinks, lowering their heads as Cunnings walked past them and exited the alehouse. Not long after, her father had followed suit.

They'd given it another five minutes—enough time for George to reach his phaeton—before they acted.

Making their way outside, they'd peeked to the right, ensuring George was out of sight, before veering off to the left.

Wells hadn't come close to keeping up with her pace.

Breanna huddled in the phaeton, watching the elderly butler hurrying toward her, blood pounding in her veins. There was never a doubt what she had to do.

"Miss Breanna . . ." Wells hoisted himself into the phaeton. "Are you all right?"

The poor man was sheet-white, and Breanna lay her hand over his. "No," she replied honestly. "Are you?"

Mutely, he shook his head.

"Wells, listen to me. I've got to get to Stacie. I know how exhausted you are, not to mention you're reeling with shock. I'd never ask this of you, but . . ."

Jaw set, Wells snatched up the reins. "I assume Miss Stacie is with Lord Sheldrake?"

"Yes."

"I recall the address. We're on our way."

It was still dark when the phaeton sped up to Damen's Town house.

Inside the sitting room, Stacie's head shot up, and she gently disengaged herself from Damen's arms, climbing off the chair and trying not to awaken him. He'd nodded off less than an hour ago and, after the emotional upheaval of the night, she was determined not to disturb him until it became absolutely necessary.

It was about to become necessary.

She'd expected something significant to occur ever since that feeling had come over her. She didn't know what, but the very knowledge had precluded her from relaxing into sleep.

Well, she was about to get her answer.

She peered out the window, tensing as she saw two shoddily dressed men climb out of a phaeton and dart up the Town house stairs.

Whatever she'd been expecting, it hadn't been this.

"Damen . . ."

He was awake and beside her before she'd finished uttering his name. His jaw clenched as he scrutinized their two surprise visitors. "Who the hell . . . ?"

"You don't know them, then?"

"No. I don't know who they are or what they want. But I'm sure as hell going to find out." He stalked over to the small corner desk, unlocked the top drawer, and extracted a pistol. Clutching the weapon in his hand, he headed off, pausing only to glare at Stacie. "Stay here—out of sight," he ordered. "These men might work for your uncle."

She opened her mouth to protest, then thought better of it. "All right. But be careful."

"I will."

Stacie listened as Damen strode down the hall and yanked open the front door. She couldn't keep herself from venturing as far as the sitting room threshold, peeking around the corner to watch.

"Who are you?" Damen was demanding. He flourished his pistol, blocking the doorway, and whoever was standing at it. "What are you doing here at this hour?"

"Damen." Breanna's voice was muffled but urgent. "It's us."

20

Stacie was across the threshold and down the hall in a heartbeat.

"Breanna!" She grabbed her cousin's arms, pulling her into the entranceway, and staring in amazement as she assessed Breanna's unexpected attire. Her gaze shifted to the tall, shabbily dressed man behind her, and her eyes widened. "Wells? Is that you?"

"Yes, Miss Stacie. Indeed it is."

"Why on earth are you dressed like that?"

It was Breanna who replied. "We followed Father to his meeting place. We saw and heard everything: who he met, what they talked about—oh, Stacie . . ." She stared at her hands, realized they were still shaking.

"You . . . what?" Anastasia gasped. "Are you all right?"

"Were you followed?" Damen interrupted to demand. "Is anyone after you?"

"No, we weren't followed and yes, we're fine." A pained pause. "Physically."

Damen leaned past them, peering suspiciously out into the night and seeing nothing but a deserted street. "Let's not take any chances. Don't stay out in the open. Come in." He gestured for Wells to enter, shutting the door behind him, then leading the way to the sitting room. "I'll pour you each a drink. You look as if you've seen a ghost."

"More like a demon," Anastasia muttered. "A demon named Cunnings."

"You know?" Breanna's head jerked up as she sank into a chair.

Anastasia nodded, glancing over at Damen, who was pouring drinks at the sideboard.

"So, it really is Cunnings." He handed a glass of Madeira to Breanna, then one to Wells, a bitter scowl darkening his face. "Yes, we knew. My contacts uncovered some ugly facts about him. But I suppose I needed confirmation."

"You have it." Breanna tugged off her cap, her burnished tresses, for the first time, a bit disheveled. "He's my father's informant. That, and a great deal more."

Anastasia was too unsettled to sit still. She paced about the sitting room, looking from Breanna to Wells, a thousand questions crowding her mind, clamoring to be asked.

Her curiosity was diverted when she saw Wells lean his head wearily against the wall, looking so utterly depleted that it broke her heart.

"You're spent, my friend," she said softly, walking over and guiding him into a cushioned armchair. "You need rest."

"I'll get rest," he stated flatly, taking a healthy swallow of his drink. "*After* all this is resolved. Don't worry about me, Miss Stacie. I'm hardier than I look."

"Wells was heroic tonight," Breanna declared. "I don't know how I would have managed without him."

"Tell us what happened. How did you come to follow Uncle George? What did you overhear?" Stacie began blurting out her stream of questions.

Quickly, Breanna filled Stacie and Damen in on the talk she'd had with her father, on the plan she and Wells had conjured up, and on where it had taken them.

"So you actually saw Uncle George and Mr. Cunnings together?"

"Oh, we more than saw them," Breanna affirmed. "We sat at the table next to them. We eavesdropped on their entire conversation." She took an unsteady sip of Madeira, then lifted her chin, met Stacie's intent gaze. "Stacie, there's no easy way to tell you this. So, I'm not even going to try to soften the blow. Father's hiring an assassin. He means to have you killed."

A ponderous silence filled the room.

"Killed," Anastasia repeated woodenly—although her surprise was less acute than Breanna's. Any man who'd sell his niece—or any woman, for that matter—as a whore, was capable of anything. "What about Rouge? What happened to Uncle George's plan to export me?"

"Apparently, Father's fear that you're closing in on him, figuring out the full extent of his criminal activities, has overshadowed all else. He's convinced you're still in England. Probably to finish the investigation you began, and see him in prison. Either that, or . . ."

"Or?" Anastasia prompted.

"This is just a feeling on my part. But, judging from some of the things Father said to me, I suspect he's contemplating another reason you might have dropped out of sight—a reason that intimidates him almost as much as your plans to incriminate him."

"And what's that?"

"I think he's afraid you're with child—Damen's child. That would be almost as destructive to him as being found out. With the exception of prison, the rest of his sentence would be the same: he'd lose Uncle Henry's inheritance, control of Colby and Sons, and, of course, Damen. As for Rouge, Cunnings solved that problem for him."

"Cunnings did?" Damen echoed, a vein throbbing at his forehead. "How?"

"By making some adjustments to my father's original plan. He offered to find Father a substitute for Rouge—one of the bank's female clients who, as he put it, won't be missed. That way, Father can collect his huge fee *and* get his hands on those things he'd need Stacie dead to acquire."

"I don't believe I'm hearing this."

Breanna nodded bleakly. "I don't believe I'm saying it."

Damen rubbed the back of his neck, trying to come to terms with everything he was learning. "You said George is hiring an assassin. How is he managing that?"

"He's not." There was genuine pain in Breanna's eyes, spawned by the realization that she was about to deliver a cruel blow. "Cunnings is."

Shock jolted through Damen's body, and he recoiled from its impact. *"Cunnings?"*

"Yes. I'm sorry, Damen. But Cunnings is the one with this particular contact. Father instructed him to make the arrangements."

"How the hell is an officer at my bank acquainted with a paid killer?"

Breanna spread her arms helplessly. "He didn't say. In fact, he was very secretive about the matter. When Father asked to meet with this man, Cunnings said no, that this assassin would do business only through him."

A muscle was working furiously in Damen's jaw. "What's Cunnings getting in exchange? A huge amount of money?"

"Several thousand pounds, plus ten percent of whatever Rouge pays Father. Oh, and one thing more." Breanna swallowed. "A seat on the Board of Directors at Colby and Sons."

"Which Uncle George will have sole ownership of, if I'm eliminated." Twin spots of red tinged Anastasia's cheeks. "That monster will then have just what he wants, what he's always wanted—to triumph over Papa, and to wrest away everything Grandfather held dear: his company, his name, and everything good our family represents."

"Not to mention acquiring Uncle Henry's inheritance," Breanna reminded her. "And Damen, who Father assumes will seek solace in my arms once you're gone." A bitter gleam flashed in her eyes. "Does that course of events sound familiar?"

"It's the path he took when he married your mother," Anastasia supplied, gripping the folds of her gown as if by doing so she could stem her rage. "He's decided Damen will do the same: love a woman he can't have, and marry her closest replica."

"Exactly. Father all but admitted that to me during our argument tonight. Which reminds me . . ." Breanna shoved her hand into her pocket, extracted the miniature portrait. Its frame was somewhat mangled, but the image inside remained clear as day. "I found this in Father's study after he left tonight. He'd obviously hurled it at the wall." She stretched out her arm, offered the portrait to Stacie. "I believe it's self-explanatory."

Stacie took it, her eyes widening as she recognized the likeness. "Mama," she murmured, angling the picture for inspection. "He's kept a portrait of her all these years?"

"And destroyed it the very day he decided to destroy you."

"I can't listen to this another minute." Damen strode over, refilled his drink. "Not without riding to Medford Manor and choking that son of a bitch with my bare hands." He sucked in his breath, then released it, fighting for the restraint necessary to resolve things. "However, we still have one problem—the same problem we've had since the onset. Proof. Or lack thereof. What concrete evidence, other than hearsay, do we really have against George?"

"I believe we can tie the viscount to Mr. Cunnings," Wells put in, his color somewhat restored from the Madeira. "I gave Miss Breanna the address of the courier who delivers messages between the two of them. Surely that will help."

"Thank you, Wells," Damen replied, staring broodingly into his goblet. "Unfortunately, it's not enough. Oh, I have more than enough proof that Cunnings is involved in personal business with George." He gestured toward the pile of papers on the end table. "My contacts supplied me with dates and times when that courier ran personal deliveries back and forth between Medford Manor and my bank—at Cunnings's authorization. And Cunnings has been living like a prince, buying property, jewelry for women, you name it."

Damen's hands balled into fists. "The problem is, we still haven't gotten hold of documents that directly incriminate George. Nor have we closed in on any of his colleagues to the point where we could squeeze a confession out of them, one that would implicate George, as well. If we went to Bow Street, had them seize George, he'd slip right through our fingers. They'd have only our testimony, and a few suspicious actions, to go on. Doubtless, George would have Bates exert some judicial influence—Bates, who's nearly as crooked as he is. After which, George would walk out a free man."

"What if we had a confession?" Anastasia interrupted. "A confession made directly to the authorities?"

Three pairs of eyes riveted to her.

"Stacie, have you lost your mind?" Breanna responded. "Father would never confess—not when he's sober and never to the authorities."

"He might. If he didn't know he was confessing."

"You've lost me." Breanna inclined her head quizzically in Damen's direction. "Do you know anything about this?"

A dark scowl. "Only that I'm not going to like it." He set down his drink, folded his arms across his chest, and leveled his stare at Anastasia. "Let's hear your plan. And Stacie—it had better not involve you."

Her chin jutted up. "I'm already at risk, Damen. As of tomorrow, a hired assassin will be out hunting me down. How long do you think I can hide in your Town house?" She rubbed her palms together, growing more determined the more she contemplated her plan. "Breanna, did Cunnings say anything to Uncle George implying Damen played a part in my disappearance?"

"Cunnings is convinced that Damen isn't involved. He's satisfied that Damen believes you're really on your way to the States."

"Excellent. I suspected as much, given Damen's acting performance today at the bank. So whether I dropped out of sight because I'm pregnant with Damen's child or because I'm close to exposing Uncle George as a criminal, he thinks I haven't yet gone to Damen with the news."

Still baffled, Breanna nodded.

"What if I found the evidence I was looking for? What if I got hold of exactly what it would take to throw Uncle George into prison?" A smile curved Anastasia's lips. "I'd share that proof with Damen immediately, wouldn't I?"

"But we don't have any proof."

"Your father doesn't know that."

Breanna's brows drew together. "Do you want me to plant a seed in Father's mind?"

"Absolutely not. He'd never believe you. Uncle George already knows your loyalty lies with me. No, we'll let Cunnings take care of that for us."

"How?"

"That's easy." Anastasia grinned. "Remember our pact. I'll go to the bank in the morning, pretending to be you. I'll insist on seeing Damen, alone, in his private office. Mr. Cunnings will be unbearably curious about the nature of my visit—pardon me, *Breanna's* visit. Damen and I will make sure he overhears every word of our private talk. I'll tell Damen that Anastasia contacted me, saying she found the evidence she was searching for, but that she was reluctant to deliver it to Bow Street without first getting my—Breanna's—permission. After all, turning over this evidence would mean sending Breanna's father to prison, and thereby tainting the Colby name, neither of which Anastasia felt right doing without securing Breanna's consent first. Being the moral person Breanna is, she'll fully support Anastasia's decision once she sees the evidence."

Stacie turned to Damen. "Damen, you'll gallantly refuse to have Breanna meet Anastasia alone. You'll arrange to be there with her when she reads Stacie's evidence—which will be, say, at the docks, at ten o'clock that night. You'll tell Breanna that, once this damning proof is in your hands, *you'll* be the one to turn it over to the authorities, sparing both her and Anastasia any potential risk. Cunnings will hear this entire plan. He'll rush off to contact Uncle George, alerting him to the fact that he'd better intercept whatever evidence Anastasia has before she shares it with you and Breanna—and you present it to the authorities. Uncle George will panic. He'll arrive at the docks at nine-fifty P.M.—he's *always* prompt, and this time he'll want to be early so, hopefully, he can grab Anastasia, destroying her and her proof before you and Breanna even lay eyes on it. Sure enough, you both won't have arrived yet, giving Uncle George just the advantage he needs. When I show up, as myself, we'll have a little scene. I'll provoke him into admitting what he's done. It shouldn't be hard, given his high opinion of himself and the fact that he believes we're alone."

A triumphant smile lit Stacie's face. "What Uncle George won't know is that Bow Street has been alerted to the situation, and has men hiding behind the warehouses and listening to every word that's spoken. Once he's confessed, they can take him away. Now, are we all ready to enact my plan?"

"Absolutely not." Damen sliced the air with his palm. "Your plan neglects to take into account a few minor details. Such as, what if this assassin Cunnings hires is watching the bank when *Breanna* visits? What if he figures out it's you, not she, who's calling on me, and he decides to carry out his job then and there? He's a professional killer, Stacie; there's no guarantee you can fool him."

"We don't have to try." Breanna's eyes were glittering precisely like Anastasia's. "Stacie will stay here, in your home, safe. *I'll* come to the bank."

"And what will you tell your father?" Stacie demanded, hands on hips. "Before he thrashes you, that is?"

"I'll tell him nothing. I won't see him. I'll spend the remainder of the night right here. Then, I'll borrow one of your gowns, take our phaeton, and ride to the bank as soon as it opens."

Anastasia's jaw dropped. "And how will you explain your absence at Medford Manor?"

"I won't have to." Breanna's lips curved, and she explained to them how she'd stuffed her bed to make it look slept in. "My lady's maid will peek in, and think I'm still asleep. By the time she realizes her mistake, I'll have finished my business in London and be on my way home. Given the speed of your courier—Cunnings's courier—Father will have received his warning message before I return, so he'll already know where I've been. Beating me for it would be counterproductive: it would only alert me to the fact that he's aware of my plan, which would give me the opportunity to warn Stacie. So he'll save my whipping for *after* he deals with her." Breanna's smile widened. "But, as we all know, there won't be any 'after' for Father. He'll be en route to Newgate."

"And if he brings a weapon?" Damen demanded.

"Father's no marksman," Breanna assured him. "I'm a far more accurate shot than he is. He's also a coward. That's why he's paying an assassin to do his dirty work, rather than taking care of things himself. When it comes to violence, Father uses his fists, not a pistol."

"Which brings me back to the assassin." Damen's scowl deepened. "Obviously, Cunnings will alert him to our plan at the same time he alerts George. He'll respond by being right there at the docks waiting for Stacie to show up."

"I'm sure he will be," Anastasia concurred. "But Cunnings will also instruct him not to shoot me until Uncle George gets the written evidence he's there to collect. So I'll be safe until that happens. And once this assassin sees Bow Street swarming about, I doubt he'll rush forward, pistol aimed and ready."

"It's bloody risky," Damen said, with a hard shake of his head. "I don't like it."

"You'll be there to safeguard me," Anastasia reminded him. "Bring your own pistol, if it makes you feel better. Give me one, as well. But this is the only way we're going to catch Uncle George. Before he makes sure I'm . . ." She wet her lips, not eager to finish her own sentence.

"Dammit," Damen bit out, only too well aware of Stacie's implication, and the fact that she was right.

"What about Wells?" Anastasia suddenly realized aloud. "He's been at his post every morning for three decades. If he and Breanna stay here overnight, he'll be glaringly absent at dawn. That will make Uncle George suspicious."

"That's true." Damen rubbed his chin, considering the issue thoughtfully.

"I told the viscount I felt ill," Wells protested. "He won't be surprised if I'm not up and about at dawn."

"We can't take that chance," Damen replied, studying the tired but determined butler. "Listen to me," he continued gently. "Don't be stubborn. You're exhausted. You need some rest. And Stacie's right—you'd better be at the entranceway door tomorrow morning. Even if George believes you're ill, you can't be sure he won't check on you. If he does, and finds you missing, he'll most certainly become suspicious, especially since he knows full well how deeply you care for Anastasia and Breanna. That's a risk we can't take."

Seeing the butler's oncoming protest, Damen held up his palm, warded it off. "If you want to help us, go home. I'll arrange for an appropriate change of clothes. Then my driver will take you to Medford Manor. He'll use the closed carriage, so you can get a few hours' sleep on the way. It will be later than usual when you reach your post—which is understandable, given how ill you felt the night before—but the important thing is that you'll be there. Everything must seem in place."

"That's perfect," Breanna agreed. "If Wells goes home, I won't have to face Father until ten o'clock tomorrow night. I'll stay here, drive the phaeton to the bank, then return here, spending the rest of the day with Stacie. I'll fill her in on what happens at the bank, keep her inside and out of view—" A pointed, no-nonsense look at Stacie. "—until it's time for us to leave for our rendezvous at the docks. In the meantime, Wells can tell Father I left Medford Manor right after breakfast, took the phaeton, but mentioned nothing about where I was going. Once Father receives Cunnings's message, he'll know my destination, and why I didn't disclose it to Wells."

She gazed pleadingly at the butler, appealing to him in a way she knew would ensure he went home, got the rest he so desperately needed. "Please, Wells. You'd be sparing me Lord knows how severe an argument and how painful a beating. Do it for me."

The butler's protective instincts won out, just as Breanna knew they would. "Very well, Miss Breanna. If it will shield you and help Miss Stacie, I'll do as Lord Sheldrake asks." He rose, looking tenderly from one girl to the other. "I'll do my part," he assured them, his voice quavering a bit. "And then . . . I'll pray."

As always, the House of Lockewood opened its doors at 9 A.M.

And, as always, Cunnings was there at half after eight, doing his paperwork in preparation for the day.

His first client arrived promptly at nine.

A half hour later, their business together was completed.

Leaning back in his office chair, Cunnings nodded, satisfaction gleaming in his eyes. "Excellent. You'll take care of it, then."

A smug smile curved the lips of the man sitting on the opposite side of the desk. "For such an enormous sum and an even more enormous challenge? Of course."

"Good." Cunnings felt a surge of triumph, a premonition that, at long last, he was about to come into his own. "I've given you all the information I have. I realize it's not much, but . . ."

"It's all I need."

"I rather suspected as much." Cunnings rose, handing the man a sheet of paper. "By the way, here are the figures you requested. If you glance at them, you'll see . . ." His head snapped up as a din from the hallway accosted his ears.

"Please, Graff. Hurry. I left Medford Manor at the crack of dawn in order to get here this early. I must see Lord Sheldrake now—no matter who he's meeting with. My business simply won't wait."

It was Breanna Colby's voice, Cunnings realized. Clearly, she was standing just outside his closed office door, or rather, rushing by it. She sounded breathless, and terribly distressed.

"I alerted Lord Sheldrake to the urgency of your visit, my lady," Graff was reassuring her. "He's agreed to see you at once. I assure you, I'm walking as quickly as I can."

"Good. And please see that we're not disturbed."

Her voice moved in the direction of Damen's office, and Cunnings took an inadvertent step toward the door, wondering what the hell this was all about.

"That's Breanna Colby, Anastasia's cousin," he muttered, half to himself, half to his visitor. "I'd better find out why she sounds so flustered. Maybe she's heard from her cousin. Will you excuse me?"

"By all means. I'll wait here, in case there are developments I should know about."

"Good idea." Cunnings scooped up some paperwork. Then, he crossed over, opened his door, and wandered casually into the hall.

Graff was on his return trip, shaking his head in puzzlement as he headed back to his post.

"What was that commotion?" Cunnings inquired.

"Lady Breanna," Graff supplied. "She has some critical business to discuss with Lord Sheldrake." An exasperated sigh. "Women can be so excitable at times." He shrugged, continuing on his way until he disappeared from view.

Cunnings moved down the hall, pausing a few feet from Damen's office. He leaned against the wall, scanning his papers as if he were actually reading them, in the event someone walked by or Sheldrake abruptly emerged.

The marquess's door was shut nearly all the way, a slim crack being the only open space.

It was enough—not for observing, but definitely for eavesdropping.

"She's *here?* In England?" Sheldrake was asking incredulously.

"Yes," Breanna replied. "Apparently, she'd uncovered information that implicates Father in some horrible crimes. But she had no proof. So she pretended to leave the country, only to stay right here and gather the evidence she needs to send him to Newgate."

"I don't believe this." Sheldrake sounded badly shaken. "Is she all right? Did you see her?"

"She's fine. And, no, I didn't see her. She sent a messenger to Medford Manor late last night, instructed him to throw pebbles at my window until he got my attention. I was lucky. Father had gone out after midnight and Wells was feeling ill and had retired early. I slipped downstairs and met the messenger at the door. He gave me Stacie's note. Then, I sent him on his way, quickly, before Father could return and ask questions. No one saw him but me."

"Did Anastasia's note tell you where she's staying?"

"Only that she's somewhere in London. Her note said that knowing her exact whereabouts might put me in danger."

"Did she tell you what proof she had?"

"Not specifically. Just that it would shock me and strip Father of everything—including his freedom. So it must be despicable. In any case, Stacie insisted that I see it with my own eyes and decide what I want her to do. She won't turn the evidence over to the authorities without my permission." Breanna drew a shaky breath. "It is, after all, my father she'd be relegating to Newgate. Not to mention the scandal this entire affair would cause our family."

"Lord," Sheldrake muttered. "Whatever George did, it must be contemptible. Otherwise, Anastasia would never ask you to betray your own father."

"Exactly."

"What do you intend to do—or need I ask?"

"I'm going to support Stacie's decision," Breanna responded instantly. "Our grandfather would want nothing less. If Father is guilty of some horrible crime, he should be punished. The Colby name will survive, and ultimately prevail." A troubled pause. "But Damen, to be honest with you, I'm terrified of what Father will do to me if he finds out I'm involved. Despite my false show of bravado—waving that pistol around as I did—I'm truly afraid of the man. I don't know why I ran to you, but the truth is, I had nowhere else to turn."

"You did the right thing." Sheldrake's voice was taut with strain. "I'll help you. Tell me when and where Anastasia expects you to meet her."

"Tonight. At the London docks—the deserted southwest section nearest the Tower. At ten o'clock."

"Fine. I'll go with you."

"What?" Now Breanna sounded panicked. "But, she's expecting only *me*. If she sees someone else, she might bolt."

"Not if that someone is me. I love her, Breanna. Anastasia knows she can trust me." Sheldrake paused, blowing out his breath slowly, thoughtfully. "On the other hand, you have a point. Between the night and the fog, she'll see the silhouette of a man and, unless I have time to call out and let her know it's me, she'll take off. The best thing would be if we both went. You can coax her out, and I'll be there to lend my support—to both of you."

"And what about the evidence?"

"I'll take it directly to Bow Street. You and Anastasia will wait for me in my carriage. We won't venture back to Medford Manor until the authorities have arrested your father."

"After which we'll all be safe." Breanna emitted a shaky sigh. "I don't know how to thank you."

"No thanks are necessary." A hesitant pause. "I suggest you spend the day in Town. Feel free to use my house as your own. Shop, call on friends, do whatever you most enjoy. But don't ride back to Kent. The last thing you need is a confrontation with your father. Answering his questions was bad enough when you knew nothing. Now that you've actually heard from Anastasia, I'm not sure you'd be able to successfully lie about it. And if George should suspect . . ."

"Say no more," Breanna interrupted, an audible tremor in her voice. "I can't face Father. Not now, knowing what I know, planning what I've planned. I'll do just what you suggested—stay in Town, then go to your house until tonight's meeting." A rustle of material, alerting Cunnings to the fact that Breanna had risen, was heading for the door.

He edged back toward his office, head cocked as he listened to Sheldrake and Breanna's parting words.

"I'll see you tonight," she murmured.

"I'll be home in plenty of time," Sheldrake vowed. "We'll be at the docks promptly at ten."

Breanna opened the door, stepped into the hallway.

The area was deserted.

"How did it go?" Stacie pounced on Breanna the instant she walked into the Town house.

Her cousin grinned, slipping off her gloves as she strolled toward the sitting room. "Like a perfectly acted play."

"Cunnings was there?"

"He arrived at half after eight, just as Damen said he would. By the time I dashed into the bank, he was ensconced in his office with a client."

"You're sure he heard you?"

"Oh, he heard every word," Breanna stated confidently. "I began my speech when I was right outside Cunnings's office—the third door to the right, just as Damen instructed me. Poor Graff," she added, laughing. "He's never seen me so overwrought. I think he was torn between consoling me and choking me to death."

Anastasia's eyes sparkled. "It sounds like you were very convincing."

"Oh, I was. But then, so was Damen. Once Graff delivered me to his office—after which he darted off like a prisoner who'd been granted his freedom—both Damen and I played our parts superbly. At first, we waited."

"Three minutes, as planned?"

Breanna's brows lifted. "It only took two. We shut the door all but a crack, positioned ourselves near enough to be heard, and watched the outside wall. Less than thirty seconds later, we saw Cunnings's shadow hovering on the wall not ten feet from Damen's office. That's when I launched into a recounting of my dilemma."

"And Cunnings didn't budge?" Anastasia prodded, circling Breanna like an anxious parent. "The entire time you and Damen talked, he stayed outside and listened?"

"Up to the very last word, yes. In fact, I actually spent an exaggerated moment shaking out my skirts to give him enough time to get back to his office. When I emerged, he was gone."

"Wonderful," Anastasia breathed. "Then, by now, the note is on its way to Uncle George, and Damen is on his way to Bow Street."

"Yes, and a paid assassin is out combing the streets of London looking for you," Breanna reminded her, all humor vanishing.

Rather than terror, Anastasia felt a surge of impending victory, a sense that the end was in sight. "Yes, but he won't find me. Not until we want him to." Her eyes glittered with anticipation. "At which time, Bow Street will grab him."

"And if he spies them first and escapes?"

A careless shrug. "Then, after tonight, it's *he* who will be the hunted. With Uncle George in prison and Cunnings a cornered rat—pressured into revealing the names of his contacts—this assassin is all but captured."

Breanna nodded, trying hard to share Anastasia's optimistic appraisal.

Still, she thought, an uneasy prickle crawling up her spine. Gut instinct warned her it wouldn't be that simple.

21

❦

*I*t was nine forty-five.

George steered his phaeton through the last of the rutted roads that led to the docks, gripping the reins more tightly as he neared the end of his journey. The fog was too thick to see clearly, but he could smell the Thames, hear the screech of gulls circling overhead. He was trembling, whether with apprehension or relief that this would finally be over, he wasn't sure.

Cunnings's message had been terse and to the point. Anastasia would be here tonight, carrying with her some unknown proof that was damning enough to send him to Newgate. Cunnings had alerted the assassin, who would be there to give her a proper farewell, *after* she'd relinquished the evidence to George.

How Cunnings had learned about Anastasia's impending appearance was the infuriating part.

Breanna.

George's insides clenched with rage every time he contemplated the fact that it was *his daughter* Anastasia was meeting with, *his daughter* to whom Anastasia was turning over this proof.

His obedient little Breanna meant to betray him.

She actually intended to turn him over to Bow Street, relegate him to prison—and at her precious cousin's bidding.

Well, he'd deal with Breanna and her lack of loyalty later, after the proof was in his hands and Anastasia ceased to be a problem.

Then there was Sheldrake.

The fact that he was joining Breanna here tonight was the main reason George had arrived so early. It was imperative that Anastasia's evidence be destroyed before Sheldrake could see it. That was the only prayer George had of seeing his plan through, regaining all that was his, and still acquiring Sheldrake as a son-in-law. Oh, the marquess would never really trust him again, of that he was certain. But Damen Lockewood was a pragmatic man. And without proof, he wouldn't do anything to ruin George, not given the strong history that existed between their families. Nor would he allow whatever indiscretions George might or might not have committed to cloud his opinion of Breanna. After all, even if her father wasn't all Sheldrake had hoped, that was in no way Breanna's doing. She was as honorable as the day was long. Sheldrake knew that firsthand. He might not love Breanna, but he most certainly liked her. Moreover, despite Anastasia's intrusive presence hovering between them, he and Breanna had grown much closer these past weeks.

And they'd grow closer still as a result of Anastasia's tragic death. Why, within a few short months, Breanna would probably become Mrs. Damen Lockewood.

The very notion eased George's rage.

But not his trepidation.

He had to carry tonight off perfectly. He'd get the proof from Anastasia, hold it high over his head so the assassin could see it, then watch Anastasia take her last breath.

With any luck, he'd be gone by the time Sheldrake and Breanna arrived. If so, the marquess would never know he'd been here, much less that he was involved in Anastasia's shooting. As her uncle, he could grieve beside Sheldrake at her funeral. After which, the marquess would need some time to mourn her death—a period of bereavement Breanna could help him through.

If things happened that way, then everything could turn out just as he'd planned.

But if not, if Breanna and Sheldrake burst into view before he had time to bolt, he'd play the scene of a lifetime. He'd rush over to Anastasia's lifeless body, lament her untimely passing, caused by a smuggler's stray bullet. Hell, he'd shed real tears if he had to. Between those tears, he'd explain how Anastasia had summoned him, expressed her regret over being too impulsive, believing him guilty of trying to wrest away her inheritance, only to find she'd been wrong. The proof she'd been so sure was incriminating had turned out to be false.

It had been her intention, he'd claim, to offer him a formal apology at tonight's meeting with Breanna— a meeting she'd scheduled before she realized her mistake.

But now she was gone . . . and it was too late . . .

George's lips thinned into a grim line. No matter what happened here tonight, he had to convince Sheldrake or, at the very least, give him pause, make him contemplate the possibility of George's innocence. He *had* to.

Reaching the end of the road, George pulled the phaeton over and left it behind a warehouse.

He'd go the rest of the way by foot.

Warily, he headed toward the Thames, trying to see through the fog and make out the shape of a woman moving along the docks.

All was still.

Pebbles crunched under his feet, and the smell of the river grew stronger, the silence thicker.

The Tower of London was just on the other side of this section of warehouses, he thought, veering to his right. She had to be hiding near here somewhere.

He peered around the corner of the first building he reached, eyeing the deserted area beyond, strewn with empty bottles and a few scurrying rats.

"Breanna?" a tentative voice called. "You're early."

A slender shadow eased out of the shadows about twenty feet away from where George stood. She took a step, then halted when she saw the larger frame of her arrival. "Damen?" she tried. "Is that you?"

"Yes," George hissed back, his whisper too fleeting to be differentiated as his and not Sheldrake's.

"Where's Breanna?" Anastasia took a few more cautious steps in his direction.

It was enough.

"With Sheldrake, I presume," George replied in his normal tone. He lunged forward, grabbed Anastasia's arm. "What's the matter?" he bit out, seeing the shock register on her face. "Aren't you pleased to see your uncle?"

"What are you doing here?" she managed, struggling to free herself.

"You know the answer to that. I'm here to collect what's mine."

"I don't know what you're talking about."

"Stop lying, Anastasia." He dragged her to him, his eyes blazing with rage. "And don't play games with me. Whatever proof you've found, I want it. I want it *now.*"

"And then what?" Anastasia shot back, abandoning all pretense. "Will you throw me on the nearest ship to Calais, ship me off to Rouge?"

George started, but recovered himself quickly. "You are well-informed, aren't you?" He glared at her, loathing the rebellious glint in her eyes that refused to be extinguished, despite the fact that she was obviously afraid. "So bloody defiant. I pity the man Rouge would have sold you to."

"*Would have?*" Anastasia stopped struggling, went very still. "Does that mean you've reconsidered? That you're not going to sell me as a whore?"

A thoughtful pause. "Perhaps not. *If* you give me that proof you have." He glanced about, seeing no documents in her other hand. "Where is it?"

"You're frightened," Anastasia taunted softly. "I don't blame you. Selling women as chattel to warm the beds of strangers. Stealing from the company your father founded. Plotting to stage your niece's death so you could get her inheritance. I'd be frightened, too. Especially if that same niece had evidence of my crimes. Not to mention confessions by Lyman and Bates. Why, as we speak, both those men are signing statements incriminating you. Then again, what choice did they have? With proof that Lyman accepted illegal payments from you *and* that Bates supplied you with workhouse girls to export to the Continent as whores, your two colleagues were desperate to save their own skin. They happily turned you over to Bow Street in exchange for leniency."

"*Shut up!*" George shouted. His rage was spiraling out of control. He could feel it. "*Shut up and give me that proof!*"

"Why should I? I'm not stupid. Neither were Lyman and Bates. They realized that, as accomplices, their necks weren't pulled nearly as tight in the noose as yours is. You're the head of everything." Anastasia's smile was mocking. "As for their loyalty—it didn't extend as far as sacrificing their own freedom. Especially since their incentive to do so has worn a bit thin. Let me think—how long has it been since you paid them what they're owed?"

George drew back his arm, struck Anastasia across the face with such force that her head snapped back. "You lying bitch," he snarled. "Lyman and Bates would never confess. They're as involved with Rouge as I am."

"Not quite," Anastasia refuted, teeth clenched against the pain shooting through her cheek and down her neck. "Granted, Lyman supplies the ships, and Bates the women. But it's *you* Rouge communicates with; *you* who orchestrates all the exchanges. And it's *you* who reaps the largest profit. Also, neither Bates nor Lyman are stealing from their companies or attempting to steal from their dead brother."

"That money is mine!" George bellowed through the savage red haze coursing through him. "All of it. Henry's, the company's. I'm entitled to it. And I intend to have it—the minute I get you out of the way."

"Why are you entitled to it? As compensation—because Papa stole Mama? He didn't steal her, Uncle George. She loved him."

With a violent curse, George's free hand whipped out, wrapped around Anastasia's throat. "Your mother was a whore," he roared, his fingers biting into her tender skin. "*You're* a whore. Whatever Rouge had in store for you was too good. You should be thrashed until you bleed, taken until that brazen spark is snuffed out of your eyes, the life snuffed out of your body. And I intend to see that it is." He began walking, dragging her toward the warehouses with him. "Damn you, Anastasia—where is that proof? Do I have to choke you to death to get it?"

A silhouette lunged out of the shadows, and a fist shot out, slamming George in the jaw and sending him reeling. "Get your hands off her, Medford," Damen commanded, shoving Anastasia to safety and advancing toward a wild-eyed George.

"Sheldrake," he gasped.

Damen's fist shot out again, this time sending George toppling to the dirt. "You filthy bastard. I'd like to kill you here and now."

"Don't, Lord Sheldrake." A uniformed Bow Street runner strode out, gesturing for two of his colleagues to follow. "It's not worth dirtying your hands. We'll see that the viscount gets what he deserves. We have everything we need to do that."

The three officers stalked forward, yanking George to his feet, then grabbing his arms, jerking them behind his back.

"You arranged this?" George managed, looking bewilderedly from Anastasia to Damen. "Both of you?"

"*All* of us, Father." Breanna walked forward, coming to stand beside her cousin.

"*Breanna?*" George's eyes looked like they were going to bug out of his head. "You?"

Her nod was emphatic, bitter tears glistening on her lashes. "How else would Mr. Cunnings have known where and when to direct you?"

George swallowed convulsively—once, twice. "You're saying . . . this morning . . . your visit to Sheldrake . . . your conversation . . ." His eyes widened in sudden realization. "The evidence Anastasia has . . ."

"All fabricated," Breanna supplied. "At least until we get into your private files to confirm it. We simply set the trap. You walked into it." She signaled to the Bow Street men to take him away. "Maybe now Grandfather can rest in peace."

She turned her back to him, his furious verbal assault falling on deaf ears, growing more indistinct as Bow Street dragged him off.

Her head held high, Breanna turned her attention to Stacie, who was standing in the circle of Damen's arms.

"Are you all right, sweetheart?" he was asking, tracing the red marks on her cheek with gentle fingers.

"I'm fine," she assured him, kissing his palm. "I'm more than fine. I'm thankful and I'm relieved."

"You were incredibly brave," Breanna declared.

Anastasia gazed proudly at her cousin. "So were you. My ordeal lasted only a few minutes. Yours lasted a lifetime. Your inner strength never ceases to amaze me. Right down to the way you just faced your father, told him the part you played in his capture, when you could so easily have stayed in the shadows, spared yourself the ugliness of his reaction. And why? Because it was important to you that he knew of your commitment, not only to doing what was lawful and right, but to our family and to Grandfather." A glowing smile. "You're the most courageous woman I know."

"*One* of them," Damen corrected her. "I'm holding the other." Anger slashed his handsome features. "I almost charged out and beat George senseless when he hit you. But I promised Bow Street I wouldn't interfere until they signaled to me that they'd gotten enough of a confession to do what they had to." His voice grew husky. "I'm sorry he hurt you."

"It was worth it," Anastasia replied fervently. "Because now he'll never hurt anyone again. Also, as Breanna just said, Grandfather can finally rest in peace. As can Mama and Papa." She reached up and kissed Damen, then turned to hug Breanna fiercely. "Let's go home."

She took a few steps, Breanna and Damen following suit.

Breanna had no idea what made her glance back. All she knew was that that eerie sensation she'd experienced earlier returned, crawling up her spine like some odious insect, propelling her to act.

She could feel a pair of eyes boring through her.

She pivoted. Her fingers slipped reflexively into her pocket, as her gaze swept the docks beyond the warehouses.

A silhouette emerged from the fog. A glint of metal flashed in the night.

It was a pistol.

Breanna never hesitated.

In one smooth motion, she whipped out her own pistol, aimed, and fired.

A scream of pain split the darkness. The dark figure grabbed his hand, his gun thudding softly as it struck the ground.

He bent, recovering his weapon just as Damen whirled around, pulling out his own pistol.

Damen never had the chance to shoot.

The silhouette melted into the night.

"My God," Anastasia breathed, shock reverberating through her. "The assassin. But I don't understand—why would he go ahead and kill me when he obviously wasn't going to get paid?"

"He must not have seen Bow Street," Breanna murmured, still staring at the spot where the armed killer had stood. "The fog is thick. He must have heard Father's voice, then saw the three of us standing alone. I guess he assumed the proof had been confiscated and the deal was still on."

"He'll find out the truth soon enough," Damen muttered, equally shaken. "If he survives that wound you just inflicted. Judging from his scream, it was pretty bad."

"Bad, but not fatal," Breanna corrected. "The bullet struck his hand. I saw him grab for it. The important thing is that I stopped him from doing what he came here to do. When he finds out Father's been arrested, he'll seek an assignment elsewhere."

"Oh, Breanna." Anastasia went to her cousin, grasped her arms. "Do you realize you just saved my life?"

Still trembling, Breanna smiled, although a fine mist veiled her eyes. "Consider it repayment, then. For all the times you saved mine. Beginning with that night we made our pact."

Cunnings was working later than usual.

It was half after ten, and he was still at the bank, perusing the files to select just the right woman to send Rouge.

Once he found her, he'd haul her onto that ship himself, arrange for her immediate passage to Rouge. That would certainly earn him extra points with Medford. Why, the viscount would be eternally grateful for his assistance. After all, as of tonight, Medford would be mourning the death of his precious niece. He couldn't very well conduct business. Cunnings, on the other hand, could. So he'd visit Medford Manor, pay his respects, and offer to take care of the whole process. Rouge would get his shipment, Medford would get his son-in-law . . .

. . . and he would get his spot on the Board of Directors.

Leaning over his desk, Cunnings doubled his efforts, smiling as he imagined Sheldrake's expression when he learned they were going to share equal roles at Colby and Sons.

Finally. He'd have all the wealth, influence, and position he deserved.

Cunnings's thoughts were interrupted by the telltale click of his office door—a click that told him he was no longer alone.

His head shot up, and he started as he saw who his visitor was.

"What are you doing . . . Dear Lord!" he exclaimed, jumping to his feet as he saw the stream of blood flowing from the man's hand, seeping through the torn forefinger of his glove and trickling down his wrist, saturating his coat sleeve. "What the hell happened?"

"Breanna Colby happened," the man snapped, sweat pouring from his face as the pain of his wound lanced through him. "The little bitch shot me."

"She shot . . ." Cunnings wet his lips with the tip of his tongue, his mind racing. "Before or after you killed Anastasia?"

"I didn't kill Anastasia, you stupid fool. It was a trap. Bow Street was there. Anastasia goaded Medford into confessing everything aloud. They took him away."

The color drained from Cunnings's face. "Medford arrested? Then why did you . . . ?"

"I never fail, Cunnings. Money or not. I waited for the perfect moment. Then I acted." Fury darkened his sweat-drenched face. "I didn't make a sound. I don't know how the bitch knew I was there. But she did. I would have killed them both—one bullet per cousin—if Sheldrake hadn't gotten in the way."

"Sheldrake saw all this?" Cunnings asked with a sick sense of dread. "He heard Medford's confession?"

"Every word." A determined glint flashed through his physical agony. "Including the part about you."

"Christ." Cunnings sank into his seat, burying his head in his hands. "How the hell will I . . . ?"

The click of a trigger. "You won't."

Again, Cunnings's head snapped up. This time, his eyes widened with terror as he saw the pistol aimed at him, the assassin's blood trickling from his mutilated forefinger, which hung limply beside the gun's barrel, his middle finger against the trigger.

"You're the only one who can identify me," came the icy assessment. "You'd give them my name in a heartbeat."

"No," Cunnings whispered. "I wouldn't."

"You would." A wince, and the man swallowed, fighting to combat the excruciating pain. "Besides, I've never failed before. Until now. And you're responsible."

"Please . . ."

A bitter smile curved the man's lips. "Don't worry. My failure is only a temporary setback. I'll finish it. At the same time that I torture and kill the bitch who did this to me." A mock salute with his good hand. "Goodbye, Cunnings."

The shot echoed through the walls of the bank.

The assassin slipped into the street, ducking into an alley and doubling over with pain.

Cunnings was taken care of. In addition, the intriguing set of notes on his desk had been confiscated, to be put to use at a later time.

Now he had to get this wound fixed. Not in England. Somewhere else. Somewhere where they didn't know him. He stared at his saturated glove. The wound was bad. His entire forefinger had been severed. He'd had to shoot Cunnings with his middle finger. It was awkward. He'd need his weapon modified. Fine. He'd take care of that, too—*and* master the new weapon. There were no other options. His craft, his incomparable skill, would overcome this setback. He was a genius. And no amateur chit was going to take that away from him.

He'd do what he had to.

After which, his first order of business would be to come back and even the score, take care of that bitch. She'd die slowly, with the maximum degree of anguish.

Completing tonight's unfinished business would be part of that anguish—relatively easy to accomplish. Those two damnable cousins were rarely apart.

Another agonizing pain shot through him, and he emitted a muffled groan. He groped in his pocket, pulled out a handkerchief, then gritted his teeth as he tied a ruthlessly binding tourniquet around the wound. There. That would have to do, at least until he could get himself to a doctor.

He needed passage on the next ship leaving for the Continent. He had no time to waste.

But he'd be back. Lady Breanna Colby could count on it.

Epilogue

❧

The south gardens at Medford Manor had never looked more exquisite. Despite the fact that summer was at an end and the cooler days of September had arrived, the blossoms had never been brighter, the oaks' branches never more green.

Or perhaps it only seemed that way to Anastasia.

"My, you're looking euphoric," Breanna teased, as they strolled toward their favorite oak. "That wouldn't be because next week at this time you'll be the Marchioness of Sheldrake, now would it?"

With a glowing smile, Anastasia gazed about the gardens. "It just might. Actually, I pinch myself each morning to make sure I'm not dreaming. For weeks I wondered if the time would ever come when we all could put our fears behind us, when the nightmare we've been living would stop haunting us, and we could bid the past good-bye. I guess I'm only now starting to believe it's possible."

"Oh, it's possible, all right," Breanna assured her. "And no one deserves the resulting happiness more than you and Damen." A twinkle. "What's more, I think your betrothed agrees. In fact, judging by the way he stares at you when he thinks no one is watching, I suspect he might just drag you down that aisle to become his wife."

"He won't have to. If Wells doesn't restrain me with a firm grip, I'll probably run to the altar at breakneck speed."

Laughter bubbled up in Breanna's throat. "That might be one shock too many for our guests. Most of them still haven't recovered from your unorthodox business proposals at your coming-out ball. And now—a streak of silver and white, rushing down the aisle to accost her bridegroom—I don't think they're quite ready for that. Why, dozens of swooning guests would litter the aisle, blocking your return path."

Anastasia grinned. "Shocking the *ton* yet again. It sounds appealing. But for Wells's sake, I'll control myself. He's nervous enough about giving me away. But I can't think of anyone Grandfather would rather have represent him or Papa at my side."

"Nor can I. Wells is the perfect choice." Breanna glanced about them, savoring the beauty of the garden. "And this is the perfect spot for your wedding breakfast. There are so many happy memories here. It's fitting that we add one more—one extraordinarily important one."

"I agree." Anastasia reached the oak, traced its bark lovingly as she gazed up at the canopy of leaves. "Not to mention that if the guests become too tiresome, I can always scoot up here and try again to touch the sky."

A reminiscent smile touched Breanna's lips. "Don't stretch too high. You'll fall and reopen that scar of yours. And I have no intention of tending my cousin's injuries on her wedding day." Tenderness softened her features. "Besides, I think your climb will be unnecessary. The way you and Damen feel about each other, you're closer to heaven than any oak could take you."

Anastasia nodded, twisting a tumbled strand of hair about her finger, a look of wonder in her eyes. "I always knew love would be wonderful. But I never imagined *how* wonderful—not until Damen." Concern darted across her face, and she regarded her cousin with probing intensity. "Breanna, I want the same for you. I want you to find someone who loves you every bit as much as you deserve. I want your heart to skip a beat every time he walks into the room, and to pound furiously every time he takes you in his arms."

Breanna gave a tolerant shake of her head. "Stacie, I know what a romantic you are. And I love you for it, and for wanting me to be happy. But please try to understand. I *am* happy. Oh, I want all those things you just described—someday. For now, though, I'm so thrilled to be free. Free from Father's cruelty, free from the isolation he imposed on me. For the first time, I can do things like meet new people, visit their homes. I can invite other young women to tea. Why, Lady Margaret Warner and her friends aren't nearly as snobbish as I thought. These diversions may seem frivolous to you, but that's because you've been able to do them all your life. I haven't. So, I don't mind waiting a little longer to meet the man of my dreams."

A grudging sniff. "Damen said you needed time to come into your own. He likened you to a butterfly emerging from its cocoon." Anastasia rolled her eyes, folded her arms across her breasts. "The insufferable man is right again."

Breanna's eyes sparkled. "This marriage is going to be a lifetime of fireworks. Neither you nor Damen will ever be bored. Nor will I, just watching you." She gathered up her skirts and lowered herself to the grass, relishing the fact that grass stains were no longer a horrifying prospect, but a welcome result of a brush with nature. "I, in the mean-time, will have the chance to flap my gossamer wings. You have no idea how excited I am."

"I think I'm beginning to." Anastasia dropped unceremoniously to the grass beside her. "Will you be all right while Damen and I are away? Three months is a long time for us to leave you alone."

"Alone?" One of Breanna's brows shot up in amusement. "I have a houseful of servants who are as elated about being released from bondage as I am. And I have Wells looking out for me—Wells, who's more of a father to me than my own ever was. I'm fine, Stacie. I promise you. There are no lingering scars from Father's actions. He and his colleagues are locked up. Cunnings is dead, and his paid assassin gone. Rouge has pulled up stakes and vanished. The ordeal is over. I want you and Damen to leave on your wedding trip as planned. Open that wonderful new bank of yours. Take long moonlight walks in Philadelphia. And try not to start another revolution—that is, during those scant hours when you're not abed." She blushed at her own comment, blurted out before she could censor it.

Anastasia dissolved into laughter. "The butterfly is already out of its cocoon," she observed. "By the time Damen and I return, you'll be soar-ing the skies like an eagle." She took Breanna's hand in hers. "We'll be back before Christmas. Then, as soon as we return, we'll hold a huge party at Medford Manor—to celebrate the holidays and both of our twenty-first birthdays. By that time we'll both be of age."

"Yes we will." Breanna plucked a blade of grass, an air of gravity set-tling over her. "I'll miss you, Stacie," she said softly. "Not so much on your wedding trip, but after. We're finally reunited after ten long years. Selfishly, I suppose I'm not ready to say good-bye. Even if you're only off to London, where you and Damen will be living. It's still not the same as having you here."

Anastasia swallowed deeply, her grip on Breanna's hand tightening. "I'll miss you, too. Terribly. And I'll miss Medford Manor." Tears blurred her eyes as she gazed, once again, across the acres and acres of beloved grounds. "Part of my heart will always be here. Because you, Wells, Mrs. Rhodes—and everyone from Mrs. Charles to Lizzy—are my family. And family is the most precious gift life has to offer. No matter where I go, Medford Manor will always be home . . ." She broke off, a certain conversation she and Damen had shared on a moonlit balcony resurging like the tide.

Is it possible to miss home even when you're right there in it?

Yes. When that home is no longer the same as the one you remember. And the one you remember is the one you miss.

And then the second conversation, the one they'd had in bed, after their long hours of lovemaking.

I think about that money often, about what Breanna and I can do with it that would ensure Grandfather's wishes are carried out. I feel as if the answer is right here in our own backyard, only we have yet to see it. But whatever it is, it has to be something that would bind our family together, not only now but for generations—actually, forever, if I had my way . . . a uniting force, a means to entwine Breanna's and my futures, and the futures of our children.

I think you've just begun to answer your own question. The rest will come with time. You and Breanna will see to it.

Once again, the brilliant Marquess of Sheldrake was right.

Anastasia jerked upright so abruptly that Breanna started. "That's it!" she exclaimed, jumping to her feet, shading her eyes as she peered across the manicured grounds. "That's absolutely it!"

"What's it?" Breanna demanded, rising as well.

"Grandfather's money. *That's* what we'll do with it." Anastasia turned, gripped both Breanna's hands in hers. "Damen said the answer would come with time, and it has. Breanna, let's build another manor, several more manors, right here on these grounds. There are hundreds and hundreds of acres here, more than enough to accommodate a half-dozen houses. The first will be for Damen and me—our new home. Oh, I know his Town house is right near the bank, but this is one inconvenience I know he won't mind suffering. Besides . . ." Her grin was impish. ". . . I have a feeling my soon-to-be husband will be spending a lot less time at his desk and a lot more time working at home. Building a home in Kent will ensure that."

She paused, only to suck in her breath. "Anyway, after our new manor is complete, we can wait awhile, then begin construction of the others—the ones for our children and their families. Each manor will have plenty of privacy, yet be part of the growing Colby circle. What do you think?"

Breanna's mouth finally snapped shut, and joy exploded across her face. "I think you're more brilliant than Damen, after all." She whirled about, surveying the grounds, then turned and hugged Anastasia fiercely. "Choose the spot for your manor," she urged, drawing back to regard Stacie with spiraling exhilaration. "Now. Immediately. If we hire an architect right away, he can begin while you and Damen are on your wedding trip. You'll be able to move in that much sooner."

An emphatic nod. "Damen will be here in an hour. I'll talk to him the minute he arrives."

Anastasia fell silent, feeling a sense of rightness so profound it made her ache. Slowly, she raised her eyes to the heavens, sharing the feeling with the man who'd inspired it.

"He knows, Stacie," Breanna whispered, following her cousin's gaze.

"Grandfather already knows. He's sharing our joy, just as he always will."

Breanna's words sang inside Anastasia's heart a week later when, on the arm of a proud, beaming Wells, she walked down the aisle and joined with the man she loved.

The chapel was filled, the approving murmurs and stares all directed at her as, clad in a shimmering gown of silver and white, Anastasia took Damen's hand, declared her vows to him, and he to her.

The wedding breakfast, held in the very spot where Stacie and Breanna once climbed, and where they'd made their all-important decision last week, was a veritable paradise of flowers, an endless stretch of manicured greenery.

One that was theirs forever, Anastasia reflected joyously, separating herself from the throng of guests long enough to gaze across the grounds, to savor the fact that her future with Damen lay right here.

"Admiring the site of our new home?" Damen asked huskily, coming up behind his bride and wrapping his arms about her waist.

"Treasuring it," Anastasia amended, leaning back against her new husband's solid strength.

"I love you, Lady Sheldrake," Damen murmured solemnly, burying his lips in her hair. "More than you'll ever know."

Anastasia turned, gazed up at him, all the love in the world shining in her eyes. "And I love you. More than I ever dreamed possible."

A wicked gleam. "Enough to slip away from your own celebration?"

An impish grin. "Definitely enough." She traced his lapel with her fingertip. "See? If our new manor were already completed, we wouldn't even have to waste time riding to London."

"If our manor was already completed, I would have whisked you into it an hour ago."

Anastasia searched Damen's face, a trace of anxiety clouding her own. "You really are pleased about the way Breanna and I are spending Grandfather's inheritance, aren't you?"

A look of fierce pride darkened Damen's gaze. "I'm more than pleased. I'm so bloody proud of you I could burst. You picked the most fitting tribute, the most rewarding investment in yours and Breanna's future that your grandfather could ever wish for. He was blessed to have you. And now, so am I."

Tears dampened Anastasia's lashes. "Damen . . ."

"Come, my beautiful bride," he breathed, brushing her lips in a soft, poignant caress. "It's time to seal our vows in the most magnificent way possible." He glanced beyond her, at the very spot where their manor would soon stand. "Those workmen had best toil round the clock," he muttered. "Because by the time we return from our wedding trip . . ." An insightful spark flickered in his eyes, and he drew Anastasia to him, his hands settling on her waist, his thumbs skimming the layers of her wedding gown that covered her now flat abdomen. "Let's just say that my Town house is far too cramped for what I have in mind."

A watery smile. "And what is that, my lord? A dividend from our joint venture?"

"Oh, more than one, Mrs. Lockewood," Damen assured her. "This ultimate partnership we just committed ourselves to is going to reap more rewards than you can begin to imagine." He held her stare, his expression profound, utterly certain. "In fact, my instincts tell me that we're going to give your grandfather every bit of the extensive, loving family he prayed for."

THE
SILVER COIN

❦

To my own grandfather, whose special feeling for me is enduring, and whose belief in family inspired the character and strength of Breanna's and Anastasia's grandfather. Like the late viscount, my grandfather continues to watch over us, with a love and pride that will live on forever.

1

❖

London, England
December 1817

She was going to die.

It was only a question of when.

He sat calmly at a far corner table of the London coffeehouse, sipping his tea and gazing out the window as he contemplated the busy cobblestone streets. London looked the same as always. It was chillier than when he'd left, with winter closing in. The fog had transformed from a clammy blanket to a raw mist—a mist that thickened as it mingled with the puffs of cold air emerging from the mouths of scurrying patrons and plodding horses. Everyone seemed in a hurry, including the shopkeepers who stepped outside in rapid succession, glancing about for any last-minute customers, then locking up for the day. One by one, they turned up their collars and hurried home to their waiting families.

How touching.

How convenient.

The throngs of people, while providing an interesting scene for an early evening diversion, made it easy to remain unnoticed. He'd intentionally picked this coffeehouse—one whose customers were primarily artists and authors, none of whom would have the slightest idea who he was. So he remained, a solitary gentleman enjoying his solitary late-day tea.

And if, by chance, one of his colleagues happened to wander in, spot him at his corner table, that colleague would doubtless offer his greetings, inquire where his lordship had been, and learn about his prolonged business trip abroad.

Given his status and position, his explanation would be accepted without question or doubt.

Ah, anonymity. It came in many forms, each one of them satisfying indeed.

He set down his cup, tugging his gloves more snugly into place and studying his cloaked hands—his right one, in particular. The German physician had been remarkably skilled, he mused, turning his palms up, then back down again. Same size. Same shape. Right down to the tapered fingers. With his gloves in place, it was impossible to tell that his right forefinger was a mere replica of what it had been. Oh, it couldn't bend at the knuckle, of course—wood never did—but he had no cause to bend that forefinger anyway. Not anymore. Now he had a substitute: his middle finger—a trigger finger impeccably trained, ready to perform on command. He also had a new weapon, one fashioned especially for him, made by the same craftsman who'd designed and constructed the original. Both weapons were unique. But this new version was a stunning, one-of-a-kind achievement. Mastering it had taken every ounce of his skill and concentration, given his physical impediment. But master it he had—as brilliantly as he'd mastered its predecessor—and almost as quickly.

Yes, the weapon—and the proficiency to use it—had been acquired within a month of leaving England. But conquering the pain—*that* had taken every day of the three long months he'd been away.

Still, it would surge to life, sometimes so acutely he nearly screamed aloud. It would never truly leave him. That he knew. Not even for a day.

But it also wouldn't stop him.

Nothing would.

As if to taunt him, the front door of the coffeehouse opened, admitting a cold blast of December air. He winced as the chilling wind shot through the room, found him in his corner, and set off the throbbing in his hand. Gritting his teeth, he waited for the worst of the pain to subside, bitterly acknowledging that the winter months were going to be excruciating. Cold intensified the dull ache that gnawed relentlessly at him, sharpening his agony with a piercing stab.

He had no choice but to endure it.

Damn the winter.

Damn the pain.

And damn Breanna Colby.

He finished his tea, cursing silently as the hot beverage did nothing to warm away his agony. A drink. That's what he needed. A good, stiff drink to dull the throb.

Tossing some coins on the table, he left the establishment, shoving his hands in his pockets as he made his way through the tangle of people to the nearest tavern.

Inside, it was dark and smoky, but he paid little attention to his surroundings as he ordered a brandy. He tossed it down in three gulps.

The liquor worked wonders, burning through his system and making its way to the raw nerve endings at his knuckle.

When all this was over, he vowed, he'd spend winters somewhere warm, somewhere where the pain was bearable. There he could live in seclusion. There he could savor his victories.

Especially the one hovering just ahead—his ultimate triumph and long-awaited revenge. Doing away with that miserable bitch who'd done this to him, condemned him to three months of agony and a lifetime of physical torment.

She'd pay for each and every day he suffered, each and every night he'd awakened, drenched in sweat, pain spearing through his hand, shooting up his arm. Oh, yes, she'd pay. First, by watching her precious cousin die at her feet, then by waiting, wondering, when the bullet meant for her would find its mark.

It wouldn't be immediate. Oh, no, it would be prolonged. Torturing her had to be savored. He had to terrorize her to the point where she'd be crazed with fear.

Until she realized, with a final surge of panic, that she couldn't escape him.

Until she understood he never failed, never missed his mark.

Until she knew it would take one bullet, and one bullet alone, because he never needed a second.

And until she knew that he was watching her, toying with her, deciding when and where to end her wretched life.

Oh, Lady Breanna Colby, by the time I kill you, you'll beg to die.

And die you will.

2

Kent, England

The grounds of Medford Manor were alive with the sounds of activity, as a large crowd of workmen hammered and sawed, moving about the shell of what was becoming an elegant house—one that stood directly across the grounds from the existing one.

Bricklayers stood on scaffolding, spreading mortar and laying the final bricks of the structure, while carpenters hoisted up beams and rafters, nailed them into place. Stonemasons were constructing the marble fireplaces that would stand in each of the numerous bedchambers and meticulously shaping the stones that would define the sculptured footpaths and entranceway steps.

Breanna eyed the scene from thirty yards away, folding her arms across her breasts and nodding definitively.

Anastasia and Damen's home was well under way.

It hadn't been an easy feat to accomplish—not given the speed with which they wanted everything done. For starters, Breanna had sped up the process by doing a few quick sketches—based on what she knew of her cousin's tastes and what she suspected of Damen's—the week before their wedding. She'd shown the sketches to the soon-to-be newlyweds—and gotten their instant and unconditional approval.

Then again, Breanna had reflected with a smile, they were so absorbed in each other, she doubted they'd even studied her sketches. In fact, they'd probably have made a fuss over them even if she'd flourished pictures of a giant chamber pot and enthusiastically heralded them as sketches of their new manor—a manor that was destined to be the most exquisite home in all of England.

Ah, love.

Well, Stacie and Damen were more than entitled to that love. Lord knows, they'd been to hell and back waiting for the day they could wed. And it had come—a perfect day that united a perfect couple. As for the sketches—it didn't matter whether they'd truly seen them or not. Breanna's instincts told her they'd be pleased.

That very day, she'd taken action. The best architects had been hired, as well as the finest craftsmen, with the understanding that the Marquess and Marchioness of Sheldrake's home was to be completed as quickly, as possible without compromising quality.

Everyone had taken that order to heart and, within days, plans had been drawn up. Those plans were approved on the day before the wedding—by Breanna. *That* she'd only agreed to do after Stacie had all but begged her. It seemed the bride-to-be was far too excited to sit still and look at drawings, and besides, she'd added brightly, Breanna was the artistic one in the family. So didn't it make sense for her to look over the plans? Finally, Breanna had relented, and taken over the task herself. As a result, everything proceeded on schedule and, on the day Stacie and Damen left for their wedding trip, a work crew arrived at the site and construction began.

The way things looked now, the manor would be finished before the Season began in March.

And not a minute too soon, Breanna thought, smoothing her hair as she strolled through the gardens, watching the structure take shape. Damen had made it abundantly clear that he intended to fill that house with children—as soon as nature permitted. Knowing Damen and Stacie . . . well, Breanna wanted this house ready.

She fingered the folds of her mantle, nodding her approval as she angled her head this way and that, watching the manor take on detail and dimension. Nothing too elaborate. Just a roomy, airy, lovely home, filled with light and love.

Especially love.

She smiled, thinking with more than a little excitement that Stacie and Damen should be returning from the States any time now. They'd been away nearly three months, and Stacie had promised they'd be back for Christmas.

The wedding trip had been an exciting one, according to the letters Breanna had received. Fidelity Union and Trust—Stacie and Damen's bank—had opened its doors in October and was already thriving. Judging from the newspaper clippings Stacie had included with her letters, the bank was the financial triumph of Philadelphia, a perfect merging of the Lockewoods and the Colbys. Enough so that the new Mr. and Mrs. Lockewood weren't needed at all, and could spend their entire time enjoying Philadelphia, attending an occasional party, or in utter seclusion.

Breanna's smiled widened as she pondered all Stacie had said—and all she hadn't said. She'd written pages and pages on how wonderful it was to share with Damen the city in which she'd lived for ten years, the people, the sites. But she'd said suspiciously little about the secluded aspects of the trip.

It didn't take a scholar to figure out why. Given the passion that sizzled between Stacie and Damen . . . well, suffice it to say that it was good there hadn't been *too* many parties for them to attend. She doubted they would have had the strength to walk, much less dance.

In any case, Christmas was now only a few weeks away. And, since Stacie always kept her promises, she and Damen would already be on their way home. Breanna could hardly wait to see her—and to see her face light up when she beheld her soon-to-be-completed house.

The first step of their grandfather's dream.

Breanna's gaze lifted to the heavens, and she could almost feel her grandfather's reassuring presence. How overjoyed he'd be—Stacie and she sharing the grounds of Medford Manor, giving birth to their children here. It was precisely what he'd want, the lasting bond between the Colbys that he'd prayed for when he'd gifted her and Stacie with their coins.

The realization never failed to bring tears of joy to her eyes.

Breanna turned toward her own house—the house she shared only with her staff since that dreadful day in August when Bow Street had taken away her father, locked him up in Newgate.

Even now, the events of that day made her ill, just as her father's crimes made her shudder. He was a cruel and unforgivable man, and whatever small amount of feeling she'd held for him had been extinguished when she'd learned what he'd done—*and* what he'd intended to do. She'd closed off his room the morning after his arrest, a tacit sign to the servants that he was no longer part of her life.

They'd followed her lead, said nothing despite the lurid articles carried by the newspapers—articles that described the full extent of the Viscount Medford's unscrupulous dealings and his lifetime incarceration for attempted murder.

No words were necessary, not between Breanna and the beloved staff who'd raised her. They'd gone through the same gamut of emotions she had, at least with respect to the shock and horror. As for the sorrow and the shame, those were hers alone to bear. He'd been, after all, only their employer, while he was *her* father. It had taken her some time to come to terms with that, but it was behind her now, and the emotional scars would heal.

In the meantime, she was free—free from her father's menacing presence. It was as if a great weight had been lifted from her shoulders, allowing the real Breanna to emerge in an unencumbered way she'd never believed possible, and for that her staff cheered silently beside her. They were, after all, truly her family—the only real family she'd ever had, except for her beloved cousin, Anastasia.

Reaching the manor, Breanna paused, seized by the sudden urge to celebrate. For the first time ever, life seemed perfect, rife with promise. Stacie was happily married and on her way home, a holiday season loomed ahead—filled with house parties and laughter—and she herself had a full life to lead. One she'd tentatively but successfully initiated as soon as the trauma—and the scandal—of her father's arrest had begun to die down.

She'd been prepared to be ostracized. Most especially by the *ton*. But, to her surprise, people were more sympathetic to her plight than she'd realized, somehow coming to the conclusion that her only offense was being George Colby's daughter—a bitter twist of fate rather than a character flaw. One by one, callers began coming by; first, matrons whose kind hearts compelled them to soothe and comfort her. Then, their daughters—young women she'd met at the few parties she'd attended two Seasons ago.

And then, the major turning point had occurred. Lady Margaret Warner, who'd been affable toward Breanna since Anastasia's coming-out last summer, had come to call. Lady Margaret's visit was a signal to the inner circle of young noblewomen who followed her example—a signal that it was socially acceptable to associate with Breanna Colby. Tacitly, she instructed them to follow suit. They began visiting Medford Manor in a steady trickle—to gossip, yes, but eventually, upon learning of Breanna's artistic talents, to show her their needlepoints, to ask her opinion of their sketching. And, when she responded with warmth and encouragement, they began inviting her to their homes as well.

Breanna was amazed at her own transformation. In fact, she discovered she was not at all the loner she'd believed herself to be. Instead, she was hungry for companionship—companionship she could receive and reciprocate, now that her oppressive father was gone.

In no time at all, she had friends, homes to visit, events to attend. Her days were no longer spent in lonely isolation—arranging and rearranging her porcelain figures, sketching, and reading. Guests arrived several times a day, including even an occasional gentleman or two. No one particularly enthralling. Then again, she wasn't looking to be enthralled. All she wanted was a bit of youthful merriment: some conversation, a stroll, perhaps even a little flirtation; the very things she'd been denied.

So what if the gentlemen were a trifle bland, acceptable rather than exhilarating? Exhilarating had never been a trait she was attracted to, anyway. Stable, even-tempered, well-mannered—that was what she felt comfortable with.

Still, she *was* becoming a bit bored, feeling oddly restless these past few weeks.

Well, all that would vanish the instant Stacie returned.

Our house party, she thought suddenly, her foot poised on the first entranceway step. *The one Stacie proposed before she left.*

Excitement flared inside her. *How could I have missed this opportunity?* she mused, recalling her cousin's idea to celebrate both their comings-of-age with a gala party at Medford Manor. Stacie hadn't specified a date. Well, now was the perfect time. Stacie's twenty-first birthday had arrived in October, and her own had occurred just last week. Plus, the celebration could be not only in honor of their birthdays, but in honor of Stacie and Damen's homecoming. And it would herald the holiday season.

It was ideal. The more she thought about it, the more enthused she became. In fact, she'd sit down with Wells right now, begin a guest list. Invitations could be sent out in a matter of days. But would that be enough time, with Christmas a mere fortnight away?

Gathering up her mantle, Breanna scooted up the steps, bursting through the front door and colliding with Wells at his post.

"Oh, Wells, I'm sorry."

The butler straightened, smoothing his uniform and tossing her a look that was more amused than it was bothered. "It's quite all right, Miss Breanna. Although I must admit that, for a moment, I thought Miss Stacie had returned."

Breanna's eyes sparkled, and she laughed aloud. "Not yet. But any day now. That's why I was in such a hurry. Do you remember that house party Stacie and I toyed with having when she returned? What would you think about planning it now, and making it a homecoming, holiday, and birthday celebration all rolled into one? I know, I know," she rushed on, as Wells opened his mouth to reply. "It's not enough notice to give our guests. I should have done this sooner. But it completely slipped my mind. Perhaps if I hand-delivered the invitations myself, it would soothe enough feathers to make the party possible?" She shot Wells a hopeful look.

"I doubt it," he replied.

Her entire face fell. "Very well then. We'll host the party after the holidays."

"We'll do no such thing." Wells readjusted his spectacles. "Not after all the work we've done."

Breanna's brows drew together in puzzlement. "Pardon me?"

"Mrs. Charles and I. We waited until half of November was gone. When you didn't begin planning the party, we did. The guest list was completed by the first of December, and invitations went out last week. Mrs. Rhodes is hard at work on the menu, and I believe she and Mrs. Charles have hired the musicians as well. The day after Miss Stacie arrives home, you and she can pick out the fabrics for your gowns.

They'll be ready within a week. Of course, anything I've forgotten, including any last-minute touches, will be left to the two of you."

Disbelief flashed across Breanna's face, and laughter bubbled up in her throat. "Would you care to tell me when this party will take place?"

"The twenty-eighth and twenty-ninth of December. That will give Miss Stacie and Lord Sheldrake plenty of time to arrive and settle in, and all of us a chance to enjoy a quiet holiday as a family before our guests descend upon us. It will also give you a chance to breathe before your stream of callers arrive on New Year's Day." Wells's lips twitched. "The same stream of callers that filled those rare hours when you weren't overseeing the building of Miss Stacie's new home. Why, it's no wonder you were too busy to remember your wish to hold this party—and to plan it."

Breanna stopped laughing only long enough to toss Wells a sheepish look. "You're right. And I'm sorry." She stood on tiptoe, kissed Wells's lined cheek. "You, my friend, have rescued me more times than I care to count. You're a constant source of amazement."

A corner of his mouth lifted as he took her mantle, hung it away. "You and Miss Stacie keep me young. Exhausted, but young." He turned back to her, growing sober. "However, there is one difference. Miss Stacie has found the future your grandfather prayed she'd find. She's happy, whole. But you—I worry about you, Miss Breanna. You're still searching. You rarely consider your own happiness. So it's up to me to do it for you."

"By happiness I assume you mean properly wed," Breanna noted dryly. She gave Wells's arm a squeeze. "Well, stop worrying. I barely give marriage a second thought."

"I know. That's why I worry."

She chewed her lip to keep from chuckling at his forlorn tone. "I hate to shatter your dreams, Wells, but if you've planned this party in the hopes that I'll meet my future husband there, you're bound for disappointment. I'm doubtless acquainted with all the guests you've chosen to invite. And, as I conjure up a memory of each one of them . . ." She wrinkled her nose. "Let's just say it's unlikely I'll be making any wedding plans this coming year." A sudden notion struck, and she arched a suspicious brow in Wells's direction. "I *do* know all our guests, don't I, Wells? You haven't arranged any chance encounters with potential suitors?"

He sighed. "Unfortunately, no. Although not for want of trying. It's just that all the eligible gentlemen I had in mind are unavailable; either because they're away or because they have the poor judgment to be involved with other women—women who are unquestionably less remarkable than you. However, I'm hoping that Lord Sheldrake will be able to suggest—"

"No," Breanna interrupted. "I don't want Damen playing Cupid."

"But—"

"Absolutely not." She gave a vehement shake of her head. The gesture loosened one of her smoothly coiffed auburn tresses enough to send it toppling to her neck—a condition she promptly rectified by tucking the tress back beneath its pin. "I'll leave my future to fate. And so will you," she added meaningfully.

Before Wells could further his argument, a knock sounded at the front door.

Breanna pivoted about, eyeing the door quizzically. "Are we expecting anyone?"

"Perhaps fate," Wells suggested wryly.

A grin. "Then by all means, let her in."

Wells complied, turning the handle and swinging the door wide.

A uniformed messenger stood on the step, turning up his collar against the winter chill. "I have a package for Lady Breanna Colby," he announced to Wells, gripping a box in both hands.

"I am she." Breanna stepped forward, accepting the package and examining it curiously. "I wonder who it's from," she murmured, waiting until the messenger had received his shillings and gone before investigating further.

"One of your suitors, perhaps?"

"I don't have any suitors, Wells," she corrected, wriggling the top off the box. "I merely have . . ." Her voice trailed off as she peeled back the paper, looked inside. "What in the name of . . ." She placed the box on a low table in the hallway, and lifted out two small dolls, both with red hair and green eyes. The dolls wore identical pale-blue day dresses. Each frock was torn in the same spot—on the left side of the chest—and was marred by a bright spot of what appeared to be red paint.

Red paint that looked for all the world like blood.

"Who sent these?" Wells demanded, scowling at the dolls.

A cold knot of dread was beginning to form in Breanna's stomach—a knot she couldn't explain but that tightened more with each passing second.

Her heart thudding faster, she reached back into the box, snatching up the small square note that had been propped against the dolls' heads so as not to go unnoticed.

She unfolded it, wetting her lips with the tip of her tongue as she steeled herself.

The words leapt out at her, and she read them twice, icy fear slashing through her in ruthless talons. "Oh my God." She dropped the note, all the color draining from her face as she backed away.

"Miss Breanna?" Wells was visibly alarmed. "What is it?" He picked up the card. Adjusting his spectacles, he read aloud, " 'Did you think I'd forget you? Never. It's retribution time. I'm back to even the score. One bullet. That's all I need. One for each of you. First your cousin, then you. Soon. So tremble, Lady Breanna. Tremble and wait.' "

3

"*T*ell me the entire story again. As calmly as possible."

Cecil Marks leaned against the desk, tugging at his scarlet waistcoat and trying to ignore the din taking place behind him as a group of thieves were dragged into the Bow Street office, struggling and swearing. He'd been a Bow Street runner for three years now, and he still preferred combing the streets for criminals to actually bringing them in and having to contend with the chaos. But given the recent murders that had occurred here in London and the investigation that had ensued—well, he had no choice but to stick close to the home office.

He glanced down at his writing tablet, then back at the white-faced young woman who stood before him, wringing her hands as her elderly butler tried to comfort her. This was the last thing he needed after the kind of day he'd had. He'd questioned a half-dozen suspects, pored over pages of facts—and he wasn't in any mood to soothe the fears of an overwrought woman.

Then again, Lady Breanna Colby wasn't just any woman.

A lady in the true sense of the word, she was. Marks remembered that from last time. And a real beauty, to boot. Hair like burnished copper and eyes like chips of jade. Delicate and, at the same time, almost regal. Marks recalled the way she'd watched him lead her father away, her head held high, her eyes bright with tears she refused to shed, grief and shame she refused to display. It was rare to meet a woman who possessed that much restraint, much less one who was emotionally strong as well as beautiful.

Yes, she was a survivor, all right. Except that right now Lady Breanna looked ready to come apart at the seams.

Marks could well understand why. Hell, he'd be unnerved, too, if he were in her place. The problem was, he had no time or resources to devote to her situation. Not when the whole matter boiled down to a mere threat.

"My lady," he replied, after listening to her second recounting of the story. "I know you're upset. But unless someone's actually tried to hurt you, my hands are tied. Unless, of course, there's something you haven't mentioned? Something more substantial this man's done? If so, tell me and I'll get right on it."

Breanna drew an unsteady breath. "That's just it. He hasn't actually *done* anything—yet. But it's clear he intends to."

"You say he sent you this package." Marks jerked his thumb toward his desk, where the opened box lay. "Those two dolls and a note."

"Not just two dolls," Breanna corrected. "Two disfigured dolls. And it's not just a note, sir. It's a threat. Surely you can see that."

Marks twisted around, examined each doll for the third time, then scanned the note. "I admit, whoever sent this is warped, even unbalanced. But as for proof that he's going to kill you—"

"Mr. Marks, please don't patronize me. You of all people remember what happened the night my father was arrested—or rather, *after* he was arrested."

Marks cleared his throat. "You're talking about that shooter."

"He wasn't just an arbitrary shooter. He was paid to kill Anastasia, hired by my father—through his informant—to do so. When I shot him in the hand before he could shoot Stacie, he bolted. Obviously, he realized he might be exposed, so he killed Mr. Cunnings—the one person who could identify him—then vanished."

"We *believe* he killed Cunnings," Marks amended, scratching his head. "The killer was never found, nor was any proof of his identity." Seeing the anguish on Breanna's face, he felt a pang of guilt. "But, yes," he conceded, "we're pretty sure Cunnings's murderer was the same man who took a shot at your cousin."

"And I maimed him."

Marks's lips thinned into a grim line. "I understand why you'd think this message was from him. Maybe it was. Fine, it probably was. The question is, what can we do about it? We couldn't find him three months ago. What makes you think it'll be any easier to find him now?"

"The fact that he's surfaced." Breanna gripped the folds of her gown between her fingers, an earnest pucker forming between her brows. "Sir, I don't work for Bow Street. I'm not presuming to tell you how to do your job. But isn't it possible this man dropped out of sight long enough, not only to wait for your investigation to die down, but to give his wound time to heal? That he's only now able to resume his work? His note certainly makes it sound that way."

"I agree. It does sound as if he was waiting to be up to snuff before he contacted you. But that doesn't mean he'll be any easier to catch than he was before. Think about it, my lady. Paid killers don't operate out in the

open. Nor do they advertise in newspapers to find clients." Marks flipped
his notepad shut. "What's more, they don't take jobs without monetary
compensation—*major* monetary compensation. With your father in
Newgate, no one's interested in paying this assassin to kill you or your
cousin. So why would he take the risk? Why would he chance getting
caught in exchange for nothing? He wouldn't."

"My instincts tell me otherwise."

"No rudeness intended, my lady, but I'm in the middle of some pretty
ugly murder investigations. I can't abandon those cases in favor of your
instincts."

Breanna made a frustrated sound. "I realize that. I'm not asking you
to abandon anything. I read the newspapers. I'm aware of how busy you
are. All I'm asking is that you probe this matter a bit—perhaps after
hours." She pressed her lips together, squaring her shoulders in that regal
way she had. "I'm sorry if that sounds presumptuous. But remember,
mine isn't the only life that's at stake. My cousin's is, too. I'm sure her
husband, Lord Sheldrake, would appreciate any assistance you could
provide in eliminating a potential threat to his wife."

Lady Breanna's pointed comment wasn't lost on Marks. He knew
damned well who the Marquess of Sheldrake was, how prominent he
was in London business and society. He also knew he was the
"Lockewood" of the House of Lockewood—the most influential merchant bankers in England, maybe even in the whole damned world. Not
to mention that the House of Lockewood was the very place where
Cunnings, Sheldrake's right-hand man, had been murdered. Murdered
because he'd been instrumental in an ugly plot that sacrificed lives and
undermined the marquess himself.

Yes, if the assassin truly had resurfaced, Sheldrake would definitely
want him found, want all the loose ends of the nightmare tied up. Most
especially because the assassin's target had been Lady Anastasia Colby,
now the Marchioness of Sheldrake. And everyone knew how much
Damen Lockewood adored his new bride . . .

Hell, Marks thought, eyeing Lady Breanna with a kind of grudging
respect. This woman wasn't only resilient and beautiful. She was smart,
too.

"All right." He gave a terse nod, "I'll do some checking—as much as I
can given what's going on here. I'll start with the messenger service that
delivered the package to your home. After that, I'll review the details of
Cunnings's murder. Maybe I can turn something up."

His tone said otherwise.

"Perhaps if you speak to Mr. Cunnings's colleagues," Breanna suggested. "I know you did that right after he was killed. But that was three
months ago. Maybe someone can provide you with new information. Who

knows? It's possible one of Mr. Cunnings's less reputable associates— male or female—saw him with this man but didn't think anything of it at the time. Until now, when you mention that the suspect you're searching for dropped out of sight for the past several months and has only now resurfaced."

Marks arched a brow. "That's a bit far-fetched, wouldn't you say?" He averted Breanna's protest by holding up his palm. "I said I'll try. And I will. But I'm not promising anything." He shifted impatiently, eager to resume work on his current murder investigations. "Give me a few days, maybe a week. When I'm finished poking around, I'll ride to Kent, tell you what I've found out."

"Thank you, sir." Breanna gestured toward the desk. "Shall I leave the note and package with you?"

"Hmm? No. Take them with you. They'd probably get lost in the shuffle here. If I need to see them again, I'll let you know." Marks gave Lady Breanna what he hoped was a reassuring smile. "Go home now. And try not to worry. The chances are this madman got just what he wanted: he scared the wits out of you. And that will be that."

Across the street from Bow Street's office, the well-dressed man turned up his collar, moved casually away, and continued walking.

Excellent, he thought, a smug smile curving his lips. *She's gone to Bow Street. They can't help her, of course. They've got nothing. But she's frightened. Good. She has reason to be. And this is only the beginning.*

He rounded the corner and disappeared.

"I doubt Mr. Marks will help us much," Breanna commented a few minutes later, leaning her head wearily against the carriage seat. "I feel thoroughly patronized. Worse, I'm not even sure he believed me at all."

"Oh, he believed you," Wells returned in a tight voice. "Your situation is just not, in his opinion, a matter of urgency. He'll do what he can. If not for your sake, for Lord Sheldrake's." Pursing his lips, Wells added, "Miss Breanna, I held my tongue in there because my frustration would have done you more harm than good. But now that we're alone, I want you to know I don't intend to entrust your safety entirely to the Bow Street runners. Whether or not I'm overreacting, I plan to hire additional guards."

Grimly, Breanna nodded. "I think that's wise, particularly since there are so many comings and goings at Medford these days. With all the activity necessary to complete Stacie and Damen's new home . . ." A painful sigh. "For the first time, I'm relieved she's away. That means

she's out of danger. Hopefully, Mr. Marks is right and this will all turn
out to be nothing more than a scare. If that's the case, Stacie won't even
have to know about it. She's so audacious, I shudder to think how she'd
decide to handle things. And if he's wrong . . ." Breanna swallowed.
"Let's just say that if he's wrong, if the assassin means to carry out his
threats, there will be plenty of time to fill Stacie in when she arrives
home. In the meantime, she can remain blissfully unaware."

Far away, on a ship bound for England, Anastasia Lockewood awakened with a start. Her eyes snapped open, and she sat up, perspiration
breaking out on her brow.

"Sweetheart?" Damen shot up like a bullet. "Are you going to be sick
again?" He swung his legs over the side of the bed, reaching for the
chamber pot as he spoke.

"No." Anastasia waved the receptacle away, shuddering as she contemplated how many times she'd needed it on this trip home. "I'm fine.
Really." She wrapped the sheet around her, drawing up her knees, and
resting her chin atop them. "At least physically."

Relieved, Damen resettled himself beside her, smoothing back her
hair and pressing his lips to her bare shoulder. "Then what is it?"

"I don't know." Anastasia frowned, staring about their modest cabin
and wondering how many days it would be before they docked in
London. "But I have the most uneasy feeling. Something's not right at
home."

Scowling, Damen murmured, "With Breanna, you mean."

"Yes. With Breanna."

Damen nodded. He knew better than to question his wife's connection
with her cousin. He'd seen firsthand how attuned to each other they
were. They were more like sisters, twins in fact, than they were like
cousins—in far more ways than merely their striking physical resemblance.

"We're almost home," he soothed. "Breanna must realize that. Maybe
she's feeling the same restlessness you are. Maybe that's what you're
sensing. After all, we have been away for months."

"I suppose so." Anastasia sounded distinctly unconvinced. "Breanna's
probably anticipating our homecoming as much as I am." A pause. "Her
birthday was last week," she continued, as if trying to persuade herself
that Damen was right. "She's finally of age. I wonder if she's planning
the party we talked about before I left."

"I'm sure she is. In fact, I'm sure she's exhausted. Between planning a
house party and handling the initial construction of our home by herself—
I'm sure she's counting the days until we're there to lend a hand."

"That's true." Anastasia relaxed a bit. "Even with the staff's support, she's doubtless buried in details, determined to oversee all the preparations herself."

"Um-hum." Damen slipped his arms around Anastasia's waist, laid a possessive palm on her still-flat abdomen. "On the other hand, maybe she senses you have an announcement for her."

His wife shot him a wry grin over her shoulder. "If so, she's probably lining the grounds with chamber pots. I can't seem to take ten steps without needing one."

"That's only because of the motion of the sea. The ship's doctor assured me the sickness will ease once you're home, with both feet planted firmly on land."

Laughter danced in Anastasia's eyes. "He would have assured you of anything to calm you down. You've interrupted him six times a day for reassurance that everything I'm experiencing is normal. The poor man probably bolts his door at night, for fear that you'll burst into his cabin and accost him with yet more questions about your pregnant wife."

Not the least bit contrite, Damen chuckled, tugging his wife down to his chest. "I'm allowed to worry. I'm a new husband *and* an expectant father. I'm also insanely in love with my wife—a wife who, for the past three weeks, has either swooned or been sick every time she's stepped out of bed."

"Then perhaps I should stay on it—or rather, in it." Her attention diverted by more scintillating matters, Stacie feathered her lips across her husband's chest, nuzzling his nipples as her fingers trailed down the hard planes of his stomach. She smiled as she felt his heart rate quicken. "After all, I'm fine when I'm reclining. Better than fine, in fact." Her hand slid lower, found its goal, and her fingers surrounded Damen's erection, caressed him in light, teasing strokes. "So if you want me to feel better—"

"Say no more." Features stark with desire, Damen rolled her to her back, covered her mouth—and her body—with his. "You couldn't feel any better," he murmured huskily. "You already feel too damned good."

"Show me," she whispered, twining her arms around his neck.

Damen proceeded to do just that, breathing love words against her skin, into her lips, as he penetrated her slowly, exquisitely, melding their bodies into one.

Their lovemaking was as shattering as ever, pervading every pore of Anastasia's body, touching every inch of her soul, leaving her weak, bonelessly sated.

But afterwards, wrapped securely in Damen's arms, sleep evaded her.

Unbidden, the uneasiness crept back, latching its disturbing tentacles into her mind. And, like the relentless queasiness that plagued her, it refused to be shaken.

Something was wrong, she concluded, stirring fitfully on the bed.

Her gaze shifted to the cabin's tiny porthole, and she willed the winds to propel them swiftly to England.

Breanna needed her.

She had to get home.

4

❧

The headline of *The Times* was quite disconcerting.

It seemed that, try though they would, Bow Street could not definitively prove who had killed two prominent noblemen.

Although, after carefully questioning dozens of people—servants and associates alike—they did have their theories.

This should be fascinating, he thought, settling back in his dining-room chair and skimming the article beneath the headline.

His brows raised in interest as he read on.

While the murders were still unsolved, Bow Street had begun to alter their original theory that the crimes were linked, at least so far as sharing the same assailant. Instead, the police were now speculating that, while one crime probably inspired the other, the two murders had been committed by different killers. And not by two hardened criminals, but by two women, each with the same relationship to the victim *and* the same motivation to do him in.

Women?

Now that was an intriguing notion.

Leaning forward, he read on.

Evidently, Bow Street was coming to suspect that the wives of these renowned noblemen were, in fact, the murderesses they sought. The women in question might or might not have devised their plans together, but their motivations were doubtless the same: greed and a yearning for freedom.

He continued, almost laughing out loud as he followed Bow Street's reasoning.

The fact was that both wives had mysteriously disappeared at the same time their husbands had been shot. Initially, it was presumed that they'd been kidnapped. But now, more than a week later, no ransom notes had surfaced, nor had any trace of the women or their whereabouts been uncovered. So it was looking more and more like they'd killed their husbands, then run off, perhaps with other lovers, most likely taking with them some private source of wealth—be it cash or jewels—that no one other than they and their husbands knew about.

How clever, he thought, his teeth gleaming with amusement. *What would we ever do without Bow Street and their unmatched genius?*

The article concluded by assuring everyone that the authorities were hard at work, determined to apprehend the perpetrators.

What a waste of time, he reflected, folding the newspaper in half and placing it on the table. *Bow Street will never find them. No one will. They've vanished forever.*

He was just biting into his second scone when a knock sounded at the dining room door.

His butler entered. "Pardon me, m'lord, but a gentleman from Bow Street is here to see you. A Mr. Marks. He insists on speaking with you personally."

A flicker of apprehension—one he kept carefully concealed.

Slowly, he chewed and swallowed his food, then dabbed at his mouth with a linen napkin. "Does he now?" He rose, a frown creasing his brow as he smoothed his gloves into place. "Did he state what his business was?"

"Something about John Cunnings, sir. Apparently, the authorities are speaking to all his associates again. I have no idea why."

Ah, but *he* did know why. He knew precisely why.

Or, more specifically, *who.*

Breanna Colby.

"I see," he replied, his mind racing.

Marks's visit had to tie in to the trip Lady Breanna had made to Bow Street three days ago. The miserable bitch. She'd obviously accomplished more than he'd realized, done a better job of convincing the police to help her than he'd anticipated.

Still, this conversation had to be strictly routine. Bow Street had no evidence to link him to Cunnings—not then or now—and certainly none to link him to their current murder investigation. They were searching for runaway wives, for heaven's sake, not reputable gentlemen.

He'd do nothing to sway their way of thinking. Nor would he antagonize them. To the contrary, he'd be warm, gracious, utterly cooperative.

And Marks would leave no wiser than when he arrived.

Lady Breanna was another matter entirely. She had to be punished for her brazen act.

The very notion made excitement surge through his blood. He'd find a means of punishment that would intensify her fear beyond measure.

And, as a result, heighten his exhilaration even more.

"Sir?" the butler prompted. "What shall I tell Mr. Marks?"

"By all means, show him in," he replied graciously, clasping his hands behind his back. "I'll answer any questions he has."

And then I'll deal with the lovely Breanna Colby.

Four days later, Bow Street delivered its report.

Marks arrived at Medford just before lunch. He propped himself against the sitting-room door frame—a blatant indication that this wasn't going to be a lengthy visit—and relayed his findings to Breanna and Wells.

Thoroughly, meticulously, he read through the entire list of interviews he'd conducted, and their outcomes. He'd spoken with every conceivable one of John Cunnings's associates, from the women he'd squandered his illegally acquired money on, to the men he'd done business with, to his neighbors, to those few friends he'd had. No one knew anything about an assassin, nor did they know of anyone who'd want to kill Cunnings. In fact, they knew nothing more about Cunnings's illegal dealings than they had three months ago—which was nil, other than whatever they'd read in the newspapers.

Having concluded his report, Marks straightened and smoothed his scarlet waistcoat. "That's all I have, my lady." He shut his notebook. "Have you received any more threats?"

Breanna shook her head. "No."

"Then I'd say you're in no immediate danger. Nor is your cousin, Lady Sheldrake. Besides, the point is moot. We have nothing more to go on."

"But Mr. Marks—"

"I've done everything I can, my lady." His mouth set in grim lines. "I can't justify spending another hour on this—not with the current murder investigation I'm involved in. My suggestion is: be careful. Don't go out alone. Tell your cousin the same when she returns from her wedding trip. I noticed you hired some guards. Good idea. The more security you have the better. That'll scare this lunatic off—*if* he plans to carry out his threats. Which I don't think he will." With that, Marks tipped his hat. "Good day, my lady."

He crouched down in the bushes by the roadside, watching as Marks drove through the iron gates and curved onto the road leading away from Medford Manor.

Good. Bow Street's finished. She's on her own now. Which means I can strike whenever I wish. I won't rush it. The time has to be right ...

* * *

It was two days later when the carriage bearing the Lockewood family crest turned off the road, heading toward Medford.

Inside the carriage, Anastasia frowned as the iron gates loomed into view—along with two burly men posted on either side.

"Who are they?" she demanded, scooting to the edge of her seat and eyeing them. "And why are they standing so rigidly at the gates—as if they're sentries?"

"I don't know." Even Damen looked perplexed, his brows knitting as one of the two men gestured for their driver to stop.

The driver complied, and the man approached the carriage.

"I'll need your names, please," he began, peering inside the window. "Then you'll have to wait to be announced . . . oh forgive me, Lady Breanna. I didn't know you'd gone out." He bowed, backed away from the carriage, and waved them on. "Drive right through."

"But I'm not . . ."

Damen stopped Anastasia with a gentle squeeze of her arm. "Thank you," he called to the guard, gesturing for their driver to continue on his way.

"Why did you silence me?" Anastasia demanded, turning to her husband. "He thought I was Breanna."

"I know," Damen responded. "I wanted it that way. It got us inside faster, without further explanation. The sooner we reach the manor, the sooner we find out what the hell's going on here."

Anastasia opened her mouth to reply, then gasped, her attention captured by another, far more enticing, sight. She pointed out the window as the carriage rolled down the drive toward the house. "Damen, look." Her eyes widened, and she stared at the graceful structure to their left, workmen swarming all around it. "That's our house—and it's already standing. Why, it's practically completed."

"I'll be damned." Damen shook his head in amazement, as stunned by the progress that had been made during their absence as was his wife. "Breanna must have had these people working day and night."

"*Breanna* must be working day and night," Anastasia amended. "If I know her, she's overseen all this construction herself. In fact . . ." She scrutinized the area carefully, searching until she saw the bright spot of burnished color that was her cousin's hair. "There she is!" She whipped around. "Dixon, stop," she instructed the driver.

The bewildered driver brought the carriage to a screeching halt.

"Take our bags to the house," Damen advised him, stifling a grin. "We'll follow on foot."

"Yes, m'lord." Dixon alighted, intending to properly assist his passengers, only to have Anastasia fling open her door, knocking him flat on his back as she leapt down from the carriage herself.

"Oh, Dixon, forgive me. Are you all right?" she asked anxiously, relief flooding her face as the driver squirmed to a sitting position.

"Fine, m'lady," he assured her, brushing dirt off his uniform.

"Thank goodness." She gathered up her skirts, looking like a Thoroughbred at the starting gate. "Then if you'll excuse me . . ."

She didn't wait for a reply.

She took off at a run, shouting, "Breanna!" and waving her arm.

Damen swung down from the carriage, offering a hand to the half-crouched, half-sitting driver. "Don't be too hard on yourself, Dixon," he consoled, his lips twitching as he helped the still-dazed driver to his feet. "Keeping up with my wife is next to impossible."

"Yes, sir. Thank you, sir." Dragging his sleeve across his brow, Dixon stared after Anastasia's rapidly moving figure. Then, with a hard shake of his head, he jumped back into his seat and drove on.

Chuckling, Damen watched Stacie rush toward her cousin, shouting over the din and waving frantically.

Breanna glanced up, spotted her, and broke into an immediate run. "Stacie!"

The cousins embraced, laughing as they broke apart, saw all the workmen gaping at them, and realized what a spectacle they were making.

"You're home. I can't believe it!" Breanna grasped Stacie's hands, surveying her from head to toe. "You look wonderful. Positively radiant. Marriage agrees with you." She glanced beyond Stacie and smiled as Damen approached them. "And here's the man responsible for your radiance. Welcome home, Damen."

"Breanna." He kissed her hand, then gave her a warm hug. "It's so good to see you."

"Home, indeed," Stacie piped up, moving excitedly about as she assessed the manor that was fast taking shape. "I can't believe what you've accomplished. My God, have you slept since September?"

A hopeful look lit Breanna's eyes—eyes that seemed unusually puffy, lined, with heavy dark circles beneath them.

For reasons of her own, she disregarded Stacie's question in lieu of her own. "Do you like it? I was half afraid you'd object to the artistic liberties I took. But you were so preoccupied before the wedding, and I couldn't get you to sit still and look at the sketches. And with winter nearly upon us, we had to lay the foundation right away. Either that or we'd have to wait until spring, which would mean your home wouldn't be ready until next fall. I couldn't bear having you in London until then. So I got things started. You'll do all the decorating yourself, of course."

"Of course *not*," Stacie corrected. "I have no talent at decorating, and you know it. I need your help—with every last piece of furniture." She gazed at the half-finished manor again, her eyes growing damp. "You did all this for us . . . Breanna, what would I ever do without you?" She gulped back a sob.

Breanna blinked in surprise. "Stacie, you're crying. Why?"

"Because I'm touched. Because I'm so glad to be home. Because I missed you. Because I can't believe how much you took on while we were away. Because—"

"That's not what I meant," Breanna interrupted, inclining her head in puzzlement. "I know why you're happy. And I'm as thrilled as you—that you're home, that you like what I've done. But you never cry. At least you never used to."

"That was then," Stacie informed her ruefully, dabbing at her eyes. "This is now. I seem to be doing a fair amount of crying these days. Crying and swooning and retching. It's completely unlike me."

Their gazes met.

"You're with child." Breanna's words were a statement, not a question, and she seized Stacie's hands again, staring insightfully at the spot where her mantle covered her abdomen, as if she could see through to the changes beneath. "I knew it. Oh, Stacie, I'm so happy for you." She hugged her cousin, then Damen, tears glistening on her own lashes. "I'm going to be an aunt. Not a second cousin, mind you, because as far as I'm concerned, you're my sister, not my cousin. So, this babe will call me Aunt Breanna." She grew serious for a moment. "Are you all right— you and the babe?"

"*We* are. But Damen's not." Anastasia shot her husband a teasing look. "He's been overwrought the entire trip home. The ship's doctor nearly tossed him overboard several times. Not to mention that the doctor was the first one to disembark when we docked. He nearly knocked down three elderly women in his haste to get away. By now, he's probably at some out-of-the-way alehouse, in a drunken stupor and planning how to avoid the House of Lockewood for the next six months."

Breanna laughed—a small, strained sound. "I'll take that as a warning. Wells will make sure Damen has a full snifter of brandy each night before bed to calm his nerves." Her expression grew hopeful. "That is, if you stay here. You will stay here, won't you? You won't go to London? I know it'll mean less privacy for you, but—"

"I've already sent our driver on to the manor with our bags," Damen interceded, dismissing her concern with a wave of his arm. "Knowing how much Stacie missed you, I'd never think of separating you two again. Besides, this way we can take over supervising the building of our home. Correction, *I* can take over supervising the building of our home. Stacie is to get no closer to the construction than we are now. Please,

Breanna, I'm counting on you to keep an eye on your cousin during the hours I spend at the bank. I'll be forever in your debt."

Anastasia rolled her eyes. "I'm pregnant, Damen, not incapacitated. Fine." She held up her palm to ward off his tirade. "I'll be as docile as a lamb."

"That'll be the day."

"I'll take care of Stacie." Breanna smoothed her hand over her hair— and Stacie could have sworn her fingers shook. "You have my word, Damen. I'll never let any harm befall her. Never."

Breanna's oddly somber tone, her seemingly extreme reaction struck an uneasy chord in Stacie's mind. But before she could open her mouth to respond, her cousin had rushed on.

"I have so much to tell you," she declared, feeling Stacie's quizzical stare, and averting her gaze to avoid it.

Nonetheless, Stacie saw the worried shadow flicker across her face.

"We're hosting that party you and I discussed," Breanna informed her brightly. "Right here. The week after Christmas. Wells, Mrs. Charles, and Mrs. Rhodes planned the whole thing. It will be a holiday party, birthday celebration, and welcome-home gathering all in one. I'm sure it will be the talk of the *ton*. In addition, we've also been invited to a dozen holiday parties elsewhere. Of course, you'll have to tell me which invitations you want to accept and which you don't—"

"Breanna." Stacie had had enough. This sort of aimless babbling was as unusual for Breanna as crying was for her. It was time to get to the bottom of this.

Silencing her cousin's chatter, Stacie lifted Breanna's chin and studied her—closely—for the first time. No, she hadn't imagined the dark shadows beneath Breanna's eyes, nor the strain tightening her face. And her cheeks, when she wasn't smiling, were pale.

"What's wrong?" Stacie demanded. "And don't tell me 'nothing.' I won't believe you. I've had the oddest feeling for over a week now—like something ominous was going on here. Tell me what's happened."

Shoulders sagging, Breanna gave up the pretense.

"I prayed I wouldn't have to tell you," she said, lacing her fingers tightly together. "I prayed it would all be resolved by the time you got home. But it isn't. And now, there's a babe to consider . . . so you have to know."

"Know what?"

"A little over a week ago I received a package—a package and a note." A weighted pause. "They were a warning."

"A warning?" Stacie echoed. "From whom?"

"From the man Father paid to kill you."

"What?" Stacie blanched. "From that assassin who tried—?"

"Yes."

"How can you be so certain?" A muscle flexed in Damen's jaw. "What was in the package? What did the note say? What kind of warning?" Damen's questions sliced the air like a knife, and he slid a protective arm about his wife. "Breanna, I think you'd better tell us everything."

With a weary nod, Breanna did, eliminating none of the details, including the trip she'd made to Bow Street and the lack of information they'd turned up. "But I know in my gut it was *he* who sent them. I think Bow Street agrees, even if they've washed their hands of the matter."

"That explains the extra security," Anastasia concluded aloud. *"And* my uneasy feeling."

"Yes. Wells arranged for guards."

"How can Bow Street just dismiss such blatant evidence?" Anastasia asked, twisting around to gaze up at her husband.

"No crime has been committed," Damen returned quietly, his forehead creased in thought. "Did they talk to the messenger who delivered the package?"

"Yes." Breanna nodded. "He had no contact with whoever sent it. The lad was given the box by his supervisor when he reported for work. And, according to the supervisor, the package was left, along with an envelope containing delivery instructions and a ten pound note, on his doorstep."

"Then Bow Street's exhausted their clues. Also, judging from the headlines of the newspaper we bought in London, they're consumed with this murder investigation." Damen pursed his lips. "There's got to be something we can do. And there is always the chance Marks is right—that this madman will stop his threats as quickly as he started them."

"You don't believe that," Stacie said quietly.

Soberly, Damen met her gaze, deliberately masking the full extent of his worry, yet unable to demean what they had together by offering her a barefaced lie. "No. I don't."

A heartbeat of silence.

Breanna drew herself up—a gesture that proclaimed she was battling her own fears, and determined to master them. "This is the first day I've ventured out since Mr. Marks delivered his report," she admitted. "I've been too alarmed and too preoccupied to go about my business. But when I awakened this morning, I made a decision. I refuse to become a prisoner in my own home—*again*. Father's gone. No one's going to do to me what he did.

"Besides," she continued, the edge in her tone softening, giving way to anticipation—and more than a touch of eagerness. "I was impatient to come out here and see how much work had been done on your home." She clasped Stacie's hands, hoping against hope that she and Damen might still salvage the pleasure of watching their new home take shape—a surprise she'd relished giving them long before the threatening package arrived. "Let's not let this ruin your homecoming. Come. I want to show you your new manor—or at least the portion of it that's completed."

"Of course." Anastasia tossed Damen a beseeching look—one that spoke volumes. She was asking him to grant Breanna the measure of peace she needed—for the moment. There would be plenty of time to dwell on the horrid possibilities suggested by the threatening package. But for now, it was time to savor the joys of being home. For all their sakes.

"All right." Damen's taut nod told her he understood, although he did pause long enough to scan the grounds with an unsettled eye. "But," he added, unable to totally dismiss the worry that still gnawed at him, "after that I want to inspect those dolls and read that note."

"Of course." Breanna agreed at once, more grateful than she was unnerved. "Oh, and Damen? If you could convince Wells that your being here means there's another strong and able-bodied man to see to our safety, I'd be forever in your debt. That poor man has taken on the roles of guardian, overseer, and sentry. I worry about his strength holding out."

"I'll talk to him the minute we get to the manor." Damen's lips thinned into a tight, unyielding line. "As for you and Stacie, nothing and no one will get near you. You can count on that." He cleared his throat, deferring this conversation for later. "Now, let's take a tour of our home."

He guided the two women forward, pausing only long enough to peer over his shoulder, his penetrating gaze raking the grounds in one more exhaustive sweep.

Other than the crew of workmen toiling in their immediate vicinity, everything seemed quiet.

Safe, he thought. At least for now.

5

So this is Lady Breanna's bedchamber.

He smiled darkly, hovering near the doorway and surveying the feminine decor.

Immaculate mahogany furniture. Canopied bed. Pristine bedcovers. An array of tiny porcelain figures decorating the nightstand, dresser, and fireplace mantel.

Orderly, delicate, and intact. Just like its owner.

She wouldn't stay intact for long.

He caught a glimpse of himself in the looking glass, and smiled at the bizarre image he made. Workman's clothes. They hardly suited him. Still, the disguise had gained him entry to the estate. He'd known today would be the day. The minute he heard the gossip in London—that the Marquess of Sheldrake had returned from his wedding trip—he knew she'd finally be leaving her sanctuary today. If only to show the partially finished manor to the newly married couple.

She'd surprised him by leaving the house early—even before her cousin arrived. Evidently, she'd grown tired of being cooped up. Or perhaps it was that more than a week without threats had made her bold. Either way, she'd strolled across the grounds, venturing over to the construction site.

Giving him the perfect opportunity to lie in wait.

And then, when Anastasia and her new husband arrived, to do what he'd come here to do.

The ladder he'd taken from the shed had proved most useful. He'd propped it against the rear of the house—the side facing the wooded section of property—and climbed into a hall window on the second floor.

From there, he'd made his way to Breanna's room.

He rubbed his gloved palms together, moving slowly from the mantel to the dressing table. Idly, he fingered first one object, then another. He had to choose wisely. Something personal. Yet nothing she'd miss. Also, something intimate.

He lifted the silver-handled brush, then changed his mind. No. She'd notice that immediately.

The porcelain figures.

He prowled about the chamber, studying the dozens of tiny glass statues, wondering which would be least missed.

None of them fit that bill.

The lady was a collector. She obviously took great pride in her treasures. If any one of them disappeared, she'd realize it was gone.

No. It had to be something else.

He glanced into the modest sitting room beyond.

A sketchpad sat neatly on the desk, beside which lay a quill, some pencils, and a pile of papers.

She was a good artist, he mused, flipping through the book. The sketches were all of rooms, all in different stages of completion. A bedchamber, with a large, four-poster bed. An impressive walnut library whose shelves were lined with books. A sitting room. A nursery. Each page contained notes on recommendations for carpets, drapes, paintings, and other personal touches, bearing in mind "Stacie's" favorite colors and textures.

Obviously, these were Lady Breanna's ideas for the manor being built across the way.

He shook his head, flipped the pad shut, and replaced it. Instead, he reached for the loose pile of papers alongside it.

Ah. Other sketches, ones that were far less defined than the first set. Clearly, these were abstract doodlings, done during thoughtful moments, then torn away as extraneous. A bouquet of flowers. A ship sailing the ocean. Snow falling around a manor, blanketing the grounds in white.

Lingering over the winter sketch, his eyes glittered triumphantly. The starkness. The long stretch of bare snow. Yes. This one would do quite nicely.

He folded the sketch, slipped it into his pocket. Swiftly, he rearranged the contents of the desk so they looked undisturbed.

Now for the intimate item.

For this, he needed something that would make her feel truly invaded. Invaded and, once he'd added his personal touch, terrified.

He didn't hesitate. Going over to the dresser, he eased open the drawers until he found what he sought.

A chemise. White. Unadorned and untainted.

Untainted—for now.

He stuffed the undergarment beneath his coat, then mindfully shut every drawer.

His job done, he slipped out of the bedchamber and retraced his steps: through the hall, out the window, down the ladder.

He returned the ladder to the shed, where he gathered up some tools— tools he had no idea how to use but that seemed functional enough for one who was supposedly building a house. After all, he had to look the part of a workman, in the unlikely event someone stopped him.

Keeping his step loose-limbed, he made his way through the wooded portion of the estate. Cap pulled low, he threw continuous sidelong glances to his right and left, ensuring he was alone.

He was.

This might be the last time he'd be able to enter the manor via this route, he reflected. Once his gifts had been delivered—clearly divulging his unwelcome visit—guards would doubtless be swarming the estate, posted on this section and *every* section, rather than just at the front gates as they were now. That diligent butler would see to it.

Ah, well. He had other means of entry. More traditional means.

Means Lady Breanna herself had offered him.

He'd just eased onto the main path and was about to head toward his concealed carriage, when he heard the voice.

"You there! What are you doing?"

He froze, his hand immediately slipping into his pocket, closing around his pistol.

Slowly, he pivoted about, keeping his head down—low enough so his face remained hidden, but not so low that he couldn't see his potential adversary from beneath the cap's rim.

One glance told him that this stocky, uniformed person was not a workman.

Fine. That meant he wouldn't know anyone on the crew—a fact that might just spare his life.

Staring at the dirt, the assassin assumed the role his clothing pro- claimed him to be. "I need a drink," he muttered. "I've been layin' bricks all morning."

"A drink?" Rather than sympathetic, the man sounded assessing. "It's scarcely midday."

An adversary with a conscience, he thought, fingers gripping the pis- tol more tightly. Not a promising sign.

Still, he'd make one last attempt.

"Yer right, sir." He took a half-step backward, appearing to retreat even as he purposefully kept his quarry in view. "I'll get back to work, get me ale at quittin' time."

He waited for a reaction, impatiently hoping the man would continue along, make this easy on both of them.

It didn't happen that way.

The man's eyes narrowed suspiciously. "You don't look too eager to go back. In fact, you look more like a fleeing thief than a thirsty workman." He stepped forward, his hand sliding to his pocket—and doubtless his weapon. "You're coming with me. We'll soon find out who you are."

"Now that's where you're wrong." Jerking up his head, the assassin simultaneously whipped out his gun—flourishing it before the other man could even begin to grope for his. "You *won't* find out who I am. No one will."

The guard's eyes darted from the assassin's face to his pistol, widening in fear as he realized he'd fatally underestimated his opponent.

A cry formed on his lips.

It was never uttered.

The single bullet penetrated his heart.

He was dead before he hit the ground.

Rather than feel relieved, the assassin felt a surge of annoyance. How irritating, he contemplated, eyeing the lifeless man crumpled at his feet. Now he'd have to dispose of the body *and* stage a reason for the shooting. After all, he couldn't have Bow Street discover the guard here, thus introducing the possibility that the murder was tied to Medford Manor—and to the package Lady Breanna had received. That might cause them to reopen her case.

No. He had to remove the body, place it elsewhere. Somewhere and in some manner that would provide an explanation as to why this man— one who happened to be on his way to do a guard shift at Medford Manor—would be killed.

But move it where? And why would someone kill this fellow in cold blood?

The answer was as obvious as it was ironic, because the victim himself had provided it.

A robbery.

He'd make it appear that the killing was the result of a theft, that the guard had resisted the bandit's demands—and paid for it with his life.

Swiftly, he glanced about, made sure he was still alone, undetected. He was.

Further, the pounding and hammering, still reverberating from the construction site, was deafening enough to ensure that the sound of his gunshot had been drowned out—a lucky break, since the pistol crack would normally have been audible from this distance.

In conclusion, he had enough time to properly arrange things.

That determined, he crouched down, rifled the guard's pockets. The first thing he did was to confiscate the man's weapon. Just as expected, it was an average flintlock pistol. Unimpressive and unimaginative.

He spared it but one disparaging glance before shoving it into his own pocket, to be disposed of later. Then, he helped himself to the thin wad of pound notes and handful of shillings he found in the man's coat. He grimaced as he extracted a plain, well-worn timepiece. Cheap and tawdry. Ah, well. He'd bring it home and destroy it, so there would be nothing to trace back to him. True, it would be a nuisance. Still, it was a necessary nuisance, if he wanted to protect himself and convince the authorities that this murder had indeed been the result of a theft.

He tore the guard's coat in two spots, mussed his shirt and waistcoat. Minutes later, he dragged the body onto the path. He trudged the exact route the guard would have taken to reach his post, hauling the body a respectable distance before hiding it in the bushes on the roadside halfway between the rear portion of the estate and the front gates.

With a distasteful frown, he brushed dirt off his gloves, simultaneously retracing his steps until he reached the isolated spot where he'd left his carriage.

How irksome to have wasted his talents in so demeaning a fashion, he brooded, climbing into the driver's seat, taking up the reins, and guiding the horses onto the deserted path.

On the other hand, the guard seemed of good stock. True, not a member of the gentry, but not a gutter rat either. He had morals, dignity. He'd probably raised his children that way.

Perhaps he had a daughter. A daughter on the threshold of womanhood, maybe even a virgin. Now *that* might be worth looking into.

The assassin's irritation vanished. He'd have to find out the dead fellow's name, get some information on his background, his family. Then, he'd decide whether or not this was worth pursuing.

That line of thought reminded him that there was probably a message awaiting him from the Continent—a message whose contents he was eager to read.

He urged his horses into a trot.

Jamie Knox's body was discovered two hours later.

Known for his punctuality, Knox was missed within twenty minutes of the time when he'd been expected to report for duty at the front gates. And since he only lived a mile away and traveled to work by foot rather than by carriage, it seemed logical to send a groundskeeper to his cottage to find out what was keeping him.

His puzzled wife assured the servant that Jamie had left for work at the usual time. That fact aroused everyone's suspicions—enough to check out Knox's walking route more thoroughly.

It was one of the young gardeners who found him, coming upon Knox's lifeless body in a thicket of brush.

Wild-eyed, the lad backed away from the corpse, taking off for the front gates at a dead run. In a voice trembling with tears and dread, he blurted the situation out to the guards.

Pandemonium broke loose.

Breanna had just arranged for tea to be served in the sitting room, and Wells was congratulating Anastasia and Damen on becoming expectant parents, when the ruckus outside reached their ears.

"What on earth is going on?" Breanna murmured, moving aside the sitting-room curtain and peering out. She started. "Something's wrong."

She dropped the curtain, her face pale as she turned to Wells.

"I'll find out," he said at once.

"I'll go with you," Damen added quickly. He jumped up from the settee and followed Wells into the hall.

Anastasia and Breanna exchanged glances. Then, without a word, they left the sitting room, joining the men as they headed for the front door.

The pounding started before Wells could reach his post.

He hurried forward, flung open the door.

"What is it?" he demanded, meeting the grave stare of Albert Mahoney, the head of the security staff he'd personally hired to safeguard the estate.

"One of my guards," Mahoney replied, not mincing any words. "Knox. He's been killed. Shot to death."

"Oh my God." Breanna's hand flew to her mouth. "Here?"

"No, ma'am. On his way to work." Mahoney swallowed, turning to face Breanna with a tight, drawn expression. "From what we can tell, he was robbed. His money's missing. So's his timepiece. And, of course, his gun. He must have been grabbed from behind, which would explain why he didn't have a chance to draw his weapon. My guess is he fought back. And the thief shot him."

"How close to our gates?" Anastasia demanded. "Where exactly did you find him?"

Seeing Anastasia for the first time, Mahoney blinked, his head whipping from Anastasia to Breanna and back again.

"Mr. Mahoney, this is my cousin—the Marchioness of Sheldrake," Breanna managed, her voice shaky. "And her husband, Lord Sheldrake, head of the House of Lockewood. I'm sure you've heard of him."

"I have." Mahoney gave a half bow. "An honor to meet you both. Sorry it has to be under such grim circumstances."

"As are we," Damen replied.

"Speak freely, Mr. Mahoney," Breanna advised him. "Both Lord and

Lady Sheldrake are aware of why you've been hired. They know the entire story, since it affects them, too."

"Very well." The guard nodded his compliance, turned to address Anastasia. "We found Knox in the bushes off the path leading to the manor—around the curve, about halfway between the rear of the estate and the front gates."

"And you say he was shot—by a thief." Damen frowned. "How do you know it was a thief?"

The guard gave an uneasy cough. "We don't *know* anything, not for sure. No culprit's been found. Still, Knox's valuables were missing. So my guess is, it was a thief. Unless you have proof that says otherwise."

"I don't." Damen raked a hand through his hair.

"No attempt was made to break into Medford Manor," Mahoney reminded him. "So I doubt it was the intruder we're guarding against."

"Unless the intruder never got a chance to break in because Knox scared him off first. Or unless he had no intentions of breaking in, but was just scrutinizing the estate, watching Breanna's comings and goings. There are a dozen 'unlesses.' But none of them is worth a damn. They're pure speculation—not enough to get Bow Street to ride out here, much less to take action." Damen began pacing about the entranceway.

Mahoney eyed him speculatively. "I've sent for a constable, sir. He'll take all the information and make arrangements for the body. If there's anything you think he should know—"

"No." Damen halted, gave a hard shake of his head. "There's nothing. Nothing but a bad feeling. And that's not evidence."

"No, sir, it's not." Mahoney cleared his throat. "If you'll excuse me, I'll get back to my post. I've got to calm everyone down, make sure the constable arrives—"

"Go." Damen gestured for the guard to leave. "Do what you have to."

"Did Mr. Knox have a family?" Breanna broke in, her fingers laced so tightly together, they ached.

"Yes, m'lady. A wife and two grown sons."

"His wife . . . she's been told?"

A terse nod. "Her sons live nearby. They'll help their mother out, to the best of their abilities, anyway. But they have families of their own and—"

"Tell Mrs. Knox we'll take care of her expenses," Breanna interrupted. "*All* her expenses, from a proper funeral to whatever she needs—clothing, food—anything. And please, tell her how sorry we are." With a choked sound, she averted her head.

"I'm sure she'll appreciate that. I know my wife would." Mahoney paused, staring down at the tips of his shoes. "Lady Breanna, if you'll forgive me for speaking out of turn, stop blaming yourself. Knox knew the risks of his job. We all do. Most of the time we beat the odds. But once in a while—we don't. The thief pulled the trigger, not you."

Unsteadily, Breanna nodded. "Yes . . . the thief."

A heavy silence descended.

"I'll be going now," Mahoney said at last. "If you need me, send for me."

Wells shut the door behind the retreating guard. "You don't think it was a thief," he said to Damen, a statement rather than a question.

Damen's stare was brooding. "If it was, his appearance was extremely coincidental, wouldn't you say?"

"Yes, I would."

Breanna spun around, faced the men. "You think it was . . . *he*. Well, so do I."

"I think it *might* have been he," Damen corrected her gently.

"If it was, his message is clear," Anastasia pronounced, worry glittering in her eyes. "He's showing us no guards can keep him away."

"Then we're prisoners." Twin spots of red stained Breanna's cheeks, and she looked almost as angry as she did fearful. "We can't go out, we can't protect ourselves . . ." She shot Wells a purposeful look. "We certainly can't have that party. It's too risky. We'll have to cancel it."

"Even if we do, that's still no guarantee we'll be stopping him from doing whatever it is he intends to do." Anastasia's palm drifted automatically to her abdomen as if to protect her unborn child from harm.

Damen followed her motion, and felt his gut clench. Perhaps they were all overreacting, letting their imaginations run wild. But for his family's sake, for the sake of his own peace of mind, he couldn't take that risk.

Abruptly, he made a decision.

"I've got to ride into Town." He reached for his topcoat.

"To Town? Why?" Quick as a wink, Anastasia was beside him. "Damen, what are you planning?"

He caressed her cheek, kissed the bridge of her nose. "I want to speak with someone. Someone I think can help us."

"Who?"

"Royce Chadwick." Damen shrugged into his coat. "You don't know him. He couldn't make it to our wedding; he was out of the country. But he's an old acquaintance of mine. We attended Oxford together. From there, he went on to the military. He was a brilliant strategist during the war with Napoleon. Since then, well, let's just say he's gone on to become the best at what he does."

"Which is?"

"He finds people—people who either can't or don't want to be found."

"Royce Chadwick," Wells repeated. "Isn't he the Earl of Searby's brother?"

"Yes. Although Edmund and Royce are about as alike as tea and spirits."

"Indeed." Wells was frowning now. "If gossip stands me correctly, the earl's brother is a reckless fellow—a bit *too* wild and daring."

Damen's lips curved. "Yes, Royce is not your staid ballroom type. He lives by his own set of rules. But he's incredibly shrewd, he's honest, and he's smart as a whip. And, as I said, he's the best man I know at finding people who have vanished—people even Bow Street can't find."

"Such as people who choose not to repay their loans?" Stacie guessed, astutely determining how Damen knew of this Royce Chadwick's work firsthand.

"Exactly." Her husband smiled, admiring her keen insights—insights he'd come to know and love. "He's done some fine work for me *and* my bank." Pausing, he framed Stacie's face between his palms, bent to kiss her shining crown of hair. "Stay put," he ordered. His glance lifted to include Breanna. "Both of you. In this case, it's better to be overcautious. Wells, don't let either of them out of your sight. I'll be back later today—with a plan."

6

Royce Chadwick lived and worked on Bond Street.

His home, which also served as his office, stood in a row of three-story, gated Town houses, all of which exuded an aura of understated wealth and power—an aura that both commanded a second look and, at the same time, demanded privacy.

A description one could just as easily ascribe to Royce.

He and Damen had met at Oxford. The two men had developed an immediate affinity for each other, despite the fact that their philosophies of life differed sharply.

Damen was a pragmatist. He met life head-on, confronted its challenges, and emerged from them wiser, surer, and farther along the path to his own success.

Royce created his own challenges.

Bold, defiant, he took on the world, unwilling to accept the status quo, loath to compromise. He lived on the edge, pushed the rules as far as they could go—and then some—a fact that nearly got him expelled from Oxford on more than one occasion by the narrow-minded administration who ran it.

But, damn, he was brilliant. Brilliant and, in his own way, honorable. True, he was unconventional, driven by demons he never discussed. And yes, he lived by his own code of conduct, conduct that too often got him in trouble. But he never used people, never took advantage of those less intelligent or weaker than he. On the contrary, he was a loner, relying upon his own ingenuity and cunning to get him what he wanted—partially because he was a man of integrity and partially because he refused to settle for the mediocrity offered by others. He probed, he challenged, yet he drew his own figurative line—a line he wouldn't cross to reach his ends.

In short, reckless or not, Royce Chadwick was a fine man—one Damen admired and, at the moment, needed.

Pulling his carriage alongside the house, Damen swung down, hastened up the steps, and knocked.

An older man with ice blue eyes, silver hair, and a cloaked expression
answered the door. "Yes? Ah, Lord Sheldrake." His thin lips pursed so
tightly they seemed to disappear into his face. "Forgive me, sir, I didn't
realize you had an appointment."

"Don't apologize, Hibbert. I didn't."

Damen stepped into the entranceway, knowing he had his work cut
out for him. Trying to talk his way past this man was akin to single-
handedly taking on an army. Hibbert was more than Royce's butler, more
even than his steward and his clerk. He was all three—*and* a veritable
sentry who stood between his employer and the world. Plus, he was
Royce's right hand, his advisor, ofttimes his eyes and his ears. Hibbert's
distinguished, elderly appearance stood him in good stead when he was
helping Royce gather information. No one suspected that beneath the
aged, benign exterior lurked the intelligence, cunning, and agility of a
fox.

"Is Royce home?" Damen demanded without preliminaries. "Because, if so, I need to see him. Now."

Hibbert arched a brow. "It's not like you to become overwrought, my
lord."

"That's because I'm usually here because someone's threatening my
money. This time someone's threatening my wife."

A sharp intake of breath. "I see." Hibbert studied Damen for one long,
thoughtful moment. Then, he nodded. "Have a seat in Lord Royce's office.
You know where it is. I'll see if I can free up some of his time."

"I'd appreciate that." Damen strode down the hall, turning into the
cluster of rooms Royce used for his work. He stepped into the outer
office, bypassing the settee and pacing over to the bookshelves. He
tapped the volumes impatiently, not really seeing them, then walked over
to the window and gazed out.

Damn, he hoped he was overreacting. Maybe it really had been a thief
who'd killed Knox. Maybe it wasn't that demented assassin. Maybe the
incident was totally unrelated to the package Breanna had received.
Maybe neither she nor Anastasia were in danger.

Then again, maybe they were.

"Hibbert's right. You aren't yourself."

Damen turned, grateful as hell to see Royce Chadwick lounging in the
doorway. "No, I'm not."

"Welcome home." The tall, broad-shouldered man straightened, folding his arms across his chest and studying Damen through penetrating
midnight blue eyes that were so dark people often mistook them for
black. "Congratulations, albeit belatedly, on your marriage. I'm sorry I

missed the wedding. It couldn't be helped. I was halfway back from India." Royce ran a hand over his square jaw, missing nothing of his colleague's distress. "For a man who just returned from his wedding trip, you look wretched. Marriage too much for you?"

"Hardly." Damen wasn't in a lighthearted mood. "In fact, I'm beginning to wish that Stacie and I had never come home. She was finally safe. The biggest worry I had was seeing how weak she became after perpetually kneeling over the chamber pot—"

Dark brows shot up. "Kneeling over the chamber pot? Does that mean you have another announcement to make?"

"As a matter of fact, yes."

A low whistle. "I'm impressed. After only three months of marriage. No wonder you enjoyed your trip so much." Royce gave Damen a mock salute before moving into the room, crossing over toward the inner office and gesturing for Damen to follow. "Double my congratulations, then."

"Royce, we need to talk." Damen entered the room, shut the door behind him.

"So I gathered. Hibbert said it was urgent." All humor having vanished, Royce perched against the mahogany desk, turned his watchful gaze back on Damen. "He also said that it concerned your wife. Judging from your agitation, it must be serious."

"It is. At least I think it is." Damen paused, drew a slow breath to compose himself.

"Sit down. I'll get you a drink." Royce indicated the armchair by his desk, then went to the sideboard, poured two glasses of Madeira. "Here. Drink this. You obviously need it. Then, tell me what's wrong. I've never seen you so unnerved."

"I've never *felt* so unnerved." Damen tossed off the contents of the glass. "Then again, I've never cared as deeply about anyone as I do about Stacie. And now, with the babe on the way . . ." His head came up. "Royce, I want you to find someone for me."

Royce's eyes narrowed. "Who?"

"That's the problem. I don't know. I don't know his name, where he lives, or what he looks like. I'm not even sure he's in England—although my instincts scream out that he is. All I know is that I need him found. Found and locked up."

Slowly, Royce sipped at his Madeira. If he was taken aback by Damen's request, he kept his surprise carefully hidden. "Start at the beginning. Not with what you *don't* know, but with what you *do* know. The circumstances that brought you here, the basis for your apprehension."

A terse nod. "I'm sure Hibbert told you who I had him checking into for me while you were in India."

"The Viscount Medford. Yes, he told me. He also told me that Medford owed money everywhere, to everyone. And that he was recouping it by involving himself in some pretty shady business dealings— shadier, as it turned out, than any of us realized. But Medford's in prison now. So he's hardly a threat." A heartbeat of a pause. "Does this have to do with what happened right after his arrest? That assassin Medford hired through Cunnings—the one who showed up at the docks to do away with your wife?"

"You heard about that, then."

"The minute I set foot on English soil. Does that surprise you?"

Damen shrugged. "Not really. Some things can't be kept quiet. Do you know all the details?"

"I asked a few questions at Bow Street. They filled me in. This paid killer aimed at your wife, but before he could shoot, he was maimed by her cousin. He fled the scene, stopped off at the bank to silence Cunnings—permanently—then vanished. Is that close enough?"

"All but the last. He didn't vanish—at least not for good."

Royce's glass paused midway to his lips. "He's back."

"It damned well looks that way." With that, Damen told Royce about the note and package Breanna had received, her subsequent trip to Bow Street, and the precautionary security Wells had hired. He concluded by relaying the news that a guard had been killed earlier today, describing where Knox had been when the alleged thief came upon him.

Royce listened intently, swirling the contents of his drink, his brow furrowed in thought. When Damen finished, he took a deep swallow of Madeira, then placed the glass on his desk. "I can see why you're worried," he said. "As for Bow Street, I wouldn't expect much help from them. They're up to their necks investigating the murders that are throwing the *ton* into a frenzy. Not to mention that you've given them no real proof to go on. Which doesn't mean the threat to your wife and her cousin isn't real, only that you can't count on Bow Street to hunt this assassin down."

Damen leaned forward. "I agree. The question is, can we count on *you* to hunt him down?"

Pensively, Royce rubbed the back of his neck. "This is an ugly situation, Damen."

"Since when has that deterred you? Usually, the greater the challenge, the more determined you are to go after it. Hell, this should really intrigue you—an unknown assailant, a crime that could happen anywhere, anytime. It's just the kind of danger you thrive on. So what's stopping you?"

"This crime involves lives. Lives of people you care about."

"That should motivate you, not frighten you off."

"I'm not frightened. I'm realistic. Locating a faceless, nameless assassin is not exactly my specialty."

"An assassin is nothing more than an exceedingly violent criminal. And understanding criminals' minds is precisely how you manage to track them down."

"The criminals I track have names and faces," Royce reminded him. "You're talking about something entirely different."

"Surely you've met men who enjoy killing. All those years in the military—there must have been some soldiers who actually enjoyed pulling the trigger."

In response, Royce's jaw set, his dark eyes glittering harshly. "I've met men who enjoy killing others *and* men who thrive on destroying others without actually killing them. And not just in the military. So, do I understand a mind like this assassin's? Yes. But you know the way I work, Damen. My tactics involve taking risks—big risks. I won't jeopardize your wife's life."

"Stacie's life is already in jeopardy."

Silence.

Damen slammed his glass to the desk. "Does this mean you refuse to help me?"

Royce studied the naked pain on his friend's face, swore quietly under his breath—and relented. "No. I'll help you. I'll do as much as I can. As much as you'll let me," he amended. "You might not like my ideas, *or* my methods. Not when it comes to a matter this close to your heart."

"I'll take that chance."

Nodding, Royce rifled through some pages on his desk. "The other problem I have is that I'm in the middle of another case—one I took on weeks ago. I can't walk away from that."

"I wouldn't ask you to. Handle both cases at once. Set up an office at Medford if you need to. Bring Hibbert. I don't care. Just find this lunatic before he . . ." Damen bit off the rest of his sentence, too sickened to utter it.

"He's not a lunatic," Royce countered quietly. "Let's begin with that. At least not in the way you mean. He's unbalanced, yes, but he's very controlled, very methodical, very intelligent. He couldn't be a professional assassin unless he was. He's got to be thorough, well-organized, and have excellent timing. Which means his mind is quick, maybe even as quick as his pistol. To relegate him to the role of madman would be a grave error in judgment—one that could cost you dearly." Royce's lips pursed in thought. "I want to see that letter. And the dolls. I also want to talk to Lady Breanna, hear everything she remembers about the night her father was arrested, or rather, *after* he was arrested and the assassin showed up." A wary stare. "Tell me about her."

"Who? Breanna?"

"Yes. Is she fragile? Will I have an hysterical female on my hands? Is she a swooner, one who'll collapse each time I ask a question that triggers a memory? Or is she a wailer, one who will drench three handkerchiefs before I find out everything I need to?"

Despite the gravity of the situation, Damen couldn't stifle a smile. "You don't have a very high opinion of women, do you? Odd, considering, from what I've seen over the years, they have a *very* high opinion of you. They gravitate to you like flies to honey—until you tire of them and move on."

"On the contrary, I have a very high opinion of women. They're ideal companions—both in bed and out—splendid conversationalists and, before you berate me for not giving your wife the credit she's due, occasionally fine business partners. In fact, I often suspect that women are smarter than men—smart enough to know that it's best to hide that fact from our easily shattered self-esteem. But when it comes to emotions, all that wisdom goes straight to hell. They whine, they weep, they cajole, they pout. When that happens, I become exasperated and walk away. I'm not the comforting type. Nor the type who's easily moved or manipulated. So I'm asking you, what is Lady Breanna like? Particularly now, when she's under duress?"

"She's a remarkable young woman," Damen replied honestly. "She's been through a lot, particularly these past few months. Finding out what her father was capable of, weathering the scandal that followed his arrest—she's been astonishingly strong. I don't think you have to worry about her weeping or swooning. She's not inclined to do either."

"Good." That determined, Royce rose to his feet in one fluid motion. "I'll ride to Kent with you, attempt to make some sense out of this—at least enough to keep your wife and Lady Breanna safe while we figure out who this killer is and when he's going to strike."

"How long can you stay?"

"Just overnight. I've got to get back here by tomorrow, tie up some loose ends. I promised Edmund I'd spend Christmas with him and his family. Then, if necessary, I'll return to Lady Breanna's estate. I take it you're staying there rather than here in Town?"

"Yes." A terse nod. "Christmas. I'd almost forgotten about it." Damen frowned, speaking half to himself. "Breanna wants to cancel her party."

"What party?"

"She and Anastasia both just turned twenty-one. They planned a party to celebrate that and the holidays."

Royce grew thoughtful. "Canceling it might be unwise."

"Why?"

"Let me read that note. Then I'll answer your question." Royce inclined his head. "When is this party scheduled to be held?"

"On the twenty-eighth and the twenty-ninth of December. But now, with Jamie Knox being murdered—"

"As I said, let me read the note. After that, we'll make a decision about the party." Royce gestured toward the door. "Go home to your wife. I'll fill Hibbert in, then follow in my own carriage."

"Fine." Damen stood as well, giving Royce a grateful look. "Thank you. I'm in your debt."

"Not yet you're not. If we figure out who this killer is, stop him from hurting anyone else—*then* you'll be in my debt."

7

The guard held up a commanding hand.

Royce reined his horses to a stop, waiting patiently at the gates of Medford Manor for the expected interrogation.

Two uniformed sentries approached his phaeton slowly, carefully, each of them keeping one hand inside his pocket, doubtless clutching his pistol lest it be needed. The first guard held up a lantern, using its light to better make out Royce's features in the growing darkness of the evening.

"Can I help you, sir?" he inquired, reaching Royce and staring him down with a hard, no-nonsense look.

Who could blame him, given that one of his men had been killed that very day?

"My name is Royce Chadwick. The Marquess of Sheldrake is expecting me."

The guard studied Royce for another moment—presumably matching his physical appearance to the description Damen had provided. Clearly satisfied with what he saw, he relaxed. "Yes, my lord, he is. Go right through." He gestured for the other guard to open the gates.

A minute later, the gates made a grating sound, and swung wide to admit Royce's phaeton.

Nodding politely, Royce led his horses on, guiding them down the long drive leading to the manor. He took the opportunity to look around, taking in as much of the scenery as twilight would permit.

He could make out the construction site, a broad area that would soon house what appeared to be an imposing dwelling. That would be Damen's new home, Royce reflected. Hibbert had reported to him that the marquess planned to move to his wife's family estate once their new manor had been completed. Evidently, the construction was coming along nicely. But it was far from finished.

Which meant that workmen would be coming and going from the

grounds at an alarming rate. And that, in turn, meant the assassin could more easily find his way onto the estate, lose himself in a crowd of people.

The most logical thing for Royce to do was to shut down the construction—at least for now. On the other hand, he might be able to use that accessibility to Medford Manor to his advantage. He wasn't sure yet. But he wasn't ready to close any doors—not until he had every shred of information in his possession *and* the time to evaluate it.

Rounding the drive, Royce brought his phaeton to a stop, and swung down to his feet. He'd reviewed the details of the case with Hibbert before leaving London. Then, he'd mulled them over during his two-hour ride to Kent. The package Lady Breanna had received, the too-coincidental murder of the guard—the whole situation had a very unpleasant taste to it. Instinct told Royce that Damen's worries were well-founded. The question was, could they find this animal, stop him in time?

Mounting the front steps, he knocked.

A distinguished older man with spectacles answered the door, and a look of consummate relief swept across his face as he scrutinized their visitor, determined who he was. "Lord Royce," he stated.

"Yes."

"Come in." The butler stepped aside. "My name is Wells. Lord Sheldrake's been expecting you. According to him . . . that is, I'm praying . . . truthfully, we're *all* praying that you can help keep Miss Breanna and Miss Stacie safe." Wells cleared his throat, abruptly remembering his place—and his composure. "Your room is already made up. I'll have a footman carry in your bags." He extended his hand to take Royce's topcoat.

"Thank you." Royce shrugged out of the thick wool coat, handing it over. He assessed the butler quickly, although little insight was needed to see that this man was loyal to the core, and deeply attached to the two grown women he still considered to be his young charges.

That would be an asset and a liability.

It meant that Wells could be counted upon for any and every form of assistance. He could also, however, be counted upon to let his feelings interfere with his objectivity.

And *that* could be a problem.

Then again, Damen suffered from the same affliction. He was so bloody in love with his wife, not to mention doubly protective of her now that she was pregnant, that it was dubious whether or not he could be counted upon to act with his customary pragmatism.

Which left the women.

Royce frowned. Lord help him if Damen's wife wasn't every bit as bold and strong-willed as he'd described her. And as for Lady Breanna, well, she'd better be more than remarkable. She'd better have the internal strength of a soldier about to march into battle.

"I'll show you to the sitting room," Wells was saying. "The family is gathered there. Lord Sheldrake thought you'd want to speak with them before you freshened up for dinner."

"He's right. I would."

Royce followed Wells down the hall, glancing about as he did.

Medford Manor was spacious and warm, an appealing combination of aged beauty and modern freshness. Twin staircases with curving, mahogany banisters, divided by a rich Oriental carpet, were accented with low tables filled with vases of holly sprigs and snowdrops and, hanging on the walls, intricate needlepoints depicting sunsets, children playing in the snow, and colorful gardens.

Interesting. It was as if several generations had had a hand in fashioning this place, each adding its own strokes to the canvas, yet together creating a painting that blended together as naturally as dawn and day.

He was growing more and more curious about the cousins he was about to meet. He knew little about them, other than the fact that they strongly resembled each other, and that Anastasia had been raised in the States—Philadelphia, if he correctly recalled. She must be extraordinary for Damen to have fallen so hard, so fast, not to mention brilliant for him to have entered into a business partnership with her—a partnership that, according to Damen, had been forged on his respect for Anastasia's business acumen rather than his personal feelings for her.

Where did Lady Breanna fit into all this? Royce mused. She *hadn't* been raised in America. She'd been raised right here, by a father who'd effectively sealed her off from the world, relegated her to the manor while he tried to manipulate her future in order to cling to his own. A father who'd turned out to be, not only a felon and a scoundrel, but a cold-hearted bastard who'd resort to murder to achieve his ends.

What effect had that had on her?

He was about to find out.

"Lord Royce has arrived," Wells announced in the sitting room doorway.

All three of the room's occupants rose.

"Royce, come in." Damen moved forward, his arm wrapped around the waist of a beautiful young woman with delicate features, jade green eyes, and auburn hair that tumbled, unbound, about her shoulders. "This is my wife, Anastasia."

Boldly, Anastasia Lockewood appraised Royce as he approached, kissed her hand.

"Lady Sheldrake. It's a pleasure."

"I'm happy to meet you, my lord," she replied, still studying his face.

"I didn't even know of your existence until today. But, based on Damen's description of the investigations you conduct for him, I have the feeling you helped fit together the pieces to a very ugly puzzle several months ago that ended up saving my life. For that, I thank you."

Royce inclined his head with interest. A straightforward, candid woman—now *that* was refreshing.

"You're welcome," he responded with a hint of a smile. "But I'm afraid I can't take credit for the investigation you're describing. I was in India when Damen sought me out. My associate is the one who did the probing."

Damen's wife smiled, an open, infectious grin. "Then please thank him for me. As for you—your associate's skill speaks just as highly of you. After all, you chose him. And only the cleverest of businessmen are shrewd enough to ally themselves with equally clever partners. Just look at Damen."

A chuckle. "I see what you mean." Royce's gaze shifted, as a flash of color and movement from beside the settee caught his eye, drew his attention to the room's final occupant.

He found himself gazing at a woman who appeared, at first glance, to be a very close replica of Anastasia.

At second glance, he realized she was no replica, but an original.

Breanna Colby was a portrait come to life, all flawless lines and subtle hues—and yet, decidedly inaccessible.

She was nothing short of exquisite—a graceful, delicate, punch-in-the-gut beauty. True, her features were seemingly identical to her cousin's. Still, they were somehow different. Or perhaps it was the personality he could sense hovering behind the vivid coloring and fine features that made it so.

To begin with, Breanna's eyes, the same jade green as Anastasia's, were softer, more remote than her cousin's—as if she were guarding a part of herself she was reluctant to share, reserving judgment while letting you know you had to earn the right to be allowed in. Her expression was thoughtful, speculative, but carefully schooled. And her hair, that same glorious auburn color as Anastasia's, was upswept, perfectly arranged atop her head without a single strand mussed or out of place. She was lovely, proper, self-contained—a lady through and through.

Abruptly, Royce knew why Damen had said Breanna would never weep or swoon. This was a woman who kept her emotions in check. Her feelings, her thoughts, certainly her fears, would remain private, known only to her and to the select few she chose to trust.

He could even guess why.

She'd survived George Colby.

But he'd left his mark—in ways others could only imagine.

Yes, there was more to Lady Breanna than met the eye. *Much* more. Royce was willing to bet his life on it.

Damen cleared his throat, alerting Royce to the fact that he'd been staring. "Royce, may I present Lady Breanna Colby. Breanna—Lord Royce Chadwick."

"Lady Breanna," Royce said politely, bowing at the waist, then walking over to kiss her hand.

"Welcome to Medford Manor, my lord." Breanna's tone was measured, her voice soft, lilting. Whereas Anastasia's crisp English inflections had been muted by years in America, Breanna's speech was utterly precise, the epitome of refinement.

Royce's lips grazed her knuckles. "Your home is lovely."

"Thank you. Not only for the compliment, but for your kind intentions." She hesitated, then added, "I appreciate your riding out here so late in the day. Damen seems to think you can help us."

Royce straightened, one brow arching in question. "But you don't?"

She rubbed the folds of her lavender day dress between her fingers. "I'm not certain. It's not that I don't trust Damen's instincts. I do. It's just that—"

"It's just that I'm a total stranger and you're uncomfortable with me."

Surprise flashed in her pale green eyes, and she gave a self-conscious nod. "Exactly."

"I understand your reluctance. But, I assure you, I know what I'm doing. *How* I do it, now that's a different story. You might not care for my methods, especially since they can get a bit risky. What I suggest is this: let me take a look at the package and note you received, ask you a few questions. After dinner, we'll discuss my strategy. If you don't care for it, I'll leave."

"And we'll be right back where we started," Damen put in tersely.

Breanna gave a resigned sigh. "That's certainly true. Very well, my lord. We'll try it your way." She crossed over, retrieved a box from the end table, and brought it to Royce, shuddering with distaste as she handed it to him. "This is what he sent."

Royce opened the box, carefully examining each doll before replacing them, turning his attention to the note.

He read it through three times before lifting his head, meeting Breanna's anxious stare.

"Sit down," he advised, gesturing toward the settee. "I want to hear everything you remember about what happened the night your father was arrested. Beginning after Bow Street led him away."

Breanna inclined her head, frowning a bit. "Aren't you going to react to the dolls and the note?"

"Yes. *After* I've gotten all the facts. Now have a seat and tell me about your confrontation with this assassin." Royce glanced up, speaking to Anastasia and Damen as Breanna settled herself on the settee. "I want to hear the entire story from Lady Breanna's point of view. No interruptions. Once I've finished, I'll ask each of you if you remember anything different from or in addition to what she's said."

"In other words, keep quiet," Anastasia supplied.

Royce perched on the arm of the settee, folding his arms across his chest and turning his full attention to Lady Breanna. "Go ahead."

She wet her lips, lowering her lashes and staring at the rug as she mentally traveled back to the night in question. "The Bow Street runners led Father off. Damen, Stacie, and I stayed behind on the docks for a moment. I suppose we needed reality to sink in, to convince ourselves that the whole nightmare was truly over. I was weak-kneed with relief that Stacie was safe. She'd taken a terrible risk dragging that confession out of my father. Finally, we started to leave. Stacie walked first. Damen and I were right behind her. I got the oddest feeling . . ." She made a vague gesture with her hand. "I can't explain it. I just sensed a pair of eyes boring into me. I whirled around—and reached for the pistol I'd been carrying. That's when I saw him."

"You saw him," Royce repeated. "How clearly?"

"Not clearly at all. He was some distance away. It was late at night, and the fog was fairly thick. What I saw was the silhouette of a man, and the glint of his pistol. I saw him raise the pistol, aim in Stacie's direction. I knew exactly who he was, and what he intended to do. I had to stop him. So I shot. I scarcely remember that moment. All I remember is knowing I had to do something or he'd kill Stacie. There wasn't time to call out and warn her. There was only time to act. So I did."

"Then what happened?"

"He screamed. His pistol struck the ground. I heard it. He clutched at his hand. Then, he bent, groped for his gun. That was when Damen drew his own weapon. The killer turned, stumbled away. After that, the night literally swallowed him up."

"He never said anything? Never shouted anything at you?"

"No. I never heard his voice—other than the scream of pain."

"And his appearance? What can you remember about that?"

"Only that he was tall. And somewhat lean, in terms of his build. I couldn't make out his features, or even his hair color."

Royce stroked his chin thoughtfully. "And the only one who knew this killer's identity was John Cunnings. Unless . . ." A penetrating look. "You're sure your father couldn't shed any light on this? I understand that visiting him in Newgate would be unpleasant for you, but . . ."

To Royce's surprise, Breanna's chin came up, and she negated his statement with an adamant shake of her head. "No, my lord, you don't understand. And I don't mean how unpleasant it would be to brave Newgate. I mean how unthinkable it would be to face Father. However, that's irrelevant. Because I'd do precisely that—anguish or not—if I thought it would help. But it wouldn't. Father can't tell us anything. I know that firsthand. You see, Wells and I were in the pub when my father met with Mr. Cunnings, instructed him to hire that killer."

"Were you?" Royce could feel his interest peak. "You overheard their conversation?"

"Every word. My father pressed Cunnings about meeting this associate of his. Cunnings refused. He insisted on being the sole contact. He said his associate preferred it that way. No name was ever mentioned. Whoever this gunman is, only Cunnings knew his identity. Which is why Mr. Cunnings himself is now dead."

"The assassin had to eliminate him. I agree." Royce's fingers stilled against his jaw. "Let's get back to this meeting between your father and Cunnings—the one you overheard. Tell me what else Cunnings said, besides refusing to divulge the killer's name. What other specifics about him did he mention?"

Breanna knotted her hands in her lap. "Cunnings said he'd known him for quite some time. He implied that the man's accomplishments were impressive. Cunnings assured Father that no matter where Stacie was hiding, his associate would find her and kill her. He described him as an expert tracker and an even better shot. Oh—and he added that he was expensive. *Very* expensive. The implication was that he was worth it, that he was accomplished in his line of work. Does that answer your question, my lord?"

"As a matter of fact, it does." Royce glanced down at the note he still held, reread its message. Then, he rose, lowering the piece of paper and leveling a grave stare at Breanna. "This man is dead serious about his threats, my lady. You were right to be afraid."

She flinched, but didn't look away. "I suspected as much."

"I'm sure you did." Royce frowned, wishing he had a different evaluation to relay. He didn't normally experience personal feelings when it came to the people involved in his investigations. But in this case . . . hell, in this case, it was more than money or finding missing relatives that was at stake—it was lives. What's more, he couldn't help but admire the way Lady Breanna was holding herself together, especially since he'd just confirmed her worst fear: that she was the ultimate target of a killer. Her inner strength was remarkable. Yet, at the same time, there was something about her—something disturbingly vulnerable—that made Royce wish there were a way to spare her this ordeal.

But there wasn't.

The only way to maximize her odds of survival was to be as honest as possible, to let her know exactly what she was up against. And then to offer his services to protect her.

Roughly, he cleared his throat. "The only mistake you made was to assume the assassin would disappear from your life. He never would. His arrogance wouldn't let him. He believes he's superior, that no one can thwart him. You challenged that belief. Not only that, you had the audacity to maim him—who knows how badly. My guess is you put him out of commission for a while, which would explain his absence these past few months. He was probably nursing his wounded hand, recovering his marksmanship to its full potential. Now he's back. He's had months to harbor his rage and thirst for vengeance. He's determined to put you in your place, and punish you for what you did." A swift glance at Anastasia. "*After* he finishes the job he took on but never completed."

Breanna made a soft sound of surprise. "Are you saying he wants to hurt Stacie, not simply as retaliation against me, but to prove he's the ultimate master at killing people?"

A terse nod. "Not only killing people, but completing his assignments. He wants to prove to you, to the world, to himself, that he never fails. The marchioness represents a failed execution—his first, if I had to venture a guess. He won't leave a stone like that unturned."

Damen swore. "So the reason he's back—"

"Is to kill your wife *and* Lady Breanna. In that order." Royce didn't mince words. "But first, he wants to torment Lady Breanna. To make her feel the maximum amount of anguish and fear. That will restore the sense of power he feels he's lost."

Breanna came to her feet, and began moving restlessly about the room. "Tell me, my lord," she said at last. "Is there nothing we can do?"

Royce weighed his answer carefully. "In my opinion, the best way to hold him at bay, to keep him from striking while we figure out who he is, is to pointedly ignore him."

"I don't understand."

"He's expecting you to come apart at the seams. He can scarcely wait for that to happen, in fact. So you must deny him the satisfaction. You have to retain your composure at all costs, to pretend you're unbothered by his threats. You have to make him believe his actions aren't having the desired effect. That will force him to keep trying, which buys us more time. If he doesn't think he's successfully terrorized you—or terrorized you severely enough—he won't move on to the next step of his plan."

"Which is killing me," Anastasia clarified.

"Yes."

"There's only one problem with that, Royce," Damen inserted. "While I'm relieved as hell that it will deter him from coming after my wife, won't it make things worse for Breanna? Won't it infuriate him if she remains so totally unruffled, intensify his obsession to try—and succeed—in terrorizing her?"

Royce nodded. "Yes. He'll become bolder, more violent in his demonstrations. He'll also become angrier, more frustrated. The positive consequence of that is it might cause him to make a mistake." A weighted pause. "The negative consequence is that it will make him that much more dangerous. Especially to Lady Breanna, who's the main target of his rage. I won't lie to you. There's risk involved here—high risk. On the other hand, there's risk involved right now. A professional assassin is determined to murder these two women. The only way to eliminate the danger is to eliminate the killer. Which is just what I'm trying to do. Whether you choose to do things my way—that decision is yours."

Silence descended, suffocated the room like a heavy blanket.

Breanna was the first to speak.

"You said you'd discuss your strategy with us after dinner. Does that mean you have a specific plan in mind?"

"I have the first steps of a plan, yes."

"I'd like to hear it."

Royce pursed his lips, considering her request. As a rule, he never shared unfinished strategy with anyone other than Hibbert. But in this case, with both these women's lives at stake, didn't he owe them an explanation, if for no other reason than to let them make a decision as to whether or not they chose to put their safety in his hands?

"All right," he conceded. "But remember, I have yet to review everything we've just discussed. I also haven't heard Damen's or your cousin's recollections of the night you shot the assassin. Further, I have some remaining questions. For example, we haven't even touched on the subject of the murdered guard. Some of the details of my plan won't be worked out until I'm satisfied I have all the information I need—*and* until you've decided whether you'll go along with my methods."

"Fair enough." Breanna smoothed a hand over her hair. "Putting those issues aside, tell us your ideas. Your *preliminary* ideas," she amended.

Anastasia interrupted with an exasperated sound. "You both act as if we have all the time in the world. How do you know this madman will be patient while you sort out your plan? Shouldn't we be *doing* something—*now?*"

Royce flashed Anastasia a tolerant look, unsurprised by her reaction. Having sized up Damen's wife, he'd guessed she'd be the impatient one, the one who was unwilling to wait. "I don't think our time is unlimited," he clarified. "But no, we shouldn't be doing something. Not unless it's the *right* something. If Lady Breanna takes my advice, stays calm and *outwardly* unbothered by what's happened thus far, it will buy us more than a week to close in on this man. I can almost guarantee it. The way his mind works—he won't kill until the stage is set precisely as he means it to be."

Breanna paced slowly about the settee as she considered his words. Then, she raised her head, regarded him through wary, questioning eyes. "You keep talking about my behaving a certain way, acting a certain part. You believe he's watching me."

"At every possible opportunity, and without alerting the guards—yes."

She paled a bit, but didn't flinch. "And how do I show him I'm unaffected by his threats?"

"You go on with your life—taking certain necessary but subtle precautions," he added. "You've already hired additional guards. Hire more. After all, a man was murdered just outside your estate. It's only natural for you to seek protection. Get Wells to situate guards all around the periphery of the estate. After that, go about your business."

This time it was Damen who reacted, tensing as if he'd been struck. "Go about her business?"

Royce's nod was definitive. "In a manner of speaking. Of course, it's expected that Lady Breanna will be distressed by the guard's death. No one will be surprised if, until the highwayman who's allegedly responsible is caught, she chooses not to leave the grounds. Also, it's assumed she'll want to spend time with her cousin, who's only just arrived home. The two women should stroll out to the construction site each day—with you at their sides, of course. After all, it is your house, too, that's being built. You'd obviously want to see it take shape."

"You don't think we should call a halt to the construction?"

"No. At least not yet. We don't want to take away every opportunity this assassin has to creep onto the grounds, and to blend in, undetected. The more rope we give him, the more likely he is to hang himself."

Damen started, swearing under his breath. "That's insane. Now you're tempting fate to an absurd degree, Royce. I don't like it."

"I didn't expect you would," Royce replied calmly. "But that's how I'd handle things—*if* I end up handling things." He offered no further explanation. But it was clear that, unspoken or not, he'd demand absolute control if he were running this investigation, and that he wouldn't diverge from his rash tactics, despite Damen's objections. "In the meantime," he continued, "what my role would be over the next few days would be to check out as many local shops as possible, see if I can determine where those dolls were bought. *And* who bought them." A frown. "Although I don't hold out much hope. At least not initially. The assassin probably bought them far enough away so they couldn't be easily traced."

"What about extending your search?" Anastasia demanded.

"I will. After the holidays. Christmas is next week. It makes no sense to travel to shops that will be closed. And speaking of Christmas," Royce added, "the three of you should share a private family celebration." He paused, turned to meet Breanna's gaze. "And after your private celebration, you must hold your party, as planned."

Breanna's eyes widened, and she sucked in her breath. "You want the party to take place, in spite of the killer? Or maybe I should say *because* of him. You really do believe in taking risks, don't you, my lord?"

"I believe in outwitting my enemies. That involves taking risks."

"Risks?" Damen bit out. "You're not only inviting the bastard onto Breanna's grounds, now you're inviting him into her house."

"Maybe." Royce weighed that possibility carefully. "I suppose he could use the opportunity to slip by the guards and into the manor. But it's a hazardous step for him to take. He might sneak in to leave another of his gifts. But he wouldn't use the occasion to hurt Lady Breanna or your wife. Not with so many potential witnesses around. Such extreme carelessness would, in his mind, be unacceptable, beneath his level of genius." A defiant glint lit Royce's eyes. "Still, if he does slink into the ballroom or gaming rooms, I'll be ready for him."

"You will?" Breanna exclaimed, her delicate brows arching.

"Um-hum." Royce was as surprised as Breanna by the offer he'd just extended. He hated large house parties. They bored him. He hadn't attended one in years. An occasional ball or two during the Season, gambling at White's and at the more lucrative horse races—those were the extent of his social appearances. Yet, suddenly, he knew he'd made the right decision by opting to attend Breanna's party. It was the only way to keep things looking normal, while at the same time shielding Breanna and Anastasia from unwarranted danger.

"You've got to hold that party," he stated flatly. "Otherwise, the entire *ton* will be abuzz and the assassin will catch wind of the fact that he's unnerved you. Still, I'm not completely reckless. I realize you'll need protection. So consider that protection granted. I'll delay checking out the more remote shops about those dolls until after all your guests have left. Instead, I'll ride to Medford Manor in time for the festivities. If the assassin *should* show up—he'll be properly greeted."

"By you?"

A corner of Royce's mouth lifted. "I know it's boorish to arrive at a holiday gathering without an invitation. But, should you decide to retain my services, that's exactly what I intend to do."

"I see." Lady Breanna acknowledged his statement, and for the first time Royce saw a trace of humor light her far-too-serious eyes, warming them to a rich, shimmering jade. "Well, thank you for warning me."

He nodded slowly, feeling a keen surge of anticipation at the prospect of bringing down this killer and putting that luminous glow back in Lady Breanna's eyes. "You're welcome."

8

Christmas morning—the perfect time to arrange a shipment.

An uncommon quiet settled over the London docks, the normal rush of activity suspended as workers joined their families to attend mass. Hoists and winches were silent, ships swayed lazily in the chilly waters with few crewmen aboard to attend them. Tiny snowflakes sprinkled about, covering the docks in a diaphanous veil of white and adding to the unnatural sense of stillness hovering over the Thames.

The assassin's footsteps echoed as he crossed the alley dividing the cluster of warehouses. He glanced about, smiling as he took in the deserted buildings and path, contemplated all the sailors and workmen now gathered in church.

What a pity that they were ignorant of the brilliant strategy taking place just beyond.

He'd done a thorough job. Organized just the right crew to convey his cargo. Selected excellent merchandise. Readied the choice assortment without leaving a mark—*any* mark that might detract from their worth.

And made all the arrangements right out in the open, while the residents of London were deep in prayer.

The instructions to his men hadn't taken long. This was his regular crew—a crew that had worked for him in the past, and were far more afraid of him than they were of the authorities. Fear was a splendid motivator. It ensured loyalty in a way that even money could not. Because if there was one thing stronger than greed, it was the drive for self-preservation.

Everything was in place—at least for this crop of merchandise.

What a lovely New Year's gift his cargo would make for three fortunate gentlemen.

There would be another delivery sent on its heels. Plans were already in motion.

Yes, the week ahead looked promising indeed. Another target to hit, another shipment to begin arrangements for, and—most exhilarating of all—in four days a trip to Medford Manor.

A trip he'd counted on making with the utmost discretion. After all, there wasn't a prayer Lady Breanna would throw open her gates to hundreds of guests. Not now. Not after the dolls, the note, the guard. The party would, of course, be canceled.

But it hadn't been.

His anticipation faded, transformed to the anger that had been boiling inside him all week long, intensifying more with each passing day. He gritted his teeth, pondering the unexpected response—or rather, *lack* of response—Lady Breanna had displayed to last week's events. That maddening little bitch. Rather than quaking with fear, she'd spent her days strolling the grounds with her cousin and Sheldrake, laughing and chatting as if all was right with the world. Despite the fact that that guard had been killed at the portals of her home, she *still* hadn't panicked, hadn't canceled her holiday gathering and locked herself in her house.

There was only one explanation that made sense, he reminded himself, resorting to the same logic he'd used all week to bring himself under control.

She hadn't made the connection.

It was more than plausible. After all, he *had* done an exceptional job of making the murder look like the work of a highwayman. She'd obviously believed his ruse, dismissed the incident as being unrelated to the package she'd received. Yes. That's what had happened. It made sense, not only in comprehending Lady Breanna's behavior, but Sheldrake's, as well. The marquess's mind was far too sharp not to have considered the possibility that the two incidents were related. And, given his romantic attachment to his wife, it was unthinkable he'd subject her to danger. Therefore, he must have examined the evidence and determined that whoever sent those dolls to Lady Breanna had not been the same person who killed the guard outside her estate.

The assassin's lips curved, his good humor restored.

How delightful. He'd outwitted the entire family.

More fools they.

Actually, he was wasting his time feeling angry. Because, disappointed though he was that Lady Breanna wasn't yet shivering with terror, he was equally pleased at what that meant for him. Now he could accomplish this next part of his plan with great ease. He wouldn't have to sneak into Medford Manor, or resort to forcible entry. He'd simply stroll through the front door, right along with the other guests, choose the appropriate moment to leave the gift he'd brought for her ladyship.

After discovering this memento, she wouldn't be laughing.

No, on the contrary, she'd be overcome with horror, gripped with fear. Any hopes she'd entertained that the dolls were an isolated incident, that the guard's death was a coincidence, that she was safe in her own home, would be dashed.

He could hardly wait to see the terror in her eyes.

A gust of wind struck him and he winced, fitting his gloves more snugly into place, then shoving his hands in his pockets. Damn, how he loathed the cold.

Almost as much as he loathed *her.*

It was fitting the two would come together, that she'd die during winter.

A twig snapped and, reflexively, he turned up his collar, pulled the brim of his hat lower, shielding his face from view.

An instant later, two people—a young man and an even younger woman—darted by, sparing him not even a second glance. Giggling, they darted into one of the warehouses, the heated look in the young man's eye revealing precisely what was going to occur inside that wooden shed. The lad paused, assessed the area—deserted but for the assassin's retreating figure—and, having ensured their privacy, shut the warehouse door.

The assassin kept walking, head lowered, feeling a pang of envy. Ah, the pleasures that young couple were about to enjoy.

It was times like these he missed Maurelle.

Just thinking of her made his pulse quicken in a way no other woman could begin to equal.

Even after all these years.

He could still remember the first time he saw her. It was a sultry summer evening more than fifteen years ago, and she'd been coming down the stairs of that dilapidated brothel right outside Paris. He'd been pacing back and forth just across the street—whether by chance or by fate—driven there by the internal demons that pumped through his blood. Restless, consumed by a lethal hunger only he understood, he'd been eyeing the brothel, trying to decide if sex would ease the yearnings pounding inside him.

That's when she'd emerged.

She was easily the most striking woman he'd ever seen—thick black hair, huge dark eyes, offset by the palest of skin, all crowning the most lush, desirable body any woman could boast. The instant he glimpsed her, all his inner turmoil had converged, slamming forcibly from his brain to his loins.

He'd paid for a full night. He'd used every minute of it. But when morning came, he was no more ready to say good-bye than he'd been twelve hours earlier. He wanted her again—and not only for a night.

There was something insatiably exciting about Maurelle, something rich and dark and exhilarating that aroused him beyond bearing. Something that clawed inside him and drew him back to her side, night after night, week after week.

Perhaps it was because, even then, he recognized her as his equal.

She was his equal still.

A slow smile curved the assassin's lips.

Life had an ironic way of working out.

Royce couldn't hide his relief when the time finally came to leave his brother's estate. It wasn't that he didn't enjoy spending Christmas with Edmund and Jane. They were good, decent people—if somewhat dull—who tried their best to make him feel welcome. The highlight of the visit was romping about with their three sons: Thomas, William, and little Christopher. Thomas—actually Edmund Thomas, heir apparent to his father's title—was five years old, and far more interested in climbing trees than he was in acquiring the skills necessary toward being the Earl of Searby. William, four years old and no less energetic than his brother, kept dragging Royce off to play in the snow, pelting his uncle with snowballs. And Christopher, at just shy of two, was a virtual whirlwind of activity, toddling from room to room on his stubby little legs, sending vases and crystal crashing to the floor in his wake.

The hours spent with his nephews were a welcome reprieve for Royce. Frolicking about kept his mind off the two cases he was now working on—the one involving Viscount Ryder's missing illegitimate daughter, and the more recent one involving Lady Breanna Colby.

Both cases centered around women, and both were frustrating as hell.

Ryder was old, in broken spirits, and searching for an unacknowledged bastard daughter who had unexpectedly become his sole living heir. One short month ago, Ryder's son Nathaniel had succumbed to a severe bout of influenza, dying suddenly, unmarried and childless, leaving Ryder with no one to inherit the family name and title. The problem was that the aged viscount knew less than nothing about his illegitimate daughter, other than the fact that she'd been conceived in his home—the product of a torrid liaison with a fetching chamber maid who'd been discharged the moment she became with child—and born in the back room of a London workhouse. Glynnis Martin, the chamber maid in question, had sent word to him of the babe's arrival, adding that she'd named their daughter Emma, after her grandmother. Ryder had destroyed the note and never responded. As of now, he could remember no additional details surrounding the child's birth.

A pathetic lack of information, indeed.

As a result, Royce had nothing to go on—not a description or an address where he might find either mother or daughter. He'd gone straight to the workhouse where Emma had been born, knowing even as he did that it was an exercise in futility. Sure enough, the institution provided as few clues as he'd anticipated. The attendants there had seen dozens of bastard children brought into the world in just such a fashion and, as a result, kept no records of their whereabouts. One of the established matrons who'd been at the workhouse for more than two decades thought she remembered someone matching Glynnis Martin's description. If her memory served her correctly, the young woman in question had arrived at their doors some eighteen years ago, hugely pregnant, and given birth to an infant daughter. She'd sent a note off to the child's father and waited to hear from him. When she didn't hear, she became despondent. One night about a week later, she took the infant and disappeared.

Vanishing into anonymity.

Just like the assassin threatening Lady Breanna.

This new case bothered Royce even more than Ryder's did, no doubt because of the longstanding friendship and respect that existed between him and Damen. Royce felt doubly compelled to find a solution, to protect Damen's wife.

And to protect her cousin.

Both investigations were plaguing him, beating relentlessly at his brain.

Dashing about in the snow with three energetic nephews did wonders toward alleviating that.

It didn't, however, make being at Searby any easier.

Then again, that house held nothing but dark memories for him—memories that no amount of revelry could erase.

So, it was with a great deal of relief that, on the day after Christmas, he bid Edmund and his family good-bye and took his leave.

He and Hibbert—who had traveled with him to Searby—stopped in London overnight, long enough to gather up the Ryder file and check out the few remaining shops in Town he had yet to investigate that stocked dolls as part of their merchandise and might or might not have sold two red-haired ones in the past fortnight.

None of them had.

The following morning found the two men packed, settled in Royce's carriage, and on their way to Kent—first to check out a half-dozen shops in that shire, then to proceed on to Medford Manor.

The final lap of the journey was silent, as Royce contemplated his unsuccessful attempts to learn who'd sold the killer those dolls, much less the identity of the man who'd bought them. He'd gotten nowhere fast. And his initial time had run out, as the Colby party was scheduled to begin tomorrow.

Unbidden, he found himself wondering how Lady Breanna had fared during his absence. Not bodily, for he felt confident she was safe—for the time being. Instinct told him her assailant had more emotional torment in store for her before he acted. But mentally—had her nerve held out? And physically—had her stamina held out?

He had a staunch feeling the answer to both questions was yes. Lady Breanna was a remarkably strong young woman.

He'd seen that strength mirrored in those carefully guarded jade-green eyes when she'd stood beside Damen and Anastasia last week, on the morning he'd left her estate, and officially asked him to take on her case. Quietly, graciously, she'd voiced her understanding that this meant she agreed to adhere to his tactics, that she'd follow the procedure he'd outlined for her between then and the day of the party. She'd concluded by expressing her appreciation for his time and effort, then wished him a joyous holiday and sent him on his way.

Royce had listened to her formal speech, watched her self-contained expression as she spoke. Once again, he'd been struck by the sure knowledge that there was far more to Breanna Colby than met the eye, far more that hovered beneath that exquisite, genteel veneer.

He was more determined than ever to help her.

Yet, so far, he'd accomplished next to nothing.

After first leaving Medford Manor for London—prior to his visit to Searby—he'd not only called on numerous local shops in Town to ask about the dolls, but he'd dropped in at Bow Street, spoken to Marks about whatever information had been amassed on Cunnings's murderer, his potential link to the Viscount Medford, and now his link to the threats being sent to Lady Breanna.

As Royce suspected, Marks was more than willing to turn over his file, which contained details on the conversations he'd had with all those he'd questioned about Cunnings—both then and now. The Bow Street runner looked conscience-stricken and at the same time relieved to learn that Lady Breanna had hired Royce to follow up on the matter.

Royce understood both reactions.

Marks's relief was because he was being pressured to devote all his energies toward solving the murders of the local noblemen. And his attack of conscience was because he'd been unable to help Lady Breanna, unable to find out the name of the predator who was stalking her.

How could Royce fault him, either for his priorities or his regrets? He well understood that rueful expression on Marks's face. He had the uncomfortable feeling he'd be wearing a similar one himself when he told Lady Breanna he'd uncovered nothing of importance as of yet. She seemed to have the same effect on everyone, inspiring a surge of respect and a rush of protectiveness that made people want to slay dragons for her. And if that reaction was unusual for Marks, it was unprecedented for Royce.

That fact notwithstanding, Royce had left Bow Street armed with Marks's reports—reports that were nothing more than routine chats with all Cunnings's friends and colleagues. Fine. He'd pored over them during his evenings at Searby, then kept them close by for reference. And now, after having spoken with shopkeepers throughout London, he and Hibbert had covered six or seven shops in Kent. Those visits had, as he'd suspected, yielded no information on the purchase of the dolls. Wherever the killer had bought them, it hadn't been in Town or in Kent.

The bastard was too clever for that.

"We'll be arriving at Medford Manor in about ten minutes," Hibbert announced, shooting Royce a sideways glance. "Would you care to discuss your somber mood?"

Royce shifted in his seat, crossed one long leg over the other. "The truth? I'm not looking forward to looking Damen in the eye and telling him I've got no news on who's trying to kill his wife."

"Did you think you *would* have news—after doing only a few days of preliminary digging?"

A scowl. "No. I didn't."

Hibbert arched a brow. "Are you sure it's Lord Sheldrake you're uncomfortable facing? Or is it Lady Breanna?"

Royce's scowl deepened. "I don't appreciate having my mind read, Hibbert. Not even by you. But if you must know, no, I don't like telling a twenty-one-year-old woman that a professional killer—one with a brilliant mind and a burning desire to terrorize and kill her—is closing in and I've done nothing to outmaneuver him or find out who he is." Staring broodingly at his portfolio, Royce added, "I've been unusually slow at turning up answers to young women's dilemmas these days."

Hibbert sniffed. "Ryder's daughter is like the proverbial needle in a haystack. We're not only searching for an eighteen-year-old girl who could be anywhere, we're searching for one whose father has never laid eyes on her. We have no description, no point at which to begin. The viscount hasn't so much as contacted Glynnis Martin since he impregnated her and discharged her nineteen years ago. He even destroyed the letter she sent him announcing their daughter's birth. Why, for all we know, Emma Martin doesn't even know her father's name, much less that he's alive and searching for her."

"That's irrelevant. It's *we* who are searching for *her*, not the other way around. *We* know *her* name and that her mother dropped out of sight immediately after having her."

"Glynnis Martin could have left England."

"With what money?"

"Fine. Then, she could have moved to another shire, changed her name."

"That shouldn't stop us from finding her—*or* her daughter."

"It won't stop us. But it might slow us down. Our men are exploring all the avenues you defined. We're waiting to hear back from them. We're also waiting for word on whatever death records they can get their hands on. Not that I hold out much hope. We have almost two decades and an entire country to cover, with only a name and a description of Glynnis Martin to go on. She's had eighteen years in which to die. So, for that matter, has her daughter."

"Damn." Royce pressed his fist into the seat cushion, leaving a deep imprint in the soft cloth. "I don't like being thwarted—not even for a few weeks. I don't intend to allow it. By New Year's Day we're going to have information leading us to Ryder's daughter."

"I see." Hibbert leaned back in his seat, eyeing his employer speculatively. "And Lady Breanna? Are your plans for our progress on her situation equally ambitious?"

"Yes." Royce's jaw set, his tone as unyielding as his claim. "We're going to find that bastard who's after her, Hibbert. We're going to find him soon."

"For Lord Sheldrake's sake," Hibbert supplied helpfully.

"Don't bait me. Yes, for Damen's sake. Also for his wife's sake, and Lady Breanna's sake. Hell, for *my* sake. I'm not going to lose. Not this time."

"*This* time?" A wry grin twisted Hibbert's lips. "As I recall, you haven't lost at *any* time."

"No," Royce concurred, staring out the window as the iron gates of Medford Manor sprang into view. "I haven't."

9

From the sitting-room window, Breanna watched Lord Royce's carriage round the drive, feeling a surprising sense of relief and an even more surprising sense of excitement at the realization that he was back.

But then, why should she be surprised at the relief that seeing him evoked? Royce Chadwick represented her only hope of finding and eliminating the assassin who was hell-bent on inflicting his vengeance on her and Stacie.

She'd been living a walking nightmare ever since that package had arrived, her entire body taut with fear every time she and Stacie left the house. Even with Damen perpetually by their sides, it was terrifying to know that somewhere—doubtless within scrutinizing distance—a brilliant marksman waited, gauging the right time to end their lives.

Yet he didn't strike—just as Lord Royce had predicted.

Damen's friend certainly knew what he was talking about.

True, his methods were risky, leaving both her and Stacie susceptible to attack. Still, the tactics he'd outlined were unarguably logical—the result of an astute mind that understood its adversary.

Perhaps that was the part she found exciting. Dangerous or not, Lord Royce's reasoning was fascinating, and listening to him detail his strategy had strengthened her conviction that he was the right person for the job. He possessed all the awareness and creativity Bow Street lacked—and the courage to see it all through.

She was curious to hear what he'd found out during his absence.

Letting the curtain fall back into place, she gathered up her skirts and made her way across the sitting room. She was halfway down the hall when Wells opened the front door, and Lord Royce and an elderly, silver-haired man walked in.

Damen's footsteps echoed from the second-floor landing, and he strode down the stairs, reached the main level, and cut across

Breanna's path, never even noticing her as he headed toward the doorway.

"Royce. Hibbert." He greeted both men tersely. "What did you find out?"

"We spoke to numerous shopkeepers," Hibbert began. "And Lord Royce paid a visit to Bow Street. After our initial inquiries—"

"Nothing," Royce interrupted with an adamant sweep of his arm. "We found out nothing." His chin came up and he met Damen's anguished gaze. "But we will." He handed Wells his overcoat with a nod of thanks. "Have there been further incidents?"

"No." It was Breanna who answered, walking forward to join the men. "It was just as you said. The three of us went about our business, Wells checked the mail every day, and—other than the responses to our party invitations that continued to pour in—we received nothing from that . . . that . . . man."

Royce turned toward her, his midnight blue eyes sweeping her briefly from head to toe, as if to assess her true state of mind. "Good," was all he said. Without averting his gaze, he gestured toward the older gentleman beside him. "My lady, this is Hibbert, my most trusted associate."

"Good afternoon, Mr. Hibbert," Breanna replied with a curtsy. "And since no one can tell my cousin and I apart, I'll spare Lord Royce the embarrassment by introducing myself. I'm—"

"Lady Breanna Colby," Royce finished for her. "I beg to differ with you. I have no trouble telling you apart."

There was something about his tone that made hot color tinge Breanna's cheeks. "My apologies. It seems I've underestimated you."

"It would seem so." A corner of Royce's mouth lifted. "However, it would also seem that I've embarrassed you. So I, too, must apologize. Your apology, by the way, is accepted."

Unexpected amusement danced in Breanna's eyes. "Then I'd be a boor not to accept yours—which is just what I suspect you were counting on me to say. You're quite a maneuverer, my lord. It's no wonder you're successful at getting what you want. Very well. Consider your apology accepted."

Royce continued to gaze steadily at her. "Thank you. You're very gracious."

Hibbert cleared his throat. "Lady Breanna," he said with a bow, his pale stare assessing her in one swift motion. "It's a pleasure."

"Thank you. And welcome to Medford Manor." Catching her lip between her teeth, Breanna grew serious, mulling over Lord Royce's blunt announcement that they'd learned nothing new. "So the dolls weren't bought in London. I'm not surprised."

"Neither am I." Royce glanced curiously about. "Where is the marchioness? I got the distinct impression your cousin never missed out on anything."

Breanna's forehead creased in concern. "She doesn't. Unfortunately, she hasn't been sleeping well. She's upstairs, resting."

Royce frowned. "Is it anxiety that's keeping her awake?"

"No, my lord." Anastasia descended the stairs, shaking her head as she did. "It's not anxiety. It's pregnancy." She smiled, an illuminating gesture that drew attention away from her pallor, the dark circles beneath her eyes. "In fact, I've thought of a new and practical way to barricade our door to unwanted guests. Line the entranceway with chamber pots. They'll seal off the house, and I promise they won't go to waste."

"A novel idea," Royce chuckled. "I'll give it thought." He repeated his introductions, this time presenting Anastasia to Hibbert.

The older man looked intently from Anastasia to Breanna and back again. "Astonishing," he murmured, having properly acknowledged Damen's wife. "And you're not twins?"

"We're not even sisters—at least not by blood," Anastasia explained. "Our fathers were twins. Our mothers were sisters, and they, too, looked a great deal alike. The resemblance between Breanna and me is unusual, but not impossible. And as far as being twins . . ." She tossed Breanna an affectionate smile. "In our hearts, we are."

"I see."

"When will your guests start to arrive?" Royce asked.

"Tomorrow morning." Breanna glanced at Wells, who nodded his agreement. "Anything you want to know about the guest list, see Wells. He arranged the entire party without mentioning a word to me."

"The decorating, the arrangements, all the finishing touches are Miss Breanna's gift," Wells refuted proudly. "She brings beauty to everything she touches."

"I'm not surprised." Royce's head came up, and he inspected the festive greenery more closely—the boughs of holly and sprigs of mistletoe that decorated the entranceway and halls, the freshly arranged vases of snowdrops and ivy that sat atop every table.

"Everything looks lovely," he murmured. "Warm, inviting, and incredibly beautiful." He meant it, too. Each carefully placed adornment, each colorful wreath emanated the elegant taste and grace that was Lady Breanna.

The notion of anything threatening such beauty was unthinkable.

Brow furrowed, Royce turned to Wells. "I'll need to see the guest list. I'm sure most of the names will be familiar to me. You've hired extra guards?"

"They're stationed all around the perimeter of the estate and near every door to the manor," Wells replied.

"Good. Then if it's all right with you, I'll have a word with the head guard—Mahoney, I believe it was—after I review the guest list. I want everything in place when the guests start to arrive. Most especially, I want the guards poised and ready tomorrow when darkness starts to fall. The big ball is tomorrow night. I don't want any surprises."

Damen shot him a worried look. "You think that's when the killer might strike?"

"I don't think he'll strike at all. What he might do is visit. If he does, I'll be prepared."

"I hope to God you know what you're doing, Royce."

Royce's gaze remained steady. "I do."

The sound of yet another approaching carriage split the quiet of night.

"I hope we haven't made the biggest mistake of our lives," Damen muttered, retying his cravat for the third time. "There are over a hundred people downstairs already. The entranceway doors are opening and closing ten times an hour. The French doors in the ballroom are all slightly ajar to let in some air."

"And there are dozens of guards marching around the estate with loaded pistols," Anastasia reminded him, walking over to fix the cravat Damen's valet had long since abandoned. "Damen, you have to stop worrying. We all agreed Royce's plan was the right one. Even Wells couldn't convince us there was another way. Because there isn't. The fact is, Breanna and I are at risk. We're going to be at risk until this killer is found and stopped. And it's up to us to do that." She smoothed her hand across her husband's jaw. "Besides, wasn't it you who sought out Royce Chadwick, brought him here to help?"

"Yes, God help me, it was."

"And we all agree he was the right person for the job—extreme methods or not." She grew thoughtful. "Actually, I think it's uncanny the way he understands this killer's mind. If he's right—"

"It's if he's wrong that worries me." Damen threaded his fingers through his wife's hair, caressed her cheeks with his thumbs. "It doesn't just worry me, it scares me to death."

Anastasia's sharp jade eyes searched his face. "You don't think he's wrong. You trust him. You'd never be working with him if you didn't. What's more, *I* trust him. So does Breanna. We all believe in his abilities." She let her hand slip down her bodice, placed her palm on her abdomen. "Believe me, I know what's at stake. That's why we've got to go through with this."

Damen's eyes darkened. "Half of me keeps hoping that madman has vanished," he muttered, laying his palm over Stacie's. "We haven't received a single communication from him in over a week."

"According to Royce, he was waiting to see if Breanna went through with the party. Well, by now, he's seen guests flocking to Medford Manor. So he knows—or believes—she's brushed off any worries she might have had. He'll be reacting to that soon."

"And that's supposed to appease me?"

"No. It's supposed to make you realize that the only way to catch this killer is to lure him out. This unnatural calm is more frightening than anything else. It's like knowing there's a terrible storm coming—one that's going to strike at any moment and destroy everyone you love. Only it hovers, gathers force, and circles like some kind of predatory hawk." Anastasia shuddered. "This waiting, bracing for the assault—it's unbearable."

Damen gathered her close, tucked her head beneath his chin. "I know." His embrace tightened. "I'm not leaving your side tonight. I don't care how you explain it. Tell everyone I'm insanely worried about your condition. Say whatever you want to. But don't expect to eat, talk, or dance unless it's with me."

His wife smiled against his waistcoat. "You've become very possessive, my lord. It's a good thing you're the best dancer and the most fascinating conversationalist in the room. Otherwise, I might be forced to protest."

Damen didn't smile back. "I love you," he said fiercely. "No one and nothing is going to hurt you."

Despite her independent nature, Stacie felt a surge of welcome relief, and she gave silent thanks to the heavens for giving her this wonderful man as her husband. "I love you, too," she breathed. "And I intend to keep myself and the babe perfectly safe. I promise." She leaned back, gazed up at him. "Let's try to enjoy ourselves. This *is* a celebration." Her lips twitched. "It's also the first opportunity I'll have to mingle with the businessmen I offended last summer when I asked them to finance my bank. I have quite a few fences to mend. Especially since most of those men are clients of yours."

"It's *they* who should be apologizing to *you*," Damen countered flatly. "Your idea was brilliant. Choosing to dismiss it simply because it was a woman who thought it up was their loss—and my gain. It gave me the opportunity to become your business partner. Our American bank is thriving. Believe me, sweetheart, if those men are feeling anything, it's jealousy and regret. And if any of them makes the slightest disparaging remark, they'll have me to answer to."

"My knight in shining armor," Stacie returned tenderly. "Thank you for always believing in me, and for rescuing me when I need it." A thoughtful expression flitted across her face. "That brings me to an interesting question. Damen, have you noticed anything . . . distinctive about the way Royce treats Breanna?"

"Distinctive?"

"Yes. Different from the way he treats the rest of us. Royce is a hard man, and a somewhat detached one. I suppose he has to be, given what he does. Yet with Breanna, he's gentler, more compassionate. It's not the words he uses with her, it's the tone. As if he's trying to cushion the ordeal she's going through. And the way he stares at her—like he's trying to absorb her, figure her out. I can't quite put my finger on it . . ." Stacie broke off, trying to find the right words to describe her perception.

"Are you suggesting Royce is interested in Breanna?" Damen asked with more than a trace of surprise.

Anastasia lifted one shoulder in an ambivalent shrug. "I don't think *interested* is the right choice of words. It's more like he's fascinated by her. Whether it's just a combination of attraction and protectiveness, or it's the prelude to something deeper—that I'm not sure. What's more, Breanna is drawn to him, too. I can sense it. She's thoroughly intrigued by him—on many levels. Not that she's said a word to me. She hasn't. Probably because she's still sorting out whatever it is she's feeling—if she's even aware of those feelings at all. Still, there's definitely something different about her since Royce's first visit. I can sense it."

Damen's brows lifted fractionally. "Royce is hardly the kind of man Breanna's used to. He's—"

"He's what—worldly? Experienced? A risk-taker?" Stacie's lips curved. "I know. Maybe that's just what Breanna finds intriguing." She dismissed the notion with a wave of her hand. "It's just a thought. A fascinating one to consider, though."

"In other words, you're going to be scrutinizing Breanna all night," Damen concluded dryly.

His wife's grin was impish. "She deserves to be scrutinized a bit. She certainly did the same to me when you and I first met and she was convinced we belonged together." A pointed look. "As it turned out, she was right. Then again, she and I usually are when it comes to seeing inside each other's hearts."

Damen rubbed one of his wife's auburn tresses between his fingers. "Indeed you are," he murmured, his features tightening with emotion. "And yes, Breanna was right about us. You're my life. Which is why I'm far more concerned about your safety—and Breanna's, for that matter— than I am about her romantic interests."

"All I meant was that maybe my instincts about her and Royce are also right and—"

"I know what you meant." Damen silenced her by pressing his forefinger to her lips. "And if you want to keep a close eye on your cousin all night and speculate about the prospect—however unlikely—of a future between her and Royce, feel free to do so. So long as while you're watching her, you stay close enough to my side for *me* to watch *you*. As I said, my main concern tonight is safety—yours and Breanna's."

Anastasia nodded. "I'll place *my* safety in *your* hands." Another far-away look. "I have a funny feeling I know whose hands Breanna's will be in."

Breanna studied her reflection in the looking glass, smoothing the satin trim adorning the bodice of her lilac silk ball gown, and checking for the third time to make sure her hair was in place.

It was.

Reflexively, her fingers brushed her cheeks and nape to make sure no strands had broken free of their upswept coronet atop her head. Finding no traitorous locks, she appraised the strand of pearls her lady's maid had woven through her tresses.

Her earrings and necklace were simple, gold with a dusting of amethysts in the center, left to her by her mother. She hoped the effect was enough, but she felt ridiculous doused in the amount of jewelry worn by most of her friends. So the earrings and necklace would have to do.

Her gaze shifted critically, starting at the crown of her head and descending to the tips of her slippered feet, only to retrace its path, hovering at her face and throat. Pale, unadorned, but adequate.

Why am I so preoccupied with my appearance tonight? she thought in disgust, twisting about and walking away from the looking glass. It wasn't as if she'd never attended a ball before. And this evening, for the first time, she didn't have her father to contend with.

Instead she had his hired killer.

Flinching, she walked about her bedchamber, running a fingertip over her porcelain figures and trying to calm her nerves.

Nothing was going to happen. Lord Royce had all but assured her of it. The assassin was not going to stroll into a ballroom and open fire.

Then why did she feel so ill at ease? So vulnerable?

She glanced about the bedchamber as she had a dozen times since Jamie Knox had been murdered. She'd felt uneasy since that day, as if her domain had somehow been invaded. She couldn't shake the feeling that the killer had been here—at her home. She knew it was irrational, but she could actually feel his presence. He was watching her, waiting, coiled to strike.

But he *hadn't* been here. Not inside. Not in her house, and certainly not in her room.

She'd checked and rechecked, giving in to her inexplicable need to ensure her chambers hadn't been violated.

Everything was intact.

She'd inspected every personal item on her dressing table, every porcelain figure in her collection. Most especially her two favorites: the porcelain horse she'd had since childhood, and the porcelain statue of two little girls playing together among a field of flowers. *That* was her most cherished figure, because in it was wedged the precious silver coin her grandfather had given her.

Nothing had been touched: not the figures, not the coin—nothing.

And yet . . .

Breanna steeled herself, her gloved hands balling into fists as she drew slow, steadying breaths. This was ridiculous. She was letting her imagination run wild. And with no basis. There were guards posted all over the estate, manning each and every door. Further, the people gathered downstairs were her family and friends. And *she* was their hostess.

She had to gain control of herself. She'd survived on internal strength all her life. Now was no time to lose it.

Besides, Royce Chadwick would be there.

That thought crystallized out of nowhere, and Breanna was startled at how much comfort it brought her. Despite the limited amount of time he'd spent here, Lord Royce had come to represent strength, confidence and—no matter how risky his tactics—security.

It was more than the knowledge that he was good at his job. It was an instinctive awareness that somehow he would protect her. Protect her and at the same time make her part of that excitement he exuded—an excitement she never knew existed and wanted nothing more than to . . .

Breanna squelched that thought in the making, stunned at the direction her own reflections had taken. What in heaven's name was she thinking? Lord Royce was a professional, hired by Damen to do a job. He wasn't here to . . . to . . .

To what?

With a bemused shake of her head, Breanna turned her attention to her gloves, smoothing them more snugly up to her elbows. She was beginning to think too much like Stacie, she chastised herself. It was Stacie who possessed the romantic nature, not she.

Then again, it was Stacie who'd grown up seeing romantic love first-hand, having had parents who adored each other—*truly* adored each other—with the kind of intensity she now shared with Damen.

Just thinking about Stacie and Damen—*and* the babe they'd now conceived—made Breanna's heart swell. If ever there was evidence of happily-ever-after, of two people who deserved joy and fulfillment, it was they.

If only they could keep the evils of the world at bay . . .

No, Breanna refuted silently. She was *not* going to revert back to that subject yet again. She was going to behave as tonight commanded she should—like a proper lady and hostess. It was time to stop procrastinating and get to that party.

Purposefully, she straightened her shoulders.

Then, without so much as another glance at her reflection, she marched out of her bedchamber and down the stairs to the ballroom.

10

❧

"*M*iss Breanna." Wells greeted her at the foot of the steps, beaming with a paternal pride that was as intense as if she were his own child. "You look lovely."

"Thank you, Wells." Breanna squeezed his arm, grateful that a guard had been assigned to act as butler for the evening—not only because it meant added protection, but because it meant Wells could see the fruits of his labor by stationing himself at the ballroom door.

A cluster of chatting matrons breezed by, so engrossed in their gossip that they never noticed Breanna. They hovered at the ballroom doorway— all shimmering jewels and rustling silk—finishing their whispered conversation, then hastened in to rejoin the party.

A wave of familiar nervousness accosted Breanna in a rush, bringing with it the lingering remnants of a shy child who'd stayed in the background, let her bolder, more outspoken cousin lead the way.

"Wells," she murmured tentatively, rubbing her skirts between her fingers. "Would you do me the honor of escorting me in? You know how I hate making entrances."

Wells frowned, fully aware of Breanna's reticence—and its cause. "Your father's gone, Miss Breanna," he reminded her gently. "And, yes, I know you hate making entrances. You hate anything that makes you the center of attention. Well, tonight you *are* the center of attention—you and Miss Stacie. This party is in your honor. I refuse to pretend otherwise."

He cupped Breanna's elbow, guided her toward the ballroom. "In the eyes of the *ton*, I'm a butler. Which doesn't bother me a bit. I take great pride in my position. Besides, you and Miss Stacie view me as family, and that's all that matters. My point is, I won't escort you. That would cause those women who just passed by here to swoon, which would, in turn, detract from your entrance. What I *will* do is announce you—just as I announced Miss Stacie and Lord Sheldrake. How would that be?"

Breanna studied the throngs of people, the movement of light and color as laughing couples whirled about the dance floor, helped themselves to plates of food and glasses of punch. There were easily a hundred and fifty people already filling the room.

Her gut clenched.

"Please, Miss Breanna," Wells urged, resorting to the one tactic he knew would work. "Do it for me."

How could she not? Especially when he was looking at her like a proud father about to present his treasure to the world.

"All right, Wells," she managed. "Let's get this over with. Once everyone stops staring at me, I'll be fine."

"You're already fine," he countered. "You're far more than fine. In less than one minute, you'll be swamped by admirers, most of whom will be totally unworthy. I, myself, shall keep an eye on things, make sure you're not pestered by any one suitor for too long. Should you need further reinforcements, Miss Stacie and Lord Sheldrake are directly to your right, chatting with Lord and Lady Dutton and the Earl and Countess of Geldrick. Actually, they're not chatting. Both men are frantically trying to make amends to Miss Stacie for their stupidity in snubbing her business proposition last summer. And Miss Stacie is having fun watching them squirm. She's already done the same to the Duke of Maywood, the Marquess of Radebrook, and the Viscount Crompton."

Breanna couldn't help but laugh. "Thank you, Wells. For pointing out where I can find a safe haven and for giving me that status report."

"Your safe haven. I'm glad you brought that up." Wells's humor vanished, and his uneasy gaze traveled the room. "Lord Royce is near the French doors. So are two guards. The others are positioned everywhere on the estate. Given that a third nobleman was murdered in London last week, no one will question the added security. In fact, they'll be grateful for it. So relax and have fun. All will be well."

Soberly, Breanna nodded, sickened by the reminder of what was fast becoming an epidemic of killings. Three men had now died, and their wives had vanished. The whole situation was terrifying. Between that and the fear surrounding her own dilemma . . .

Her worried thoughts were interrupted by Wells trumpeting, "May I present this evening's other lovely honoree, Lady Breanna Colby. While I realize Lady Breanna is your hostess, I am temporarily relieving her of that role—long enough to ask you to join me in wishing her a very happy birthday."

Wells's utterly unconventional announcement yielded a round of laughter and a host of good-natured wishes. It also did wonders for easing Breanna's unsettled state—a state that had escalated from mere anxiety over a public appearance to blind fear over armed killers.

"You're incorrigible," she told Wells affectionately, grateful as always for his innate understanding of her. She knew he'd very intentionally made her entrance more relaxed and less ceremonious. And she loved him for it.

Drawing a slow breath, she walked into the room, greeting her guests as she did, finding that it was infinitely easier than expected to act the part of hostess. Many of her guests approached to thank her for considerately adding so many guards to the estate since, as expected, they were all terribly nervous about the string of murders taking place.

Breanna scarcely had time to answer before she was swept up into a whirl of activity, being claimed for a dance, then moving from one partner to another. She found herself wishing she could stop long enough to take a breath and exchange a word with Stacie.

Not that her cousin was any more idle than she. Dressed in an exquisite gown of bottle-green silk overlaid with French gauze, Stacie was holding her own kind of court. With Damen adhered firmly to her side, she was politely accepting the stammering apologies of a half dozen businessmen—apologies, Breanna suspected, that were motivated by equal doses of regret over their missed profit-making opportunities and worry over the glares they were receiving from Damen Lockewood, whose bank was at the heart of all their ventures.

As she circled the dance floor with the arrogant and handsome Lord Percy Gilbert, Breanna caught Stacie's eye, saw the amusement there, and nearly laughed aloud. Those poor men. They didn't stand a chance.

The strings fell silent, and Breanna was just about to excuse herself and head toward Stacie and Damen when she heard a soft, feminine voice ask, "Breanna, may I speak with you?"

She turned, surprised to see Lady Margaret Warner waiting impatiently beside her.

As the most sought-after young woman in the crowd, Margaret never approached anyone, certainly not at a ball. She waited for *them* to approach *her.* Ever coy, friendly but not eager, Margaret was always surrounded by far too many friends and admirers to break free and chat. True, she and Breanna had become friends over the past months, but doing needlepoint together and seeking her out at a ball were two different things entirely.

"Margaret." Breanna hid her surprise well. "Of course." She smiled at Lord Percy. "You'll excuse us?"

"Of course he will." There was that flirtatious charm Margaret exuded so well. She gazed intently at Gilbert, batted those long, irresistible lashes, and murmured, "His lordship understands that we ladies have things to discuss. You don't mind, do you?"

Gilbert bowed, an anticipatory gleam flashing in his eyes. "Of course not."

"I knew you'd understand." She touched his arm, ever so slightly. "Thank you."

With that, she led Breanna off, guiding her close to the musicians so whatever they discussed would be drowned out once the dancing recommenced.

The next set began and Margaret came to a halt, pivoting about, the skirts of her blush-colored gown swirling about her ankles like a pastel cloud. "This ball is delightful," she told Breanna with an unexpectedly warm squeeze of her hands. "The whole party is a stunning success."

"I'm glad you're enjoying yourself." Breanna offered her new friend a genuine, if puzzled, smile. She waited, wondering what the real reason was behind Margaret's unprecedented behavior.

She didn't have long to wait.

"Tell me," Margaret whispered, leaning closer to Breanna as if to share a coveted secret. "I'm dying to know. How did you do it?"

"Do what?"

A puff of tinkling laughter. "You needn't be modest. Not with me. I'm duly impressed. So tell me, how did you convince him to come?"

"Convince *who* to come?" Breanna was beginning to feel like a total idiot.

The look Margaret gave her did nothing to erase that feeling. *"Who?"* she repeated incredulously. "Why, Royce Chadwick, of course. He's refused every invitation since returning from India. And last Season he made only three appearances, none of them for more than an hour. Yet you managed to lure him to your party. How did you do it?"

Breanna followed Margaret's line of vision, easily spotting Lord Royce conversing with a group of gentlemen. Then again, Lord Royce would be easy to spot anywhere, even in a large crowd such as this. His height and build, his powerful presence, those hard, dark, dangerously handsome good looks—especially clad in formal evening clothes—were enough to attract any woman's eye.

Clearly, they attracted *every* woman's eye. And Margaret Warner was no exception.

"I . . ." Breanna wet her lips with the tip of her tongue, desperately trying to think of a reply. She recalled Lord Royce mentioning that he rarely attended parties, but it never occurred to her that his appearance here would cause such an extreme reaction.

Then again, it should have occurred to her. Judging from the look on Margaret Warner's face, Royce Chadwick was not only *noticed* by every breathing unattached female in the *ton,* he was coveted by them, as well.

"Don't keep me in suspense," Margaret hissed. "Tell me. Have you known him long?"

"He's a friend of Damen's," Breanna finally replied, realizing that she couldn't stand there gaping and saying nothing forever. "I believe they're business associates." She prayed that wasn't a confidential tidbit she'd just revealed. But Lord help her, she had to say something.

"So you're not acquainted with him yourself." Margaret's face fell. "I was hoping you could put in a kind word . . . that is . . ."

Breanna understood precisely what Margaret was hoping. The question was, how did she respond?

She was mulling it over when Royce Chadwick looked up, staring directly toward the musicians and finding her with an ease that made her suspect he knew exactly where she was now, and probably where she'd been from the instant she entered the ballroom.

His midnight blue gaze locked with hers.

The impact was staggering, like a blow knocking the breath right from her lungs, and Breanna had to fight the urge to gasp in air. Instead, she merely stood there, unable to look away, watching as he made his way across the room, heading purposefully toward her.

"Breanna?" Margaret repeated, obviously unsettled by Breanna's silence, as well as by the fact that she had to humble herself in a fashion that was utterly foreign to her. "Have you met him or not?"

"Yes," Breanna heard herself say. "I've met him."

"Ah." Margaret released a heartfelt sigh. "Then Anastasia *has* introduced you. Good. Would you do me the same favor? I mean, I've actually been introduced—twice—and even shared a dance or two with him. But it can't hurt to refresh his memory. It would certainly ease my way—some idle chatter, a waltz, maybe even a moonlight stroll. After that, the rest should go smoothly."

Breanna scarcely heard what Margaret was saying. Because at that moment, the very man her friend was plotting to snare was reaching their sides.

"Good evening, Lady Breanna." Royce bowed, lifted her gloved hand to his lips. "Thank you for inviting me to this lovely party."

Breanna's heart began slamming against her ribs and, suddenly, she knew why she'd reacted so strongly.

This was a different Royce Chadwick, not the implacable man who hunted down criminals, understood their minds. This was an elegant, polished nobleman who blended in with the *ton*—polite, sociable, alarmingly charismatic. No—not just charismatic. Seductive. Desirable. Exciting in a way that had *nothing* to do with outwitting an enemy.

This man was more dangerous than the one she'd originally met.

"I'm delighted to have you, my lord," she managed, then felt hot color rush to her cheeks at the implication of her own words. She found herself praying it was only her heightened senses that were causing her to view her comment in such a lascivious fashion.

If Lord Royce perceived anything out of the ordinary, he didn't show it. "I'm delighted to be here."

Thank heavens. He'd missed it.

"You're flushed," he added with offhanded ease. "May I get you some punch?"

He hadn't missed it. Or if he'd missed the indecent connotation of her words, he certainly hadn't missed her flustered reaction to them.

Once again, Breanna summoned her now-faltering inner reserve. "Yes. Thank you. I do feel warm. I suppose it's all the excitement." From the corner of her eye, she spied Margaret, inching purposefully closer. "Lord Royce, are you acquainted with Lady Margaret Warner? If not, let me introduce you."

Royce's smile was the essence of gentility. "Lady Margaret and I have met. How are you, my lady?" he inquired.

"Very well, thank you, my lord. And, yes, I do recall our introduction. It was last year, during my first Season." Margaret lowered her lashes and moistened her lips—ever so scarcely—prompting Breanna to wish she could master the fine art of flirting as well as her friend.

"Will you excuse us?" Lord Royce was asking Margaret, simultaneously gripping Breanna's elbow. "Our hostess deserves something cool to drink."

"Of course." Whatever disappointment Margaret was feeling she kept carefully in check.

Royce led Breanna across the room and over to the punch bowl. "Here." He offered her a glass. "This will help."

Help what? Breanna wanted to ask. Her hand trembling, she accepted the glass, drinking down the entire goblet in an attempt to cool her throat and calm her nerves.

"More?" Royce asked.

It was only fruit juice, flavored with a little Madeira, a bit of champagne, and an insignificant amount of brandy, Breanna reminded herself. She nodded, swallowing the second glass almost as quickly as she had the first, then reaching eagerly for a third.

She was three-quarters of the way through with that glass when Royce murmured, "I think you should take a few breaths before going for a fourth."

He sounded amused.

Breanna glanced up at him.

He *looked* amused.

"I suppose so." Breanna wondered what his amusement was based on:

was it her nerves, her excessive thirst, or that stupid remark she'd made about having him?

She'd have to find out in order to make the appropriate amends.

"My lord," she began, grateful that the area they were standing in was unoccupied. The last thing she wanted was to make a fool of herself in front of all her guests. And as it was, she could already feel the warming effects of the punch drifting through her, making her question whether she'd underestimated the amount of liquor that was mixed in with the fruit.

"Royce," he amended.

Breanna's head snapped up. "Pardon me?"

"My name. My *given* name. It's Royce. Not my lord. Nor Lord Royce. Just Royce."

She studied his face: the bold features and hard, square jaw, the thick raven-black hair and broad forehead over the twin black slashes of brows and midnight blue eyes. And the decisive mouth that was used to issuing orders—and having them obeyed.

Her gaze lingered there, studying the subtle curve of his lips.

She wondered what it would be like to kiss him.

God help her, she was foxed.

She was also still staring.

"My name," he repeated, those incredible lips moving ever so slightly, his deep baritone huskier than it had been before. "It's Royce."

She tore her gaze from his mouth, met his hooded stare. "It wouldn't be proper for me to address you that way."

He leaned negligently against the wall, regarding her with a kind of lazy curiosity. "Why not?"

"We scarcely know each other."

"Anastasia calls me by my given name. And she knows me precisely the same amount of time as you do."

That comparison elicited a fond smile. "That's Stacie. She's far more unconventional than I."

"I think you're more unconventional than you realize—more unconventional than that conventional veneer of yours allows."

Breanna's eyes widened, and she gaped at him silently.

"Ah, a waltz," Royce commented as the strings began to play. He straightened, took her near-empty glass, and set it down on a tray. "May I have the honor of sharing it with you? Once you've recovered from your shock, that is." He extended his hand, his gaze darkening, looking directly into hers. "By the way, I don't blame all these men for fighting over you. You're breathtaking."

Instinctively, Breanna placed her fingers in his. "Yes," she managed, first answering his request for a dance. "And thank you."

"Splendid. And you're welcome." He guided her onto the dance floor, his fingers burning through the fine material of her glove—and her gown—as he led her into the waltz.

For the first time Breanna understood why some people considered this dance to be scandalous. Then again, most people hadn't drunk three glasses of Regent's punch on an empty stomach before attempting it. Still, it was unlike any dance she'd shared with any man this evening. The steps, the motions, even the proximity—those were all the same. And yet . . .

"So far, so good," Royce murmured.

Breanna blinked, finding it suddenly difficult to focus on his face. "What's so far, so good?"

A corner of his mouth lifted. "Your party. The fact that there haven't been any unwelcome guests all day, nor thus far tonight."

"Oh." She nodded, wishing the punch had done more to eliminate the knot of dread this topic incited.

Royce seemed to sense her distress, because he frowned. "I'm sorry. I didn't mean to bring up this subject. You've been living with it too much as it is."

"That's your job. Besides, it's not something I can forget."

"Maybe you should—at least for a while." Abruptly, Royce halted, capturing Breanna's elbow and drawing her off the dance floor.

She blinked, wishing she weren't so dizzy and puzzling over how two and a half glasses of punch could wreak so much havoc. "I felt fine before," she announced.

"It takes time for the spirits to hit." Royce guided her forward, and she felt a blast of cold air strike her face and arms. Abruptly, she realized they were standing just outside the French doors. "Come with me," he urged. He led her onto the balcony, nodding as they passed the guards. "Lady Breanna and I are going to get some air," he said quietly. "We won't go far. And I have my pistol."

"Fine, my lord. We're here," replied one guard, a big, burly fellow whose size alone was intimidating.

"Where are we going?" Breanna asked, stumbling a bit and wrapping her arms about herself as her teeth began to chatter. "It's cold."

"I know. The cold air is good for you." Even as he spoke, Royce was shrugging out of his coat. He wrapped it around her, covering her bare arms and enveloping her in a layer of woolen warmth. "Better?"

"Yes." She felt odd, like she was floating, gloriously numb to the anguish of the past weeks. "I think I'll drink more often," she announced.

Royce chuckled, snaked an arm about her waist as she teetered on her feet. "I wouldn't suggest it. You don't hold your spirits too well."

"I guess not. A bit of fruit punch and look what happens to me."

"Fruit punch?" Royce echoed dryly. "There are several bottles each of Madeira and champagne in Regent's punch, not to mention a pint of rum, and a quart of brandy. No wonder you're foxed." He scanned the area, led her over to a small rock garden that was lined with shrubs— enough to ensure privacy but not isolation—and came complete with a small, outdoor bench. "Sit."

"All right." Breanna sank down, leaning her head back and staring up at the sky. "The stars are waltzing."

"Really? Who's leading?"

She didn't smile. "You're mocking me. I'm not too foxed to realize that. I suppose I can't blame you."

"I'm not mocking you." He stood beside the bench, hands clasped behind him as he stared off into the darkness. "I'm teasing you. I want you to smile."

"I do smile."

"Not often enough."

She twisted around to look up at him. "And how would you know that?"

"The same way I know you're less conventional than you think. And the same way I know you need relief from the worry you've been carrying around."

"Oh." Breanna's heart gave another of those little skips, and she wondered if Royce realized how excruciatingly charismatic he was, how powerful an effect he had on women.

"Royce?" she tried, finding it wasn't so hard to say his name after all.

"Hmm?" His smile told her he approved.

"Margaret wants you." She blurted it out without preliminaries or warning—even to herself. "She asked me to put in a good word for her." Pausing, Breanna's brow furrowed in thought. "I should do that."

Another chuckle, this one husky. "Should you?"

"Yes. And quickly. Because Margaret has a great deal of competition. Apparently, dozens—scores of women—want you." Even as she spoke, Breanna wondered who in God's name was saying those things.

"Are you one of them?"

Royce's question, uttered with a fierce but quiet intensity, penetrated her clouded mind, made it swim even more. Her head dropped back against the bench-top, and she stared blindly into the night, struggling to regain her senses. "Your eyes are that color," she noted in a whisper. "That same midnight blue. Almost black. Ebony with a sharp tinge of color—color that makes them all the more riveting. It's hard to look away from eyes like that."

"Breanna." He was standing in front of her. He caught her arms, drew her to her feet, and tilted up her chin with his forefinger. "Answer my question."

She wet her lips, felt the coat he'd enveloped her in slip from her shoulders, topple to the bench.

Odd, but she was no longer cold.

"It's not fair of you to ask me that," she murmured. "Not when I'm foxed."

"You'd never answer me if you weren't."

She couldn't deny the truth of that. "You're right." Stunned, she watched her own gloved fingers reach up, trace the hard curve of his jaw. "I wouldn't answer it. I also wouldn't do this." Her fingertips brushed his lips as she'd longed to do before, felt their warmth even through her glove. "Let me ask you the same question, my lord."

"Royce," he corrected her, his voice even huskier than it had been before. "And go ahead."

"Royce. Do you want me?"

Sparks glittered in his midnight eyes. "Yes, I want you. You have no idea how badly. More than I realized. Much more than I should." He turned his lips into her palm. "Does that answer your question?"

Mutely, she nodded.

He kissed the pulse at her wrist. "Then answer mine."

Breanna felt a rush of warmth that had nothing to do with the punch. "Yes, I want you," she admitted, intentionally giving him the exact words he'd given her. "You have no idea how badly. More than I realized. Much more than I should."

She saw the triumph flash across his face an instant before he gripped her arms, drew her to him.

"Good," he said fiercely.

He paused only to lift each of his hands to his mouth, yank off his gloves with his teeth, and toss them to the ground—all the while staring at her, devouring her with his gaze.

Then, he crushed his mouth to hers.

If the impact of his gaze was stunning, the impact of his kiss was fatal.

Breanna gasped, clutching at his waistcoat as Royce's lips ravaged hers, possessing her in a series of deep, drugging kisses she felt to the depths of her soul. Their mouths fused, parted, fused again, and this time his tongue penetrated her, awakening her to an intimacy she'd never imagined. She followed his lead, opened her mouth to his, shiveringly accepting his tongue's caresses, then eagerly returning them in a way only the blissful effects of alcohol would allow.

Royce growled deep in his chest, and his arms closed around her with staggering force, pulling her flush against him. He kissed her again, more deeply still, cupping her head in his hands and angling his mouth to allow his tongue deeper penetration.

"Put your arms around me." He breathed his command into her lips, kissing her senseless while she complied.

Realizing she'd been clenching at his waistcoat to keep from collapsing, Breanna unknotted her fists, glided her palms up the hard planes of his chest, feeling his muscles contract beneath the fine material of his shirt. His shoulders flexed beneath her fingertips, and she stroked his neck lightly with her forefinger, lingering there to feel the warmth of his skin.

Royce must have sensed her need, or perhaps even shared it. Another harsh sound vibrated in his chest, and he dragged his mouth from hers long enough to capture her hands in his, yank off her gloves in a few quick tugs. "Now," he muttered, flinging them aside and bringing her arms back around his neck. "Touch me. Let me feel your hands on my skin."

Longing welled up inside her, and she gave in to it, brushing her fingers against Royce's neck, then letting her palms discover the corded muscles and smooth flesh.

A jolt of reaction shot through him, and his eyes darkened to near black. "God," he rasped, stunned disbelief registering on his face. "My God." He bent to take her mouth again, his arms contracting like bow strings, bringing her up and into him. The thin silk of Breanna's gown did nothing to hide the hardening contours of his body, but rather than freezing with horror and shame, she felt herself melt, soften as if to fit more snugly against him.

The world was spinning out of control, and Breanna never wanted it to stop. She explored his throat, slipped her fingers beneath his cravat to feel the heat of his flesh, then glided them through his hair, savored the silky texture. Her own hair had come undone, she realized absently, sighing with pleasure as Royce's hands captured the toppling auburn waves, savored their texture before tangling in them, lifting them away so he could stroke the nape of her neck, the exposed skin of her back and shoulders. God, these sensations were too exciting to withstand—yet unthinkable to abandon.

She pressed closer.

"Breanna."

Something inside him seemed to snap. He cupped her bottom, crushed her lower body to his as he ravaged her mouth, his tongue rubbing against hers until she thought she would die. Her breasts were tingling with sensation, her entire body heavy with longing, liquid heat pulsing through her with each plunge of his tongue, each nudge of his hips.

Almost violently, Royce tore himself away, biting off a curse as he lowered her feet to the ground, steadied her against the bench—an arm's length away.

Gasping in air, they stared at each other.

"Are you all right?" Royce demanded, his fingers digging into her arms.

Reflexively, Breanna nodded, inclining her head in dazed noncomprehension. She was still awash with sensation, her mind and body reeling with discovery, her mouth clamoring for his.

"Royce?" She said his name in question, in bewilderment. When he didn't answer, she blinked to clear her head, to make out the expression on his face.

His handsome features were taut, strained, a muscle working furiously at his jaw. His midnight eyes were blazing with sparks, and his forehead was dotted with sweat, despite the evening's chill. His teeth were clenched, his breath coming in hard rasps, sending erratic puffs of vapor into the night sky. He looked livid—no, not livid, tormented, as if he were fighting some harsh internal battle.

An internal battle over her.

Another long minute passed, and the cold began sinking back into Breanna's bones, causing her teeth to chatter.

Royce swore again, snapped into action. He bent, scooped his coat off the bench and wrapped it around her, rubbing her arms to warm them. "I'm sorry," he said hoarsely. "I don't know what came over me. I know that's no excuse, but it's the only one I've got." His hands glided up to cup her face, and he inspected her closely, frowning as he surveyed her disheveled tresses. "How do we fix your hair?"

Automatically, Breanna's hands came up, discovering the extent of the damage. "I can manage." At his dubious expression, she forced a weak smile. "I've had practice."

That made his eyes narrow. "Have you now?"

She realized instantly how he'd perceived her remark. "Not *that* kind of practice." She swallowed. "My father insisted on my looking immaculate at all times. That wasn't easy to manage, especially when I was a child. I learned how to readjust my hair in record time. Watch." She stepped back, smoothing loose waves of hair back up, twisting and braiding them until they'd reformed their original sleek coronet.

"I'm impressed." Royce was studying her from beneath hooded lids.

"Now all I need are these." Breanna stooped, picked up her gloves, and gracefully tugged them on. "There. As good as new."

"Just like before," he said in an odd tone.

"No," she replied quietly, meeting his probing stare. "Not just like before."

Silence.

Breanna gazed up at him, taking in the warring emotions crossing his face as he struggled with whatever internal demons were plaguing him. She wouldn't ask him what they were—that wasn't her right. She, better than anyone, knew the need to keep one's thoughts, one's conflicts, even one's memories private.

Memories like the ones they'd just made.

Dimly, she wondered why she didn't feel the shame she knew she should. She had, after all, behaved like a total wanton. Yet she felt more alive, more exhilarated, than she'd ever felt in her life. Was that because the full extent of what she'd done hadn't had time to sink in yet, or was it because what she'd done had felt so incredibly right?

So magnificently, incredibly right.

"Stop looking at me like that," Royce commanded roughly. "Or you'll be back in my arms before you've caught your breath."

"What makes you think I don't want that?"

She heard him inhale sharply. "Breanna, you're playing with fire." A weighted pause. "We both are."

"Fire." Her gaze remained steady on his. "Yes, that's what it felt like."

"I *don't* want you to get burned."

"All right," she whispered. "Just singed then."

"Damn." He gripped her waist, pulled her closer and took her mouth in one long, blazing kiss. "You should be slapping me," he muttered, his thumbs just grazing the underside of her breasts. "Pulling away, calling me a bastard, and slapping me."

"Is that what I should be doing?" She shivered, totally focused on the tantalizing motion of his fingertips.

"Yes." The kiss deepened, his tongue moving slowly, seductively against hers. "You should." His thumbs shifted, brushed her hardened nipples once, then stroked them in slow, teasing circles.

"Oh, God." Breanna's knees were shaking, pinpoints of almost unendurable sensation shooting from her breasts to her loins. She shrugged Royce's coat off her shoulders, let it drop, then stepped closer, wrapped her arms around his neck.

Royce shuddered, his entire body going rigid as he shaped and caressed her breasts. Each caress grew hotter, more urgent, more intimate.

His trembling hands reached for the top of her bodice.

"Breanna." He lifted his head slightly, his eyes molten with desire. "If I touch you, I'll take you. Right here. Right now. On this bench. With the entire *ton* carousing just inside those walls." His hands made the return journey to her waist. "I've got to stop."

"I know." Her eyes slid shut, a shivering sigh escaping her. "I know."

Royce caught her chin between his fingers, and her lashes lifted to see him studying her face for a long, searching moment. "Are you going to remember this later?" he demanded. "When the Regent's punch has worn off?"

A soft smile touched Breanna's lips. "I'll remember it," she assured him. "And the punch wore off long ago."

11

❧

Stacie glanced over at the French doors for the tenth time in the last half hour, nearly sagging with relief when she saw her cousin stroll in on Lord Royce's arm.

Finally. Breanna was back. Back and safe.

Thank God. No one had hurt her.

Then again, her protector had been by her side.

Besieged by a rush of curiosity, Stacie met Breanna's eyes, spied a definite sparkle that hadn't been there before, and had to fight the urge to rush over and ask what had happened during that stroll in the glittering winter moonlight.

Winter. And Breanna had stayed outside for thirty minutes without her mantle.

Interesting. She didn't look at all cold.

"Stacie?" Damen's voice was tender, but his grip, tightening ever so fractionally about her waist, was telling her in no uncertain terms that she'd better stay put.

Damn, the man knew her so well.

"Yes?" She gave him a sweet, innocent look, turning her attention back to the small group surrounding them—a group that had, in the short minutes while her mind had wandered, expanded from Lord and Lady Dutton and the Earl and Countess of Geldrick to include the Viscount Crompton and Lord Arthur Landow.

"The viscount was just commenting on how radiant you look," Damen prompted.

Anastasia felt a twinge of guilt when she saw the concern furrowing Lord Crompton's brow—and Lord Landow's, for that matter. Like Dutton and Geldrick, both these men had strong monetary ties to the House of Lockewood and both were uneasy about offending Damen. True, they'd rejected her request for financial backing last summer—as had every other businessman she'd approached. Still, that did nothing to shed doubt on their integrity, only on their open-mindedness. Like all Damen's clients, these were honorable men—the viscount a retired military general who'd served in the Napoleonic Wars, and Lord Landow a wealthy manufacturer whose products were sold both here and abroad.

By nature, Stacie wasn't cruel. Needling these men for missing out on a superb business opportunity was one thing. Forcing them to humble themselves, as they had been doing since the party began, was quite another. Enough was enough. The last thing she wanted was to add insult to injury by making Lord Crompton think he was being snubbed.

"Forgive me, my lord," she told him, relieved to see the intense consternation on his face ease a bit. "I appreciate your gracious compliment." Her mind raced, and she quickly came up with the ideal explanation for her rudeness *and* for Damen's constant presence at her side—a reason they'd like far better than their current belief: namely, that he was looming over them to retaliate, to make them squirm for offending his wife.

Sometimes the truth came in handy. Now was one of those times.

She shot Lord Crompton a grateful look. "Your kind words couldn't have come at a better time—especially when I know I look anything but radiant. I haven't slept in weeks, nor have I kept down a meal. That's actually why I missed hearing what you said. I was feeling light-headed."

Crompton now looked concerned. "Have you seen a physician?"

"Every day on the ship home," she replied with a smile. "Much to his dismay." She inclined her head, turned her smile up at Damen, whose twinkle told her he knew exactly what she was doing—and that he approved. "My illness is for the most wonderful of reasons. Damen and I are expecting a child."

"That's splendid." The viscount relaxed, raised his glass. "Congratulations to you both."

"Yes, congratulations," Landow echoed, as pleased by the congeniality of her tone as he was by her news. "What a delightful announcement." His good wishes—and his gaze—were clearly directed at Damen.

"I agree," Damen responded, drawing Stacie closer to his side. "I'm elated."

"He's also exceedingly anxious and protective," Stacie confided, tossing a you-understand glance at Lady Geldrick, in the hopes of eliciting the countess's support. It was well known that she and the earl were very much in love, and that she had gifted her husband with their second son just five months ago.

"That poor doctor couldn't wait to see the last of us," Stacie added, still speaking to Lady Geldrick. "Damen paid him three visits a day to verify that the symptoms I was experiencing were normal. And, as you can see, he refuses to budge from my side."

"Well, of course he does." It was Lord Geldrick who chimed in first, nodding vigorously and giving Damen a look of genuine sympathy. "It's your first child. I don't blame you a bit for your concern, Sheldrake."

"You shouldn't," his wife teased, her eyes twinkling. "You acted the same way when I was with child—especially the first time." She leaned forward, touched Stacie's arm. "Best wishes to you both. And don't worry about feeling ill. The sensation will pass in a few months. After that, you'll be hungry enough to eat three banquets a day."

"I'm relieved to hear that." As she said it, Stacie realized it was true. She also realized how good it felt to speak with another woman about her condition—something she hadn't yet done. In fact, she'd been so worried over the killer stalking her and Breanna that she hadn't stopped to give much thought to the more normal concerns surrounding pregnancy.

As if on cue, a wave of light-headedness accosted her, made her teeter on her feet.

"Stacie?" Damen felt the motion, whipped about to face her. "What's wrong?" Lines of worry tightened his face. "You're white as a sheet."

"I'm fine—really." She blinked to clear her head. "Just a bit dizzy."

"We're sitting down." He was already guiding her away from the group. "If you'll all excuse us."

"Certainly," Lord Crompton said, backing away to let them pass. "Tend to your wife, Sheldrake."

Damen intended to do just that. He drew Stacie over to an airy corner of the room, then eased her into a chair. Turning toward the hallway, he signaled Wells with his eyes.

The butler was beside them in an instant.

"Miss Stacie? Are you ill?" he demanded.

"No, Wells, just dizzy." Stacie wished the room would right itself.

"You've eaten almost as little as Miss Breanna did today," Wells admonished with a frown. "And *you're* eating for two. I'll bring you a plate of food."

"Good idea," Damen answered for her. "And something cool to drink. *Not* laden with spirits."

"Of course not, my lord." Wells sniffed. "I wouldn't think of it."

"Of course you wouldn't. Forgive me, Wells." Damen raked a hand through his hair. "I guess I'm more unnerved than I realized."

"I understand. No apology is necessary."

"Would you both stop staring at me as if I'm on the verge of death?" Stacie demanded, looking from one man to the other. "The guests will start thinking I have some rare disease."

"I'll be very discreet," Wells assured her. He glanced about the room, took in the merrymaking. "Believe me, no one has even noticed us. They haven't any idea what we're talking about."

Even as he spoke, Lady Dutton was passing the news of Stacie's pregnancy on to the Marchioness of Radebrook.

By the time Wells arrived back from the refreshment table, there wasn't a guest in the room who didn't know that the Marquess and Marchioness of Sheldrake's first child was on its way.

"I'm so glad we're being discreet," Stacie said in amusement, after the twelfth person had congratulated her. "Wells, you should know by now there's no keeping a secret in the *ton*."

"Maybe it's better this way," Damen muttered purposefully to his wife, simultaneously smiling his thanks at the retreating Duke of Maywood, who'd come over to offer his best wishes. "At least the guests are keeping you so busy you can't dash off to interrogate Breanna. That *was* where you were headed when you nearly collapsed at my feet, wasn't it?"

"Yes." Anastasia knew better than to insult her husband by lying. "Or rather, I was *considering* inching my way over to Breanna." Her curious gaze returned to where her cousin was still chatting with Royce. Breanna was obviously unaware that Stacie was feeling light-headed, or that the room was abuzz with news of her near-swoon. In fact, Breanna was unaware that anything out of the ordinary had taken place. Odd, considering how attuned to each other she and Stacie were. It would take a major distraction to preoccupy Breanna to the point where she wouldn't sense that an event involving Stacie had taken place.

Evidently, Royce Chadwick was such a distraction.

"Damen, surely you noticed—"

"I noticed." Damen followed his wife's stare. "But I think you're reading far too much into it. Royce is keeping an eye on Breanna—a practical idea under the circumstances. He knows I'm attached to your side for the night. You need no further protection. Breanna, on the other hand, is alone. So, he's serving as her sentry."

"Indeed," Wells agreed with a sniff. "There could be no other explanation for it."

"A sentry." Stacie rolled her eyes at the two men. "I see. And as her *sentry*, Royce took her for a half-hour walk on a night that's so cold no one else would dare venture out and he'd therefore be assured of complete privacy."

"No," Damen countered. "Knowing Royce, he probably took her for a walk to try to keep her mind off her anxiety. Breanna's coping with an enormous emotional burden. Not only is she grappling with her own fears, she's terrified for you and the babe."

"That's true." A pained expression crossed Wells's lined face. "Miss Breanna feels responsible—unfounded though her guilt might be—for jeopardizing you all. She feels that if she'd never taken that shot—"

"I'd be dead right now," Stacie stated flatly. "Breanna saved my life. I've told her over and over again that she's not responsible for the threats of a madman. But she won't be appeased until he's found and stopped. Nevertheless . . ." Stacie broke off, still studying Breanna pensively. "None of this has any bearing on what's happening here tonight. After all, worry wouldn't bring a glow to Breanna's cheeks, nor would her overly acute sense of responsibility cause tendrils of her hair to topple."

Wells frowned, puzzled. He polished his spectacles, then shoved them back on, peering worriedly toward Breanna. "Miss Breanna's hair looks fine to me."

"*Fine?* Wells, you know Breanna. Her hair is never fine. It's perfect. Except now. Even from this distance, I can distinctly see a few curls sagging at her nape." Stacie arched a brow, first at Wells, then at Damen. "What shall we attribute it to?" She paused for effect, then snapped her fingers in mock deduction. "I know—the wind!"

Damen's lips twitched, as much at Wells's vigilant glower as at Stacie's observation. "You made your point. Fine, maybe there is something going on between those two. But whatever it is, you're not going to find out about it until you've eaten and drunk every drop of that." He gestured toward her plate and glass.

"Whatever you say, my lord." She gave him a beatific smile and returned to her refreshment. "Stop glaring, Wells," she berated gently, sipping at her punch. "Breanna's a grown woman. She's entitled to share a chaste embrace with an enigmatic man—especially when that man is one we've entrusted to safeguard her life. Besides, aren't you the one who wanted Breanna to find someone special?"

"I didn't have a reckless womanizer in mind."

"If Royce is a womanizer, he's abandoned that trait tonight." Stacie took a small bite of her lemon tart. "He hasn't so much as danced with another woman. Only Breanna. As for reckless . . ." Another bite. "I wouldn't describe personal, full-time guard service as reckless behavior, would you?" She shot Wells a look. "I know you worry about Breanna. But give Royce a chance. He might surprise you." With that, she polished off her tart, dabbing at her mouth with a napkin.

"Ah, word about your condition just reached Breanna," Damen noted, watching Lady Dutton insert her plump figure between Breanna and Royce, then begin chatting excitedly. "Let's see, Breanna now knows you're with child, which she already knew, and she's about to find out that you're dizzy."

As if on cue, Breanna's head came up, and she whipped about to face Stacie.

Her cousin gestured to her that she was fine, that she was eating, and that Breanna could safely go about her business.

Visibly relieved, Breanna concurred, turning back to Lady Dutton—*and* deliberately ignoring the questioning look that flitted across Stacie's face as she glanced meaningfully from Breanna to Royce and back again.

"I'll have to get my answers later," Stacie concluded with a sigh. "Breanna's too private to confide in me during the ball." Shelving her curiosity, Stacie watched Lady Dutton move on to the next group to share her news. "I'm so glad we're providing the evening entertainment," she muttered. "My pregnancy is the topic of conversation among our guests."

"That's not necessarily bad," Damen replied, cradling her gloved hand between his. "At least they're discussing something other than the murders Bow Street is investigating. *That* topic has dominated the party thus far, and dampened the mood of the ball. Good news must feel like a welcome balm to everyone."

"The situation is terrifying," Stacie murmured, placing her empty glass and plate on the tray of a passing footman. "This is the third murder in a fortnight. Certainly Bow Street can't still suspect the men's wives. Three wives—three *young* wives scarcely older than I am—capable of murdering their husbands? I doubt that's possible."

"Yet all three women have disappeared," Wells reminded her.

"Maybe they were kidnapped," Stacie suggested.

"Possibly." Damen pursed his lips thoughtfully. "Then again, if they were kidnapped, where are the ransom notes? And who would the kidnapper expect to extort money from if the husbands in question are all dead?"

The assassin brushed by in time to hear Sheldrake's last comment, and a hint of a smile touched his lips at the knowledge that he was responsible for Sheldrake's bafflement and for the fear pervading the *ton*.

Good, he thought, heading down the hall, away from the ball and toward the servants' quarters. The marquess was as baffled as the detectives, and *he* was an exceedingly intelligent man, far smarter than the Bow Street runners. So, if he couldn't figure out the mystery of those noblemen's deaths, neither would they.

Then again, Sheldrake wouldn't be contemplating the London murders for long. The deaths of three strangers would soon pale in comparison to his own loss. In a matter of days, maybe weeks, the poor man would have his own, very personal, grief to deal with.

Pity Sheldrake had to be involved. Ah, well. He'd married the chit *and* made things worse by falling in love with her and now filling her with his child. He'd have to suffer the consequences. He'd have to nurse a broken heart and reacquaint himself with the life of a bachelor.

Because Anastasia Lockewood would die. The babe she was carrying would die.

And then that bitch of a cousin of hers would die.

The assassin paused when he reached the flight of stairs at the darkened rear of the house. It was deserted.

Excellent.

He took the steps purposefully, but not so as to call attention to himself—just in case anyone was watching.

He rounded the second-floor landing, and headed directly for Lady Breanna's bedchamber, still thinking about the snatches of conversation he'd overheard between Sheldrake and his wife.

It wasn't a shock that, with this third murder, the *ton*—and Bow Street itself—would begin to doubt the merit of their original theory that the wives of the murdered noblemen were responsible. The killings were adding up. Only a dolt would believe that these women had *all* killed their husbands. Instead, Bow Street would doubtless assume that the three women were being held for ransom.

Which was another reason he'd abandoned his plan to use Knox's death to his advantage—a decision he'd made even before discovering the victim had only sons. Knox was a working-class fellow, a security guard with a modest income. If a woman in his family were to suddenly disappear like the noblemen's young wives, it would contradict the notion that ransom was involved. Not to mention, Knox's murder had taken place too close to Medford Manor. And if his death were linked with the others, someone might get suspicious and tie the crimes to the threats Lady Breanna had received.

Someone like Royce Chadwick.

The assassin felt a warning tremor ripple through him.

Seeing Chadwick here had been an unexpected surprise—and not a welcome one. The man was clever—far brighter than everyone at Bow Street. He was also a rebel, certainly not the type to attend holiday gatherings. So why was he here?

At first, he'd attributed Chadwick's attendance to his friendship with Sheldrake, not to mention the fact that he was still poking around the *ton* to see if he could uncover information on Ryder's bastard daughter. Observations of Chadwick throughout the day seemed to support that theory. Sticking close by him during the day's events—the morning ride, the midday meal, the afternoon card games—and listening closely to what he discussed had yielded no cause for alarm. Chadwick's topics of conversation were predictable: business ventures, the likely contenders at Newmarket this spring, the trip he'd taken to India. Interdispersed with the discussions were frank inquiries of the men he had yet to formally question—inquiries about whether or not they knew anyone who'd employed a chamber maid matching Ryder's paramour's description.

It seemed Chadwick's intentions were innocuous, at least so far as *he* was concerned.

But tonight, watching the way he hovered around Breanna Colby . . .

Could Chadwick be here for another reason?

Could he be here to keep an eye out for him—the killer threatening Anastasia and Breanna's lives?

No, he silently concluded, reaching Lady Breanna's room. Royce Chadwick hunted down missing people; he didn't investigate murders. Besides, after seeing the heated way he stared at Lady Breanna at tonight's ball, it was obvious that if Chadwick had any other motive for being here, it was to get Lady Breanna into his bed.

As for the lady in question, she seemed interested enough. Maybe that explained her damnably good spirits.

The familiar anger knotted his gut.

He loathed her for her laughter, for her vitality, for her well-being. He loathed her for still being alive.

But that wouldn't last long.

He would kill her now if his hatred had its way. Fortunately, his brilliant mind and iron discipline kept him in check. The stage hadn't been properly set. Unfinished business remained—namely, Anastasia Lockewood. More important, Breanna hadn't suffered nearly enough. Not *nearly* enough. Tonight had demonstrated that. She was so infernally happy—greeting her guests, drinking her punch, strolling outside with Chadwick.

All that gaiety would vanish the instant she walked into her room tonight.

With that, he focused on the business at hand.

Pausing outside her bedchamber door, he scanned the hallway. Deserted. The guests were at the ball. Ladies Breanna and Anastasia were otherwise occupied. The guards were safeguarding the estate from intruders.

But he had no need to intrude.

On that ironic thought, he turned the door handle and crossed the threshold. Shutting the door behind him, he reached swiftly into his pocket to extract his little surprises.

The room carried her scent—sweet, floral—the lingering fragrance of her customary perfume.

He could picture her, cheeks flushed with excitement as she'd readied herself for her ball. Lighthearted, enthused.

She'd be neither when she went to bed tonight.

If she went to bed. She wouldn't be able to sleep. She'd feel violated, numb with shock, quaking with terror.

The image was exhilarating.

He crossed over to her nightstand, having decided it was the best place to leave his tokens. Not as intimate as the dressing table, perhaps, but far closer to the bed, and more visible from the doorway. Illuminated by a single lamp, his gifts would render their full impact the moment she walked in. They would make her feel all the more vulnerable—draped across her nightstand, just brushing her bedcovers.

With a bitter smile, he went to work, arranging the reminders just so.

Five minutes later, he let himself out of Lady Breanna's bedchamber and retraced his steps to the ball.

He was just about to enter the ballroom when he heard the argument.

Not an argument exactly, but a heated debate. Quiet but intense. Fervent enough to capture one's attention—if one was listening. And he was listening, especially given the repeated use of the name "Lord Royce."

The dispute was taking place in the front hallway. And the men involved were Wells, the efficient Colby butler, and Hibbert, Royce Chadwick's trusted manservant.

Whatever this discussion pertained to, it was worth eavesdropping.

He meandered toward the entranceway, threading his way through the tangle of guests moving in the opposite direction. Alone, he hovered near the staircase, an inconspicuous guest enjoying a bit of solitary time at a crowded party. Then, in one thoroughly unobtrusive motion, he slipped into an alcove behind the staircase. He pressed close to the wall so as to see but not be seen.

"I run this household," Wells was stating flatly. "When a message arrives, *I* deliver it."

"And *I* work for Lord Royce," Hibbert retaliated icily. "When a message arrives addressed to him, *I* deliver it."

"Deliver it, or read it?"

"Both."

The two servants glowered silently at each other, each standing his ground, yet each managing to retain the requisite amount of composure.

"I'll take full responsibility for my actions," Hibbert pronounced with arrogant certainty. "I—and *only* I—know this is what my employer expects of me. If you're so disturbed by my conduct, I suggest you go and summon him. But in the meantime, I intend to see that letter."

"As you wish." Wells's jaw was clenched so tight it looked as if it might snap. He slapped the missive into Hibbert's hand and walked around him. "I'll summon Lord Royce at once."

"Fine." A rustle of paper as Hibbert slit open the letter. "I respect your principles. I'm equally principled—and equally loyal to my employer. As you'll soon find out."

"We shall see." Wells marched by, heading directly to the ballroom, presumably weaving his way over to the French doors.

Two or three minutes passed.

Abruptly, Royce Chadwick emerged, preceding Wells, and crossing directly over to where Hibbert stood, openly reading the contents of the letter.

"What is it?" he asked his manservant quietly.

"One of your avenues paid off." Hibbert turned to face his employer, his tone no lower than normal. Clearly, whatever was in that missive was not of a confidential nature.

"Which one? The list of noblemen I gave you to follow up on, or the list of wealthy matrons who help out abandoned women?"

"The latter. It's Lady Barton, the seventy-year-old matron you suggested contacting in Berkshire. She's been abroad, and only just returned. One of our men spoke with her. She remembers Glynnis Martin, went on and on about how pretty she was, how desolate she was left alone with her babe. It seems Lady Barton sent her to an elderly dowager's home—a Dowager Duchess . . ." Hibbert glanced at the message, "of Pearson."

"And the babe?"

"She went with her mother. Glynnis was hired as a paid companion. As far as Lady Barton knows, she and her daughter are still living at Pearson Manor in Berkshire."

"Excellent." Chadwick was triumphant. "This party will be over tomorrow night. I'll ride to the duchess's home straight from here. With any luck, I'll have news of Ryder's daughter for him by the first of the year."

"Fine work, my lord."

"Thanks to Lady Barton." Chadwick clapped Hibbert on the shoulder. "Come. This calls for a drink."

"In the ballroom?"

"Of course. Where else?" Chadwick paused to glance at Wells, who was looming behind them like a vigilant sentry, far enough away to ensure their privacy, but nearby enough to assert his position in the household—and to clearly demonstrate his disapproval over Hibbert's behavior.

"It's all right, Wells," Chadwick assured him. "I appreciate your diligence, but Hibbert was following my orders. He's instructed to read my mail. He also knew I was expecting this letter. So you can relax."

Wells nodded, although his back remained stiff. "As you wish, my lord."

"Would you care to join Hibbert and me for a drink?"

The butler cleared his throat. "No, thank you." He slanted a purposeful look at Hibbert. "I wouldn't feel right."

Chadwick shrugged. "Suit yourself." He gestured toward the ballroom. "Let's go, Hibbert."

Hastily, Wells interceded, taking an inadvertent step to block Hibbert's way. "My lord," he addressed Chadwick respectfully. "It really isn't appropriate—"

"I realize that." Chadwick was already in motion, his heels echoing as he bypassed Wells and headed toward the party. "But as you've probably heard about me, I rarely give a damn what's appropriate and what's not. I'm going into the ballroom for a drink. And Hibbert is joining me." He paused, angled about to face Wells. "My invitation still stands. You can make it a threesome."

"I think not, my lord."

"Fine. Until later then." Chadwick continued on his way.

Hibbert gave a dry chuckle as he followed behind his employer, ignoring Wells's censuring glare. "I don't expect the guests to be any more pleased than Wells is."

"Probably not. They'll probably be outraged. But they won't be surprised."

"And our hosts?"

Chadwick paused again, this time mere yards away from the stairway alcove. "Damen's known me for years. He won't even flinch. As for Anastasia, she might just applaud. And Breanna . . ." A poignant pause as Chadwick contemplated the woman he'd been squiring about all evening. "Breanna will be as gracious as she always is—no matter how taken aback she might be. And behind that proper veneer, she'll be smiling."

Maybe, the assassin acknowledged silently from his hiding place. *But she won't be smiling for long.*

12

❧

$\mathcal{B}$reanna climbed the stairs, feeling equal measures of exhaustion and exhilaration.

The remaining hours of the ball had passed by in a haze. Through most of that time, she'd longed for nothing but the solace of her room. She needed to ponder exactly what had happened between her and Royce tonight and, more importantly, exactly what it meant.

She might be inexperienced, but she wasn't naive. Nor was she stupid. What she and Royce had shared had, by absolute standards, amounted to no more than a very heated kiss, something Royce might indulge in with countless women. But she *didn't* indulge in it with countless men. She'd never even yearned for that intimate a contact, never imagined herself capable of it.

Not until tonight.

So while Royce might have already dismissed the encounter, summed it up as the result of one slightly tipsy woman falling prey to his charms, she couldn't be so blasé.

She'd realized from the start that she was drawn to him, that he affected her in a way no man ever had. That in itself had been an intriguing discovery. But out there tonight, clasped in his arms, she hadn't even known herself. She'd been alive, uninhibited, hungry for more. What's more, now that reason had resumed, she still couldn't seem to summon one iota of remorse or shame.

Confusion, on the other hand—*that* she was feeling in abundance.

Understanding Royce's feelings, his motives, was imperative.

But more imperative was understanding her own.

She gazed longingly down the hall at Damen and Stacie's room, wishing Stacie were still awake to talk, that her curiosity had won out over her fatigue. Normally, it would have. But pregnancy was taking its toll and, after a long night of merrymaking, she'd been exhausted. Despite her protests, Damen had taken her up to bed several hours ago.

Even through drooping eyelids, she'd cast one questioning look after another at Breanna, obviously dying to interrogate her about what had happened.

That Stacie knew something had happened wasn't an issue. Awareness had been written all over her face—at least enough so that Breanna could see it.

What was Stacie thinking? How would she interpret Royce's behavior, and his reaction to Breanna's? How would she explain Breanna's uncharacteristic actions? What advice would she offer?

Breanna would have to wait to find out.

Glancing at the clock on the mantel in the hall, she sighed. It was almost 4 A.M. The last of the guests had retired over an hour ago, followed shortly thereafter by Wells. She'd feigned going to bed just so he would do the same. The poor man was spent and, knowing him, he intended to be at his post by eight o'clock in the morning—just in case he was needed. Royce and Hibbert had gone up at about the same time, deep in discussion over the letter they'd received earlier.

It was just as well. Breanna wasn't sure how to act around Royce after that ardent embrace they'd shared, and she was almost relieved when his attention was diverted by news of Lord Ryder's daughter.

She had to smile, recalling the *ton*'s reaction when Royce had strolled into the ballroom, Hibbert at his side. Dozens of flies could have found homes in the gaping mouths throughout the room. Even Lady Dutton had stopped gossiping for a full minute, a rarity indeed. Breanna had caught Stacie's eye, seen the twinkle there. And, beside her, Damen, his lips quirking as if to say: that's Royce for you.

As for Royce, he was clearly aware of the stir he was causing. It was obvious from the arrogance of his stance. Equally clear from that stance was the fact that he didn't give a damn *whom* his actions offended.

Good for you, Breanna had found herself thinking. She could only hope that Hibbert's boldness would rub off on Wells. If anyone deserved to be treated like an equal, to *demand* such equality, it was Wells, who was more a father figure than a butler.

In any case, Royce had paused only to find her with his gaze, ensure she was all right. Then, he and Hibbert had launched into a discussion of Lord Ryder and locating his daughter. Between that conversation and the various colleagues who waylaid Royce for other reasons—having not seen him since his return from India—*and* the five or six women who inserted themselves in his path, insisting on saying hello, Royce was monopolized for the rest of the ball.

On the other hand, there were at least a half-dozen times when

Breanna had felt his compelling stare find her, penetrate her with its intensity . . .

By three o'clock the house had fallen quiet, hushed but for the remaining footmen who were scurrying about, cleaning up and readying the manor for the new day.

Left alone, Breanna had wandered down the hall to the sitting room, curling up on the settee and savoring the darkness, just thinking over the turbulent events of the past fortnight. All that had happened, all that was still happening—the threatening package, Stacie's pregnancy, the murders plaguing Bow Street and paralyzing the *ton*, and now Royce Chadwick in all his complexity—was enough to make her head spin.

Having resolved nothing, she'd gone up to bed.

She reached the door to her room just as the clock chimed four. Everyone was asleep. Even her lady's maid, who had been instructed to retire early, given how late the ball was expected to run.

The manor was silent.

All the guests would sleep until noon, she reflected, turning the door handle. All but Stacie. Thankfully, Stacie would be up and about by ten. Sooner, if her lurching stomach demanded the chamber pot. Then they could talk.

Contenting herself with that fact, Breanna eased open the door, and shut it softly behind her. As always, she'd left the lamp on her nightstand turned down low, offering her more than enough light to guide her way. She moved directly toward it, intending to turn it up higher while she undressed.

She took one step and froze.

A white chemise lay draped across the nightstand, its lacy edge just touching the bed. A dark splotch of color stained its center, and an unfamiliar object sat alongside it.

Dread curling inside her like dark tendrils of smoke, Breanna walked over, cautiously placing one foot in front of the other as she approached the nightstand.

Her hand was shaking as she turned up the lamp.

Light flooded the nightstand, and Breanna let out a low cry, her hands flying reflexively to her mouth as if to stifle the sound.

The chemise was hers. The dark splotch marring the garment was red. Bright, vivid red.

Blood red.

Her horrified gaze shifted, took in the other object atop the nightstand.

It was a figure, a porcelain figure. At least it had been, before it was defaced. She bent over to examine it more closely, unable to bring herself to touch it. The figure wasn't one of hers. She'd never seen it before. It depicted two women standing on an elaborate pedestal base.

Red smears had been painted on both women's bodices near their hearts, and expressions of torment had been etched onto their faces.

Violently etched.

She sank onto the bed, her knees shaking too badly to support her. He'd been here. *Here.* In her room, going through her dresser. He'd taken her undergarment, tampered with it in a vile, sick manner. And the statue. Obviously meant to symbolize her and Stacie. Shot, bleeding.

Dying.

Oh, God.

Breanna fought the urge to scream, to race down the hall and awaken Stacie and Damen. There was nothing they could do. Not tonight. Whoever this madman was, he was long gone. He'd taken advantage of the chaos generated by the party and found a way to slip into the manor.

How had he known which room was hers?

She knew the answer to that even as she asked herself the question.

He'd been watching the house. For weeks, probably. And now he'd gotten inside. Inside and upstairs. To her room.

She couldn't stay here another minute.

Jumping to her feet, Breanna nearly ripped the door off its hinges, then bolted out. Wild-eyed, she surveyed the empty hallway, reminding herself again and again that there was no one here. Not now.

Another quick glance toward Stacie's room.

And another dismissal of the notion to awaken her.

Tomorrow morning was more than enough time for Stacie to hear about this. Nothing could be gained by alerting her now—nothing except a selfishly attained peace of mind for Breanna. And that she wouldn't allow. Her peace of mind wouldn't begin to offset Stacie's distress. She'd have to face this soon enough anyway. She needed her sleep. So did the babe. It wasn't as if she was in any immediate danger. For tonight, she was safe. Damen was with her, their door was bolted, and no one could get in. Even if someone was still lurking in the house. Which, given the intelligence of the assassin, who knew the number of guards lying in wait for him, was doubtful.

No, awakening Stacie was out of the question.

So until morning, this problem belonged to Breanna.

She'd never felt more alone in her life.

Wells. Maybe she'd awaken Wells.

Who would do—what? Comfort her, just as Stacie would. But nothing more. He'd have no better idea than she how to handle this intrusion. And he was nearly as exhausted as Stacie.

Which left no one to turn to.

No one except Royce.

His name sprang to mind, eliciting a surge of relief so acute, Breanna sagged against the wall. Royce. He was here. He'd predicted this very thing might occur. He'd know what to do.

With that thought, she gathered up her skirts, nearly running down the hall, veering around the corner to the wing that housed his chambers. Unlike the other guests, Royce hadn't been assigned to the guest wing. He'd suggested Wells put him and Hibbert in the main section of the house, just in case events happened that warranted their attention—attention he'd want to provide without alerting the other guests.

Thank heavens he'd thought of that.

Reaching the door of his room, Breanna knocked. *Please,* she prayed. *Let him be in there. Let him be awake, or at least hear my knock and wake up. Please.*

As if in answer to her prayers, a muffled voice called out, "Yes?"

"Royce . . . it's Breanna." She wet her lips with the tip of her tongue, fighting for some measure of composure. "I need to see you. Now. It's urgent."

"I'll be right there." There was nothing muffled about his tone now. He sounded awake and completely alert.

Breanna heard rustling sounds, an indication that Royce was donning his clothes. Although, at the moment, she wouldn't care if he walked out in his nightshirt. As long as he walked out.

As if on cue, the bolt turned, and the door swung open.

Royce stared at her intensely, his dark hair tousled, his shirt half-buttoned, tucked haphazardly into his breeches. "What's wrong?" he demanded, his gaze tightening with concern as he took in her ashen expression and trembling hands.

"My room," she said, amazed that her voice could sound so calm when her insides were twisting. "He was there. Sometime tonight. While I was at the ball. He left me some . . . things. I couldn't bear touching them. I couldn't even bear staying in the room, knowing he'd been there. I didn't know what to do, who to tell. So I came here."

"You did the right thing." Royce retreated into his chamber, opened his nightstand, and yanked out a pistol. "Then Anastasia doesn't know?"

Mutely, Breanna shook her head. "I didn't want to frighten her. I came straight to you."

"Good." Royce returned to her side, silently assessing her emotional state. "Breanna, are you all right?"

"Yes. I'm fine."

Without thinking, he caught her shoulders, tugged her against him. "You don't have to be so bloody strong," he muttered, brushing his lips through her hair. "You're afraid. You have reason to be."

She swallowed, fighting the urge to sink into his strength, fighting the more unnerving urge to cry.

She'd been taught since childhood never to fall apart in front of others. And she never did.

Why then, did she long to now?

"He won't hurt you," Royce said in a low, hard tone. "I won't let him."

Those simple words meant more to her than she could possibly explain. "Thank you," she whispered.

Royce drew back, tilted up her chin so he could see her face. "Would you be able to go back to your room if I went with you? I need to see what he left. I also need to look over the room, just in case he left any clues. And you're the only one who can tell me if something looks different in any way—added, moved, or touched."

Slowly, Breanna sucked in her breath, then nodded. "Yes. If that's what I need to do, I can do it."

An odd emotion glinted in Royce's eyes—something akin to admiration and a touch of amazement. "Good. Let's go." He paused, his knuckles drifting lightly over her cheek. "I'll be right beside you. You won't be alone."

Another nod, this one shaky. "I'll remember that."

He led the way, his pistol clutched by his side, Breanna right behind him. She could feel her insides clench tighter and tighter as they neared her bedchamber. She slowed, longed to stop. But she refused to give in to the impulse. Royce was right. This inspection was essential.

As if reading her mind, Royce glanced behind him. Studying her face, he reached out to capture her hand, gently leading her the remaining steps to her room.

They stopped in the open doorway.

Breanna crossed the threshold, and prickles of fear shot up her spine. The room she'd always regarded as a sanctuary was now a place to fear. Numbly, she wondered if she'd ever feel safe within it again.

"They're on the nightstand," she told Royce, halting just inside. "Both of them."

He gripped her elbow, drew her into the room. "I'm here," he said softly.

"I know," she replied, understanding just what Royce's assurances were meant to convey, and why he was offering them. "And you need me to be here, too. I have to come in—*all* the way in—or I can't help you, and you can't do your job." She forced herself to move deeper into her chambers, walking toward her bed as if in a dream. "There." She pointed at the nightstand, her head swimming with reaction. "Those are the things he left me."

Royce went ahead, examining the chemise and porcelain figure in the glow of lamplight. His expression was intense, never changing as he inspected the tainted objects more closely. "This chemise—is it yours?"

"Yes. I recognize the buttons. It's mine."

A nod. "The color is only paint. Not blood."

"I realize that. And the women are only porcelain, not human. But the message is clear nonetheless."

Royce's mouth thinned into a grim line. "It certainly is." He straightened, scanning the rest of the quarters. "Was anything else disturbed?"

Breanna studied the room as closely as her dazed mind would allow. She slid open each bureau drawer, checked inside her wardrobe and nightstand, even scrutinized each and every one of her porcelain figures. "Nothing else was touched—nothing I can detect."

"And nothing's missing?"

"No." Breanna crossed over to her desk, picked up the sketch pad and flipped through it. None of the drawings of Stacie's house had been tainted, no pages torn away. Beside the pad, her pile of unrelated sketches was stacked neatly, just as it had been earlier.

She eased open the desk drawers. Each one was precisely as she'd left it, all her quills and pencils intact. "It looks as if he only took the chemise."

"What about the statue? Was it originally on your nightstand? Or did he remove it from the bureau or fireplace mantel in order to place it beside the chemise?"

"Neither. It isn't mine. I've never seen it before in my life."

That detail seemed to disturb Royce more than anything else. His dark brows drew together, and his eyes narrowed in troubled concentration.

"What is it?" Breanna asked. "Why does that upset you so much?"

Royce opened his mouth to reply, then hesitated, reluctance written all over his face.

"Please, Royce," she requested quietly. "Don't hide things from me. I don't want to be protected. I want to know. I *need* to know. Why are you bothered by the fact that that porcelain figure isn't mine?"

His sober gaze met hers. "Because the fact that he chose to bring such a statue here, to use it to make his point, is too perfect to be a coincidence. He obviously knew you collect porcelain figures."

"How would he know . . . ?" All the color drained from Breanna's face. "You think he was here before this? That he'd invaded my room before tonight?"

An unwilling nod. "My guess is, yes. It would explain the appearance of this statue. It would also explain how he found the time to deface your chemise. He wouldn't want to carry paint with him, nor would he want to linger an instant longer than necessary. So he didn't. He probably slipped into your room at an earlier date—most likely before the additional guards were assigned—took the chemise, and left. He did his handiwork on it at home, bought and defiled the statue, then placed both things on your nightstand tonight. He wouldn't need more than five minutes to accomplish that."

Breanna could feel her insides lurch, and for one horrible moment she was afraid she was going to be sick. "He *was* here," she whispered. Awareness dawned, crept through her like some odious insect. That feeling she'd had—that nagging perception that had plagued her all week— it hadn't been groundless.

It had been accurate.

"I sensed it." Her panicked gaze darted about the room. "Ever since the day Mr. Knox was killed. I thought I was overreacting. But I couldn't shake the uneasy feeling that came over me every time I was in my room. I tried to attribute it to nerves, but after what you just said . . ." She broke off, pressing her palms together as if the very action could hold her emotions in check. "I know he was here."

"The day Knox was killed?" Royce jumped on her words, contemplated them thoroughly before giving a hard nod. "That makes sense. A *lot* of sense. The killer could have slipped in here that afternoon, taken the chemise, and been in the process of leaving the grounds when Knox came upon him. It would explain why Knox got shot."

"But why did the killer come here?" Breanna felt cold, so very cold—a chill that radiated from the inside out. "Just to take something that belonged to me? Or did he come to shoot me and, when my being out strolling the grounds made that impossible, settled for stealing my chemise to torture me instead?"

"No." Royce refuted the latter. Walking over, he pressed her cold hands between his. "He had no intention of killing you. He came for the chemise. He also wanted to familiarize himself with you—your tastes, your weaknesses. He was searching for the best ways to terrorize you."

"He found them." Breanna curled her fingers in Royce's—and felt her core of inner strength waver. "I can't stay in this room tonight," she blurted, unable to keep the words from tumbling out. "I just can't."

"That's not an option." Royce saw the terror flash in her eyes, and he shook his head, negating her fear. "What I mean is, you're *not* staying here. Not only tonight, but any night. Not until we find this animal."

Breanna started, her insides lurching again. "You think he'll be back?"

"Eventually," Royce said honestly. "But not to kill you. He has more to accomplish first. He's not finished tormenting you. And we're not going to give him the opportunity to do that to the point where he's ready to move on to the next stage of his plan." The phrase *to kill Anastasia and you* hung between them, echoing as clearly as if Royce had spoken it aloud. "Breanna," he added fervently, his grip tightening as he watched the expression on her face. "We're going to hunt him down. *I'm* going to hunt him down. I promise you that."

"How?" Breanna heard herself ask.

"He bought that statue somewhere. Just like he bought those dolls somewhere. I'm going to find out where. I have contacts all over England. I'll send them to every shire, every bloody town if I have to. But I *will* find this killer. You've got to trust me."

A shaky nod. "I do."

"In the meantime," Royce continued, "if he does manage to get back inside the house, he won't find you in your chambers. I'm moving you into the room next to mine. Hibbert and I will take turns guarding your door. You'll never be unprotected."

"Stacie." Breanna's thoughts were racing. "What about Stacie? She's in danger, too."

"Anastasia is safe. Damen's with her. The assassin would never enter their room and take the chance of alerting her husband."

"But if he shot her before Damen awakened, or if he decided to shoot Damen, too . . ."

Again, Royce shook his head. "That's not his plan. He's only after you and Anastasia. To close in on her, knowing full well her husband would be at her side and would, therefore, have to be eliminated, would be unacceptable. This man only kills those he means to—unless an unexpected victim like Knox gets in his way. In that case, killing is unavoidable. But to plan his strategy—his *ultimate* strategy—knowing the stage wasn't set precisely as he wanted it to be; to burst in with the foreknowledge that someone other than his intended victim would be there? That would be amateurish.

"Besides which, he'd never shoot Anastasia from inside the manor. He knows he'd be caught—if not by Damen, then by someone else who heard the shot. He'd want you and Anastasia isolated, away from prying eyes and alert ears. Remember, demonstrating his cunning is as much a part of this bastard's thrill as demonstrating his skill. No. I'm convinced that if he went to your chambers again, it would either be to leave something else to terrorize you or, at the very worst, to watch you when you're unaware."

"To . . . watch . . . me?" Breanna managed. She shuddered. "You mean while I sleep?"

"Yes."

"I see." Breanna recognized she was on the verge of totally breaking down and, desperately, she struggled to bring herself under control.

Royce was offering her an alternative, a means to remain safe. She wouldn't reward him by sobbing like a child.

That thought prompted another.

"You said you and Hibbert would alternate standing outside my door," she said, her voice stronger, steadier. "That won't be necessary. The killer won't find me if I'm in a different wing of the house. Besides, I refuse to impose on you. You weren't hired as guards."

Royce raised her chin with his forefinger, those midnight blue eyes delving deep inside her. "That's my choice to make. Not yours." He released her. "Now collect your nightclothes and whatever else you need. We're getting you out of this room."

13

❧

$\mathcal{B}$reanna's temporary quarters were bare, void of personal touches and bedding.

Royce took care of that problem quickly and efficiently, carrying in a few blankets and pillows from his chambers to her new one, then building a healthy fire to warm away the winter chill.

Breanna couldn't seem to stop shaking, no matter how high the flames were fanned. She hugged herself tightly, trying to conceal the severity of her tremors, clenching her teeth to disguise their chattering.

"That'll do for tonight," Royce announced a half hour later. He stepped back from the fireplace, setting down the iron poker. The room was still barren, unlived in. But, barren or not, it was far safer than Breanna's.

His gaze flickered to Breanna, then to the window. "It'll be light in a few hours. You'd better get some sleep."

Sleep?

That word brought Breanna's head up, and her stomach twisted into knots as she realized the implications of Royce's suggestion.

He wanted her to lie down, to close her eyes, to rest.

And he intended to leave her alone so she could do that.

Impossible.

Before she could stop herself, she'd reached out, clutched Royce's sleeve with her fingers. "No."

He glanced down at her hand, his own expression unreadable. "No?"

"I can't sleep. Not yet. Not alone. No, that's not what I meant," she amended hastily, hot color flooding her cheeks.

She sucked in her breath, tried again. "What I meant is, could you stay awhile? Just to talk," she added in a rush. "It's just that . . . that is . . ." This was even harder than she'd expected. Turning to someone for help—someone other than Stacie or Wells—it didn't come easily to her. "I'm not quite ready to be alone with my thoughts," she admitted at last. "Not after tonight's incident."

Royce smiled faintly, plucked her fingers from his sleeve, and brought her palm to his lips. "Was that really so difficult?" he murmured.

"Yes."

His smile faded, and his gaze intensified. Tersely, he nodded, as if in understanding. "I suppose it was." He guided her over to a chair, eased her into it. Then, he gathered up the blankets, spread them out over her, one by one, until she was totally enveloped. "I'll stay. We'll talk. Under one condition. You curl up under those blankets. We've got to warm away that chill of yours. You're shaking like a leaf."

Breanna looked sheepish. "You noticed."

"Noticed?" He leaned over her, his hands gripping the chair arms on either side of her. "Your teeth were clenched so tightly, I was afraid your jaw would snap. And your fingers were biting so deeply into your gown sleeves, I was afraid the material would wear away. Does that answer your question?"

Her lips twitched. "I suppose it does."

Royce's knuckles caressed her cheek ever so slightly. "You're an astonishing woman, Lady Breanna Colby. Tell me, does that inner strength of yours never falter?"

Breanna swallowed. "I'm not certain how to answer that."

"That doesn't surprise me." Royce studied her intently. "You're not even aware of how extraordinary you are. Every woman I know would be close to hysteria by now—crying, clinging, fainting dead away. But not you. You do none of those things. No matter how terrified you are, how dire things get, you stay strong."

"That's not strength," Breanna replied honestly. "It's self-control. I was raised to always exhibit it. After all these years of reinforcement, I suppose it's part of me."

An odd look crossed Royce's face. "I understand that reality only too well." He straightened, turned his attention back to the fire.

He might have been referring to *her* reality, to his knowledge of her father's crimes.

Somehow Breanna sensed otherwise.

The reality he was referring to was his.

And the self-control was one he understood firsthand.

Watching the stiffness of his posture, Breanna once again resisted the urge to pry. "I appreciate all you've done tonight, all you're still doing. I needed your assistance—badly. Regardless of how you perceive me, I'm not really all that strong. My blood ran cold when I saw that chemise."

Royce relaxed, lowered himself to the rug by the fire. He stretched out his long legs, propped himself up on one elbow. "You're every bit as strong as I believe. If you weren't frightened by what happened here tonight, you'd be a fool. Don't confuse intelligence with cowardice."

"All right. I won't." Breanna tucked the blankets beneath her chin. "How do you think he got in?"

"That's a good question." Royce frowned, the light of the flames reflecting off his face, illuminating the hard angles and accentuating his pensive expression. "He could have slipped past the guards by climbing into one of the arriving guest's carriages and riding all the way to the manor. If he was dressed in black, he could have scaled his way to the second floor after that without being seen. Or, he could have smuggled himself into one of the delivery vehicles and ridden to the rear of the house, then crept up the rear staircase while the ball was under way. No one would have noticed him. All the activity was taking place in the front sections of the manor. Or . . ." Royce broke off, midnight sparks glinting in his eyes.

"Or?" Breanna prompted.

He raised his gaze to meet hers. "Or he could have simply presented his invitation at the door and walked in."

Breanna stared, her eyes growing wide as saucers. "You're suggesting this killer might be one of my guests? Someone we knowingly invited to this party?"

"I'm not suggesting it. I'm simply not ruling it out. After all, what do we know about this person? Only that he's a master at his craft and that he has a twisted, albeit brilliant, mind. That description could apply to anyone, in any walk of life."

"Including the *ton*." Breanna gripped the blanket with icy fingers. "If he *is* one of our guests, then he's still in the manor. He's here right now, sleeping under my roof, planning to do Lord knows what."

"*If*," Royce emphasized. "It's a slim chance, not a likelihood. None of your guests is exactly a stranger. Most of them have done business with Colby and Sons for years, including a fair number who were close acquaintances of your grandfather. Not to mention that a good portion of them, *I'm* acquainted with—well enough to doubt they're killers."

"That doesn't eliminate the possibility that he's here. So how can we either dismiss or confirm the notion? Should we begin questioning everyone?"

"Definitely not." Royce shook his head. "If we do, and if it happens we're on the right track, we'll only incite the killer in ways we'd be best off not doing. My reputation is not exactly a secret. If the assassin realizes I'm involved, that I'm actively looking for him, it would push him in a dangerous direction. He needs to believe he's in control. Let's let him think that. We'll find out what we want to know—subtly. Very subtly."

Royce paused, his mind racing. "I'll do some nosing around tomorrow before the first guests begin to leave," he decided. "Better yet, I'll have Hibbert do it for me. He has a way of getting information out of people without their realizing they've revealed anything. I'll concentrate on finding out where that statue was purchased. And the dolls, too. The killer won't notice any of that. He's too busy planning the next step in his scheme to terrorize you." A muscle flexed in Royce's jaw. "I'm going to beat this bastard at his own game.".

"You certainly understand his mind," Breanna noted quietly.

Something cold and bitter flashed in Royce's eyes. "I've known others like him," he responded. "Predatory geniuses obsessed with their own superiority. Some call themselves assassins. Some don't. And some don't kill—at least not in the bodily sense, nor in ways one could describe as criminal. But their minds are twisted and their means destructive as hell—at least to those who are unfortunate enough to be their victims."

Like you? Breanna almost blurted out.

She bit her lip to silence the question, although she knew in her heart the victim Royce was alluding to was himself. And not in a professional capacity. Whoever had hurt him wasn't among the military personnel he'd dealt with. It was someone else—someone closer to him. She, better than anyone, recognized the signs.

So where did that leave her? True, she didn't want to pry. But, given her own life, was it possible she could help?

"I don't know very much about you," she ventured, broaching the subject cautiously, giving Royce as much or as little room as he chose to take. "I know only what Damen's told me."

"I'm not given to discussing myself," Royce returned bluntly. He angled his head to study Breanna's face. "Neither are you, I would imagine."

"You're right. I'm not." She rushed on without allowing herself time to reconsider and change her mind. "I'm also not given to extreme shows of affection. Tonight proved to be an exception—at least for me. Maybe it should be for you, as well. If not physically, then verbally."

A hint of a smile. "Maybe it should. All right, what would you like to know?"

"Only what you're comfortable discussing." Beneath the blankets, she drew up her legs, rested her chin atop her knees. "You said you spent Christmas with your brother and his family," she tried carefully. "Are you and he close?"

A shrug. "Not particularly. Edmund is a good man. His wife, Jane, is a decent woman. They're content in their roles as the Earl and Countess of Searby."

"Content. In other words, dull," Breanna surmised, her lips curving a bit. "Your brother sounds like most of the men I'm acquainted with. And now, having met you . . . I can't imagine you'd have much in common with him."

"I don't," Royce admitted. "But his sons are incredible—three bundles of energy. The hours with them are worth all the boredom. They're even worth spending a few days in that house. *On occasion,*" he qualified. "Too often and I'm besieged by the ugliest damned memories . . ." Abruptly, he broke off.

Breanna recognized the bitterness in his voice, the pain and resentment in his eyes. She'd experienced those emotions all too often herself, incited by only one person.

That helped make her assessment of Royce easy.

It had to be his family. Not his brother, whom he talked about without anger. His parents. Most likely, his father—unless his mother was an unusually tyrannical woman. Yes, his father. That had to be who was behind Royce's bitterness. Breanna would be willing to bet on it.

"These memories—were they of your father?" she tried quietly.

"One and the same," was the sharp retort.

It was the only confirmation she needed.

"My guess is that he was much like mine," Breanna ventured. "Domineering and cruel. Edmund is one result of such a father. He must have turned out as I did: malleable, self-contained. And you? You're too dynamic for that. You veered off in the opposite direction. You're the rebel, the one whose will was strong enough to fight back."

Royce stared into the flames, and for a moment Breanna thought he didn't intend to reply.

She was on the verge of apologizing for overstepping her bounds when he said, "For the record, you're nothing like Edmund. Self-contained, maybe, but not malleable. And definitely not dull. As for me, I wasn't always as strong as you implied. I was once a frightened child. *Very* frightened. You see, my father's philosophy was to bludgeon us into what he called 'being men.'"

"He beat you."

"Oh, the beatings were the easy part. They were quick, they were predictable, and all they could hurt was my body. So I endured them. Edmund couldn't—not that I blame him. His passive nature was no match for my father's brutal resolve and vile temper. He crumpled by the time he was six, conformed to my father's wishes. That, combined with the fact that he was the heir apparent, freed him from my father's exercises in abuse. In my case, the exercises took a new form—a series of challenges my father provided for me to overcome."

"Challenges?" Breanna felt an unpleasant sense of foreboding. "What kind of challenges?"

"The kind supposedly designed for me to prove myself, but which, in fact, were designed to prove my father's dominance and to destroy my will. When I was five, I was ordered to ride a wild stallion who had a history of throwing and trampling his owners. My orders were never to fall. Each time I failed to stay in the saddle, I was whipped. And each time I cried, I was forced to endure an additional hour on the stallion's back.

"When I was six, I was locked in a cramped closet and told to find my way out. If I dared fail or call out for help, the next space I was locked in would be more cramped, harder to escape. And when I was seven, I was given books to read—in various languages—and told to memorize them. When reciting them back, I was denied one meal for each mistake I made. That usually meant going days without food. Shall I continue?"

"No." Breanna shook her head, bile rising in her throat. "How did you get through it?"

"By becoming resourceful, learning never to fail. Every challenge my father hurled in my face, I mastered. Of course, that made him angrier. Which meant his challenges grew harder and his punishments more severe. He was determined to break me. It became his obsession. He was brilliant, vicious, and relentless. But, as you so astutely guessed, my will was stronger. I withstood his brutality for twelve long years. Then, I left for Eton. After that, I rarely came home. And once my mother died, I stopped coming altogether."

"Your mother?" Breanna's head came up. "Didn't she intrude?"

"I wouldn't let her. Do you know what he would have done if his wife defied him? He would have brutalized her."

"But you were a little boy."

"I was a *resilient* little boy," Royce corrected. "She was a broken, defenseless woman. I did what I had to. If anything, it made me stronger."

"Stronger, perhaps," Breanna concurred softly. "But scarred. And I don't mean physically. Your wounds are entrenched—permanently. I know that firsthand."

"My wounds?" Royce shook his head. "I don't regard them as such. Probably because I don't regret what they made me. I suppose, in a way, my father did me a service."

Something about Royce's words touched something inside her. Perhaps it was the similarity of their upbringing, perhaps it was the conclusion he'd reached—one Breanna understood and shared with regard to herself. Perhaps it was respect for the man he'd become.

Or perhaps it just was.

On sheer impulse, Breanna squirmed out from beneath the blankets, lowered herself onto the rug beside him. "Now I understand what you meant by those who destroy without killing. I also see why you're determined to outwit your enemies, even if it means taking risks—maybe *especially* if it means taking risks. Your father provided a service, all right. But not for you. For the rest of us—the people you help." She reached out, trailed her fingertips across his jaw. "Thank you for confiding in me. You're a fascinating and complex man, Royce Chadwick."

The impact of her touch was jarring. Undercurrents of sensation radiated through them both, jolting them from candid revelations to naked awareness.

Abruptly, the mood in the room altered.

Royce went taut, his gaze finding hers, delving inside her in a way that made her breath catch.

"I *am* a complex man," he said roughly. "I'm also a hard man. Despite how you perceive me, despite my concern for you *and* my attraction to you, I'm not given to tenderness or sentiment. They're not in my nature."

"But compassion is." Breanna's heartbeat had begun to accelerate.

"Compassion, yes. Compassion *and* passion." His reference was pointed, an intentional effort to assign a name to what he was feeling. Not for his sake. For hers.

He was trying to shock her into realizing they were alone in a bed-chamber in the dead of night, where there was no one nearby to ensure they restrained themselves.

His efforts failed miserably.

"Passion—definitely. As I discovered earlier." Breanna had no idea where her bravado was coming from. She only knew it was there. She also had no idea what she was striving for by flagrantly baiting him as she was. She only knew that she had to see where it led.

Her thumb just grazed his lips.

"Breanna, stop." Abandoning all subtlety, Royce caught her wrist, tiny sparks flaring in his midnight gaze. "You're not foxed now. And you're playing a dangerous game."

"Yes, I recall. Fire, you said. And I said I wanted to get singed."

"And *I* said you were going to get burned."

She swallowed, wet her lips with the tip of her tongue. "Maybe it's time I learned to take some risks."

Royce's eyes narrowed on her face. "Not these kind. Not with me. I don't normally display the gallantry I did in that garden tonight."

"Of course not. That would be a show of sentiment—something you're not given to."

He was losing and he knew it. Breanna could actually see him weaken.

"Stop provoking me," he commanded. "Don't you understand what I'm trying to tell you?"

"What you mean is, trying to warn me about." Breanna eased closer, her heart slamming against her ribs. "Yes, I understand."

Royce sucked in his breath. He released her wrist, then rose to his knees, his fingers, of their own volition, gliding into the strands of her upswept hair. "This is a mistake."

"Is it?"

"Yes. You're unnerved by what happened tonight. You're feeling vulnerable."

"I'm feeling many things." Breanna tilted back her head, studied the hard angles of his face in the firelight. "But right now, vulnerable isn't one of them."

"Damn," Royce hissed. He leaned forward, sliding his palm around to cup the nape of her neck, and drew her closer, staring down at her with an expression that sent live flames licking through her. "This *is* a mistake. An unprincipled, reckless mistake."

Breanna gripped his shirt, raising up until their lips were inches apart. "I don't care."

With a harsh sound, Royce dragged her against him, crushing her mouth to his. There were no preliminaries this time. His lips devoured hers, parting them for the intimate invasion of his tongue. He delved deep, angling her head to give him greater access, taking her with heated, suggestive strokes of his tongue.

He twisted her around until he could lower her to the carpet. Then, he stretched out alongside her, half atop her as he continued his hot, drugging kisses. His tongue captured hers, caressed it in dizzying strokes, and his hand moved restlessly down to cover her breast.

Breanna was caught up in a vortex of physical awakening. When Royce's hand found her breast, she whimpered—a soft sound that Royce caught with his mouth. His thumb found and teased her nipple, circling it until it hardened and throbbed beneath his touch. She wound her arms around his neck, threaded her fingers through his hair. She was lost in sensation, in the sheer excitement of discovery.

Royce tore his mouth from hers, moved down her neck, her throat, searing her with each hungry caress. His lips closed around her nipple, tugged at it through the silk of her gown, and Breanna's eyes slid shut, her breath expelling in a rush. She clutched Royce's head, held him against her to prolong the pleasure. Shuddering at her touch, he stopped, but only long enough to reach behind her, undo the tiny row of buttons down her back.

He tugged down her bodice, his fingers automatically shifting to the ribbons of her chemise. "Tell me to stop," he ordered, his voice hoarse.

"No." Breanna shook her head from side to side, desperate to experience whatever magnificent sensations hovered just beyond her reach.

"Breanna."

Her lids snapped open, and she met Royce's molten gaze.

"Tell me to stop," he repeated, already tugging the first ribbon free.

"I won't," she said breathlessly. "I can't."

With a stifled oath, Royce dispensed with the final barrier that separated him from his goal. He parted the sides of her chemise, and an awed expression tightened his features before he lowered his head, captured her taut nipple between his lips. "You're so beautiful," he muttered thickly, cupping her other breast as he sampled its mate. "And your taste . . . God, this is an even bigger mistake than I thought."

Breanna didn't answer. She couldn't. Everything inside her was concentrated on the sensations storming her body. Royce's mouth on her skin . . . his hands . . . his breath . . . She wondered if pleasure this acute could be withstood.

Reflexively, she held him, wrapped her arms around his back. His shirt, which he'd haphazardly donned when her knock had awakened him, was half-free, only partially tucked into his breeches. She took advantage of that, slipping her hands beneath the shirt, gliding her palms along the warm, hard planes of his back.

Every muscle went rigid beneath her caresses.

"Breanna." He uttered her name in a hoarse rasp, his tongue lashing at her nipple even as his hands left her, moved to unbutton the front of his shirt.

Then, he was covering her, the hot, hair-roughened skin of his chest rubbing against her breasts.

This time, Breanna couldn't help but cry out. The sound was short-lived, because Royce was kissing her again. She opened her mouth eagerly to his, and he cradled her head in his hands, devouring her lips and shifting to increase the friction of his body against hers. Breanna savored every exquisite sensation, her nipples tightening painfully, liquid heat coursing through her.

"God, I want you," Royce muttered, burning a trail of kisses down her neck, nuzzling the valley between her breasts. "I want to bury myself so deep inside you that . . ." He stopped abruptly, as if the impact of his own words had suddenly registered. Forcing up his head, he stared down at her, his eyes burning with desire, his breathing harsh, uneven, tremors of reaction rippling through him.

Almost violently, he tore himself away, rolled to one side. "Dammit." He sat up, raked a hand through his hair. "Goddammit."

"Royce?" Breanna turned her head, stared at the rigid lines of his back.

In reply, he pivoted, his hot gaze raking her bare torso once before he pulled the sides of her chemise together, helped her sit up.

"I obviously do have the ability to be gallant twice in one night," he said, his voice still thick with desire. "Then again, that shouldn't surprise me. Not when it comes to you."

Breanna blinked, trying to still the swimming in her head. "I didn't want you to stop."

Royce's mouth thinned into a grim line. "I know you didn't. Not right now. Tomorrow would have been another story."

"Would it?"

"Yes." Royce buttoned his shirt in a few harsh motions. Then, he turned, yanked up Breanna's bodice and clasped her shoulders in his hands. "Breanna, you're beautiful. And I don't mean only physically, although Lord knows I can't keep my eyes, or my hands, off of you. You're beautiful to the core. You emanate something I can't begin to describe. But you need—you *deserve*—a hell of a lot more than a quick tumble on the floor. And you deserve it from someone who can offer it to you. Someone who has the depth of emotion to offer it to you."

"I see." With shaking hands, Breanna reached around to button the back of her gown. She was still too dazed to form a coherent thought. But she wasn't too dazed to recognize Royce's implications as untrue, even if he himself didn't realize it. "So, along with my life, you're now protecting my virtue."

A weighted pause. "I'm trying. Not very successfully, it seems." Royce shook his head in amazement. "I didn't count on this. I've never . . ." Unsteadily, his knuckles caressed her cheek. "It seems tonight was an exception for me, too. I *don't* lose control. Tonight, I did."

He rose to his feet, shoved his shirt into his breeches. "It's almost dawn. Try to sleep. I'll be right outside your door. We'll talk before breakfast. Then we'll tell Damen and Anastasia about the assassin's visit to your room." Extending his hand to her, he helped her up, then brought her fingers to his lips, his hard-edged demeanor softening a bit—whether at the mention of tonight's trauma or the memory of what had just happened between them, Breanna wasn't certain. "Will you be all right?" he murmured.

Breanna nodded. "I'll be fine." She studied his face, saw the intimate look in his eyes—a look he wasn't even aware of—and wondered if perhaps she didn't have her answer. "Good night, Royce."

A whisper of hesitation. "Good night." He turned, walked out of the room, glancing back at her briefly before shutting the door in his wake.

Breanna stared after him for a long time. She heard him drag a chair into the hall, place it against her door, and settle himself for the remainder of the night. Just knowing he was out there, safeguarding her against the madman who wanted her dead, brought her more than a small measure of relief.

Relief and a great deal more.

On that thought, Breanna gathered up the blankets, made herself a cozy bed by the fire, and snuggled into it.

Somehow this spot felt more comforting than the bed. Probably because she'd just shared it with Royce.

She had much to mull over. And, whether he knew it or not, so did Royce. She'd felt his reluctance when he'd dragged himself away from her. And she'd seen his ambivalence, his bewilderment, when he bid her good night.

They'd both encountered sides of themselves tonight that they hadn't known existed. What that meant, where it was leading, remained to be seen.

But one thing was certain. For a man obviously experienced with women, Royce Chadwick was as confused as she.

Not so when it came to the assassin. There, Royce knew precisely what he aimed to do. He was hell-bent on capturing his adversary, determined to succeed.

Unfortunately, so was the assassin.

An icy chill shivered up Breanna's spine.

Lord only knew what tomorrow would bring.

14

"I can't believe I'm hearing this."

Damen stalked about the sitting room that adjoined his and Stacie's bedchamber, pausing beside the settee where his wife and Breanna sat. He slammed his fist against the ornately carved frame. "That madman invaded Breanna's bedroom while a ball was going on, and left those sick, mutilated . . ." He broke off.

"Yes." Royce leaned back against the tightly closed door, arms folded across his chest.

It was early—half past ten—and very few of the guests were awake. Still, Royce had chosen the privacy of Damen and Anastasia's quarters in which to have this talk.

"You must have been terrified," Stacie murmured, turning to study her cousin anxiously. "Why didn't you awaken me?"

"I considered it," Breanna confessed. "But there was nothing you could have done. Besides, you needed your rest. You were exhausted. And I knew you were safe. Damen was with you."

"I sat outside Breanna's door all night," Royce assured Stacie quietly. "Her *new* door," he amended. "I've moved her to the room next to mine. I don't want her in her usual bedchamber—not until the killer's caught."

Damen's mouth thinned into a grim line. "You're saying you expect him to be back."

"Maybe. *If* he ever left."

"You think he's hiding at the manor?" Stacie gasped.

"No. Either he slipped out the same way he slipped in, or he's here at your invitation."

A stunned silence filled the room.

"You believe he's one of our guests?" Damen demanded.

Royce shrugged. "What I believe isn't important. What I do, *is.* I have to investigate every possibility. It would be foolish to overlook anything, however remote." He picked up the disfigured statue he'd brought to show them, and turned it over in his hands. "Whoever and wherever he is, our killer's message is clear. But each time he delivers that message, he leaves clues along with it. The chemise is Breanna's. But this porcelain figure isn't. He bought it somewhere, just as he did those dolls. I intend to find out where. *Someone* will remember who bought these items."

"I assume you'll be leaving Medford Manor, then," Anastasia concluded. "When, tonight? Or sooner, before the party ends?"

Royce scowled. "I'm not going anywhere until every guest is gone. After that—" He hesitated, visibly troubled. "I must go to Berkshire, check into the whereabouts of Ryder's daughter. I'm not happy about it, not in light of what's happened. But I have an obligation . . ." Unconsciously, his gaze flickered to Breanna.

"Royce, go to Berkshire," she said, her voice steady, rife with conviction. "If Lord Ryder's daughter is alive, he deserves to meet her. Family is a gift. If my grandfather taught Stacie and me anything, it's that. We'll be fine. Besides, you have to start somewhere checking into shops. Why not start in Berkshire? Maybe that monster bought the statue there."

Royce nodded, and Breanna could feel Stacie's scrutiny as she stared curiously from her cousin to Royce and back.

"All right," Royce conceded. "But I'm only covering the shires right around London. The rest I'll have my men take care of. I'll ride out to Pearson Manor tonight, get my answers on Glynnis Martin. Tomorrow at dawn I'll travel down to Ryder's home in Sussex. Along the way, I'll check out the shops. I'll be back here by tomorrow night, or the next morning at the latest. Also, I've decided that Hibbert will stay behind. I want him here, guarding your door. That will ease my mind considerably."

"Yours, maybe, but not Wells's." Breanna attempted a smile. "He and Hibbert are both rather territorial. It should be interesting to see them living under the same roof and sharing responsibilities."

"They'll work it out." Royce didn't smile. He set down the statue, turned to face the three of them. "Listen to me, all of you. I can't stress enough how important it is for you to act normally. What that means is, I want *no one* playing detective, interrogating our guests." He shot a meaningful look at Anastasia. "Leave the questioning to Hibbert and me. We have a whole day to probe. Don't impede us and endanger yourselves by doing anything stupid."

"Stacie?" Damen prodded, giving his wife's shoulder a gentle tap. "Do you understand what Royce just said?"

She rolled her eyes. "I'm neither deaf nor dense. I heard. And I'll do what Royce said."

"Breanna?" Royce pressed.

"I've already assured you, I won't interfere."

"Good. Then let's go downstairs. Your guests should be arising any time now. Damen, find a way to stay with Anastasia and Breanna. Use the excuse you conjured up last night—that you're a nervous father-to-be. No one will question it."

"And no one will try to kill either of the women if I'm there, since my presence isn't part of his plan," Damen finished for him.

"Exactly." Royce's nod was terse.

"Fine. Then it's needlepoint and tea for me." Damen placed a protective hand on each of the women's shoulders. "I'll leave the riding and shooting contests, and the gaming tables, to you and Hibbert."

A fine layer of snow prohibited the men from holding their more ambitious races on horseback.

That suited the assassin just fine. It gave him a better opportunity to study Royce Chadwick.

Something wasn't right.

First of all, the man was too damned relaxed, something Chadwick never was. Which led him to believe it was all an act, being put on for someone's benefit. But whose? Lady Breanna's? And if so, why? Was it because he was trying to seduce her or because he was acting as her knight in shining armor? Did he know about what she'd found in her bedchamber last night? Had she told him? If so, was he coming to her rescue, helping her find out who her tormenter was?

It was the only thing that made sense.

Added to that was the fact that Hibbert had made three appearances among the men today. That unto itself wasn't unusual, given how unorthodox Chadwick was about his manservant. Still, there was something about Hibbert's demeanor—a fine tension only the sharpest eye could discern—as if the elderly butler was delving for something.

Or someone.

Hibbert was subtle, nondescript. *He*, on the other hand, was more. He was brilliant. Nothing got by him. Certainly not the casual inspection of an elderly manservant.

Then there was Lady Breanna.

She hadn't slept a wink. The dark circles beneath her eyes told him that. Still, she was up and about, fresh and lovely in her yellow morning dress, her hair perfectly coiffed, as always, and her smile intact.

Inside, she had to be quaking.

But, dammit, he wanted to see her crack.

What was keeping her in check? Certainly not her own reserves. It had to be Chadwick.

Damn him to hell.

The assassin shoved his hands into his pockets, feeling that familiar rage boil up inside him. He'd been curtailing it for days now. But it was intensifying, refusing to be quieted. It spilled over, surged through his veins, pulsed through his blood. He gave in to it, savoring its fire, although outwardly he knew his veneer was intact. No one watching would know the fury lashing through him.

He had to act. To vent his rage before it consumed him.

It was a good idea anyway. He could use the physical exertion. It would keep him razor-sharp for when he eliminated the Colby women. He'd view his next victim as target practice. He'd arrange things perfectly. Everyone would make the obvious, terrifying assumption that this latest murder was tied to the three unresolved crimes that had preceded it. Except for Lady Breanna, who'd be gripped by the horrifying prospect that this new killing was unrelated to the others, that it was a brutal warning just for her.

No one would guess it was both.

As for the killer's identity, that would feed right into the *ton*'s natural inclination to believe there could never be a murderer among them. So deviant a mind must belong to a common criminal.

The stupid fools. There was nothing common about him.

A smile curved his lips as he visualized the pandemonium that would ensue. Both guests and hosts would be thrown into a panic. As a result, his remaining hours at Medford Manor would be thoroughly enjoyable.

Enjoyable but hectic. Too hectic to act.

He'd wait a day or two before absconding with the grieving young widow. Then, he'd ride to her home, grab her from there.

And have a lovely piece of merchandise to ship to Calais.

He glanced about, pleased to see that the gentlemen had split up, since riding conditions were not optimum. Some of them had remained outside to fish or shoot, some were heading inside to play whist. And some were going off by themselves, to enjoy a late breakfast or a strong brandy.

No one would remember who was where, and who was missing.

It was time to lure his target out to die.

Lord Richard Hart found the message in the pocket of his coat.

He had just left the manor, and was about to join a group of men who were fishing at the stream, when he discovered the folded slip of paper. Puzzled, he pulled it out, smoothed open what looked to be a sheet of feminine stationery. An anticipatory glint lit his eyes as he read the words, and the signature.

Ten minutes later, he was on horseback, galloping off to his destination.

He eased forward in his saddle, excitement rippling through him. He'd always been lucky with the ladies. Even now, at forty-five years of age, women were drawn to him. They were attracted to his still-firm physique, his natural charm, and, of course, his staggering fortune. He'd been approached by many women, with every offer from a swift, one-time liaison to a long-term mistress. He'd accepted more than his share. Rarely did the identities of those who approached him come as a surprise. He had a sixth sense for knowing when someone wanted him. But never in his wildest dreams had he guessed that Lady Breanna Colby was among them.

He smiled, urging his horse to pick up speed. According to her note, she wanted to meet him on the far western side of the estate, away from the guests and the construction, where she knew they could be utterly alone.

Her only stipulations were that he told no one he was coming and that he brought the note with him, so she could destroy it and eliminate any chance of discovery. Their tryst, she'd declared, had to remain a secret.

That was fine with him. The less people who knew, the less chance there was of his new wife finding out.

The notion of Lady Breanna wanting him, yearning for him, made his pulse race. True, this was one time he hadn't guessed, hadn't had an inkling of her desires.

But Breanna Colby was the ultimate lady, a woman who kept her feelings and her desires hidden.

The realization that he was to be the one to free them made his mouth water.

He glanced back at the manor, secure in the knowledge that his young, inexperienced wife was sitting among a cluster of women, chatting on some inane subject. Her youth and virginity, which a few short months ago had seemed so incredibly appealing, had quickly lost their luster. She was malleable enough, but passive, passionless. As a result, he was fast growing tired of having her in his bed.

Lady Breanna was different. Inexperienced, perhaps, but not passionless. After all, she was the mirror image of her cousin. And the heated expression on Sheldrake's face when he looked at his wife spoke volumes, proclaimed the exquisite Lady Anastasia to be all fire and initiative in bed.

So it would be the same with her cousin.

Lord Hart's smile broadened triumphantly as the rows of hedges

Breanna had described loomed into view. This must be where she was waiting. It was at the very edge of the estate, a few dozen feet from the road. The hedges were sheltered, private. Ideal.

He brought his mare to a halt, peering about in the hopes of spotting a glint of yellow. He well remembered the lemon-hued gown she'd been wearing at breakfast, and his loins tightened at the thought of removing it.

"Lady Breanna?" he called out. "I'm here, as you requested."

No reply.

Realizing she must be nervous, he yanked out the note she'd sent him, waved it in the air. "See? I've brought your message. No one knows my whereabouts. So there's no reason for self-restraint."

That yielded the desired results.

A glint of color flashed from the hedges.

But it wasn't yellow.

It was silver.

Hart scarcely had time to turn before the pistol fired. And he never realized he was going to die before the bullet found its mark.

Excellent, the assassin thought, watching Hart's body drop to the ground like a stone, the note fluttering to his side. A perfect shot. If any of the guards heard it, they would assume it was one of the gentlemen out gaming. Their job was to protect against intruders, not scrutinize those already present at Lady Breanna's invitation.

Still, he had to be prudent. He waited—just long enough to peer about and be sure no one was approaching. Satisfied that he was alone, he crossed over, sparing the body not even a glance as he leaned past it to scoop up the note.

Stuffing it into his pocket, he slipped into the hedges and made his way back to the manor.

It wasn't until late afternoon that the victim was missed.

His wife had assumed he was with the gentlemen, and each of the gentlemen had assumed he was with either one of their colleagues or one of their colleagues' wives.

But just after three o'clock, a group of men began looking for him. An afternoon thaw was allowing for a fox hunt and, fine sportsman that Hart was, they wanted him to join. Upon scanning the grounds, they noticed the mare wandering about. She was saddled, but minus a rider. The men were puzzled. As a result, Lord Percy Gilbert, who'd spied the mare first, rode her back to the stables to make an inquiry. He talked to a young stableboy, who readily told him that Lord Hart had taken her out hours ago.

A search got under way.

Forty-five minutes later, Lord Crompton spotted the body.

"Over there," he called, pointed toward the hedges.

The men hurried over, gathering around as the viscount squatted down, checked for a heartbeat, a whisper of breath, anything that indicated Hart might still be among them. But his body was cold and still, the smear of blood across his shirt telling them this was no riding accident.

"He's dead," Crompton declared grimly, rising to a standing position. "He was shot in the chest." Pale but composed, Crompton scanned the grounds, years in the military having accustomed him to staring death in the face. "The killer could have fired from there," he suggested, indicating the rows of hedges that offered a fine place from which an assailant could strike without being seen.

"Or he could have fired from the road." The Duke of Maywood gestured in that direction. "It's no more than twenty-five feet away, just past those trees. That makes a lot more sense to me. He could have hunched down by the roadside and waited for a victim to show up, to get close enough to be within firing range. But to sneak onto the estate? The killer would never have gotten past all those guards—and not only once, but twice—before he committed the murder and after."

"I agree," Lord Percy concurred, wiping sweat off his brow and glancing about apprehensively. "And if he did fire from the road, maybe he's not finished. He could be hiding nearby, waiting to shoot another one of us. Let's get back to the manor. We'll send the guards to collect Hart's body and take a look around."

Pandemonium did indeed ensue—as soon as the news reached the manor.

The men argued and muttered among themselves, the women wept and wrung their hands, and Lord Hart's young widow needed to be revived twice with smelling salts. It took the guards thirty minutes to get the full story from the men who'd discovered the body, and even longer to collect the body and search the area.

No assailant was discovered—not in the hedges, and not by the road.

The next hours passed in a frenzy, as the panicked noblemen battled each other to dispatch messages to Bow Street, demanding that action be taken and offering huge sums of money for any runners willing to leave Bow Street and ride out to this shire or that in order to protect them and their families from harm.

Wells was equally frantic, trying to calm down their guests and simultaneously summon enough footmen to accommodate all the outgoing messages. Hibbert stood off to one side, keeping a clear view of both the hallway and the sitting room, unobtrusively studying the guests' individual reactions while awaiting a signal from Royce.

Inside the sitting room, Royce was watching Breanna from across the way, making sure Damen stood with her and Anastasia as they spoke to Mahoney, tried to learn all they could about what had happened.

She was shaken. Badly shaken. Especially after last night's violation—which none of the guests knew about. Ironically, if they did, they'd be relieved. Frantic to get away from here, but relieved. *If* they drew the same conclusion Breanna had drawn.

She believed that Hart's murderer was the assassin who was after her, not the criminal terrorizing Bow Street with his string of aristocratic killings. Royce believed she was right. Clearly, it was another message from that bastard, one that foreshadowed what he intended to be her fate. She was terrified, and with good cause. Worse, there wasn't a damned thing he could do about it.

Nothing except find the killer.

He stared over her head, gazing out the window and noting that the guards who'd been searching the grounds were returning to their posts. They'd done all they could. Their job was to keep other incidents from occurring.

And his job was to pick up where they left off.

He turned toward the hallway, signaled Hibbert with a look.

A short while later, the two men were scrutinizing the area near the hedges where Hart's body had been discovered.

"Are you concerned that the guests might see us, ask questions about our motives?" Hibbert asked.

"No." Royce shook his head. "At this point, anyone who knows me knows I'd be compelled to look around. That's my nature. It would be more out of character if I *didn't* do so." He paused, glanced at the row of hedges, then angled his head to gaze off toward the road. "I'm not convinced the killer shot Hart from outside the estate. He might have. But there's no real evidence that he did. He could just as easily have shot from those hedges."

"Agreed." Hibbert turned up his collar, and followed Royce's line of vision. "You're still contemplating the possibility that he's here. That he's one of Lady Breanna's guests."

"I can't eliminate it."

"No, you can't. But you can't prove it either. There's just as good a chance he's out there," Hibbert made a sweep with his arm, "watching Lady Breanna and lying in wait."

Royce scowled, unable to dispute Hibbert's reasoning. "He's smart as hell. He intentionally chose this spot to shoot Hart, so we'd find ourselves in precisely this dilemma. He's trying to make it look as if he's the murderer of those noblemen, rather than the killer after Breanna. Dammit!" Royce clenched his fists at his sides. "How can I leave her alone after this?"

"You don't have a choice. Every guest at the party is aware of your plans to ride straight from here to Berkshire, to try to reunite Ryder and his daughter. If you alter those plans, there will be questions. Those questions could prove dangerous, especially if the killer *is* among the guests. Besides, from what you told me, Lady Breanna insisted you go. She wants you to bring Ryder and his daughter together." Hibbert studied Royce's expression. "I could go to Berkshire for you. It would be risky, but we could try to come up with some plausible excuse—"

"No." Royce shook his head. "You're right. I have to go. But Hibbert . . ." Royce fixed his friend with an unyielding look. "Don't leave Breanna's door tonight, not for an instant. Or tomorrow night, if I'm still not back. I don't think he'll guess she's changed bedchambers—I've asked Damen to make the room look lived in, to turn up the lamp in the evening and douse it at night, just in case that animal is watching. But if none of that works, if he should figure out that she's sleeping elsewhere and come looking for her, I want him to have to go through you."

A grim nod. "And so he shall."

The party ended early, an aura of morbidity settling over the manor as, one by one, the vehicles were brought around and the visitors took their leave.

Inside the sitting room, Royce hovered at the window, watching the activity taking place outside in the drive. Hibbert stood behind him, listening to the sounds of muffled voices and slamming doors that indicated the guests' departures.

Both men were waiting for Wells to come in and report that the party was officially at an end.

At last, the butler walked in, wearily proclaiming that the final carriage had driven away.

"Thank you, Wells." Royce was already in motion, crossing over to leave the room. "Where's Lady Breanna?"

"In the library, my lord," the butler supplied. "Just as you asked. With Miss Stacie and Lord Sheldrake."

"Good." Royce veered off down the hallway. "I want you and Hibbert in there, too."

Five minutes later, they were all assembled.

Breanna shut the novel she'd been pretending to read, and met Royce's hard stare.

"Everyone's gone," he said, addressing all the room's occupants, but looking directly at Breanna. "From this moment until whenever we find the killer, there are to be no more callers. None. Not even on New Year's Day."

"Callers?" Damen interrupted, bolting to his feet. "I want to take my wife and Breanna and get as far away from here as possible. My God, Royce, this assassin not only invaded Breanna's room, he shot and killed another man right under our noses. I won't just sit here and wait for him to do the same to Stacie and our unborn child."

"Those are your emotions talking, not reason," Royce observed quietly. "You know as well as I do that running would be a mistake. It would turn the women into moving targets. This man is a professional. He's hell-bent on killing Anastasia and Breanna. He'd follow them to the ends of the earth. They'd never be safe. They'd forever be looking over their shoulders. And one day—he'd be standing there. Is that what you want for your wife? For your child?"

Slowly, Damen sank back down into his chair. "No."

"Then listen to me," Royce urged. "Fleeing is not the answer. The answer is to eliminate this bastard permanently. Which I intend to do. The women must stay put. I know it's frustrating. But it's the safest way—the only way."

"I see your point," Damen murmured reluctantly.

"Good. As I said, from now on, no callers are to be admitted. To keep speculation from forming, keep tongues wagging. Make it public that Anastasia is still feeling ill, that's she's far too weak to entertain guests—and that her condition has worsened since Lord Hart was killed on her estate. Breanna, as expected, will be attending to her, as will you. Until Anastasia's health improves, no callers will be received."

Anastasia forced a smile, however strained. "This pregnancy of mine is becoming more than a blessing. It's becoming quite useful in manipulating people to suit our purposes."

Royce didn't smile back. "We'll use whatever we have, do whatever it takes. I want to rob the killer of every opportunity he might seize to get through those gates." He rubbed his palms together. "Which reminds me, the construction is set to resume after New Year's Day. That will have to be delayed. Blame the cold weather."

"Consider it done," Damen agreed at once.

"I'm leaving for Berkshire within the hour," Royce continued. "The sooner I dispose of the Ryder matter, the sooner I'll be back. I'd rather stay. But if I do, and if the killer discovers my change of plans, he'll start drawing his own conclusions. If he should figure out I'm hunting him down, he might lash out." A harsh edge laced Royce's tone. "That would be fine, if I were the one he was lashing out at. It would be more than fine. I'd welcome the chance to meet him head-on. But it's not me he'd vent his rage at."

"It's me," Breanna said quietly.

"Yes." Royce's gaze held hers. "He'd find another way to terrorize you. Right now he's appeased. He thinks he's winning. I'd rather he keep thinking that, until I get back. Then, we'll show him otherwise. But not until then."

"The *ton* thinks Hart's shooter was the killer Bow Street is looking for," Damen muttered.

"Our assassin wanted them to think that. He's shrewd as hell. This way, he terrified Breanna without arousing a shred of suspicion. Hopefully, his victory today will ensure us a short lull as he waits to assess Breanna's reaction. She's got to keep him wondering."

"How do I do that?" Breanna asked.

Royce's stare delved deep inside her. "Stay in the manor. Don't even let him see you, much less gauge how you're holding up. It will buy us time." A pause. "May I see you alone before I leave?"

"Of course." Breanna rose, smoothing the folds of her gown as she did. "We can talk in the green salon."

"I don't think it would be proper to—" Wells began.

"Oh, dear." At that exact moment, Anastasia jerked upright, looking like a rabbit about to bolt. "My stomach is beginning to lurch. It's my own fault. I haven't eaten since breakfast, and when I'm empty, I . . ." She clamped her lips together, as if stifling a wave of nausea.

Wells was already in motion. "I'll bring you some food. I'll be back in a minute."

He was gone in a heartbeat.

"Well done," Damen commended drily. "You accomplished just what you wanted to."

"I did, didn't I?" Stacie returned with a self-satisfied nod. She shot Royce a beatific smile. "You see? I told you my pregnancy was becoming useful. Now go. Before Wells comes to his senses and figures out what I've done—and why. And he *will* figure it out. He always does, as Breanna will attest."

A hint of amusement lurked in Royce's eyes. "I'm sure. Thank you for your warning, and your clever diversion."

He guided Breanna into the hallway, led her across to the green salon, and closed the door with a firm click.

All humor vanished, leaving only the raw emotions of fear, gloom—and something quite the opposite of both.

"Breanna," Royce said quietly, leaning back against the door and studying her beautiful, composed features. "I know you're terrified. But I promise you, this won't last much longer. I'll find him. You have my word."

Breanna drew a shaky breath. "I can cope with the terror. But this is the second man who's died because of me. *That* I can't endure."

"Sweetheart." Unaware he'd even uttered the endearment, Royce walked over, framed her face between his palms. *"You* didn't kill them. *He* did."

"I know. But his hatred for me prompted him to do so. That makes me responsible, even if indirectly."

Royce felt his insides tug—with compassion, with understanding, with something more.

Gently, he drew her against him, pressed her cheek to his coat. There was something about this woman, a beauty that was unique by its very design, its very extent, that made him wonder if perhaps he did have a heart after all.

"Hibbert has instructions to watch you like a hawk. You'll never be alone. No one except he, Wells—and, of course, Damen, Anastasia, and I—know you've changed rooms. Oh, and your lady's maid. I told her your chambers were being redecorated. I showed her your temporary quarters, and instructed her to tell no one of their location."

That brought Breanna's head up. "What possible reason could you give her for making that request?"

"Discretion." A corner of Royce's mouth lifted. "I told her you'd chosen that particular room because you wanted to be near me."

Breanna stared at him for a moment, a pink tinge spreading up from her neck to her throat. Then, she began to laugh. "You're the most outrageous man I've ever met."

"I know." His thumbs caressed her cheekbones. "And you're the most extraordinary woman *I've* ever met." He lowered his head, brushed her lips with his—and broached a subject he'd vowed to himself to avoid. "I'm sorry if my actions last night hurt you. I didn't mean for that to happen."

"Which part are you sorry for?" Breanna murmured, making no attempt to pull away from his embrace. "Are you sorry for what we did? Or for the way you behaved afterward?"

"That depends on when you ask me."

Breanna lay her palm against his jaw. "I'm asking you now."

"Now?" Royce savored the pleasure of her touch, fought the urge to drag her against him. "Right now, my conscience is warring with my instincts. My conscience is sorry I let things go so far. And my instincts are sorry I stopped when I did, that I didn't make you mine as I've wanted to do from the moment we met."

A teasing smile. "I prefer your instincts to your conscience."

"So do I." He kissed her again, a slow, dizzying exploration of her mouth. "We'll talk about this when I return. In the meantime, be careful. Stay inside. I'll be back by the morning after next, at the latest."

Slowly, Breanna nodded, her fists clenching in the folds of his coat. "I will. But Royce?"

"Hmm?"

"Hurry."

15

❧

$\mathcal{H}$e lurked in the brush, waiting until Chadwick's carriage had pulled away.

It was no surprise that Hibbert wasn't in it. As he'd suspected, Chadwick had left his faithful manservant behind, no doubt instructing him to safeguard Lady Breanna's life.

How noble.

The rage he'd hoped to assuage boiled up inside him once again, stronger, more relentless, than it had been before he pulled the trigger, ending Hart's life.

And that rage was aggravated by Royce Chadwick.

The man was an unwelcome complication. He was too inferior to be a threat, but not too inferior to be a nuisance. He was delaying the inevitable, helping to ease Lady Breanna's terror.

He was involving himself in a war he'd never win.

Clearly, he thought himself clever—leaving Medford Manor as scheduled, heading off to Berkshire to try finding Ryder's daughter. He believed it would convince his adversary that he wasn't acting as Lady Breanna's protector. But the fact that he'd left Hibbert behind said otherwise. It said that Chadwick was coming back.

So the fool hoped to match wits with him.

He was doomed to failure.

It was time to demonstrate that fact.

His mind racing, he massaged his hand, which throbbed beneath his glove after all the hours spent outdoors in the cold. The pain was worsening. He needed to warm it away, to soak his hand beneath some hot compresses in order to ease the knuckle that supported his wooden replica of a finger.

Not yet. Not until he resolved this issue.

But how?

In a flash of insight, he had his answer. Not just any answer, but a
brilliant one—one worthy of great genius—its ramifications as exhilarating as its goal.

What a splendid way of putting Chadwick in his place, and furthering
his own ends in the process. It would send Chadwick a message and, at the
same time, divert the fellow's energies elsewhere—probably straight to
Bow Street. Of course, that would mean a greater risk of discovery. Then
again, greater risk meant greater excitement. No battle was worth pursuing
if the opponent was totally unworthy or the odds of losing nil. By giving
Chadwick this demonstration, leading him to a whole different set of
answers, it would even the score.

It would also enhance the next shipment by one.

And why not deliver that shipment himself?

Instantly, rage was transformed to anticipation, the thrill of battle
mingling with another, equally enticing thrill.

Maurelle. *She* could ease the demons raging inside him, make him
forget the agonizing pain in his hand.

And he could bring her the excitement she craved, satisfy her in ways
no other man ever could.

Why hadn't he thought of this before? It was just what they both
needed—a profitable cargo and each other.

Not wasting a minute, he crept back to his phaeton, slapped the reins,
and rode off.

He was careful to keep a mile span between his carriage and
Chadwick's. He knew where he was headed—to Ascot, where, if his
exceptional memory served him correctly, Pearson Manor was situated.
He didn't recall the precise location, but he'd attended a ball or two there
when the dowager's husband was still alive. If need be, he'd stop at some
local pub where the ale was cheap, and the patrons poor enough, greedy
enough, to sell him a bit of harmless information, such as directions—
for the right price, of course—after which they'd forget his visit *and*
him. Either way, he'd find the dowager's home.

The easier method, of course, would be to keep Chadwick in sight, let
him lead the way.

But Chadwick's instincts were too good.

And it wouldn't do for him to know he was being followed.

An ironic smile lifted his lips. Interesting. The pursuer being pursued.
More than interesting. Ingenious.

The elderly, white-haired Dowager Duchess of Pearson listened atten-
tively as Royce presented his facts. Her thin hands folded in her lap, her
pale blue eyes unreadable, she sat, straight-backed, in the library chair,
waiting until the entire story had been told.

Then, she sighed, her already-lined face creasing further with uncertainty.

"I've protected Glynnis for eighteen years now," she murmured, her tone weary with age and pain. "There's a part of me that would like to keep on doing so. I'd like to send you away, to tell you to advise Lord Ryder that he's lost any right to speak with the mother of his child, much less the child herself. But Glynnis is a grown woman, and a mother. In addition, my own circumstances have changed drastically in the last few months. So I'll let her decide for herself what she wants to do."

Tactfully, Royce refrained from prying, although he did wonder what circumstances the dowager was referring to. "You'll let me speak with her?"

"Yes. I will." Her posture stiffened and her pale eyes narrowed on Royce's face. "But let me warn you, Lord Chadwick. Glynnis's feelings for your client have long since changed from love to resentment, maybe even to hatred. I wouldn't expect a warm reception."

Royce had to admire the woman's loyalty. Moreover, he had to agree with her assessment of Ryder's actions. He'd been a selfish, arrogant fool. The difference was that *now* he knew it. Age had granted him its unique wisdom, opening corridors of his mind that had, at one time, been shut. And one thing that wisdom had afforded him was the realization that blood ties did matter, and that human emotions transcended the bounds of class or monetary status.

In short, he was sorry. Deeply sorry. And while it was much too late to make amends with Glynnis, perhaps it wasn't too late to form a bond, however tenuous, with his daughter.

"I appreciate your honesty, Your Grace," Royce said respectfully. "I have no illusions, nor false hope. I want only a chance to speak with Miss Martin, to explain to her where things stand."

"So be it." The dowager summoned her butler, who came directly to the library.

"Yes, madam?"

"Please ask Glynnis to join me."

"Of course." The butler withdrew, looking not the least bit surprised by the request.

"Glynnis has been my companion since she came to live here," Lady Pearson explained to Royce. "She reads to me, walks with me in the garden, and, as of late, keeps me company when I'm confined to my quarters—which is more often than not. It's rare that she's not by my side."

Royce leaned forward on the settee, studied the emotion on the dowager's face. "You care a great deal for Miss Martin."

"She's like a daughter to me," was the shaky reply. "If this were a year ago I would have refused to let you see her. But now . . . I'm in failing health, Lord Royce. According to my physician, I haven't much time. I also have limited funds to bequeath to Glynnis. My poor late husband made some bad investments before he died and what little he left me went to running the estate. So, if there's a future for Glynnis—a good future—somewhere else, I won't stand in the way of her pursuing it. *If* it's what she wants."

A knock interrupted them.

"Come in."

"You sent for me, Your Grace?" Glynnis caught sight of Royce, and halted, looking hesitantly at her employer. "I'm sorry. I didn't know you had company."

"Come in, Glynnis." The dowager beckoned to her. "I'd like you to meet Lord Royce Chadwick. The matter that brings him to Pearson Manor concerns you."

A startled blink. "Very well." Glynnis Martin entered the library, approaching the settee with a shy yet curious demeanor. "My lord." She dropped a curtsy.

Having risen to his feet, Royce bowed. "Miss Martin. A pleasure." He straightened, eyeing her closely and seeing a woman who had once undoubtedly been quite lovely, with thick pale hair and wide gray eyes. But time and experience had taken their toll, and she now looked worn, resigned, her luster faded, her beauty diminished into plainness.

"What can I do for you, sir?" she inquired politely.

For an instant, Royce considered asking to speak with Glynnis alone, then abandoned the notion. To begin with, the dowager would never agree. Further, he sensed the elderly matron might turn out to be an ally, rather than an obstacle.

"Please, sit down," he began, gesturing toward the chair beside the dowager's. "As it happens, I've been searching for you for weeks now. Actually, for you and your daughter."

In the process of settling herself, Glynnis went rigid. "Emma? Why would you be searching for her?"

"On behalf of my client," Royce said gently. "Emma's father."

Shutters descended over Glynnis's eyes. "What do you know of Emma's father?"

Royce lowered himself back to the settee, speaking as frankly and objectively as he could. "I know who he is—the Viscount Ryder. I know you were employed in his home when Emma was conceived. I know he treated you abysmally when you told him you were with child. I know he abandoned you, and ignored your message informing him of Emma's birth." A weighty pause. "And I know that he's aging now, and deeply remorseful for what he's done. He realizes he can never make up for his callousness and negligence. But he wants to try—if not with you, then with Emma."

"Just like that." Glynnis Martin gave an incredulous shake of her head. "He seduced me, threw me out when I conceived his child, and denied that child's existence for eighteen years. And now he's remorseful. Tell me, my lord, how am I supposed to react? With compassion?"

"I'd be lying if I said yes to that," Royce stated bluntly. "Were I in your shoes, I'd probably hate the man. But your scars aren't really the issue here."

She looked taken aback, both by Royce's unexpected support of her plight and by his equally unexpected bluntness. "I see." She cleared her throat, her defensiveness visibly abating. "If my scars aren't the issue, then what is?"

"Emma is." Royce didn't diverge from his straightforward approach. "Look, Miss Martin. Despite all the insults we hurl at him, Lord Ryder *is* Emma's father. And—if it makes any difference at all—I can honestly say his regret at having rejected her, and you, is very real and very acute. He realizes he was a stupid, selfish fool. He also realizes he can't undo what's been done. But he's old, he's alone, and he's aware that his life is drawing to an end. He'd like to meet his child, to try to afford her—and himself—the chance to form some kind of relationship, however tenuous, before he dies. He'd also like to leave her his title, his estate, and his fortune—which is considerable."

Glynnis emitted a soft gasp. "I—I'm stunned. I had no idea." She pursed her lips, recovered herself. "But Emma is not for sale, my lord."

"I never assumed she was," Royce responded, unsurprised by Glynnis's reaction. She was clearly a proud woman, and a protective, devoted mother. All of which he admired—and planned to use, not only to his client's advantage but, whether Glynnis Martin knew it or not, to hers and her daughter's.

"I assure you," Royce continued, his tone and gaze unwavering, "that Lord Ryder has no desire to purchase your daughter. He's not luring her with the promise of money. He's simply offering her all that's his to give." A profound pause. "I'm a very good judge of character, Miss Martin, especially when it comes to my clients. The viscount has no ulterior motives, nor is he stupid enough to believe he can buy Emma's loyalties. He just wants to give her her birthright—and perhaps afford himself a measure of peace, a sense of having left something behind that's real and lasting. Surely you can understand that?"

Glynnis averted her gaze, indecision warring on her face.

"I believe that if you give this some thought . . . ," Royce pressed.

"I'm not sure I want to."

"Why?" Royce inquired gently. "Because you might find yourself softening?"

"Glynnis," the dowager interrupted, reaching out to take the younger woman's hand in hers. "Listen to me. You're angry. You have reason to be. I share your anger and hurt, as I have from the day you told me what the viscount had done. But I'm a great deal older than you. And I have a perspective you have yet to acquire. Age changes people. They suddenly see things clearly that, in the past, they were blind to. I think that's what's happening here."

"You expect me to forgive him?" Glynnis asked her employer in amazement.

"Of course not. I expect you to think of Emma. Don't let your bitterness, however justified, cheat her out of what's rightfully hers. You'll regret it."

"What's rightfully hers," Glynnis repeated bleakly. "The viscount's money."

"There's a lot more involved here than money," Royce put in.

"Such as what? A title? Status?"

"You're missing my point. Greed is clearly not in your nature, so I'd be a fool to use it as an incentive to sway you into accepting Lord Ryder's request. I'm urging you to do so for a number of reasons: to give Emma a sense of heritage—something meeting her father would permit; to give her the formal acknowledgment she has been denied all these years; to ensure her future, so she's never out in the cold, alone and abandoned, the way you were." Royce paused, glancing down at the carpet before lifting his gaze to meet Glynnis's. "And last—despite what you've claimed, despite what we've *both* claimed—to offer a shred of charity to a lonely old man. Pain and resentment aside, she is his daughter, Miss Martin."

Her expression softened, and Royce watched her innate decency prevail over her bitterness. "Yes, my lord. I know she is."

"Discuss it with Emma," he suggested. "She's young, but she's hardly a child. I think she deserves the right to know her father has asked to see her, don't you?"

Wearily, she nodded. "Considering how often she's asked me questions about him—yes. She does."

Satisfied with the results of this first meeting, Royce made to rise. "I'll go then, give you a chance to talk with her. I'm staying at a local inn, so I can return—"

"Wait." Glynnis came to her feet in a flourish. "I appreciate how considerate you're being. But I know my daughter. The instant I tell her about this, she'll want to talk with you. So, if you don't mind waiting, I'll get Emma now. Just give me a few minutes alone with her. Then, I'll bring her to you. I'd be grateful if you'd explain the situation to her exactly as you did to me. Would that be too inconvenient, my lord?"

"No, of course not."

In truth, Royce couldn't be more pleased. If he could eliminate a night of waiting, that might enable him to cut his trip by a full day. And get him back to Medford Manor by tomorrow night.

"Thank you," Glynnis was saying. "I'll get Emma." She turned to the dowager, frowned as she noticed the trembling of her hands. "Your Grace? Perhaps you should retire now. You're exhausted."

The elderly woman nodded, even that gesture appearing to tire her. "If Lord Royce doesn't mind waiting alone, I think I will."

"Please, go up with Miss Martin," Royce said, assessing the situation quickly, and stepping forward to kiss the dowager's quivering hand. "I apologize for tiring you."

"Don't apologize," she said, her fingers tightening briefly in Royce's. She raised her eyes to his, and he saw the shimmer of tears glistening there. "You've brought me just what I needed. Now I can leave this world in peace. Thank you, sir." With that, she accepted Glynnis's arm, leaning heavily against her as she came slowly to her feet. Pausing, she gestured weakly toward the sideboard. "Help yourself to a brandy. It will warm away the winter chill."

"I will. Thank you." Royce watched the two women walk away—Glynnis supporting the dowager's frail, aged frame—and he felt strangely moved by what had just taken place.

He blinked, stunned by his own reaction.

When had he started succumbing to sentiment?

He didn't need to explore that question to know its answer.

Breanna.

The thought of her brought his mind back to returning to Medford Manor by tomorrow night.

Swiftly, his mind raced, laying out plans. He'd reason with Emma now. Hopefully, if she was as curious about her father as Glynnis had implied, she'd agree to ride to Sussex and meet with him late tomorrow morning. That would give Royce the early morning hours to check out the Berkshire shops, and the remainder of the afternoon—after leaving Ryder's home—to cover the shops in Sussex. From there, he'd ride on to Surrey, chat with the shopkeepers before closing, then ride directly to Kent before nightfall.

To Kent—and to Breanna.

Royce gritted his teeth, acknowledging to himself that he had a lot to ponder with regard to Breanna Colby. Tonight, he promised himself.

When he was alone in his room at the inn. There, he'd devote serious thought to what in the hell was happening between them, where this fixation was leading.

And what in God's name he was feeling.

It was half past ten o'clock that night when Stacie shut the door to Breanna's temporary quarters, leaned back against it as if to bar her cousin from leaving, and announced, "All right, Breanna. That does it. I'm not waiting another instant. We've made up the room. We've brought in your sketches, your needlepoint, and all your favorite porcelain figures. It's as much home as it's going to be. Now talk to me."

Breanna turned, placing her final statue—the horse she'd had since childhood—on the fireplace mantel. She raised her brows quizzically. "You know as much as I do. Damen is turning up the lamp in my chambers, then coming here to escort you to bed. Hibbert is sitting right outside this door, planning to guard it for the night. Wells is standing at his post like a stubborn sentry who refuses to rest. You and I are both expected to get some sleep, after which—"

"That's not what I'm talking about and you know it." Stacie folded her arms across her breasts, giving her cousin a pointed look. "I've waited since the ball. And I'm not budging until you tell me what's going on between you and Royce Chadwick."

A flush stained Breanna's cheeks. "Oh . . . that."

"Yes. That." Stacie inclined her head. "It's even more serious than I thought. I can tell just by looking at you."

Sighing, Breanna perched at the edge of her bed. "I don't know how serious it is. I only know that I feel as if I'm being tossed about in a windstorm and I can't seem to break free or catch my breath. What's more, I'm not sure that I even want to."

"That sounds suspiciously like love."

Silence.

Stacie came to sit beside Breanna, taking her hand in hers. "Are you in love with Royce?"

Breanna gave a helpless shrug. "I've known him less than a fortnight."

"That doesn't answer my question."

"I know." Breanna stared down at their joined hands. "I think about him constantly. When he's in the room, I can scarcely look away. When we talk, it's as if we understand each other completely, despite the fact that we're so very different in so many ways. And when we touch . . ." A pause, as Breanna struggled to give voice to such intimate feelings. "When we touch, I lose myself entirely. I ache. I burn. I want things I never even imagined wanting. No, not wanting—needing. It's as if there's a whole different me inside, a person I don't even recognize but one Royce seems to know. Does that make any sense?"

"Oh, yes." Stacie exhaled sharply. "A lot of sense." She tucked an unruly strand of hair off her face. "You're in love with him, Breanna. The question is, what are you going to do about it?"

A thoughtful pause. "I have no answer for you. Because I'm not sure how Royce feels about me."

"Find out," Stacie advised. "Better still, help *him* find out. I think you'll both be pleased with the results."

"We're in the midst of hunting down a killer. Surely I should wait—"

"No, you shouldn't." Stacie gave an adamant shake of her head. "Love doesn't wait. Not even for danger to subside. Aren't you the one who taught me that not too many months ago?"

A flicker of memory danced in Breanna's eyes. "It appears my own advice is coming back to haunt me."

Stacie's grin was smug. "Yes. Pity, isn't it?"

At that same moment, Royce was hovering just inside the entrance-way at Pearson Manor, patiently answering the last of the two dozen questions Emma had fired at him since agreeing to meet her father the next day.

She was a delightful young woman. Much, Royce suspected, as her mother had been in her youth. She was charming, inquisitive, and lacking in artifice—her golden hair unbound, her gray eyes keen and intelligent. She'd been without a father her whole life. At last she was being offered an alternative. And she was eager to explore it, if somewhat cautiously, for all the right reasons.

"Will he expect me to move in right away?" she asked Royce, concern lining her face. "Because I can't make that commitment. It depends upon my mother's plans, the dowager's health and, truthfully, how well the viscount . . . my father," she corrected herself, "and I get on together."

"Lord Ryder has no expectations, Emma," Royce replied in total candor. "He'll be elated that I found you, and that you agreed to see him. After that . . . I'm sure he has his hopes, but they're not demands."

"He has no right to demand anything," Glynnis put in quietly.

"You're right." Royce met her gaze, seeing the kind of bleakness that resulted from having her youth stripped away, along with whatever hopes and dreams she'd possessed. Now those dreams belonged to her daughter, and it was clear that, while the dowager might think of Ryder's offer as a future for Glynnis, Glynnis regarded it only as a future for her daughter.

For her, there was only the present—or whatever was left of it when the dowager passed away.

"Mother, will you ride to Sussex with Lord Royce and me?" Emma was inquiring, trying to include her mother in this all-important step.

Royce knew the answer to that before Glynnis spoke it.

"No, Emma. I won't. I can't. Her Grace needs me."

Emma studied her mother speculatively. "That's not the only reason, is it?"

Glynnis drew a slow breath. "It's a very important reason, but, no, it's not the only one. This is one journey I can't take with you. It's one you *must* take in order to move ahead with your life. But, in my case, it would be like slipping backwards, into a past I've finally managed to put behind me. As I said, you have to go. But I can't."

Understanding flitted across Emma's face, and she hesitated, torn between loyalty to her mother and desire to complete a circle that, for her, had never been closed.

"Don't even consider changing your mind." Glynnis obliterated her daughter's dilemma in one fell swoop. She went to Emma, placed a gentle hand on her shoulder. "You must meet him, form your own opinion. He's your father. He's looked high and low for you. You'd never forgive yourself if you refused." Glynnis paused, weighing her next words carefully. "I'll never stop being your mother, Emma, no matter where either of us goes. But I've made my choices. It's now time for you to make yours. Do you understand what I'm saying?"

A solemn nod.

"Good. Then go upstairs and pack. It will be day before you know it."

Emma squeezed her mother's hand. "Thank you." She turned to Royce. "And thank you, my lord."

"You're welcome, Emma." Royce opened the front door, having tactfully retreated to it during the private moment between mother and daughter. "I'll see you tomorrow at ten." His gaze flickered to Glynnis. "Good night, Miss Martin."

She managed a small, if weary, smile. "Good night, my lord. I appreciate your searching so hard for Emma, and for offering her a chance to meet her father."

Royce should have felt satisfied as he descended the front steps of Pearson Manor.

But he didn't.

Instead, he felt uneasy.

He paused at the foot of the drive, glancing behind him and watching the lights go out, one by one, as the footmen readied the house for slumber.

Emma was excited about her upcoming adventure. Glynnis was resigned to, if not thrilled by, the unexpected opportunity that had presented itself to her daughter.

The situation was as positive as it could be, given Ryder's deplorable conduct eighteen years ago. As a result, Royce's assignment with the viscount was nearing an end—a successful end. Which was just what he'd hoped for.

So what the hell was bothering him?

Puzzled, he walked toward his phaeton, trying to analyze the unsettled feeling he had deep in his gut. On the verge of climbing into the driver's seat, he paused, turning once again to study the manor, intent on determining the reason for his restlessness.

Everything looked calm, the household settled in for the night.

He pivoted slowly, peering across the grounds, scrutinizing the shadows of trees, the thin layer of fog that was unfolding to hide the moon from view.

All was still.

Still frowning, Royce swung into his seat, unable to explain or shake free of his uneasiness.

Maybe it wasn't Ryder's case at all. Maybe it was worry over Breanna that was plaguing him.

Accepting that as a very real prospect, Royce slapped the reins, guided his carriage onto the road. Anything was possible, he mused, especially when it came to Breanna. It went without question that he wouldn't feel totally at ease until he was back at Medford Manor, overseeing her safety himself.

And catching the bastard who was after her.

He had a feeling sleep wouldn't be forthcoming—not for hours, if at all.

He steered his phaeton toward the village inn.

He waited until the last distant echo of hoofbeats had faded, and the road leading to Pearson Manor was silent.

Chadwick was gone.

The fool should have listened to his instincts, checked out the grounds to see who was lurking about. Not that it would have mattered. He wouldn't have found him.

Well, it was a moot point now. Chadwick had left. Only until morning, judging from the snippets of conversation he'd overheard when the front door opened. Tomorrow morning, he'd be back to take the girl to her father.

Or so he thought.

Slipping his gloved hand into his pocket, the assassin closed his four good fingers around the pistol. His other arm tightened around the horse blanket he carried—one that would serve two purposes tonight.

He'd have to strike swiftly, abandon some of his finesse in lieu of speed and skill. Ah, well. One had to be adaptable, especially when one's attack was spontaneous, one's tactical planning limited to a few brief minutes.

His timetable was excitingly tight—and not only in terms of his invasion of Pearson Manor.

After leaving here, he had to ride to London, make last-minute arrangements with his crew, then rush off to collect the final piece of his cargo.

He also had a package to send off to Medford Manor, the contents of which would ensure Lady Breanna's terror remained at a peak during his two-day absence.

All of this had to be done by daybreak, when his ship would be sailing for Calais.

An almost insurmountable challenge.

One he'd relish—and master.

Soundlessly, he moved toward the manor.

Glynnis Martin stood by the window, listening to her daughter shove a few final items into her bag, then snap it shut, having readied herself for the trip.

Emma was going to her father.

The thought felt more strange than it did upsetting. Perhaps that was because so many years had passed, taking much of the hurt and anger with it. Or perhaps it was because whatever fervent emotion she'd once possessed had long since drained away, given freely and lovingly to her daughter and the dowager.

Eighteen years had passed. Emma had grown to be a secure and level-headed young woman. The dowager had grown to be a trusted mentor and to depend upon Glynnis for friendship, for companionship, for strength.

But now, Her Grace's life was ending.

Emma's, on the other hand, was beginning.

And she?

Most of the time, the only thing she felt was tired. So many years had passed, taking with them her vitality and her hope, leaving behind only a sort of passive acceptance and prayer that Emma's life would be better.

Maybe that prayer was about to be answered.

Emma was young. She could find the energy and the will to forgive— both of which Glynnis lacked. As for the viscount, he'd be captivated by his daughter. Now that he'd taken this important step, decided to acknowledge Emma as his own, Glynnis was certain of that. He wasn't an evil man, only a weak one. And once he met Emma; saw his own charm, sharp mind, and melting smile reflected in her—he couldn't help but love her.

And he could offer her so much that Glynnis couldn't.

Perhaps she'd grown too soft-hearted. Or perhaps she'd just grown weary of battling an emptiness that had lapsed into futility.

"Mother?" Emma came up behind her. "Are you sure you're not upset that I'm going?"

"No, Emma. I'm not upset. In fact, I'm glad—for many reasons." She sighed, wondering how to explain to her daughter that she lacked what was needed to propel Emma into adulthood, that she hadn't the enthusiasm, the means, or even the energy to do so. "I'm tired, Emma," she began, starting to turn. "Sometimes I find myself wishing I could just close my eyes and . . ." She broke off, her words dying on her lips as she spied the intruder.

"And what—sleep?" the man in black inquired. He flourished his pistol, crammed the blanket against its muzzle. "I'm delighted to oblige."

The shot was muffled by the thick wool.

But the result was no less effective.

Glynnis Martin slumped to the floor.

The assassin was beside Emma before she could scream.

Dropping the blanket, he grasped the barrel of his pistol, brought the butt down against the side of her head. Dispassionately, he noted the shocked look in her eyes go dazed, then fade into nothingness.

She sagged forward, unconscious.

He glanced down at her, frowning a bit as he studied the lump already forming on the side of her head. He hated damaging the merchandise. Still, youth was an astounding thing. She'd heal by the time it mattered.

Resuming his work, he leaned over, dragging the blanket over Emma's head and pulling it down around her until she was fully covered. He'd tie her up later, when he was a safe distance away—long before she awakened.

Sidestepping Glynnis's body, he swung Emma over his shoulder, making his way from the room and reversing the path he'd carefully taken to get to her—down the shortest corridor of the servants' quarters and out the rear door of the manor.

Royce Chadwick would be so disappointed, he mused ten minutes later, tossing Emma's unconscious form into his carriage, and climbing in beside her.

As for the Viscount Ryder, he'd be positively despondent.

Unfortunately, there would be no one to carry on his title and his name.

Both would simply have to die when he did.

16

Royce stalked across the small room at the local inn, pouring himself a brandy and tossing it off in an effort to relax.

It wasn't like him to be so unnerved, he thought, unbuttoning his shirt and flexing his back muscles. But he felt unusually on edge, as if he were needed.

Could Breanna be in trouble?

No. He dismissed the notion, not out of fear, but out of pragmatism. Hibbert would never let anyone get to her. Besides, this assassin they were dealing with wasn't interested in storming Medford Manor, alerting the entire staff to his presence. He was interested in isolating Breanna, making her beg for her life before ending it. And that was only after terrorizing her and murdering Anastasia.

The prospect made his blood run cold.

Worry. Fear. Protectiveness.

He was even more personally involved in this case than he'd allowed himself to fathom.

And it wasn't because of his friendship with Damen.

It was because of his feelings for Breanna.

Feelings. That in itself was uncharted territory. The only feelings he'd known until now had been uncomplicated ones—determination, anger, compassion, lust. Those he could deal with; those he understood. Anything more, he'd never received nor learned how to give.

And this preoccupation, this desire to protect, this bloody sense of being off-balance—not only had he never experienced these sentiments, he'd never believed himself capable of them.

Obviously, he was wrong. Whatever emotional deficiencies he thought he suffered from as a result of his upbringing were not entirely irreparable.

But, whatever sentiments he could cultivate, were they enough?

Slowly, Royce sank down onto the edge of the bed, somehow aware that he'd gotten to the heart of his misgivings, his reticence to care for Breanna.

She was all he'd told her she was—beautiful to the core. Yet all that beauty had gone unnurtured for twenty-one years. She'd spent her entire life deprived of the very caring she so naturally offered others. True, she had Anastasia, and a houseful of servants who adored her. But she deserved more. She deserved a man who cherished her as Damen did Anastasia. She deserved a man who recognized her for the exquisite and rare flower that she was, and offered her all that was necessary to make her bloom.

And he? Here he was, slamming into her world like a thunderstorm, taking advantage of her fear and vulnerability, causing her—unconsciously or not—to depend on him. And then, disregarding her innocence, intentionally coaxing forth her natural sensuality, seducing her with words, acting as if he had the right to be that man.

He'd known he wanted her, probably from the first instant he set eyes on her. But what had happened between them last night—whether or not it was the result of the raw emotions generated by the assassin's visit—had been dumbfounding. He'd never experienced anything like it. He was no stranger to passion or its nuances; he'd explored them with more than his share of women.

But last night he'd been drowning. Holding Breanna in his arms, feeling her skin against his, he'd damned near lost control, torn off the rest of their clothes and buried himself inside her. And judging from the look in her eyes, the flush on her cheeks—she would have let him.

God help him, what was he doing? What was he thinking? He had no right to toy with her this way, not unless he was willing, able, to give her everything she needed.

They were so very unalike.

Except for the ways in which they were the same.

And even in their differences, she seemed to see inside him, understand him with a clarity that was startling.

He'd confided things to her he'd never spoken of before. His childhood was a distant memory, a painful precursor to the man he was today. His father was dead. And whatever hold he'd had over Royce had died long before that.

The hold, yes. But the residual pain?

Scars, Breanna had said. Well, maybe she was right. Maybe he hadn't escaped without some of those, even if he was stronger for it, more sure of who he was.

He was hard, detached. He'd told that to Breanna last night. And it was true. Too true, perhaps.

The problem was, he wasn't detached when it came to her. With her, he was in over his head.

Why and to what extent—those were the questions that needed answering.

Was he in over his head because he'd never met a woman as incredibly beautiful, both inside and out, as Breanna—a woman who was so strong and at the same time so delicate, whose depth of passion even she had yet to fathom, much less explore? A woman he wanted almost beyond bearing, certainly beyond resisting? A woman he wanted to protect and devour all at once?

Or, as he was beginning to suspect, was the reason he was in over his head something far deeper?

He'd best find some resolution—soon. Because if he wasn't the right man for Breanna, if he wasn't capable of being all she needed, he had to get away from her—fast. If last night was any example of what happened when they were together, he couldn't rely upon his self-restraint. Despite his best intentions, despite his supposed iron will, all she'd done was look at him, touch him, and every shred of reason had vanished.

He shouldn't go back to Medford Manor at all, certainly not to sleep in the bedchamber right next to Breanna's.

But that insight wasn't going to stop him.

He wasn't leaving until he found that son of a bitch who wanted her dead.

Morning brought with it a blistering headache from too much brandy, and little in the way of resolution.

Still, Royce was dressed and out early, riding to several local villages in the hopes of finding either the shopkeeper who'd sold the dolls or the one who'd sold the statue. Berkshire was a strong possibility—close enough to be accessible to Kent, near enough to London to be bustling, filled with enough shops for the assassin to find an unobtrusive one in which to make his purchases.

The dolls continued to be a lost cause. They were too common, several similar ones having been sold in each of the five shops Royce visited.

The porcelain figure yielded far better results.

It happened in the third shop Royce strolled into. The store, which sold various novelties and trinkets for women and their dressing tables, was tucked away in a village halfway between Ascot and Reading. Sure enough, Royce spotted a row of small porcelain figures near the back of the store.

He summoned the shopkeeper, an amiable enough fellow named Barker, and questioned him about the specific statue he was hunting for.

Halfway through the description, Barker's entire demeanor changed, and he became wary, shifting uneasily from one foot to the other. "I might have seen the statue you're talking about. Why are you asking?"

"Why are *you* unnerved by my asking?" Royce challenged, realizing the man knew something and using the most aggressive tactics possible to scare the information out of him. "Is there some reason you don't want to discuss that particular statue—some reason that might get you into trouble?"

"Yes. No. Not in the way you mean." The man blanched, taking in Royce's powerful build and gauging the distance between him and the door.

"I wouldn't bolt. It's a bad idea." Royce tapped his pocket, made it clear he was armed. "If you'd prefer we could continue this conversation at Bow Street." It was a bluff, but he suspected it would yield the desired results—*if* Barker's fear was the honest kind.

It was.

"Are you a constable or something?" Barker asked hopefully, visibly heartened by the mention of Bow Street.

"Or something." Royce's stare bored through him. The man wasn't a criminal. But he *was* scared. The question was, why? Had he been threatened by whomever bought that statue?

"You're not under suspicion," he continued, offering just enough information to assure Barker's cooperation. "Quite the opposite. It's possible you could help me find someone who's, shall we say, shady. What can you tell me?"

By now, Barker looked more than convinced. "I know the porcelain figure you mean. There's actually a whole group of them similar to the one you described. They're all of two women who look like sisters doing different things together—gardening, sewing, picking flowers. The entire set was on display and for sale. But not in my shop, in my cousin's. His store is in Canterbury."

"You said the figures *were* in your cousin's shop," Royce repeated, furious with himself for missing the obvious. The arrogant son of a bitch bought the statue in Kent. Right out from under their noses. He'd assumed they'd never check the local shops, since they'd already checked there once, for the dolls.

He'd been right. They hadn't.

"So your cousin sold the statues," Royce probed, determined to get some facts, however limited. "I'll need the name and address of his shop. How recent were the purchases made? How many of the porcelain figures sold? Will he have a record of the sales?"

The shopkeeper waved away Royce's questions. "I can give you Henry's address. But it won't help. He doesn't have any record of the sales. Normally, he would. He keeps fine records. But the statue you're asking about, along with the other half-dozen from that collection, was stolen."

"Stolen?"

"Yes. That's why I got nervous when you asked about the statue. I thought you might be a friend of the thief's."

"Hardly." Royce's mind was racing. "When were the statues taken?"

A thoughtful look. "About ten days ago, I'd say. Henry went home, locked up as usual first. When he opened up the next morning, the statues were gone. Whoever stole them went to a lot of trouble. Cut a pane of glass from the door and let himself in. Perfectly neat pane, too. You'd think he'd smash the glass, climb in and grab all he could, then run before he got caught. No. This thief, whoever he is, cut a square just small enough to fit his hand through. He took nothing but the statues— not even the money Henry keeps in the front drawer." A shrug. "Makes no sense to me. Not to the local constables either. They've been at Henry's shop already. They found nothing."

It makes perfect sense to me, Royce thought silently. *This bastard needs to be superior at everything he does.*

Aloud all he said was, "Thank you for your help, Mr. Barker. I'll still need your cousin's name and the address of his shop, just so I can talk to him and have a look around."

"Sure." The shopkeeper scribbled down the information. "You never said who you were," he commented, eyeing Royce curiously as he handed over the slip of paper.

"An investigator," Royce replied tersely. "And if I find out anything about your cousin's property, I'll let you know. I'll also let Bow Street know how cooperative you were."

The man stood up a little straighter. "Happy to oblige, sir. I hope you catch the man."

Royce's jaw clenched. "Don't worry. I intend to."

Royce's day went from bad to worse.

He arrived at Pearson Manor on schedule, only to see the scarlet coats of two Bow Street runners in the entranceway. The men's backs were to him as they spoke with the dowager's butler. They were nodding, scribbling notes in a pad as the butler mopped at his brow with a handkerchief.

An ominous knot coiled in Royce's gut.

"What's wrong?" he demanded, taking the front steps two at a time.

The men turned. Royce recognized Marks right away, as well as Carson, a younger lad who'd been with Bow Street a little more than a year.

"Chadwick. I'm glad you're here," Marks greeted him tersely. "We sent a messenger to the inn to find you, but you'd already left. I understand you were scheduled to take Emma Martin to the Viscount Ryder's home today."

"That's right."

Marks glanced swiftly at the butler, who looked as if he were about to swoon. "You can go now. I'll send for you if I need you."

"Thank you, sir." The man practically bolted.

"Marks, what the hell is going on here?" Royce repeated.

"Emma Martin is gone."

"Gone? Are you saying she's run off?"

"I'm saying she's gone. I don't know under what circumstances. She's gone, and her mother is dead. Shot to death in her daughter's room. Sometime last night, it looks like. No one here saw or heard anything. Except, I suspect, the girl. And she's missing."

Royce tasted bile. "What about the dowager?"

"She wasn't hurt—at least not by the shooter. But the news of Glynnis Martin's death was too much for her. Her Grace died a half hour ago."

"Dammit," Royce muttered, his hands balling into fists at his sides. "Goddammit."

Marks scratched his head, studying Royce's reaction. "As you know, Berkshire's not exactly our territory. But when we heard who Emma Martin really was, where you were taking her today—"

"It occurred to you that this murder might be tied to the others you're investigating. The ones involving the London noblemen."

"Exactly."

"Except why would the killer shoot Ryder's mistress?" Carson interjected to ask. "That doesn't fit into his pattern. Why kill the woman?"

"Damned if I know." Marks's answer was candid, his shrug as uncertain as his words. "None of us has any idea what's inciting this lunatic. He's killed four men and kidnapped their wives. Maybe Ryder's next on his list and he came here looking for him. News is all over Town about Chadwick figuring out who the viscount's daughter is. Maybe the killer thought Ryder would come here to claim her, rather than the other way around."

"You're thinking that when the killer broke in, he went straight to Emma's room to find Ryder. And that Glynnis Martin was there and saw him, so he shot her." Carson nodded. "Makes sense."

"It doesn't explain Emma's disappearance," Royce pointed out, although he was already forming his own theory—and it bore no similarity to anything Marks was going to come up with.

"She is Ryder's blood relation," Marks tried. "A mistress isn't bound by blood or marriage. A daughter is. Maybe he grabbed her for ransom."

"But who'd pay that ransom if Ryder was dead?" Royce countered. "For that matter, who's paying the ransom for the other women who were kidnapped? Their husbands' beneficiaries?"

Marks shrugged again. "I don't know any more than you do, my lord. We haven't seen a single ransom note yet—not in any of the four cases."

"Four?" The number finally sank in, and Royce's head came up. "Why are you including Hart in your count? He was killed at Medford Manor, which is in Kent, not London. And his wife wasn't touched."

"Lord Hart was shot in Kent, but his home's in London," Marks corrected. "Everything else about the crime fit the pattern exactly. The target was a nobleman; the method, a gunshot to the chest. As for Lady Hart . . ." A slight hesitation, and Marks exchanged glances with Carson. "This isn't public knowledge yet, Chadwick. We're trying to keep it quiet as long as possible, to avoid mass hysteria. But under the circumstances, you should know. At the same time we got word about what happened here, we got word that Hart's widow disappeared from her London Town house last night. Both crimes happened sometime between eleven P.M. and dawn."

Royce sucked in his breath. "The kidnapper got past Hart's guards?"

"Yes. Just as he did here. Just as he always does. It's like he's a mind-reader or a genius of some kind. He times it perfectly, so he gets by the guards and goes unseen by the staff."

A genius of some kind. Gets by the guards. Goes unseen by the staff. The same method—a gunshot to the chest.

Realization exploded inside Royce's skull.

Of course. It all tied together. It didn't explain the kidnappings, but it sure as hell explained the murders, and the precision with which all the crimes were committed.

He'd assumed Marks and Carson were exploring the wrong path. They weren't. What they were doing, was exploring only *one* of the right paths.

He knew the other.

Royce's brain began pounding with details, one after the other, as pieces of the puzzle fell into place. The murders—when they'd begun happening, the deliberation with which they were committed—it all fit. All but the missing women. That motive was yet to be revealed. But the rest?

The rest spoke volumes.

All the killings, with the exception of Glynnis Martin, had been target practice for the killer.

Because that killer and the assassin tormenting Breanna were one and the same man.

The bastard was toying with the authorities while he honed his skill for the ultimate prize.

And that prize was Breanna.

As for Glynnis Martin's death, that had been retaliation, a taunting reminder of who was the master.

That reminder was aimed, not at Breanna, but at him.

Obviously, the assassin had guessed what he was about. Having over-heard what Royce intended him to overhear—that he was riding to Pearson Manor to bring Emma Martin to her father—the killer had somehow deduced the rest: that Royce would be returning to Medford Manor, that he'd taken on the role of Breanna's protector.

He knew. The son of a bitch knew everything.

And he was warning Royce to stay the hell out of this—or else.

"Chadwick?" Marks pressed, his eyes narrowed on Royce's face. "Have you come up with something we missed?"

Royce schooled his features, resisted the urge to blurt out his suspi-cions. To do so would be a mistake. Bow Street couldn't help Breanna any more now than they could before. They needed proof. He had none to offer. All he had was gut instinct. And, however certain that instinct was, it still wasn't proof.

Plus, there was another reason for his silence.

He wanted to get that son of a bitch himself.

"Chadwick, what's on your mind?" Marks demanded.

"I was thinking of Ryder," Royce replied, turning their attentions toward a different concern. "If he is this killer's next intended victim, he'd better be warned."

Marks nodded. "We'll ride straight to Sussex from here."

"Ryder's expecting Emma, not you," Royce said grimly. "I sent him a missive late last night, explaining that I'd found her and that I'd be bringing her to his estate this afternoon. Now, instead of meeting his daughter, he'll be confronted with news of her kidnapping. Not to men-tion the remorse he'll feel over Glynnis's murder."

"We'll handle Ryder." Marks shot Royce a pointed look. "Leave him and his safety to us. That's our job. Yours was finding the girl—which you did."

"Only to lose her again—and this time not to the safe haven provided by her mother." Royce frowned. "I'll leave Ryder to you. But as for Emma, I'm starting a new search. I intend to find her. That's what I'm being paid to do."

"*After* we find the killer."

"Agreed. The killer comes first." Royce chose his words with care, deliberately avoiding a blatant refusal to leave the detective work to them. Not because he agreed with Marks's assessment. Nor because he intended to stay out of Bow Street's way. But because he knew in his gut that the assassin wasn't after Ryder.

No, the son of a bitch had made his point, right here at Pearson Manor today. Now, Royce would be willing to bet that he'd be returning to circle his true quarry like the vicious predator he was.

Royce's gut clenched tighter.

Let Bow Street guard Ryder.

He was speeding back to Breanna as fast as his phaeton could travel.

17

❧

*B*reanna had been on edge all day.

She'd tried doing her needlepoint, then abandoned it after pricking herself three times. She'd then turned to her sketches, but couldn't seem to get the colors right. Finally, she picked up the novel she'd been reading, and found herself staring blankly at the words.

The tension was beginning to get to her.

She tossed down the book, smoothing her hair and glancing at the clock.

Just after four—ten minutes later than the last time she'd checked.

Sighing, she left the bedchamber for the third time since lunch.

Hibbert jumped up from his chair the instant she emerged. "My lady?"

"I'm fine, Hibbert," she assured him, touched by the concern she heard in his voice. "Losing my mind, but fine." She rubbed the folds of her gown between her fingers. "You haven't received word from Royce, have you?"

The barest hint of a smile touched Hibbert's carefully schooled features. "No. Nor do I expect to. He'll finish his business and ride back here as quickly as possible. If not tonight, then tomorrow."

"I suppose." Breanna nodded. "He's probably reuniting Lord Ryder and his daughter as we speak."

"That could very well be." Hibbert gestured down the hall. "Your cousin and her husband went down for tea a few minutes ago. Lady Sheldrake said you should feel free to join them."

"Thank you. I will." Breanna paused. "And so will you."

"Pardon me?"

"Oh, come now, Hibbert." This time it was Breanna who smiled. "Certainly a man irreverent enough to join his employer for a drink in the middle of a ballroom isn't shocked by the notion of joining my family for tea."

"Good point, my lady." One brow rose fractionally. "I am rather thirsty."

"Besides, Wells will be there. The two of you can resume glaring at each other like two male cats fighting for their territory. That should please you."

Hibbert actually chuckled. "A rousing activity, I agree. Very well, you've convinced me. Tea it is."

They were halfway down the stairs when the knock resounded at the front door.

At his post, Wells stiffened. He threw a quick glance at the sitting room, then turned to fix his stare on Breanna, noting that Hibbert was one step behind her.

"I'm armed, Wells," Hibbert said quietly, reaching for his pocket. "Go ahead and open it."

With a terse nod, Wells yanked open the door.

Mahoney stood there, a parcel in his hands.

"This was just delivered to the front gate," he said without preliminaries. "It's for Lady Breanna. The messenger had no idea who sent it. It was left on his employer's doorstep, along with a ten pound note."

"Like the last time." Breanna felt everything inside her go cold. Outwardly, she remained calm, continuing to descend the steps. She put one foot in front of the other, watching Wells and Mahoney stare up at her, seeing Stacie and Damen walk out of the sitting room and into the hall, where they, too, turned anxious gazes to her.

The scene unfolded as if it were a dream.

More aptly, a nightmare.

"You don't have to open it, Miss Breanna," Wells interceded, planting himself between her and Mahoney as if to stave off the inevitable.

"That's true," Mahoney concurred. "I can just toss it out."

"No," Hibbert refuted. "You can't. We have to know what's in there." He made his way to the doorway, leaned around Wells, and took the box from Mahoney. "Thank you. We'll deal with this from here."

Mahoney shot Wells a quizzical look, waiting for official instructions.

This time there was no argument. Wells nodded. "Hibbert's right. We'll deal with the matter. You can go, Mahoney. Thank you for bringing the package to us."

He shut the door behind Mahoney's retreating figure, his face ashen as he stared at the box in Hibbert's hands.

"I'll open it, Hibbert." Breanna took the package, which was about the length and width of a portfolio, though twice the thickness, and fairly light of weight.

"Are you sure, my lady?"

"Yes. I'm sure. It's addressed to me." A slight tremor rippled through Breanna's fingers as she tugged off the paper and string, pulled off the lid.

Inside was a smaller box, cushioned by what appeared to be just a rumpled sheet of paper.

It wasn't.

Setting the box on a table, Breanna smoothed out the folds of the rumpled page, and realized it had come from a sketch book.

Her sketch book.

She recognized at once what *had* been her drawing—an expanse of snow-covered ground, flakes falling everywhere, Medford Manor in the background.

Two women had been added to the picture.

Both had green eyes and auburn hair. Both stood, side by side, pain etched on their faces.

Both had blood trickling from the bodices of their yellow gowns to form crimson puddles on the snow beneath them.

"Oh, God," Breanna whispered.

"That's supposed to be us." Anastasia had come to stand beside her cousin, and her voice was choked with horror.

"It's my sketch." Breanna wet her lips, struggled for composure. "At least it was. I drew everything in this picture except the women. And the blood." She swallowed. "It was in my room, in a pile of unrelated drawings. That's why I didn't notice it was missing."

"He must have taken it when he broke in," Hibbert concluded. He took the sketch, frowned at the detail. "These gowns are identical to the one you were wearing yesterday," he told Breanna. "The lemon color, the lace around the sleeves—he had to have seen it. He was either a guest at the party or nearby enough to study you at close range."

"I'll open the smaller box," Wells announced firmly. "Miss Breanna's been through enough."

He walked to the table, removed the inner box and raised the lid.

A puzzled expression crossed his face. "A blanket?" he muttered, reaching inside and lifting out what appeared to be a child's quilt.

"There's something wrapped inside the blanket," Hibbert informed him. He went over, carefully unfolding the layers until he revealed a miniature wicker basket, within which lay a tiny doll—an infant doll—its head smothered by the quilt, its eyes tightly closed.

Pinned to the basket was a note that read: *Lady Anastasia's babe will never see the light of day. Mother and child will die. You, my dear, will watch. Then I'll have the pleasure of watching you die. It's almost time, Lady Breanna. Your bullet awaits.*

From behind her, Breanna heard Stacie's harsh gasp of distress.

She turned, automatically striving to comfort her. "Stacie." She gripped her hands, feeling ill at the sight of her normally dauntless cousin literally quaking with fear. Stacie had gone sheet-white, and was staring at the note with a wild-eyed expression, her control on the verge of snapping.

"I'm all right," Stacie managed, squeezing Breanna's hands in return, before gratefully leaning back into her husband's comforting embrace.

"He's not going to get near you," Damen said fiercely.

"I know." Stacie blinked back tears. "And when it's only me he threatens, I can handle it. But our child . . ." Her voice quavered.

"We knew the threats would continue," Hibbert said in a quiet, calming tone. "And that's all these are—threats. He's heightening your fear. But he's no closer to touching either of you than he was before. Try to remember that."

"Damen, I'm not feeling very well." Stacie lay an unsteady palm on her stomach. "I'm going to lie down."

"I'll go with you." Damen shot Wells a we'll-talk-about-this-later look.

Stacie paused to glance anxiously at Breanna. "Will you be all right?"

"Of course." Breanna wondered where that composed voice was coming from. "Take Stacie to your room," she instructed Damen.

Watching the two of them climb the staircase, seeing Stacie unconsciously caress her abdomen as if to protect her unborn child, Breanna couldn't help but feel a surge of guilt. Logically, she knew the emotion was irrational. She'd shot that assassin to save Stacie's life. Still, it was because of her that Stacie and the babe were in danger.

And she felt helpless to eliminate it.

Her gaze flickered over the basket and the sketch, and she shuddered, turning away.

"Come, my lady," Hibbert urged, walking over to take her arm. "Let's have that tea we discussed. Wells," he added, without a trace of the usual goading. "Join us."

"Certainly." Wells took Breanna's other arm, and the two men escorted her into the sitting room.

They'd barely poured the tea when a frantic banging began at the entranceway door.

"Now what?" Wells sprang up, rushed to his post.

Breanna clenched her hands in her lap, almost afraid to wonder who it was.

She heard the door swing open.

"Lord Royce." Wells sounded as relieved as he did surprised. "You're back early. Thank heavens."

"Is Breanna all right?" Royce's voice was closer, his heels echoing as he strode down the hall. "Where is she?"

"In the sitting room. And she's . . ."

Royce was through the sitting-room door before Wells could finish. His gaze found her immediately, and Breanna was stunned at the intensity of her relief. *Thank God,* she found herself thinking fervently. *Thank God he's back.*

"Has he been here?" Royce demanded, looking from Breanna's haunted expression to Hibbert's strained one.

"He sent another package," Hibbert replied. "It arrived a few minutes ago."

"But he himself didn't show up, strike directly in any way?"

Hibbert inclined his head in question. "No. What's happened, my lord?"

"A lot." Without elaborating, Royce went directly to Breanna, sat down beside her. He took her hands in his, frowning at how icy cold her skin was. "Breanna?"

She met his gaze, determined to stay strong. She wouldn't fling herself into his arms as she longed to do. Nor would she give voice to the wealth of emotion churning inside her—the numbing terror, the crippling worry, the weak-kneed relief.

The surge of love.

"His gift was even more unnerving than the last," she said with as much dignity as she could muster. "But I'm fine."

Royce's stare delved deep, and she had the uncomfortable feeling he could see clear down to her heart.

"Come here," he ordered softly. Without a word, he drew her against him, pressing her cheek to his coat and rubbing her back in slow, soothing strokes. "Still determined to take on the world alone, I see."

Breanna said nothing. But she couldn't resist the need to lean on him. She sank into his strength, her hands balling into fists as she fought the urge to do something she rarely did—not even when her father beat her.

She fought the urge to break down and sob.

If Royce sensed her turmoil, he said nothing. He merely held her, met Hibbert's gaze over the top of her head. "Tell me about the package."

Hibbert complied, describing the entire event from the moment Mahoney knocked on the door.

Royce scowled, rubbing his chin over the smooth crown of Breanna's hair. "Listen to me," he told her quietly. "He's aiming for your vulnerabilities. He knows how much you care for Anastasia. That's why he sent the message about her babe. He wants you to feel twice the terror you would if it were only your own life at stake."

"Then it worked, because I do." She drew back, gazed up at Royce. "What if we can't find him? What if he never gives himself away?"

"We will. And so will he." Royce gripped her shoulders very gently. "He's figured out I'm involved. And he's not happy about it. He's taking action to stop me. That means taking risks. Which makes it more likely he'll give himself away."

She blinked. "How do you know all that?"

Royce hesitated, and Breanna could see him trying to assess her state of mind.

"Tell me," she commanded. "What's happened? Why did you come rushing back the way you did?"

"I was afraid he'd get here first. And I'm unsure of his state of mind right now. Although my guess is, he's gloating."

"Get here? What makes you think he left?"

"Because he was in Berkshire and in London. He followed me to Pearson Manor. And after I left there last night, he killed Glynnis Martin and kidnapped Emma."

For a minute, Breanna wondered if she'd heard right. "What?" She forced the room to right itself. "You'd better explain."

Royce did, beginning with his interviews with the dowager and Glynnis and Emma Martin, moving to Emma's decision to go to her father, and then touching on the uneasiness that had besieged him upon leaving the manor that night. He culminated with what had happened this morning, when Bow Street gave him the shocking news of Glynnis's murder and Emma's disappearance.

"I don't understand," Breanna replied, attempting to sort out all Royce had just said. "Why would you assume the assassin did this? It sounds more like the work of that killer Bow Street's looking for."

"It is. They're one and the same."

"Yes," Hibbert murmured behind her. "It would seem they are." He rose, pacing about for a minute before turning to face Royce thoughtfully. "All the noblemen died the same way?"

"Yes. A bullet to the heart."

"Just like the dolls, the chemise, and now the sketch," Hibbert responded. "The blood on all of them is painted in the chest area." He pursed his lips. "You think the murders were all part of a game?"

"More like target practice. Except Glynnis. That was a message to me."

"He wants you to stay away."

"Exactly."

Breanna stared from one man to the other. "He killed people as *practice?*"

Royce didn't insult her by softening the truth. "Yes."

"You didn't tell your theory to Bow Street, I presume," Hibbert said, more a statement of fact than a question.

"No. I have no proof."

One of Hibbert's brows rose. "Not to mention that you want to catch this blackguard yourself."

"Not to mention that," Royce concurred, a cold light glittering in his eyes. "There's a missing piece, though."

"The kidnappings."

"Right. That's the other thing Marks told me. The news hadn't gotten out yet, but apparently Hart's wife was kidnapped last night, too. So now all the victims have missing wives."

"Except Ryder, who has a missing daughter." Pensively, Hibbert stroked his chin. "Ransom makes no sense. Who would pay it?"

"That's what I want *you* to tell *me*. Check out all the victims. Find out everything you can: who'd inherit if their wives were gone, who drew up their wills, who had a grudge against them—anything that might give us some answers. This assassin doesn't do anything at random. Everything is planned with the utmost precision. He specifically chose his victims, just as he chose to kidnap their wives. There's got to be a reason why. Which means there's a common thread among the victims, besides the fact that they were all of noble birth."

"Glynnis Martin wasn't of noble birth. But then, I notice you've omitted her from your reasoning."

"Bow Street thinks the killer came looking for Ryder and killed Glynnis when she spotted him."

"And you think he killed Glynnis to warn you away from Lady Breanna."

"I know he did."

"I agree. What's more, he probably took her daughter to best you."

"Or to divert me from Breanna."

"Yes—or that." Hibbert pondered his impending task. "I'll begin looking for the common link among the victims. All but Glynnis Martin. I'll assume his motive there was to get at you."

"A wise assumption." Royce looked about restlessly, spied Wells hovering in the doorway, his expression stricken. "Wells, I'll need to see the sketch. And the basket." He hesitated, turned to Breanna. "Do you want to go upstairs and lie down? You don't have to go through this again."

"No." Breanna gave a hard shake of her head. She might be dazed, overwhelmed by all she had to process, but about this point she was adamant. "I want to stay here. I need to help resolve my own fate, as well as Stacie's and her babe's."

"All right." With a flicker of understanding, Royce signaled to Wells to get the package, then waited while he complied.

"The killer had to have been here," Royce murmured, after carefully studying each item. "Not just outside the gate, or on the grounds, or even stealing in and out of Breanna's room. He had to have been in the manor for a substantial period of time. Enough time to see Breanna up close, memorize the details of what she was wearing. He also had to have been at the party to hear news of Anastasia's announcement. It's too soon for outsiders to know about her pregnancy. The party just ended last evening. The package was left on the messenger's doorstep before daybreak. And the killer spent the night rushing from Berkshire to London. So he didn't stop to eavesdrop on street corners."

"Not to mention that he had to have been here if he followed you to Pearson Manor," Breanna added. "How else would he have known you'd located Emma Martin, and that you intended to ride out to see her? You got that message during the ball. Only those present knew about it."

"True."

"So where do we begin looking?" Breanna demanded. "Do we go back to our plan to interrogate the guests?"

"*We* don't do anything," Royce replied pointedly. "Hibbert and I do. We didn't have much of a chance to question anybody before Hart was killed. We'll have to rectify that. Before that, we'll eliminate any other possibilities, however small: workmen who still have access to the grounds, drivers who delivered provisions for the party, even Mahoney's guards. Anyone who could gain entry to the estate."

"You don't really think any of those people is the killer, do you?"

"No. I think the killer is on your guest list." Royce scanned the note. "This was penned by an educated man. It's well-written, polished. I don't know too many workmen with the kind of privileged lives that would afford them a formal education. That, combined with the effortless way he got into your room and onto the grounds to kill Hart, his knowledge of what went on at the party—I'd say it looks more and more likely that the killer was one of the guests. Still, I don't want to overlook anything."

Breanna sank back against the settee, bile rising in her throat. "The very thought of him chatting with my family, laughing with us, eating with us, maybe even dancing with—"

"Breanna, stop." Royce pressed a silencing forefinger to her lips. "There's no point in speculating. It saps strength and wastes time. The important thing is that we find him." He rose, gave the box back to Hibbert. "Find out all you can about the victims," he instructed. "Wells, before Hibbert leaves, give him a list of everyone, from delivery boys to final members of the construction crew, who had access to the grounds this week. Also, tell Mahoney I want to see him. I plan to interview each of his men separately."

Hibbert nodded. "You'll guard Lady Breanna's door tonight, I presume?"

"Oh, yes." Royce's jaw tightened fractionally. "I'll be there. I intend to use those hours to pore over the guest list and do some thinking. Between what you find out for me tomorrow and what I figure out on my own, I intend to come up with some answers."

18

❧

*T*he brothel was posh, significantly more elegant than the dingy one outside Paris where she'd worked as a girl.

Then again, she'd been a child then, grateful for a place to sleep and a few francs in her pocket. She'd have done anything to keep from starving, even work in the Maison Fleur, offering her body to any soldier who could pay for it.

She'd come a long way since those dark days at Maison Fleur, when Napoleon's rise to power was at its peak. She'd clawed her way out of poverty, demonstrated herself to be a shrewd businesswoman. She'd taken a new name, bestowed it upon Le Joyau, the luxurious establishment of which she was now the proud proprietor.

She hadn't expected to see Ansel again.

Their affair had ended long before the war. They came not only from different countries, but from different worlds. It was one thing when he'd been merely a patron. In bed, they'd been equals. He'd paid handsomely for her time; she'd provided the extravagant levels of sexual gratification he craved. But when feelings had intruded, complicating the relationship and transforming it from lust into passion into something even more—something strong enough to compel him to keep her in his life—everything had changed.

Suddenly they were no longer equals. Suddenly, he was demanding that she become an aristocrat's mistress—a role she found far more demeaning than that of whore. Being someone's "kept woman" would strip her of her independence, a condition she couldn't abide. After all, she was as proud and vital as he, his match in every way.

Which was what he found so fascinating about her.

She'd never said good-bye. It would have been too overwhelming. He would have been infuriated. His rages were difficult enough to control, although she knew just how to do so. In her own way, her fires burned as fiercely as his. But he would have misconstrued anything she said, taken it as rejection—and *that* would have pushed him too far. No, it was better to simply drop out of sight, allow him to conjure up whatever excuse his brilliant, arrogant mind chose to.

His finding her again, particularly now, had been a spectacular surprise. Because now her circumstances were different. Now, she could meet him on her own terms. She was financially independent, mistress of her fate, in the prime of life and in extraordinarily high demand.

Not only was their reunion exhilarating, but its timing was *bonne chance.*

Or, if not luck, an unexpected but welcome series of circumstances.

Either way, he was back in her life—a life that was already thriving and now promised to soar.

Draped across the sheets of the lush, oversized bed, Maurelle sighed, stretching her arms overhead and feeling that bone-weary contentment only Ansel could ensure.

Beside her, he exhaled sharply, releasing whatever lingering fragments of tension still plagued him.

"Better?" she murmured, tipping up her chin to study him.

He smiled, a rare gesture that reached up to his enigmatic eyes. "Much. Finally."

She laughed, rubbing her thigh against his. "It did take more vigor than usual to quiet your rage. You've been in my bed for hours."

"And I'll be here hours more." He pulled her over him, his anger transformed once again into that bottomless lust that made their reunions so frenzied and so satisfying.

He drove into her with a violence she found thrilling, and her eyes slid shut, her body tightening as if to meet his violence with her own. He groaned, impaling her again, battering her with the force of his thrusts.

This climax was even more shattering than the last.

Afterward, she leaned up on her elbow, her hair a dark curtain sweeping his chest. "You really are edgy," she murmured, when she was able to catch her breath. "Usually your job drains you. Not so this time. To whom do I owe my good fortune—or need I ask?"

He regarded her from beneath hooded lids. "I won't rest until she's dead. The torture is taking longer than expected. She's acquired a knight. He has to be diverted—or eliminated."

"I see." Maurelle nodded, leaned up to nibble on his chin. "So that explains the rapid delivery of this shipment—and the fact that you came with it?"

"Partly. The rest is simply because I missed you." His good hand reached up, fingers combing her hair off her face. "It's been too long. And I don't intend to let you slip away again."

Maurelle smiled, shifting to bring him more fully inside her. "I'm not going anywhere." Seeing the familiar scowl, she added, "I told you why I left last time, darling. I felt unworthy. Things are different now. I won't be disappearing."

"Soon I'll be here to stay," he told her, the scowl fading as quickly as it had come. "We'll spend the winters where it's warm. And summers we'll spend anywhere you want—Paris, the Far East—anywhere."

She trailed her finger down his chest. "Will I be enough excitement for you, I wonder."

"I could ask you the same."

"Oh, yes, quite enough." A melting smile. "We're well-matched, you and I. In business and in bed." Thoughtfully, she contemplated his promise for the future. "Until the day comes when you're here for good, I'll have to settle for these visits. How long can you stay in Paris this time?"

His hand stilled its motion. "Only a day. I must complete things." A flicker of interest crossed his face. "It should be fascinating to see what Lady Breanna's protector has done during my absence. If he's half as clever as I suspect, he's probably looming over the desk of that Bow Street runner Marks, telling him the killer who shot Glynnis Martin is the same one who's hunting down Breanna Colby."

Maurelle started. "If that's true, won't Bow Street be closer to finding you?"

"Not at all. Linking the two killers tells them nothing. Chadwick has to uncover my flawless plan—and my equally flawless aim. My guess is, he'll figure out the latter—eventually. He won't deduce the former."

"In other words—?"

"In other words, you're quite safe, my love. Chadwick will make the connection between the precise method I used to murder those noblemen and the one I intend to use on Lady Breanna. My gifts alone should have shown him that. As to who I am, why I chose those particular men, and, most particularly, my relationship with you, that he'll never piece together. But, if he should, I'll either have finished my business in England and be here with you permanently, or he'll be silenced, permanently. Either way, raising the stakes has made this a much more exciting chase. Don't you think?"

"It certainly sounds that way." She inclined her head, more curious than worried. She knew Ansel and he was too brilliant to leave any stone unturned—most particularly any stones that might endanger her. "What about Bow Street?"

"Bow Street?" A scornful laugh. "They're less of a threat than Chadwick. By the time they've absorbed all the information his lordship provides, decide what to do with it, you and I will be sailing the world."

"Mmm. That sounds heavenly." She gave him a quizzical look. "Chadwick—is that the name of Lady Breanna's knight?"

"Indeed it is. Lord Royce Chadwick. Eminent locator of missing people." The hard edge had crept back into his voice.

"Really?" Maurelle kept her tone light. "Then I have more than Lady Breanna to thank for your fervor. It seems I have Lord Royce Chadwick to thank, too."

A brooding stare. "Excitement comes with its price, Maurelle. So if you're probing to find out if my earlier rage extended to Chadwick, I'll save you the trouble. The answer is yes. The man might represent a challenge, but he's also an unwelcome intrusion. I look forward to either besting him or killing him—whichever comes first."

Sensing it was time to change the subject, Maurelle settled herself closer. She could still feel the undercurrents of violence rippling through him, and she draped herself over him, cloaking him like a comforting blanket. "Obviously, some of that rage and excitement are still lingering. Give me an hour to regain my strength. Then, I'll burn away the rest."

He didn't answer. He just lay silently beneath her, savoring her softness and continuing to twine his fingers in her hair.

The clock ticked on, and he felt her breathing even into slumber.

It was times like this when he realized just how much he needed her. He rarely let himself ponder that fact. It only served to remind him that she was his weakness—his *only* weakness. But he knew in his gut that's precisely what she was. What's more, she knew it, too.

She was far too smart to betray him.

However, she was also far too smart not to perceive—and to use—her power over him.

And, oh, what power it was.

He'd been vibrating with fury when he arrived in Paris. He'd been that way from the moment he saw Chadwick's carriage leave Medford Manor—without Hibbert in it. Did they take him for a fool? They now knew otherwise. He'd beaten them at their own game.

Winning hadn't helped. He'd still felt that burning emotion churning in his stomach, pounding through his veins. Neither the murder at Pearson Manor nor the kidnapping of Emma Martin and Lady Hart had appeased it. He'd sailed from London immediately and, upon reaching Calais, he'd ridden for Paris like a wildman, his two pieces of cargo in tow.

It was only now, after hours in Maurelle's bed, that he felt the anger recede, the tension seeping from his body like the blood would soon seep from Lady Breanna's.

No one, nothing, did that for him but Maurelle.

He could hardly wait to have her forever.

Idly, he wondered how long it would take Chadwick to figure out the identical methods he'd used to kill all his victims. Probably not long. The bullet wounds were in the exact same spot on each body. One bullet. One clean shot, directly to the heart.

He never needed more than that.

Chadwick would become a permanent fixture at Bow Street, urging them to listen to his theory. They wouldn't, of course, not right away. Breanna Colby's hardships were not their problem, nor was the death of Glynnis Martin who, in their estimation, was nothing more than a servant. Their attention would be focused on investigating Hart's missing wife, tying together the four murders that mattered.

Pleading his case would keep Chadwick busy.

He'd have to stay in London, a substantial distance from Medford Manor.

Leaving only Hibbert to contend with.

The thought brought a tight smile to his lips. The old man didn't stand a chance of stopping him. Neither did that aged butler Wells. The same for Sheldrake. The marquess was a gifted banker, but an inept opponent.

Within the week, Sheldrake's wife and unborn child would be dead.

And then . . . Lady Breanna.

Ah, that reminded him. He had a purchase to make while he was in Paris. Maurelle would do the honors. After which, the gift would accompany him back to England.

Where it would be delivered to Breanna Colby's door.

Something was nagging at Royce.

Sitting outside Breanna's door, he shifted his weight, stretched his legs out in front of him and resettled himself in the chair. Intently, he stared at his journal, poring over the details about the killer he'd listed.

Some of those notes applied to the assassin who'd killed four noblemen. Some applied to the assassin who intended to kill Breanna.

Being that those men were one and the same, there had to be a link.

But what?

He was convinced the killer had been a guest at Breanna's party.

That certainty had come after repeatedly reviewing the names of the workmen and delivery companies that Wells had provided, then speaking with Mahoney and each of the guards—and eliminating them all as suspects.

So the guest list was the key.

Royce scanned it again, wishing some name would jump out at him as the logical choice.

It didn't.

He leaned his head back against the wall, temporarily abandoning his notes to contemplate what he knew about the assassin.

He was educated. He was well-bred, a member of either the gentry or the *ton.*

Which meant that financial status factored heavily into his life. And *that* meant that, if his own financial status were threatened, and he could somehow gain access to all the victims' funds, it might provide a motive for murder.

That avenue, Royce had already explored. Farfetched or not, he'd pursued it throughout a good portion of the evening. He realized the question of access to the victims' funds would have to wait until Hibbert returned with whatever information he uncovered. But, in the interim, Royce had set out to learn who might be experiencing financial trouble.

He hadn't far to go for his answers. No one knew more about the status of people's finances than Damen. Not only was he at the heart of England's banking community, virtually every one of the guests had funds at the House of Lockewood.

Damen had spent two full hours reviewing all the names on the guest list. He'd compared them with his personal sources as well as his banking records.

Not one of the partygoers fit the bill.

Not that Royce was surprised. Instinct told him that greed had little to do with this. This was showmanship in its truest form. A show of power, superiority, and control, coupled with the vindictiveness and rage of a twisted mind.

He knew the type well. He'd dealt with it many times, and could spot it in a heartbeat.

But it had never been this brilliantly concealed.

Which brought him back to his notes.

He leaned over the page, staring at the words he'd jotted down.

A man paid to kill. Yet one who was willing, no *eager,* to kill for reasons other than money, at least in the case of Breanna.

If the assassin's nature was as Royce suspected, it wasn't money that drove him. It was power. Which explained why he'd killed four other victims to taunt Breanna and hone his skills for her demise. But the *particular* victims he'd chosen—now that was another matter.

Why had he selected those specific noblemen? What the hell did they have in common?

Royce's eyes narrowed on the page. He had the distinct feeling he was overlooking something that was staring him right in the face.

Dammit.

He was just about to start poring over the facts anew when Breanna's door opened a crack. "Royce?"

He pivoted in his chair. Breanna hovered in the doorway, looking a trifle uncertain. She was still fully dressed despite the fact that it was nearly 3 A.M.

"I thought you were asleep." Royce frowned, rising to his feet and taking an inadvertent step toward her. "Is something wrong?"

"No, nothing's wrong." She wet her lips with the tip of her tongue, then blurted out, "You told me to ask for help when I need it, not to take on the world alone. I'm having trouble settling down. My mind is racing. I'd like someone to talk to." A dignified pause. "If you don't mind."

He rubbed the back of his neck, reminding himself that this was the second night he hadn't slept, that his reserves and his self-restraint were severely worn. He had long hours of work ahead of him, and being alone with her was a terrible idea, especially in light of the fact that he was still grappling with his raw, unresolved feelings for her.

He was about to say no, to point out all the reasons why he couldn't do as she asked. Then, he met her gaze, saw how much this expression of need had cost her. To turn her away would be like a harsh slap in the face.

To her, and perhaps to himself.

"I don't mind," he replied, gathering up his notes and stepping into the room. "I'm hitting my head against a brick wall right now anyway."

Breanna nodded, smoothing her hair in that proper way she had—a way that belied the astonishing sensuality he knew hovered just beyond reach.

Beyond everyone's reach but his.

He squelched that particular line of thought, determined to give her whatever comfort she sought.

"I built up the fire," she told him, shutting the door and rubbing her arms for warmth. She crossed over, indicating the two armchairs she'd pulled over to the hearth. "Is this all right?"

"Perfect." Royce waited politely until she was seated, then followed suit. "The fire feels wonderful," he murmured, realizing even as he said it that it was true. "Just what I needed."

A flash of guilt flickered across her face. "You're cold and you're exhausted. You haven't slept in days. I feel terrible—and responsible."

"You're not responsible; the killer is. And you've tried sending me away three times already. It's not going to work. I'm not leaving you alone. So let's drop that particular subject."

"Very well." Her back was rigid, her palms pressed tightly together as she stared into the flames.

Clearly, she was distraught, whether or not she chose to admit it.

"Breanna . . ." Royce leaned forward, gently touched her arm. "I'm on the verge of figuring out something important. I'm just not certain what it is—yet. But I will be. Hibbert will be back tomorrow, and between the two of us . . ."

To his surprise, Breanna rose abruptly, shaking her head and waving away his explanation. "That's not it. That's not what I wanted to discuss." She whirled about to face him, her fingers knotting in her gown as she spoke, her chin coming up in a purposeful gesture that seemed to contradict her nervousness.

"The next few days are going to be an emotional nightmare," she proclaimed, her words frank and deliberate. "I don't want to have this discussion then, not when the assassin is closing in and you might misinterpret my feelings to be something less than they are, or worse, to try unduly to protect those feelings *and* me. I want to have this conversation now, when I'm still strong and in control and you realize I mean what I'm saying, and that you also realize I won't fall apart from the conversation's outcome."

She gave Royce no chance to respond.

"Having said that, I have to add I'm a novice at this," she confessed, never averting her gaze, although twin spots of red stained her cheeks. "But then, so are you—not at the physical aspect, since I know you're quite seasoned at that. I'm referring to the emotional aspect. That part's as new to you as it is to me. Well, neither of us has much experience at speaking our hearts. And since one of us has to have the courage to go first, and since your scars are apparently more extensive than mine, I decided that someone should be me."

This time she did pause, but only to draw a slow, unsteady breath. "I'm falling in love with you, Royce. And whether you laugh in my face or bolt from the room, I have to tell you so. What's more, I believe you have feelings for me, too—deeper feelings than you choose to. If I'm right, tell me so. Then, take whatever time you need to decide what you want to do about it. If I'm wrong, or if what you're feeling is simply lust and not love, just say so. I've endured a great deal in my life. I won't shatter. But having lived amid secrets, I know I'd much rather face the truth than cling to a lie. So tell me what you're thinking, and what you're feeling. Not about the assassin. About me."

She broke off, watching his reaction, a flushed but expectant look on her face.

Royce just stared, wondering if he'd ever been rendered so off-balance. This was Breanna, casting aside propriety and self-restraint, not in the throes of passion, but to speak her mind. She was relaying her feelings with all the dignity she possessed and a directness that came with great effort.

His first coherent thought was how incredibly proud of her he was. What she'd just done had taken an amazing measure of courage—a measure of courage he was a stranger to.

Ironic, he was reckless, daring, downright formidable when it came to his enemies. He was also the consummate risk-taker. Yet, when it came down to it, she was far braver than he.

His second thought wasn't a thought at all. It was a surge of feeling so strong it nearly felled him—as did the realization that accompanied it.

She might be falling in love with him, but his fall was already complete.

All that was left was to acknowledge it, to her and to himself.

Slowly, he rose, watching the firelight turn her hair to an auburn blaze as he reached out, framed her face between his palms. "You've given me candor. Let me give you the same in return." His voice sounded hoarse to his own ears. "I thought about you every minute I was away. I told myself I wouldn't hurt you, that if I couldn't be everything you needed, I'd walk away. But I won't. I can't. Because, whether or not I believed myself capable, whether I can give you every fragment of emotion you deserve, whether it happened so fast I never saw it coming, I love you. I love you in a way I never imagined, much less experienced." His thumbs caressed her cheeks. "Does that answer your question?"

"One of them, yes." Breanna gave a shaky nod. "The next question is harder. What do you want to do about it?"

"What do I want to do about it?" Royce's reply emerged with a will all its own, having formed somewhere inside him that required no conscious awareness. Yet even as he spoke the words, he knew they were true. "I want to protect your life with my own. I want to immerse myself in your beauty every moment for the rest of our days. I want to drag you off to the nearest church and make you my wife."

Two tears slid down Breanna's cheeks. "I didn't expect . . ." She brought herself under control. "I didn't expect an answer. Not right away. I told you to think about it."

"I don't need to. My answer won't change." He captured her tears with his thumbs. "Don't cry. Just consider my proposal. I know I'm not the staid, conventional man you expected to marry. But—"

"I don't need to consider it. I accept." Breanna stood on tiptoe, brushed his lips with hers. "I love you. I want nothing more than to marry you. As for the last . . ." Her eyes sparkled through her tears. "Since I met you I discovered something about myself. I loathe convention. It bores me to death."

"Does it?" Royce was still reeling with the impact of what had happened, all he'd just discovered about himself. Feeling almost giddy, he caressed Breanna's nape, continuing to let his impulses guide him. "May

I test that claim in a way I've wanted to since the first instant I laid eyes on you?"

"By all means."

His fingers glided into her hair, caressing the satiny crown before—in slow, exacting motions—he began tugging out the pins, tossing them randomly about until her auburn tresses tumbled free.

He threaded his fingers through them, draping them around her, then capturing her shoulders, pulling her to him. "Beautiful," he murmured. "Now come here."

She stepped closer, and his arms encircled her, brought her up against him. "No one's ever seen your hair this way—free, uninhibited—have they?"

Breanna's breathing was unsteady. "No. Not my hair, and not me."

"Good." He lowered his head, covered her mouth with his.

The kiss was slow and hot and deep, and Breanna's soft sound of pleasure vibrated through them both. Royce gathered her more closely to him, savored her taste, the softness of her lips, the exquisite feel of her tongue as he possessed it with his own. She leaned into him, molding the contours of her body to his, wrapping her arms around his neck and wordlessly showing him how much she loved him.

Royce responded with a hard tremor, lifting her up and into him until there was nothing separating them but the impeding layers of their clothing.

The kiss went on and on, ending only to begin anew, generating fiery currents that flowed between them, intensified more and more with each passing second.

It was Breanna who eased away, leaning back a fraction, and staring up at him with jade eyes that were smoky with passion. "Royce?" His name was a wisp of sensation against his lips.

"Mmm?" He could barely speak.

"I really wanted to give you time to think about our future."

"I know. I didn't need it."

"That's not what I'm getting at." Her fingers trailed across his jaw, drifted down the side of his neck. "When I asked what you wanted to do about the fact that you love me, I meant it in the more immediate sense." A suggestive pause. "As in, what do you want to do about your feelings *now?*" Her lips traced the path her fingers had taken, feathering kisses along his heated skin. "Right now."

Royce's eyes slid shut, her vivid invitation making hot need explode in his loins. "Breanna . . ." His fingers tangled in her hair, intending to move her away from him but never quite doing so. "I promised myself I wouldn't—"

"Break that promise," she whispered.

All Royce's good intentions crumpled. "You want to know what I want to do about my feelings?" he rasped, his palm moving down to cup her breast, his thumb teasing her already hardened nipple. "I want to lay you down by the fire and bury myself inside you."

She shivered, stifling a cry as she shifted herself more fully into his hand. "Follow your instincts. They've always served you well." Blindly, she pushed open his coat, slid her palms up the front of his waistcoat.

"Breanna—"

"Don't be noble, not this time." She unfastened his buttons one by one—first his waistcoat, then his shirt. "It took all my courage to bare my heart to you. Please don't shield yours from me now." She slipped her fingers inside his shirt, caressed him tentatively. "Protect me when I need it. Not when I don't."

He felt her delicate touch on his skin, and the last of his resolve disintegrated into dust. "Sweetheart . . ." He forced out the words, determined to say them before it was too late. "This time I won't be able to stop."

Her smile was tremulous. "I'm glad."

"Are you?" It was a lost cause, and he knew it. He was already reaching around to dispense with the buttons of her gown, frantic to have her in his arms, under his body. "First, we should be talking about the future. What you need, what you deserve."

"We'll do that later. What I need now is you."

Something inside Royce snapped.

He swept Breanna up into his arms, placed her on the rug in front of the fire, and followed her down. His mouth devoured hers, leaving it only to blaze kisses down her throat and neck to the top of her bodice. His fingers finished their task, and he tugged down her gown, his mouth continuing its journey even as his fingers shifted to the ribbons of her chemise.

His lips surrounded her nipple, and he tugged at it, first through the barrier of her chemise and then beneath it. He lost himself in her flavor, his tongue lashing across one hardened peak and then the other, and he reveled in her cries of pleasure, the uninhibited motions of her body.

His hands were shaking as he dragged away her clothing, tearing the delicate material in his frantic haste to have her naked.

When he finished his task, he sat back on his heels and stared.

She was breathtaking, more beautiful than even his fantasies had evoked. There were no words profound enough to express his feelings, so he settled for making love to her with his eyes, drinking in the glow of her skin by firelight, the perfect curves and hollows that she'd offered only to him.

God, he was blessed.

"Royce?" She reached for him, not with uncertainty, but with eagerness. "Please—"

"Have you any idea how beautiful you are?" he choked out, letting his hands explore her, stroking upwards from her legs to her hips, then higher to cup her breasts, whispering over the tender points of her nipples. "Any idea?" He absorbed her quivering sigh, his hands retracing their journey, this time pausing to caress her thighs, to part them to his touch. "You humble me." He brushed the auburn cloud that beckoned him, first lightly, then more intimately, his fingers opening her, gliding inside to explore the velvety folds.

She was so perfect, Royce thought he'd die from it. He repeated the caress, and Breanna cried out, arching against his hand, her entire body responding to the new, unbearably erotic sensation.

Royce's fingers slid deeper, pushing into her gradually, his entire body pulsing with a need so acute, he actually wondered if he might spill himself before ever getting his breeches off.

Breanna provided that answer.

When she inadvertently tightened around him, warm and wet, tiny tremors shimmering through her, he regained control—only to feel it slipping away again.

Shoving himself to his feet, he tore off his clothes, scarcely giving her time to breathe before he covered her body with his. He moved against her, torturing himself with the motion, then kissing her fiercely as he repeated it.

Breanna undulated beneath him, rubbing her breasts against his chest, urging her lower body up to his, and wrapping her arms around his back.

"Don't." He shuddered. "God, Breanna, don't."

"Why?" she whispered breathlessly. "It feels so good."

He tore his mouth away, stared down at her through a red haze of passion. "Because I want you too much. I'm not going to be able to hold back." Another shudder. "I already can't hold back."

"I don't want you to." She caressed his spine, traced the taut muscles of his back. "Please, no holding back."

"I'll hurt you."

"No you won't." She arched restlessly beneath him. "Tell me what to do."

"Just . . . yes . . . ," he grated out, as her thighs parted beneath him. He nudged them farther apart, settling himself in the cradle between them, his rigid shaft finding the heated entrance to her body.

"Like this?" she whispered, raising her knees to hug his flanks.

"God . . . yes." He was already crowding into her, his hips moving reflexively, blatantly ignoring the dictates of his mind, which warned him how small she was, how delicate and tight. As if to further test him,

Breanna melted around him, hot and clinging, stretching to take him deeper, her soft moans of pleasure obliterating any hope his mind had of regaining control. "Sweetheart . . ."

"Make love to me," she breathed, her hands gliding down to the base of his spine, as if that motion alone would be enough.

It was.

Cupping her bottom, Royce pushed into her, reached the barrier of her innocence, then thrust beyond it. He sank into her, sweat drenching his body as he buried himself inside her the way he'd burned to do from the start.

Breanna tensed, instinctively biting back her cry of pain—which gave Royce the strength he needed to wait.

"Don't," he said fiercely, raising his head to look deeply into her eyes. "Don't hide what you're feeling—not your pleasure or your pain. No holding back." Deliberately, he repeated the same phrase she'd spoken to him.

Slowly, she nodded, her body relaxing even as she did. "It doesn't hurt anymore," she murmured, wonder in her eyes. "It feels so . . . oh . . ." She cried out, this time with pleasure, as Royce drew back slightly, then pressed forward, sinking deeply into her.

"So incredible?" he finished for her.

"Yes. Incredible." She urged his mouth back to hers. "Don't stop."

"I couldn't if my life depended on it." He kissed her hungrily, beginning an exquisite motion of plunge and retreat that made the world spin away in a torrent of sensation.

Instinctively, Breanna understood the rhythm, and her hips lifted, undulating to meet each one of his quickening downward strokes.

A roaring commenced in Royce's head, a passion he'd never known mingling with a love he'd never imagined, his every nerve ending attuned to Breanna, and to the engulfing culmination that hovered just beyond their reach.

"Royce . . ." She was frantic now, her inner muscles taut, slick with need, her nails scoring his back as she struggled for that elusive peak she couldn't yet fathom but was desperate to capture.

Beyond conscious thought, Royce simply reacted, hooking his elbows beneath her knees and pulling her legs up higher around him, opening her fully to his possession.

He penetrated her with one deep, inexorable stroke, then another—this time caressing her inside and out, only to do it again and again and again.

Breanna plunged over the edge.

She arched wildly, a dazed, stunned look widening her eyes as she reached the pinnacle of sensation, and fell.

Royce covered her mouth with his, swallowing her sharp cry of pleasure and shuddering as her hard spasms gripped him, spiraling out from deep inside her—quickening in pace, intensifying in strength—clenching his engorged shaft until he could take no more.

He climaxed violently, his own release slamming through him with the force of a blow. Biting back a shout, he gave in to the wildness, his hips moving convulsively as he poured himself into her, each burst of completion more powerful than the last.

The moment seemed to go on forever, tiny aftershocks of Breanna's climax rippling over him, triggering yet another burst of wetness as the last of his seed emptied into her.

Then . . . peace.

Royce collapsed on top of her, his head dropping into the crook of her neck, his body blanketing hers. The room was silent, but for the crackling of the fire and the harsh, rasping sounds of their breaths.

Sanity returned in increments and, slowly, Royce became aware of his surroundings. Beneath him, Breanna sighed, her legs unclenching and sliding down to sink into the rug, her arms going lax around him. Her breathing was still ragged and, abruptly, he realized she was trembling.

"Breanna?" He tried, unsuccessfully, to lift his head, and settled for murmuring in her ear instead. "Sweetheart?"

"Mmm," was the muffled reply.

"You're shaking."

"And you're astonishing."

He smiled at the dreamy quality to her voice. "That compliment belongs to you. I think I'm half-dead."

"No, you're not." Her fingers trailed lightly down his back. "I can vouch for that."

He kissed her neck. "Am I crushing you?"

"Only in the most wonderful way."

Forcing himself to move, Royce rolled to one side, taking Breanna with him and keeping their bodies tightly joined. Then, he groped around until he found the blanket he'd seen lying near the armchair, pulling it over them until they were securely covered. "How's that?"

"Ummm," she responded, snuggling closer and rubbing her thigh over his with that innate sensuality he found so unbearably arousing. "That's perfect."

He cupped her face between his palms, studied her intently. "Does it hurt?"

She shook her head, sending masses of her newly freed hair tumbling about. "Not even a bit. It feels," she wriggled slightly, taking him deeper into her, "more right than I can say."

Royce felt his body leap in response—an astounding fact considering that minutes ago he thought himself incapable of moving, much less making love.

More astounding was the emotion that accompanied it.

"Breanna," he said, determination lacing his words. "I meant what I said earlier. We need to talk. To make plans. The minute I eliminate that bastard who's after you, I'm dragging you off and putting a wedding ring on your hand."

She traced his lips with her fingertips. "You'll get no argument from me." A pause. "Although *I* really meant it when I said I didn't expect you to decide our future right away. Love is one thing, marriage quite another. You're a very independent man, Royce. I don't want you to feel as if you're sacrificing that independence."

"If you're telling me not to need you, don't bother. It's too late." Royce kissed her fingertips. "I don't feel less independent. I feel lucky." A heartbeat of a pause. "And I want to give you everything you deserve."

"Including a depth of emotion you're still not sure you're capable of," she replied astutely. "Well, you might not be sure, but I am. And I happen to be a very wise woman."

Royce chuckled, tangling his hands in her glorious auburn hair and kissing her tenderly. "Yes, you are."

She wrapped her arms about his neck. "I love you," she whispered.

Royce's eyes darkened with emotion. "I didn't realize what I was missing. Now I do." His palm slid around to caress her nape. "You're the most beautiful, courageous—"

"Surprising?" Breanna added with a shaky laugh. "I've never been so forward in all my life. I still can't believe I just seduced you."

One dark brow rose. "Is that what happened? Funny, I recall it being very mutual."

"But I initiated it. I think there was a part of me that knew it would happen the minute I stepped into the hallway." She gave a dazed shake of her head. "My heart was pounding when I walked out there. Because I was determined to tell you that I love you. I'm sure you've guessed I'm rarely so audacious. In fact, I can only think of one other time I shocked myself as thoroughly as I did tonight."

"When was that?"

"When I held my father at gunpoint."

Royce propped himself on one elbow, feeling more intrigued than stunned. "Was that when he was going after Anastasia?"

A nod. "He planned on selling her. He meant to ship her off to some animal named Rouge, who sold women as prostitutes. And he was going to beat me until I told him her whereabouts. I couldn't allow any of that. Something inside me just snapped." She inclined her head, gazing thoughtfully up at Royce. "I often relive that moment. And I wonder what I would have done if he'd disregarded my threats and continued advancing toward me. Would I have pulled the trigger? I honestly don't think I could have—not then. Maybe because he's my father, and maybe because I hadn't yet actually heard him hire an assassin to do away with Stacie. If I already had, or if I'd seen Father either hurt Stacie or shove her onto that ship bound for Calais, my anger might have won out over my reticence. I don't know."

She inhaled shakily. "But with the assassin, it's different. He's a cold-blooded killer who's made it flagrantly clear he intends to murder Stacie and her unborn child. In his case . . . Royce, I think I could shoot to kill."

In response, Royce's jaw clenched. "I know you could," he replied, that fierce mixture of pride and protectiveness welling up inside him. "But you wouldn't be able to do it fast enough. I'd beat you to it. Because I'm the one who's going to kill that bastard."

A tiny shiver went through Breanna, as if some premonition told her that's precisely how it would happen.

Blindly, as if to ward off the ugliness of their discussion, she reached up, twined her arms around Royce's neck. "No more." She tugged his mouth down to hers, obliterating all talk of the assassin by rekindling the beauty they'd just shared. "No more talk about him tonight." She pressed closer, shifting her hips ever so slightly, drawing Royce into her melting warmth. "Tonight is ours," she whispered. "I want nothing else to intrude."

Royce responded with an overwhelming urgency, his body hardening to rigid fullness, swelling to fill hers. "It won't," he murmured, rolling her to her back, pressing deep inside her. "Not tonight. Not ever."

19

❧

"You're saying there's no connection among the victims, at least not financially," Royce stated, taking a healthy swallow of brandy and leaning against the sitting-room mantel, regarding Hibbert, who'd just returned from his investigative excursion.

"None." Hibbert settled himself in a chair, and glanced through his notes. "Except that they all lived in London and were all affluent."

"What about their wills?"

"Four separate solicitors drew them up. I spoke with all of them. They had nothing substantial to offer in the way of information. As for the beneficiaries, none were common among the victims. Each of the wives stood to inherit first. But, in the event the wives died before they did, each gentleman made different provisions. In two of the cases, the estates were bequeathed to grown daughters by a previous marriage, in one case to a grown nephew. In the case of Lord Hart, it was left to a son he'd sired with one of his mistresses."

Royce frowned. "Nothing to the children they shared with their current wives?"

"There were no children with their current wives. That was the only other link I found among the four noblemen. Their wives were significantly younger than they, and had been married a relatively short period of time—three years or less. My guess is that's what led Bow Street to suspect the women were involved. They had huge fortunes to gain and long years in which to enjoy them."

"Have any of the beneficiaries pressed to collect their money?"

"No." Hibbert shook his head. "They're all wealthy in their own right, other than Hart's illegitimate son, who ran off years ago and took to the sea. The other three are waiting patiently. They're more interested in finding out who killed the victims and kidnapped their wives than in claiming an inheritance."

His frown deepening, Royce stared off into space. "So the men all had young wives—wives who disappeared, taken by a kidnapper who's made no attempt to get at their husbands' money." He took another swallow of brandy. "Which brings us to the question, if the killer isn't holding these women for ransom, what did he do with them? Murder them? If so, why haven't the bodies turned up? If not, what would he want with them?"

Abruptly, Royce broke off, his own words finding their mark.

Realization struck hard, and the missing piece fell into place.

"Dammit," Royce bit out, slamming his goblet to the sideboard. "It's been right in front of me all this time and I never saw it." He turned, his hard stare finding Hibbert. "We've been assuming the men were his intended victims. They weren't. They were merely sport—as I said, a sick game of target practice to ready him for Breanna. It's their wives who were his true marks. *They* were the ones he wanted. And, as you discovered, they're the ones with something in common—their youth, their childless state."

Hibbert gave him a puzzled look. "You've lost me."

"Something Breanna said last night just sank in." Royce began prowling about, his forehead creased in thought as he polished his theory. "Or rather, two things she said in the same breath. She referred to overhearing her father arrange for the assassin to kill Anastasia, and she referred to having to bear the knowledge that he intended to sell her cousin as a prostitute."

"We knew both those facts."

"Yes, but we didn't look for the common link between them. We never directly tied the assassin to Medford's selling of women. But there is a tie, a strong one—Cunnings."

Hibbert's head came up, his eyes narrowed as he caught his employer's implication. "It was Cunnings who Medford paid to hire the assassin. So we know Cunnings and the killer were well-acquainted. We also know that Cunnings was aware of Medford's business of selling women. Which means he could very well have mentioned that fact to his colleague."

"Cunnings was more than *aware* of what Medford was doing," Royce corrected. "From what I remember of the Bow Street report, he was right in the thick of things. While he went about hiring the assassin, he was also trying to provide a substitute for Anastasia—another nobly-bred young woman to send to Paris. That way, Anastasia would be eliminated, and George Colby would still get paid by his French buyer. Cunnings knew he'd be handsomely rewarded for managing both."

"A fact he could have boasted to the killer," Hibbert murmured.

"Right. After all, he was taking on a daunting task. Highborn ladies don't vanish as easily as workhouse women do. They're missed—*if* there's someone alive to miss them."

"You think the assassin picked up where my father left off?"

Both men started, jerking about to see Breanna standing in the doorway, her face drawn, her eyes filled with pain. "You think he sold those four women?"

"I think it's a strong possibility." Royce walked over, took her hands in his.

"But why? We've determined he doesn't need the money . . . Don't answer that," she amended, with a shiver of disgust. "The challenge. Winning. God, this is sickening."

"But it makes sense," Hibbert said quietly, glancing at his notes. "As you pointed out, none of the wives had yet borne children—which probably means they were fresher, more youthful-looking, and therefore more desirable to whomever purchased them. None of them had relatives, other than parents who lived far away and represented no threat to the assailant."

"All but Emma Martin." Royce raked a hand through his hair, another glimmer of insight taking shape. "That miserable bastard not only bested me by killing Glynnis and stealing her daughter, he furthered his own sick scheme in the process."

"Emma must have been among his latest shipment." Hibbert nodded. "I agree. Which brings to mind another fact. All the women lived in London, which made them easily transportable to the Continent. All except Emma. My guess is she was dragged there by the killer, who then sent her off along with Lady Hart."

"Sent off to whom?" Breanna asked. "Has that Rouge person my father dealt with resurfaced? Or is there someone else buying these women?"

"I don't know. But since Emma and Lady Hart were kidnapped two days ago, the shipment that included them had to have left between then and now. We'd better act fast." Royce was already in motion, crossing the threshold into the hallway. "Wells," he called, summoning the butler. "Where's Damen?"

"He's upstairs with Miss Stacie," Wells reported. "I didn't alert them to the fact that Hibbert had returned. It's after eleven o'clock and Miss Stacie is exhausted. I assumed we could disturb them if it became necessary."

"It just became necessary," Royce informed him. "Get Damen. Tell him to come down here, and to bring every bit of information he accumulated on that M. Rouge who was buying Medford's cargo."

Wells blinked. "Is Rouge the killer?"

"No. But he might know him." Royce turned back to Hibbert. "One of us has to ride to London. I want to check the manifest of every ship that has sailed in the past few days. Perhaps something will strike us as suspicious. Or maybe someone at the docks will even remember Emma Martin or Lady Hart, if we describe them."

"Pardon me, Lord Royce, but I have a suggestion." Wells had paused on his way to the stairs. "Neither you nor Hibbert has slept in days. What's more, the docks will be practically deserted until daybreak, with no one either knowledgeable enough or sober enough to talk to. My advice is to go to bed directly after your meeting with Lord Sheldrake. That applies to Hibbert, as well. I'll stand guard outside Lady Breanna's room tonight. After a decent night's rest, you can ride to London."

"Thank you, Wells, but I . . ." Royce broke off, realizing how absurd it would sound for him to say he trusted no one other than himself when it came to Breanna's safety.

A look of gentle understanding touched Wells's features. "I've protected her for twenty-one years, sir. I'm certain I can continue to do so— during those rare times when I'm needed."

"You'll always be needed, Wells," Breanna said softly. She gazed reassuringly at Royce. "I'm in excellent hands. Do as Wells suggested and get some rest."

Royce nodded. "All right—*after* I've spoken with Damen."

"I'll get him at once." Wells hurried up the stairs.

"Breanna," Royce said, turning his attention back to her. "I know Bow Street questioned your father thoroughly when they brought him in. Did he tell them anything specific about this French contact of his, this Rouge?"

"No." Breanna shook her head adamantly. "Just as Father never met the assassin, he never met Rouge. Their only contact was by post. Rouge was very careful to keep it that way. Evidently, he's the one who originally sought my father out, not the other way around. The way Father described it, Rouge sent him a letter, said he had a proposition he thought could benefit them both. He was aware of my father's financial woes. He was also aware of the fact that my father would go to any lengths to resolve those woes. Father responded at once, and their alliance began."

"You're sure your father was telling the truth, that he wasn't concealing anything?"

Breanna sighed. "My father is a coward, Royce. If there were any chance of lessening his own punishment by blaming someone else, he would jump at the opportunity. So, yes, I'm sure he was telling the truth."

"Then there's no point in my wasting time at Newgate. As for

Rouge's knowledge of your father's desperation and lack of ethics, he could have picked that up anywhere—at a club, a tavern, right here in England, or in Paris from a chatty English visitor. There were certainly enough people who knew Medford's ways." Royce pursed his lips, thinking. "Let me hear what Damen knows. Then, I'll get some of my less reputable contacts involved."

"Less reputable contacts—you mean, criminals?"

Breanna sounded more intrigued than shocked, reminding Royce yet again that she was far stronger than her delicacy suggested.

A corner of his mouth lifted. "Yes, but not hardened killers. Just seedy types who have more wits and brains than scruples. They get me information, I pay them well."

"Snitches, you mean."

"Yes."

"That makes sense. After all, finding unscrupulous people is what you do."

"Indeed it is. And one thing I've learned is that there's no one better equipped at ferreting out a criminal than another criminal."

"Which is certainly what we're dealing with here," Breanna replied bitterly. "Whether it's Rouge or someone else, we're dealing with an animal, someone who buys women."

At that moment, Damen strode down the stairs, his mouth drawn in a grim line. In his hand was a letter.

"Wells stayed upstairs," he announced. "I want him guarding our bedroom door. Normally, Stacie would have beaten me down the stairs to take part in this conversation. But she's asleep—the first real rest she's gotten in days. She never heard Wells knock, and she didn't budge when I left the room. I've never seen her sleep so deeply. Frankly, I'm worried sick about her."

"She's under a lot of strain, Damen," Breanna said, trying to soothe him—and herself. "This pregnancy was difficult to begin with. And now, fearing for her babe, her strength is depleted. As soon as we stop this assassin . . . as soon as we . . ." Her voice quavered, and she broke off, averting her gaze.

"Breanna, I'm sorry," Damen responded at once. "This has been hell for you. I didn't mean to be insensitive."

"You weren't." Swiftly, Breanna composed herself. "I'm as worried about Stacie as you are. But I truly believe Royce will catch this monster."

"I intend to. Is that all the material you have on Rouge?" Royce interrupted, pointing to the letter Damen held.

"Yes." Damen handed the correspondence to Royce. "It's an explanation from Dornier, the manager of my Paris branch. As you know, Rouge and Medford used the House of Lockewood—both the London and Paris branches—as hubs through which to send messages. Cunnings was their intermediary. When I attempted to check out Rouge, I contacted Dornier for my initial answers. That's his reply you're holding. Go ahead and read it."

He waited while Royce complied.

"According to Dornier, Rouge himself never made an appearance at the bank," Royce muttered as he skimmed the letter. "Everything was forwarded to an address in Paris . . . 4 Rue La Fayette. Rouge was never seen by anyone—not even the messenger, who was instructed to slide the letters under the door and leave."

"Exactly. That's as far as my investigation got. I advised Dornier to hire someone to follow the messenger the next time he arrived for Rouge's mail. But next time never occurred. Medford was caught, and Rouge simply dropped out of sight."

"Seemingly."

Damen's brows drew together. "Seemingly? Does that mean you suspect he's still involved in all this?"

"Someone is." Swiftly, Royce recounted his latest suspicions to Damen, explaining what he'd pieced together about the assassin and his overseas dealings.

"But we have no idea if the person receiving these women is Rouge," Damen noted when he'd finished. "Or even if he's receiving them in France."

"No, we don't." Royce rubbed his chin thoughtfully, altering the subject slightly. "Let's talk about the night Cunnings was killed. Do you recall what Bow Street found on his desk when they discovered his body?"

"Of course. Stacks of files detailing our bank's clients—including their personal histories. That came as no surprise. He was looking for a substitute to send Rouge in place of my wife."

"Now let's talk about what Bow Street *didn't* find. Isn't it likely that Cunnings was making notes on what he read in those files? That he was jotting down enough pertinent details to allow him to make the proper selection?"

Damen exhaled sharply. "You think the assassin took those notes when he killed him?"

"If Cunnings had boasted about how difficult his challenge was, how certain he was that he could master it by finding the ideal candidate for Rouge? Absolutely."

"Let's assume you're right. In that case, the assassin either has a different buyer or he and Rouge are contacting each other directly. Because John Cunnings is dead, and no one else in my bank is a criminal."

"I agree." Royce turned to Hibbert. "Get the right men out there to dig up what we need. I want details on anyone even remotely suspected of buying or selling women."

Hibbert nodded. "Should they focus primarily on England and France?"

"My instincts say yes. In any case, no farther than the Continent. The assassin would want immediate results. His nature wouldn't permit him to wait months while his cargo sailed to the Far East or to India. But give me until morning. Once I visit the docks, I'll know exactly where we should focus our efforts. Someone's going to tell me what ships sailed and where they went these past two days. Then, I'm going to pore over those manifests. And with any luck, I'll find something that will help narrow down our search."

Royce left at daybreak.

Breanna heard him go, and she wanted more than anything to rush into the hall and see him off. But Wells was at his post outside her door, and he wouldn't think too kindly of a public display. Especially since he didn't even know of her wedding plans.

So she settled for listening to Royce's deep baritone, quietly conferring with Wells, thanking him for watching over Breanna and assuring him he'd return as soon as he could.

The morning hours were intolerable.

Not only was the knot of tension in her stomach coiling tighter with each passing moment—almost as if she sensed the assassin was closing in—but Breanna felt as if she would burst if she didn't share her secret with Stacie.

She was pacing in the hallway when her cousin wandered downstairs for breakfast, and Breanna pounced on her, dragged her into the sitting room.

"Breanna, what is it?" Stacie demanded, blinking at her cousin's uncharacteristic impatience. "Has something happened? Damen told me what Royce figured out last night. He also said Royce was riding to the docks first thing today. Have you heard from him?"

"Not yet. He's still in London." Breanna shut the door, leaned back against it. "Stacie—"

"I can't believe I slept through all the excitement. I suppose I just—"

"Stacie!" Breanna broke in, unable to wait another instant. "There's something I want to tell you. Something that has nothing to do with the assassin. But I'm going to explode if I wait any longer."

Stacie's entire demeanor changed, and a spark of anticipation lit her eyes. "This is about Royce."

"Yes." Breanna watched her cousin's expression. "I told him I love him." A pause. "Are you shocked? Because, if so, here's something even more shocking. He loves me, too."

Joy erupted on Stacie's face, and she rushed over, hugged her cousin fiercely. "Shocked? Why would I be shocked? I knew it! I knew it the first time I saw you two together."

"I appreciate your faith," Breanna laughed. "Did you happen to hear what I said about who initiated these declarations? *I* did. I called Royce into my bedchamber and announced that I love him."

Stacie drew back, approval shining in her eyes. "Good for you. If you're waiting for me to be astounded, don't. I know all about that inner resolve of yours. You're as strong and determined as I am. It was only a matter of finding the right man to bring out those qualities."

Breanna smiled. "I've found him. And, Stacie, he's asked me to marry him."

"You said yes, of course."

"I did." Breanna lowered her voice to a conspiratorial whisper. "And then I seduced him."

This time Stacie's jaw dropped. Recovering herself, she began to laugh. "Now I *am* impressed. Although having seen the way Royce looks at you, I doubt you had to work very hard."

"True enough." A becoming flush stained Breanna's cheeks. "Stacie, I know how frightening everything in our lives seems right now, how terrified we are for the future of your babe. I have no right to feel these bouts of joy—but I do. In fact, I cling to them. It's as if they're all I have to keep from going mad."

"Listen to me." Stacie gripped her cousin's hands tightly. "Don't you dare apologize for the joy you feel. Being in love with Damen was the only thing that kept me sane when your father was hunting me down. Happiness is something to seize, to revel in. And that's precisely what we're going to do. You and I are going to use these endless hours of confinement to plan your wedding. Just think how elated Grandfather would be."

"You're right. He would." Breanna swallowed past the lump in her throat. "You'll be my bridal attendant, of course."

"Naturally." Stacie grinned. "And I promise not to carry a chamber pot down the aisle with me."

They'd just started making plans when the sitting-room door nearly burst from its hinges, and Damen and Wells exploded into the room.

"Hibbert was right. They're in here," Wells said, sagging with relief.

"Why did you leave the room without me?" Damen demanded, glaring at his wife. "I thought you were still abed."

Stacie sighed. "Damen, you finally fell asleep. It was half after nine. I couldn't bear to awaken you. So I came downstairs for some breakfast."

She exchanged glances with Breanna, and grinned. "Which I still haven't eaten, by the way."

Now Wells looked totally stricken. "You haven't? I'll bring you something at once."

"Wells, wait." Breanna rose, going over to him and laying her hand gently on his forearm. "Forgive me for detaining Stacie. But I had a very good reason." She paused, searching for the right words. "You and I have a very special bond, my dear friend. You've protected me from my father my whole life, even those years when Stacie was in America. You've been my friend, my rescuer, and, in all ways that matter, my family. So I have a request to make. Actually two requests. Royce has asked me to marry him. It would mean a great deal to me if you'd give us your blessing. Also, I'd be honored if you'd walk me down the aisle, give me away to the man I love."

Moisture actually glinted in Wells's eyes, and he swallowed twice before replying. "I'm not surprised by the announcement. But I am overwhelmed by the requests." He covered her hand with his. "Lord Royce is a fine man. He loves you deeply. Your grandfather would be overjoyed. And so am I. So, yes, you have my blessing. And just as I stood in for your grandfather once, gave Miss Stacie to Lord Sheldrake, I'd be elated to do the same for you and Lord Royce."

"Thank you." Breanna rose up on tiptoe, kissed Wells's cheek, then turned to accept Damen's congratulatory hug. "Now," she informed the two men, "you may feed my poor starving cousin."

They all laughed, and the very sound of it felt wonderful after the strain of the past few weeks.

It also made them crave normalcy even more.

Normalcy was not yet to be.

They were all enjoying their late breakfast when Hibbert walked into the dining room, a sober expression on his face.

"Hibbert, what is it?" Breanna was on her feet. "Is it Royce?"

"No, my lady. He has yet to return from London." Hibbert flourished a small box. "This was just delivered to the front gates. Mahoney brought it up."

"Oh, no."

"Actually, I'm not surprised to see it. I'm more surprised it's taken so long to arrive. Considering the killer's desire to intensify your terror, I would have thought he'd be increasing the frequency of his reminders by now." Hibbert paused, giving Breanna a measured look. "Do you want to open it, or shall I?"

"I'll do it." Breanna walked over, saw the familiar penning of her name on the box. This parcel was smaller than the last, about the size of one of her porcelain figures.

Taking a few deep, calming breaths, she tore it open.

Inside was a bottle of perfume—a pear-shaped bottle, its glass facets carved atop a gilded mount, its design intricate.

Its color blood red.

The note lay beneath it.

Death's sweet scent is upon you, Lady Breanna. Retreat is impossible. So is rescue. Tell your warrior his efforts are in vain. Urge him to give up the battle or his blood will spill, too. Either way, you and Lady Anastasia are doomed. Your walls cannot protect you any longer. I've toyed with you, let you believe you were safe. That's over. Precious hours remain until I strike. Your blood is my vengeance.

20

*B*reanna pressed her lips together to still their trembling. "This note not only threatens me and Stacie, it threatens Royce, as well."

"Good," Hibbert stated with some satisfaction. "That means Lord Royce has unnerved him."

She started. "Is that what it means?"

"Of course." Despite his show of nonchalance, Hibbert was rereading the note, clearly bothered by its contents.

Before Breanna could question him further, he'd turned his attention to the bottle. Pensively, he studied it, then opened its elegant gilded stopper to waft the fragrance under his nose. "An interesting scent. Jasmine and rose, I should say. Which probably means it was produced in Grasse. And the glass bottle—Louis XIV–style—definitely French."

Breanna stared. "How do you know so much about perfume?"

Hibbert gave her one of his hints of a smile. "About five years ago, Lord Royce had a client who was an apothecary. The gentleman had invented a promising recipe for a new fragrance. Before he could produce and sell it, a competitor of his stole it and ran off. The thief changed his name and was halfway through Italy before we caught up with him. In the interim, we had no way of knowing whether or not he'd already reproduced the fragrance and was selling it. As it turned out, he wasn't. He was looking for an isolated spot where he'd never be found before starting his business.

"To get to the point, our client gave Lord Royce and me quite an education before he sent us off. We learned what type of bottles were manufactured where, what ingredients originated in individual provinces, even the names of specific jewelers in France, Germany, and Austria who were famous for setting precious stones on the more ornate bottles." Hibbert ended his explanation, glancing back at the bottle in his hands. "The gilding here is sophisticated, as is the design of the base. I'll wait for Lord Royce to confirm it, but I'm fairly certain this bottle was crafted by one of three jewelers in Paris."

"So we know the killer favors French perfume," Damen stated flatly.

"The question is, does he also favor working with French business associates?"

"Are you implying the perfume was some kind of payment from his contact?" Breanna demanded.

"More like some kind of purchase." Hibbert returned the bottle to its box. "I doubt whoever bought those women would take the time to forward a bottle of perfume as a token of thanks. And if he did, he'd send gentleman's cologne, not women's perfume." A thoughtful pause. "After Lord Royce returns, I think I'll take a quick jaunt down to Dover. I want to see if I can find out anything about the passengers who arrived from Calais this morning. Dover is a quieter port than London—far too risky to use when one is shipping questionable cargo but ideal if one is crossing the Channel, on a return trip to England alone."

Breanna drew a slow breath. "You think the killer actually went to Paris and bought the perfume himself?"

"It would certainly explain why we haven't heard from him these past few days. Perhaps he arranged a business meeting with his associate. He could have traveled from London with his cargo, delivered it in person, met with his contact, bought the perfume, then left Calais and sailed for Dover."

"And now he's back. Ready to carry out the final stages of his plan."

"In his mind, yes."

"He's implying he can get to Stacie and Breanna whether they're inside the manor or not," Damen said quietly, skimming the note. "Is that true?"

Hibbert met his gaze head-on. "I don't know, Lord Sheldrake."

"But you think it might be." Damen got his answer in the silence that ensued. "Dammit, Hibbert. You and Royce said they'd be safe if they didn't venture out."

"And they were. *Then*. He wasn't ready to kill yet. He wanted only to taunt Lady Breanna, to draw out her torture. Which he's obviously still doing. But the tone of this note is more ominous than the others. He went out of his way to address exactly what you just mentioned—the safety of your wife and Lady Breanna if they stay indoors. He's announcing that he's stripping away that safety. Also, he's now specifying a matter of hours before he acts, rather than alluding to some imminent but vaguely in the future time frame. He's running out of patience. And eventually . . ." Hibbert drew a slow breath. "The problem is, I don't know when eventually will be."

*   *   *

Royce was on edge when he returned to Kent.

He'd interrogated enough people to find out that no one had seen any suspicious cargo being loaded at London's docks over the past several days. He'd also seen enough manifests to know that ten ships had left port that were large enough to hide the kind of cargo he was looking for—namely, at least two unconscious women. Maybe more. He had no way of knowing whether the killer had shipped the five women en masse or separately.

All the merchant ships that fit the bill were headed for distant ports, with brief stops on the Continent. Every one of them had captains of impeccable standing, who always verified the contents of their cargo, and whose honor and decency would never permit them to carry women in their holds.

Which left the smaller packet ships.

The manifests here were sketchier, so it was quite possible that someone using a phony name had arranged to ship illegal cargo by listing that freight as sacks of wheat, coal, or something equally innocuous. Or, perhaps the killer worked with a crew of his own choosing—a crew he paid to do his bidding. In which case, the entire manifest could have been falsified.

There was no way of telling.

Not unless Royce awaited those ships' return. And some of them were not scheduled to sail back into London for months.

Breanna didn't have months.

Besides, every instinct in Royce's body was screaming that the cargo he was searching for had been shipped to Calais. It made absolute sense. Calais was nearby. It promised immediate results for the assassin. Most of all, it gave him the ultimate satisfaction—another demonstration of his superiority. In short, John Cunnings had failed. George Colby had failed. *He,* on the other hand, would not.

Fine. So Calais was the likely destination. But to whom was the cargo being delivered? To Rouge? Or had Rouge been replaced by someone else? And how did Royce get to that someone?

Before leaving the docks, he interviewed a line of crane operators and porters. Some knew the crewmen who worked on those smaller ships. A few knew the captains.

But it was one wiry old fisherman who supplied Royce with the morning's most significant tidbit of information.

The old fellow recalled a packet ship that had sailed two days ago, just after sunrise. The reason he remembered it was that none of his longshoremen friends—the ones who usually worked the early shift— were there to attend it. Which was odd, almost like none of them knew it was scheduled to sail. Curious, he'd watched the crew hoist a few bags on board, then untie and cast off, as if they were in a great hurry to get going.

Unfortunately, he didn't know any of the crew members personally, other than by face, so he couldn't tell Royce much about them. And he knew nothing about the ship's destination or when it was scheduled to return.

However, he did recall one thing, and that was the ship's name. It was called the *Triumph*.

Royce acted on that immediately. He issued strict instructions—along with a twenty-pound note—to one of the wharf rats he gave occasional work to, ordering him to advise Royce the instant the *Triumph* sailed back into port.

It might be nothing more than a coincidence. On the other hand, it might lead to the kidnapped women.

The problem was, it wouldn't lead to the assassin—not fast enough to stop him.

Time was running out.

By the time Royce reached Medford Manor, he'd made a decision. Someone had to go to Calais. Armed with a description of the missing women, this someone had to be subtle enough and shrewd enough to ask the right questions, investigate this matter from the receiving end in the hopes of finding the buyer, which, in turn, could lead to the assassin.

Unfortunately, that someone couldn't be him.

Because the hunt would take several days at least, especially since it meant following leads from the port of Calais to wherever those women had been taken. And he wouldn't, couldn't, leave Breanna for that amount of time.

Hibbert, however, could.

Royce drew his carriage up to Medford's iron gates.

Rather than just waving him on, Mahoney approached the carriage, simultaneously gesturing for his men to begin opening the gates.

"There was another delivery late this morning," he told Royce. "I left it with Hibbert. I thought you should know."

Nodding tersely, Royce waited only until Mahoney had backed away. Then, he slapped the reins and sent his carriage racing down the drive.

He mounted the front steps two at a time.

"I'm glad you're back," Wells greeted Royce, flinging open the door at once.

"Mahoney told me about the package," Royce replied, his gaze darting about, searching for Breanna. "Is everyone all right?"

"Yes, my lord." Wells didn't pretend to misunderstand. "Lady Breanna and Lady Anastasia are in the library playing cards with Hibbert and Lord Sheldrake. I felt more comfortable guarding the door. But now that you're back . . ." He made a sweep with his arm. "I'll join you."

Royce strode down the hall, veered sharply into the library, Wells only three paces behind him.

Breanna looked up, and Royce nearly sagged with relief at the sight of her, unharmed, outwardly composed as she played her game of whist. "Did you learn anything?" she asked softly, laying down her cards.

"Nothing concrete. I'd rather discuss the package first."

"As would I." Hibbert rose, abandoning the game to cross over, hand Royce the box they'd received hours ago. "I'd like your opinion."

Royce read the note through twice, his frown deepening as he did. Then, he turned to the bottle, looking it over quickly before opening the stopper, sniffing the fragrance. Replacing the stopper, he studied the bottle more closely.

"This will narrow down the search," he muttered. "The women are not only in France, they're in Paris. Or not far from it."

"So you agree that's where you'll find the jeweler who designed this bottle."

"No. That's where *you'll* find the jeweler who designed this bottle." Royce's stare bore into Hibbert's. "I need you to do this for me. I'm not leaving—not now. The situation here is far more immediate, and more dangerous, than the one at the receiving end."

Damen jumped to his feet before Hibbert could reply. "You're saying he's about to—"

"Damen, stay calm," Royce interrupted quietly. "I don't think it's a matter of hours, although he wants us to believe it is. But I do think he's losing patience."

"Then what's stopping him from shooting?"

"I am." Royce lowered his head, reread the note. "Not actively, but by what I represent—the ultimate contradiction. On the one hand, my involvement is plaguing the hell out of him. He wants me to get scared, back away. On the other hand, he wants me to figure out what he's about, and to confront him. That way, he gets to enjoy the challenge—and to win. Without that, I'm just another obstacle to eliminate, which would be a great disappointment. So he'll wait a bit longer, see what I do."

Royce looked up, his mind racing. "In the meantime, he has no idea we've linked him to Medford's selling of women. If he sees me leave the country, he'll assume I succumbed to his threats. He'll feel momentary triumph, then great disappointment. That will lead to restlessness and then rage. All his anger will focus on the one person he blames for everything: Breanna. *That's* when he'll act. *That's* when Anastasia's—and then Breanna's—lives will be at greatest risk." A pause. "And *that's* why I'm staying right here."

Anastasia took Damen's hand in hers, interlaced their fingers. "That makes sense," she said, addressing Royce but speaking to her husband. "And it makes me feel much more secure."

Royce was studying the package wrapping. "This was dispatched from here in England?" he asked Hibbert.

"Yes." Clearly, Hibbert realized his employer was thinking along the exact same lines as he had. "And it's the first package Lady Breanna's received since the doll and the sketch came, two days ago."

"He went to Paris. He bought the perfume there."

"Yes, and now he's back in England." Hibbert rubbed his palms together, making swift plans. "I'd intended to wait for your return, after which I was going to ride down to Dover, glance over the manifests of this morning's arriving ships. I'll follow through on that. After which, I'll take the first packet to Calais, then ride on to Paris. I'll find out everything I can."

"I have a strategy to help you do that." Royce's gaze drifted back to Breanna. "Hibbert, go pack a bag," he instructed his friend. "Include some formal clothing. I'll explain the details later."

"Fine." Hibbert looked distinctly unsurprised by Royce's abrupt dismissal. Rather, he glanced about, leveling a pointed gaze, first at Wells, then at Anastasia and Damen, before delicately clearing his throat and heading for the door.

"A subtle hint," Stacie noted, coming to her feet. "I think my cousin and her *betrothed,*" she emphasized the word, "would like a moment alone. Come, gentlemen," she told Damen and Wells. "You may both escort me to the sitting room. We have wedding plans to continue making." She paused as she walked by Royce, rose up to kiss his cheek. "You, my lord, are a very lucky man. You're also perfect for Breanna, just the man I prayed she'd find. I wish you every happiness." A tremor crept into Stacie's voice, the only indication of her persisting fear. "May your brilliant tactics prevail, so you can share a long and happy future."

"Thank you, Anastasia." Royce squeezed her shoulder gently. "And I agree—my luck is incredible. As for the future, it *will* be long and happy for us all. You have my word." He turned to Damen. "As do you."

Damen shook his friend's hand. "I echo Stacie's sentiments—with one additional comment. Perhaps now you'll begin to understand why I'm irrational when it comes to my wife."

A corner of Royce's mouth lifted. "I've already begun."

"My congratulations as well, sir," Wells said with an approving nod. "I was wrong about you. I should have listened to Miss Stacie's instincts. You're a fine man. I wish you and Miss Breanna great joy."

"Thank you." Royce was torn between gratitude and amusement.

He waited until the door had closed and he and Breanna were alone before asking, "What exactly was Wells wrong about?"

Breanna smiled as she walked toward him. "Oh, Wells thought you were a little too wild and daring to be suitable for me. I think he also feared you were a bit of a womanizer."

"Did he?" Royce reached for her, pulled her against him. "The wild and daring I can't argue with. As for being a womanizer . . ." He tilted up her chin with his forefinger. "The only woman I want is you." He lowered his head, covered her mouth with his. "I'm consumed with you, Breanna Colby," he murmured into her parted lips. "I think about you all day, burn for you all night. And I worry about you every minute I'm away."

"Then don't go." She twined her arms around his neck. "Guard me personally. Especially at night. The closer you are to me, the safer I feel."

A chuckle vibrated through him. "Is that so? Then we'll have to see how close I can get."

"Tonight?"

"Tonight," he promised.

"Perfect. Because I just remembered we have something to celebrate." Breanna brushed Royce's lips with hers. "Today is New Year's Day."

"That's right. It is." Royce's arms tightened around her, and he molded the contours of her body to his. "No wonder the docks were so quiet. I'd completely forgotten."

"So did I." She shivered, pressing closer. "But now that I've remembered, I must say I much prefer this method of celebrating to the line of gentlemen callers I originally intended to receive."

"I'm relieved. Otherwise, I'd be calling out a lot of men." He silenced her response with his mouth, kissing her until she was trembling in his arms. "I hope you got at least a little sleep last night. Because tonight you won't be shutting an eye. And it won't be fear keeping you awake. It will be me."

"How enticing." Breanna's eyes glowed. "I'll leave the door unlocked."

Ten minutes later, Hibbert packed his final article of clothing and snapped the bag shut.

"Do you think I should contact Girard as soon as I arrive in Paris?" he inquired.

"Definitely." Royce was perched at the edge of a chair, his posture rigid as he issued Hibbert's instructions. "You know how good Girard is. His instincts are exceptional."

"Almost as good as yours," Hibbert commented, a statement of fact rather than acclaim. "I agree. He's our most valuable contact in the area. Very well. I'll stop in and see him before I visit the jewelers. How much do you want him to know?"

"Whatever you can tell him in a half hour. Don't waste your time or his. He already knows about the assassin. I've asked him to do some checking, to see if he can find the physician who treated that wounded hand."

Hibbert pursed his lips. "I never thought of that. But it makes sense. He didn't dare have an English doctor look at his wound. It would be too risky."

"Not to mention that if the trigger finger's as damaged as I suspect—enough to make him drop out of sight for months and then compel him to return just to kill Breanna—he'd need a physician of extraordinary skill. An expert."

"Perhaps he first met his business contact while recuperating abroad," Hibbert suggested. "Whether by chance or intent.".

"Most likely intent. Pose that notion to Girard. Then tell him, in addition to the doctor, to start digging for whoever's been buying the women, whether it's Rouge or someone else. In the meantime, you trace the perfume. Just let Girard know what you're doing so he can watch your back."

"You mean, Lord Hobson's back," Hibbert corrected dryly. He quirked a brow at his employer. "I think I'll enjoy playing the part of a nobleman."

"I'm sure you will." Royce rose, thinking through the final steps of his plan. "You know what to say in those letters?"

"Of course." Hibbert grasped his bag, swung it off the bed. "I'll take care of things at my end. You just keep everyone here safe." A penetrating look. "Including yourself."

"I intend to." Royce glanced restlessly toward the window. "He's out there, Hibbert. I can feel it. If only I could force him to confront *me,* to vent his rage at *me,* rather than Breanna."

Hibbert studied Royce for a long, thoughtful moment. "You've taught me well. So let me give you some of your own advice. A bit of apprehension is healthy. It's what keeps our wits sharp and our senses honed." A profound pause. "However, this is more than mere apprehension. It's fear. That's because the stakes are personal. Very personal. The life of the woman you love is at risk. So you're terrified— terrified and determined to protect her, even at the expense of your own life."

Royce's head came up. "And you take exception to that?"

"No. I admire it. But I'm not the issue here. The killer is. He'll use your vulnerability to his advantage. If he so much as senses the intensity of your feelings for Lady Breanna, it will make things worse for her. Don't let him know how much she means to you, my lord. Don't."

Hibbert's words echoed in Royce's head all evening. He knew his friend was right. The worst thing he could do was alert the killer to his feelings. Lord only knew what kind of leverage that would provide.

Which meant only one thing.

Royce had to keep his distance from Breanna. Not just when they ventured outside or stood near windows, in full view of the world, but inside, as well. The killer's latest message had made it clear he had access to the house—a taunt that might or might not be true. Consequently, Royce couldn't take chances. Moments such as the one he and Breanna had shared earlier had to cease.

Except in one place: her bedroom.

It was the only detail Royce was convinced the killer hadn't yet discovered—that Breanna was sleeping in different quarters. He, Damen, and Wells had been careful to continue making her room look lived in, especially at night. Obviously, they'd been successful. The assassin's actions, or lack thereof, told them that. If he'd been aware of the switch, his arrogance would have insisted he throw it in their faces. He'd either have invaded Breanna's new quarters or at least made some terrifying reference to doing so in his notes.

He hadn't.

Which meant he didn't know.

And *that* meant that Royce and Breanna still had the nights.

Starting with tonight.

Royce didn't even bother dragging a chair into the hallway when he positioned himself outside Breanna's door. He was far too restless, too fidgety, too rife with energy to sit still.

He was also frantic to hold Breanna in his arms.

He spent the first part of the night pacing outside her door. And the minute the house fell silent, he reached for the door handle, let himself in.

Breanna was sitting on the bed, sketching by the thin filaments of moonlight that drifted through the window. Other than that and the glow of a crackling fire, the room was unlit, cast in shadows.

For safety.

And for him.

She looked up when he entered, putting aside her sketchpad and rising to her feet. "I'm glad you're here."

Royce caught his breath. She was wearing only a thin nightrail and robe, both of a sheer ivory silk, the lacy edges of the robe barely touching, loosely tied.

She smiled, reaching up to tug the first pin out of her upswept hair. "I left this task for you," she added softly.

Restless energy exploded into raw hunger.

Royce turned the key in the lock with such force he wondered if he'd snapped it in two.

He hoped so. In that case, they could stay here, locked away together, forever.

He couldn't stop staring at her. Staunchly, he fought to control the tidal wave of desire that surged through him, all his earlier tension converging, crashing through his loins.

"Royce?" Breanna took a step toward him, opened her arms.

Restraint vanished.

Royce scarcely remembered closing the distance between them. All he knew was dragging Breanna against him, seizing her mouth with more urgency than he knew he possessed. He tugged the pins from her hair, gathering handfuls of it as he continued kissing her. Her robe dropped to the floor, her nightrail followed, and Royce savored the exquisite silkiness of her skin as he lifted her, placed her on the bed.

He felt her fingers on the buttons of his waistcoat, but he couldn't wait. Stepping away, he tore off his clothes, coming down over her the instant he was naked.

Breanna let out a soft moan of pleasure, rubbing her breasts against his powerful, hair-roughened chest. She clung to him, understanding and sharing his urgency, wanting to savor every moment, to savor him, yet frantic to feel him inside her.

"Later," he muttered, answering the conflicting emotions waging inside her. "We'll go slowly later. Now, I've got to have you." He was already wedging her thighs apart.

She felt him tense, as if remembering how new this was to her, and her breath caught as his fingers found her, slid inside to assure him of her readiness.

She was more than ready for him.

Royce shuddered heavily as he encountered her satiny wetness, stroked her softly.

Breanna seized his wrist, pushed his hand away. "Later," she whispered, echoing his sentiments.

Royce's gaze darkened to near black. His hands slipped under her, gripping her bottom and angling her to receive him, his rigid shaft probing the entrance to her body.

He entered her in one slow, inexorable thrust, pushing as deep as he could go.

Breanna cried out, arched to meet him, her entire body softening and opening to take him, to sheathe him inside her. She whimpered in protest when he left her, only to cry out again as he pushed forward, filled her even more fully than he had the first time.

"Does . . . it hurt?" Royce could barely speak.

She shook her head, her arms tightening around him. "Don't stop."

"Stop?" Royce was moving again, each lunge of his hips sending skyrockets of sensation shooting through her. "I'd die first."

There were no more words then, nothing but the harsh rasps of their breath, the frantic kisses and caresses, the broken sounds of need, the grating of the bedsprings beneath them as their motions became more frenzied, wilder, more abandoned. Royce lost himself inside her, and Breanna tossed her head on the pillow, the pleasure too acute to bear, the tension coiling tighter and tighter until she thought she'd die of it.

It peaked . . . and unraveled in a rush, throbbing spasms of completion radiating out from inside her, clenching again and again, contracting frantically around his engorged length.

Royce gave a hoarse shout, throwing back his head and groping for the headboard. His fingers closed around the bedposts, his knuckles turning white as his own climax slammed through him. His hips moved convulsively, pushing him into her, heightening her contractions as he met each one with a scalding burst of heat.

Breanna bit her lip to keep from screaming. She could feel him spurting into her, sensations so erotic they retriggered her spasms, sent them spiraling even higher than before.

When it was over, they collapsed, neither capable of moving. Breanna sank into the bed, reveling in Royce's weight, the inadvertent shudders still racking his body, the final drops of his seed trickling into her.

"I love you," she whispered, pressing her lips to his shoulder.

He swallowed, an audible sound in the silence of the room. "You have no idea," he answered hoarsely. "No idea." Reflexively, his arms closed around her, as if that act alone could keep her safe. "I'm going to spend a lifetime showing you." He raised his head, stared deeply into her eyes. "Beginning tonight."

Breanna smiled, smoothed damp strands of hair off his forehead. "You've made an extraordinary start."

He caught her hand, brought her palm to his lips. "That's all it was—a start." He rolled to one side, taking her with him. "I just want to hold you, feel you against me, for a minute."

"And then?"

"Then, I'm going to make love to you the way you deserve to be made love to, the way I still haven't mustered enough control to do."

A sated sigh. "I've no complaints."

His expression singed her. "You'll have even fewer by morning."

"I'm intrigued."

"Are you?" He bent to kiss her, cradling her head in his hands as he made love to her mouth. His lips moved slowly over hers, circling and tasting, nudging them apart for the intimate invasion of his tongue. He teased her with light, shivery strokes, awakening every surface of her mouth, his tongue gliding over hers in unhurried, lingering caresses, until her breath was coming faster and she was clinging to him, desperately trying to escalate the pace.

Clearly, the minute was up.

Still, Royce kept himself in check, although his body swelled inside hers, throbbed in a way that told her what this delay was costing him. But he didn't give in, waiting until she was frantic before letting the fire of their kisses take over.

Breanna's inner muscles softened and tightened around him, her body reflexively asking for more.

Maddeningly, Royce refused.

Rather than begin the rhythm she craved, he withdrew, separating their bodies and dragging his mouth away from hers.

"Royce . . ." She whimpered a protest, but he ignored it, his lips burning an open-mouthed trail down her neck, her throat. He kissed her shoulders, the spot where her heart was racing, then down to the upper swell of her breasts. He savored each curve, moved lower, letting his warm breath tease her nipples into aching points, then grazing them with fleeting brushes of his lips and tongue.

Breanna's nails were digging into his shoulders when Royce gave in. He slid one arm beneath her back, arched her up to his mouth and drew her taut nipple inside, tugging and releasing, tugging and releasing, then lashing across the hardened peak with his tongue. He didn't stop until she was twisting on the sheets, chanting his name in harsh, broken gasps, and even then only to shift to her other breast, lavish it with the same attention.

Drowning in sensation, Breanna cried out, her insides clenching with every pull of Royce's lips. The urgency was building again, that desperate need for release, and she caught his head between her hands, trying to tug him upward, to urge him over her. If he didn't cover her, fill her, she'd die.

He let her ease his head from her breasts, but ignored her unspoken plea. Following his own compulsion, he caught her wrists, held them away.

His mouth continued its path, down her waist, across the hollow of her abdomen to her thighs.

She had no time to think, or even to wonder.

Releasing her wrists, he draped her legs over his shoulders, bent his head, and sank his tongue into her.

Raw, unimaginable sensation jolted through Breanna, and she shoved a fist into her mouth, knowing there was no other way to silence her scream. She'd never imagined anything like this in her life. She was dying . . . dying.

Royce intensified the torture, making love to her with his lips and tongue, tasting her, savoring her flavor. His fingers glided high up inside her, moving seductively to heighten her pleasure. She tried to wrench away, to keep herself from flying apart, but he was relentless, unbearably precise, finding where she needed him most and deepening his caresses.

"Royce . . ." It was a primitive sound, one she didn't recognize, even though it came from her.

"Let it happen," he commanded in a voice thick with desire. "God, your taste. Let it happen."

It was already happening. Breanna couldn't stop it. It was a dark roaring wave that boiled up inside her, crashed down over her, drowning her in its wake. She sobbed aloud, giving in to its power, her entire body wrenching beneath the spasms.

She felt Royce's grip tighten as he heightened her pleasure, tasted every nuance of her climax. Then he was on her, in her, his own control shattering as he surged deep, spurting hotly into her, rasping her name with each pulsing burst of release.

This time recovery took longer. Breanna felt dazed, stunned by the magnitude of what had just happened, and by the intensity of her own body's response. *My God,* was all she kept thinking. *My God.*

Eventually, Royce raised up on his elbows, his breathing still unsteady as he gazed down into her face. "You're mine," he said fervently. "And I love you."

Tears shimmered in Breanna's eyes. "I never imagined it could be so . . . so . . ."

"Nor did I."

His implicit meaning made what they'd shared that much more profound.

"I wish we could hold back the morning," Breanna whispered, realizing how silly she sounded, how unlike herself, and yet unable to stem the words or stop herself from feeling them. She was no longer the woman she'd been a month ago. Now, she was a woman in love. And she was terrified that the faceless killer out there would shatter all the wonder she and Royce were only just discovering.

That . . . and worse.

Royce kissed her tenderly, his thumbs caressing her cheeks. "The morning is hours away."

"But it *will* come. And when it does—"

"When it does, we'll face it," Royce murmured. He rolled onto his back, taking Breanna with him and pressing her head to his chest. He sifted his fingers through her hair, staring quietly at the ceiling. "He's waiting for me to make some kind of move. And I will—as soon as I think of the best way to lure him out."

Breanna tensed, and she raised her head, her eyes wide with fear. "Lure him out? But, if you lure him out—"

"I'll kill him," Royce finished quietly.

"He's an expert marksman," Breanna returned in a small, shaky voice. "Killing is his craft, his passion." A hard swallow. "If anything happens to you . . . Royce, I'd rather take one of his bullets. It would destroy me far less."

"Stop it." Royce drew her mouth down to his, kissing her with a ferocity that strove to burn away all the frightening possibilities that lay ahead. "Nothing is going to happen to you. *Or* to me. I won't let it."

Breanna nodded, willing her surge of fear to subside. "I know you won't." She caressed his jaw, watching the unyielding look in his eyes and saying a silent prayer.

Let this nightmare be over, she prayed. *Let us all be spared. But if something has to go wrong, if someone has to die at that monster's hands, don't let it be Royce. Keep him safe. And please, please, protect Stacie and her babe. If it has to be someone, let it be me.*

Royce studied the play of emotions on her face, and his features hardened, as if he knew just what she was thinking. "Come here," he commanded, pulling her more fully atop him, draping her hair around them like a shimmering curtain. "You wanted to hold back the morning," he reminded her in a low, urgent tone, framing her face between his palms. "Well, so do I." His hips lifted, pushing his lower body upward until his rigid length surged fully inside her, possessed her. He withdrew, then repeated the motion, gritting his teeth and waiting only until her glazed eyes and soft moan told him he'd eclipsed her fears—for now. "And I know just the way to do that."

21

❦

"*L*ord Hobson. I like that idea."

Philippe Girard chuckled, pouring two brandies and giving one to Hibbert before settling himself behind his desk. "Please. Have a seat." He waited until Hibbert had lowered himself into one of the plush mahogany armchairs that decorated Girard's elegant office. "Was this new identity your idea, or Chadwick's?"

"It was Lord Royce's." Hibbert sipped at his drink, an expression of wry amusement on his face. "But I've taken to it quite nicely."

"*Évidemment.* So I see." Another chuckle as Girard set down his goblet, leaned forward to study Hibbert intently. "You've been to the three jewelers?"

"Yes. Right after I left here this morning."

"Forgive me for not speaking with you at that time." Girard's smile vanished, and his dark brows drew together. "I had no idea you were here. My clerk is new, or he would have recognized your name. He certainly would have known Royce's. Either way, he would have interrupted my meeting. It won't happen again."

Hibbert waved away the apology. "Your clerk was just doing his job. He was most efficient. He took down my name, gave me an appointment for half after two, and saw me to the door. That gave me a chance to do my preliminary investigating."

"And you found the right jeweler?"

"In less than an hour. I followed my first instinct and went to Passeur on Avenue De Villiers. I was right."

Girard's lips twitched. "You're becoming as arrogant as Chadwick. And as shrewd. Passeur does indeed craft elaborate bottles for the most discerning customers." He rubbed a palm over his clean-shaven jaw. "Now what?"

"As I suspected, the bottle is exclusive to Passeur. It's also quite expensive. Only five customers have purchased it—quite regularly, in fact. As luck would have it, all five live here in Paris."

"You have all their names, of course."

"Actually, they have mine—or rather Lord Hobson's." Hibbert enjoyed the perplexed look that crossed Girard's chiseled features. "Another of Lord Royce's fine ideas—one that was acceptable to Monsieur Passeur. As anticipated, the jeweler is an ethical man who refused to divulge the names of his customers. Lord Royce's plan spared him the necessity of doing so."

"I'm intrigued. Please, go on."

Hibbert complied. "Through Passeur, I sent off five urgent messages, one to each customer. I told them I was in a delicate predicament. I'd spent one unforgettable night with a beautiful woman whose name I neglected to take, but whose scent I could never forget. I confessed that I'd traced the perfume in the hopes of renewing our acquaintance during my brief trip to Paris—no matter what the price. I closed by asking if they might know this woman and, if so, could I prevail upon them to urge her to contact me—immediately, as I'll only be in Paris for a day or two. And I provided my name and the name of the inn where I'm staying."

This time Girard threw back his head and laughed. "In other words, you appealed to the passion so typical of the French."

"Yes. And the greed so typical of criminals." Hibbert gave an offhanded shrug. "I expect I'll hear from several very irate husbands."

"I'm sure you will."

"When I find the source of this bottle, it's possible I'll need your help. Depending upon who that source is, of course."

"Consider it done." Girard polished off his brandy, and eyed the empty glass speculatively. "You're hoping this will lead to whoever is buying the women who have been kidnapped."

"Exactly."

A terse nod. "Then I suspect I'll be hearing from you. In the meantime, I have your descriptions of the women in question. I'll see what I can find out. Oh, and I should be hearing back any day now on my inquiries regarding the physician Chadwick's looking for."

"Good. Because it's possible the killer first met his business associate en route to or from that physician."

"That makes sense." Girard organized his notes. "With any luck, all these pieces will be found while you're in Paris, and you and I will be able to assemble them." Girard shot Hibbert a curious look. "This isn't Chadwick's usual type of case. Nor is he going about it in his usual detached manner. Is that because Sheldrake's a friend of his? Or is it more?"

Hibbert's expression never changed. "Lord Royce and the marquess have known each other since their days at Oxford."

"*Oui.* And Lord Royce and Lady Breanna have known each other less than a month. Yet I get the distinct feeling Chadwick's determination has a lot more to do with her than with Sheldrake."

Another bland look, although Hibbert knew his employer wouldn't object to Girard knowing the truth. Still, baiting him was far more enjoyable. "I'll let Lord Royce answer that question himself, when you see him."

"Ah, and will my answer be in the form of an invitation, perhaps?"

"It might be." Hibbert rose, gathering up his things. "*If* you help solve this case."

Girard stood, a broad smile on his face. "You drive a hard bargain—*Lord Hobson.* However, being that I wouldn't want to miss out on what I'm fast coming to believe will be Royce's wedding day, I'll see what I can do." Abruptly, all levity vanished. "Good luck with your search, Hibbert. But be careful. You don't know what you're dealing with—yet. When you do, come to me."

Hibbert's nod was equally solemn. "I will."

By late afternoon, three replies, one incensed husband, and one round woman well past middle years with an eager gleam in her eye had arrived at Hibbert's inn.

The woman was both hopeful and persuasive. She spent twenty minutes assuring Lord Hobson they'd spent a torrid night together—one she'd be thrilled to repeat, with or without payment.

Hibbert sent her home to her husband.

The second arrival—an incensed man who introduced himself as Monsieur Blanc and then called Hibbert every French obscenity he was able to recognize, and a few he couldn't—swore that his wife was faithful and that if Lord Hobson ever contacted her again, he would shoot him.

Hibbert sent him home to his wife.

He then ordered a brandy, collected his three written messages, and took them upstairs to his room.

He tore open the first message.

It was written by an insolent butler, who informed Lord Hobson that the Duc had received his note, but had elected not to reply for personal reasons. He added that it would be highly indiscreet for Lord Hobson to press the matter, as it would offend the Duc, his wife, and his mistress, for whom the perfume was purchased.

Hibbert contemplated the butler's meaning for only a minute before putting aside the reply. It didn't warrant further attention. His instincts told him it rang true. Besides, the specifics would be easy enough to check out.

He turned his attention to the other two replies.

One was from a Mademoiselle Chenille, who regularly purchased the perfume for her grandmother, most recently as a Christmas gift. She expressed regret at not being able to provide Lord Hobson with the answers he sought, and wished him the best of luck. She added that she was leaving Paris the day after tomorrow, first to visit her grandmother in the hospital, then to return to the convent at which she'd soon be taking her vows to God. But if Lord Hobson had any further questions, he was free to contact her there. She closed her letter by blessing him, and providing him with the name and address of her religious order.

Hibbert winced, and refolded the note. It was replies such as these that made one feel guilty about using deception as a means to get at the truth. Then again, it was decent young women like Mademoiselle Chenille whom he and Lord Royce were trying to protect through their actions. So in the end, it was worth it.

He would, of course, verify the story—if it came to that. But he had little doubt she was telling the truth.

Which brought him to the last reply.

This note was penned in a flowery, feminine hand, and Hibbert's discomfort vanished, his instincts roaring to life when a hint of the fragrance he was searching for drifted to his nostrils.

The recipient had taken the time to dab her letter with a provocative touch of the perfume he'd mentioned. That meant she was interested.

The question was, was he?

Slipping his finger under the flap, Hibbert opened the letter, and read:

Lord Hobson, I'm fascinated by your letter. We should meet. I'll be at the front steps of Notre-Dame at seven o'clock, wearing your perfume.— Maurelle Le Joyau.

Maurelle Le Joyau.

Hibbert reread the name and the note, then glanced at his timepiece. Half after five. That gave him enough time to catch Girard before he left the office, find out more about the lady in question.

After which, he'd be on his way to the cathedral.

Maurelle Le Joyau was an extraordinarily beautiful woman—every bit as beautiful as she'd been described.

Her thick black hair was swept off her face, emphasizing her fragile, fine-boned features and wide, dark eyes. Her costly silk gown and fur-lined pelisse cloak were the height of fashion, and her diminutive height and build made her look like a china doll swathed in expensive material.

She looked young, vulnerable—the kind of woman a man would want to protect and, at the same time, to possess.

Hibbert studied her impassively as he approached the front steps of Notre-Dame, thinking that all the information he'd been given didn't do her justice. She was breathtaking. Without a doubt, she could pass for a woman a decade younger than her thirty-two years. She had an untouched quality to her beauty that was unmistakable.

Except that she happened to be the owner of a very elite, very expensive Paris brothel.

"Lord Hobson?" She gave him a dazzling smile, inclining her head just so as she stepped toward him.

Hibbert played his part, scrutinizing her with an element of longing, and an equal amount of regret. "Miss Le Joyau?"

"Yes."

He bowed, brought her gloved fingers to his lips. The perfume—he could smell it even in the crisp evening air. "I'm as disappointed as I am entranced," he confessed. "I wish I could say we've met. But as we both know, we haven't." A charming smile. "Although, to be honest, I wish it was you I was searching for. The young woman I recall was wearing your exact scent. Still, she doesn't come close to matching you in beauty."

Maurelle flushed accordingly, although Hibbert was aware that her show of maidenly shyness was just that: show. Indeed, at the same time that she attempted to preoccupy him with her allure, she was assessing him with a shrewd but subtle thoroughness the average man would never have perceived.

Hibbert perceived it.

"*Merci.* What a lovely compliment," she murmured, her English punctuated with a soft French accent. "However, now that we meet face to face, I have to sadly agree you're a stranger to me, as well. Still, perhaps I can help in your search." She tucked a tendril of hair off her face. "You're English. Yet your message said you met this woman in Paris. May I ask when?"

Interesting that she didn't ask *where,* Hibbert noted.

His brows raised in a semi-hopeful gesture. "Why? Do you know another woman who wears that scent?"

"Possibly. But I don't know *you* well enough to say."

"Ah, you're being cautious." Hibbert nodded his understanding. "I don't blame you. One can't be certain whom one is speaking with these days. Well, I assure you, I'm an honorable man. Lonely, but honorable. What would you like to know? My name is Albert Hobson. I live in Surrey, but I also have estates in Yorkshire, Dorset, and Devon. I'm a man of considerable means, and can provide handsomely for the young woman in question. As for when I met this mystery lady, it was last summer. I was in Paris on business."

"I see. She must have thoroughly impressed you, to still be in your thoughts six months later. Yet you didn't get her name."

"Unfortunately not." Hibbert gave a discreet cough. "I'm not sure how to say this delicately, but it was an arranged evening. I'd had a fair amount to drink when the liaison began. I can describe her to you, if that would help."

Maurelle lowered her lashes. "You're very frank."

"Have I offended you?"

Her lashes lifted. "No. I prefer candor to evasiveness." Another pause. "I'd like to hear more about you, and about this woman you're seeking."

"Indeed. I'll tell you anything about myself you wish to know." Hibbert shivered a bit, turned up the collar of his coat, and glanced about. "It's cold. Can I take you somewhere warm where we can talk?"

She rubbed her gloved palms together, still inspecting him closely— his expensive clothing, his cultured demeanor. *"Oui,* my lord," she said at length. "I believe you can. You can take me to my establishment. There, we'll continue our chat."

Le Joyau looked more like an opulent manor than a brothel.

The entire dwelling was furnished in rich blue velvet and carved mahogany, its drawing rooms warm and cozy, each with a cheery fire burning and adorned with plush sofas and drapes of gold brocade.

Maurelle escorted Hibbert into one of the rooms, after giving their coats to a sophisticated young woman at the door, who greeted mademoiselle and her guest politely, then went off to get them some refreshment.

Hibbert warmed his hands by the fire, thinking it was no wonder affluent men came here. With very little effort, they could pretend they were calling on a virtuous lady, rather than buying a prostitute for the night.

"My lord? Won't you have a seat?"

He turned, his smile back in place, and noted that Maurelle had situated herself in the center of the sofa. Even now, in her establishment as she called it, she looked anything but what she was. Straight-backed, her skirts draped formally around her, she looked like a young woman awaiting her beau, her hands folded primly in her lap, her expression warm but not seductive.

"Thank you." Hibbert crossed over, sat down on the sofa—a respectable distance away.

"I should begin by asking if you're shocked by where I've taken you." Maurelle beckoned to the woman who'd greeted them at the door, gesturing for her to leave the two goblets of brandy and plate of cakes on the table beside her. At the same time, she never averted her gaze from Hibbert. "I should, but I won't. You see, my lord, I'm as straightforward as you are. And I think we understand each other well enough to continue this discussion without the annoyance caused by silly displays of ignorance. It only wastes time—time you could be spending with the right woman."

"I agree."

"Besides," Maurelle added, handing him a goblet. "Since the perfume you used to trace me is fairly exclusive, I suspect you've been here before, probably while I was away. *Quel dommage.* Had I been at home, I would have personally seen to your satisfaction. But since I wasn't, I'm glad one of my ladies was able to give you such a memorable night. Even if you were too deep in your cups to remember her name or where you could find her."

"Indeed." Hibbert waited until Maurelle had lifted up her own goblet. "Shall we toast, then? To renewed acquaintances and new friendships."

Maurelle raised her glass, and the two of them drank.

"Now," Hibbert continued, his lips curving. "What else can I tell you about myself? My age? My success rate at White's or at Newmarket? Or would this character reference suffice?" He reached into his pocket, pulled out a thick wad of pound notes.

Her eyes gleamed. "That's an excellent start, monsieur. Why don't you describe this young woman to me."

Hibbert stared broodingly into his drink. He had to begin as generally as possible. After that . . . well, if things went well, after that he'd make the challenge more interesting. "She had a beautiful smile. Her hair was pale—blond or light brown. Her eyes were light, too—gray, maybe blue. Mostly what I recall was her scent. That and . . . her considerable other charms."

"I see. That's all you remember?"

"I'm afraid so."

"Hmm." Maurelle's lovely brow furrowed as if she were baffled, but Hibbert could see that her mind was completely unclouded—and racing. Clearly, she was pleased with what she'd heard, since his recollection was vague enough to fit a half-dozen women, any of whom she could douse in perfume and send to him—in exchange for a small fortune. "And for how long would you require her—one night? Two?"

That was his cue. It was time.

With a sorrowful smile, Hibbert said, "I would require her for much longer than that. However, given the type of woman we're referring to, one night will be fine."

"I don't understand," Maurelle returned with a genuinely perplexed look. "I thought you wanted . . . ?"

"What I *want,* and what's available to me are two different things." Hibbert tossed off his brandy, glad he'd had the presence of mind to fill his stomach with a large meal before leaving his inn—just in case he needed to lessen the effects of any liquor he'd consume.

Heavily, he set down his glass, taking in her uncertain expression, and attempting to explain. "I'm a realistic man, Miss Le Joyau. Candid, as you yourself said. I know my attributes . . . and my limitations. I'm well past fifty. I'm not displeasing to the eye. But I'm hardly able to capture the fancy of a beautiful, well-bred young lady. I can pay for a roomful of women. But the one I truly want can't be found at a brothel, no matter how elegant."

The tiniest flicker in Maurelle's eyes was his only indication that what he'd said had struck a chord.

Calmly, she reached for a piece of cake, nibbling at it as she asked, "And what type of woman is that?"

He waved away her question. "Please, my dear. You're not required to listen to my fantasies." He peeled off several hundred-pound notes, pressed them into Maurelle's hand. "Where shall I await my liaison?"

"S'il vous plaît—in a minute." Maurelle set the bills aside, her fingers closing around his. "My job is to see that you're happy. If there's something more you need, just ask for it."

He quirked a brow. "Forgive me, but what I need is not something you can provide."

"Let me be the judge of that."

"Very well." Hibbert averted his gaze, staring off toward the fire. "It's quite simple. I'd like a companion. Not just for a day, or a week. For an extended period of time, maybe even for the rest of my life."

"But you object to paying for her," Maurelle guessed softly. "You want her to fall in love with you."

A dubious laugh. "That's a delightful notion. But I'm not impractical enough to expect it. No, I don't object to paying. Love isn't the issue."

"Then what is?"

"Breeding. Breeding and chastity."

Silence.

"I see our discussion has reached an end," Hibbert said, glancing over to give Maurelle a rueful smile. "I didn't mean to offend you. But you did ask. Now perhaps you'll understand why I didn't want to pursue the subject."

"I'm not offended." Maurelle caressed his fingers. "Just so I understand, monsieur, you're saying you'd prefer to buy one of my ladies for an indefinite period of time—if she's well-bred and untouched?"

"Nobly bred and untouched," Hibbert corrected. "Any companion I acquired would have to be of the same class as I am. And, at the same

time, young and beautiful." The warmth left his face. "I hope you're not toying with me, Miss Le Joyau. I might be lonely, but I'm not stupid."

"I'm not toying with you, my lord."

"Then why are we pursuing this discussion?"

"Because I might be able to supply you with precisely the companion you want." Maurelle withdrew her hand, suddenly all business. "For the right price, that is."

"Do we understand each other?" Hibbert asked bluntly. "I'm referring to a noblewoman. A young lady born of the peerage. And a virgin. Someone who's never lain with a man before."

"I know what a noblewoman is, my lord. Just as I know the definition of a virgin."

"And why would I find either, much less both, in a brothel?"

"Because the young woman I'm thinking of just arrived, this week in fact. She has yet to entertain her first client." Maurelle leaned forward, obviously sensing a windfall. "I would give you a guarantee, of course. I have my reputation to consider."

Hibbert remained dubious. "Suppose I accept your guarantee. You've assured me of her innocence. What about her roots?"

The barest of pauses, as Maurelle adjusted her story ever so slightly. "She's English, like yourself. Her late father was a viscount. He died, leaving his family destitute. Until recently, she lived with her mother. Unfortunately, her mother died, too. The girl came to Paris, penniless and alone. I took her in."

He permitted himself to appear hopeful—wary, but hopeful. "What does she look like?"

"As luck would have it, she's just what you're seeking. She's lovely. Like the woman you came in search of, she, too, has pale hair and eyes. She's just eighteen. I was going to put her to work tonight, but . . ." Maurelle bit her lip thoughtfully. "I could change my mind—*if* I were properly persuaded."

"You said she was alone." Eagerness laced Hibbert's tone. "That means she has no ties. Could this arrangement be permanent?"

"As permanent as you wish."

"Let me meet her."

Maurelle hesitated, well aware she now had the upper hand. "We haven't agreed upon a price."

"If she's all you say, you may name your price. I'll give you every pound in my pocket, and a signed note for the rest. I'll have my banker authorize the remaining funds the instant I return home. But first—I must meet her."

Maurelle squeezed his hand, her own eyes glowing with the triumph of victory. *"Naturellement.* I'll bring her to you. You won't be disappointed."

"I'm sure I won't be."

Hibbert remained in his seat, glad for his own ability to remain unreadable. He felt a surge of relief, supplanted only by his deep-seated anger and disgust. He knew only too well who Maurelle would be bringing out to meet him. He also had an excellent idea of the state she'd be in. It was up to him to disregard that state, to keep her in the dark long enough to get her out that door with him—for her own sake.

After which, he'd tell her the truth, reassure her fears, and elicit her help.

And somehow convince her to be strong for a little while longer.

"Here we are, my lord." Maurelle guided a lovely young woman into the room—a woman whose description perfectly matched the one Lord Royce had provided of Emma Martin. Her ashen complexion and terrified expression told Hibbert she'd been warned not to do anything to discourage her potential buyer—probably at the risk of physical harm, or worse.

"This is Emma," Maurelle supplied. "Emma, please greet Lord Hobson."

"Hello, Emma," Hibbert said gently, coming to his feet.

"Sir." Emma gave a brief curtsy, her eyes downcast.

"She's a little shy," Maurelle explained. "Under the circumstances, I'm sure you can understand why."

"Indeed I can." Hibbert forced himself to go through the motions. He clasped his hands behind his back, walking around Emma and inspecting her as one would a prize Thoroughbred. His smile widened with each passing minute, although it sickened him to see the way she was trembling.

"You're a very charming young lady," he complimented. He raised her chin with his forefinger. "I hear you're English."

Her lips quivered.

"I won't hurt you," he said quietly. "You've nothing to fear."

A lone tear slid down her cheek.

Enough was enough. Hibbert could take no more.

His gaze lifted to Maurelle, and he gave an emphatic nod. "Pack her things."

22

$\clubsuit$

Why didn't he *do* something?

Breanna's insides clenched, an overwhelming sense of desperation claiming her.

She hovered near her bedchamber window, peeked out from behind the drape, and scanned the darkening skies.

He was lurking out there somewhere.

But where?

It had been two days since he'd sent that perfume. His note had said precious hours remained until he struck.

So where was he?

Had he guessed what Hibbert was about, where he was going and why?

No. If that were the case, he'd have reacted.

Was he watching them, peering through windows and gauging their fear, waiting for it to peak before he acted?

Was *that* the cause of his utter silence? Was he doing it intentionally to heighten her agony? Or was he plotting something horrifying, anticipating the exact moment in which to strike?

And if he did strike, what form would it take? Was he going to send them another of his threatening gifts, or had the time come when he meant to step out of the shadows, make an attempt on Stacie's life?

Dear God, she was losing her mind.

Dragging in a breath, Breanna pressed her palms together, determined to bring herself under control before she went down to dinner. She couldn't let Stacie see her like this. Her poor cousin was frightened enough as it was, more so since that last note had arrived. For the past two days, she hadn't had a minute's reprieve, not an instant to lose herself in something other than the danger to her life. Now Damen *never* left her side, not even allowing her to make solitary trips from their bedchamber to the sitting room or to walk down and visit Breanna in her chambers. He guarded her round the clock and, during the scant hours when he slept, he arranged for Wells to take over. The butler was as steadfast as Damen, appending himself to Stacie like a shadow and escorting her about.

Breanna didn't blame them. She was as worried as they.

And still the nagging thought persisted: What if the killer found another way? What if he got to Stacie despite all their precautions? What if . . . ?

No. Breanna gave an adamant shake of her head. She wouldn't let her thoughts wander in that direction. If she did, she'd break down entirely.

She moved about the room, watching the early evening moonlight wash the furniture, and wondering how a winter night could look so lovely and, at the same time, feel so terrifying.

As if in search of something to combat the fear, to reinforce all the joy and hope in her life, she paused by the bed. Lovingly, she ran her fingers down the post and over the bedcovers, eliciting the familiar surge of warmth that accompanied her memories of the hours she had spent in Royce's arms.

Their lovemaking had gotten more frantic each passing hour over the last two nights, as they both wordlessly sought the wonder and peace that only their joining could bring. Afterwards, they'd lie in each other's arms, talk until dawn—about anything and everything but what they feared most. Instead, they shared pieces of their pasts, learning more about each other and planning a future Breanna only prayed would happen.

Unfortunately, morning always came.

With the daylight hours, everything altered drastically. Even though Royce guarded her closely, he stayed at arm's length, appearing more like her sentry than her future husband. The two of them never touched, never even sat close together. Not because of protocol. Because of the assassin. If he could see into the manor, he could see them. And Royce was adamant that he not know what they meant to each other.

Breanna complied without question, although her reasons for doing so were different than Royce's. *He* was protecting *her. She* was protecting *him.*

The tension at Medford was becoming unbearable.

Royce spent long, concentrated hours reviewing the guest list, then comparing his updated facts to the reports that arrived daily from his contacts, after which he'd amend the list accordingly. Some of the guests' names were struck, others were labelled with a question mark as Royce went through the laborious process of verifying and eliminating in order to determine the assassin's identity.

The rest of the household was beginning to crumple.

Stacie had dark circles beneath her eyes, and Damen looked like death. Wells was haggard from lack of rest. Even Mahoney and his guards were testy, beginning to wonder if the intruder they were being paid to stop would ever come out of hiding so he could be captured.

The overall effect was maddening.

Each day the assassin didn't strike heightened everyone's sense of terror. Each of them silently wondered where he was, what he was thinking, what he was planning.

At the same time, they dreaded their answers.

Breanna prayed Hibbert would return soon, bearing *something* that would lead them in the right direction.

Most of all, she prayed Royce would get the killer before the killer got to him.

Sighing, she crossed the bedchamber, seeking her greatest tangible source of comfort.

Her porcelain figure.

Not just any figure, but her most prized one—the statue of the two girls picking flowers.

The one that held her silver coin.

Breanna lifted the statue and touched the coin, reliving the moments when her grandfather had gifted it to her, and its mate, the gold coin, to Stacie.

He'd wanted so much for them. He'd wanted their future.

Dear God, how she wanted to give that to him.

"Breanna?" Royce hovered in the doorway, his tone gentle. "It's almost time for dinner. I'll walk you downstairs." A pause. "Are you all right?"

"Of course." She forced a smile to her lips before turning to face him. "I was just thinking."

He didn't look one bit fooled by her pretense. He walked deeper into the room, then spied what she was holding. "We have a few minutes. Would you like to tell me whatever it is you're conveying to your statues?"

"Not all my statues," she corrected softly. "Just one in particular."

"Ah." He walked over, studied the porcelain girls amid the flower bed. "Does that figure have special meaning?"

"Yes. Very special." This time her smile was genuine. "Do you remember the coins I told you about? The ones Grandfather gave Stacie and me when we were six?"

He nodded. "Silver for you, gold for Anastasia."

"With Medford Manor engraved on both, so we'd someday find our way back home forever—obstacles or not. It was Grandfather's way of reminding us what was important. And that something is family." She worked the coin free. "I keep it here, in this statue. The girls remind me of Stacie and me." She held out her hand. "Would you like to see it?"

"I'd be honored." Royce took the coin, turned it over in his palm. "It's the perfect symbol for you and Anastasia. Your grandfather was a very wise man."

"Wise and loving. I always wished he'd been my father instead of my grandfather." She swallowed, stared down at the floor. "I never want to disappoint him. In a way, I feel that by endangering Stacie and me—and most especially his future great-grandchild—I have."

"That's ridiculous." Royce glanced about the shadowy room, then over at the window. Convinced it was dark enough so they couldn't be seen, he reached for her, took her in his arms. "Your grandfather could be nothing but proud. You're a remarkable woman."

"Extraordinarily special," Breanna murmured, ribbons of memory drifting through her mind. "That's how Grandfather always referred to Stacie and me."

"I couldn't agree more."

Breanna gazed up at Royce, her smile returning as she recalled the other pivotal event that had occurred on the day her grandfather gifted them with their coins.

"I can't attest to how special we were, but we were certainly resourceful," she confided. "Do you know what we'd done just minutes before Grandfather gave us the coins? We'd made a pact. We vowed that whenever one of us got into trouble—the kind of trouble that would go away by our switching places—we'd do so."

Royce chuckled. "And did you ever carry out that pact?"

"Oh, several times." Breanna's eyes twinkled. "Beginning that very night. It was Grandfather's birthday. We'd sneaked outside to play. My dress was covered with mud. My father would have beaten me senseless. Stacie was wearing the identical frock. She played me to perfection."

"And you? Did you pretend to be her?"

"Yes. I loved every minute of it. It was the first time I ever spoke my mind without fear of punishment." Breanna laughed softly. "And that wasn't the only time we switched places. We did it again this past summer—every day for weeks. It was during the time when Damen and Stacie were falling in love. My father wanted it to be me Damen was courting. And so it was."

Now Royce was grinning. "It was really Anastasia?"

"Absolutely." An exaggerated sigh. "Keeping my cousin's hair intact was the hardest part. Stacie can't go five minutes without sending, first strands, then tresses, toppling down. She's hopeless. Still, to be with Damen, she managed."

"I'm sure she did. I wish I'd been here to see it." Abruptly, Royce's amusement vanished. "I wish I'd been here to see everything. I'd have broken your father's jaw for ever laying a hand on you. And I'd have put a bullet through that son of a bitch he hired to kill Anastasia." Royce's gaze hardened. "I'll get my chance yet."

Fear knotted Breanna's stomach—the same fear that paralyzed her every time he made that claim. Reflexively, her fingers gripped his coat. "I saw several reports arrive for you today," she said, reverting back to the topic they tried so hard to avoid. "Did your contacts provide any answers?"

Royce's arms dropped to his sides, and he raked a frustrated hand through his hair. "Yes and no. This process is so damned tedious. Remember, there were two hundred fifty people at your party, two hundred forty-nine of whom are innocent. I've eliminated over half that number."

"All from the information your snitches provided?"

"That and my own knowledge of the guests." Royce rubbed his palms together, explaining the basis for his reasoning. "For example, one hundred four of the party goers were women. That leaves one hundred forty-six. Of those, over half have the wrong build—they're either short, brawny, or just plain fat. That brings us down to sixty-three. Here's where the reports come in. From what I'm reading, a good percentage of the men have alibis, either for the times when one of the murders occurred or for the night last summer when Anastasia was almost shot. Every few hours more information arrives, and I update my facts. Right now, I've narrowed the search down to thirty-four."

"You're amazing." Breanna shook her head in wonder. "Is this the kind of work you did in the military?"

"Yes. Whitehall relied upon what they called my deductive skills. During the war with Napoleon, I went back and forth from London to the Continent, depending on where I was most needed. The War Department knew I was good at reasoning out the enemy's strategy. I'd compile all the facts, consider the personalities involved, and make a prediction as to their intentions. My projections were usually right."

"That doesn't surprise me. You're brilliant." Breanna inclined her head quizzically. "What happened when the war ended? How did you decide to keep doing this?"

"Fate decided for me. Near the end of my service, I was approached by a general I'd worked with during my months in France. As a commander, he was admirable. I had great respect for him. As a man, he was inflexible and overbearing. When he sought my help, he was worried sick about his son, a junior officer who'd disappeared during battle and whose body was never recovered. I went about trying to find the boy. I analyzed the circumstances, talked to his associates, and figured out what I'd suspected from the start: that the general's son was a deserter. Not because he wasn't loyal to England, but because he didn't have the strength to stand up to his father."

"His father wanted him to follow in his footsteps, to pursue a career in the military," Breanna guessed.

"Right. And he had no stomach for it."

"I don't need to ask why you felt committed to the situation."

"No, you don't. The similarity to my own upbringing was definitely there—*with* some important differences. The general wasn't cruel, whereas my father was. This man truly loved his son. By the time he came to me, he would have willingly accepted his son's decision, just so he could have him home, alive and well. That worked in my favor. When I tracked down the boy, he was frequenting a seedy brothel on the outskirts of Paris. He refused to go home, said it would kill his father to hear he'd deserted his country. So, we reached an agreement. We never revealed what had really happened. Instead, our story was that he'd been captured by the French, but had escaped and was trying to make his way back to England when I found him. This spared his father embarrassment and him imprisonment. In return, I insisted he announce to his father that he didn't want to stay in the army, and then resign his commission."

"Did your plan work?".

"Beautifully. Everyone was happy."

"Including you." Breanna caressed his jaw. "You're a fraud, my love. You claim to be hard and removed, but I know it made you feel wonderful to give that boy something you never had." Her gaze was rife with compassion. "I'd have felt the same way."

"Yes, you would have." Royce kissed her fingertips. "In any case, word of mouth took over after that."

A smile. "In other words, the general raved to everyone about your brilliant rescue of his son, and suddenly scores of influential people had someone they needed you to find."

"Scores?" Royce chuckled. "That's a bit of an exaggeration. But, yes, it happened something like that."

A sudden thought struck Breanna. "You've never failed, have you?"

"Never."

"No wonder you were so determined to fight your feelings for me. Love is a daunting challenge, especially for a man who believes he has no depth of emotion—a man who never fails. Success would be far from guaranteed. That's unnerving, and risky."

Royce's knuckles caressed her cheek. "It was worth the risk."

"The risk is over," she murmured. "You've triumphed yet again."

"This time it was pure luck." His jaw tightened. "With my next challenge, it won't be."

Breanna knew just what path his thoughts had taken.

"Royce—"

"I'm not going to do anything stupid," he assured her, his tone as rigid as his jaw. "But I'm also not going to lose. Not this time. The stakes are too high. I'm going to figure out who he is. And then I'm going to kill him."

An urgent knock at the door brought their conversation to an abrupt halt.

"Lord Royce?"

Breanna blanched. "It's Wells. He sounds upset."

She was across the room before Royce, yanking open the door. "Wells? It's not Stacie, is it?"

The butler shook his head, far too preoccupied to worry about the impropriety of Breanna being alone in her room with Royce. "Miss Stacie is fine. Another box just arrived. It's downstairs."

Royce took Breanna's arm. "Let's go."

The box was small, the size of a book, and addressed, as always, to Breanna.

Stacie and Damen were waiting in the hallway, and the five of them crowded into the sitting room, where Royce pulled the drapes closed before nodding for Breanna to unwrap the package.

She did so in a sort of numbed state, peeling back the paper to lift out a porcelain figure. It depicted the same two women as the previous statue, only this time they were sitting side-by-side on a sofa. Across their laps was a pale blue quilt, and their hands were poised, preparing to sew on some lacy trim.

Crimson paint had been slashed across the quilt and the lace, staining both a sickly shade of red.

More blood.

This time the blood led to the women's hands.

Instantly, Breanna saw why.

Their right hands had been mutilated, the index finger of each broken off, saturated with red paint.

A note lay beside the statue, penned in the same bold, defined hand as always.

I can feel your terror. It makes my vengeance complete. I'm here, Lady Breanna. My pistol is aimed at your cousin's heart. Sheldrake can't save her. Nor can Chadwick save you. His reconnaissance is inferior. There's no time. A bullet takes only seconds.

Succumb to your fate. The battle is lost.

My finger . . . your life.

23

Hibbert waited until he'd ushered Emma into his room at the inn.
Then, he told her everything.

For a long moment afterward, she stared at him in disbelief. Then, she broke down, harsh sobs racking her body as she absorbed the realization that her nightmare was at an end. She wrapped her arms around herself, tears coursing down her cheeks as she wept.

"Come. Sit down." Hibbert led her to a chair, handing her his handkerchief and laying a reassuring hand on her shoulder. "Can I get you anything?"

She shook her head, battling for her sobs to subside. "Forgive me," she choked out. "I just never thought . . . She said you were buying me. She warned me that if I breathed a word of the truth, she'd find me and—"

"You don't need to explain, and certainly not to apologize. I'm just grateful I got here in time. Lord Royce was distraught when he went to fetch you at Pearson Manor and learned what had happened."

She gulped. "That monster—he killed my mother."

"Who?" Hibbert couldn't help himself, not when it came to this. "Who killed your mother, Emma? Did you see him?"

"Yes." An unsteady nod. "I saw him. I'm the only one who did. The other women—the ones who were locked in that room with me, whose husbands were killed—they never saw his face. But I did."

"Those other women, they're all at Le Joyau?"

Another nod. "We weren't all shipped at the same time, but, yes, we were all there. *They* still are."

"Locked in a room together?"

"Yes. They're not with Maurelle's women. That's because they're for sale. Not for a night—forever. Like I was. Maurelle said I'd bring the highest price because I was so young and because I was untouched. But she was expecting a fortune for them, too. They're noblewomen and not much older than I am." Emma buried her face in her hands. "She's selling them like chattel."

"We'll get them out." Hibbert squatted down beside the chair. "Emma, I know you're still in shock. But I need your help. That man who shot your mother has killed many times. He's threatening to kill again. We've got to stop him. So, please, tell me everything you remember about him, everything you can."

"I only saw him for a minute," she said, raising her head, a haunted look on her face. "But I'll never forget his eyes. They were like chips of ice. Empty and unfeeling."

"What did he look like? Describe him."

A horrified shudder. "He was tall. And very fit. Not stout or pudgy like most men his age. More like you, only not thin—muscular. I could feel his strength when he dragged me around." She squeezed her eyes shut. "I don't remember anything else. Except that his hair was dark, and graying at the temples. He was wearing all black." She drew a quivering breath. "He shot Mama through a blanket. Then he hit me. The next thing I knew, I was in a canvas bag in the cargo hold of a ship. I was unloaded in Calais, then taken here by carriage. He let me out a few times, but I was blindfolded. So I never actually saw him again."

"What about his voice—can you describe it?"

Another tremor ran through her. "Cold. Clipped. I'd recognize it if I heard it again. I think we all would."

All. That brought Hibbert back to the matter at hand. He needed to get those other woman out of that brothel.

And he needed to get Maurelle under lock and key.

"Did he deliver you to Le Joyau personally?"

"Yes. The women who work there said he and Maurelle were friends."

"Friends?"

"More than friends."

"I see. And did they refer to him by name?"

"No. Even Maurelle never said his name. She just called him 'my noble assassin.' She seemed to find that amusing."

"Did she?" Hibbert replied thoughtfully. That told him a great deal about Maurelle. It told him she was aware of how her lover was providing her with saleable noblewomen.

Maurelle Le Joyau was a bitch, and even harder than he'd realized.

It was time to consider his options. The sooner he acted, the better. Maurelle needed to be stopped before she could sell any of the other women. She also needed to be escorted to England, where Royce could pry information out of her—information that would lead him right to the "noble assassin."

On the other hand, none of this could be done hastily. Hibbert knew better. He couldn't risk alerting Maurelle before he'd freed those women. It was too dangerous. If she had any idea what he was planning, she'd either move the women, or silence them. The timing had to be right. He needed the element of surprise.

And he needed help.

He glanced at Emma, saw her teeth chattering, tears still flowing down her cheeks, and he knew she couldn't be left alone. Not only for compassionate reasons, but for practical ones. He couldn't be sure she was coherent enough to understand that she wasn't to leave this room under any circumstances.

He'd summon Girard.

Quickly, he went to the nightstand, picked up the paper and quill.

He only prayed he was in.

Girard arrived at Hibbert's room at the inn just before midnight.

His eyes widened when he saw Emma, curled up asleep on the bed, two blankets wrapped around her to calm the chills that had racked her body for nearly an hour.

"Mon Dieu," he muttered, rubbing a palm across his jaw. "No wonder your message was so urgent." His eyes narrowed as he studied Emma, noting her age, build, and features. "My guess is that this is the girl Royce was searching for—the daughter of Lord Ryder."

"Yes." Hibbert spoke quietly, although Emma showed no signs of stirring. Having endured a week of hell, she'd fallen dead asleep, and was totally unaware of Girard's arrival. "I found her in Maurelle Le Joyau's brothel," Hibbert continued. "She's on the verge of emotional collapse. That's why I couldn't leave her here alone."

"Has she spoken to you?"

A terse nod. "All the kidnapped women are at Le Joyau. I'll give you the details. After that, I'll need that help you offered."

"Consider it done."

It was nearly 4 A.M. when Emma stirred.

She pushed herself up on one elbow, and for a brief instant, she looked like the innocent young woman she'd been a week ago, before the assassin destroyed her life.

Then reality intruded, and she went rigid, her eyes snapping open to survey her surroundings.

Relief flooded her face when she saw Hibbert sitting in the chair by the desk.

"It wasn't a dream. You really did take me away from there. Thank God." Her gaze flitted to Girard, who sat on another chair, this one blocking the door against intruders.

She struggled to a sitting position, her brows drawing together in concern.

"It's all right, Emma," Hibbert assured her. "This is Monsieur Girard. He's a friend of Lord Royce's. He lives here in Paris. He's come to help us."

Emma relaxed. "You're French?"

"Mais oui." His smile was gentle. "And you're a very strong young woman. You've endured a great deal. But it's over now. Hibbert and I will see to it."

She managed a small smile. "Thank you."

Hibbert stood, fetched a tray from the nightstand, and offered it to her. "I had some tea sent up. It's probably cooled off a bit, but I think you should drink it. There are rolls, too. I want you to eat. You've got to regain your strength."

Emma's lashes lowered as she contemplated the tray on her lap. When they lifted again, there were tears in her eyes. "I hope my father turns out to be as fine a gentleman as you are."

Hibbert felt an uncustomary surge of sentiment. "Your father is very fortunate to be getting you as a daughter. And, yes, he's a decent man. I think you'll like him. I know he'll be very relieved to learn you're all right."

A spark of curiosity lit her eyes. "You know the Viscount Ryder?"

"I assist Lord Royce with his work. So, yes, I'm acquainted with the viscount."

"Will you tell me about him? Later, when all this is over and the other women are also safe?"

Hibbert and Girard exchanged glances. It was no surprise that Emma Martin needed something to cling to. Nor was it a surprise that her thoughts had turned to her sire. He might be a stranger to her, but he was all she had left. What *was* surprising was that, after all she'd been through, she was caring enough to postpone her own needs and think of others.

Lord Ryder was luckier than he knew.

"There's no need to wait until after the rescue," Hibbert replied. "It's not even dawn. Once Girard and I have worked out a plan, I'd be pleased to tell you whatever I know about the viscount."

Some color was beginning to return to her cheeks. "I'm grateful." She poured herself some tea, took a sip. "What can I tell you that would help?"

"Three things," Girard responded, rising to his feet and pacing about.

"First, when is the best time to break into Le Joyau? Should we wait until evening when the women are . . ." He broke off, gave an awkward cough.

"It's all right, Mr. Girard," Emma assured him with a quiet dignity that tugged at the heartstrings. "Thanks to Mr. Hibbert, I was spared being defiled. Nonetheless, I lost my innocence at that brothel. Beforehand, actually—when that animal shot my mother. Yes, the best time to break into Le Joyau is when Maurelle's women are working. Not before midnight, because most of them are still doing their more formal entertaining in one of the parlors. But afterwards, when they've retired to the bedchambers to earn their pay." She pursed her lips thoughtfully. "Sometime between one and three A.M. That way, you'll avoid those patrons who choose to depart early," contempt laced her tone, "to return home to their wives."

Girard nodded, averting his gaze out of some instinctive respect for this decent young woman. "Can you think what the best way would be for us to get in?"

She gave a bitter laugh. "I don't need to think. I *know* the best way for you to get in. It's the same way I dreamed about escaping through every moment of the day I spent in that particular room." She shuddered, took another long sip of tea. "There's a window in back, on the ground floor. It leads to an empty storage room. That's the room where the killer first brought me. Later, Maurelle dragged me down the hall and put me in with the other women she means to sell."

"How many rooms did you pass along the way?"

Emma frowned, trying to recall. "Not many. It was very quiet in that area of the house. Maurelle wanted it that way. She had to be sure that, if any of the women cried out, nothing could be overheard by her patrons."

Girard's disgust was evident. "I understand. Tell me, Miss Martin, did you happen to notice if the window in that storage room was locked?"

"As I said, I planned my escape at least two dozen times. So, yes, I studied the window, and its lock. It's actually a latch. Not a very strong one. A man could definitely break it. Also, the window is hidden by some ivy. That makes it hard to find." She set aside the tray. "When do you plan to break in?"

Surprise darted across Girard's handsome features. "Why?"

"Because I want to be there. I can show you where the window is, and where the women are being kept. I can also help keep your presence a secret. When you first burst in, those women are going to be terrified. Someone is bound to scream. But if I go in before you, explain what's about to happen, they'll be prepared."

Girard's jaw dropped. "You would do that? You'd go back there, after all you've been through?"

"For this? Yes." She gazed from Girard to Hibbert. "When shall we go?"

"Tonight." Hibbert's mind was already racing. "It must be tonight. The sooner we grab Maurelle, the sooner she'll lead us to the assassin. Time is running out."

"That leads me to the third question," Girard continued, nodding his agreement. "Miss Martin, where are Maurelle's chambers?"

"They're in a separate section of the house. But you won't find her there. She doesn't retire until daylight, after all the night's payments have been collected. She reads all night in the front parlor—the one I met Mr. Hibbert in. The only exceptions are when she's away, and when her noble assassin visits. But he's not at Le Joyau now. So she'll be in the salon, not her chambers."

"I'll get the women," Girard told Hibbert quietly. "I'm sure you want the pleasure of seizing Mademoiselle Le Joyau."

A terse nod. "She'll be accompanying me back to England," Hibbert informed him. "You keep the women here in Paris. Find a safe place for them. Until the killer is caught, it's not safe for them to go home. We can't run the risk of him finding out they've escaped. That includes you, Emma."

Her shrug was sad. "That's fine. I'm not sure I'm ready to go home and face a future without my mother."

"I'll make the arrangements," Girard agreed. His gaze drifted to Emma, and there was an intensity in his eyes that was palpable. "You'll be cared for and safe."

"I appreciate that."

"Emma, one more question," Hibbert concluded. "You said the assassin is gone. Do you remember when he left, and how long he stayed at Le Joyau on his last visit?"

She squeezed her eyes shut. "One day spilled into the next. I didn't see him leave. It must have been several days ago. As for how long he stayed, I overheard Maurelle's women whispering about how she was closeted in her chambers for a whole day with him. Oh—I also heard some gossip about him coming back next week, after he finalized some urgent business."

"Urgent business," Hibbert repeated grimly. "I can guess what that is. And we must prevent it from happening."

The next porcelain figure arrived at Medford the following night, just after sunset.

It, too, was part of the set of statues that had been stolen from the Canterbury shop—the set depicting two identical women. This time, the women were posed arranging white flowers in a vase. A quiet, tranquil scene.

Except that the flowers had been stained with red paint, as had the women's gowns over their hearts.

The same monstrous touch as last time had been added.

The women's right hands had been stained red, and their right forefingers had been hacked off.

The accompanying note read: *Flowers for Lady Anastasia's grave. Even flanked by Sheldrake and Wells, she'll die. Like an arrow to its target, my bullet will bypass their ranks and find her heart. One bullet. Then one for you. Severed finger, severed lives.*

The household was still reeling from that delivery, when the next one arrived the following afternoon. It was another statue, similar in design, identical in disfigurement, and with a similarly ominous note.

Royce was becoming more and more troubled by the pattern.

His instincts told him that the assassin planned a steady stream of these deliveries until all the statues had reached their mark.

After which, he planned to strike.

If that shopkeeper, Barker, was correct, there were seven statues in all. Which meant only three were still remaining to be delivered.

Time was running out.

So was Royce's patience.

He'd narrowed things down as best he could. There were twenty-five names remaining on his list. Caution decreed he wait until he'd cut that number in half before confronting the suspects.

But caution had never been his strength. He was a risk-taker by nature. He pushed the boundaries and then some. That was how he'd survived as a child, and that was how he achieved his success as an adult.

In this case, however, the risk was acute. By aggressively pursuing the killer, he'd be making himself a walking target. And by doing so without having a damned good idea who the killer was, he'd be relinquishing the upper hand, leaving his own back exposed to attack.

Jeopardizing his life.

Before now, he'd have met that challenge head-on.

But now, there was Breanna—Breanna and their future together.

How could he put that future on the line?

He couldn't.

Except that, fairly soon, he'd have to. There would be no other option. Because if it came down to a choice between Breanna's life and his, there was no choice to make. He'd die before letting that bastard hurt her.

So, if the stream of statues finished arriving at Medford before he finished conducting his investigation, he'd be forced to take action.

By stepping into the middle of things, he'd disrupt the assassin's plan, break his building momentum. Not only that, he'd also divert the assassin's attention from the women to him, acting as a decoy of sorts. He'd venture out to the front gates, announce to Mahoney that he'd narrowed down the list of suspects to three, all of whom he was on his way to confront. On that unnerving note, he'd ride off like the wind. And, like a vicious dog who'd been thrown a piece of meat, the killer would veer off after him, ready to attack his more immediate and dangerous enemy.

The killer's identity would still be unknown.

But he'd be called off Anastasia and Breanna, focused on stopping the man who was threatening to best him.

And when the moment of truth arrived, when the son of a bitch emerged to silence and outwit him, Royce would have his chance to obliterate him.

One chance.

It was a risk. A big one.

The question was, who could shoot first?

Given equal odds, Royce's answer would have been different. But the odds weren't equal. Not when he had no idea who the enemy was. The full advantage lay with the killer.

If there was just a little more time. If Royce could pare down the list to, say, five or six, strengthen his position.

Then he could make his move.

A confident move.

With vehement determination, he returned to his analysis.

Another tortuous day passed.

The next afternoon arrived, menacing skies and icy temperatures matching the somber mood that permeated the house.

Breanna moved about the sitting room, fluffing some cushions, brushing some invisible dust off the wood, and trying to calm her nerves.

She couldn't bear the tension any longer.

She glanced over at Royce, who sat on the settee, his head bent over his work, and watched him slash another three names off the guest list.

She was going to go mad.

Wandering over to the window, she perched at the corner of the ledge, peering around the curtain and surveying the frosty grounds.

A moving object caught her eye, and she squinted, focusing on it and waiting until she could make out who it was.

It was Mahoney, approaching the house at a brisk pace.

Dear God, could it be *another* package?

Breanna held her breath, waiting to see if he clutched a parcel in his hands.

He didn't.

Instead, he had a letter. That meant that another of Royce's contacts had come through, providing an additional bit of information.

She stole another cautious peek at Royce. He looked haggard, his handsome face lined with strain. She couldn't remember the last full hour's sleep he'd had. He was obsessed with his pursuit, relentless in his investigation.

He was also only human.

And Breanna wanted desperately to help him.

She was the only one who could. Hibbert was away. Stacie was the assassin's immediate target. Damen and Wells had to stick to Stacie like glue—just in case—and the guards had to stay, armed and ready, at their posts.

She *had* to do something.

Scrutinizing Royce, Breanna knew this was her chance—maybe her only chance. He was engrossed in a report, not concentrating on her. Besides, it would never occur to him that she'd do anything impulsive. As a rule, impulsiveness was not in her nature.

He was about to learn that every rule had its exceptions.

Slowly, Breanna eased toward the sitting-room doorway. She and Royce were virtually alone in this part of the house; she knew that. The servants were scattered about, in the kitchen or upstairs, performing their duties. Stacie was napping. Wells had gone up an hour ago, to relieve Damen so he could shut his eyes for an hour. No guests were expected, nor would Mahoney allow them through the gates, so it didn't matter that the entranceway was temporarily unattended.

It was now or never.

She slipped into the hallway, hurrying to the front door and opening it before Mahoney could knock.

The head guard looked startled. "Lady Breanna?" he guessed, taking in her neatly coiffed hair. "Why are you attending the door?"

"It's all right, Mr. Mahoney," she assured him. "Everyone is taking a much-needed nap. I don't want to disturb them." She indicated the letter. "Is that for Lord Royce? I'll see that he gets it the minute he awakens."

"Yes, it is. But . . ." Mahoney frowned, as if uncertain what to do. He peered into the deserted hallway, then glanced swiftly back over his shoulder, scanning the grounds in uncomfortable scrutiny. Clearly, he was worried about leaving his post for so long.

In the end, he decided it was best to get back to the gates and do what he'd been hired to do, rather than to stand here and argue with her lady-ship.

He placed the note in her hand. "Here. Now please—go inside."

"I will." With a grateful smile, Breanna complied, shutting the door and leaning back against it.

She tore open the envelope.

The information was terse, but pivotal.

Apparently, Royce had contacted some of his more technically knowledgable men, instructing them to uncover any gunsmith who had the ability to construct a sophisticated and unusual weapon—one designed for a four-fingered man. This reply, from someone named Rogers who was clearly an intelligent, reliable source, stated that he'd found such a gunsmith, although he no longer worked as such—at least not formally. His name was Wilkens, and his shop had been in London. But he'd shut the shop down hastily after finding out that Bow Street was on their way to ascertain whether or not he was supplying weapons to criminals. Now officially retired, he'd just spent several months abroad, and had returned to settle down at his home in Maidstone. An address was provided.

Maidstone? That was only an hour's ride from here.

Breanna put down the letter on an end table and scooted across to col-lect her mantle. Finally, she could do something to help Royce. She'd go and speak with this Wilkens, find out if he was the one who'd crafted the assassin's pistol. She'd do it subtly, of course, ask him questions without alerting him to her intentions. Now that she considered it, she'd probably get farther than Royce would, anyway. The gunsmith, unlawful or not, would be more apt to let down his guard with a wide-eyed young woman than a formidable-looking man.

She reached for the door handle, and hesitated.

The assassin was out there. What if he saw her?

Of course he'd see her—if he hadn't done so already. Her job was to use that fact to her advantage. She knew he wasn't ready to kill her yet. Not with Stacie still alive. So she'd have to do something to satisfy him that she was going somewhere imperative, and for some plausible rea-son.

She'd better make this convincing—for all their sakes.

On that thought, she left the house, shut the door quietly behind her.

She held her breath the entire time she waited for the phaeton to be brought around. It was eerie standing outside in the open, knowing she was being watched, praying she'd accurately assessed the killer's inten-tions.

Her heartbeat accelerated, and she tensed, half-expecting a shot to ring out, to cut her down where she stood. At the same time, she listened for noises sounding behind her—noises that would indicate Royce had discovered her absence and come storming from the house to drag her back inside.

She prayed that wouldn't happen. Because if the assassin saw Royce rush to her rescue, exhibiting the emotion she knew he would, Lord knew how he'd react. He might just decide to further torture her by killing the man she loved—the very thing she'd been trying to prevent.

Never had a phaeton taken so long to arrive.

Finally, it did—without incident.

She thanked the footman, climbed into the seat, then took up the reins and led the horses toward the front gates.

Whatever she said had to be believable—not only to Mr. Mahoney, but to the killer.

One thing she'd learned from surviving two decades with her father, dodging his anger and avoiding being beaten, was that the most convincing lies, the ones you desperately needed to work, were the ones that stuck closest to the truth. The further from the truth you strayed, the more nervous you became and the more likely you were to slip up.

So be it.

She braced herself as she neared the gates, slowing down as Mahoney stepped in her path, holding up his palm and barring her exit.

He approached the phaeton, a stunned expression on his face. "My lady, what in heaven's name . . ." He broke off, inclining his head and staring at her, obviously trying to ascertain if she'd lost her mind—the only logical explanation he could come up with for her to attempt this insane antic.

"I'm not mad, Mr. Mahoney," she supplied, making no attempt to hide her apprehension. Not only was it genuine, it was necessary that she convey it to the assassin. Her gaze darted about, in a very real attempt to ensure her safety and, at the same time, to let the assassin see her sense of urgency. "I must ride out," she announced to Mahoney. "That last correspondence you delivered said there was a second letter—an important one—that should have been delivered along with it. I've got to go after that messenger, catch him right away."

Mahoney's stunned expression didn't change. "With all due respect, my lady, you're hardly the one who should be going after—"

"Mr. Mahoney—please!" Breanna interrupted, her voice and hands shaking. "I realize I should be in the house. But I don't want to take the time to awaken the men. By then, the messenger will be gone. And I certainly can't send Stacie—the initial threats are on her life. It's got to be me." She tightened her grip on the reins. "We're wasting time arguing. If you let me go now, I'll be back in minutes. The longer we wait, the longer it will take to return."

"My men will go." Mahoney turned, raising his arm to issue the order.

"No!" Breanna reached forward, grabbed his sleeve. "That would mean fewer guards to protect Stacie. And if anything happened to her . . ." She sucked in her breath, assuming a tone she rarely used. "Mr. Mahoney, I don't want to put it this way, but I am mistress of this house. If I have to, I'll order you to let me pass. Now, open those gates, before the messenger rides all the way back to London."

Mahoney hesitated another moment. Then, he complied, waving his arm and ordering the guards to open the gates. "I'll give you a half hour," he informed her. "Then, I'm alerting Lord Royce."

She didn't pause to argue. She simply nodded, then slapped her reins and led the horses on.

She sped down the road, then veered west toward Maidstone.

The assassin watched her go with some interest and an unforeseen tinge of respect.

He hadn't expected her to be so brazen. Nor so clever. She'd correctly assessed his determination to adhere to the order in which he meant to carry out his plan. In an odd way, she was baiting him. Well, he wouldn't let her win by giving in to the temptation to shoot her down now, when she was alone and unguarded. Her cousin had to die first—first, and right in front of Lady Breanna's horrified eyes.

He'd made that clear. Nonetheless, she was taking a risk, lest he change his mind.

And all to go after a messenger, to get her hands on that second letter.

Then again, if the information in the letter was *that* important, it would warrant such prompt attention, risk or not. Her reason was sound.

It was also a lie.

From the thick branches of the tree he'd just scaled, he could see her phaeton, heading southwest.

London was northwest.

And, based upon the fact that she'd just intercepted one of Chadwick's messages—a message that probably provided answers to a piece of the puzzle he'd fully expected a worthy opponent like Chadwick to investigate—he had a fairly good idea where she was riding.

And to whom.

Pity. He'd hoped Wilkens could have remained a mystery for a while longer—long enough to speed this process to its natural conclusion while sparing the poor fellow's life. Now, it would set things back a few hours, not to mention forcing him to find another gunsmith, one with as great a flair for the creative as Wilkens had.

It couldn't be helped. Lady Breanna was too fetching, Wilkens too susceptible to beauty, too easily duped, to be relied upon to keep his mouth shut.

Swinging lightly to the ground, the assassin eased through the trees, making his way to the road, then the hidden brush beyond, where his own carriage was concealed.

A sudden, pleasurable thought struck, made his eyes glitter with anticipation.

He knew a back route to Maidstone. He'd beat Lady Breanna there by twenty minutes, take care of his task, and get back to Medford Manor ahead of her—*and* Chadwick, who'd undoubtedly go rushing after her the minute that guard gave him the news of her departure. As for the guards, they'd be frantically searching for her ladyship, cursing themselves for ever allowing her to go.

Leaving the manor vulnerable to attack.

24
❧

"*Y*ou let her do *what?*"

Royce nearly struck Mahoney, visibly controlling himself as the head guard delivered word of Breanna's departure.

Mahoney mopped his brow. "I had no choice, sir. She ordered me—"

"I don't care if she held you at gunpoint." Royce drew a slow breath, biting back his anger in lieu of reason. "Where did she go?"

"After the messenger."

"*What* messenger?"

"The one who sent you that last piece of correspondence, the one I brought to the door right before Lady Breanna left." Mahoney swallowed. "She took it from me herself, said she'd give it to you when you woke up."

"She didn't. And I wasn't sleeping." Royce scanned the hallway, and spied the letter on the end table. He snatched it up, read through it quickly. "This says nothing about another message. It says . . ." He came to the word Maidstone, and his jaw snapped shut. "God, no."

He nearly knocked Mahoney down in his haste to leave. "Go inside. Tell Lord Sheldrake that I think Breanna's ridden to Maidstone. Post a few guards outside Anastasia's chambers. Then get the rest of the guards to begin a search, just in case I'm wrong and Breanna's gone elsewhere. We've got to find her."

The cottage was quiet.

Breanna brought her phaeton to a halt, taking a minute to compose herself and review her story before approaching Mr. Wilkens.

She had to seem pathetic, to weep real tears as she told him her fabricated story of the tragic accident that had claimed her father's trigger finger. She'd scatter in as many facts as possible, confess that her father had been involved with unsavory types. She'd say that out of desperation,

she'd used those contacts, taken unorthodox steps to find out who the most qualified gunsmith was to craft a new pistol for her father, who was confined to Newgate, and desperate to escape.

An ironic smile touched her lips. Who'd ever have thought her father's unscrupulous dealings would serve her so well?

She climbed down, gathered up her skirts, and marched to the door.

Her first knock went unanswered.

So did the repeated ones that followed.

Oh, God, he has to be home, she thought fervently. *He has to be.*

Resorting to something she never would have considered, Breanna turned the door handle and entered.

The door swung open.

"Mr. Wilkens?" she called.

No response.

Breanna stepped into the small, cluttered house, praying the gunsmith was either asleep or hard of hearing. Just so long as he was home. She made her way down the hall, calling out his name as she did. She paused at each room, stepping inside and checking to see if he was there.

The door to the sitting room was shut.

"Mr. Wilkens?" she tried hopefully, twisting the handle and giving it a push.

The door wasn't locked. But it wouldn't budge.

Frowning, Breanna shoved at the wood, only to be met with the same resistance. Finally, she threw her weight against it, jarring the door until it shifted enough to let her squeeze through.

A blast of cold air accosted her from the open window in the far corner of the room.

She shivered, drew her mantle more tightly around herself as she stepped inside.

A scream froze in her throat.

Wilkens's body lay on the floor, a stream of blood trickling from his chest, pooling on the floor beneath him.

He was dead.

"Dear God," she whispered, pressing her fist to her mouth. "Oh, dear God." She backed away, unable to stop staring at the man's lifeless form as she inched toward the hall.

Powerful hands grabbed her from behind.

This time her scream broke free, and she began struggling violently against whoever held her captive.

"Breanna, it's me." Royce swung her around, seized her shoulders in his hands. His eyes were nearly black with anger, his features taut with worry. "Are you all right?"

"Royce." She sagged toward him, happier to see him than she'd ever been to see anyone in her life.

"Reckless little fool," he muttered, dragging her against him and holding her with arms that shook. "You scared the hell out of me."

She gripped the lapels of Royce's coat. "He's dead," she managed, gesturing toward the sitting room. "Shot like the others."

Keeping one arm snaked tightly around Breanna's waist, Royce leaned past her, peered inside. Frowning, he released Breanna long enough to check Wilkens, verify he was dead.

"That son of a bitch beat us here," he pronounced, rising to his feet, noting the open window. "And not by much. Wilkens couldn't have been shot more than a half hour ago, judging from the body. Somehow that bastard knew where you were headed. He used the window to escape."

Breanna was trying to steady her breathing, to clear her head. "How could he know my destination? He didn't read Rogers's letter. It was sealed when Mahoney delivered it. He must have seen through my story about pursuing the messenger." Her voice quavered. "It's my fault this man is dead."

"No." Royce drew her against him, stroked her hair. "Wilkens was doomed the minute Rogers's note was delivered to Medford. Had I received it first, I would have done precisely what you did—ridden to Maidstone to question Wilkens. The assassin is smart. He knew I was checking into the gunsmith who crafted his pistol. He'd have seen where I was headed, and put two and two together. He'd have dashed on ahead of me, killed Wilkens before I had the chance to talk to him. Just as he did with you. The only difference is, *I* would have been the one in danger. Which is how it should have been."

Royce buried his lips in her hair. "Dammit, Breanna, don't do that to me ever again. I was terrified." He paused, realized she was trembling. "Let's go home. Anastasia is probably frantic by now."

That had the desired effect.

"Stacie knows where I've gone?" Breanna asked, worry supplanting shock.

"By now, yes. I told Mahoney. The whole household is probably in turmoil. And the guards must be scouring Kent looking for you."

Breanna's grip on his coat tightened. "If so, they won't be guarding Stacie."

"Yes they will." Royce eased her worry, his knuckles gently stroking her cheek. "Damen and Wells are with her. They're both armed. I had Mahoney post guards outside her room, as well. No one will get by them."

"We've got to go." Breanna was already heading for the door.

Royce escorted her to the phaeton, stopping only to harness his mount to the front, alongside the horses who'd guided her here. "I rode here on horseback. It's the only way I could gain the time I needed. We'll ride back together. I'll hail a local constable along the way, tell him about Wilkens's body."

Breanna nodded mutely, sitting in a numbed state as Royce turned the phaeton around, headed for home.

An icy premonition began forming deep in her gut.

It spread, crawling up her spine, intensifying as their carriage neared Medford Manor.

She'd known that premonition before. It had struck last August, an instant before the assassin stepped out of the shadows, took a shot at Stacie.

He was closing in, nearing the moment when he'd complete his unfinished execution.

Abruptly, Breanna seized Royce's arm. "Royce, I've got to get home. Now."

Royce studied her terrified expression, instantly slapping the reins to comply. "What is it?"

"It's the killer. He's getting close to Stacie."

Lady Anastasia would wait.

The assassin's lips curled in a mocking smile as he peered around the corner of the hall, watched the two guards standing rigidly in front of the marchioness's door.

Putting them there had no doubt been Chadwick's doing. He was making sure Lady Anastasia stayed safe while he dashed off after her cousin. Well, Chadwick needn't have worried. It wasn't time for her ladyship to die—not yet. Not without her wretched cousin there to watch the life drain out of her. That would defeat his whole purpose, take the satisfaction out of his revenge.

No, this visit would serve a different purpose. This visit would be to deliver his ultimate gift to Lady Breanna.

Getting inside the manor had been pathetically easy.

The guards were dashing about like frantic mice, leaving gaping holes in security.

He'd made his way across the grounds, then slipped inside via the servants' quarters. He'd waited in the shadows, assessing the area to ensure it was clear. Not surprisingly, it had been. Lady Breanna's loyal staff was undoubtedly combing the house, room by room, looking for a sign of where their mistress had gone.

He'd scaled the stairs, then hovered in the alcove off the landing before easing his way down the hall to scrutinize Lord and Lady Sheldrake's chambers.

Scornfully, he turned away, wondering if the guards actually thought him stupid enough, amateur enough, to lunge for the door with them standing outside it. Perhaps they were novices. He was not.

He moved furtively toward Lady Breanna's chambers.

Noiselessly, he twisted the door handle and walked in.

It took him ten seconds to realize something wasn't right. The room looked far more barren than before, a sense of abandonment hovering in the air.

He scanned the room swiftly, realizing at once that the porcelain figures were gone, as were the other personal touches.

Lady Breanna had been moved elsewhere.

Rage boiled up inside him.

The little bitch had changed rooms, and she'd done so successfully, without alerting him. She'd obviously staged her regular evening routine so he'd think all was as usual.

She'd pay for this victory. Pay dearly.

Where were her new chambers?

He didn't have to rack his brain for an answer.

Chadwick. He'd moved her closer to his room, put her somewhere he could keep an eye on her.

A triumphant glint flashed in his eyes.

Their little deception had just ended. Now, it was his turn to gloat.

Breanna burst into the house.

She gathered up her skirts, dashing up the stairs and down the hall to Stacie's room.

The two guards looked startled by the commotion. But, seeing who was causing it, they relaxed, very relieved to see Lady Breanna home, unhurt.

"Is my cousin all right?" she demanded.

"Yes, ma'am," one guard replied. "We've been posted outside her room for over two hours now."

"And no one's tried to get in?"

He gave an adamant shake of his head. "No one."

At that instant, the door was flung open, and Stacie bypassed Damen and Wells, stepping into the hallway and giving Breanna a fierce hug. "I heard your voice. Thank God, you're all right."

Breanna nearly wept with relief. "My sentiments exactly. I had the most awful feeling. I thought that . . ." She broke off, drew a steadying breath. "It doesn't matter. What matters is that you're safe."

"*I'm* safe?" Stacie asked in amazement. "*You're* the one who went out in the open, left Medford Manor to ride to Maidstone. Why? Who was in Maidstone?"

Before Breanna could reply, Royce came up behind her. "I'll answer your questions, Anastasia," he said quietly. "I think Breanna needs to lie down."

Even as he spoke, Breanna realized her knees were shaking. She felt weak and wobbly, the aftermath of discovering a murdered man's body, then fearing for her cousin's life, more severe than she'd realized.

"I . . . Yes, I think I should lie down—for a few minutes," she added, seeing the concern on Stacie's face. "I'm fine. Just spent."

Royce gestured to one of the guards. "Walk Lady Breanna down to her room. Stay outside the door until I get there."

"Of course, m'lord."

Breanna shot Royce a grateful look, then turned, headed toward her new chambers, the guard by her side. All she needed was a few minutes to herself—time to lie down, put a cool compress on her pounding head. Then she'd be fine, ready to go back and discuss where things stood now that the gunsmith was unable to tell them anything.

She nodded politely at the guard, opened the door to her room, and shut it behind her. She was relieved to know he was out there. Still, she loathed this need for confinement. She couldn't wait for the day she could come and go again as she pleased.

If that day ever came.

Unbidden, the image of Wilkens's lifeless body flashed in her mind, and she fought back the sickness that rose in her throat.

How many more people would die before this nightmare ended? How much longer would this assassin's rampage continue?

Distraught, she crossed over, turned up the lamp on her nightstand to offset the effects of the intensifying dusk.

A horrified scream lodged in her throat, and for a moment, she actually stopped breathing.

In the center of the bed lay a white glove. The glove had been impaled by a sword, which was now imbedded deeply in the mattress. It had been driven all the way through the glove's index finger. Three-quarters of that finger had been sliced off. Red paint was splattered everywhere, staining the bedcovers and trickling onto the carpet. On either side of the glove sat a statue—both from the same set as the previous statues. Once again, the women had been disfigured, their right index fingers lopped off, their right hands and the front of their gowns covered with bright crimson stains.

On the pillow, lay a note. It read:

Your strategy was a mistake. You changed quarters to outsmart me. Instead, you enraged me. I'm an expert tracker. And you're a fool. Your evasive tactics have now guaranteed Lady Anastasia a more agonizing death. Listen to her screams, as her life drains away. Your cousin's time is up. Her blood is on your hands. My satisfaction will come when I see yours flow. The invasion is about to commence.

Die, Lady Breanna.

For a long moment, Breanna just stood there, paralyzed, besieged by a sort of white shock. She stared at the note, the glove, the crimson splotches that looked so much like blood.

Hysteria bubbled up inside her.

Then, the dam burst, and she shattered.

Letting out a low cry of pain, she covered her face with her hands, tears coursing down her cheeks. Her entire body shook with the impact of her sobs, everything converging in an unendurable knot of anguish that tore her entire soul apart.

She couldn't take anymore.

She sank down on her knees on the rug, fear and agony converging, slashing through her in clawing talons. Her sobs tore at her, emerging in low, wrenching gasps as she rocked back and forth, emotionally surrendering to that which she could no longer fight.

As if from far away, she heard the door open.

"Breanna, my God, what is it?" Royce crossed over, then stopped. A muffled oath escaped him as he saw what had occurred.

He lowered himself to his knees, enfolded Breanna in his arms. "Shh," he murmured, cradling her to him, feeling her tears drench his shirt. "I'm here, sweetheart. I'm here."

"I'm s-sorry," she sobbed. "I j-just can't be strong anymore."

"You don't have to be." Royce's grip tightened, and he squeezed his eyes shut, aching for what this was doing to her. This incredibly strong, resilient woman, this woman he loved to the core of his being, had been pushed beyond human limits.

At that moment, Royce loathed the assassin with a murderous hatred so powerful, he could have torn him apart limb from limb, killed him with his bare hands.

"I'm weaker than you b-believed me to be," Breanna whispered, in a broken voice that tore at Royce's heart. "I-I didn't mean to disappoint you."

"You didn't disappoint me," he returned fiercely. "You're every bit as strong as I believed. And as brave. Everyone has a breaking point, Breanna. Everyone. Most would have reached theirs long ago." Royce's furious gaze raked the bed, darkening as it settled on the mutilated glove. "There's no one alive who wouldn't crumple after walking in and seeing that."

Breanna nodded, her sobs beginning to lessen from the sound of

Royce's soothing voice, the feel of his arms around her. "I was right about his being in the house," she managed, her muscles relaxing as Royce stroked her back in slow, soothing circles. "Seeing the guards must have stopped him from going after Stacie. Instead, he went to leave me those . . ." a shudder, "things. And he found out I'd changed rooms."

"The guards weren't his only deterrent. You kept him from going after Anastasia."

She leaned back, gave him a teary, quizzical look. "I?"

"Yes. Your not being here." Royce brushed his lips across her cheeks, taking her tears with him. God, how he wanted to comfort her, give her his strength. "Remember, the bastard wants you present when he takes aim at Anastasia. He knew you were in Maidstone. So shooting your cousin was out. That wasn't the reason for his breaking in here today."

"Leaving me his most hideous gift was."

"Yes." Wisely, Royce omitted telling her his theory about the statues, that he believed the assassin was delivering the remaining three figures, then striking.

Two of those remaining figures were now sitting on Breanna's bed. Which left one.

"Royce . . ." Breanna pressed her wet face against his shoulder. "I can't stay in this room another night. I don't know where to go, what to do."

"Stay with me." He rose, gently easing her to her feet. "Not just tonight, but every night until this ordeal is over. I don't give a damn what protocol dictates. You're sleeping in my bed, by my side. What's more, not only will Wells agree, he'll hand-pick the guards who stand outside our door. But sweetheart," he added, trying to give her a measure of peace. "I don't think he means to break into your room again. This was his final appearance."

Rather than relieved, Breanna looked more unnerved, fear darkening her eyes. "That's what terrifies me. It's like this was a culmination of sorts. And, if so, he's about to shoot Stacie."

"To *try* to shoot her," Royce corrected. "He won't succeed." He walked over to the bed, picked up the note, and reread it carefully. "Something about these notes keeps nagging at me," he muttered. "I'm going to line up the whole lot of them and read them together." He turned his attention back to Breanna. "*After* we get you settled." He went back, tilted up her chin. "Better?" he asked softly.

A slow nod. "I've never lost control so totally," she murmured self-consciously, her hand fluttering over her hair. "You must have thought I'd gone insane when you walked in and saw me on the floor, weeping like that."

"Stop it." Royce caught her hand, tugged it away from her hair, and brought her palm to his lips. "I thought we'd broken down that ludicrous wall of self-restraint by now."

Her lashes lowered. "We have."

"Breanna, do you trust me?"

Her head shot up. "You know I do—with my life."

"Then trust me with your vulnerabilities, as well. I promise, I'll protect them."

Breanna's eyes misted. "You're such a wonderful man," she whispered.

"I'm a man in love." Royce kissed her tenderly. "And, by the way," he added with a twinkle. "You *have* lost control so totally. You do so every night in my arms."

She flushed, his teasing comment having the desired effect, melting away a bit of the past hour's horror. "You're right."

"And have you ever regretted it?"

"Never."

"Then don't regret this either." He enfolded her against him for one brief, intense moment. "I'll never let anyone hurt you," he said in a raw voice. "Not physically or emotionally. You have my word." He released her, guided her toward the door. "Now, let's get you out of here."

Outside, the assassin watched the room go dark.

Chadwick was taking her out of there, hiding her elsewhere.

It didn't matter.

There was no need to invade her bedchamber again.

He'd selected a different battlefield for her death.

25

❧

*R*oyce made Breanna drink an entire glass of Madeira, then ordered dinner for two to be served in his chambers.

Instructing two guards to remain outside his door, he left Breanna only long enough to tell Anastasia, Damen, and Wells what had happened, as well as what provisions he'd made.

He'd dealt with their distress as expediently as possible, answered their questions with terse directness. Then, he informed them they'd discuss this tomorrow, after Breanna had gotten some sleep.

"Royce, is she all right?" Anastasia had asked anxiously.

"She's badly shaken. But you know how bloody strong she is." Royce had frowned. "How strong she *insists* on being. I'd let you see her, but I want you to stay put. I'm going to go over those letters the killer sent. Maybe there's something there that will point me in the right direction. We'll discuss it at breakfast."

With that, he'd left them. Wells, as he'd suspected, was more relieved than shocked to learn where Breanna would be sleeping. The safety of his beloved charges was more important than his adherence to protocol. After quietly thanking Royce for caring for Miss Breanna, he'd summoned two footmen, ordered them to clean up the violated bedchamber immediately; removing all traces of the break-in, but saving the defaced items for Lord Royce's later inspection.

Royce had returned to his room, expecting to find Breanna huddled by the fire. Instead, she was sitting at the desk, scrutinizing the assassin's notes.

She looked up when he entered, her composure fully restored, her brows knit speculatively. "I was paralyzed when I first read tonight's message," she murmured. "But now that I examine it with a clear head, one of the killer's phrases triggered a memory—a memory of something Mr. Cunnings said to my father at their meeting in the tavern."

"The meeting you eavesdropped on."

"Yes. The one at which they made arrangements for the assassin to execute Stacie."

"Go on," Royce urged.

"I remember Father asking about the assassin's credentials, and Mr. Cunnings assuring him there was no one better at tracking people down and killing them—no matter where they were hiding. Cunnings's exact words were that the assassin was an expert tracker and an even better shot."

" 'An expert tracker'—the very words the assassin uses here." Royce walked over, reexamined the notes with that in mind. "Interesting. And maybe not as straightforward as I originally thought."

"What do you mean?"

"I realized from the start that every one of these messages sounded like a battle call. But I just assumed it was this arrogant bastard's way of making you feel like he was the hunter, and you the prey. But looking at it in light of what Cunnings said—maybe there's more to it than that."

Breanna twisted around to gaze up at him. "Like what?"

Royce's eyes narrowed, a flash of insight illuminating their midnight blue color. "Maybe that's what's been bothering me. These notes are all full of military jargon: retreat, flank, reconnaissance, strategy; and phrases like 'evasive tactics' and 'the invasion is about to commence.' "

"True," Breanna concurred. "I wouldn't have recognized the ones you just mentioned, having never served in the military, as you did. But even I know that words like battle, warrior, and ranks are combat terms."

"So maybe we're overlooking the obvious," Royce concluded. "Maybe this isn't just an arbitrary choice of analogies. Maybe it's based on the killer's personal experience."

Breanna rose slowly. "He had to get his training somewhere. What better place than the army?"

Royce was already yanking out the guest list, grabbing a quill. "I'll make a list of these twenty-two remaining names. First thing tomorrow, my contacts will check into every one of their backgrounds, see who's served." He frowned. "Offhand, I see three or four names this could apply to. Obviously, Crompton was a general. He tells that to anyone who will listen. Radebrook was an officer in the infantry. Landow spent a few years in the horse artillery, if I'm not mistaken. The Duke of Maywood served, too—I believe in the cavalry. His enlisting was a big scandal, since he was heir to his father's dukedom. He only served a few months before his father won out and he returned."

"When did all this happen?"

"Fifteen or more years ago. I was young, away at school. All I recall is the gossip surrounding the event. I have no idea how adept any of these men are at shooting, or if there are others on this list who are equally competent. I want every name looked into, every military man found. I want to know where they were stationed, what branch they served in, details of their service records. We'll line up the information, compare it to the traits I've established for this killer, and see if we come up with some plausible matches. Then, I'll pay visits to all those matches. I'll accuse each man of being a murderer, if need be, tell them I have evidence of their crimes, just to gauge their reactions. All of them will call me out. Only one will follow me back to kill me. I don't care how damned risky it is. Not anymore. It's the only way I'm going to get at the truth in time."

Breanna was about to protest, when a commotion from downstairs met their ears.

Voices. Slamming doors. Treading feet.

Breanna went sheet white.

Royce whipped out his pistol, moved slowly toward the hallway. "Stay put," he ordered Breanna. "Don't go near the door or the windows. I'll find out what this is about."

He was halfway to the door when the knock sounded. "Lord Royce?" one of the guards called. "Mr. Hibbert's back. He needs to see you immediately."

Royce and Breanna exchanged glances. "Tell Hibbert to come directly to my chambers," Royce instructed the guard.

"Yes, sir."

Three minutes later, Hibbert walked in, looking rumpled and tired, but rife with purpose. "I have some crucial information and even more crucial cargo . . ." He broke off, spying Breanna leaning against the desk. "My lady," he acknowledged. His forehead creased with worry as he saw the frightened state she was in. "What's happened?"

"A great deal," Royce answered for her. "But all that can wait. Something obviously took place in Paris. Were you able to learn who bought that perfume?"

"Bought not only the perfume, but the women, as well," Hibbert corrected.

Breanna gasped. "What?"

Hibbert swiftly relayed the details of what he'd discovered: Maurelle's identity, her relationship to the assassin, her part in the sale of the women. He told them about Emma, how he'd bought her from Maurelle, and how she'd assisted him and Girard in rescuing the others.

"Is she all right?" Breanna asked. "And the other kidnapped women— are they unharmed?"

"Other than being badly shaken, yes. Fortunately, we got there before any real damage had been done. The first thing I did was to grab

Mademoiselle Le Joyau. Then, I questioned her employees, only to find out that none of them had any more information on the killer than Emma did. Their description of him matched hers, as did the fact that they knew him only as the noble assassin."

"My God," Breanna managed.

Hibbert rubbed his palms together. "I escorted Mademoiselle Le Joyau out of her establishment and into a carriage headed for Calais—at gunpoint. We boarded the first ship to Dover. As for the kidnapped women, Girard is keeping them in Paris until it's safe for them to return. And Maurelle Le Joyau," he concluded with a tight smile, "is downstairs in the servants' quarters, being looked after by three guards. I'll take you to her whenever you wish."

Royce rubbed the back of his neck pensively. "So the assassin's partner is a woman. Tell me about this Maurelle Le Joyau."

"Obviously, she's French. She's also exquisitely beautiful and equally cunning. She was more than charming to Lord Hobson. Especially when she saw how wealthy he was. To Hibbert . . ." A mocking smile. "She's refused to speak a word since we left Paris. Girard is running a check on her background and history to see what he can find out. He said he'll dispatch his findings posthaste. Oh, he also said to tell you that the physician who treated the assassin's finger was a doctor named Helmett. He's German-born, extremely wealthy, and successful. He's a genius at reconstructing limbs. He's also on an extended holiday. But it seems no one knows where he's gone or when he'll be returning."

"Convenient. Hopefully, we won't need to hunt him down. Not with Mademoiselle Le Joyau at our disposal. She'll lead us to the killer more quickly than his physician." Royce's features tightened into fierce lines, his predatory stance making him look like a wolf about to close in on a sheep.

"Stay with Breanna," Royce instructed Hibbert. "Keep her in this room—with you by her side, and the guards outside the door. As for Mademoiselle Le Joyau, I want to see her. *Immédiatement.*"

Hibbert nodded. "I thought you might."

Royce took a step, then halted, as a troublesome prospect struck home. "Did you and Mademoiselle Le Joyau arrive in an open carriage?"

"No." Hibbert had obviously anticipated this question. "I hired a closed carriage. And when we neared Medford Manor, I insisted that Mademoiselle Le Joyau lie down beneath the opposite seat, covered by some blankets. She wasn't pleased. Nevertheless, my pistol ensured her cooperation. I smuggled her in the rear entrance, the blanket over her head. Believe me, my lord, no one saw her arrive."

"Excellent." Anticipation glinted in Royce's eyes. "That means her presence at Medford is our little secret. Fine work, Hibbert. That resolved, it's time for me to pay mademoiselle a little visit. Where in the servants' quarters can I find her?"

"In the vacant room next to Wells's quarters." An ironic lift of Hibbert's brows. "I hate to admit it, but Wells has proven himself to have stamina, a quick mind, and fine instincts. All of which," he added, with a quick sideways look at Breanna, "I will deny having said, should anyone feel compelled to tell him." A hint of a smile. "In any case, given Wells's abilities, I thought it best we restrict Mademoiselle Le Joyau to an area he can oversee—when he isn't guarding Lady Sheldrake's door."

"I agree." Royce paused only long enough to go to Breanna, frame her face between his palms. "Will you be all right?" he asked tenderly. "I won't be gone long."

"I'll be fine," she assured him, actually able to force a smile, thanks to Hibbert's light banter. "Hibbert will take excellent care of me. And I'll fill him in on what happened here since he left. Now, go. I'm itching to hear what this Maurelle Le Joyau has to say. *If* she'll say anything, that is."

Royce's jaw clenched. "Oh, she'll say plenty—beginning with that bastard's name. Because if she doesn't . . ." He sucked in his breath. "Let's just say she won't like the consequences."

Royce stalked into the tiny room in the servants' wing firmly intending to intimidate Maurelle Le Joyau into telling him everything, even if he had to choke the information out of her.

Two things stopped him.

One, was his immediate assessment that this was no ordinary woman.

Despite her fragile appearance, Maurelle was impervious as steel, her chin held high, her dark eyes mocking him and any attempt he'd make to extract information from her. She wouldn't relent, his instincts proclaimed, not even if he thrashed her. Violence didn't frighten her. Knowing her relationship to the killer, she was probably accustomed to it—witnessing it and, quite possibly, enduring it. So, threats would be wasted.

And then, there was the second thing.

Royce had seen this woman before.

He wasn't quite sure where. But the instant he laid eyes on Maurelle Le Joyau, he was certain of it.

She didn't know him.

There wasn't a flicker of recognition on her face, not even before she had time to school her features. She simply sat at the edge of the chair, her hands folded primly in her lap, her taunting stare daring him to do his worst.

Instantly, Royce abandoned his plan to take the harshest, most direct avenue possible, to go in for the kill simply because they were running out of time.

A different approach was in order with this woman—one she wasn't used to. The direct approach. No tricks, no casually asked questions she was too smart to answer, and definitely no browbeating.

He'd learn far more about her this way.

And in the process, figure out where he'd met her.

"Hello, mademoiselle," he greeted, shutting the door behind him and leaning back against it. "My name is Royce Chadwick."

A glint of interest. "Ah, so you're the infamous Lord Chadwick." She inclined her head, appraising him thoughtfully. "You're not what I expected."

"Really?" Royce purposely abandoned his sentrylike stance, strolling over to pull up a chair directly across from her. "What did you expect?"

"An older man. One with more wrath and less charm."

Royce leaned back in his seat, crossed one long leg over the other. "How did you form this opinion? From what Hibbert told you?"

An arrogant smile, one that confirmed Royce's belief that she was far too shrewd to fall into a trap. "No. Mr. Hibbert and I didn't discuss you at all. *Au contraire,* my lord, you need no discussion. Your reputation precedes you. It travels all the way to the Continent—even to establishments like Le Joyau."

"I'm flattered." Royce tried to place her voice. He'd heard it before—briefly. But mostly what he recognized was her face. Where had he been when he'd seen it?

"Maurelle—may I call you Maurelle?" he inquired politely.

"*Mais oui.*" She gave a careless shrug. "Suit yourself. You're in charge here."

"As you were at Le Joyau."

"*Certainement.*"

Royce drummed his fingers lightly on his leg. "I don't enjoy playing cat and mouse, Maurelle. I suspect you don't either. So why don't I refrain from insulting you? I want the name of the noble assassin. And you're going to give it to me."

Maurelle didn't bat a lash. "You're insane if you believe that."

"Why?" Royce demanded. "Are we engaged in some sort of contest? A battle of wills? Are you determined to best me, just as your friend is?"

"You flatter yourself, my lord. You mean as little to me as you do to him. You're just an obstacle, nothing more. So, no, I'm not trying to best you. As for him—let's say our motives are quite different. He has his, and I mine."

"And what are yours?"

"To protect him. Which I will do, no matter what you do to me."

Maurelle rose, shook out the folds of her gown, and braced herself before him, as if preparing for a vicious beating. "I'm sure you require proof. So go ahead. Do your worst. You'll find out I'm true to my word."

Royce feigned shock, letting his jaw drop a notch. "You'd endure physical abuse just to protect a lover?"

Anger flashed in her eyes. "He's not *just* a lover. In fact, the word 'just' never applies to him. He's not 'just' anything. He's extraordinary."

"You're in love with him."

A brittle stare. "Did you think women like me didn't fall in love? That because we've been with hundreds of men over the years that there could never be one that actually meant something? If so, you're a fool."

"I'm no fool, Maurelle." Royce stood, steadily meeting her gaze. "I was just making a statement, not a judgement. You're in love with this man."

"*Oui*—now more than ever."

Now more than ever? An interesting choice of phrases.

How long had these two known each other?

Royce pursued the question from a nonthreatening angle. "As for your bedding hundreds of men, I was under the impression that you're the proprietor of Le Joyau. Do you entertain customers, as well?"

"Only him. That part of my life is over."

Just the answer he wanted.

So, Maurelle Le Joyau had been a prostitute before graduating to her more lucrative role. Had it been at the establishment now known as Le Joyau, or had it been elsewhere? And when had she met the assassin— before or after she changed roles?

Royce had to tread carefully to get his answers.

"Tell me, Maurelle, how would your noble assassin feel if he knew you were once a common whore?"

A throaty laugh. "I assure you, I was never common—no matter how shabby my surroundings. I was always a treasure. A coveted treasure— worth everything a man had and more. There's no one like me. Not then, not now, not ever. No one understood that better than he."

She'd given Royce both his answers. Her days as a prostitute had been spent somewhere else. Somewhere shabby. And the assassin had already known her there.

"So he's familiar with who you are," Royce acknowledged, diverting her attention from the fact that she'd just supplied him with vital infor-mation. "What about you, Maurelle? Do you know what he does? How he gets you the women he delivers?"

That scornful look returned. "Ah, you're hoping to deliver a crushing blow. To shock me into revealing his name. Don't bother. Yes, Lord

Chadwick, I know what he does. I know how he rids the women I sell of their family ties. And I know what he intends for your friend Lady Breanna. Death—one bullet to the heart." Her brows arched in sardonic question. "He's a superb marksman, wouldn't you say?"

Royce forced his features to remain impassive, fully aware she was trying to goad him into an emotional reaction. "Indeed he is. A filthy animal, but a superb marksman."

"Now you're trying to provoke me, monsieur. That won't work on me any more than it just did on you."

"I'm impressed. You're a formidable adversary." Royce studied her closely, focusing on her face. What was it about her? Her features, her mannerisms. The utter self-confidence of her stance.

No matter how shabby my surroundings . . . I was always a treasure. A coveted treasure . . .

Abruptly, an image flashed through Royce's mind—a younger, less sophisticated Maurelle, but Maurelle nonetheless.

The pieces slammed into place, the scene replaying from start to finish.

He had his answer.

It was time to do something with it.

Unaware of the direction Royce's thoughts had taken, Maurelle played right into his hands, assuming she was taunting him.

She stretched her arms high over her head, then covered her mouth to stifle a yawn. "If you're not going to beat or brutalize me in any way, I'd like to get some sleep." A mocking smile. "May we continue this interrogation tomorrow?"

Royce nearly laughed aloud. Maurelle was waiting for him to fly into a tirade. While, in truth, he was delighted to comply with her request. He was impatient to get out of that room, itching to put his new realization to work.

Still, he couldn't arouse her suspicions.

Feigning irritation, he gave a curt nod. "As you wish. But tomorrow begins quite early here. Don't expect to get much sleep."

Maurelle looked amused. "I can do with very little sleep, my lord. It's a necessary talent in my business. *Bonne nuit.*"

No, Maurelle, Royce countered silently, making his way from the servants' quarters. *Not bonne nuit.*

Fini.

His first stop was Damen and Anastasia's room.

There, he explained the situation in a few terse sentences, then requested Damen's help. Damen offered it instantly.

The message was written and, ten minutes later, was in the hands of a footman who was rushing it to Damen's swiftest courier. The attached note from Damen instructed his envoy to dispatch Royce's message to the Continent within the hour.

It would be in Paris by morning.

Satisfied that the wheels were in motion, Royce headed directly to his quarters, where Breanna and Hibbert were discussing the events of the past few days while eyeing the door, waiting for Royce to reappear.

They both jumped up when he walked in.

"Did Maurelle tell you anything?" Breanna burst out.

Triumph gleamed in Royce's eyes. "Far more than she realized."

"Then she gave you enough to figure out the killer's name?"

"Definitely not. Maurelle Le Joyau is as tough as they come. And smart. She'll die before exposing the killer. Especially since it's clear she's in love with him."

Breanna gave a bemused shake of her head, puzzled by the victorious expression on Royce's face. "What *did* she say?"

Swiftly, Royce relayed their conversation.

When he was finished, even Hibbert looked baffled. "I see where your questions were headed. You wanted to find out about her past, figure out where and when she and the assassin met. Hopefully, Girard will do that for us."

"Oh, he'll definitely do that for us. Very effectively, with the help of the note I just sent him."

"A note," Breanna repeated, sensing this piece of information was directly tied to whatever was making Royce feel so encouraged, "telling him what?"

"That I've encountered Mademoiselle Le Joyau before tonight. And that I remember exactly where and when that was."

Even Hibbert stared. "You've met?"

"Not officially, no. Which makes it all the better, as she has no memory of me, while I have an excellent memory of her. She was the main attraction in Paris some years ago—at least to a very confused young man who was reluctant to return with me to England and to his anxious father. I had to drag the boy out of that brothel, so taken was he with his paid companion's beauty and numerous charms. I never knew her name—we weren't exactly formally introduced. But I never forget a face. It's she, all right."

By now, Breanna had caught on. "You're talking about your first case—the one you told me about. That junior officer you found for his father the general. The man you located at a seedy brothel outside Paris."

"Maison Fleur," Royce supplied. "That was the name of the brothel. I don't know whether or not it's still standing. But when it was, Maurelle Le Joyau worked there. Their clientele were chiefly soldiers."

"Including the assassin," Breanna declared.

"Right." Royce rubbed his hands together. "Damen arranged for his fastest courier to get my message to Girard. We'll have Mademoiselle Le Joyau's complete history in a matter of days. In the meantime, tomorrow my men will start compiling information on all the men on the guest list who have military records—which will reveal exactly who was stationed near Paris, and when. Between that and what Girard tells us, we'll figure out the identity of our assassin."

"But will it be in time?" Breanna asked.

Royce shot her an uneasy look, trying to ascertain how much she'd deduced.

"Royce, I know you're trying to protect me." Softly, she answered his unspoken question. "But I'm not stupid. That animal is taunting us by delivering a stream of those porcelain figures—the ones stolen from the shop in Canterbury you told me about. If there really were only seven statues in all, then he's down to the last of them. And after that . . ." She shuddered. "After that, there will no longer be a reason for him to wait."

"We'll give him a reason." Royce went to her, seized her shoulders in a tender but determined grip. "Remember something, sweetheart. Now we have something he wants—a bargaining tool to dangle before him."

"Maurelle."

"Right. My guess is, he's as involved with Maurelle as she is with him. Which means he's vulnerable when it comes to her. And his vulnerability is our weapon."

"How can we inform him we have her if we don't know who he is?" Breanna asked.

"There are ways," Royce returned quietly, thinking he'd parade Maurelle Le Joyau across the front lawn at gunpoint, shouting out that she was his prisoner in order to get the assassin's attention, if need be. "Some of those ways are riskier than others. But let's not get ahead of ourselves. The last statue hasn't arrived yet. Until it does, we have time. Let's use that time. Maybe we'll have our answers by then."

"What are you planning?"

"I'm going to interrogate Maurelle Le Joyau. I'm bound to learn something, however small. Maybe I'll run Cunnings's name by her, or even your father's. She might know something about them."

"How?"

Royce cleared his throat. "Men are known to be less guarded when they're in a woman's bed. They talk more openly. Maurelle knew about you—she taunted me with the fact that her assassin meant to kill you with one bullet. That means he said something, not only about his plans, but about his belief that you and I are involved. Why else would she expect me to react to your intended fate?"

"I see."

"I might learn enough to strike a few additional names from the guest list. At the same time, I'm going to send a deluge of letters out to my contacts—as many as I can write tonight and tomorrow. That will keep messengers rushing on and off the estate, which, in turn, will keep the assassin wondering what the hell is going on. It might also interfere with his ability to get close to the manor. I'm buying time, Breanna. Just a day or two. By then, I'll have what I need."

"Unless the last statue arrives first. In which case, our time has run out."

Royce's jaw clenched. "In which case, so has his."

26

❦

$\mathcal{T}$he next day passed in a frenzy of activity and a knot of tension.

By nightfall, two dozen messages had gone out, five had arrived, and no packages had been delivered.

The distraction had done its job.

As for Maurelle, she was as unyielding as ever. She staunchly refused to discuss her lover, other than to hail him as a genius and declare her commitment to him.

Still, Royce chipped away at her reserve, finding out tidbits of information about their relationship—enough for him to realize this was a longstanding liaison, formed over many years, and that it centered around a sick preoccupation with each other that Maurelle viewed as love.

Love between a murderer and a heartless bitch who sold women.

The whole notion made Royce sick.

It was late at night when he finished interrogating Maurelle. After that, he began amassing the initial information that his contacts had provided. It was sketchy, but it did enable him to eliminate ten names, men who definitely hadn't served in the military.

That still left twelve.

He could hardly wait to get his hands on the thorough background checks of the possible suspects. With a modicum of luck, those reports would arrive at Medford Manor by late tomorrow.

It was half after three when he finally crawled into bed.

Breanna was awake, her nightrail tangled from tossing about, trying to sleep.

Royce reached for her, gathered her against him, and held her tightly.

"I wonder if I'll ever shut my eyes again," she whispered. "Or if he'll haunt me forever."

"He won't. It's almost over." Royce pressed his lips to her shining crown of hair, feeling that now-familiar surge of protectiveness and need. "And the instant it is, I'm dragging you off somewhere and marrying you."

She smiled against his chest. "You won't have to drag me. I'm as eager as you." She continued talking, desperate to forget the present, to cling to the hope of their future. "There's a little church about a mile from here. I used to walk there a lot when my father was away. Actually, I discovered it as a child, with Grandfather. He took me there for the first time when I was eight. My father and I were visiting Medford, and Father had flown into one of his rages. I was desperate to get away from him. The church is so peaceful and lovely; it has a sort of quiet dignity about it that reminds me of Grandfather. It conjures up special memories of him for me. I'd love to get married there."

"Then we will." Royce tilted up her chin, brushed her lips with his. "We'll ride there the day this nightmare ends, speak to the vicar. I'll get a special license, if need be. We'll be married as soon as Wells and Anastasia are finished organizing the kind of wedding you deserve."

Breanna swallowed. "Do you think I'm foolish for wanting something traditional?"

"I never think you're foolish. I think you're beautiful. And I think you're entitled to the most perfect wedding day any bride ever dreamed of."

The raw emotions of the past few days converged, welled up inside her, and Breanna felt a sharp need to relieve them, to lose herself in a way only Royce could ensure. "Royce," she murmured, her voice unsteady. "Make love to me. Please."

She felt his sharp intake of breath, sensed her own urgency come alive in him. He unbuttoned her nightrail, pushed it down and off, and tossed it to the carpet. Then, he pulled her against him, kissing her fiercely as he rolled her beneath him.

"Forget everything," he muttered thickly. "Everything but how much I love you, and how right it feels when I'm inside you."

Breanna complied, wrapping her arms around him and opening her body to his.

The rest of the night was theirs.

The reports began arriving after lunch.

Four more names were eliminated by the time late afternoon tea had been served.

"That leaves eight," Royce announced, looking around the sitting room, where Breanna, Anastasia, and Damen were seated, with Hibbert manning the doorway. "All with lean bodies, graying temples, and around forty-five or fifty years of age."

Damen nodded, taking Stacie's hand in his. "Let's analyze each one of them, see if we can make an educated guess as to which one is the killer."

"No." Royce gave an adamant shake of his head. "I've purposely avoided doing that. Our views on all these men are subjective. Whoever this killer is, he's a master at deception. He's managed to fool us, and the rest of the *ton* for Lord knows how long. Let's get all the facts. *Then,* we'll analyze."

Restlessly, Damen nodded. "You're right. I'm just losing my mind."

"I have a feeling we're on the verge of something," Anastasia murmured. "I'm not sure why, but I do."

"So do I," Breanna concurred. "So it must be true."

Ten minutes later, Wells rushed into the sitting room, waving an envelope.

"Lord Royce," he said, proffering the letter. "This just arrived from the Continent. Lord Sheldrake's envoy delivered it. It's from your colleague, Mr. Girard."

"Good." Royce went taut, snatching the envelope and tearing it open.

His eyes widened as he read, first with surprise, then with realization. "Damn," he said, rising slowly with a sharp exhalation of breath. "This is unbelievable."

"What?" Damen bolted to his feet, too. "What did Girard find out about Maurelle Le Joyau?"

"Did he confirm that she worked in that brothel—Maison Fleur?" Anastasia questioned eagerly.

"Indeed he did." Royce skimmed the letter again, then lowered it to meet the five expectant stares glued to him. "She worked at Maison Fleur for over a decade, until about four years ago. She began her career there, as a young girl in her teens. She formed quite a reputation among Wellington's men. Over the next eleven years, she made a bloody fortune servicing them in bed. Enough to buy the townhouse that's now Le Joyau and redecorate it from top to bottom, turn it into a plush abode. She hired some girls who were almost as much in demand as she was, and opened the doors to Paris's most elegant brothel."

"And?" Breanna prompted, recognizing the look on Royce's face, impatient to hear the rest.

"And it's no wonder Girard was finding it so bloody hard to uncover anything about her past before my message arrived. Without knowing she worked at Maison Fleur, it was virtually impossible to dig up a single detail on her history. Maurelle covered her tracks like a seasoned criminal. It's as if she appeared out of nowhere four years ago." Royce paused, filled in the most essential piece. "Because at the same time that she acquired Le Joyau, she acquired the name she christened it with."

"Her real name isn't Maurelle Le Joyau?" Breanna demanded.

"No." Royce shook his head, his midnight gaze glittering with sparks. "Her real name is Maurelle Rouge."

A heartbeat of silence followed Royce's revelation.

Then, the impact sank in, and everyone began talking at once.

"Maurelle Rouge . . . M. Rouge," Breanna breathed. "My God, it was her all along."

"No wonder my men couldn't find George's Paris contact," Damen realized grimly. "It never occurred to any of us *he* was a *she.*"

"Right." Royce's lips thinned into a pensive line. "Apparently, Maurelle renounced the name Rouge when she left Maison Fleur. She only uses it for buying and selling women. The rest of the world knows her as Maurelle Le Joyau."

"Wait." Anastasia held up her palm. "If this is true, if Maurelle is Rouge, and if the assassin was intimately involved with her when she was using her real name, then his establishing a business relationship with her at this particular time makes sense. The night he shot John Cunnings, Cunnings was searching for a woman to ship to M. Rouge— even if he didn't know who M. Rouge was."

"But the assassin *did* know who she was," Breanna finished for her. "He would have recognized the name when he saw it. He would have seized Cunnings's notes. And he would have planned to pursue things with Maurelle when he got to the Continent."

Stacie frowned. "The only problem with that theory is that Royce believes the relationship between the killer and Maurelle is longstanding, not sporadic. So why would he need Cunnings's notes to figure out what she was up to? Why wouldn't she just have told him? She seems to be aware of all his sinister activities. Why wouldn't he know of hers?"

"Unless . . ." Royce pursed his lips thoughtfully. "Maurelle keeps making references to her feelings for the assassin being more powerful than they've been before. She emphasizes that she loves him now more than ever—almost as if she's had time apart from him to realize the depth of her feelings. Maybe, at some point, they severed ties. I don't know when, or for how long, but maybe they lost touch. Maybe he never knew her as Maurelle Le Joyau—until he found Cunnings's notes and went in search of M. Rouge. Maybe they only recently rediscovered each other."

"But if they're so deeply involved, what would make them sever ties?" Breanna wondered aloud. "Could he have frightened her off?"

"No." Royce shook his head. "Maurelle is as cold-blooded as they come. She doesn't frighten easily. If they ended things, even for a while, it wasn't because she was afraid of him. Maybe it was *he* who had his reasons. I don't know. But it certainly gives me another angle to pursue.

I'll see what I can find out." A hard smile curved Royce's lips. "I have a great many more facts now, and some strong leads to pursue. Not only Maurelle's tie to the killer, but her tie to Viscount Medford. Maybe I can learn the fate of all those poor women she did sell."

Maurelle was thumbing through a novel when Royce walked in.

She glanced up indifferently, noting his arrival, then tucking her legs beneath her on the chair and resuming her reading.

Royce shut the door with a firm click. "Put down the book."

His icy tone gave her pause.

She arched a brow, surmising from the unyielding set of his jaw, the brutal determination in his eyes, that he was angrier than he had been previously, and more purposeful.

"Very well." She tossed aside the novel and eyed him expectantly.

"Sit up." Royce barked out the command.

She complied, uncurling her legs and lowering her feet to the floor, shaking out the folds of her gown as she did. "There. Is that to your satisfaction, monsieur?"

"Nothing about you is to my satisfaction," he returned, folding his arms across his chest. "But all that's about to change. We're about to have a very informative chat."

Her expression hardened. "You're wasting your time. I won't give you his name."

"Forget *his* name. Let's talk about *yours*—Mademoiselle Rouge."

A flicker of surprise, if not alarm. *"Bon.* Now I *am* impressed, my lord. I see how you earned your reputation."

"And I see how you earned yours—beginning fifteen years ago at Maison Fleur." Royce crossed over, dragged up a chair and sat directly across from her. "You met your lover then, when you were no more than a prostitute. You held his—and scores of other soldiers'—attention for years."

Silence, but the proud tilt of her chin told Royce he was right.

"Let's discuss a more recent matter, then," he suggested icily. "You were Viscount Medford's Paris contact. He sent you the women you sold."

Maurelle's sniff was haughty. "Medford was pathetic. So was his merchandise. They were nothing more than workhouse women—common and unrefined. Worse, they were drained of youth, beauty, and vitality. In short, they had nothing to offer. What affluent customer would pay to buy such refuse?"

"Clearly, you found buyers."

"A few. No one worth the trouble."

Royce clenched his teeth, fighting back the urge to shake Maurelle senseless and make her realize these were human beings they were discussing. He stifled the impulse. Losing control would only weaken his position. Besides, pleas for humanity could do nothing but fall on deaf ears when it came to this bitch.

"Would you like *their* names, monsieur?" Maurelle taunted, clearly perceiving at least some fraction of Royce's outrage. "Those I'd be happy to provide. And who knows? Maybe you could find the lowlifes I dealt with, rescue the pathetic wenches Medford provided from their lustful hands."

"You graduated beyond lowlifes," Royce shot back instead, his voice devoid of emotion. "As of your last correspondence with Medford, you'd stepped up to aristocratic buyers."

"I improved the caliber of my merchandise and my patrons. But no thanks to Medford. He sent me nothing. He's an insipid fool. He deserves to rot in Newgate."

"So you turned to your lover instead. He took over out of lust for you and the thrill of executing people. He's even rich enough to forego the money. Lucky you. He probably gave you every pence of the profits. Pity you two had lost touch, or he might have served as your business partner from the start. Then, you'd never have had to turn to a weakling like Medford."

With that, Royce arched a sardonic brow. "Obviously your charms aren't quite as acute as you believe. Your beloved assassin was able to stay away from them for years. What was the problem, Maurelle? Were you beneath him in station? Was that what made him leave you at Maison Fleur, cut you off?"

Anger flared in her eyes. "You're grasping at straws. You're also insulting me. So rather than listen to your offensive words, I'll put an end to them. I'm the one who severed the relationship, not he. I was foolish. I didn't want to be a nobleman's property. I vanished. He found me. I won't make that mistake again. I believe that answers your question, *n'est-ce pas?*"

Royce's eyes narrowed as he digested that tidbit of information. Purposefully keeping her from pondering how much she'd revealed, he segued back to the previous, and less inflammatory, subject. "How did you and Medford start working together?"

"*We* didn't start. *I* did. That fool never even met me, much less knew who I was. He knew only the name M. Rouge. Which was how I wanted it. As for why I approached him, it was a wise business decision. I had the money-making scheme. He had the connections and the desperate need for money."

"How did you find out about that?"

Maurelle's mocking smile returned. "Men are fools when in the throes of passion. My girls listened and often encouraged their patrons to talk. What they learned convinced me that Lord Medford was a fine candidate for what I had in mind. He knew influential people who could supply him with ships and cargo. He was deeply in debt and taking stupid chances to recoup his losses. I gave him an opportunity to do that. He jumped at it."

"And when you heard he got caught by Bow Street?"

She shrugged. "I'd already arranged for M. Rouge to drop out of sight. Lord Sheldrake was digging around, trying to find out who I was. Medford's going to Newgate only reinforced my decision. It was time for Rouge to go on holiday."

"But that's not what happened. Instead, your lover showed up and helped you resurrect the role, and the business of selling women. Only now the quality of women was elevated to a higher standard—and the means of acquiring them, murder."

"*Oui.* Exciting, wouldn't you say?"

"Depraved, I'd say."

A purposeful knock sounded at the door.

"Yes?" Royce called.

Hibbert stepped into the room. "The confirming documents you've been awaiting just arrived, my lord. I thought you'd want to know."

"I do." Royce was already heading for the door. He turned, shot Maurelle a glittering, triumphant look. "We'll continue this shortly, Mademoiselle Rouge."

Royce's lips curved as they rounded the corridor of the servants' quarters, strode toward the sitting room. "That bluff worked nicely. It's the first time I've seen Maurelle look worried since she arrived."

"I'm hoping it won't be a bluff, sir. If these reports tell us what we expect, we'll have our answer. Then we'll need Miss Le Joyau only to verify it." He frowned. "She won't do that willingly. We'll have to be very convincing."

"We will be." Royce bore down on the sitting room. "And she'll tell us exactly what we need to know. Her loyalty to her lover will ensure it."

The reports were comprehensive.

Eight of the remaining twelve men had served in the military. However, three of those had done so either during the wrong years or in the wrong places, and were stationed too far from Paris to be viable choices.

Which left five men who could be the assassin.

Damen stood beside Royce, poring over the five names as Wells and Hibbert stood on either side of the settee, flanking Anastasia and Breanna, who sat upon it, eagerly awaiting some answers.

"Maywood? He's afraid of his own shadow," Damen muttered. "His father browbeat him until the day he died. He balks at the slightest risk of losing money, much less lives. No. I don't see it. And Crompton's one hell of a shot, but he's also eccentric as hell. He talks so much about his days as a general, we can all recite them by memory. If he'd been involved with a woman like Maurelle, she'd have been the high point of his tales. A cold-blooded killer? I can't imagine it. Radebrook, I'm not sure of. He's quiet. He doesn't talk much about himself. It says here his aim is exceptional. Maybe——"

"He's married," Royce interrupted. "Happily married. And the father of three, two of whom are still young enough to live at home. That makes him the least likely candidate of the bunch. Our killer is a loner. He's not a family man. Nor is Maurelle the type to share. I'd strike Radebrook before I struck anyone else."

"Fine. That leaves Arthur Landow, who's uneasy about squashing a bug, and James Fairwood, who I didn't expect to be listed here. He always talks of himself as a naval officer."

"He was a naval officer." Royce was rereading the pages. "After Napoleon crushed our navy, he switched to the army. Apparently, he's an expert marksman."

Damen slammed his fist against the mantle. "So where do we go from here? How do we figure out which one it is?"

"We don't." Royce began organizing the reports into five separate, carefully-labelled folders. "We let Maurelle act as our bloodhound."

A startled look. "Royce, you've spent the past two days telling us how staunch Maurelle is when it comes to refusing to betray her lover. Do you honestly believe that by waving five files beneath her nose you're going to goad her into blurting out his name?"

"No." Royce carefully lay the most damning pages atop each report, before closing the files. "I believe that by leaving five files beneath her nose I'm going to goad her into acting to protect him."

Breanna's chin came up. "You're using her love for him to trap her into giving him away. You're going to leave her alone in the room with those files. Instinctively, she'll go over and read the report on her lover. She won't be able to help herself. She'll want to see what facts you've compiled, how close you are to finding the man she loves."

"Exactly." Royce shot Breanna an admiring look. "You've become quite the sleuth, my love."

"You've trained me well. Too well." Breanna rose, walked over to him. "Royce, it's a mistake. Not the idea, the execution. If you casually leave those files lying about in Maurelle's room, she'll know you're up to something. She won't go near the reports. And what will you do? Kneel outside her door all night, peeking through the keyhole, hoping she'll relent?"

Royce's brows rose in surprise. "You have another way?"

"Yes." Breanna nodded, lifting her chin in a gesture that was becoming more and more natural for her to make. "Let me go in there and get the results we need."

"No." Royce was already shaking his head. "Absolutely not. You're not going anywhere near that bitch."

Gently, Breanna lay her hand on his forearm. "We only have one chance. If she figures out we're uncertain, she'll never give anything away. I can throw her off-guard. You can't. Her defenses go up whenever you walk into that room. You're a man—and a brilliant one, at that. I'm a woman—a gentle, delicate, weak-minded woman." Breanna's lips twitched at her own description. "Maurelle will have no regard for me. She'll assume I'm faltering, on the verge of collapse. I'll use that to my advantage."

Anastasia had perked up and was nodding her agreement. "Breanna has a point. Maurelle is used to battling wits with men, not women. I doubt she believes any woman is as strong as she, much less a soft-spoken, composed woman such as Breanna. If anyone can prove Maurelle wrong, it's my cousin."

"Royce," Breanna pressed, her jade gaze holding his midnight one. "I'll get what we need."

Royce swallowed. "How?"

Her lips curved. "I'm a very good sketcher. And, as you just said, I've also become an excellent sleuth. Between the two—I have a plan."

Maurelle was moving restlessly about the room when the door opened.

She turned, eager to confront Lord Royce, to probe until she found out just what had incited that arrogant smirk he'd worn when he left her an hour ago.

Did he really have confirming documents, or had Hibbert been lying, trying to incite a reaction from her? The older man was an excellent actor. He'd fooled her once. He wouldn't fool her again.

She forced herself to look nonchalant, to watch casually as Lord Royce entered the room.

But it wasn't Lord Royce who stepped into the chambers.

It was a woman. A very pretty, very genteel woman, whose unusual coloring and haunted expression left little doubt as to her identity.

"Bon." Maurelle folded her arms across her breasts, studying the woman she knew to be her lover's ultimate execution target. She was clutching some folders tightly to her body—folders she seemed unaware of holding.

Interesting.

"Lady Breanna Colby, *oui?*" Maurelle inquired.

"*Oui.*" Breanna halted to lean back into the hallway. She glanced about furtively, searching the area in a most thorough fashion. Then, she gestured to that wretched butler of hers, who magically appeared out of nowhere and proceeded to hover just outside the door. "Stand guard," she instructed him in a fierce whisper—one Maurelle managed to overhear. "Don't let Lord Royce know I'm in here. He thinks I'm behaving irrationally, letting my emotions rule my head. But he doesn't understand. I must try this my way. I must." She inhaled sharply. "Knock twice if you see him approaching."

Waiting only for her butler's assent, Lady Breanna shut the door and faced Maurelle.

"I had to see you," she announced in a small, shaky voice. "No matter what Lord Royce says, I refuse to believe any woman could remain immune to another woman's anguish. Not in this case. Not if she fully understood it."

Maurelle kept her features carefully schooled, although her gaze flickered to the folders clutched in Breanna's arms. What was in them? Was this some kind of ploy?

Doubtful. The insipid girl's state of mind was far too precarious for Chadwick to entrust her with his work. Still, those folders had to contain something. But what?

She had to find out—for *his* sake.

"Go ahead," she replied carefully. "I'm willing to listen."

Breanna swallowed, clearly fighting for control. "I won't denounce you for loving this man. I can only guess you've never seen the side of him I have. I've come here to share that side of him with you, in the hopes that you'll realize what he's capable of, and that you'll help me stop him." Tears glistened on her lashes. "I don't want to die, Maurelle. I'm twenty-one years old. My life is just beginning. Please, help me."

"What is it you intend to share with me that will plead your case— your words, your fears?"

"No. My proof." Breanna began crossing over toward the desk.

Halfway there, she paused, becoming aware of the five files she still gripped. With a shudder of revulsion, she tossed them down on the table alongside the wardrobe, keeping only some loose papers in her hand as she made her way to the desk.

"Proof?" Maurelle followed her automatically, her dark gaze focusing on the pages Breanna was spreading out on the desktop.

"Yes. His letters to me. The ones that describe what he intends to do to me, and to my cousin. My cousin is with child, Maurelle. And he knows it. He means to kill her unborn babe. He specifically says so."

"Does he?" Maurelle controlled her amusement, her glance shifting from the letters she already knew of to the files Breanna had abandoned near the wardrobe. "Those files—are they also proof?"

Breanna looked up, followed Maurelle's gaze, and shuddered again. "Those are what *Lord Royce* calls proof. They're facts, dates, and worst of all, drawings, for me to go over." Her voice trembled. "I can't do that. It's too painful. Especially seeing his face again. I realize Lord Royce has narrowed the search down to five men, and that I'm the only person who can identify the killer—other than Emma, who's too dazed to speak, much less confront the man who killed her mother."

"You've actually seen him?" Maurelle asked, keeping the fear out of her voice.

"Twice." Breanna lowered her lashes, her entire body trembling as she spoke. "The night I shot him, and several days ago, when I left the estate. The first time it was dark, so all I could make out was his build. But the other day, I saw his face, his features, the coldness in his eyes. I can't brave that again. I've described him to Lord Royce. I can't help it if my description could apply to any of those five noblemen. I just can't bear looking at him again."

"I find it odd that you'd need to," Maurelle said carefully. "If you really saw him in such great detail, why didn't you recognize him? Surely you've met him at one social gathering or another."

"Lord Royce said the same thing—a dozen times. But, as I told him, my father kept me isolated. I never attended a full London Season. So, I wasn't formally introduced to anyone. The gentlemen are all a jumble of faces."

"I see." Maurelle's mind was racing, trying to find a way to use that to her advantage.

Slowly, she began backing toward the wardrobe.

Lost in her own pain, Breanna buried her face in her hands, weeping softly as she spoke. "I'm begging you, Maurelle. Read these letters. Tell us his name. Don't make me go through any more than I already have. Please . . . spare me. Spare my cousin. And most of all, spare her unborn child, who's innocent and deserves a chance at life. Please."

Maurelle halted beside the files. "Read me the letters," she ordered. "Let me hear this firsthand. I can't believe the man I love would kill an unborn child."

Eagerly, Breanna complied, drying her eyes with a handkerchief, and composing herself enough to pick up the first note, read its contents aloud.

By the time she'd reached the final, dooming letter, Maurelle had completed her perusal, and her work—silently, rapidly, and as thoroughly as time would permit.

The information she had the chance to skim was equally damning to all five men. Any of them could be her noble assassin.

The drawings were another matter entirely.

Fear had prickled up her spine as she realized how accurate the visual depictions were, how easy it would be for Lady Breanna to identify her stalker by looking at his likeness.

Destroying the drawing was unthinkable. So was defacing it enough to disguise his features. Either of those steps would alert Chadwick to the fact that she'd tampered with the file, not to mention leading him to precisely the man she was determined to protect.

So how could she save him, buy him enough time to kill this interfering bitch and vanish?

There was only one way. It was risky, but it was a chance she had to take. After all, the chit had said she wouldn't know one man from the other.

In one swift motion, Maurelle had opened his file, plucked out his picture, and slipped it into the file behind it. Then, she'd stepped away from the reports.

Lady Breanna was reading the final phrase of the last letter. That alerted Maurelle to the fact that she hadn't time to get back over to the desk, where she was supposedly still standing, without calling attention to herself. Even an overwrought fool like Lady Breanna might become suspicious if she saw her enemy standing so close to a report that would condemn her lover. And the last thing Maurelle wanted was to arouse her ladyship's suspicions.

She acted on impulse.

Reaching for the wardrobe, she grabbed at the first item of clothing she could find. A night robe. Fine. She'd feign distress, make it look as if what she'd just heard had upset her so greatly, she couldn't stay still and bear it. She had to busy herself to keep from breaking down.

And what more logical outlet for her anguish than donning her nightclothes, retiring to bed to bury her pain?

Breanna was staring at the page in her hands, her breathing unsteady as she fought back tears. When she finally looked up, Maurelle was unbuttoning her gown in dazed, jerky motions, watching her with a shocked expression.

"Now do you understand?" Breanna beseeched her.

"*Oui.*" Maurelle kept her voice low, shaken. "How could I not?" She stepped out of her gown, untied the ribbons of her chemise. "I never imagined . . ." She finished undressing, then, with trembling hands, shrugged on the absurdly pristine night robe that had been left for her. "I don't know what to do," she confessed. "To betray him . . . It's not only love. I'm afraid."

"We'll protect you," Breanna assured her quickly. "We'll keep you safe until he's caught. Please, help me. If not for my sake, for the sake of Anastasia's babe."

That, ostensibly, clinched it.

Maurelle nodded, pain twisting her lovely features. "I will." She pressed her palms together, summoning up all her courage. "No unborn child should be killed without ever tasting life." A heartbeat of a pause. "His name is Arthur," she whispered, forcing out the words. "Arthur Landow."

She watched relief sweep Breanna's face.

Slowly, she counted to ten.

It was time for her seemingly virtuous move.

"Lord Royce will want your verification," she informed Breanna, dabbing at her eyes. "He's a man, and will never understand your qualms about viewing the drawings. But I'm a woman. I do. So, while I know you must confirm what I've told you, I don't think you should subject yourself to doing so—not alone." She crossed over, picked up Landow's file, holding it so Breanna could see his name penned in bold letters across the front. "Here. Do it now. With another woman beside you for comfort. Then, you'll never have to do it again." She tugged out the sketch she'd placed atop Landow's, flourished it before Breanna's horrified eyes. "Is this not he?"

Breanna stared at the drawing. Her gaze shifted to Maurelle's compassionate expression, and she shuddered, biting her lip to stifle a sob. "Yes. It's he." She turned away from the sketch. "Put it away. I never want to see him again."

"*Mais oui.* I understand." Maurelle hurried back to the stack of files, slipping her noble assassin's sketch back in its proper place before laying Landow's file atop it.

Maurelle picked up the entire stack of reports. "Why don't you give these to your butler right now? He can turn them straight over to Lord Royce, and you need never see Arthur's face again." A shaky pause. "Just as I won't."

Breanna stood, gathering up the letters and walking over to Maurelle. "Thank you, Maurelle," she said fervently, taking the files from her. "I know how difficult this was for you. But you did the right thing. Just as I knew you would." She opened the door, gestured for Wells to approach. "Take these," she directed him. "Give them to Lord Royce. Tell him I have his answers. I won't need to see these sketches again."

27

❧

Everyone was gathered in the sitting room when Breanna and Wells walked in.

Breanna's ashen expression was no longer feigned, but very real.

"It's done," she stated simply, her voice more hollow than shaken. "We finally know who he is." Her gaze flickered from one beloved face to the next, finally settling on Royce. "Viscount Crompton," she supplied. "He's the assassin."

"You're certain." Royce's words were more statement than query.

"Yes." Breanna nodded, interlacing her fingers tightly in front of her. "Maurelle went first to his file. She looked at it twice, once before and once after she skimmed the others. Then, she removed my sketch of Crompton from his file and slipped it into Arthur Landow's. She brought Landow's file over to me, made sure I saw his name on it, and flourished the drawing of Crompton, admitting to me that Arthur Landow was indeed the man we sought. Once I acknowledged recognizing his face, she put the sketch back where it belonged and told me I need never look at it again." Breanna exhaled slowly. "It's Crompton."

Royce crossed over, enfolded Breanna in his arms. "You're astonishing," he murmured. "I'm so proud of you." He tilted up her chin. "Are you all right?"

"I'm fine," she replied. "A bit numb, but fine."

"Crompton," Damen repeated. "I never would have believed he had the presence of mind, much less the coldheartedness, to do this."

"I told you," Royce responded. "This killer is a master at deception. Crompton assumed you'd think him too eccentric to be the culprit. He was right. None of us guessed."

"I don't think I've ever seen him without his gloves," Anastasia commented. "Not before or after Breanna shot him. Then again, I'd have no reason to. The only times I've seen him have been at formal or sporting events."

"Shooting," Breanna clarified.

"Yes, shooting . . . no, wait. That's not true." Anastasia sat up abruptly.

"You've seen him without his gloves?"

"No, but I've seen him outside Medford. It was right around the time Damen and I were about to expose Uncle George. Crompton was at the House of Lockewood . . ." She turned to gaze at her husband. "Meeting with John Cunnings. I remember because Cunnings came to your office looking for the viscount's portfolio."

"He met with John often," Damen concurred. "In fact, most of the time. He sought me out for large investment decisions, but on a day-to-day basis, he dealt with Cunnings."

"Obviously, discussing more than finances," Royce modified caustically.

"So what do we do now?" Damen demanded. "We know who the killer is. Why don't we just ride over to his estate and grab him?"

"That would be the worst thing we could do," Royce refuted. "First of all, Crompton isn't spending much time at his estate these days. He's here, watching Breanna. And if he knew we were on our way to seize him, he'd simply vanish, the way he did last time." Royce paused, his worried gaze shifting from Breanna to Anastasia and back.

"Only to resurface Lord knows when to finish what he started." Breanna completed Royce's unvoiced thought aloud.

"Yes."

"I see your point." Damen swallowed. "Then, how do we stop him?"

"We lure *him* to *us*. We taunt him, anger him, and turn this little cat-and-mouse game around."

Stacie looked intrigued. "How?"

Royce's jaw set, that purposeful gleam returning to his eyes. "I'll have one more chat with Maurelle. Who knows? Maybe I can even unearth a few more details while her tongue is loose—which it will be, as long as it's Landow she thinks she's betraying. At the end of that time, I'll let her know just how badly she underestimated Breanna. I'll toss out Crompton's name, and let her choke on it. Then, I'll help myself to an article of her clothing—preferably something intimate—and I'll leave her in the guards' capable hands."

"You're going to send the clothing to Crompton," Breanna murmured. "Let him know we have Maurelle."

"You're damned right I am. I'm going to flaunt that fact as crudely as I can. Let him think I'm bedding his precious Maurelle, violating the one thing he cares about. He'll react. I guarantee it. He'll go berserk. All his precision, his brilliant strategy, will be cast to the wind. Gut emotion will take over. Even his hatred for you will be temporarily forsaken. He'll want to free Maurelle, slit my throat for having her. And I'll be ready for him when he tries."

Breanna raised her chin another notch, studied Royce's face. "It had to come down to this, didn't it?" she asked softly. "From the very beginning. It was going to end in a final battle between you and him. You'd have it no other way."

"No, I wouldn't." Royce met her gaze. "From the very beginning? Maybe. Maybe not. I don't know. But from the day I fell in love with you? Definitely. So if you're asking if I'm arranging things this way so I can meet him face-to-face, personally pull the trigger to end his wretched life, the answer is yes. I wanted to wait until the odds were with me. They finally are. And Crompton is a dead man."

"I understand," Breanna said in a tremulous voice. "But, Royce, I love you." She lay her palm against his jaw. "I can't lose you."

"You won't." He turned his lips to kiss her fingertips. "Sweetheart, I'm not doing this out of arrogance." His tone gentled as he gave voice to that which they already knew. "The truth is that you and Anastasia will never be safe as long as Crompton's alive."

"I know." Breanna wet her lips with the tip of her tongue, weighing her next words carefully. "Your letter has to be convincing. Maurelle's chemise, even doused in her scent, won't be enough. Remember, he sent me a bottle of that same perfume. We could be using that to fake Maurelle's capture."

"True." Royce nodded, eyeing Breanna speculatively as he realized she was leading him somewhere in particular. "I intended to include a lock of her hair. I'd parade her across the front lawn so he could see her for himself, if it weren't so risky. Given the frenzy he'll likely be in, he might go off like a loose cannon, firing blindly at everyone in sight. I won't take that chance."

"You don't need to." Breanna spoke calmly, her decision made. "Send the chemise and the lock of hair. Make the letter as provoking as you can. And when you do, mention the birthmark on her right breast. It's in a spot only a lover would know about." She flushed. "I'll describe the exact location to you when you write the letter. But that should get you the response you're looking for."

Royce stared at Breanna in amazement. "How did you have the presence of mind to—?"

"I didn't. It just so happens that Maurelle used undressing as a means to conceal the fact that she'd been looking through the files. She changed into a nightrobe while I was in the room. The birthmark is very conspicuous."

"And you call me brilliant." Royce kissed her triumphantly, unbothered by their audience. "This is almost over," he said, raising his head to include Anastasia in his assessment. "Hold on a little longer."

Royce strode into Maurelle's chambers and shut the door behind him.

She smiled inwardly, seeing the victorious gleam in his eye. Her ruse had worked. Chadwick now believed that Arthur Landow was her noble assassin.

Excellent.

"May I help you, monsieur?" she inquired, folding back the bedcovers. "I was just about to retire for the night."

Royce glanced at his pocket watch. "It's not even dinnertime."

"I'm fatigued." Maurelle smoothed her hand over the sheets. "Your friend Lady Breanna exhausted me."

His jaw tightened fractionally. "I heard that Lady Breanna had been in to see you. And while I wish she hadn't subjected herself to that, I can't deny I'm pleased by the results."

"I thought you would be."

"Funny, you didn't seem to me to be the type one could reach through compassion."

"People aren't always as they seem."

"No, they're not." Royce paused, rubbed his palms together. "In any case, I'm glad you relented. It will be easier on everyone."

"Is that why you're here?" Maurelle inquired, gripping the bedpost. "To ease my fears?"

"No. Frankly, I don't give a damn about your fears."

She smiled. "I appreciate your honesty, monsieur. So tell me, what can I do for you?"

"You can answer a few questions. I want as much evidence against Landow as I can get before I send Bow Street over to arrest him."

Warning bells sounded in her head, and her gaze turned wary. "What kind of evidence?"

"His relationship with Cunnings—what do you know of it?"

Ah, that. Inwardly, she relaxed. Cunnings was dead. He couldn't deny Landow's guilt. Therefore, the closer she stuck to the truth, the better.

"Arthur knew John Cunnings for quite some time," she replied.

"So Lady Breanna overheard Cunnings tell her father. He said he'd seen the assassin's . . . Landow's," Royce corrected himself, "accomplishments for years."

"That's true. From what Arthur explained, he needed a contact to arrange the jobs he took on."

"The executions, you mean."

"Yes. Cunnings was perfect. He knew scores of people through his position at the House of Lockewood. You'd be surprised to learn how eager some supposedly honorable men and women are to rid themselves of family members that stand between themselves and their fortunes."

"I don't doubt it."

"The bank itself made an ideal meeting place. No one suspected anything unscrupulous was going on during their meetings. After all, Arthur was a client—a good one." Her lips curved. "And a smart one. He eavesdropped on Cunnings's conversations enough times to realize he was willing to compromise himself for money. He confirmed that fact by keeping an ear to the ground and learning Cunnings was spending more than he had, courting women with expensive jewelry, buying homes he couldn't afford. In short, John Cunnings was willing to do anything to support his expensive habits. Arthur offered him that opportunity."

"Hmm." Royce stroked his jaw thoughtfully. "In other words, Cunnings got a percentage of Landow's fee on the clients he referred?"

"Exactly." Maurelle sighed. "I'm sorry Monsieur Cunnings had to die. I have a soft spot in my heart for him. After all, it was through him that Arthur came back into my life."

"So Landow did find you again through Cunnings's notes."

"*Oui.*" Maurelle lowered her lashes, reminding herself that she was supposed to be feeling guilty, torn by her own betrayal. "Arthur didn't come directly to Paris. First, he went to Germany, to visit that brilliant Dr. Helmett. Wilkens, the gunsmith, met them there. Arthur had surgery." A thought struck her, and she eliminated the quickest and most logical way for Landow to prove his innocence. She had to buy Ansel time— time to finish his mission and vanish. "The surgery was so successful, his finger is as good as new."

"Is it?" Royce looked surprised. "Then why is he so eager for revenge?"

"Because it took some time to regain his muscle control. And being in control is more important to Arthur than anything else. He was at a disadvantage for months. He had to master the new weapon Wilkens crafted in order to shoot. Also, he can't bear the thought of being bested, especially by a woman."

"I see." Royce nodded, acknowledging the truth of her words. "Where is Helmett now?"

Maurelle swallowed. "Arthur killed him. He had no choice. He didn't expect Dr. Helmett to react so strongly when he heard Arthur boast of his plans to do away with Lady Breanna."

"Ah. The good physician threatened to alert the authorities?"

"Yes."

Royce inclined his head. "By the way, Wilkens is dead, too. Did you know that? Your lover killed him a few days ago."

"No, I didn't. But I'm not surprised."

"I didn't expect you would be. He seems very adept at eliminating anyone who might give him away."

"He is." She bit her lip. "That's why I'm so frightened. If he should learn I've betrayed him—"

"Oh, he will," Royce assured her cheerfully. He glanced at his time-piece again. "This very night, as a matter of fact." He stepped aside, yanked open the door. "Hibbert, I could use your help."

"My pleasure." Hibbert strolled in, walking over to jerk Maurelle's arms behind her back. "Go ahead, my lord."

Maurelle's eyes widened as she saw the razor appear in Royce's hand. "Are you mad? I've told you everything you want to know, and in return you're going to slit my throat?"

"No. You're not worth it." Royce crossed over, quickly shearing off a lock of her hair. Wrapping it in his handkerchief, he glanced about the room, spying the pile of clothing Maurelle had left on the chair near the wardrobe. He went over, rifled through it until he found her chemise. "This will do." He crumpled it up, tucked it beneath his arm. "Let her go, Hibbert."

Hibbert complied, shoving Maurelle away from him as if she were an odious insect. He headed to the door, Royce directly behind him.

"Oh, Maurelle." Royce paused on the threshold, arching a brow in her direction. "In case you're wondering, I'll be sending off your chemise and your strand of hair, together with a very provocative letter." His teeth gleamed. "Crompton should have it before midnight. That's Ansel Crompton, by the way, not Arthur Landow. Then again, you already know that. Your attempt to save him was valiant. Speaking of which, Lady Breanna asked me to thank you. She appreciated your switching those drawings. You played right into her hands and helped ensure Crompton's downfall."

If Royce needed any further proof, the look of sheer panic on Maurelle's face provided it.

Her anguished cry, "Ansel," echoed through the halls as Royce and Hibbert walked away.

Crompton was applying the final touches of red paint to the last porcelain figure when the messenger galloped up his drive.

He frowned, wondering who could be contacting him this late at night.

Ah, Maurelle, he thought, his frown vanishing. No doubt she was summoning him, eager to have him back in her arms, her bed.

Well, she hadn't long to wait. By tomorrow at this time, Lady Anastasia and Lady Breanna would be dead, and he'd be on his way to Paris.

He held the statue away from him, admired his own handiwork. The two women were leaning over a book, clutching it as they read together. And they were smiling—placid smiles that seemed incredibly out of place when one considered their fatal injuries and mutilated hands.

Satisfaction glinted in his eyes. He'd severed both women's right index fingers, trickled bloodlike paint over their hands and the book's binding, and added a final red splotch over their hearts.

His final gift to Lady Breanna. It would arrive in the dead of night.

Tomorrow morning, it would be time.

He'd planned it all very carefully. The guards changed shifts at 6 A.M. As always, that stout, uncouth sentry posted on the far side of the estate would have been drinking his secret cache of ale from sometime after midnight, and would have nodded off no later than half past 5 A.M. That left thirty minutes—more than enough time to climb the sturdy oak he'd been using for his comings and goings, and slip onto the premises. From there, he'd creep toward the manor, hide in the thick brush, and eventually ease his way around the house until he had a clear view of the sitting room.

Then, he'd wait.

Sometime between 10 and 10:20 A.M., both Lady Breanna and Lady Anastasia would appear—heavily guarded by Chadwick, Sheldrake, and those two old codgers, Hibbert and Wells.

Did any of them actually believe they could scare him off or—an even more ludicrous thought—block his shot?

If so, they were bigger fools than he'd realized. *They* weren't what had kept him from striking before now. His battle plan was. He'd devised it. He meant to carry it out.

The first step had been to terrorize Lady Breanna.

That step was complete.

Now, it was time for the second step. Lady Anastasia had to die— right at her cousin's feet. For that, he needed no more than fifteen seconds. And he'd get those seconds, the instant Sheldrake stepped away from his wife.

Lady Anastasia would be dead by ten thirty.

Then came the tricky part—step three.

He had to isolate Lady Breanna. It wasn't enough to kill her. If it was, he'd simply shoot her right after he did away with her cousin. No, he had to first ensure that she knew precisely who he was, what he intended to do to her. He had to close in on her like a tiger stalking its prey, see the stark terror in her eyes as she realized her life was about to end.

He needed to see her crawl, to hear her plead for her life, sob for mercy.

Then, he'd blast away her life with one long-awaited shot.

It wouldn't be that difficult to get her alone. The house would be in an uproar once Lady Anastasia fell down dead. People would scatter. Chadwick would rush outside, determined to find the killer.

Taking Lady Breanna with him to ensure her safety.

That's when he'd make his move. He'd grab her the instant Chadwick turned his back.

No, this wouldn't be difficult at all.

A knock on the front door broke into his thoughts, reminded him of the messenger's arrival.

Carefully, he lined his desk drawer with a handkerchief, then placed the statue upon it, sliding the drawer shut to conceal it. He'd write the note later. For now, he wanted to read Maurelle's words of love.

He left his study, made his way to the entranceway.

His butler had just accepted a small package from the messenger and was shutting the door. He looked up, saw the viscount approaching.

"For you, sir," he announced.

"Excellent. Thank you." Crompton took the parcel, glancing at it as he retreated to the privacy of his study. He'd expected a letter. Had Maurelle sent him a gift?

He locked his study door, lowered himself to the settee, and unwrapped the package. A carnal smile touched his lips as Maurelle's fragrance greeted his nostrils. He lifted out the perfume-scented chemise, amused by Maurelle's uncharacteristically girlish gesture. Evidently, she missed him as much as he missed her. But she needn't have gone to such extremes to tell him so. She, of all people, knew he needed no enticement. Not when it came to her. His desire for her was compulsive, a gnawing in his belly that seemed never to fade.

He brought the chemise to his face, inhaled deeply, and felt his body throb to life. Another day. That's all it would be. Then he'd be with her. And not just for a brief interlude. For the rest of their lives.

He lowered the garment, intending to restore it to the box.

A lock of hair tumbled out of the folds.

His brows arched in surprise. Maurelle's hair? Why on earth . . . ?

The note caught his eye. It was neatly penned, but not in Maurelle's hand.

A warning bell sounded in his head, and he tensed, snatched up the page.

Crompton, it read. *Your maneuvers were good. Mine were better. To the victor go the spoils. In this case, the spoils are the prisoner I've taken. And I do mean taken. Not once, but repeatedly. Her body is too lush to resist—especially that erotic birthmark just under her right nipple. I salute you for your taste in women. Maurelle Rouge is one woman I'd never sell. She's extraordinary. Insatiable, but extraordinary. She keeps begging for more, insisting that my charms exceed yours. Yet another victory, wouldn't you say?*

Crompton's skull was hammering so loud he could scarcely think, his body shaking with a rage like none he had ever known.

Chadwick had Maurelle. His intimate description left no room for doubt. That filthy bastard was bedding *his* Maurelle.

Damn him. Damn him to hell.

Crompton dragged his sleeve across his forehead, sweat trickling down the side of his face as he forced himself to read on.

Did you think I'd summon Bow Street? Think again. I want no intermediary. It's just you and me, Crompton. Except the roles have now reversed. You're the mouse and I'm the cat. I've hunted you down. Now I can torment you as you tormented Lady Breanna. I've already stripped you of everything—your anonymity, your unblemished success record, even your woman. Concede defeat. Or die by my hand. The war is over. The best man has won. —Chadwick

A roar of denial exploded from Crompton's chest. He bolted to his feet, crumpling the note into a ball and hurling it and the box across the room.

He raked both hands through his hair, pacing about in an effort to comprehend what had happened, *how* it had happened.

Chadwick knew who he was. He knew who Maurelle was. He'd called her Maurelle *Rouge.* Worse, he'd kidnapped her, forced her to act as his whore. She'd never have gone willingly. He had to have brutalized her.

Had he also brutalized her into revealing her lover's name?

No. Maurelle would never betray him. Not even if she were tortured.

Then how had Chadwick figured it out? How had he gotten his hands on Maurelle to begin with?

Hibbert.

That wretched old fool had been in Paris. He must have found Le Joyau, seized her there.

Which meant he'd found the women. *All* the women.

Emma Martin. *That's* who'd given him away. She was the only one who'd seen his face.

He'd kill her later. After he took care of the others.

He stopped pacing, forced air into his lungs. He had to think, to come up with a plan. Chadwick wasn't sending Bow Street here. He was too pompous, too cocky.

Too smart.

He knew bloody well that if Bow Street showed up here, the man they sought would find a way to elude them, to drop out of sight and, as a result, be back in a position of control. Instead, Chadwick was trying to lure him out, to goad him into showing himself.

Oh, he'd show himself, all right. But not in the reckless way Chadwick expected.

He'd rethink his strategy. He'd get into that house. He'd rescue Maurelle.

And then he'd kill every last one of them.

28

❧

*H*e arrived at Medford as originally planned, at half past 5 A.M.

It had taken all his self-control to wait out the night, to restrain himself from rushing right over there and breaking down the front door, firing at everyone until he found Maurelle.

But that's what Chadwick assumed he'd do. The son of a bitch was lying in wait.

As a result, the only thing to do was to outmaneuver him.

Oh, the best man would win, all right.

And Chadwick would be dead.

Crompton jumped down lightly from the oak tree, glancing behind him at the sleeping guard. Scornfully, he noted the half-empty bottle clutched in the man's fist.

Pathetic fool.

Turning away, he crept across the grounds, his black clothes invisible in the darkness of night's final hours.

He reached the manor.

This was where his original strategy ended, and his modified one began.

He squatted down in the bushes, remaining in the rear of the house rather than inching around front, as initially planned.

He edged his way along the outside wall, raising up a bit when he reached the kitchen window. He peered through, checking to see if the staff had appeared to begin preparing breakfast.

A cook and two scullery maids were moving about, starting their morning routine.

Splendid. Just enough people to suit his purposes, not so many as to obstruct his entry.

Silently, he dropped to the ground, choosing a spot next to the rear entrance—one with just a spotty number of evergreen shrubs. It wouldn't do to choose a denser patch. His goal was to cause a disturbance, not to burn the whole manor to the ground.

He struck the match.

It took two minutes for the fire to leap high enough to be seen, and for the fumes to be smelled as they seeped beneath the windows and door.

The kitchen staff reacted.

One of the scullery maids shrieked and dropped a frying pan, pointing to the curling wisps of smoke.

The cook grabbed a kettle of water and doused the area, only to realize the source of the fire was outside.

She flung open the door, wringing her hands as she saw the flames.

She swung around, shooing the two maids away, and gesturing toward the inside hallway.

The three servants dashed off to alert the household.

Crompton waited ten seconds. No more, no less. Then, he slipped inside, making his way straight to the pantry and concealing himself in a dim, barren alcove within it.

He pulled up a stool, sank down on it. Alert yet unmoving, he settled himself for the long hours that lay ahead.

He was an expert at lying in wait. It was one of the skills that had made him the fine general he was. He knew how to outlast the enemy, to create the illusion that the danger was gone.

Only then would he strike.

By 7 A.M., the flames were doused.

By 10 A.M., the guards had given up patrolling the area. Having spied no one suspicious lurking about, they'd come to the conclusion that the fire was indeed an accident and bore no connection to the intruder they were guarding against.

Chadwick wasn't so certain.

He hovered at the scene, scrutinizing the shrubs and muttering to Hibbert, who had accompanied him outside to search the area.

Eventually, they let themselves in through the kitchen.

"Go back to Breanna," Chadwick instructed his manservant. "I don't want her left alone."

Hibbert frowned. "You suspect Crompton did this?"

"I don't know. It's winter. The air is cold and dry. A spark from the kitchen might have started the fire. So, it could be a coincidence. But I'm not taking any chances. If Crompton is behind this, he's on the grounds. I'm going to alert Mahoney's men, have them search every inch of the estate, not only this immediate area. After that, I'm heading down to the servants' quarters to see what Maurelle is up to. If Crompton did break into Medford, she's the reason why."

"I agree." Hibbert nodded briskly. "I'll watch Lady Breanna. Lord Sheldrake is with his wife. And Wells is standing guard outside Maurelle's room, just in case. He's been there since he awakened."

"Good. Putting Maurelle in the room next to his was wise. He can keep a close eye on her." Chadwick was already heading out. "I'll check in with you later."

"Fine."

The two men left. Quiet ensued.

The day wore on.

Slowly, the ordinary routine resumed, tension ebbing away as hour gave way to hour and no further incident occurred.

At last, the sun set.

Darkness fell, settling over the manor with the customary impatience of January.

The evening meal was served. The kitchen staff completed their work, washed the last of the evening dishes, and doused the lights.

The lower level fell silent.

Just above the pantry, the family chatted in the library, the distinct sounds of Lady Breanna's lilting tones and her cousin's more Americanized accent drifting to the floor below, interdispersed by comments issued in Sheldrake and Chadwick's deeper baritones.

It was time.

Inside the cramped alcove, Crompton stood, stretching his arms and legs to restore feeling. He winced at the throbbing pain that gripped his finger, which was raw and stiff after the prolonged day he'd spent in this chilly room.

Soon that pain would be vindicated. Then, he'd sail off to a warm climate where the sun would ease his physical torment.

But first, he had to rescue Maurelle.

She was alone now. He'd watched the house often enough to know the evening routine. Wells would be posted at the entranceway—especially at this point, when they were anticipating the delivery of the final statue—and Hibbert would be stationed in the hall between Wells and the family, adding his presence for extra security.

That was fine. They weren't his targets—yet.

Of course, there was always the chance that Chadwick had kept guards posted outside Maurelle's door. However, that prospect was unlikely, now that this morning's threat had been removed and there was no reason to believe the noble assassin was anywhere near Maurelle, much less on the verge of rescuing her. Chadwick wouldn't want to waste the men, not when they could be patrolling the perimeter of the estate, or standing guard over Lady Anastasia and Lady Breanna.

A bitter smile curved Crompton's lips.

Cautiously, he crept out of the pantry and through the kitchen, made his way to the servants' quarters.

The wing was deserted. Not a surprise, given that the staff was doubt-less either retiring for the night or upstairs preparing their employers' chambers so that they might do the same.

Nonetheless, his fingers closed around his pistol to ready it, most par-ticularly when he rounded the corner that led to the butler's quarters.

Wells's chambers were silent. Clearly, he was upstairs at his post.

Crompton relaxed his grip, moving to the door next to Wells's.

It was locked.

Ever so slightly, he jiggled the handle to make sure. Yes. Definitely locked.

He glanced about, ensured he was alone.

Then, he knocked—a hushed little rap.

No answer.

He tried again, this time louder.

"Have you lost your key, monsieur?" Maurelle's icy voice sounded from within. "Don't bother getting another. I have nothing more to say to you."

That was all Crompton needed.

He pulled out a blade, slipped it into the keyhole, and gave a hard flick of his wrist.

A telltale click told him he'd accomplished his goal.

He turned the door handle and stepped into the room.

Maurelle looked up from the chair, her features set in hard, unyielding lines. "I just said I'm finished speaking to . . ." Her mouth snapped shut, and she gave a start of surprise as she saw who her guest was. "Ansel." She rushed over, gripping his arms and peering wildly over his shoulder. "Are you insane? You're playing right into Chadwick's hands."

"No. He's playing into mine." Crompton shut the door, capturing Maurelle's chin in his gloved hand and tilting up her face so he could study it. "What methods did he use to force you? I'll prolong his death one painful minute for every time he took you."

Maurelle's brows drew together. "What are you talking about? He didn't bed me. Is that what his letter said? He was baiting you, Ansel. He cut a lock of my hair and took my chemise. But he never laid a hand on me."

Thunderclouds erupted on Crompton's face. "He described your birthmark. The one here." He touched her breast.

"My birthmark." Maurelle glanced down at herself in puzzlement.

"How could he . . . ?" Abruptly, her head snapped up, and her eyes blazed with anger. "That bitch Lady Breanna. She was in here while I was changing. She must have given him a description." Worry supplanted rage. "Chadwick arranged this. So he must know you're here. He'll kill you."

"No. He doesn't know I'm here and, no, he won't kill me." Fury rippled through Crompton's body in violent currents, intensifying as he realized how Chadwick had duped him. "I have no intentions of letting him win."

"But he set this whole thing up so—"

"Yes." Crompton's confidence returned as he reevaluated the events of the day. "He managed to deceive me. But I've outmaneuvered him. This morning, he suspected I broke in. But I've since convinced him otherwise. He now thinks the household is safe and secure. Which gives me the advantage."

Crompton seized Maurelle's hand, led her to the door. "Chadwick's amateur tactics are over. I'm getting you out of here. Then, I'm coming back and completing things once and for all. I'll execute Lady Anastasia the way I should have in August. Then, I'll make her wretched cousin beg for mercy. And once I have, I'll fire a shot through her heart right in front of Chadwick, show him how pitifully he's failed in his attempts to protect her."

"And Chadwick?" Maurelle's eyes were glowing with smug anticipation.

"He'll die next," Crompton vowed, hatred etched on his features, pervading his tone. "I'll relish that moment. Then, I'll do away with Wells and Hibbert, and whoever else gets in my way, including Sheldrake." He paused, the taste of victory on his tongue. "I won't have further need of the House of Lockewood anyway. You and I will be sailing away this very night."

Maurelle nodded eagerly. *"Oui.* I can hardly wait."

Inside the next room, Wells stood, taut and ready, his fingers gripping the door handle.

He forced himself to wait, to follow Lord Royce's instructions to the letter.

He remained still, listening as Crompton exited with Maurelle, their footsteps moving toward the rear of the house, then fading into silence.

Instantly, he rushed from his room and upstairs to the library.

"He freed her, my lord," he announced breathlessly to Royce. "They just left the house. Through the back entrance, I think."

"Excellent." Royce checked his pistol, a fierce light glinting in his eyes. "Let's give them a minute. I want Crompton a healthy distance from the manor, for Breanna and Anastasia's sake. Then, the rest is up to me."

"No." Damen stood, snatching up his own gun. "It's up to *us*. I want him dead as much as you do. Besides, it's you who's been goading him. If he sees you, he'll go after you with a vengeance. You'll need help."

Royce gave a terse nod.

Breanna bit her lip, exchanging a quick, worried glance with Stacie.

Before either woman could speak up, Hibbert announced, "Wells and I are coming, too." He flourished his weapon.

"Definitely." Wells produced the pistol Hibbert had provided him. "This isn't a question of honor, my lord," he advised Royce. "The viscount could be anywhere. The grounds are vast. And I know them better than anyone."

"You're right," Royce concurred. He went to Breanna, gripped her shoulders. "You and Anastasia go upstairs to my chambers. Tell two of the guards to stand outside the door. Stay put. That's just to be on the safe side, since Crompton assumes you're in the library. But he's thinking of Maurelle right now, not you. So he'll be heading away from the manor, not toward it."

"Very well," Breanna murmured.

Stacie couldn't bear her passive role another instant. She jumped up from her chair. "But, Royce, I want to—"

"Stacie." Breanna's quiet admonishment silenced her. "Let the men do what they have to. Otherwise, Crompton will escape." She met her cousin's gaze, and a current of communication ran between them. "It's best this way."

"All right." Stacie ceased her protests.

Breanna rose up, kissed Royce gently. "Be careful."

"I will."

Soberly, Breanna watched her future husband walk away, along with three men who meant the world to her.

She waited only until she and Stacie were alone. Then, she whirled about to face her cousin.

"What are you planning?" Stacie hissed.

"I'm planning to stop Crompton and protect the men we love."

"How?"

"By doing what we do best." Breanna heard the front door shut, and she grasped Stacie's arm. "Come on. We must work quickly."

She hurried into the hall, snatching the two dark mantles that belonged to her and Stacie. "Put this on," she instructed Stacie, tossing her one of the wraps and shrugging into the other. "After that we'll . . ." Abruptly, she stopped, a self-deprecating expression darting across her face. "What was I thinking?" she murmured, her gaze falling to Stacie's abdomen. "Your babe. I won't endanger your child." She gave an adamant shake of her head. "I'll manage this alone." That done, she reached up, began tugging pins out of her hair, releasing the upswept knot and letting it tumble free.

"No, you won't." Stacie yanked on her own mantle, realization mingling with fierce determination. "We're switching places," she said, a statement of fact more than conjecture.

Breanna hesitated.

"Breanna, you need me for whatever it is you're planning. Besides . . ." Stacie laid a protective palm over her abdomen. "My going after Crompton won't mean endangering my babe. It will mean saving it. Destroying that man is the only true protection I can offer my child. Right now he—or she—is at risk. It's my responsibility to eliminate that risk. In short, you need me, and I need to do this. So, tell me, shall I put up my hair? We are switching places, right?"

"Yes and no," Breanna told her, relenting. "We're each being both of us."

Stacie paused in the midst of buttoning her mantle. "You've lost me."

Breanna faced her, drew a slow breath. "Crompton will never leave Medford for good. Not as long as we're alive. So if he flees with Maurelle, we'll go right back to living in perpetual fear and uncertainty. I can't bear that thought. Nor can I bear the thought of what he'll do to Royce and Damen if he finds them before they find him. We have to eliminate that possibility."

"How?"

Another pause. "Stacie, this plan borders on reckless."

"Not as reckless as letting Crompton escape. That would be akin to a death sentence—for us and my babe."

"You're sure you want to—?"

"I'm sure."

Breanna nodded, knowing there was no changing Stacie's mind, equally sure that, were it she who was pregnant, she would make the same choice—for her child's sake. "We're going to lure him back. We're going to provide the viscount with exactly what he wants: us. The only problem is, he won't know which of us is which. And that will pose a major obstacle to that consummate plan of his. Remember, he means to kill you first. With one bullet. No mistakes."

"True," Stacie concurred, understanding dawning on her face. "And he can't very well do that—not with utter certainty—unless he's sure it's me he's firing at. Why, he could be undermining his entire plan, killing you first. It would reverse his order *and* deny him the sick pleasure of torturing you further, making you watch me die. That would be unthinkable after all his meticulous planning."

"Exactly. To a man like Crompton, certainty is everything. And how can he be certain? He'll see two Anastasia's: you," Breanna altered her voice, dropped her clipped accent in favor of Stacie's Americanized tones, "and me." She finished shaking out her tresses, her hair tumbling over her shoulders, loose and uninhibited like Stacie's. "It's risky, but it's the only way we can protect the men we love, and be sure Crompton doesn't vanish, only to keep terrorizing us."

"I agree." Stacie nodded, her mind racing. "We'll have to stay far enough apart so Crompton believes we're each alone, yet nearby enough to appear at a moment's notice—so that whichever one of us Crompton spots first can be quickly joined by the other."

"Right." Breanna finished her preparations. "Once we've done that, we'll have to challenge his pride without pushing him over the edge. We'll simply remind him that if he were truly the master shot he claims to be, he'd know which of us was which. We'll point out that to fulfill his plan, he has to shoot Anastasia first with Breanna watching—and that he has to kill us with only one bullet apiece." She raised her chin. "We'll each take a pistol. The minute Crompton turns away from one of us and provides the other with a clear shot, that Anastasia will fire." Breanna's gaze grew intense. "Stacie, I asked myself this question days ago, and answered it. Now I'm asking you—can you shoot to kill? Because I can."

Stacie's palm strayed back to her abdomen, caressed her unborn child. "Oh, yes, Breanna. When it comes to the Viscount Crompton, I can shoot to kill."

29

*B*reanna walked slowly through the thatch of trees on the south side of the estate.

Her instincts told her that Crompton would use this avenue to escape. Stacie had concurred.

If anyone knew the grounds of Medford Manor better than Wells, it was they. They were the ones who had played here as children, found hiding spots, climbed trees. And they were the ones who knew the densest areas in which to conceal oneself.

They'd intentionally left their hoods down. Their hair—a bright, burnished auburn—glittered in the moonlight, highly visible even in the darkness of night.

Gripping the handle of her pistol, Breanna placed one foot before the other, her heart hammering as she surveyed the deserted grounds. Every shivering leaf, every whoosh of wind made her jump, her stomach knotting as she contemplated what she was walking into.

Worse, what she'd talked Stacie into walking into.

Her cousin was with child. What if this plan went wrong? What if Crompton was no longer exacting, in control? What if he went wild, shot them both? What if . . . ?

No. She clenched her teeth, forced herself to stop thinking that way. Stacie's babe was in danger whether or not they enacted this plan, and it would continue to be in danger as long as Crompton lived.

They had to stop him.

A twig snapped behind her, and everything inside Breanna went numb. A sort of sickening, fatalistic awareness came over her, and she knew.

The moment of reckoning had arrived.

As if in a dream, she turned, not the least surprised to find the Viscount Crompton leaning against a tree, eyeing her calmly.

"You've made this far too easy," he commented, adjusting his gloves and watching dispassionately as she raised her pistol with a trembling hand. "Don't be absurd. You can scarcely hold that weapon, much less fire it." His arm snapped up, and the glint of his pistol flashed as he aimed it at her heart. "Whereas I . . ." A biting smile, and Breanna could see the madness in his eyes. "I'm a perfect shot."

He watched her frantically scrutinize the area beside him, and easily read her thoughts. "You're searching for Maurelle. Did you propose to hold her at gunpoint in the hopes of bringing me to my knees? Don't bother. You'd be dead before you finished aiming. Besides, she's off the estate. I made sure she was safely ensconced in my carriage before I came back to get you and Lady Breanna." His features hardened. "Now put down the pistol. Or I'll make your execution so painful, so prolonged, you'll beg for death." His middle finger hovered over the trigger. "You can die quickly. Or you can die with agonizing slowness. The choice is yours. Make it."

Breanna sized up her options, which were nil. She could try to shoot him, but it would be suicide. He could elude her bullet by simply stepping behind the tree, whereas she was utterly exposed, and standing before an expert marksman. Her only hope was to throw down her gun and keep him talking until Stacie arrived.

"Very well." She tossed her pistol to the grass.

"A wise choice," Crompton informed her dryly. "You would have failed, and died a horrible death doing it. Whereas I never fail."

"You did last August," Breanna reminded him, careful to use Stacie's voice. "My uncle hired you to shoot me, and you didn't."

Hatred twisted Crompton's features. "That was because of your wretched cousin. By the way, where is she?" he added, his middle finger pressing closer to the trigger. "Wherever you are, she can't be far behind. And I'm determined she should watch this."

As if in answer to his own question, his head jerked around, and he stepped backward, shifting to aim his pistol to the left, while keeping Breanna in his sight. "Come out, Lady Breanna," he invited icily, angling his head to survey the area from which Stacie was obviously approaching. "I can hear you. Ah, now I can see you," he determined with great satisfaction. "Therefore, I'll coax you out in a more convincing manner." With that, he fired—one shot—and Breanna jumped, stifling her shriek. Dear God—Stacie.

What had he done?

A cry of surprise and a thud followed the shot, and Crompton smiled cruelly, beckoning Stacie forward. "See?" he taunted with a vicious glare. "I can do it without mutilating your finger the way you did mine." His jaw clenched. "Now get out here and join your cousin."

Anastasia stepped out, her eyes wide with stunned apprehension, her hands unscathed, but devoid of a weapon.

Crompton's shot had sent it hurtling to the ground.

Which left both women unarmed.

Despite that fact, Breanna nearly collapsed with relief when she saw that Stacie was unharmed. They were in trouble. But they were alive.

Someone had to have heard that shot, she told herself. Wherever the men were, they would rush to Stacie's and her aid.

Crompton was too obsessed with killing them to consider that fact. So, it was up to them to keep him occupied until help arrived.

"Get over there where I can see you," Crompton was ordering Stacie. "Next to Lady Anastasia."

Breanna saw Stacie regain control, saw the flicker in her eyes as she reached the same realization Breanna had. She did as Crompton asked, walking slowly, her chin held high. *"Next to* Lady Anastasia? I *am* Lady Anastasia."

"Unless *I* am," Breanna challenged, boldly meeting his gaze.

For the first time, Crompton became aware of their identical appearances and voice inflections, and he hesitated, looking quickly from one of them to the other. "What kind of childish game are you playing?"

"No game, my lord." Breanna didn't know where she found the strength to confront him. But she did—just as she'd confronted her father last summer.

"It's reality," she continued, hearing her own voice—no, Stacie's voice, but coming from her mouth. "We're just pointing out that either of us could be Anastasia. Or Breanna. And that presents you with a problem. You did boast you could kill each of us with one bullet—and that the first bullet was meant for Anastasia. Well, how do you intend to manage that without knowing which of us is she?"

Crompton's eyes narrowed. "I've been an expert marksman for more years than you've been alive. I've never been bested, not in or out of battle. Do you honestly believe you—two insignificant little chits—can outwit me?"

"We're not trying to outwit you," Breanna assured him, curtailing all signs of arrogance. "We're just curious. You've sent us note after note declaring your superiority, vowing your intentions and your capabilities. We're just curious how you would carry out your plan given this particular counterattack. Even if it is being launched by two insignificant chits."

A muscle pulsed in Crompton's cheek, and he turned his furious gaze on Breanna. "You've given yourself away. Breanna is a mouse. Medford made sure of it. Clearly, you're Anastasia." He paused, gauging her reaction.

"Maybe I am," Breanna agreed.

"On the other hand, maybe not," Stacie posed. "After all, my uncle has been in prison for months now. Breanna has come into her own during that time. So how can you be sure *I'm* not Anastasia? You disappoint us, my lord. You've never relied upon inferior tactics such as badgering people into providing you with answers. You've always found your own answers. Anyone can make a lucky guess. But you've always been so certain."

"You have us at your mercy," Breanna admitted with a sad shrug. "We know that. We realize we're both going to die. We only want to know how you're going to kill us without risking your entire reputation."

There was a wild light in Crompton's eyes now. "Damn you both. I won't forfeit my rank and position. I'm the ultimate marksman. I can outmaneuver anyone."

He broke off, sweat beading on his brow, the tension in his arm easing a bit as his deranged but brilliant mind raced for answers.

For an instant, Breanna thought they had won, that he was actually going to crumple before their eyes.

She was truly considering lunging for his gun, when he snapped back to attention. A sudden triumphant smile curved his lips, and his self-control reasserted itself, the wildness in his eyes dimming. His arm stiffened, his fingers gripping the pistol even more firmly than before.

"Very well," he said silkily. "Let's have it your way. I won't waste a bullet. I'll just designate a third—one per person. After all, there is a third person here to consider." He lowered his pistol a notch, aiming for Breanna's abdomen. "My first bullet will go to your child. Your unborn child." He jerked his wrist sideways, shifting to aim at Stacie's abdomen. "It will die before its mother. So bid it farewell." His arm lurched back and forth, alternating between the two women.

It was Stacie who acted, instinctively leaning over to shield her unborn babe, covering her abdomen with both hands.

Crompton inclined his head in mock tribute. "A touching show of maternal protectiveness, Lady Sheldrake. And an ingenious approach on my part. Now I *am* certain." He turned his gun on her, gestured for her to straighten. "Now that we've established my superiority and resolved this amusing deception, I can finish my business and be gone."

He raised his arm a notch, aiming for her heart.

Without thinking, Breanna lurched to the left, planted herself in front of Stacie. "The only way you're going to kill my cousin is through me," she announced in a murderous tone that was totally foreign to her. She reached around behind her, held Stacie's arm so she remained firmly in place. "I can't stop you from killing us. But I won't give you the satisfaction of doing it the way you planned. You're going to fail, Lord Crompton. At least on some level. I'm going to die first. You won't rectify last summer's mistake beforehand. Nor will I watch Stacie die. So, once again, you'll be bested."

With a vile oath, Crompton strode over, grabbed Breanna by the throat, his fingers biting into her as he flung her aside. "No, you little bitch, I won't." He moved quickly, before she had an opportunity to catch her breath, much less rise. He lowered his booted foot to her chest and pressed, pinning her painfully to the ground. "Say good-bye to your cousin," he commanded, raising his pistol and pointing it at Anastasia. "She's about to die. And then I'll finally, *finally* have the ultimate pleasure of blasting away your life."

"Think again, Crompton."

Royce's voice rumbled out of nowhere, and Crompton whipped around, pistol raised.

He was still in motion when Royce's shot rang out.

The bullet pierced Crompton's chest, sent him jerking backwards from the impact.

A look of utter disbelief crossed his face.

Then, he slumped to the ground, less than a foot away from Breanna.

Royce walked over, his pistol still aimed and ready. He bent over Crompton's body to make sure he was indeed dead. Satisfied, he helped Breanna to her feet, held her tightly against him as he stared down at the blood seeping through Crompton's coat, soaking the fine wool.

"One bullet through the heart, you bastard," he muttered. "Now rot in hell."

30

Royce's bedcovers were a tangled, disheveled mess.

"Are you sure you don't want to sleep?" he murmured, balancing himself lightly on his elbows and kissing Breanna's flushed cheeks as she lay beneath him, limp and sated.

She sighed, a dreamlike smile her only reply.

They'd been making love for hours, ever since the guards had disposed of Crompton's body and seized Maurelle as she tried to flee in Crompton's carriage. The family had stumbled back into the manor, numb with relief, stared at each other in mutual understanding and bone-deep fatigue. Then, after a few emotional hugs between Breanna and Anastasia, everyone had retired for the night.

There would be time enough for discussion tomorrow.

For tonight, it was over. And it was time for recovery—recovery and renewal.

Breanna suspected Stacie and Damen had much the same sort of remedy in mind as she and Royce did: each other. And not only out of desire. Out of a soul-deep need to reaffirm both their lives and their love.

Now, hours later, the need seemed no less pronounced.

"Would you like to sleep for a while?" Royce repeated, brushing her lips with his.

"Sleep?" Breanna echoed, as if the word were foreign to her.

"Um-hum. It's almost dawn."

"No."

"You're sure?"

"I'm sure," Breanna whispered. Her lashes lifted, and she shifted to take Royce more deeply inside her, looped her arms around his neck. "Why? Have I tired you out?"

He chuckled. "Not a chance. Not now, not ever."

"Ummm, I'm glad." She leaned up, kissed the damp hollow at his throat. "Have I told you how heroic you were tonight?"

"Yes." Royce frowned, despite the erotic pleasure shuddering through his body. "Have I told you how reckless you were tonight?"

"Repeatedly." Breanna arched her hips, eliciting an involuntary groan from the man she loved. "Can we stop rehashing it now? It's over. And thanks to you, I'm fine. We all are."

With fervent intensity, Royce tangled his hands in her hair, lifted her face to meet his burning gaze. "You have no idea how much I love you," he told her, his voice husky with emotion. "Or how terrified I was when I realized the danger you were in—the danger you'd put yourself in. God, Breanna . . ." He kissed her fiercely. "Don't ever do that to me again."

"I won't." She caressed his spine, traced the damp planes of his back with her fingertips. "I'll go back to being self-contained and conventional. Later." Her eyes sparkled as she drew his mouth down to hers. "Much later."

Much later turned into much, *much* later, and the sun was climbing the sky when Breanna finally gave in to the need to rest.

She curled quietly in Royce's arms, watching the day unfold outside his window and thanking the heavens for the simple joy of knowing she could continue to do that, day after day, savoring each moment with the man she loved.

"Later this afternoon, we'll go visit that church you told me about," Royce announced, as if reading her mind. "I'll have the license within a week. How much time do you need to prepare for the wedding?"

Breanna smiled. "A fortnight," she decided abruptly. "Any invited guests who can't change their plans to accommodate us, will simply have to miss the occasion. The loss will be theirs. The union," she added softly, "and all the joy it promises to bring, will be ours."

Royce drew a sharp breath, then tilted up her chin so he could see her face. "You know what I want," he stated flatly. "I want you, as my wife, as soon as possible. But *I* also know what *you* want."

"Do you?"

"Yes. You want a formal wedding, something traditional and refined, something to make up for all you've been denied."

"I already have that—and more. I have you. No wedding celebration, no matter how grand, could enhance that joy."

A dubious look. "Sweetheart, are you sure?"

"Very sure." Breanna caressed his jaw. "I feel as if I've been given my life back. I want to begin it in the most perfect way imaginable—by becoming your wife. I want to be Mrs. Royce Chadwick the instant I can. As for guests, everyone I love is already under this roof. Including Grandfather, who's always with us. You and I will begin our life together surrounded by love. The rest is unimportant."

"Just what I wanted to hear." Royce kissed her fingertips, the delicate pulse at her wrist. "Now that I consider it, a fortnight sounds like forever. Maybe we should make it ten days."

Breanna laughed. "Stacie and Wells will be crushed if we give them *no* time to prepare. Besides, I think the prospect of a wedding is just what everyone needs to raise their spirits. Let's allow them a couple of weeks to savor it. Is a fortnight really that intolerable a waiting period?"

"Yes. But for your sake, I'll try to withstand it." Royce pressed her palm to his lips. "It won't be easy. I need you to belong to me in every way possible."

"I do. I will. And after that . . ." Breanna broke off, sobering as a sudden, worrisome thought intruded. "Royce, we haven't discussed our living arrangements."

He arched an amused brow. "We've certainly changed bedchambers often enough. Which room would you like to officially make ours?"

Breanna's eyes widened. "You really don't mind?"

"Mind what?"

"Living here. At Medford Manor. I know your memories here haven't exactly been pleasant ones. And you do have your house on Bond Street. I was afraid . . ."

Royce silenced her with a kiss. "Did you really think I'd take you away from your grandfather's dream?" he breathed into her lips. "Never. We'll use my house when we stay in Town. As for my memories of Medford—they're more than pleasurable. They're miraculous. This is where I met you, fell in love with you, made love to you for the first time. All that outweighs everything else, even Crompton. We'll start over right here, pick a section of the house that's new to us both. A private section, where we're assured of exquisite, utter seclusion. We'll wipe out all the ugly memories, keep only the spectacular ones. We'll redecorate, order all new furniture. You can provide brand-new sketches and needlepoints. And we'll move your porcelain figures, one by one, to our new chambers, designating a place of honor on our nightstand for the statue holding your silver coin. How would that be?"

Tears glistened on Breanna's lashes. "That would be wonderful."

"Anastasia and Damen's house will be ready by spring. Their babe will arrive not long after. And the family your grandfather prayed for will be well under way." Royce's midnight gaze darkened. "If I have my way, that family will be growing faster than even he expected."

Breanna smiled through her tears. "Perhaps that wish is already under way."

He started. "Breanna, are you saying—?"

"I don't know." She rolled over until she was lying atop him, her jade eyes filled with tender promise. "But given the daring man I'm marrying, and the unconventional woman I've become, I suspect our child won't comply with tradition. We've anticipated our wedding vows. Why wouldn't our babe?" She leaned over to kiss him, waves of auburn hair tumbling forward to encompass them in a shining cocoon. "Perhaps he or she was conceived this very night."

"Perhaps." Royce could scarcely speak. The very idea of Breanna carrying his child was almost too overwhelming to bear, and his body reacted instantly, hardening to almost painful proportions. He gripped Breanna's hips, lifted them so he could lower her onto his rigid shaft. "How would you feel about increasing our chances of that happening?" he asked, his voice rough with passion.

"Now?" she managed, her own words unsteady.

"Right now." He cupped her bottom, pushed deep inside her.

Breanna's breath caught, and she nodded, sinking into Royce's hypnotic spell. "Now would be ideal."

Epilogue

Medford Manor
November 1824

*T*he two six-year-old girls peeked curiously into the dining room.

The table was set with fine china and silver, and pinpoints of light cast by the gilded chandelier danced off the crystal glasses as the seven adults raised them in a toast. Lord Ryder, the evening's sole guest, beamed from ear to ear, thanking his hosts—the Lockewoods and the Chadwicks—for all they'd done to make this day possible. Then he rose, pivoting toward the sideboard, where Hibbert and Wells stood, and offered a special thanks to Hibbert, murmuring something about the fact that without Hibbert, his Emma would never have been restored to him.

Hibbert replied in his customarily gracious manner. Then he and Wells drank, actually abandoning whatever subject they'd been heatedly debating tonight, to join in the festivities.

The footmen refilled everyone's glasses, and the chattering resumed. Royce muttered something that made everyone laugh, and turned teasing eyes on Breanna, whose cheeks were tinged with color, but who looked more pleased than embarrassed by whatever her husband had said. Tenderly, Royce pressed her gloved hand to his lips.

"It's not Christmas yet." Holly Lockewood twisted an auburn curl around her forefinger, studying the adults with curious jade-green eyes. "Are our parents celebrating something?"

"They must be. They're laughing." Her cousin, Joanna Chadwick, followed her gaze, took in the scene before them. "So's Lord Ryder. Even Wells and Hibbert are smiling between arguments. It must be an important celebration."

"Maybe. Maybe not. Our parents always laugh. And they kiss, too. A lot more than most grown-ups do." Holly gave her cousin a wise look. "Mama says it's a special kind of magic."

"Magic? What kind of magic?"

"I don't know. She says I'll understand when I'm older." Holly made a face. "Why do we always have to wait to get older? That leaves noth-ing to do till then."

"Maybe the magic comes from the coins great-grandfather gave our mamas," Joanna suggested, still pondering what her Aunt Anastasia had told Holly. "Maybe the coins have special powers."

"That makes sense." Now Holly looked intrigued, her fanciful mind dancing through the possibilities. "Gold for laughing and silver for kisses." Her brow furrowed. "We should test our idea on Cody, stick the gold coin in his fist when he's waiting for Mama to feed him," she muttered. "Maybe that will make him smile when he's hungry. He cries so loud it hurts my ears."

"That's true," Joanna agreed. "But you're still luckier than I am. At least your brother's too little to walk. Mine runs all over. And he scrib-bles on my drawings if Mama isn't looking."

Holly grinned. "Maybe we should wake up both Cody and Quinn and bring them down. Just to see what Lord Ryder would do with one squalling baby and one little boy tearing up the dining room."

"Holly." Joanna, the far more practical of the two, planted her hands on her hips, shook her head. "That would only get us in trouble."

"Well, I'm bored. We've been listening to Lord Ryder talk about his new granddaughter for an hour. That can't be what they're celebrating. She's a baby. And babies yell too much to celebrate. Besides, he already has two grandchildren. He visits them all the time in Paris."

"Maybe his daughter and her family are coming here for Christmas!" Joanna's face lit up. "I like when they come. Monsieur Girard and Papa tell exciting stories."

"Especially the one about when Monsieur Girard rescued his wife from that bad witch." Holly's eyes sparkled with her typical romantic excitement. "And then they got married and she found her papa, Lord Ryder. It's like a fairy tale."

"We can go in and ask if the Girards are coming."

"We could. But even if they are, we'll still be bored now." Holly's shoulders slumped. She paced around the hallway, her mind searching for something unique to do.

"There you are." Miss Carter, the Chadwick governess, appeared at their sides. "Joanna, it's bed time. You, too, Holly," she added, turning to face the other child, who happened not to be Holly, but Joanna. "Your parents said you could sleep here tonight since it's so late. Unless you'd rather go across the way and sleep in your own bed? I could ask Wells to walk you home."

Holly sighed, tugging at the governess's sleeve. "*I'm* Holly, Miss Carter," she informed her. "And I'd rather stay here. But Joanna and I aren't tired. We wanted to be with the grown-ups for a while."

"Oh." Miss Carter gazed from one child to the other, exasperated by the mistake she seemed perpetually to make. Then again, the entire staff made it—with the exception of Wells and Hibbert. It was virtually impossible to tell Joanna and Holly apart. With only four months separating them, the two girls could pass for twins, just as their mothers could.

With regard to Holly's request, Miss Carter knew that neither set of parents would object to having their children stay up later than usual. In fact, they enjoyed having them about. It was a pleasure seeing the genuine affection that existed between the Chadwicks and Lockewoods and their children.

"Well, perhaps a few more minutes then," she relented. "But only a few."

"Thank you, Miss Carter," Joanna agreed. "We'll come up in a little while." She sighed as the governess headed off. "She still mixes us up."

"Everyone does," Holly said with a shrug.

"Except Hibbert and Wells. They always know who's who. So do our parents."

Holly's entire face lit up. "That's it!"

"What's it?"

"What we can do for fun. Remember what Mama told us about the game she and Aunt Breanna used to play? Let's change dresses. Then let's go into the dining room and try to fool everyone. You be me and I'll be you. Just like our mamas used to."

"They even fooled Wells."

"We will, too. We'll fool everyone."

The girls rushed down the hall to the blue salon, where they quickly changed frocks, slippers, even hair ribbons.

"Make your hair messier," Holly instructed. "Mine never stays as neat as yours."

Joanna nodded, tying her ribbon, then tugging out a few strands of burnished hair, letting them topple to her cheeks. "How's that?"

"Perfect." Holly's eyes glowed. "Now let's go in there. Remember to keep twisting those loose strands of hair around your finger. Papa says I do that all the time."

"And you bring in that new sketch I made," Joanna urged. "The one of the pond. I promised Mama I'd show it to her tomorrow. But tonight would be even better."

Holly's nod was filled with enthusiasm. "You left it in the library for the ink to dry. We'll get it on our way to the dining room. C'mon."

Five minutes later, Joanna and Holly poked their heads into the dining room—a far different dining room than the one their mothers had crept into more than twenty years ago when they'd been desperate to protect

Breanna from her father's wrath. Oh, the furnishings hadn't changed much from when Stacie and Breanna's grandfather had celebrated his sixtieth birthday. But the occupants had. So had the aura they exuded. Tonight there was no tension, no arguing, no resentment permeating the room.

Tonight, there was only love and laughter and contentment.

"May we come in and listen for a while before we say good-night?" Joanna asked.

Sipping at his coffee, Damen chuckled. "For a while? You've already been listening for an hour, only outside the door."

Across the table, Anastasia laughed, beckoned the girls in. "Of course. Come in and hear all about Lord Ryder's new granddaughter. She's only a few months old."

Joanna wrinkled her nose, remembering she was supposed to be Holly. "Is that what you're celebrating?"

Anastasia nodded, although she knew what was coming.

"Does that mean she yells as loud as Cody?" Joanna demanded, rather enjoying her role as her more outspoken cousin.

Lord Ryder coughed—a cough that sounded suspiciously like a smothered chuckle. "From what I experienced during my visit there last week, yes, I must say she does yell. But not often, and not terribly loud."

"Then that's different." Joanna gave Lord Ryder a reassuring look. "I don't think you should worry. She'll probably be okay. Cody's a boy. They're worse."

"Not always," Royce inserted dryly. "The entire staff was jolted out of sleep whenever Joanna bellowed."

"Funny, it was the same with Holly," Damen concurred. "I guess too many years have passed for our daughters to recall the din they created as infants."

The girls exchanged disbelieving glances.

Ryder's lips twitched, and he nodded his white head at the girl he thought to be Holly. "Thank you. I'm relieved to hear that the shouting will be minimal. I'm sure my Emma will be, too."

"Are they coming here for Christmas?" the real Holly inquired.

"As a matter of fact, yes." Ryder beamed. "The whole family will be arriving in three weeks."

"And we'll have them over for a long visit," Breanna inserted, anticipating her daughter's request. "I'm sure Monsieur Girard and your father will keep you both up until the wee hours of the morning, telling stories." She rolled her eyes. "And now that Quinn is almost three, he'll probably want to stay up, too, along with Emma's two older ones. It should be quite a gathering."

"Don't forget Damen and Wells," Anastasia added, grinning wryly at

Breanna. "They hang on to every word, just like the children. And Hibbert's worse. He adds his own personal touches to each story."

She and Breanna laughed.

In the process of pouring himself and Hibbert a brandy, Wells gave a dignified sniff. "I thought you two had gone to bed," he questioned Joanna and Holly, striving for a measure of discipline. "Where is Miss Carter?"

"Upstairs. She said Holly and I could stay here for a little while." Holly flashed him a beatific smile, her cousin's drawing clutched in her hands. "Please don't be angry, Wells. We just wanted to see what you were celebrating. And to ask Lord Ryder if the Girards were coming to Kent for Christmas. Oh, and I wanted to show Mama this." She waved the sketch in the air.

Wells tried, and failed, to look stern. "Very well. But it's late. You and Miss Holly can visit for ten minutes."

"Well, perhaps fifteen," Hibbert interjected, then glared defiantly at Wells, who scowled back, gearing up for another disagreement.

Royce rose from his seat at the head of the table. "We'd all like to see the sketch, moppet. Come in."

Beside him, Lord Ryder rose, as well, ruffling Holly's hair as she walked by. "Your daughter is delightful, Chadwick," he praised Royce. "As beautiful and talented as her mother." He turned to gaze fondly at Joanna. "And Holly is as dazzling and fiery as you, Anastasia. It's astonishing to have two sets of such enchanting women in one household."

"I have to agree." Royce caressed Holly's cheek. "Damen and I are lucky men. Our wives and daughters are incomparable treasures." He took the drawing, placed it on the table so that Breanna and everyone else could see.

"The pond," Breanna murmured, smiling. "It's lovely. You've captured it all, right down to the two ducklings we saw there last week. We'll have the drawing framed. You can hang it in the sitting room for everyone to admire."

Joanna's heart lurched with pride, but she was careful to let Holly act out her part.

"Thank you, Mama," Holly said with all her cousin's grace and presence. Joanna was a natural lady, just like her mama. Also like her mama, she was an incredibly talented artist. She took great pride in her drawings, as Holly well knew. Bearing that in mind, she received her Aunt Breanna's praise with all the pleasure Joanna was feeling. "It's one of my favorites, too. Can we go into Town this week and pick out a frame?"

"I don't see why not." Breanna glanced at Royce, who nodded.

"How does tomorrow sound?" he asked.

"Perfect." Holly beamed, but her mind was already elsewhere.

Joanna knew exactly where.

"Papa," she chimed in, addressing Damen. "Can I go with them? I haven't visited the House of Lockewood since Cody was born. Mr. Graff promised to show me how to count the money like you do at the end of the day," she added, referring to the head gatekeeper at the bank. "Now that I'm older I'll really appreciate it. Mama can come, too," she suggested, sweetening the pot. "She can bring Cody. He hasn't even seen where you work yet."

Damen couldn't hide his amusement. "I see your point. But, tell me, what if he decides to do some of that yelling you were referring to? How will my clients feel about that?"

"I'll accompany Miss Stacie and the children," Wells offered at once. He gave a conspiratorial wink to the girl he believed to be Holly. "I'm sure that between us, Miss Holly and I can keep Master Cody amused enough to limit his shouts."

"And I'll help Miss Joanna pick out a frame," Hibbert announced to Royce. "My taste is exceptional, and you and Lady Breanna will have your hands full keeping Master Quinn from turning the shop into a woodpile."

"A fine plan," Royce concluded. "Consider it done." He grinned as the two girls tried to restrain themselves from jumping up and down. "Now, I'd suggest you both go upstairs and get some rest. We don't want you falling asleep during your excursion."

Without a word of protest, the two girls hugged their parents—both sets, so as to avoid figuring out who was supposed to be hugging whom—and curtsied to Lord Ryder. Then, they started to the door.

Abruptly, Holly stopped, deciding that so grand an evening deserved an equally grand conclusion.

She touched Joanna's arm, then gestured for her to follow.

Joanna complied, and the two girls walked back to Hibbert and Wells.

"Would you take us up?" Holly asked, her expression innocent. "Miss Carter might not have waited up, and Holly and I can't fall asleep without a story."

Wells beamed. "Of course, Miss Joanna. I'd be delighted."

"You, too, Hibbert," Joanna piped up. "I want to hear all about how you and Uncle Royce met Monsieur Girard."

Hibbert stood up tall. "That's one of my favorite stories, as well. It would be my pleasure to share it with you, Miss Holly."

Holly placed her hand in Wells's, and Joanna did the same to Hibbert.

The small entourage left the room, the girls beaming secretly at each other.

Royce waited until they'd gone.

Then, he leaned back in his chair, his shoulders shaking with laughter. "That was amazing."

"An exceptional performance," Damen agreed, his own laughter rumbling from deep in his chest. He shot his wife a pointed grin. "I wonder who they could take after."

"We had nothing to do with this," Anastasia denied at once, trying to speak between peals of laughter.

"That's true." Mirth danced in Breanna's eyes. "They did this entirely on their own."

"With no tantalizing stories from you to encourage them," Royce teased.

Anastasia and Breanna exchanged glances, and dissolved into giggles.

"They're going to be unfit to live with," Anastasia said, dabbing at her eyes with a napkin. "They not only fooled Wells. They fooled Hibbert, too."

"Has anyone ever fooled Hibbert?" Breanna asked her husband.

"Now that you mention it, no." Royce rolled his eyes. "God help us."

Lord Ryder was gaping from one of them to the next. "May I ask what you're talking about?"

"Certainly," Royce supplied. "Forgive our rudeness. What you just witnessed was a clever impersonation. Two, actually. The girl you thought was Holly was, in fact, Joanna, and vice versa. They were very convincing, if I must say so myself."

Ryder blinked. "Are you saying your daughters just switched places? And that they actually had us . . . well, some of us fooled?"

"That's exactly what I'm saying." Royce grinned. "And if Hibbert ever finds out he was duped, he'll never be the same."

"I doubt the girls will tell him," Breanna pointed out. "They'll want to savor their secret."

"I agree," Anastasia said.

Royce arched a questioning brow. "Shall we tell them we figured them out?"

"No." Both women spoke simultaneously.

"I guess we have our answer," Damen replied with a smile.

"I guess we do," Royce acknowledged.

Breanna reached over to take her husband's hand. "Stacie and I had our dreams. We've realized them all. Let our daughters have the same. Dreams can carry you a long way. As our grandfather always knew."

Upstairs, the two girls giggled as they changed into their nightgowns. They kept their voices low, since Wells and Hibbert were positioned outside the door, waiting patiently to be summoned for storytelling.

"We did it," Holly hissed. "We even fooled Hibbert and Wells."

"That's even better than our mothers did," Joanna declared proudly. *"They* only had Wells to fool."

"Let's keep pretending until we go to sleep. That way it will *really* be an accomplishment. We'll have fooled Wells and Hibbert for an even longer time, and without a roomful of people they can say distracted them—*if* they ever find out about our game. Which they won't. But if we ever do decide to tell them . . ." Holly dimpled. "Think how smug we can be."

"Okay." Joanna's eyes sparkled, the notion of besting Wells and Hibbert as appealing to her as it was to Holly. Her self-satisfaction, however, was short-lived, as another, far less enticing, thought occurred to her. "We can pretend until we go to sleep," she clarified, wrinkling up her nose. "But tomorrow I'm being me. I don't want to spend the day at the bank."

"That's fine with me. I hate galleries, and I couldn't choose one frame from another," Holly responded without hesitation. "So we'll switch back by morning."

"Agreed."

Squirming into her nightgown, Joanna wandered over to the window, staring out across the grounds that her mother had gazed at for so many years of her life. But what she saw held none of the fear and loneliness her mother had known as a child, nor the terror she'd known as a young woman of twenty-one.

What she saw was the true magic of Medford Manor, the magic her great-grandfather had hoped to convey to Anastasia and Breanna along with the coins, a magic he hoped they'd pass on to their children and their children's children.

High above, a silvery moon shimmered in the sky, and golden stars twinkled alongside it, the gold and silver hues dousing the world in light and love.

Holly came to stand beside her cousin, propping her elbows on the window sill and reveling in the same wonders as Joanna.

The two girls saw safety and security. They saw the place where they'd been born, the place in which they were growing up, the place they'd always come back to no matter what changes life wrought.

They saw exactly what their great-grandfather had always prayed they would see.

They saw home.